Critical acclaim for The White Mare

'A fine historical epic set in Roman Britain'   *Woman's Own*

'It requires a special sort of imagination to create a plausible vision of Britain at the time of the Roman conquest. Jules Watson's *The White Mare*, the first in an epic trilogy of life in Celtic Britain, rises effortlessly to the challenge' *Daily Express*

There are plenty of plotlines, but Watson keeps them nicely dovetailed and tightly laced with romantic tension, treachery and cliffhangers aplenty . . . Mightily appealing'
                                                    Kirkus Reviews

'Wanton queens and evil druids stalk the mists in a book that is packed with action. Lovers of all things Celtic will find much to satisfy in this incredible tome'   *Good Book Guide*

'This one's a cut above . . . Where Watson wins is in the detail – there's loads – plus earthy politics. As good as any about right now'   *Ladsmag*

'Watson has researched her locations and history well, but has also confidently used the latitude provided by a little-known era . . . Firmly in historical romance territory, as the love story is the main focus. This fresh and interesting page-turner is a confident and assured debut'   *Historical Novels Review*

'In the grand tradition of the historical epic, this is a tale of heroic deeds, kinship and kingship. Truly sumptuous reading'
                                                    Lancashire Evening Post

Jules Watson was born in Australia of English parents. She came to fiction via archaeology and public relations, working most recently as a freelance writer in England. She and her Scottish husband divide their time between the United Kingdom and Australia. *The White Mare* is her first novel. Visit her website at www.juleswatson.com.

By Jules Watson

The Dawn Stag
The White Mare

The White Mare

Jules Watson

ORION

An Orion paperback

First published in Great Britain in 2004
by Orion
This paperback edition published in 2005
by Orion Books Ltd,
Orion House, 5 Upper St Martin's Lane,
London WC2H 9EA

A CIP catalogue record for this book
is available from the British Library.

ISBN 0 75286 537 4

Typeset by Deltatype Ltd, Birkenhead, Merseyside

Printed and bound in Great Britain by
Clays Ltd, St Ives plc

www.orionbooks.co.uk

For Alistair, for Eremon's eyes, and more

ACKNOWLEDGEMENTS

No one can complete such an undertaking alone, and I'd like to thank all my friends and family for their love and support, particularly for not minding that I was only half-there for the last few years, since my other half was off in first-century Scotland.

To the friends who gave invaluable and encouraging editorial feedback, and helped me answer the breeches/trouser question: Amber Trewenack, Tessa Evans, Helen Jamieson, Kathryn Tenger, Claire Hotchin, Lisa Holland-McNair, and Jo Ferrie.

To Amber, who cried in all the right parts and thereby gave me hope. To my big brother Mark Thompson, for beaming with pride and unconditional love at all the right times. To my wonderful agent Maggie Noach, for believing in me so staunchly. To my editor Yvette Goulden, for understanding what I was trying to do, and all those at Orion, for treating my 'baby' with such respect.

Patricia Crooke helped me with some ideas for gaelic terms. David Adams McGilp of the Kilmartin House Museum kindly broke away from an audio-visual crisis to talk to me, and in return I promised to tell everyone about his brilliant museum in Kilmartin, Scotland, a stone's throw from Dunadd.

Great thanks go to Dorothy Watson, who generously gave me a temporary home in Australia. To Claire, Graeme and Cassie Swinney, who took me into their home during the last fraught months of editing: for barbecues, essential gin and tonics, and overwhelming generosity and love when I needed it most.

My biggest thanks come last. To Claire, who sowed the seed, believed in me with unwavering ferocity, and held my hand through absolutely every drop of blood, sweat, and tears.

And to my beautiful husband Alistair: for cooking up the best plot details over many a pint in many a pub, for reading it umpteen times and still getting emotional, for coping with my meltdowns, and above all, for unstinting love and belief. I couldn't have done this without you.

·ALBA·(SCOTLAND)
SHOWING THE FIRST CENTURY TRIBES

ORCADES
(ORKNEY ISLANDS)

SACRED ISLE
(ISLE OF LEWIS)

CORNAVII

CAERENI

SMERTAE

LUGI

CARNONACAE

DECANTAE

CREONES

THE GREAT GLEN

DUN OF THE WAVES
(INVERNESS)

CALEDONII

VACOMAGI

TAEXALI

VENICONES

TAY INLET

FORTH INLET

EPIDII ▶ DUNADD

DAMNONII

VOTADINI

DUN OF THE TREE
(TRAPRAIN LAW)

(FIRTH OF CLYDE) CLUTHA INLET

SELGOVAE

NOVANTAE

✕ ~ ROUGH LINE OF FORTS BUILT BY AGRICOLA 79 ~ 83 A.D.

PROLOGUE

linnet

She was the child of my heart, though not of my body. I remember her as a girl, running up the mountain path towards me with amber hair flying, face twisted with weeping.

I worried about her then, and how the jealous taunts of the other children could draw such tears. I feared she was weak, and would not survive what was coming. For it was both my gift and my curse to see some of her future.

Blood spattering wet sand.

A green-eyed man in the prow of a boat.

The sea closing over her head.

And last, the cries of women on a battlefield, picking their way among the dead.

I knew she had a greater destiny to fulfil, but how would it unfold? That I did not know. As priestesses, we trumpet our powers of sight, but the truth is that it comes rarely, and never clearly.

I watched the girl closely from the day my elder sister birthed her and died. I remember her grasping my finger, milky eyes seeking my face, the tuft of red-gold hair still damp from the womb ... ah, but these are a mother's musings.

What I did realize that day, was that she was one of the Many-born, who come back to live again and again. And that because of this, her gifts would be as great as her pains.

For this reason I could not help her. She had to grow into her strength. And so she did. Like the fierce salmon, she fought against the currents of people's jealousy, ambition,

1

and awe. As her legs lengthened, so her face came into its form, losing the softness that had troubled me once. I saw also that she no longer cried – and in my priestess heart I felt relief.

But in my mother's heart, I wept for her.

I could not speak about her future – the blood, the man in the boat, the battle. My role was not to guide her course, but to build her courage and insight so that she could steer her own way through what would come.

For while we are caught like threads in the Mother's loom, we still have choice. I loved her more than my life – and so I wanted her to choose her path. Perhaps I would have done differently if I had known how it would hurt.

One thing only I clung to: although my sight hinted that many dark years were coming for the people of Alba, somehow, I knew she was a link to our freedom.

History can turn on many things.

On a word.

On a sword blade.

On a girl, running up a mountain path, amber hair flying in the wind.

CHAPTER 1
leaf fall, AD 79

T he babe fell into Rhiann's hands in a gush of blood. The mother let loose one final scream of triumph and agony, and slid down the roof-post against which she squatted. Rhiann, leaning in on her knees, wriggled to get a better grip on the slippery body. Fire from the hearth glowed on waxy skin and smeared blood, and under the wisps of dark hair, tiny bones throbbed against her fingers.

'To the Mother's arms you sink. The kin bids you welcome, the tribe bids you welcome, the world bids you welcome. Come in safety.' Rhiann murmured the ritual words breathlessly; the woman's heel was digging into her ribs.

Still holding the child, she nodded to the old aunt, who eased the mother to a pallet of bracken by the hut's fire. Now mercifully upright, Rhiann brushed her hair back with one shoulder, her hands still full of the squalling baby.

The mother pushed herself up on her elbows, panting. 'What is it?'

'A boy.'

'Goddess be thanked.' She sank back down.

When the cord stopped pulsing Rhiann rested the baby on the pallet, taking her priestess knife from her waist-pouch. 'Great Mother, as the child has fed from this body, now let him feed from You. Let his blood be Your blood. Let his breath be Your breath. So shall it be.' She cut the cord and deftly tied it off with flax, then wrapped a scrap of linen around the tiny shoulders to turn the baby's face to the fire.

'Oh, lady, what do you see?'

All new mothers asked this of priestesses. And what were

3

they to reply? *This boy is not of the warrior class, so at least he will not die by the sword.*

'What will he be?' the old aunt wheezed.

Rhiann turned back, smiling. 'I see him hauling in nets full of fat fish with his da, for many years to come.' She nestled the baby on his mother's breast, leaving a last caress on his soft head.

'You'll have one of your own soon,' the aunt croaked, handing her a rag. 'They won't be picky over your suitor, our man says. Not with the King so ill.'

'Hush!' the other woman hissed from her pallet.

Rhiann forced a tight smile, wiping her fingers. 'Now,' she said to the new mother, 'brew up the woodruff twice a day, as I told you, and it will bring in your milk.'

'Thank you, lady.'

'I must go. Blessings be on you and the babe.'

The woman drew her child closer. 'And you, lady.'

Outside, the tiny hut's reek of fish and dung smoke was washed away by the dawn air. Taking a deep breath of it, Rhiann forced the old aunt's words away too, draping herself over the cow-pen to stretch her back. The bony cow lowed and scraped its flank against her fingers, and she smiled.

Many nobles at Dunadd would look down their noses at this steading: the turf roof, the driftwood fence, and crusted fishing nets. To Rhiann, though, it seemed content in its little bracken glen. The scent of brine and lilt of fisher songs drifted over the bay. The rhythm of the day was well begun for everyone, and it would be much the same as any other day. She thought about how fine a future that would be. Calm. Uneventful. Predictable.

Then a tiny figure came hurtling around the side of the house and barrelled into her legs. 'Ah!' she cried, and bent to swing the little boy into the air. 'Who is this great, fierce boar trying to run me down?'

The child could hardly be seen for dirt; she didn't know where his ragged fringe ended and his face began. He battered

4

grubby feet on Rhiann's thighs, and she held fast and tickled until he squealed.

Then the boy's sister was there, clucking in embarrassment as she took him from Rhiann's arms and set him down. 'Ronan, you scamp! Oh, forgive us, lady . . . your robe . . .'

'Eithne,' Rhiann glanced down at her stained dress, 'I was hardly clean – your new brother saw to that. Goddess knows what I look like!'

'A brother!' Eithne hid a shy smile with one hand. 'Da will be pleased. And you look as fine as you always do, lady,' she added, remembering her manners.

'Pretty,' the boy piped. 'She says you're pretty.'

Eithne looked at her feet, giving his hand a sharp tug. She was dark like her brother, with black eyes and bird-like bones. The two of them were strong in the blood of the Old Ones; the people who lived in Alba before Rhiann's tall, red-haired ancestors arrived. Common blood, as it was known.

Right now, Rhiann ached to be small and dark and common. Life would be much simpler for her then.

'Thank you for bringing the babe safe, lady. And for coming so far.' Eithne dared a quick glance at Rhiann. 'Especially with the King so sick and all.'

Rhiann's belly turned over at this, but again, she forced it away. 'When your mother knew she was bearing, I promised to come, Eithne. And I left my uncle in good hands. My aunt attends him.'

'Pray to the Goddess he gets well!' Eithne pulled something from the recesses of her patched dress and proffered it to Rhiann: a crude and dented stag-head brooch. 'Da asked me to give you this. It's good copper – he found it on the beach.'

Rhiann touched the brooch to her forehead and stowed it away reluctantly. It was tradition to pay for the services of a priestess, no matter how poor the family. Yet, by the Goddess, she had enough brooches.

There was a loud nicker from a horse tethered to the end of the fence, a light-boned mare the colour of winter mist.

Rhiann smiled at Eithne. 'Ah! My Liath calls. Give my blessings to your father, and thank him for the fine brooch.'

She drew on her sheepskin cloak, pulling the fleece close about her neck. Then she squared her shoulders and took up her pack. It was time to seek her own home.

The path inland was wreathed with mist that crept over the water meadows, choking the River Add in its bed, clinging to Rhiann's face and throat. Liath's hooves were muffled on fallen alder leaves, and all was silent and dripping.

Such a fog hid many doorways to the Otherworld. Perhaps fey spirits were floating beside her right now, just beyond her fingertips. Perhaps they would draw her through, and she would leave the dankness of Thisworld behind. Rhiann spread her hand, hoping that the air between her fingers would conjure the spirits she sought, to take her away . . .

But she caught a branch instead, and icy dew spattered down her neck. She rubbed it away, sighing. Doorways and spirits! Here, there were just rotting leaves, mist and damp, and long nights to come.

The track wound up on to a spur, and when she emerged into milky daylight she reined in. Stretching away before her, the blanket of mist hid a wide marsh, which lapped at the flanks of a lone rock crag. And rearing from the crag into the light was Dunadd – the *dun*, the fort, on the Add. On its crest, the King's Hall, where her sick uncle lay, squatted against the sun, and the pillars of the druid shrine clawed the sky with black fingers. She shivered and nudged Liath along.

Dunadd's nobles lived high on the rock above the sprawling village at its feet, surrounded by an oak palisade. As Rhiann reached the village gate, the guard came down from his tower to loosen the cross-bars, blowing on his hands, and then helped her dismount with a wary nod.

They were all looking at her warily now.

The village was just stirring, the first dog barks and curses and children's cries drifting out from under hide doorcovers.

Rhiann led Liath through the jumble of thatched round-houses, sheds and granaries to the stables. There, she threw the reins to a yawning horse-boy and hurried up the path to the Moon Gate, the entrance to the crag, leaving the village and the mist behind.

'My lady! My lady!'

It was Brica, Rhiann's maid. In the weak sun, the carvings of the moon goddess on the gate shadowed her lean, sharp face. She flew forward to take Rhiann's cloak, chittering at the mud that had splashed up from Liath's hooves. 'I've heard nothing about the King, mistress – the Lady Linnet was not back when I left. Are you well? Are you feared? You look pale . . .'

'I'm fine!' Rhiann brushed off the invasive prods of those black eyes.

Brica was of the Old Blood, too, and grew up on the Sacred Isle out in the Western Sea, where Rhiann had trained to become a priestess. When Rhiann had stormed from the island the previous year after her initiation into the Sister-hood, the eldest priestess pressed Brica's services upon her. Rhiann didn't know why, for she and the little maid had never taken to each other.

'I need to wash properly.' Rhiann spread her hands. 'Is there water?'

'Ah! Your aunt emptied the water-pot with her draughts for the King. I'll go to the well right now!' Brica handed Rhiann's cloak back and darted away, lifting her skirts from the churned mud beneath the gate.

Rhiann slowed as she passed the houses of the King's kin. Here, the air of waiting was pungent, broken only by the steady drip of dew from carved doorposts. Servants crept to dairy and well on soft feet, their eyes cast down. Somewhere, a baby wailed and was hushed.

Rhiann's heart began to thump against her ribs.

And then the great arc of the Horse Gate was looming over her, leading to the crest of the dun. Peering between the carved stallion's legs, Rhiann could glimpse a curl of blue smoke rising from the small druid shrine, on the edge of the cliff. Between gate and shrine sat the King's Hall, a sprawling roundhouse topped by a thatch roof that swept to the ground. No one moved there.

From the roof-peak hung the royal emblem of her tribe, the Epidii – the People of the Horse. It was embroidered with the divine White Mare of the horse goddess Rhiannon on a sea of crimson.

This morning, though, the breeze was as weak as the pale sun, and the pennant stirred forlornly on its post like a bloody rag.

Rhiann lived on the edge of the crag, her door facing out to the marsh. When the wind was in the south, the only sounds that carried to her were lonely bird-cries, and the beat of wings. Sometimes she could pretend she was Linnet, her aunt, who lived on a mountain with only goats and one loyal servant for company.

As Rhiann lifted her doorcover, a finger of sun outlined Linnet herself, seated on a stool before the hearth-fire. Her aunt was changed. Normally so tall and regal, now she was slumped in weariness. Her russet hair, untouched by grey, looked somehow faded, straggling from its braids, and when she raised her face, the pale, tranquil oval was lined with furrows of worry. The women of Rhiann's line bore strong bones and long, fine noses. But in pain this fineness became pinched, and Linnet looked so now. 'It is not good, child.'

Rhiann's legs gave out, and she sank on to the hearth-bench, her cloak in her lap. 'I thought you would heal him when I could not. I was sure. I was so sure!'

Linnet sighed, her grey eyes grown darker with shadows. 'I can give one more dose of mistletoe, and we will see if his heart slows.'

'Then I will go to him now . . . I'll try everything . . .'

'No.' Linnet shook her head. 'I will return to him. I just came to see if you were back.'

Rhiann leaped up, the cloak falling to the earth floor. 'I will come with you. If we both reach out to the Mother . . .'

'No,' Linnet said again, and rose, glancing at the bronze scales hanging from the rafter. Behind, glazed jars and baskets gleamed against the curved wall. 'Stay here and brew more meadowsweet for me.'

'You try to distract me.' Rhiann was breathing hard.

Linnet managed a tired smile. 'Then you have found me out. But nevertheless, I will go. I am the senior priestess.'

'But I am the Ban Cré! It is my duty to be by the King's side!'

'Brude is my brother.'

'And you loved him as little as I!' Rhiann bit her lip, for the words had flown from her heart before she could stop them. As they often did.

Linnet put a hand on Rhiann's cheek, and looked deep in her eyes. 'That is true, as the Goddess knows. But let me spare you this. Soon such choices will be in my hands no longer.'

The denial trembled on Rhiann's lips. Part of her wanted to run away from the King's sickbed; part yearned to fight for his life. And no, it was not for love, the Goddess forgive her. It was to stave off what was coming. When, as Linnet said, all choices would be gone.

Eventually, in exhaustion, she gave in, for Linnet's soothing voice and measured speech hid a backbone of iron. This was something they shared, along with their fine bones, but one of them must always back down, and this time it would be Rhiann.

After Linnet had gone, Rhiann crept to the stool and sat before her fire, watching the throbbing of blood under the pale skin of her wrist. The same blood had run in those veins all her life. How could a single man's death make it greater, more valuable?

Special blood.

The words were bitter on her tongue. For in Alba, the king's line did not run from father to son. His female kin, his sisters and nieces, carried his blood. His heir was his nephew. But of the royal clan, which had ruled for six generations, no heirs now remained, leaving it vulnerable to those other clans who desired the kingship. And now only Rhiann could bear a male of the King's blood, for Linnet took her vow of retreat long ago, and was past her time.

While her uncle stayed hale, Rhiann kept at bay the dread that one day she would be forced to mate. But as the King's death drew closer, so did her own day of reckoning. There was no heir left alive. There was only her womb.

Her special blood.

Linnet returned with the dusk. 'Another draught, and still his heart skips. I dare not give him more.' She rubbed her eyes wearily. 'I have done all I can, daughter.'

Rhiann pressed trembling fingers into her cheeks. 'But surely he can fight this, aunt. He is strong – Goddess! Fighting, eating, drinking! They were his *life*!'

Linnet shrugged in defeat. 'Perhaps all that eating and fighting harmed his heart. Sometimes the soul blazes too bright for the body, and burns it from within. I've seen it before.'

The birch fire snapped and sent up a spray of sparks, which drifted to ash against the thatch roof. Rhiann turned to face it, wrapping her arms around her thin chest. Did death follow her? Was she one of those unfortunates who were stalked by marsh-sprites, which sucked human life dry? Her own birth took her mother into the Otherworld; her father followed only five years later. And then . . . and then came that other loss, those other deaths, a year ago on the Sacred Isle . . .

The force of Linnet's gaze drew her back into the room. In the way it was between priestesses, Rhiann sensed the weight of her aunt's concern on her skin. She knew why. She knew what Linnet saw.

Once, Rhiann took after her mother's beauty, so the bards sang. They shared the same hair and eyes: amber and violet to the bards, auburn and blue to Rhiann. But now her mother's bronze mirror was buried deep in her carved trunk. Rhiann's fingers had found the deep hollows in her own cheeks, and traced the prominent bones in wrist and neck. She did not need a mirror to tell her she no longer favoured her mother. That wide mouth would be a gash across her fine bones; the long nose a sharp prow. Linnet's features were showing the strain of days; her own showed the strain of moons. Shame and grief could consume flesh, as all healers knew. So it was with her.

There was a rustle of linen skirts, and then Linnet's warm hands were smoothing back her hair. An ache sprung to Rhiann's throat, an ache that she could not give in to, for fear the tears would never stop. She hunched her shoulders, struggling to swallow it. After a moment, Linnet sighed and dropped her hand.

'There must be something we can do, aunt!' Rhiann turned to her, fists by her sides. 'Cold slows the blood . . . there will be ice on the peaks now . . .'

Linnet shook her head, fingering the moonstone pendant at her throat. 'I've considered everything. We must entrust him to the Goddess now, daughter. Only She knows the warp and weft of the loom.'

Even though Linnet must know the fate that reached for Rhiann with those words, no other comfort came, as it had not since the King's illness struck. The familiar hurt gave one great throb in Rhiann's chest.

It was then that they heard it. One piercing wail rose from the pinnacle of the crag; a soaring, lonely sound, plaintive as a curlew-call. It came from the King's Hall. It was Brude's wife. And as the rest of his women broke into their ululations, cry after cry arced down from the crest, sharp enough to pierce Rhiann's breast.

She met Linnet's eyes. The King was dead.

The hours passed in a blur of ritual wailing, and the pale, shocked faces of people crowding the King's Hall, and the tears of his daughters wet on Rhiann's neck. Eventually, Linnet ordered her to seek her bed. Under pale starlight she could barely put one foot in front of the other, and once in her house she warded off Brica's attentions and crawled on to her bed pallet.

There, face buried deep in deerskin, she sought the oblivion of sleep.

Her mind would not rest, though. All eyes would be on her now. She bit her lip to stop herself from cursing the womb she carried. Without it, she would be no more than a man. Without it, the elders would not care who she was. If only she'd been born to a tribe in the south, in what the Roman invaders called Britannia. There, kings craved sons, and looked to their wives to breed. No one cared much about royal sisters or nieces there.

She sighed and rolled on to her side, watching the sparks of the hearth through the wicker screen around her bedplace. If only she'd been born into a fisher family, or to farmers . . .

Stop thinking, she told herself. *Just sleep.*

Sleep would not bring peace, though, not on this night. As a healer, she should have known that this new grief would conjure the old; the pain that had stalked her this past year, wasting her flesh. She should have given herself a special draught to take away the visions in the night.

But she forgot.

And so, in the darkest hour before dawn, she began to dream. First came swirling visions of her uncle on his horse. She was hanging on his bridle, pleading with him to take her up before him. But his cold helm was over his eyes, and he kicked up his steed and raced away, the horse becoming a gull as it ran.

She tried to follow him, for something was chasing her, bearing down on her . . . but her legs were caught as if in mud, and she stumbled, sobbing, in a marsh . . . Then there was Linnet before a fire, spinning, endlessly spinning, her wool a pool of scarlet at her feet . . . and the skein reached out tentacles to tangle around Rhiann's legs . . .

And then, with shocking suddenness, the confusion cleared. There was a doorway in the air, and the taste of a salt breeze blew through it. It was the air of the Sacred Isle. She was back there.

And part of her realized what lay on the other side of the door, and frantically tried to wake itself. Yet it was far too late. The memories took hold of her limbs and drew her through, eager to live again ...

... Her feet crunch on shells.

Spray hangs thick on the shore, and through it swim red sails and sharp prows that are black against the sun. The acrid smell of smoke is on the wind.

Sounds drift closer. A clang as sword bites sword. The hissing whine of spears. The thud of iron points in warm flesh ...

There stands her foster-father Kell, shield raised against a tide of north-men with fierce eyes. And there, his head rolls bloody in the spume, one eye cast back to its home.

There, little brother Talen stumbles, clutching his belly as pale guts spill between his fingers, his first sword fallen on the sands. And there, a screaming woman flings herself on the boy; her foster-mother Elavra, peal of anguish cut short by burly hands around her slim throat ...

And there ... right there ... her gentle sister Marda is splayed beneath a grunting man, copper hair tangled in seaweed ...

Then she sees no more, dear Goddess, no more. Nothing but her own hands, pale as dead fish on the dark rocks as she scrambles away, sobbing. Run, Rhiann! Away from the iron-hot smell of blood, and the crackling of flames, away from the harsh shout behind ...

In the bed, Rhiann's eyelids fluttered as she tried to wrench herself out of the dream. That shout! She groped for consciousness, a cry on her lips, until at last her eyes opened and she desperately blinked away sleep.

The dazzling brightness of the dream was gone, and in its place, shifting fire-shadows on a mud wall. She couldn't move her legs, the sheet held her down, stifling her ... she would be sick. A burning rose in her gullet, like it did that day on the beach.

The day of the raid . . . yes . . . a year ago this night . . .

She clapped a hand to her mouth, gagging. The wave of nausea surged and peaked, and then subsided, until at last she lay, gasping for breath. Her family . . . her beloved foster-family . . . was torn from her heart one year ago. By day, it felt like a lifetime; in her dreams, only yesterday.

All noble children were fostered out young, to strengthen the kin bonds, and foster-kin were therefore held dearer than blood-kin. But as Rhiann only had Linnet, they had meant even more to her. Kell and Elavra had sheltered her as she began her Sacred Isle training, and taught her how to be a royal lady as well as priestess. But the entire family had died between the rising and sinking of one sun. Just one sun.

After a few gulps of air she eased her legs free and curled into a ball, hands in fists. Against the rush of blood in her ears, she could just hear the whisper of Linnet's breath from the next alcove: a tiny, innocent, ordinary sound.

So alive.

A tear trickled into Rhiann's ear, and she dashed it away. No, she must not do this. If Linnet heard one sob, she would stroke Rhiann's face and hold her hands and draw out the pain into the light. And as much as Rhiann yearned to bury herself in Linnet's arms, as she had when a child, she could not face that agony. She could never let it free.

Cold and numb was better. So she kept her silence. And Linnet kept hers.

It took a long time for the drumming of her heart to fade, and tortured images continued to sweep across her mind in lurid swirls of light. She pushed them away and fixed on her breathing. *In, out. In, out. Think slow. Think of nothing.*

She thought of nothing, for some time. But even so, the rushing was still there. Just at the edges of awareness. She raised her head.

Since the raid, Rhiann's abilities to see, to receive visions and feel the spirit world, had all but deserted her. The source

14

of her power had ebbed away, along with her family's blood on the sands. For a year, she had stumbled blindly, dead inside.

But was she feeling something now? Some whisper from the Otherworld to comfort her?

The whisper around her grew to a murmur. And then there was a far-off, swelling, reedy cry, and out of nowhere a fist of wind slammed into the house. Rhiann sank back into her furs, heartsick. It was only a storm, not a vision to help her, then. Storms like this came often this season, swift and furious, sweeping in from the sea and across the marsh to break over the lone crag.

In three heartbeats it was skirling around the rock, beating its wings on Rhiann's roof like some great, dying bird. Keening gusts clawed madly at the thatch, until the door cover slapped and cracked and bucked on its thongs.

From a gap in her cocoon of furs, Rhiann stared at the roof. The sky could weep for the dead King Brude of the Epidii, for her people, for the land.

Not for her. No one would weep for her.

CHAPTER 2

Far out on the dark sea off Alba's coast, lightning struck with a sizzling crack. Its flame lit up a single boat that foundered in the storm's fury, and the men within who clung desperately to life.

'By the balls of the Boar!' cried Eremon mac Ferdiad, their leader. 'Brace yourselves . . . now, by all the gods, now!'

His plea was drowned in a roaring rush as another wave broke over the boat's bow, and he pushed his feet into the ribs of the hull. At last the seething foam cleared, and Eremon shook the spray from his eyes.

Heart in mouth, he counted the men again. Under a clouded moon he couldn't tell who was who with any certainty. Except his foster-brother Conaire, of course, whose bulk was unmistakable. But twenty, yes, there were twenty still aboard, and the fisherman they brought to be their guide. And Eremon's wolfhound Cù still crouched at his feet, shivering. The dog hadn't even whimpered.

As Eremon's pulse slowed, he felt the now-familiar gorge rising into his throat. *Not again . . .*

He leaned over the side and retched what was left of his guts into the heaving sea. Around him his men did the same, most not bothering to lift their heads from the oar benches. Young Rori seemed to have a bigger belly than he, despite his small size, and managed to vomit an enormous slick that just missed Eremon's feet.

So much for princely dignity. Eremon wiped his mouth. The stink of piss and the sight of blood he could take, for these were part of a battlefield, part of being a warrior. He could hold his drink, too. But this? This was another world entirely. For once, his hard will could not bring his body into line, no matter how he fought.

Another wave was bearing down, and Eremon ordered the men back to bailing and rowing. He was no mariner, indeed he'd hardly set foot on a boat before. Yet common sense told him that they must keep head-on to this swell, or be lost.

In the ridiculous way of crises, at this very moment a scrap of old lore from his father's druid tumbled through his mind: *The gods' smiles bring the sun, the thrust of their swords a king's death, their frowns the thunder and wind that split the sky.*

Ha! Gods!

As the foam rushed around him, sucking at his feet, Eremon frantically shook hair back from his eyes. If the old druid was right, then he knew what he now faced, for surely only a god's wrath could conjure this storm from a calm sea!

Even the fisherman could barely cling to the tiller, his eyes glassy with terror. Eremon fought down a rush of guilt. The man had only ever sailed *curraghs*, and those little hide boats could skim lightly over such waves. This craft was a larger trading vessel: planked instead of hide hull, ten oars each side and the square-rigged sail. Not only that, but the fisherman was the most reluctant of guides, for he'd been stolen as well as the boat.

If Eremon had known the danger they were sailing into, he might have spared the man. But the day they fled Erin in a hail of arrows had been calm and bright. It wasn't until the second day that the sky darkened and the wind rose, and the fisherman began to mutter at the threatening bank of cloud that loomed up in the south.

The storm front attacked with stark ferocity, the wind, waves and rain rolling together into a grizzled beast that sprang on them, gripping and shaking the boat in its jaws. They hardly noticed as day fled into night, and they could see no more in the darkness. Their world narrowed to sound and touch and taste: wind roars and cold lash of rain; spume on their tongues; the creaking of rigging; the breaking of blisters on the oar.

Now the star wheel must have swung well towards morning. The whole sky was heavy with cloud, yellow where the moon was sinking. Like an eye, that baleful glow seemed to Eremon, the merciless eye of a god. Was it Hawen the Great Boar, totem of his tribe? Dagda the Sky God? No, more likely it was Manannán, Lord of the Sea, protector of Erin. Maybe Manannán was angry that Eremon had abandoned his own land.

Then just take me! he silently cried to the eye. *Spare my men!*

He received no answer, no slackening of the wind or softening of the sea. The next wave hit, and a great gout of water slapped into Eremon's mouth and filled his nose, and he snorted and spat and held tight until it set the boat free again in fickle disgust.

Cù was cringing as low as he could, belly and chin flat, rangy legs spreadeagled as if to grip the hull. Eremon spared a moment to pat the shaggy head, and felt the dog's tongue on his hand where a sword callous had been torn away by the damp, splintered oar. In the lull, Eremon cast a glance back to Conaire. He was rowing strongly, his thick, sinewed arms and immense back pulling with as much strength as when he was fresh two days before. True to form, Conaire was the only one not struck by the sea sickness.

Eremon managed a grin, and although Conaire's teeth flashed in the dimness, the feeble light that caught his eyes showed something else. With a shock, Eremon realized his foster-brother was afraid.

He turned back to his own oar. This was bad. Conaire had never been afraid of anything in his life – man or beast. He met every fight, every challenge, with fierce joy and laughter. But even Conaire had never been in a boat before. Eremon thought: *He doesn't believe we're going to make it.*

And then the next surge hit. The men held tight to their oars as he'd instructed, except young Aedan the bard, who would not let go of his precious harp. However, this wave was the greatest yet, and it felled Aedan with one blow, and tore him from his braced stance against the ribs of the hull. For one frozen moment he hung over the stern in a cascade of foam, scream lost in the wind.

Eremon pushed Cù away and launched himself across the oar benches, heedless of the men he was trampling. Conaire was already there, his great bulk steadying Aedan's flailing body, and together he and Eremon fought the surge until the water surrendered the bard, and he collapsed at their feet. Panting, Conaire stared blankly through his dripping fringe, eyes fixed on a place over Eremon's shoulder. Eremon took a breath and turned.

The mast, weakened by the waves and wind, had finally cracked, and now leaned at a crazy angle, sail and ropes flapping uselessly. Eremon let the breath out in one long hiss of despair. When would it end? Then he looked past the shattered timbers to twenty pairs of eyes, all turned to him for guidance.

At Rori on his oar bench, scarlet hair slick with water, chin thrust out manfully despite his quivering lip.

At grey-eyed Aedan, who cradled his harp so carefully as he retched.

At burly Finan, who had fought battles when Eremon was a baby at the teat, and who now clung fiercely to the tiller that had been abandoned by the cowering fisherman.

Around Eremon huddled the rest of his warband. Some were young warriors with hero-light in their eyes, desperate to follow a prince to glory; and others, veterans like Finan, were loyal friends of his dead father, King Ferdiad of Dalriada.

Though he was only one and twenty himself, they followed Eremon because they believed he could reclaim his father's hall from his usurping uncle, a man who wrenched it from him by sword and betraying tongue. All Eremon had managed to salvage were these twenty men and some jewels and weapons. They had barely escaped from Erin's shores alive, in that last, surprise attack on the beach.

And now death will claim us anyway . . .

'We can't keep this up!' It was Conaire, yelling in his ear above the wind. 'We have to hold, not row, or we'll be food for fish by morning!'

Eremon blinked rain away. Conaire spoke sense, but he knew that if they stopped rowing they could not keep head on to the waves, and would surely tip. Torn, he gnawed the tiny, puckered scar that worry had worn inside his lip. He must decide, and quickly.

He reached out to grip Conaire's shoulder, more for his own comfort. 'We've fought plenty of battles, and this is no different!' he cried. 'I say we row!'

Conaire's face fell, but before he could answer, there came a hissing voice, and they both looked up to see a curling wave-crest begin its deadly descent towards them. They just caught the mast before it hit, and this time, when the spume cleared, it was Finan sprawled on his back.

The tiller yawed, caught by a blast of wind, and as if waiting its chance, the sea grasped the boat and spun it wildly. They were wrenched side-on, and as the next wave swelled beneath them, the hull rose and tilted, until they were all staring into the black depths below. For an endless, sickening moment, the boat clung bravely to the wave shoulder, and every man aboard braced himself for the long fall, and the heart-stopping, icy splash.

Then the wave released them, and the boat rolled down into the trough, upright again. Finan was on his feet before Eremon reached the stern, and between them they wrenched the tiller around, desperately turning the bow back into position.

'Get to those oars!' Eremon roared, chest pounding. The terror was so great that it immediately cleared the sickness, and he gave his belly no more thought. 'Diarmuid, Fergus and Colum, keep bailing – everyone else row as if the hounds of the Otherworld are on your heels! To Alba!'

Alba of the waves, of the moors, of the mountains. Though they had been blown north, not east, he knew his goal loomed somewhere near, just out of reach. But he could not spare any thought to what awaited them there.

There was just the now: wind, black rain, and the hungry sea.

CHAPTER 3

'The funeral is at dawn in two days.'

Rhiann felt Linnet, beside her, stiffen at the chief druid's clipped words. The roof of the druid shrine was open to the clouded sky, and dull morning light striped the rain-soaked earth between the massive oak pillars. But the face of the chief druid – Gelert – remained in shadow.

He had just performed a sacrifice for King Brude's soul. Blood streaked one gnarled hand and spattered his bleached robe, and behind a half-circle of other druids, a yearling calf lay across the stone altar. At the base of each oak pillar, the wooden idols of the gods stared down with empty eyes, stained with ochre, wreathed with withered flowers. Dried petals littered the floor around their feet.

'Surely we need time to prepare.' Linnet's tone matched the druid's coldness.

Gelert dipped his hands into a bronze washbowl held by a young novice. 'All is prepared. The nobles will journey to the Isle of Deer before first light in two days. We burn him at sunrise.'

'I see grief has not slowed you, Gelert.'

The druid waved the novice away, moving forward into the sunlight. Rhiann caught her breath, as she always did when she was near Gelert. The fading tattoos on the old man's cheeks were twisted by the wrinkles that seamed his skin. The flesh of his nose had shrunk away from the bone, and it cleft his face as a prow cuts the waves. Lank, white hair straggled to his shoulders. But it was his eyes that repulsed her, and no more so than when they were fixed on her. The lashes were nearly gone, and the irises were yellow and flat, like those of an owl.

'What is the point of grief?' Gelert shrugged. 'I knew he was dying. I, at least, *saw* it. And unlike you, I have little time to indulge myself in women's grief.' Another novice appeared with a wolfskin cloak, and Gelert drew it around his bony shoulders. 'Other matters require my thought.'

Linnet folded her hands into her sleeves. 'You mean the rumours of Roman soldiers to the south. But we all know they won't come into Alba.'

Rhiann started. Lost in the depths of her misery, she'd not heard any such rumour about Romans. The invaders had been on the islands of Britain for nearly forty years now, so the lore of the priestesses said. Though they advanced north at intervals, they seemed to have stopped, content to sit and bleed their new province dry. But Alba? It was too cold and rugged for them, and the tribes too fierce. This is what Rhiann had heard around the cookfires since she was a baby. Everyone knew it.

Gelert smirked. 'Well, I would not expect women to appreciate such matters. That is why they are safely in other hands.'

Rhiann knew Linnet would not rise to this, for Gelert always spoke so to her aunt. His hatred for those of the sisterhood – those of the Goddess – had been a steady thread throughout Rhiann's life. The druids drew increasingly close to their sword, thunder and sky gods, although most of them at least still paid their respects to the female face of the Source. But not Gelert. He would sweep the whole sisterhood from the face of Alba if he could. To him, Rhiannon the Great Mother, after whom Rhiann was named, was no more than the ornamental wife of a god.

Which was even more reason for Rhiann to stop standing there, gawking as if she were a child. She was a priestess, too, and must act like one. 'What of the symbols for the King's journey-boat?' she broke in, returning to the matter at hand.

The Romans would remain a rumour, so she put them out of her mind.

Gelert turned to her, and the power in his eyes was like yellow flame spilling from two oil lamps. 'All done. While you were off delivering that fisherman's cub, my brethren were preparing the King's way. You need only grace us with your presence. Unless you object?'

She did not reply, only raised her chin.

He smiled. 'Ah, yes, our proud Ban Cré, our Mother of the Land. Our Goddess-incarnate, our royal *priestess*.' He always managed to imbue her titles with such contempt. 'The people would be so disappointed to see you fail your kinsman.'

'Of course we'll come,' Linnet snapped. 'Unlike you, we respect the dead.'

This was uncomfortably close to a lie in Rhiann's case, but she *had* tried to save her uncle's life. Not Gelert. As soon as the King fell sick, the druid had obviously set about organizing the funeral, not even waiting for the spirit to relinquish the body.

Rhiann considered that as they left the shrine. She did not expect to see Gelert grieving, but she had anticipated more respect.

Linnet's arm slipped around her waist. 'Don't let him upset you, daughter. His words do not come from the true Source.'

'He doesn't upset me,' Rhiann lied.

But the memory of those owl eyes stayed with her throughout the day.

The *bodhran* drums began at dusk, rolling from the peak of Dunadd like storm-claps, shot through with the flash of bone pipes and strident horns.

The druids were conducting their own rituals with the King's body, for he had worshipped the sword gods, paying little heed to the Goddess, and Linnet and Rhiann would stay away until they were done. Rhiann did not like the smell of druid magic. Or perhaps it was just that it always carried the taint of Gelert's soul, and she felt it keenly.

She and Linnet ate by her hearth-fire while the wailing and singing swirled outside. The first rams had been slaughtered now the long dark grew near, and the mutton broth was warm in her belly, though no more than ashes on her tongue.

That day Brica had replaced the stale rushes on the earth floor, and so at least the familiar smells of home were around her: fresh plants, herb stew and peat smoke.

She thought about the King's Hall, with its taint of blood and half-cooked meat, its gaudy banners, and walls bristling with spears and shields. The curved walls of her single-roomed roundhouse were softened by hangings woven by her mother, and only bunches of herbs and net bags of tubers decorated the rafters.

On the hearth-stone lay a deerhide bag that needed mending, and by the door rested an assortment of digging sticks, stained with mud. Hanging above them were weaving shears, and knives for herb-cutting, their blades blessed in sacred wells. On a low shelf a line of tiny wooden figurines rested: statues of the Mother Goddess, ochre-stained.

There were no hunting spears or shields propped up, no horse harness waiting for repair, no long *bracae* trousers spread on the loom by the door, half-woven.

But for how much longer? A man was going to invade her home.

As he would invade her.

CHAPTER 4

The world was still ragged with scudding cloud, and beneath a dawn sky the colour of cold ash, Eremon sat alone in the bow of the boat.

Eremon, son of Ferdiad. Rightful King of the people of Dalriada, in Erin.

The corner of Eremon's mouth lifted bitterly. *King of nothing, and no one.* He glanced at the huddle of men in the stern. Well, King of twenty good men, at least.

Over their heads, he squinted across the waves, now only rocking the hull with light, insistent slaps that nudged them shoreward. Another day and night after the storm, it was only clear now that they'd been swept north along the Alba coast, and not out into the trackless reaches of the Western Sea.

The sharp tang of brine was strong on the west wind now, but in the still air before dawn, he'd caught the scent of wet pine and mud. Earth; good, solid earth.

He idly fondled Cù's ears, too weary and heartsick to appreciate this good fortune. Then he was struck by a new thought, and sat up a little straighter. Against all odds, they'd come through the storm and were close to land. So perhaps Manannán had sent it to *test* Eremon, to know that he was worthy to take back his father's hall and rule the people of Dalriada. Maybe he could earn the blessing of the gods after all.

Eremon's hand stilled on Cù's warm head, his eyes glazing over. The storm was the first test, then – so there would be others. And he would pass every last one of them, until he returned to Erin to kill his usurper uncle, Donn of the Brown

26

Beard. He lost himself for a moment in a dream of a blazing sword, and the expression on his uncle's face when it bit him through the neck.

'Wake up!' Conaire waved a hand before Eremon's eyes, and squatted down, passing over a hunk of damp bread. Cù thumped his tail on the deck and raised his head for a sniff, then flopped back in exhaustion.

Eremon patted him, eyeing the crumbling bread with sudden, ravening hunger. After all, there had been nothing in his stomach for two days now. He tore off a chunk and chewed in silence.

'So we are near land after all,' Conaire offered. He paused. 'You were right about the oars.'

Eremon snorted, picking barley grit from his teeth. The memories of the storm were now just a hazy blur of rain, wind, and terror. He knew they had come close to passing over to the Otherworld, and even though the druids said this was nothing to fear, he'd realized just how much his body wanted to stay right here. Trust Conaire to forget it all so quickly.

Then Eremon cast another glance at his men, chewing their bread. They were worn and wet, with new bruises and oar blisters. And yet, they'd somehow made it through the storm alive. He should be thankful, and leave it at that. He cocked his head at Conaire. 'You admit that I'm right, do you, brother? Did the mast catch your head as it fell?'

Conaire grinned in answer, and stretched his long legs out along the rough-hewn planks.

The two men were an unlikely pair. Conaire had been a giant even as a babe, with hair that shone like ripe barley, and the wide, blue eyes of his people. Next to him, Eremon always felt too dark and lean. His own eyes were a shifting sea-green – the legacy of his Welsh mother, along with his hair, the deep brown of a mink's pelt. Both had marked him as different when he didn't want to be.

As a boy, Conaire had raced around in a storm of yelling and running and laughing. That exuberance did not come easily to Eremon, and less so when he realized he was a prince, and must learn how to be a king. Conaire's sire was only a cattle-lord, and Conaire could fulfil *his* expectations easily. Be as quick to fight as to jest. Hold a man's fill of ale and boar. Oh, and bed a woman as soon as physically able, which in Conaire's case was before his eleventh birthday.

But Conaire had a sense his bluff father would never have appreciated – he always knew when Eremon was brooding. So now he brushed the crumbs from his thighs and clapped Eremon on the back. 'What say we get some earth under our feet then, brother? My balls are turning bluer by the day, I swear!'

The thump set Eremon choking, and it took some moments of coughing and laughing before he could reply, by which time the dark hurt of betrayal and home had fled. Donn and revenge could wait a little while; there were more pressing issues to take care of first.

'Now that you've woken me up,' Eremon cleared his throat, 'we need to find out where we are.'

'Right.' Conaire leaped to the oar benches, and in three hops was standing over the fisherman, who was gnawing half-heartedly at a hunk of bread.

Eremon watched the ease with which his brother moved, despite his great bulk. Sometimes, just sometimes, he longed to be like Conaire: to follow some other man's orders, to ride into battle behind someone else's flying banner, giving no thought to strategy, just to fighting. Ah, to fight and become lost in blood and heat and the glorious surrender it gave . . .

He took a breath. That was not for him, especially not now. He must be a leader from the moment they landed in Alba. A prince, not – Hawen forbid – an exile.

He followed Conaire, pausing to check on Aedan and Rori as he passed. Rori was thin and pale, his freckles standing out like spots of blood on his white cheeks. Aedan was drawn and bruised, and his grey eyes were shadowed. Yet both youths straightened bravely when their prince touched their shoulders.

Then Eremon was staring down at the mottled top of the fisherman's head, which was burned the deep colour of skin that lived in the sun. Conaire was standing over him with hands on hips; plainly, he'd got nowhere.

'Where are we?' Eremon demanded.

The fisherman squinted up at him sourly.

'Answer the prince, man!' Conaire growled.

The other dropped his gaze. 'Aye, it smells like Alba's air, all right. But not the Misty Isle, we're north of that. Where, though, only Manannán knows.'

Eremon met Conaire's eyes. They must go ashore sometime soon, for they were running out of water. Chances were that they'd arrive on an island of poor fishing folk, anyway. This would suit him well, for they could rest and get their strength back before seeking out the local chieftain.

'We'll row this coast until we find a safe landing; somewhere with few people. We can hold out another day or so.' Eremon then addressed the fisherman. 'And as I promised, I'll find you a boat to return you to Erin.'

'Good!' the man spat through rotting teeth. 'Savages, the Albans are. You'll probably all be eaten alive come night—' He was silenced by the crunch of Conaire's great hand on his shoulder, and he gulped and slipped into more respectful silence.

No matter who they first met, Eremon knew they must make a show of strength. News travelled fast among the islands, and the more fear and awe they could inspire at the outset, the better. The tale would grow in the telling, and by the time it reached the local ruler's ears he would think twice about attacking them.

Or so Eremon hoped.

At the very least, they should not look like the sorry pack of refugees that confronted him now. So as they rowed towards the distant coastline, the men took it in turns to clean their weapons and faces, and comb and braid their hair. Shields were polished and tied in lines down the flanks of the boat, and spear-tips, helmets and mail shirts were burnished.

For the fifth time, Eremon checked on the three iron-bound chests strapped safely in the hull. These were filled with jewellery gathered in from a handful of secret supporters, when his uncle's challenge for the throne became a growing threat, but before Donn attacked Eremon openly. Some time before they landed, he would distribute the wealth among his men.

Safe in Eremon's leather pack was the gold circlet of his father, with its green jewel that glowed on the brow. That jewel came from a land so far to the east that Ferdiad was forced to trade a sack of gold and his favourite concubine to gain it. And wrapped in oiled hide was Eremon's own iron and bronze helmet, its crest a bronze boar, the totem of his clan, bristles stiff with attack fury.

When they were ready, Eremon leaped on to a rowing bench, and surveyed his men with an approving grin. 'I swear you all look as pretty as maids.' Then he grew more sober. 'Unfortunately, though, you must impress as men, not maids, or our lives may be forfeit before we see Erin again.'

'Not without a fight.' Finan stroked his sword.

'No, not without a good fight. Though a score of men, no matter how fine, cannot stand up to a whole people.' Eremon stared at each face hard in turn. 'You know the plan and you must follow it, every one of you. For now, I'm a prince seeking trade alliances. A lie brings dishonour, I know, but Hawen the Boar will forgive us. He wants us alive.' In a sudden burst of inspiration, he unsheathed his father's sword and held it aloft. 'This blade was named by my father, but now I give it another name on Alba's shores, in honour of Manannán, Lord of the Sea. Like His own sword, I call it Fragarach, the Answerer. And it will answer our betrayal with blood! The blood of the traitors!'

The men roared, baring their teeth, their worn faces lighting up. Some leaned over to beat a din on their shields, and others spat deadly curses at Donn of the Brown Beard. And then, breathless and fierce, they returned to their benches to row once more.

Soon the strain of a harp took up the beat of the oars, and in the bow, Aedan began a new song. Aedan's songs involved too much undying glory for Eremon's taste, especially when the reality was cold fear, the stench of battle, and a final sword thrust in the gut. And as for the maidens who swanned through the bard's tales, the reality there was similar. In Eremon's experience they were twittering birds with a love of finery and jewels; jewels that must be hard won by such as he.

But as the men relaxed into the rhythm of rowing, Eremon noted their new sense of purpose, a purpose that no storm, no betrayal, could beat out of them. He smiled to himself. The campaign against his uncle had wrought them into a warband to reckon with. Above all, they were intensely loyal – they'd proven this by being willing to follow him into exile.

Exile.

He savoured the vile, unavoidable word on his tongue again. If only there'd been more men like this, his uncle's betrayal would have ended differently. He tested the razor-edge of his sword with a fingertip. *Very differently.* Then he sighed, sheathed the sword and stowed it, joining Conaire at the oar.

In his short life, he had learned that men's hearts are seldom true. Of women's hearts, he gave no thought.

CHAPTER 5

Brica woke Rhiann and Linnet long before dawn on the day of the funeral, a lamp of tallow-soaked rushes sputtering in her hands.

By the hearth, the maid first stripped Rhiann of her bed-shift, and then with a mixture of fat and rowan ash, she painted over the blue tattoos that curled all over Rhiann's breasts and belly.

All Epidii women were tattooed at puberty, but as the Mother of the Land, the Ban Cré's tattoos represented the curving lines of power that radiated through the soil and rock, and along the rivers. The designs anchored the divine Goddess to the land and people through Rhiann's earthly body. Her tattoos were therefore the most beautiful and sacred, and must be protected by the rowan as they sent the King to the Otherworld this day.

Over a fresh linen shift, Brica dressed Rhiann in an ankle-length tunic of green wool, embroidered with scarlet flowers, fastened on each shoulder by a swan-head brooch. Over that she draped her blue priestess cloak, clasped by the royal brooch of the Epidii: two filigree horses, their eyes set with jewels of amber that matched her hair. Bronze rings glittered on her fingers and white wrists, their chased designs digging into her tender skin. Her twisted gold torc was heavy, and she felt every measure of its weight dragging on her neck.

Linnet was dressed in similar finery, and when they were ready, she surveyed her niece with approval in her eyes. Rhiann's answering smile felt bleak. She understood well how such spectacle garnered respect and power, and she was not above using it to her own advantage when needed.

But deep down, she longed to be barefoot on Liath's back, with a hot sun above her, and only dandelion seed in her hair.

'It is time,' Linnet said. 'We must go.'

And as they sprinkled the goddess figures with the daily offering of meal and milk, Rhiann thought, *Great Mother, though you no longer speak to me, at least give me strength this day. Give me the courage to face what I must.*

By light of moon and flaming torch, by foot, on horseback and chariot, it was a subdued throng of nobles that took the Trade Path downriver for Crianan, where they would take ship for the Isle of Deer, just offshore. Mist rose in ghostly wraiths from the Add, and hung in pale sheets over the marshes, softening the sound of riffling water. The alders and willows that fringed the banks dripped with dew.

Gelert had set off leading the King's chariot and the bier that held the body, so Rhiann let Liath drop back. But, sunk in a chill reverie, she suddenly realized that the chief druid had appeared silently on foot by her side. 'You should be with your uncle's body, doing your duty.'

She hunched her shoulder away. 'I do my own will, not yours.'

'Always so disrespectful!' he spat, and grasped her bare ankle in a bruising grip, making Liath shy. In the jostling crowd, no one could see. 'But not for much longer, girl. I have plans for you.'

'You have no power over me!' she hissed back.

'You and I both know that's not true.' Gelert's voice was a sibilant murmur. 'You're not witless, though you make me believe so. I've watched you shirk your duty for too long. You should have given us another heir years ago, instead of sailing off to that witch camp to dig up roots and weave your petty magic.' He inclined his owl-head staff towards the King's bier.

'Now he is gone, and it is time for the snare to tighten on you at last.'

'The people won't force me to marry!' Rhiann bit out. But they were only fine words, and her fear was a live thing fluttering in her breast.

'Try them, child! Without a king we are in grave danger from the other clans – and other tribes. Danger makes people think of their own skins, not that of a pale, bony wraith like you.'

She followed his eyes, seeing the nobles of the lesser clans of the Epidii riding so high on their horses, gaudy with their wealth, proclaiming their power. She knew they were circling for blood, hungering to take the kingship from her royal clan, even as they paid their respects. One of the contenders was right in front of her, a young hot-head called Lorn, with hair so fair it shone silver under the moon. He and his father boldly raked the other warriors over with the same slate-grey eyes as they rode.

Suddenly Gelert released her ankle, and though it throbbed, she made no move to ease it.

'I am no child, druid.' She strove for control over her voice. Priestess training was good for some things, that was certain. 'You cannot force me.'

'Perhaps not. But you always were a dutiful girl. And don't think that I haven't sensed the guilt that rides your shoulder. Duty and guilt . . . a potent mix. One that will do my work for me.'

He glided away, and she pulled her fur wrap closer about her throat.

As the wailing of women faded away, and harp string, pipe and drum were stilled, Rhiann stood with Linnet on the beach on the Isle of Deer, the waves lifting the hull of the King's boat as it rolled in the shallows. Gelert's voice, distorted by his horse-head mask, rang out as he sprinkled water from the sacred spring to the four directions, calling on his gods.

The sky over the island's dark slopes was aflame with the approaching sunrise, though they still stood in cold, purple shadow. In the faint light, Rhiann saw a mother hush her babe's strident demands, and Aiveen, daughter of Talorc, the King's cousin, smiled slyly at a warrior behind her father's back. Brude's tear-streaked daughter rubbed her nose, smearing ashes on her cheek, as her mother, hair cropped in grief, bowed her head.

Suddenly Rhiann realized that Gelert had paused, and everyone was looking at her expectantly. Talorc now waited by the bier in the boat with the dead man's sword in his hands. Rhiann stepped forward as if in a dream, taking the great scabbard flat on her palms and wading into the foam to lay it on the King's body.

The water was bone-jarring cold, but Brude himself still blazed, with silk thread and exotic cloth, amber, jet and glass rings, his beard oiled and braided, his torc as thick as his wrists. Two gold coins from Gaul lay on his closed eyes. Yet as Rhiann rested the sword across him, her hand brushed his arm, and she jerked back at the chill heaviness of his flesh.

As Rhiann returned to her place she felt the force of Gelert's gaze. He smelled her fear, she knew it. She returned his look coolly, but her only answer was the glint from the mask's eye slits, under a fringe of ochre-dyed mane.

When Linnet had laid down the King's spear, Gelert took up a flaming torch, calling to Lugh of the Shining Spear to light the way to the Blessed Isles. Sparks drifted out over the water, and as the first fingers of sunlight at last spilled over the hills, Gelert bent and lit the pyre beneath the King's body.

Flames leaped into the air with a roar, fed by the pitch that soaked the nine sacred woods, and in answer to the hungry tongues of fire, the women's wailing broke out again, and the harps and pipes skirled into life. Warriors beat their swords on their hide shields, drowning out the druid drums.

With a wave, Gelert signalled to the *curraghs* that were roped to the King's boat in the shallows. The oarsmen rowed hard, and the ropes grew taut as they drew the boat offshore.

Rhiann's gaze was fixed on the smoke, unseeing. *The King was gone.*

Desperate, she wanted to reach out and pull the boat back, have him sit up again, laugh again, bellow again. *He was gone.*

The *curraghs* cut the ropes and came racing back to shore, and the blazing boat was soon no more than a speck on the water, obscured by smoke. Dread swept over Rhiann then, and with it came a fevered vision of a man, her unknown husband, laying on her, smothering her with his rank beard, stinking of meat and sweat and ale . . . She swayed in horror. How could she ever face such an attack, night after night, for the rest of her life? She would not be able to bear it.

I won't, she thought fiercely. *I'll give them what they want and then I'll leave. Or die!*

And then, something happened to sweep these bleak thoughts away in one shocking flash of light. Something . . . impossible.

A flare of crimson and gold blazed for a heartbeat, cleaving the smoke. Rhiann shaded her eyes. Then the breeze cleared the haze for one brief moment and – there – the flash came again, so brilliant and sharp it hurt. Goddess, what was it?

Abruptly, the singing and wailing died away, and Declan, the seer thrust his way to Gelert's side. People were peering out to sea, open-mouthed. The shocked silence lasted only a moment, and then a rustling of whispers began to hiss like foam over the sand. When the flash came a third time, the rustling swelled to a fearful murmur. Time was caught, suspended on the cold dawn wind.

But death was all around this day, and fear and tension were running high. And so the first cry of terror at last spilled over. 'The sun rises again in the west! The gods have come!'

'An omen!' someone else screamed.

The panic instantly caught alight, blazing through the crowd as a spark lit to dry tinder.

'The gods are angry!' a young woman wailed. 'Oh, mercy, save us!'

Warriors were wrenching spears from their shield-bearers

and unsheathing swords, unsure whether they faced a threat from Thisworld or the Otherworld. Talorc, bellowing orders, got the men into a wavering line facing the sea, and the druids clustered closer around Gelert and Declan. But when Rhiann felt Linnet grip her hand, and saw her aunt close her eyes in the seeing way, she did the same, her senses yearning towards the strange light. *Please, Mother, just this once, let me see!*

She held her breath . . . and then a swirling picture flared into life in her mind. The spirit-eye on her brow blazed with pain, and she gasped, trying to hold the scene steady. As she did, the gasp lurched into a cry of shock. For what faced them was not, as the people feared, an Otherworld sun. It was something much, much worse: sunlight reflecting off weapons and mailshirts. A boat full of warriors, shining from head to foot, with the glint of swords in their hands.

As she registered this, terror coursed through Rhiann's veins in a bright flood, so intense that she caught her breath. *Raiders! How could I let them get so close again!* Then a second thought raced on its heels. *No! The blood on the sands . . . the screaming . . . Oh, Mother, no . . .*

She heard a low moan, and realized it came from her own throat. Beside her Linnet was swaying, her grip on Rhiann's hand growing tighter and tighter until flesh lost all feeling.

The image behind Rhiann's eyes was now clearer. There was a young man standing in the bow, dark-haired, his skin brown and clear, unmarked by the blue tattoos of her own tribesmen, his face shaven. A *gael* of Erin.

The man's green cloak was swept back to expose an immense gold torc, and under the sleeves of his embroidered tunic, arm-rings shone. The mailshirt over his tunic was burnished so that it glittered, and on his brow blazed a jewel of green fire. In one hand he held an unsheathed sword; in the other a crimson shield, bright-painted with the symbol of a boar.

At last she dragged her eyes open, daring it all to be a dream. But there it was. Goddess, it was real.

The boat was so close now that those of the Epidii without the sight could discern for themselves what the gods had brought them: a battered craft with cracked mast, and inside, a score of men with fierce eyes.

And they were making for the shore.

CHAPTER 6

I n an instant, panic broke out on the beach, as women swept up children and raced for the hill-slopes above, old people stumbling after on cold-stiffened legs. Rhiann stood rooted to the spot, her knees weak beneath her. She tried to turn, and faltered, and then Linnet's firm arms were steadying her.

'It is all right,' Linnet murmured, as if she was gentling a filly. 'We are safe, daughter. We are safe.'

Rhiann tried to gulp a breath, but the panic had taken hold, and it left no room to fill her lungs. The edges of her sight wavered and grew dark.

'Stop!'

Gelert's roar split the air, and such was the ingrained fear of him that the tide of people froze. The chief druid wrenched off his horse mask, spilling white hair over his shoulders, and thrust it into Declan's hands. Then he took back his oak staff and raised it before him. Though old, he was formidable, and for the first time Rhiann felt almost grateful for that daunting power.

The *gael* rowers had stilled their own hands, and the boat now hung suspended, the leader's cloak against the sky like the first spear of grass after snow. And then the man held his hand up, with fingers open in the trading sign of peace.

'Name yourself!' cried Gelert, raising his staff. His voice carried clearly over the water. 'You disturb a soul's journey to the west!'

'I am a prince of Erin!' the man called. His voice was fair and strong, speaking a language close to Alban, with its own strange lilt. 'We have come to negotiate a trading treaty, but were caught in the storm. Please, let us land and we will talk.'

Rhiann's mind was still spinning, and yet his words penetrated the haze of shock around her. These men were not raiders, no matter how well armed. Raiders fell upon people in surprise; they did not approach a shore defended by spears, or exchange fair words. Still, her shoulders trembled as Linnet released her.

Gelert leaned into Declan and the two druids spoke, heads close together. The chief druid turned back to the boat. 'You may land, man of Erin,' he conceded. 'But only if I bind you by your most sacred oath to do us no harm.'

Without hesitating, the man laid his sword out across both palms. 'I swear on my father's honour, and that of Hawen the Great Boar, god of our tribe, that we will not raise weapons against you.' He swung the sword back down, and broke into a sudden, crooked smile, startling in the grimness of his face. 'Be assured! I would not wear such finery to attack, honoured druid. I only seek pardon for disturbing your rite.'

Around Rhiann, people who had been crying out moments before began whispering again, and now their voices held a note of . . . admiration?

Gelert stared impassively at the man, as the boat drifted closer on the incoming tide. 'So be it, bold prince! Then you'll hand over your weapons as a surety, until we feast you.'

The foreigner's smile faded, and angry murmuring broke out among his men before he silenced them with a curt gesture. Rhiann saw that they obeyed him instantly, even though many were older than he.

'My men will give up their weapons,' the man agreed, his jaw tight. The crooked grin had fled as instantly as it had come. 'And you can have my spears – but not my sword. It is worth more to me than my life.' He sheathed the blade in a bronze-tipped scabbard at his waist. The clink as it slid home echoed across the waves. 'If I touch it, strike me down. I swear that none of my men will make a move to save me.'

The other *gaels* flinched at this, though said nothing – they

40

clearly trusted him. And it was a clever reply. Unprovoked, no Epidii warrior could harm him without losing honour. And men, of course, valued their honour even more than their horses.

Gelert slowly nodded. 'Then you may land.'

The line of Epidii warriors fell back as the boat's hull grated on the sand. Talorc, a thick-set, grizzled warrior who still sported formidable arms despite his age, planted himself before the strangers to take their weapons as they stepped ashore.

Rhiann drew her cloak closer with trembling fingers, stepping back so that she was further away from these strange men. She saw the prince take a ring from his finger and hold it out. 'I give this to you for your dead,' he offered, bowing gracefully from the waist.

The rustling of approval around Rhiann grew louder. 'He speaks fine for a *gael*!' an old woman croaked.

'He came to us as the sun,' a younger one breathed. 'The gods must favour him!'

Gelert studied the foreigner before taking the ring. 'We will offer your gift at a sacred spring. The gods will look kindly on you.' He beckoned one of the novices forward. 'Take these men to the funeral hut, and send mead.' He swivelled his eyes to the *gael* leader. 'We are soon to return home, and have little food to give you beyond cold meat. You can drink, though, and then we'll speak.'

Wide-eyed, the novice led the men up the beach to a single round-house that stood on the *machair*, the flower-starred strip of grassland that edged the sands.

Rhiann watched them pass. Now that they were close, she could see the prince's clothes, though well-made, were torn and crusted with salt. Yet he held his head as if dressed in the most expensive finery, and now that the crooked smile was gone, his dark braids framed a face that seemed carved from stone. His forehead was a smooth plane, his jaw-line clean, and high cheekbones gave his eyes an exotic, slanted cast. Yet his out-thrust chin was too sure of itself, and the eyes

41

themselves were a glacial green. Then she saw the bloodless lines on his swordhand from clenching hard the horn pommel of his sword.

Ah . . . he was lying. His face dared someone to see it, as his very hand betrayed it. Someone who could lie and look so fair was dangerous. She wondered if Gelert already knew.

Behind the leader came the largest man Rhiann had ever seen. His mop of barley hair and sky-blue eyes gave him a boyish air, yet his arms were thick as young trees, and a curved scar caught at the corner of one eyelid, pulling it down slightly and scoring his cheek. A smile hovered at the corners of his mouth, which broadened when the young women crowded forward to stare at him. Aiveen, Talorc's bold daughter, was foremost among them, her butter-coloured braids swinging.

And then there came a shy youth, hidden behind a shock of scarlet hair, neck a mass of freckles. Then a bard, pretty as a girl, with cream and roses skin that was bruised along the jaw. He limped slightly, clutching his harp to his chest as if drawing strength from it. Both of these boys were too young, surely, to be away from their mothers! But then Rhiann's eyes fell on the men who followed: all hard-bitten warriors in their prime, with sinewed arms that spoke of constant swordplay, seamed with faded scars. Likewise, their armour and weaponry shone with careful burnishing, though their tunics and trousers showed the wear of the storm.

Traders. Indeed.

As the Epidii closed in behind the foreigners, Rhiann felt a soft touch on her hand. 'Come,' said Linnet, 'walking will help your body to let go of the fear.'

Until it comes again, Rhiann thought, but accepted the arm around her shoulders. After a few steps, she glanced up, bracing herself for the pity in Linnet's eyes. Perversely, though she yearned for help from her aunt, she hated to be pitied.

But Linnet's face was white, with bright spots of rose on each cheek, and her eyes had deepened to a stormy grey. She was not looking at Rhiann at all. She was staring out to sea, past the last traces of smoke from the burning, her eyes glazed.

And then Rhiann's senses caught the smallest quiver of something else in her aunt; something entirely unexpected.

Excitement.

Eremon and his men were left alone in the funeral hut, with only one guard to watch over them. It was clear that guest laws were as sacred in Alba as in Erin. Strangers must eat before discussing their business: it was a rule that every tribe from Gaul to Erin held to.

Cold meat in a cold dawn was not ideal, though better than stale bread. The others eagerly attacked the woven willow platter of deer flesh, but under the piercing black eyes of the warrior at the door, Eremon had little appetite.

The wild blue tattoos curling up the man's cheeks and around his eyes made him look as fierce as a charging boar. The effect was heightened by the long moustache that drooped over his mouth, and his hair, limed into stiff peaks. Eremon rubbed the stubble on his own chin, which was kept shaven among his people. Those blue markings must inspire fear in battle, but he'd rather keep his own face.

Conaire had no such qualms about eating beneath those fierce eyes. He ripped off huge mouthfuls and chewed noisily, and Rori, Finan and the others followed his lead. Eremon leaned in to pick some pieces for Cù, who was laying under his feet. The hound gulped the meat from his fingers, coating them in drool.

Eremon wiped his hand on his trousers and scanned the room.

Despite his estimation that the Alban jewellery was not as ornate as his, nor their swords as fine, the walls of this hut were painted with beautifully-wrought symbols, and similar forms were sculpted into the roof-posts and beams. Some were animals: he could see the horse, the boar, and the stag, so real that their muscles flowed as if moving. Other symbols were unknown shapes; lines and curves that were also beautiful, yet meaningless to him. The same symbols were painted on a high table by the hearth, scattered with pots of fragrant oils, and dried petals of meadowsweet. There, the bier for the dead person had clearly laid.

The guard moved, and the sunlight from the doorway glinted on his spear. Eremon frowned and shifted, conscious of his own sword's weight by his side. He'd been furious about giving up their weapons, even though there was little choice. Many spears had been trained on them, and from the size of the warriors they were well within range. If only he'd seen more clearly through that smoke, perhaps they could have landed somewhere else . . .

So much for simple fisherfolk.

He gnawed at his lip. It seemed he'd just brought his men from one danger straight to another. It was not the landing he'd imagined at all. And yet, the gods had brought him here, for the boat was driven helplessly before that storm. Were They plotting his glory, or his downfall?

It is a test, he reminded himself. *The gods demand proof of your bravery. Show yourself worthy, and you'll be home next leaf-fall.*

The meat was almost gone when, from outside, he heard a burst of singing and crying, a blaring of trumpets, and thundering of beaten shields. The din grew and grew, until it echoed on the walls of the house, and Cù threw his head back and howled, his eyes wild. As the noise died away to a last throbbing drumbeat, Eremon saw the Alban warrior close his eyes and murmur fervently to himself.

He did not need to ask what had happened, for in Erin they, too, drove the spirits of the dead away like this. Now the freed soul would heed the god Lugh's call to fly away to the Blessed Isles.

Soon after, a shadow blocked the doorway: the old druid who had spoken on the beach. He was followed by a servant girl, carrying a bronze-rimmed horn cup, and the heavy, older warrior who had taken their weapons – a man almost matching Conaire's size. The servant came straight to Eremon with the cup, its two handles cast as rearing horses. The workmanship was very fine, like that of the carvings, and to Eremon's surprise the ale within was also good, with a musky flavour he'd never tasted before.

He must have betrayed himself, for the druid was smiling at him. It was not a warm smile. 'Our women make the best ale in Alba. The heather flowers give it the flavour.' The druid's voice belied his age, ringing with power and authority.

Eremon nodded carefully, and the girl took the cup and turned to lift it to Conaire's mouth. She was pretty, and Eremon saw her start and blush when she caught his foster-brother's eye. After the cup had been offered to Eremon's men, the druid wasted no more time. 'Now,' he said, gesturing to a screened alcove. 'I wish to find what you are seeking here. Come, and we will speak.'

Eremon glared at Conaire, who pulled his eyes away from the girl and followed him, wiping the traces of grease from his mouth. They joined the druid and the old warrior, easing themselves on to fur cushions on the alcove's earth floor.

Eremon began, as was his due as a guest. 'I am Eremon, son of Ferdiad. My father is King of the great kingdom of Dalriada in Erin. This is my foster-brother Conaire, son of Lugaid. We come to make new trade alliances with our honoured neighbours.'

'I am Gelert, man of the oak,' the druid returned. 'My cousin Brude, son of Eithne, is King of the Epidii, our tribe. The King is . . . away, collecting tribute in the north.'

The pause was slight, and Eremon saw the Epidii warrior glance at his druid, before turning to Eremon. Around one great arm was a fox-fur band, the same colour as his hair and moustache, though they were now frosted with grey. But his blue eyes were clear, cheeks ruddy with health. 'And I am Talorc, son of Uishne, also cousin to Brude.' He folded his arms on his barrel chest, chin thrust forward. 'You are right to seek us out, prince, for we are the foremost tribe on this coast, with many riches.'

I did not seek you out, and I see few riches, thought Eremon, keeping his face still. *And where, in truth, is your king?*

'I am surprised,' he said out loud. 'Your death rite was for a man of great standing, it seems – yet your king is not here?'

Gelert's yellow eyes glinted with anger. 'You seek trade alliances, you say?' he barked.

Eremon blinked in surprise, and nodded.

'Then your storm gods drove you to the right place, prince. Our fortress of Dunadd rules the trade route this side of the mountains. We exchange with the tin tribes in southern Britannia, and those on the Northern Sea. What can you offer us?'

Eremon took a deep breath: at least he was ready for this. 'The gold you see is only a part of our wealth,' he explained, throwing open his cloak to reveal his ornate belt and jewelled dagger-hilt beneath his mailshirt. 'Our rivers run with it, and the hills are seamed with copper. And I have men joining us with more examples of our skill. We will call on tribes all over Alba.'

Talorc's eyes were resting on the jewelled circlet on Eremon's brow.

'Of course, gold is not all,' Eremon continued, smiling. 'We have plains of barley and rich cattle herds, for our land is warmed by milder winds than yours. And we make many other things: our craftsmen are famed the world over.'

At this, Talorc could not help himself. 'So! We have the best deermeat, the finest hunting dogs, and the warmest hides!' He thumped his chest. 'Our sheep give much better wool than yours – and our women are, of course, the most beautiful.'

'I'll be the judge of that!' Conaire broke in, grinning. 'How about I show you the quality of my sword – and your women the fineness of another weapon altogether!'

Talorc's face twitched, then he chuckled and slapped his leg. 'You jest well for a *gael*,' he laughed. His eyes gleamed as he took in the breadth of Conaire's sword-arm. 'I wonder if you can fight as well as you make jokes, young colt! I was cattle-raiding when you were pissing in your *bracae*! What say I give you your sword back, and—'

An abrupt movement from the druid silenced him. Gelert was raising himself to his feet with his oak staff, frowning. Eremon saw the knobbed end was carved as an owl's head, with eyes of glittering jet, and as the druid leaned on it, two pairs of pupils seemed to fix on the prince. 'I'm sure my cousin appreciates how little time we have for such ... pleasantries. Come with us across the water to Dunadd. There we can feast you, and talk more.' His cold gaze swept Eremon from feet to head.

Caught in that druid net, Eremon felt a sudden, childish impulse to take his men and run. Run where, though? Such discourtesy would win him nothing except suspicion. No, he was being foolish. He must trust to the Boar. The breaking of hospitality laws was unheard of, and these people were not savages, plainly, no matter what the fisherman had said.

'Thank you, we'll come gladly,' he found himself saying. 'But ... you go by sea?' He could not hide his body's sudden remembrance of that roiling hull.

Gelert smiled thinly, as if he sensed the sickness that lurched into Eremon's belly. 'This is only an island: Dunadd lies across the strait to the east. We'll give you guides for your boat, for there are many rocks in the Bay of Isles. Talorc will see to it.' He turned to go, and then paused. 'One more thing. We cannot speak of the dead man for one moon. Respect this, and ask no questions.'

Eremon nodded, his face stiff.

Once Gelert was gone, the air seemed lighter. Talorc clapped Conaire on the shoulder and jumped to his feet. 'Come,' he said. In contrast to the druid, his eyes were guileless; the pale blue of a winter sky. 'Our servants will make ready for a while yet. Let's not waste the ale!'

CHAPTER 7

Eremon was glad the day had unfolded so fair, for his men came close to mutiny when he said they must take to the water again.

'It is an island,' he explained, as they clustered around the hearth in the hut, cups in hand. Talorc had left to speak to the Epidii nobles. 'There is no choice.'

'How do we know we can trust them?' This was Finan, gruff as ever.

'We're under guest laws now,' Eremon replied, with more confidence than he really felt. 'They will hold to this, as we do. And there's another thing.' He drained the dregs of his ale. 'They think I have more men coming, and that my father is a powerful ruler. They wouldn't risk a blood feud with a king.'

'They will when they find out there's no king.' Colum rubbed ale-foam from his stubbled chin.

'Then we make sure they don't find out. Look, without allies, the Boar knows how long we might remain fugitives, fighting for our lives instead of building our strength. How can I win my kingship back then?' His eyes rested on them all, one by one. No one argued.

They left the hut and crossed the sands to their battered boat, past the suspicious eyes of the Epidii warriors, and the speculative looks of their women. On the way, Eremon's attention was caught by a bloom of flame along the dark rocks that cupped the bay, and he stopped as his men carried on without him. The painted *curraghs* were being burned!

Though born and bred a warrior, Eremon had always had,

48

in his father's eyes, an unmanly attraction to the mysteries of the druids. If he'd been a commoner he might have followed that path, though any such tendencies had been driven away by Ferdiad's beatings. So he stood and watched the burning for a moment, intrigued that something so beautiful was being destroyed.

Suddenly he became aware of another standing nearby who also watched; someone with the unmistakable air of a druid, draped in a sapphire cloak, its hood up. Struck by an impulse, he opened his mouth to ask what the symbols on the boats meant, and why they were being burned.

But before he'd uttered a word, the druid whirled to face him, and he saw snapping blue eyes, huge in a white face, and a nimbus of the most extraordinary hair. 'Keep your hands off me, man of Erin!'

Her voice cut through him like a shard of ice. No one had ever looked at him like that, with blazing eyes in a face of such tense coldness. Women did not look like that. Not at him. Gaping, he stood there like a fool, as she clutched her cloak closer and hurried away. *By the gods, have I insulted a druid? How? Why?*

Conaire was suddenly by his side. 'Eremon, I've been calling! We have our guides and we're waiting for you.' A loud belch sounded in Eremon's ear, and then Conaire paused, watching the slim figure retreating down the beach. He cocked his head at Eremon and chuckled. 'You don't waste time, my brother.'

Eremon shrugged helplessly, and put the encounter out of his mind as he followed Conaire to the water. Their boat was already afloat in the pale shallows, and one of the Epidii guides was directing some of Eremon's men to hold it steady while the others boarded.

A pack of curious children jostled each other in the foam, and further back, young women eyed Eremon with interest, whispering behind their hands, as he waded through the water. He placed his sword carefully in the boat and hoisted himself in, and the women's murmuring grew louder. One of the Epidii guides shot him a sullen look.

'I am not used to your local speech.' Eremon's voice was friendly as he stowed his blade and settled to the oar. 'What are they saying?'

'They call you mac Greine, lord.' The man's voice held a hint of scorn. Plainly, he thought little of the women's fancies.

Mac Greine. Son of the sun. Eremon did not know whether to be flattered or embarrassed, for that was a name given to the god Lugh of the Shining Spear. Then he shrugged to himself, practicality winning out. If they were in awe of him, that was no bad thing.

And, though he was sorry for startling the druidess, if some were afraid of him, then that was no bad thing either.

The Alban boats were timber built, as sleek and curved as spear points, with painted animal prows. The horse was foremost among the carvings. What had Talorc said over the ale? *We are the People of the Horse.* It was a noble creature indeed – Eremon just hoped that this tribe lived up to its totem.

Despite his concerns, he could not help but feel excited. Behind him lay great darkness, and he would have to face the pain of it all soon. Too soon. For now, though, they were on an adventure in an unknown land, with a new day's sun in their faces and swords by their sides. The Boar knew what glory might come his way here; what paths might open . . .

Steady on, my boy. Just focus on getting home.

His eyes were drawn west, to where Erin lay over the horizon . . . Erin, his land, his love, with her rounded, lush hills and soft winds. A stab of longing pierced him, but then he shut the door firmly in his mind. He could not go back, not yet. The time would come, one day, and it would be the right time, under the right circumstances.

He caught the eye of the other Epidii guide, a friendlier man than the first. His skin was seamed and burned by the sun, and his face had the characteristic squint of someone who worked on the sea. Perhaps he was a fisherman.

'What island is this?' Eremon asked.

The man grinned, pleased to be superior. 'The Isle of Deer.'

'Ah.' Eremon shaded his eyes to peer up at the hazels and oaks crowding the island's glens. 'I've heard of this place even in Erin. Exceptional hunting, I believe.'

At mention of the hunt, Cù's ears shot straight up, and he looked at Eremon with a longing that was matched only by that on Conaire's face.

'Is this true, man?' Conaire demanded.

The guide nodded.

'A spot of spearwork with the dog is just the thing to right my belly!' Conaire crowed, delighted. 'When can we go?'

Eremon smiled. 'Let's get to Dunadd first.'

'Aye, but I'll take you soon,' the fisherman promised, eyeing Conaire's great arms with ill-concealed envy. 'There, the boars are so big that even you, young giant, will have trouble pulling them down!'

'You are blessed with riches!' Conaire exclaimed.

The man shrugged, his face flushed with pride. 'We are under the protection of Rhiannon and Manannán both. Rhiannon is the Lady of Horses, rider of the White Mare. She gives us the best mounts in Alba. Manannán fills our nets with fish and brings the traders.'

'We, too, revere our Lord Manannán,' Aedan put in helpfully.

The man twisted on his oar bench, sizing him up. 'Is that so? Though I bet you haven't seen the Eye of Manannán, as I have, harper! It is close now – perhaps you'll hear it roar!'

Aedan's rosy cheeks paled, and his grey eyes widened. 'An eye that roars?' he whispered. 'What is that?'

'A whirlpool,' came the devastating reply. 'It'll suck you down and spit you out in the Otherworld! You'll never come back here, to be sure!'

Aedan paled even more, and Eremon regarded him with frustrated affection. He would have preferred to leave the youth behind, for this was no journey for the faint-hearted. But Aedan leaped into the boat as they fought to leave Erin, and would not be moved. 'You are going to glory, lord!' he declared. 'And I will be there to sing your praises, and to bring your deeds back to Erin, so you are never forgotten!'

A hail of Donn's arrows unfortunately cut this stirring speech short, and in the rush to escape there was no time to argue. Now Aedan was here, though, he must do his part. So Eremon stared at him steadily, seeking to put into his eyes what he could not put into words. 'Aedan, why don't you go and liven the men up? It will keep their minds off their bellies.'

Gratefully, Aedan scrambled to his feet and joined Eremon's men in the stern. Soon the strains of his harp floated across the bow, the playing fine but not up to its usual standard.

At the first pull on the oar, Eremon's new blisters broke, and he had to grit his teeth against the pain. Then, just as the boat began to skim over the waves, he felt a queer, tingling sensation on the back of his neck. He threw a glance over his shoulder to the boat just ahead – and saw a white swan's prow, and beneath, a figure in a blue cloak. Then they cleared the rocks, and the open sea was slapping the bow in the rising breeze, and a cascade of icy water rushed over his hands.

Conaire was laughing next to him. 'You know, I could get used to this!'

Ever since the unexpected arrival of the *gaels*, Linnet had been withdrawn. Rhiann spoke with her on the beach, but her aunt's conversation had been desultory, her mind clearly elsewhere. So once the boats were on their way, Rhiann settled beneath the swan prow and retreated into her own thoughts.

Staring into the water, she wondered again how Linnet could have been *excited*, of all things. These foreigners had brought Rhiann only fear – she could still feel the aftershock of the trembling in her limbs. And then that lying brute nearly touched her on the beach. She shivered, despite the warmth of the sun on her face, and forced herself to sit a little straighter.

She could not wait to clear the sheltered bay, for the sea always calmed her. As the crystal water deepened to blue-black, laced with broken kelp, Rhiann drew the salt air into her lungs and slowly let it out, closing her eyes. The control she had to exert in public was becoming increasingly fragile. She longed to be home, where she could bury herself in bed and shut it all out.

A cry floated down from above, and she glanced up to see a curlew beating its slow way towards the marshes around Dunadd. Its voice was mournful, lonely, and she tried to lose herself in it, to send her spirit up into the air with the bird. For a moment it almost worked, and she started to drift away . . . away from her body with its hurts . . .

Then she realized that her mind was in fact anchored most firmly in her skull, and her eyes were fixed on the boat shooting up behind: the one with the men from Erin. She was close enough to see the copper glints in the leader's dark hair where the morning sun caught it. And again, she tasted the terror that had clawed at her when he nearly touched her arm.

A warrior who lied. A child murderer, a violator of women, like all the others.

Suddenly she saw the man turn, as if he could hear her. Impossible!

She frowned, twisting away to lock her gaze on the blue haze of the mainland hills, and the sun pouring through the wide cleft that sheltered Dunadd's plain. When she glanced back, the boats had drawn apart, and the man was no more than a blur of leaf-green and glittering bronze on the sea.

By the time the fleet neared the shore, Eremon's boat had slipped to the rear. Dunadd's port, Crìanan it was called, was no more than a cluster of piers and roundhouses squatting on a spur of rock. To its south, a river unravelled as it reached the bay, slicing the marsh and mudflats into ribbons of dark water.

But Eremon saw the advantage of its position immediately. Curls of surf showed the swell rolling in from the sea to the north, but the port lay on calm water, sheltered by a curving arm of land. Across this bay, a palisaded dun looked down on it with watchful eyes from a high crag.

'Is that Dunadd?' Eremon asked.

The fisherman shook his head, smiling. 'That is the Dun of the Hazels. Dunadd is up the river; you'll see.'

Eremon peered past Crìanan's piers, the crowding houses, and the *curraghs* and dugout canoes scattered on the tidal sands. Try as he might, he could not see the royal dun, only wide expanses of bronze sedge and scarlet reeds.

Dunadd.

He had heard the name in Erin: it was indeed of some trading renown. What awaited him there? He realized he was on his feet, his muscles tensed as if they wanted to spring. Or run.

The boat ground against the pier, its timbers slippery with green weed, and his men jostled to get to dry land, Cù in their wake. Eremon let them pass and held himself back, for a sense of foreboding had suddenly come upon him, like a cloud over the sun. Cù checked his headlong rush after the men and stopped, looking back at his master.

And it was as Eremon stood there, poised between sea and sky, that the icy breath of fate touched him. He suddenly knew, in his heart, it was not a joyous adventure that awaited him here. Something else wanted his allegiance. Something he would not be able to resist.

He froze. He'd not set foot on Alba yet, so perhaps this fate was not sealed.

The Epidii guides were throwing rope around pilings, and hailing those who had beached their boats. No one noticed him. He glanced over his shoulder to Erin again, hidden behind the islands, and then back to Alba's shore.

Cù whined softly, and Eremon closed his eyes, telling

himself he was being ridiculous. The salt breeze ruffled the hair at his temples, and he breathed the familiar scents of dung and peat and baking bread. It was just a place; a place like any other. How Conaire would laugh if he knew his fears!

Slowly, his breath whistled out through his teeth. Then, without pause, he forced himself to leap on to the pier, and take his first steps on Alba. *By the Boar, it's all nonsense!* he chided himself. *The sea sickness has addled my mind!*

He broke into a run, cuffing Cù around the ear as he hurried to catch up with his men. Talorc was waiting to take them to Dunadd.

Eremon's first glimpse of the Epidii dun was in clear light, so he witnessed the full effect of the gold-thatched roofs on its crest and the flying banners, warmed by the ruby glow of the marshes that surrounded it.

It was impressive, by design. The King's Hall was exposed to the full force of the sea-wind, but spectacle was far more important than comfort. Dunadd's builders well knew how their dun would look from afar.

The thudding feet and hooves of the party of Epidii nobles ahead raised flocks of teal to wheel in the air, skimming low over the moss and sedge to land in a scattering of marsh pools. The only firm ground was the path that followed the river, which had been laid with hard shell and gravel until it shone pale under the falling alder leaves.

As the path brought them closer to Dunadd, they could just make out a scarlet banner flying from the highest roof-tree, and when the wind caught it, Talorc cried, 'See there the White Mare of Rhiannon, emblem of our Royal House!' Yet Eremon caught the glimpse of a frown marring that bluff face.

Dunadd's palisade was broken only where the sheer walls of the crag made attack impossible, and even the pier, tied about with punts and canoes, was built into a whaleback of rock that reached out to the river. This dun was a mighty jewel indeed – and it looked as if it knew this, standing proud and lonely above its marsh.

'Have you seen anywhere placed so well?' Eremon breathed to Conaire. 'A single rock bounded by bog, with clear access to the sea?'

Conaire's eyes sparkled as he looked up at the rock face. 'A worthy challenge! We'd be spitted like pigs before we gained the walls!'

'Taking it by force is not what I had in mind,' Eremon said drily.

The Trade Path ran up to a gate that was guarded by twin towers. On entering the village, Eremon expected to be engulfed by the noise and smells of a busy dun: the ring of smiths' hammers and squawking of geese; children crying, women calling. But though there were people about on the pathways, the dun had a subdued air, and there was little evidence of anyone labouring at the granaries or in the multitude of worksheds. The murmuring groups of people fell quiet as the men from Erin passed under the shadows of the gate, and people stared, toddlers hanging wide-eyed on their mothers' skirts.

Talorc hurried them past the people clustering by the gate. 'The stables are there.' He waved to one side. 'You'll find that we are the best horse breeders and traders in Alba: we've an eye for fine blood. And there, you see the sheds of the armourers and iron-smiths.' He stopped and hooked his hands in his belt, cinched under an ample belly. 'Your sword is very fine, prince of Erin, but perhaps your young lads,' he smirked at Aedan and Rori, 'could do with a sturdy helmet or two. You may not find our neighbours so friendly, and some of them can bring a sword down faster than a bull can come, eh?' He jabbed Rori in the ribs with a forced jollity, and the boy blushed and ducked his head.

'Our own swords are fast enough, thank you,' Eremon responded firmly.

'Well, here's the bronze-smith, then. You're not the only ones with fine craftsmen, as you'll see.' He turned to Conaire and clapped him on the back. 'Maybe you need an amber hair pin for your lady back home, son of Lugaid!'

'I'll need more than one, then!' Conaire replied, grinning.

Rhiann left Linnet at the stables with her mount Whin, and made her way to her own house. Brica was outside, hopping from foot to foot with excitement. 'I've heard about the strangers, lady. Where are they, then? What do they look like?' She craned her neck, squinting through the gaps between the houses.

'I think they're down in the village.' Rhiann lifted the doorcover, and the maid followed her inside. 'It's nothing to be scared of, Brica. They're a trading party, that's all.' She unpinned her cloak and drew it from her shoulders.

Brica sniffed as she took it; the closest she ever came to contradicting Rhiann. 'Well, Fainne said they were from Erin and had many swords and spears. I wonder what they're doing here?' Her black eyes darted about as she hung the damp cloak over the loom to dry. 'Maybe they want an alliance? Or perhaps they—'

'I'm sure we'll find out soon enough.' Rhiann was suddenly exhausted. 'The Lady Linnet will be here soon. Have you brewed tea?'

'It's here.' Brica bustled around with the iron pot, pouring out two cups and setting it back on its tripod over the coals. The sour tang of blackberries wafted up on the steam. Then she took up a wicker basket. 'I've made mutton stew, and Nera has baked the bannocks. I'll go and get them and you can eat.'

At a nod from Rhiann, Brica disappeared outside.

Rhiann wandered to the hearth, and stirred the cauldron suspended on its chains over the fire. The nobles must be gathering in the King's Hall now, and soon, too soon, there would be a council.

But who would be the next man to be declared king, to stand on the slab of rock at the summit, one foot in the carved hollow, the stallion hide around his shoulders? A man from another clan, who forced his ascendancy with bloodshed? Or a son of her own? He would be a baby in the arms of a regent, although still the rightful king. Neither possibility was welcome to her.

She pulled up her stool and was sitting with her hands around her cup, when Brica burst back through the door, bread spilling from her basket. 'The watch cry has gone up, my lady,' she panted.

'What of it? And why have you been running?'

'Everyone is running, mistress,' Brica gasped out. 'There is a warrior in full gallop on the south road. From Enfret's dun, he is, and he bears the banner warning of attack! I heard the watch send a guard to the chief druid!'

Rhiann caught up her cloak once more and hurried to the King's Hall. There she met Linnet in the stream of people who were squeezing through the Horse Gate, for though this day they were in mourning for King Brude, news about the *gaels* had drawn many from their houses. Everyone wanted to see the gold that adorned the newcomers.

Together, she and Linnet managed to push through until they were close to Gelert and Talorc, who were standing with the men from Erin outside the hall, watching the rider approaching the village gate below.

As the messenger reined in and leaped to the ground to begin his run up through the village, Rhiann saw Gelert narrow his eyes against the glare of the sun. Declan the seer, hands clasped on his crescent staff, was also frowning. Whatever the message, the seer was worried – it did not look good. Rhiann's heart started to skip again.

At last the crowd parted for the man, and he threw himself down on one knee before the assembled nobles.

'Well?' barked Gelert, 'What is this haste for? What has happened?'

The rider could not get his words out, his chest heaving from his run. His trousers were spattered with mud, his tattoos smeared with sweat and dirt. Gelert made a sharp gesture with his hand to still the murmuring of the people around him.

'We have had news from the Damnonii to the south, my lord,' the man finally gasped out. His eyes were wide with fear.

'What news?'

'It is the men of the Eagle – the Romans!' the man cried. 'At last they have crossed into Alba!'

CHAPTER 8

Gnaeus Julius Agricola, Governor of the Roman province of Britannia, was well satisfied.

The Alban evening was unseasonably fine, and his body slave tied back the flap of his tent so that he could watch the camp going up around him. To an untrained eye, the noisy bustle of soldiers, slaves, carts and mules was chaos. To Agricola, this hive of activity was perfect order.

Hundreds of leather tents were sprouting up in rows on the plain, and between and about them, thousands of legionaries were unpacking bed rolls, lighting cook fires and digging waste pits. Far off he could see lines of men, as tiny as ants, hoisting baskets of earth on to their shoulders as they carved the ditch to encircle the camp. Rearing above the columns of diggers, the stakes of a half-complete timber palisade cast long shadows across the turf.

In the falling dusk, Agricola watched his chief engineer correct the position of a newly-erected tent. The soldier he spoke to shrugged and bent down to knock out the errant tent peg with his mallet, and Agricola's mouth firmed in approval.

'They're getting better by the day, sir,' said the engineer, coming over to his commander. 'We've nearly halved our building time.'

The man was portly, with a thatch of dark hair that never lay flat, a bulbous nose, and a quivering, extra chin. He was a figure of amusement to the other officers, and only his exceptional technical skills kept him under Agricola's command.

'Thank you, Didius.' Agricola scanned the ramparts. 'Your new gate design is working well – the extra time is worth the added security, and the further north we go, the more we'll need it.'

Didius swelled with pride, as Agricola reached behind himself and cracked his knuckles, stretching his shoulders. They were stiff after the long ride, although getting looser every day. He was nearly back to condition. The creeping softness around his waist had been stripped from his lean frame in the first weeks of marching; though not so for Didius. Agricola glanced at the man's paunch with distaste. It seemed to have a strong tolerance to exercise.

Now the engineer's attention was caught by a shout at the camp gate. Some of the mule trains at the rear of the army had bunched up, and were milling around, blocking the entrance. Tutting, Didius hurried away, his scarlet helmet-crest waving in the breeze.

Agricola closed his eyes and sniffed the heather blanketing the hill-slopes all around. There was something about this land, cold and wet as it often was, that got into the blood, even more than his last posting in Asia Minor.

And things were progressing better than he'd hoped. The Emperor had just this month sent new orders for Agricola's push into Alba – an imperative if they were to call the whole island of Britannia their own.

Ah, and wouldn't it be fine when it was theirs? It had taken thirty-six long years to subdue the wild British tribes, and with the fall of Wales, the land from east to utter west was Roman. Now it was time for the north. Leaving it to the barbarians would be a thorn in the Emperor's side; it was not to be borne.

So in one rapid strike, Agricola had penetrated deep into Alba, the spear thrust of his attack reaching as far as the River Tay, before he pulled back to the friendlier shores of the Forth inlet. Behind this line, the tribes were subdued. Only the Selgovae tribe had resisted, until the ballista bolts did their work on their great hillfort in the south. It fell with few Roman lives lost; a satisfying result.

For the rest, the ambitious Alban woman who had offered herself to the Roman cause had ensured an easy advance. Under her influence, the eastern tribes surrendered to their new ruler, and opened their lands for his armies to march straight through. Now 5,000 of the best Roman soldiers were camped on this bay, gaining their strength, for the conquest from here on would not be as easy.

'Father!' came a voice from his tent. It was his son-in-law, Publius Cornelius Tacitus. 'Come back in! I've only got as far as your advance on the Ordovices. They would not come down from their western mountains, so you went to them . . . and then what?'

Agricola remained at the door, leaning on the tent pole. The soft evening beckoned, its warm breeze nudging away the sudden memory that blew in with Tacitus's words: of freezing winds and whirling snow during that long winter campaign, two years before. 'We killed them all. You know this already.'

'Yes, but it may end up as the only record we have, so I need detail. Did the chiefs really have enemy heads on their spears? How close was the fight? How did you win?'

At last Agricola turned, regarding the youth with impatience. Tacitus was seated on Agricola's camp stool, feet on the folding map table, scribbling on a pile of vellum sheets. One finger was black with ink.

'We killed them all.' Agricola ran a hand through his clipped hair. 'That is as accurate as I can be.'

'Oh . . . very little fighting then.' Tacitus sounded disappointed.

'All the better, since it freed me to turn my attentions to the north.' Agricola came to the table and began flicking through an untidy pile of letters. 'And here we are. So, now you're back in the present you can get down to real business. You offered to be my secretary, I recall.'

Tacitus sighed, and uncurled his body to dig through the

letters, before proffering one to his father-in-law. 'Here is a dispatch from that fat old man at Lindum. He says that construction of the forum has been delayed by rain.'

Agricola raised an eyebrow, fingering the broken wax seal, and Tacitus held up his hands. 'I know, I know! I should not speak of our learned procurator so. But honestly, Father, it rains all the time in this country – since when did that hold anything up? If it did, nothing would get done. He's just wasting too much time with that German whore of his.'

'As you pointed out, don't speak so of the man.' Agricola read the letter.

Tacitus threw the other dispatches down with a sigh, then gave Agricola a winning smile. 'Can we eat now? I'm starving. I'll go through the rest of these later.'

'So long as you do it tomorrow. I'll not have you getting behind.' Agricola beckoned to the slave lighting an oil lamp by the camp bed, for within the tent, it was growing dark. 'Send a message to the legates that I will dine with them tomorrow, and order us some food. And find the lady – I wish her to join us.'

The slave bowed and left, and Agricola turned to catch a frown on Tacitus's face. 'Don't look at me like that, boy! You know why I entertain her. She's the reason we've conquered these lands so easily.'

The youth's frown deepened. 'She's a witch, not a lady,' he muttered. 'I don't trust her. And I don't—' He caught himself, compressing his lips to stop the words.

'You don't like me laying with her?'

Tacitus shifted uncomfortably; Agricola let him. He never felt the need to explain himself to anyone, and he was not about to start. The youth would have accepted his argument that the dalliance with the woman was wholly political, and gave them valuable information about Alba, for he shared Agricola's passion for conquering the north – or at least for writing a glorious tale about it. Tacitus would not understand the other reason, though: that these northern witches provided a relief Agricola's wife could never give him, Juno bless her. And this one was better than any he had come across.

'You don't have to stay,' he offered, idly scanning another letter. Tacitus was silent, looking mutinous.

Then a honeyed voice flowed into the space between them. 'You asked for me, my lord?'

The voice was dusky, speaking lilting Latin, and the woman's colouring matched her tones: hair as black and glossy as raven feathers, eyes of ebony. She wore the simple dress of her people, but her lush, rounded curves robbed the plain robes of their modesty.

Without taking her dark eyes from Agricola, she unpinned her cloak and handed it to the waiting slave, then walked in front of the new-lit lamp. 'My lord,' she murmured to Tacitus, bowing her head. She'd positioned herself so the light came through her fine linen shift. From where he was, the boy could not fail to see every part of her outlined in all of its glory.

Tacitus was far from stupid. He grabbed the unopened letters, and with a terse nod to Agricola, swept from the tent. The woman smiled slowly.

'You shouldn't intimidate him like that,' Agricola said.

'Oh, I can't help it! He's too prim!' She pouted.

'He's also family, and a tribune. You should give him the respect he deserves.'

Her pout grew deeper, until at last Agricola smiled. He was struck, as always, how a face that escaped true beauty could be so seductive. A droop at the corner of each eye gave her a heavy-lidded look, and those obscenely full lips diverted attention from a snub nose.

A second slave had arrived with the evening meal: roast duck from the marshes, barley bread and Egyptian figs, washed down with Gaulish wine. Behind him a third slave carried a steaming basin of hot water, fragrant with bog myrtle. Agricola gave the woman a seat on the bed, and they picked at their food as the slave washed their feet. Footwashing was a custom of the British tribes; the only one Agricola approved of.

'Does this cursed ground ever dry out?' He watched the water in the basin swirl with mud.

The woman waved dismissively with one hand, while placing figs in her mouth with the other. All her appetites were strong, it seemed. 'If you would not wear such shoes! Let me get you a pair of our boots. They are sheepskin: fleece inside and hide outside.'

Agricola shook his head, as the slave wiped his feet dry. 'Good, solid Roman issue is fine for me. I won't have my men thinking I'm going native. You yourself are problem enough.'

Her smile was arch as she reached out to stroke his leg. 'You won't get rid of me, though, will you? I make you happy.'

'In bed, yes.' Agricola did not flatter himself that this witch found him attractive. He was nearing forty, and a beaky nose, greying hair, and the deeply-lined face of a soldier were not what pretty young women desired. She wanted his power, that was all, and he knew it. In his life he'd seen this a thousand times. In the imperial courts of the madman Caligula and the despot Nero there'd been many such people, fed by an unending lust for power. She thought she ruled him, when in reality he would merely play with her until he'd had enough of both her body and her information. His interest in one of them would wane soon enough. He wondered, idly, which one it would be.

Her smile faltered. 'Come now, I make you happy in other ways! It was I who opened the gate to Alba for you. If my people resisted, you would have had to fight for every step!'

This was true – not that he had any intention of admitting it. 'Your assistance is always appreciated, madam, although I reward you well enough.' He touched the ring on her finger. It was an intaglio, a garnet carved into the head of Mercury. His other gifts included the best Samian tableware and fine glass goblets, and amphorae of olive oil, sweet wine, figs, and dates. He knew she lusted after such civilized things, and that this supply of goods would assure her loyalty for a time yet.

He rose to the table, took up a creased parchment and a stylus, and sat back down, unrolling the map on to his lap.

'We are here, on the south side of this inlet, is that so?' He pointed his stylus at some crude lines on the scroll. It was not a Roman map, but had been pieced together from reports by the Greeks, who received their information from the Phoenician traders before them.

The witch looked at the map, a slight frown touching her soft brow. 'Our lands end here,' she ventured, pointing. 'The tribe on the other side of the Forth are the Venicones.' She gave a tiny, smug smile. 'This is what I came to tell you. My messengers have just returned. It seems your little raid, and my . . . persuasions . . . have convinced the Venicones leaders to surrender.'

Agricola nodded, reaching out for his wine goblet. Although he was pleased, he took the news lightly. The minds of these barbarians were like quicksilver, and what they said today rarely applied the next. Yet if it was true . . . it would just make his eventual success easier, that was all. 'And what of the peoples beyond the Tay?'

The woman's eyes flickered, and Agricola fastened a cool hand on her wrist. 'Tell me the truth. My scouts will find out soon enough, and then our . . . partnership . . . will be over. Understand me?'

Her cheeks flushed, and silently amused, he watched her bring herself under control. When she was angry her eyes darkened to glittering black beads. It was most diverting. He released her wrist.

'I have little news,' she finally admitted. 'North are the Vacomagi, the Taexali – and the Caledonii. There is a weak link there, which I am pursuing, but it will take a little more time.'

Agricola sipped his wine thoughtfully. He already knew that the Caledonii tribe would be a challenge. By all reports, they were so powerful that the Greeks used their name for all the peoples of Alba.

The oil lamp sputtered in a stray gust of wind that crept

under the tent flap, and he looked into the leaping flame, tapping his stylus on the map. Vespasian's last orders were to group on the banks of the Forth. The territory to the south would remain in check, thanks to the witch. However, further north and west was another matter. He'd heard that the Highland tribes sported tattoos on their faces as fierce as their reputations.

He must send a full report to the Emperor, before awaiting further orders. Vespasian may even want to come and join him for the final push, to be there when they reached the limits of Alba and claimed all of it for the Empire. In the meantime, there was always much to do. They needed a full assessment of the terrain, a population survey of the conquered lands, and a reliable system of local food supply.

He briskly rolled the map back up. The army had been on the move for two seasons, and they'd be glad to halt for a while and build more permanent quarters.

The woman was looking around her with that studied nonchalance she often used. Abruptly, he smiled and touched her hand. Rapid mood changes were disconcerting, he'd found, and made people easier to control. Under his fingers, her skin was warm and smooth. He gestured to the slaves to take the food and leave.

The woman was smiling too, now. When the tent flap fell back into place, she took the map from his hands and placed it carefully on the table. She knew how much he valued his maps. Then, while he lay back on the bed, she took down her hair, dropping the jewelled pins into the bronze bowl by his bed, one by one. He found the faint chimes strangely compelling.

At last her hair was around her shoulders, a fragrant mass of ebony silk that reached her waist. 'Are you still hungry, my lord?'

At the purring note, Agricola pulled her down across his lap. 'I have not even begun to satisfy my appetite.'

He was surprised to see a flash of real lust in her eyes. With all of her Roman sensibilities she was a barbarian at heart, then. As a people they were ruled by the uncontrollable fires that burned in their souls. He had learned to quench his own fire with cold will, but this the tribes would never do. That was why Rome would always triumph.

In a moment, these thoughts were banished from his mind, as she sat up and stripped off her shift, guiding his hands to her heavy breasts. When she straddled him, he was enveloped in a swathe of her hair.

It smelled of the moors around them.

The lamp-flame was low and flickering when a sound at the tent flap brought Agricola instantly awake. He recognized the voice of Tacitus, speaking to his door-guard. With a hint of irritation, he eased himself from under the woman's body, and pulled on his discarded robe.

When he raised the flap he glimpsed Tacitus in the gloom, and a figure behind him with an imperial insignia on his arm. Then his son-in-law moved into a pool of torchlight, and Agricola saw his stricken face.

A thousand cries of alarm sounded in his mind. Was it his wife? His daughter?

'What is it?' he demanded.

'It is our Divine Father, Vespasian.' Tacitus was hoarse with grief. 'The Emperor is dead.'

CHAPTER 9

How much do we know?' Linnet patted Liath's nose, as the horse eagerly snuffled at her fingers.

Rhiann was leaning on the mare's stall, her cheek pillowed on one hand. She shook her head. 'Not much yet. The new messenger is up at the King's Hall. I sent Brica to find out what's going on. I just could not . . .' She shrugged.

'I understand.' Linnet reached out and tucked a stray piece of Rhiann's hair behind her ear.

The whole dun was ablaze with the news of the Romans, but amidst it all Rhiann just felt sick. The sickness had settled into a hard knot deep in her belly. It wasn't fear of the invaders, though. The King's death and the dread that came with it had muffled the alarm around her, and left her in a cold cocoon of her own making.

Next to her, Linnet sighed. 'I should have told you before, daughter, but I did have hints of this.'

Rhiann straightened sharply. 'You knew about the Romans? And you never told me?'

Linnet hesitated. 'I didn't *know*,' she stressed. 'I heard it in the tremors in the land, in the cries of the birds – but it did not come to me in the seeing bowl. You of all people know that you rarely see what you wish.'

Rhiann stared at the sun falling through the stable door, and blinked as it blurred. 'Then have you seen anything of me, my fate, aunt?'

Linnet averted her eyes. 'No, daughter.' She grasped Rhiann's hand where it rested on the stall. 'But whatever comes, I will be there for you, always.'

Rhiann heard the note of fierceness, and looked down at the elegant fingers entwined with her own. Linnet's nails were stained with traces of some berry dye, and on one finger her gold priestess ring glittered.

She knows something. A flare of hurt bloomed in Rhiann's chest.

After the raid and the murder of her foster-family, Linnet had held Rhiann on countless nights, stroking her hair, forcing down the bitter draughts that brought her back from the edge of darkness. But once Rhiann was out of danger, a gulf had opened between them, a gulf wrought by secrets and duty. They were not a mother and daughter. Linnet was a priestess, and saw things Rhiann did not; felt things that must go beyond human love. She knew that the tribe must have its heir.

How Rhiann wished she were a child again, following Linnet through the woods as she named each plant, told her what powers it had, what sickness it could cure. No man had darkened her horizon, then. No man . . . no Romans, either. They were always just a tale for the fireside, not real people at all.

Suddenly, Brica's shadow fell across her face. 'The men of the Eagle are building camps,' the maid burst out, clenching and unclenching her hands.

Rhiann let her breath out and looked up. 'What?'

'I was outside the King's Hall, and I heard everything. The Romans had been marching quickly, but just as suddenly, they've stopped. They are building a big camp with walls. They mean to stay, but they can't move around in the snows.'

'So.' Linnet straightened and moved into the light. 'Thank the Goddess: we have a respite.'

The men from Erin had been offered all the comforts given to high-ranking visitors – plentiful meat and ale, and soft bracken beds in the guest lodge. But for a week, Eremon's trade meeting had to take second place to the Roman threat.

The council sent its own scouts south to gain more news, and discovered that the Romans had indeed halted, and were building long-term quarters. After the first shock, the tribes of Alba had been given an unexpected breathing space.

The Epidii druids sacrificed a white bull to the gods in thanks for giving their land a long dark that lasted for many moons. No troops could move through the mountains in the snows and storms, not even on horses.

But rest, the tribe could not. When the icy rivers that fell from the mountains thawed, and the sun came north again, so would the Romans.

Another storm wrenched the last leaves from the trees, leaving a haze of bare branches along the river. But though it remained heavy with cloud, the days fell still once again, and Gelert sought out Talorc where he was inspecting his new chariot team along the water meadows.

'I wish you to take the *gaels* hunting on the Isle of Deer.'

Talorc frowned, and pulled the harness tighter across the black stallion's chest. 'But I should stay here, to guard the dun.'

'Take a small band of warriors. Our scouts are now posted in a circle around the Romans: we will have advance warning if they so much as sneeze. But this is just as important.'

'Why?' Talorc adjusted the snaffle, and the horse shook its head and smacked its lips. 'We have enough food.'

Gelert's golden eyes reflected the shifting clouds above. 'I have an idea to safeguard the tribe, and it requires that we take the measure of this foreign prince. Now listen . . .'

And the two heads, one red, one white, moved closer.

Conaire was delighted that they were finally going to see the fabled Isle of Deer, and Cù was so excited when he saw them making new hunting spears that he ran rings around himself, barking furiously.

'This will be more like it! I am so bored with all this talking!' Conaire squinted down his ash spear-shaft to check its straightness. They were settled on deadfall logs along the riverbank, under a sky bruised with cloud. The evening air carried the first bite of cold from the north.

'Yes, I know,' Eremon agreed, chipping bark from his shaft with his knife. 'But don't you think it's a strange time to send us hunting, when they don't know what the Romans intend?'

'I don't think so.' Conaire grinned at him. 'After all, word is that the invaders are staying where they are. So we get to throw a few spears into a boar, and then come back and do the same to Romans. Hopefully.'

'Fighting Romans was not part of my plan.'

'Ah, but you told me you wanted us to prove ourselves to the Albans, to gain allies here. That is the plan, isn't it?'

'Well, yes.'

'Then what better way to do that, but to kill some Romans for them!'

Eremon smoothed the fresh, white ashwood with a finger. 'I've thought of that myself, brother. And yet, we know that the Romans fight differently, which makes them so hard to defeat. They have discipline . . . they make their warriors act like one beast. I don't like the thought of putting my men in such danger, and all for someone else.'

'This is just the chance we need! And, anyway, don't you wish to see them fight? You studied those scraps of Greek about their tactics enough. Don't you want to see them?'

Eremon sighed. 'Yes, but . . . I wanted time to get established here, time to run things my way. I don't want anything to happen too fast. The Romans – we are talking about war, Conaire!'

Conaire rested his spear-shaft across his knee and picked up a stick to throw for Cù. 'I can't see it coming to that, Eremon. They'll just stamp around with their swords, make a few declarations, and then leave.'

Eremon had to laugh. 'And since when do you know so much about Romans?'

Cù brought the stick back, panting, and Conaire threw it

into the river reeds. 'It's what I've heard around the dun. Look,' he put his hand on Eremon's shoulder, 'try as you might, you can't plan everything. We've got to take things as they come. I say that we grasp at anything that brings you closer to your own hall – why else did we come to Alba? We've been lucky this far. And we can just as soon die in a cattle raid as in a battle with Romans.'

'Or of sea sickness.'

'Or of loneliness.' Conaire clasped his groin. 'I need a woman soon, or I'll die!'

They sat in silence as Cù came running back and then raced off again after the stick. 'I still think it's strange, this hunt,' Eremon added, picking up an iron spear-point and hefting it in his fingers.

'You think too much. They just want to get us off their hands. And we'll be bringing in meat – the last of the season, probably. Let's just enjoy it while we can.'

Eremon did not answer, but as he fitted the point into the new shaft, he was uneasy. He would be glad when they were back, and he could get on with the real reason he was here.

Which meant, of course, that he had better think of one.

CHAPTER 10

Rhiann opened one eye, glancing at Linnet's tranquil face in the purple dawn. They were walking the barley strips closest to the dun, blessing the fallow soil to let it sleep safely until leaf-bud came. Breath misting the chill air, they stepped down the furrows, harvest stubble crunching under their feet.

As Linnet had taught her, Rhiann tried to feel the Source, the universal fire of life, running through the soles of her feet, surging up from the soil. She strained to still her mind, to send her awareness down into the earth.

Imagine that you are a tree, Linnet had told the child-Rhiann, years before. *Your roots go deep into the ground, and there they find water. The Source is the water, and it flows beneath and through all things: earth and rock, tree and spring, beast and man. When you want to feel it, turn yourself into the tree, reach your roots into the ground. And you will connect, and feel it running through you . . .*

Rhiann tried and tried, picturing her legs as the roots. But the joining with the land did not come. Perhaps it would help to seek for the voice of the Mother herself. She closed her eyes, but again, it was the memory of Linnet's words that came.

The Source wears many faces, of many gods and goddesses. We call on Rhiannon as guardian of mares, Ceridwen in childbed, Sulis at the spring, and Andraste when our men go to war. But the mystery is that they are all one, child . . . an energy of Mother, the Goddess-of-all . . .

Striving with all her heart, Rhiann sought for the Mother

touch she had felt so many times before ... sought and strained ... until her eyes flew open, and she had to stop herself from crying aloud in frustration.

It was no use. Every time she tried, she was met with the same deadness. It was something else that she had lost since the raid, along with her seeing.

She pulled her wool cloak closed as a sharp gust of wind caught it. *If the Mother will not speak with me, then She has not forgiven me yet. When I've paid the penance for Kell's life, for Elavra, for Marda and Talen, for not saving them, for not getting there in time ... then She will return to me. She must.*

There was the thudding of hooves on the Trade Path, and as she looked up, startled, a party of warriors galloped by on their way to Crìanan, a pack of yapping hounds at their heels. Near the back, she caught a glimpse of the blond giant from Erin, a brace of hunting spears in his fist.

And by his side, a darker head that turned as they passed.

The hunting party returned after four days.

Gelert was in the blacksmith's forge with Belen, a tribal elder, surveying their stocks of spears and shields, when the shout went up from the watchtower. They both emerged into the smoky dusk to see a wavering line of men tramping through the gate. And then they saw what led them.

Four hunters carried a litter of willow branches tied with rawhide, and on it lay a man. As the party came closer, Gelert could see who it was: Conaire of Erin, face pale, golden hair lank with sweat, swaddled in cloaks. The prince held one hand, and his dark head was bent close to Conaire's mouth. He was so intent on the injured man that he did not look up as they passed Gelert, but although Conaire was unconscious, the druid could see that he breathed.

Gelert did not know whether to be satisfied or disappointed. Conaire showed no fear of the druid kind, from what he could see – and that made him dangerous.

He squinted, looking among the men for Talorc's great bulk, his mind racing. Perhaps Conaire had disgraced himself.

That would deal a blow to the prince's pride – which was certainly excessive. Maybe it would put the young buck in his place, and show him how much he needed Gelert's support.

The druid studied the other faces in the hunting party. The Epidii warriors were triumphant, shoulders heavy with leaf-wrapped haunches of boar meat, bloody spears in their hands. But the Erin men were downcast: a blow had befallen them.

Gelert was intrigued. Would this benefit his plan? Were the gods extending their favour once more?

Talorc was before him now, cheeks smudged with wood-ash and smelling of sour sweat. Bristles clung to his faded hunt tunic, and there was blood on his brawny arm – boar blood or man's blood, Gelert could not tell. He raised his eyebrows, taking in Talorc's flushed, excited face beneath its red moustache.

The rest of the men followed the litter up the path, and they were left alone with Belen.

'What happened?' Gelert demanded.

Talorc swung his shield over his shoulder and leaned on his spearbutt, smiling broadly. 'Ha! A thieving raid, Lord Druid! Those cursed Creones were in our hunting grounds. We came upon them late yesterday as we were leaving. We were outnumbered, but what a rout! Killed ten, we did. That Eremon lad – by the Mare, you should have seen him fight!' He broke off coughing, hawked, and spat into the mud at his feet.

Gelert gripped his staff with impatience. 'What are you talking about?'

'A drink first! Can hardly swallow.' Talorc peered around him, then cocked his shaggy head at a passing servant. 'Girl! Get me an ale, quickly!' The girl scurried off to the nearest house.

'Tell me what happened!' Gelert snapped. 'Was the son of Lugaid wounded in the raid?'

Talorc's smile faded. 'Ah, no, poor lad. The boar got him, yesterday morn. It was a huge male, and it charged Mardon.

76

Conaire jumped right in front: fair took the tusk to his balls, it seems.' He shook his head. 'Sad business, but odds are the Lady Rhiann can put him right. At least we can feast on boar for some time . . . Ah! Good.' This last was to the girl, who had reappeared with a horn cup. Talorc gulped down most of the ale before pausing with a great sigh, his lips flecked with foam. 'Now, where was I?'

Gelert's voice was quiet. 'You are about to tell me that the prince bravely killed the boar, I suppose.'

Talorc's face cleared. 'Why, yes – spectacular kill! Flew in a rage when Conaire went down, he did – I've never seen such a spear cast.' He paused to swig the ale again. 'Straight in the eye,' he added, between gulps, 'dead before it hit the ground.'

'What about the raid?' Belen broke in, eagerly twisting the encrusted rings on his thick fingers.

Talorc handed the empty cup to the servant. 'Well,' he gave an impressive belch, 'as I said, we were on our way back across the island. We'd wrapped Conaire up, and butchered the boar. Then suddenly we heard voices; a crew of Creones bucks, not taking too much trouble to keep quiet, I can tell you! Well, the Erin prince came up with a plan I could not have bettered myself.'

I can well believe that, Gelert thought, holding his impatience in check.

'Hard as steel, that one,' Talorc went on. 'His brother bleeding everywhere, and there he is, suddenly cool as can be, laying a plan to give those upstarts a beating they won't forget! We ranged ourselves out among the trees, and Eremon took to the path to challenge them, single-handed. Three attacked at once, the cowards! He lured them by retreating, and they raced after him . . . and then we poured out of the trees and fell on them!' He shook his spear. 'You should have seen the fight! Of the ten we killed, half were Eremon's trophies – and not a wound on us. They broke and ran. Ran! Can't remember when I've had so much fun!'

Belen leaned in, the fox-tails falling forward from his fur

cape. 'Talorc, what do you think of the prince now you've seen him at close quarters?'

Talorc's face was still bright with their success. 'He brought us honour, and showed courage. He's smart, too, and fights like the god Arawn himself.' He nodded slowly. 'I would rather have him and his men by our side than not, when the Romans come.'

Belen sank back on his heels, and threw a satisfied look at Gelert.

Now it was clear that Talorc was itching to be away, for the news of the raid had already spread. Throwing his checked cloak over his shoulder, he made his excuses and strode back down into the throng of people gathering at the gate tower. Soon Belen and Gelert could hear his voice booming out the tale, as his wife hung, big-eyed, around his neck.

Belen looked up at Gelert. 'Strange times, Lord Druid, strange times. Can it be the gods have sent us such a man at this time of need? A man of great ability, it is clear. Your talk of a good omen is proved right. I will call the council together, and we'll hear the tale in full.' He hurried away, his short, bulky figure disappearing into the dusk shadows between the houses.

Gelert opened his mouth to call him back, then shut it again. This was what he wanted, wasn't it? He had said to the council that the arrival of the men from Erin was a propitious omen. For he had many reasons to encourage closer relations with Eremon of Dalriada.

Deep in him, wisdom warred with avarice. The wisdom whispered that this Eremon might prove difficult to control. The twin calamities of the King's death and the Roman threat had provided Gelert with a rare opportunity to finally exert his full power over the tribe. In their terror, they were like children, looking for a father's protection. But, Gelert was a druid not a warrior. For him to become the real power behind the throne – to steer the tribe's fortunes, to be King in all but name – he still needed a man with a strong sword arm. One who owed him much; one who would depend on the Chief Druid's backing to make his name.

Yes, he needed a strong man . . . but not a hero.

Doubt writhed in his heart, until avarice rose, reminding Gelert how powerful he himself was. The prince was a beast that wielded a sword well, that was all. He was merely a warrior. He could be as easily directed as a man directs oxen at the yoke.

And then there was the girl, Rhiann.

Proud and scornful, just like her bitch mother Mairenn, who'd looked at him with the same contempt when she threw his marriage offer back in his face, all those years ago. And the girl was likewise a priestess, and equally disobedient and wilful, always preening with her so-called goddess power.

Well, he wouldn't make the same mistake with *her*. She would be yoked to the plough early, for his gods had whispered the source of her suffering, and how to increase it until she could no longer raise her face to scorn him with those blue eyes.

Mairenn's eyes.

Ah, yes, the prince could become quite a useful weapon. At this, avarice finally triumphed, and Gelert left, wondering how soon to take the young man aside.

The carvings on the gate that led to the crag flickered shadows across Conaire's pained face. 'Take us to your healer's house, quickly!' Eremon cried to the Epidii men who took over the litter. He was so intent on ensuring that they did not jostle his foster-brother that he took no notice of where they were going. Then the bearers were laying the litter down on the ground, and he looked up.

They were outside a small roundhouse near the crest of the dun, and a woman was emerging from the covering over the door. Eremon knew that hair, those fine features, from the day of his arrival.

She is the healer? He should not be surprised; many female druids were healers, after all. But she looked so young and frail; she could not be more than eighteen. Would she be good enough to save his brother?

Without a glance at Eremon, she went to kneel at Conaire's side, taking his hand. She felt his pulse, sniffed his breath, checked his eyes, and finally peeled back the pad of torn wool, sticky with blood, that covered his groin. The boar's tusk had in fact just missed Conaire's most precious organ, and gone deep into the upper thigh instead. At her probing fingers, Conaire stirred and cried out in pain, and his eyes opened.

The woman looked up at Eremon, and in place of the cold eyes on the beach, he saw the professional frown of a healer. 'How long ago did it happen?' she asked.

'Nearly two days, now.' Then the words burst out: 'Can you help him?'

Her frown deepened, and all she said was, 'Take him inside.'

Eremon barely noted what the inside of her house was like, but was conscious somewhere that it smelled different, earthier, the air tinged with the strange, sharp scents of herbs and ground roots.

The woman was confidently issuing a stream of orders to a little, dark serving woman, to put water on to boil, and to gather linseed and moss and bandages. He helped to ease Conaire on to a small pallet in an alcove divided from the rest of the room by a wicker screen.

It was crowded now, with Finan, Rori and even Aedan milling around helplessly, until the servant shooed them away, scolding like a small, wiry crow. At length, only Eremon and the healer remained by the bedside.

Eremon leaned over Conaire, his hand gentle on his brow. It was the first time his foster-brother had been conscious since crossing the strait from the island, when the boat was tossed by waves, and Conaire, groaning, had thankfully slipped away into a faint.

'When I said we should prove our strength, my brother, I

did not mean that you must try to kill yourself.' Eremon said it lightly, but his chest was tight.

Conaire tried smiling, his forehead sheened with sweat. 'I thought something big was needed.' His voice was hoarse, and he broke into a cough. 'It was a good leap.'

Eremon squeezed his shoulder. 'Yes, it was. But now I want you to put the same effort into getting well.'

Conaire could only close his eyes in exhaustion, and Eremon looked up to find the druid watching him closely, as she soaked a cloth in a bronze basin by the bed. 'You've got to help him,' he said, heedless of the plea in his voice. Let her think him weak; right now he did not care.

She answered him bluntly, but her hands were gentle as she laid the cool cloth on Conaire's forehead. 'The wound itself is not serious, otherwise he would be dead by now. But . . . wounds from the boar often turn bad. I do not know why. This is what we must fight.'

Conaire's eyes flickered open again. 'It has been long since I gave to the Boar, Eremon. Perhaps He is angry . . .'

Eremon picked up the hand that lay limply on the blanket, and held it. 'Then I will sacrifice for you! I will give him so much that his eye never falls on you again, except with favour!'

Conaire tried to smile, but the smile turned into a wince as the wound cramped again.

'I will do all I can for him,' the woman murmured. She hesitated. 'It is best for him to have quiet now. Go and make your sacrifice. The shrine is at the brow of the hill. And I will pray to the Mother of All, the Great Goddess.'

Unhearing, his eyes still on Conaire's face, Eremon muttered, 'I thank you,' and rushed off as if he did not have a moment to lose.

The night was long, as all nights were when Rhiann had this particular fight to win. The fire, banked higher than usual, threw ghoulish, leaping shadows on to the walls. But she was lost in her own world, and did not notice Brica replenishing the water, or bringing her more moss pads, or clearing bloody bandages.

This role Rhiann fulfilled gladly. To her healer's soul, all patients were equally in need of care, even this . . . this invader, this man. She had only to use her knowledge. She did not need to deal with her heart at all. It was simple. And she did it well, for this skill had been left to her. She still had this.

She murmured the required prayers over steeping golden-rod and yarrow, and sang as she ground ivy in her mortar-bowl. The man, now drenched in sweat, tossed and cried in delirium, giving long, tortured speeches about betrayals, and battles, and Erin. She listened closely, intrigued, but could make no sense of it. Did his wandering mind speak of myths long gone, or his own past?

When the wound was cleaned and packed, she dribbled sorrel in sour milk between his lips, seeking to bring down the fever. She knew that although the poison was bad, this burning was the hungry consumer of men's souls. She had seen it happen many a time, even from slight wounds.

At least this man was strong. His arms were thick, his chest wide, his midriff lean and packed with muscle. And unlike the men of her own tribe, this man's skin was smooth and hairless. For some reason this brought her a flash of memory, a memory that had not passed the borders of her mind for many moons.

Few men had she seen like this, and only one had she touched when not a healer, many years ago, back on the Sacred Isle. She felt her face flush. And why did *that* thought arise now, of all times?

She dragged her gaze to her patient's face instead, pushing the memories away. He was younger than she had first thought him, with only a faint stubble of beard on his chin. In fact, now that he was in repose, he looked little more than a harmless boy, with a soft mouth that could even be called innocent, if she ever thought of men that way.

Then her eyes fell on the white seams of scars on those

great arms, and the curving score on his cheek, and she shivered. He was no innocent boy, this one – no poet, no artist, like the man in her memory from the Sacred Isle. This man was a killer.

Just like his prince.

CHAPTER 11

Eremon hardly left Conaire's side for days. The only other place he frequented was the small shrine on the crag's crest, where he exchanged some fine finger-rings for the daily sacrifice of a ram.

It was there that Gelert sought him out in the freezing dawn.

Eremon was on one knee before the wooden image of Cernunnos, his sword across his lap. Clouds crowded in over the lip of the open roof, swelling with rain. He looked up at Gelert's step and started, before getting to his feet. 'You do not worship Hawen, our Boar God,' Eremon said, gesturing to the idol, half-embarrassed. 'But your druids told me that this is the Lord of the Hunt, and we revere him, too.'

'Come.' Gelert threw the tattered edge of his sheepskin cloak over his shoulder. 'I wish to talk privately, and the view is fine from here.'

The old man led Eremon through an archway opposite the main entrance, and out on to a rock ledge that faced west, towards the sea. They edged past a rough-hewn stone altar, smaller than the one inside the shrine, stained dark with blood that was a black crust in the dank sunrise. There, against the shrine's outer wall was an oak bench, and Gelert sat himself down and gestured for Eremon to do the same.

The marsh was still floating in mist, and from the exposed mudflats at the river mouth came the lament of a redshank, and a wavering line of geese that rose and flowed southwards. Gelert sat straight and still, so still that the only movement was his breath stirring the wisps of his white beard. Eremon decided to say nothing: the druid could break the silence first.

'You conducted yourself admirably on the boar hunt,' Gelert observed at last. 'Our people cannot stop talking of you – your bravery, your daring. I, however, was particularly impressed by your strategic abilities with the Creones bucks.'

Eremon was taken aback. The last thing he expected from Gelert was praise. 'Well, I . . . it is no more than I was trained to do.' He was at a loss for anything better to say.

'Ah, yes, your training.' Abruptly, Gelert turned to Eremon and fixed him with both eyes. They glowed like coals in the shadow of the pillars. 'I am no fool, young man. I know very well that you are hiding a secret.'

With every shred of control he possessed, Eremon forced the sudden surge of guilt away from his face, and instead put in place a puzzled frown. 'I don't know what you mean, Lord Druid.'

'Oh, I think you do. But, be assured – I am not going to ask you what it is.'

Eremon's belly uncramped, though he thought it best to stay silent.

'I can see that you are a noble's son.' Gelert waved that away as if it were of little importance. 'Your skill with weapons, your command of your men – these would be enough, but with my druid eyes I see it written into every line of your bearing, and the pride on your face.'

He said this last with distaste, and Eremon could feel himself bridling at this casual dismissal of his breeding, which he held more important than anything else. For it was, of course, all that he had now. 'I *am* a king's son, as I said. And I'm here to trade, as I said, but if your council does not meet with me soon, I will be forced to go elsewhere.'

'Yes, the question of trade.' Gelert closed his eyes, gripping his oak staff, and his voice dropped into the sibilant tones that druids used whenever they were pronouncing prophecies. The hair on the back of Eremon's neck rose. 'But there is this. You may be a king's son, but behind you I see a darkness,

Eremon of Dalriada. Something that chases you before it, that rides your shoulder like a war crow. A different reason for your arrival on our shores.' He opened his eyes, and his voice returned to normal. 'I have not discovered what your secret is yet, but I soon will. You would not like that, would you?'

Eremon's heart was hammering now, but he only said, 'I don't mean to offend, Lord Druid, but I really have no idea what you mean.'

Gelert smiled. 'I leave the trading to others, boy, but I have a . . . *proposal* . . . to make to you. You value your secret very much. And I can promise that not only will I not reveal it to anyone, but I'll protect you from any attempts by others to discover it. And make no mistake,' he leaned forward until Eremon could smell his old breath, 'I am high, very high in the ranks of the druids of Alba. You will find no better ally than me.'

Eremon could not believe what he heard, but if he said anything, he would betray himself. He realized that his hands were clenching Fragarach's fine scabbard, the chased boar design digging into his skin, and he tried to loosen his grip.

'And in exchange?' Gelert answered his own question. 'Why, strangely enough, you don't have to give anything away in this deal, for I am going to give you yet something else. Honour beyond your wildest dreams.'

Eremon had to know. 'What,' he said slowly, his tongue dry in his mouth, 'are – you – talking – about?'

But Gelert was not quite ready to come to the point, and he sat back again. 'I have a truth to tell you, prince. I was waiting until I saw what kind of man you are. But you will already have guessed. The man we were sending to the west on the day you arrived was our king, Brude, son of Eithne.'

Eremon had guessed, and wondered again why the druid had lied. Kings die – but surely the Epidii already had another king picked out, whoever he was.

'I did not want you to know this at first, for his death has, alas, made us weak. Four moons ago the warriors of our royal clan were in the south on a cattle raid, when a plague struck.

It took our king's chosen heirs – all of them. There is no man of the royal blood left who can be king – no one young enough, skilled enough, unblemished. If Brude's line dies, then the rival clans will fight each other for the kingship. My kin, Brude's kin, will be dispossessed, but even worse, the tribe will be riven from within. We cannot afford that, not now the Romans approach.'

Eremon was surprised at this tale.

'I will be blunt,' Gelert said. 'I see this darkness of yours, this secret, and I won't ask you what it is. But you are not here to trade. You have come to win a name, I can smell it. You want to prove yourself, and I will give you the chance. We need your people's strength against the Romans, and your own at Dunadd to stop our men from killing each other. We need a war leader, a man who can head our clans, who belongs to no clan.'

Eremon felt a rushing around him, and his mind reeled. He could hear, as an echo, what he had said to Conaire: *I don't want it to happen too fast.*

'So look me in the eye and tell me this one truth, boy, and I'll let it be. Do you have the men at arms to help us, as you've boasted? Will you give your sword to protect us from the Romans, and keep stability within?'

Never had Eremon's powers of guile been so tested, as when he had to look into the owl eyes of a druid such as this, and lie. But his life, and those of his men, depended on it. *Hawen, my Lord, please aid me now, if you never do again!*

And the swelling cloud above spilled over, and a few cold raindrops spattered into Gelert's eye. He reached up to rub them away, breaking their gaze. Eremon took a breath, and focused on the last question, and he knew he could answer that one truly. For Conaire had said to grasp the chance, and his twenty men, though few, could certainly help against the Romans. His skills could be used to hold a tribe together – it was what he had been trained for all his life!

'If I so choose,' he said at last, clear-eyed, 'I can.'

Gelert had been blinking, frowning, but at Eremon's words his brow smoothed.

'You spoke of a reward,' Eremon pointed out, brushing rain from his own forehead. 'For supporting you when my own shores are not in danger.'

Gelert's laugh was a bark. 'You mean something more than keeping quiet about you?' He leaned back into the shelter of the pillars, his gaze penetrating. 'Then apart from my silence, here is the fruit I dangle before you, Eremon of Dalriada. I come here today to offer you the hand of our royal princess.'

At this, Eremon was truly speechless, his mind a blank, frozen rock that could absorb nothing.

'But wait!' Gelert added. 'The king's bloodline runs through his female kin. You will not be a king yourself: only the sons of a royal woman can be so.'

'But what about your own princes? Why not choose one of them as a suitor?'

'We always choose outsiders to wed our royal women. It has been so for generations – it strengthens alliances to other tribes. Brude's mother was an Epidii Ban Cré, but his father was a prince of the Trinovantes in the far south.'

Something else began to penetrate the shell around Eremon's mind, and as if he followed his thoughts, Gelert added, 'Yes, this means that a son she bears you will be king. But he will only be of his mother's blood: his allegiance only to us.'

A king! Eremon's heart could not help but leap.

'Of course, what we want from you is more immediate. The union with our Ban Cré will make you our champion, our war leader, someone to lead us into battle. It is far too dangerous a time to allow the warriors to fight over that honour. But if we install you . . . our problem is solved.'

'But . . . you don't know my lineage, high though it is. You don't know my people. How will your council agree to this?'

'Our need forces us to be less prudent than we would otherwise be. And there is the manner of your arrival. I have convinced them that you were sent here by our gods. And we have seen you fight. It is enough, for now.'

Eremon shook his head to clear it, and Gelert leaned forward. A light drizzle was now falling, catching on his hooked nose. 'Do you have many grades of the marriage union, as we do?' At Eremon's nod, Gelert went on. 'Then the ceremony will take place as a binding to the fifth grade only; a year-marriage, a handfasting. It can easily be severed if you prove unfruitful. In leaf-bud, when the sea lanes open again, we can send to your father. If all is well, and we are happy with the confirmation of your lineage and bridal gifts, then we will make the marriage binding, to the ninth grade. A royal marriage.' He fixed Eremon with one yellow eye. 'Make no mistake, only the Roman threat would ever make us act in this haste. It took me a long time to convince the council to agree. It was your fighting prowess that turned their hearts, for they are desperate. But we will be watching you closely.'

Eremon was too dazed by what he had been told to wonder why the druid bothered to argue for him at all. 'What if all does not go well with my kin?'

'If you have lied, then we lose little.' Gelert was blunt. 'We will be stronger then, anyway. And hopefully our royal lady will be breeding.'

Eremon heard a new note in Gelert's voice just then, a most undruid-like spite, but he was too preoccupied to care about it. *So, they want me for my loins and my sword.* As the druid said, this surpassed his wildest dreams. Had the Boar sent him here for this very reason? It had to be! He desperately wanted to talk to Conaire about it. 'How long do I have to decide?'

'A day only. It is a great honour.'

'And if I say no?'

Gelert pursed his lips, surveying his domain. 'Then we'll bid you farewell, prince, and send you on your way.'

Eremon doubted that very much indeed. Gelert would discover his exile, and he and his men would be vulnerable to attack by the other tribes – and even by the Epidii. They had seen his gold, after all.

As he rose, he turned his face from the stinging rain, which had now begun to blow in from the marsh. 'I'll give you my answer tomorrow.'

'Tomorrow, and no later.'

Once Conaire was out of danger, the Erin men had been moved into the King's Hall. Brude's wife had returned to her kin with her daughters, and the house had been purified with sweet oils and fragrant smoke. At the time, Eremon wondered why this honour had been bestowed on them, but after Gelert's offer, he thought he understood.

That day he chased the myriad servants out of the hall so that he could tell his men what had transpired in the shrine. Conaire, who was resting on a fur-covered pallet by the central hearth, let out one long, low whistle.

'Well?' Eremon said.

All eyes turned to Conaire, who shifted his bandaged thigh. A boar tusk gleamed on a thong around his upper arm. 'It seems that Hawen has given us just the chance we need, brother.'

'But I'm committing us to fight the Romans!'

'It will win us more glory than any cattle raid!' Rori burst out, hardly able to contain his excitement.

'We'll be throwing in our lot with one tribe.'

'You told us that it would be the best thing.' Finan scratched his head. 'And kin bonds are stronger than trade alliances. You'll be able to call on all the Epidii kin bonds, too. Seems a good offer to me.'

'It means no trekking around in the long dark,' Colum put in – he was known for his fondness for good food. 'Who knows how long it will take to forge an alliance with another tribe?'

'But much more important than that, you'll be the father of two kings!' Aedan breathed, his eyes alight. 'You'll sire a king here, and another when you take your father's hall back. A dynasty on both sides of the sea!'

Eremon could see Aedan's mind scrambling for a song to do justice to such an idea, and despite his misgivings, he felt his own soul stir with the thought. A dynasty in Alba and Erin. Surpassing his own father. And his uncle. 'Please tell me what's wrong with this idea,' he begged faintly. No one heard him, as they fell to wondering about what it would be like to become part of the Epidii.

Eremon gazed around the King's Hall. It had been built to inspire awe. The roof-cone soared to an apex six spear-lengths above, and beneath it lay the hearth that twenty men could stand in, with iron spits to roast whole boars, and bronze cauldrons as big as bathing pits, suspended on chains. Around the hearth curved an immense ring of benches, on which they now sat, covered in soft furs and embroidered cushions, and bright hangings swept down from the rafters. No man's heart could fail to swell with the thought of ruling this domain: feasting kings, planning raids . . .

So what was wrong?

The druid's offer was the perfect solution to his problem. All he had to do was ensure that Gelert did not discover the truth next leaf-bud. And perhaps it would not matter, then. If he was in a strong enough position, perhaps he could weather that particular storm. After all, the old man might die. The girl might be barren.

And there was a thought – he had not seen her yet! Among all this talk of siring and kin bonds, he would be getting *married*. To another person. Someone he had to share a house with, a bed. No one seemed to have thought of that. It was easy for them to apportion him out as if he was a fine stallion. What would he have to say to a *wife*?

Conaire caught his eye. 'It is the chance we were looking for, brother.' His face, which had been pale since his illness, was glowing. 'The Boar provides. And Manannán brought us here on the storm! It is the best thing for all of us.'

The best thing for all of us.

Yes, that was what mattered. 'I suppose you are right,' Eremon conceded. 'It's not a trap, after all, is it?'

'No! The betrothal can be broken, once we don't need it any more.'

So Eremon agreed with his men that he would take the hand of the Epidii princess.

Whoever she was.

CHAPTER 12

'We wish to marry you to the prince of Erin.'
The words crashed into Rhiann's skull, and were tossed from side to side as if in a whirlwind. She stared up at Belen from her hearth-stool, nerveless fingers dropping the heavy spindle into her lap. At the grain quern, set on the floor by the door, Brica stopped grinding and knelt back on her heels.

Then Rhiann's eyes fell on Gelert, stooping to enter her house, and she saw triumph chasing eagerness across his face – an eagerness to see her pain. She would not give him that. She rose, clumps of unspun wool falling from her skirts. 'And when will this marriage take place?' Her voice hardly betrayed her, as she gripped the edge of her loom.

'In three days,' came Belen's devastating answer. He checked at her expression, and added hastily, 'It is to the fifth grade only, lady. When the sea paths open, the prince will send to his father, and at year-end we will conclude the full rites then, if you are willing.'

Outrage replaced the fear in her heart. 'And when exactly were you going to tell me?'

Belen paled slightly beneath her glare, and gulped nervously, his eyes straying to Gelert.

'My lady is aware of the urgency to strengthen our position,' the chief druid put in smoothly, leaning on his owl staff. 'You are overdue to be married; you know we have only been debating where to bestow your hand.' He smiled.

'But you do not even know this foreigner, this *gael*!'

'We know he is a fine fighter and leader of men, lady,'

Belen offered awkwardly, spreading his hands. 'We know he has many riches. The druid confirms he is who he says he is.'

The loom dug into her hands. 'But . . . but you did not consult with me! I do not know what kind of man he is!' She saw the blankness on Belen's face: he, like all the elders, would think this of no consideration.

'We deem this man worthy of your rank,' he answered, frowning. 'And most importantly, he has the abilities and men-at-arms that we need so sorely. We don't only have the Romans to contend with, as you know, lady. The other clans will come baying for the kingship soon. We are desperate.'

This tug on her guilt was enough to dampen Rhiann's anger, and she found her mind stumbling, yet again, over what was best for the people.

Duty. Fear. Pain.

Then one thought of self-preservation came clearly through the rest: *You must appear to agree.*

She bowed her head. 'I will make my preparations,' she murmured, not looking up until the door cover fell back into place. Then she gasped for breath, pushing her forehead into the sharp talons of the carved eagle on her roof-post.

'My lady!' Brica cried, jumping to her feet. 'The Goddess will have Her vengeance if they force you! In the old days the queen would choose her consort, and then another if she wished . . .'

'But it is not the old days any more.' To her own ears, Rhiann's voice sounded dead, and far away. The next thing she knew she was on her way to the stables, and the healer in her realized that she was in shock, real shock, for this was what the numbness was.

Distantly, she heard the cries of children playing in the tanner's yard, and from behind the forge came the squealing of a pig, the sound abruptly cutting off. She stumbled through the dyer's shed, sharp with the smell of urine, and then she was at Liath's stall.

She had no riding trousers or cloak, but it did not matter – before she could form a coherent thought, she was on the mare's bare back and nosing her through the outer gates of the village. No one stopped her, but again she felt their eyes.

Her ears folded, Liath kept to a sedate walk until Rhiann was well out of sight of the dun, held by the hands in her snowy mane. But the mare must have felt the tension in her mistress's legs, the taut muscles across her back, and once released from Rhiann's hold she was away, flying through the bare fields, north towards Linnet's glen.

Once alone among the dying bracken of the brooding hills, the fear of this day, so long denied, at last broke free from Rhiann in an anguished gasp, the strangled sound of her heart, her secret heart. But as Liath's legs drummed faster and faster, leaping out from beneath her, the gasp became a moan, and then swelled and sharpened into a cry of rage that wrenched itself from her throat, cleaving the air.

Dimly, Rhiann felt the wind clawing at her bare thighs, but the ache was nothing compared to the sheer agony of helplessness. She, who prided herself on her courage, her strength, could do nothing. She was trapped: by duty, by guilt and shame. Trapped by men who saw her as no more than a brood mare.

Then Liath was slowing to a stop, and Rhiann looked down to where her hands were clenched in the frosted mane, and they were wet with tears. Shakily, she slipped to the muddy ground beneath a dead oak furred with lichen. Liath blew her sweet breath on Rhiann's face and lowered her head to lick her legs, which were trembling from cold and the strain of gripping the mare's back.

Rhiann buried her face in the horse's warm neck, and let the tears come fully in the wake of the rage.

By the time she cantered into Linnet's yard, the wild outpouring was over, leaving behind a steely anger. 'How dare they?' she muttered, pacing the floor of Linnet's tiny, low-beamed hut, as her aunt stirred tansy tea over the fire. She whirled. 'Did you know they were planning this?'

'Of course not!' Linnet poured the water into cups and set

them to cool on the hearthstone, then offered hesitantly, 'Is he so bad, this man? He is very fair, and not old at all. He is noble. It could be wor—'

With one look at Rhiann's face, Linnet broke off.

'Any man, any marriage, is hateful to me!' Rhiann cried. 'You know this! There could only ever be one, and even then—' She bit off her words, appalled at herself.

But Linnet's senses were sharp. 'One? You mean there *is* a man?'

Rhiann gritted her teeth, shook her head. '*Was*, not is. It is nothing, a child's fancy, that is all.'

'No.' Linnet held her eyes. 'Tell me.'

Rhiann shook her head again. 'The man who tattooed me at my first bleeding, on the Sacred Isle. But that was years ago!'

Linnet sat down wearily in her wicker chair. 'Daughter, the skin painters are *meant* to rouse the girl, for it imbues the sacred symbols with power.'

'I know, aunt, which is why I have forgotten him. None of that matters now – that is not why I resist!' Rhiann passed her hand over her eyes. 'The council is not marrying me to *him*, they're marrying me to this . . . this . . . murderer, this sword-wielder!'

'Not all men are like those raiders, daughter.'

Rhiann spun on her heel and kept pacing. 'I can still invoke the law. No woman can be forced!'

'That is true, and if you take that path, then by the Goddess I will stand by your side, you know that. But . . .' Linnet bit her lip. 'This marriage is for the good of us all, especially now that we face the invaders, for without it we will fragment. It is a hard choice; and I would spare you from it, believe me. But if you say no, I see darkness and chaos for us all. That is the truth.'

Rhiann whirled again. 'And who did *you* choose, aunt, to give us our heir, when you were young? You have the same blood as me! You've never been sold to a man, I recall.'

Linnet paled. 'It was different, then. Your mother was Ban Cré. The King had many heirs. My blood was not needed.'

A shadow of grief crossed her face, but Rhiann was too angry to take it in. 'I don't want any man!' she cried again. 'And this one is arrogant, and . . . and he is lying! I can see it!'

'Rhiannon brought him to us, on the waves. He does not bode harm – I sense it, I sense it strongly.'

Rhiann stopped, clenching her hands into fists. Linnet's definition of harm differed greatly from her own, she knew that. Oh, her aunt would let no man disturb a hair on her head. But that was not the point . . . she didn't understand . . .

Linnet rose and took her hands. 'Daughter, daughter, calm yourself! You must trust what She sends you, and trust me, and the things that I cannot speak. Somehow, all will be well.'

All will be well.

Rhiann wanted to knock the cups to Linnet's feet. She wanted to wrench the shelves from the wall, shattering the pots of salves and bitter tinctures, send the loom crashing to the floor, its threads snapping, tear down the bags of dried roots from the rafters, scatter the digging sticks and the carved figurines and the pans of beeswax and crushed dyes on the table. *All will be well.*

She had spent years learning such acceptance, such calm trust, on the Sacred Isle. It was easy to find, as a child. But all of that had bled away with one ringing blow of a raider's sword across her foster-father's neck.

Linnet pulled her resisting body into her arms. 'Stay here this night. I will brew you a sleeping draught. Perhaps the Mother will make things clearer for you in your sleep.'

Rhiann drew a trembling breath. Well, she could not go back today anyway, not if all the *ban-sidhes* of the Otherworld were on her heels. Let the council worry over her, for once.

But in the darkness of the night, these proud thoughts deserted her, and the shadows on Linnet's walls seemed to draw in. She huddled deeper into the goatskins to escape them, until the draught took her at last.

And a dream from the Mother did come.

This vision was much older than the memory of slaughter; it had come to her often since her first moon bleeding. It was a secret dream, a golden dream that she'd once dared hope might come true.

There stood Rhiann, surrounded by all the people of Alba in a valley filled with light. Danger stalked the dark slopes beyond, and the harsh, high shrieks of eagles came from the mountain peaks above. But Rhiann stood at the centre, cupping the cauldron of the goddess Ceridwen in her hands, gathering the Source so that it drove back the shadows.

And by her side there stood another, a man, though she could never see his face, and he held a sword that brought not death, but protection and truth. And they had come together again, as in many lives, to bring the Source into balance.

Over the years, Rhiann had attached features to this man's face in her imagination: dark gold hair and brown eyes. *Drust.*

He was a youth when he tattooed her on the Isle; a man he must be, now. It had to be him, for he was an artist, with fine fingers – not a killer. And he was there when she bled for the first time, when the dream first came. Kissing her, touching her . . .

In her dream, she sighed and turned, cradling this one glimpse of joy to her breast.

Which was when, for this one night, the dream changed.

She was alone in a forest glade. There was the whisper of wings in the night air, and she felt the fear of the mouse as it cowers from the shadow of the owl above. The fear grew, until, in a panic, she ran, sensing always the wings beating above. 'Help me!' she cried, and suddenly on the path before her stood a beast; its eye bright, its shoulders thrusting with strength. For a moment she thought it would attack, and she felt despair, but as her feet carried her on, the beast let her go, then turned to paw the path against what followed.

Ahead of her she saw sunrise creeping through the trees. But from behind came an unearthly cry, torn from the owl's throat.

CHAPTER 13

R hiann's bed-place was empty when Linnet woke to the chinks of dawn creeping under the turf roof, but to her relief Liath was still tethered in the stable.

Not knowing when Rhiann would return, Linnet drew on her work dress and took down the muslin bags of goat-cheese that her maid Dercca had tied up to drain before she left to visit her sister. But as she ladled the curds into nettle baskets, Linnet's mind kept straying to the night before.

She could not tell Rhiann that she saw the man from Erin in a vision, that she recognized him at the moment of his arrival. To reveal that would mean revealing the other scenes she'd foreseen, and somehow Linnet felt if she did this, the course of Rhiann's life would alter, and not for the better. She wouldn't learn what she needed to, before the Otherworld called her.

You knew you must prepare her, not guide her, Linnet reminded herself. She thought she had accepted this long ago . . . yet it had not been tested, not really. And now the time of testing had come.

She sighed, teasing thyme stalks from a bunch drying on the rafter. The raid on the Sacred Isle had left Rhiann with a deep hatred of warriors, but why the girl feared marriage itself, that Linnet did not know. So long as the man was honourable – and the prince seemed so – then he bore no resemblance to the shrieking murderers branded on the poor child's heart.

Of course, if Rhiann had once felt a child's love for a boy . . . but the tattoo artists painted many girls, and many fell in love with the first to touch them that way. It was not a love to hold on to. Rhiann said she had forgotten it, so Linnet would have to believe her. This Erin prince was a different matter altogether.

Pursing her lips, Linnet stripped the thyme leaves, the sharp scent filling the room. Was the prince here for good, or ill? Was the vision of him a warning? She thought back to how she'd felt on the day she received it. No, she did not sense he was here to harm. And surely the Mother would not let him cross the waves – a realm where many die – if he was to hurt Rhiann?

She sprinkled the cheeses and wrapped them, then wandered to her loom, plucking the warp threads absently, thinking of the harsh words Rhiann had flung at her.

The girl had touched on more than she knew. For although she thought that in retreating from the world, Linnet had found her true place, Linnet had once wanted hearth and home as desperately as Rhiann wished to escape it. In the end, Linnet lost the very chance that was being offered to Rhiann now.

But, ah! She could not tell her that.

It was past midday when Rhiann returned. Linnet was feeding her goats, and she paused and set down the bucket of slops, leaning her elbows on the brush paling of the pen, as Rhiann approached. Her eyes still burned, though with wonder now, not anger.

'Come, you must eat.' Linnet drew Rhiann to the old bench set against the hut's wall, ducking inside for a honey bannock and cup of milk.

Rhiann ate silently, her eyes still far away. But finally she brushed the crumbs from her skirt and stretched her kidskin boots out. 'You were right,' she said, lifting her face to the weak sun. 'The Mother did send me a sign.'

Linnet's heart leaped. 'What was this sign?' she asked eagerly, taking in the brightness of Rhiann's eyes. But then she realized what a brittle light it was, with none of the warmth Linnet longed to see.

'It was a dream, which I have been puzzling out all morning.' Rhiann shook her head. 'But now I am clear. And listen! The Mother sent this man from Erin to be the sword in my hand – the sword to break Gelert's hold!'

'What do you mean?'

Rhiann explained the dream when she ran through the forest. 'Don't you see? The beast appeared to be a boar, and this prince has a boar crest on his helmet – I saw him polishing it while visiting his sick brother. I have been so afraid . . . but I see now that I can turn Gelert's own weapon – this prince – back on him!' She clasped her hands together. 'If I accept, I will have a husband with a strong warband, and a kingdom across the sea. If I can gain control over him, I can use him to fight Gelert on his own terms!' A grim smile touched her mouth. 'I've been weak and sad for too long, aunt. But now a weapon has come to my hands, and I can wield it, and be just as hard as any man!'

Linnet's heart sank. No one should start a marriage with a heart so full of dark thoughts. *Oh, my dearest!*

And yet . . . Rhiann had agreed to marry the prince. And the pitiful despair in her eyes, that had been slowly breaking Linnet's heart for many moons, was gone. Perhaps, over time, Rhiann would change, if he was kind and treated her well.

Please let him be a good man, Mother, the man with green eyes.

And then, just as this fine day had broken through unending cloud, her spirit lifted. The sisterhood taught that the strongest soul-healing comes when the wounded one faces the source of harm.

As man had wounded her, perhaps man would lead Rhiann back to herself.

Most marriages took place at Beltaine, the start of sunseason, and brides were crowned with flowers beneath blue skies.

But as Rhiann rode back to the dun with Linnet and Dercca two days later, she realized that this time of year was right for her union. A hoar-frost glittered on the dying sedges, and the taut air bit at their noses and fingers until they burned with cold. In the pale sky over the marsh, the geese wavered in long lines, fleeing south.

The Samhain festival was close: the end of the old year and the start of the new, when the long dark drew in and the land went to sleep in the Mother's womb. And for a new year, perhaps it was time for Rhiann to throw off the fear and weakness that had infected her for this last wheel of the sun.

Samhain was also the time when the fabric between the Otherworld and Thisworld grew thin, and the powers could cross between worlds more easily, tormenting the living with apparitions. An Otherworld marriage, then . . . a dark marriage.

I also do this for the Mother, Rhiann thought, winding her icy fingers in Liath's mane. *And if I suffer it well, and am strong, perhaps She will forgive me for not being strong enough to foresee the raid, for not being strong enough to save my family. Perhaps then she will let me see again . . .*

No one stopped Rhiann as she entered the village gates, but all those hurrying along the paths, and loading and unloading carts, and hovering in doorways, fell silent, staring. She sensed Linnet glance at her, and she kept her back straight, and Liath stepped proudly.

Brica welcomed her back with a tirade of renewed anger about the marriage. 'The lord druid is furious!' she cried, taking their cloaks and laying them out near the fire. 'He has had to put a good face on it for the *gaels*, but they must know something is wrong! The council guessed where you'd gone, but they argued about whether or not to force you. Belen said if you were so unwilling, to leave you be.'

'Did he? I'm shocked.'

'Everyone is talking,' Brica rattled on. 'Oh, my lady, you have caused a stir!'

Rhiann glanced at Linnet, and smiled. 'Good! Now Brica, I have something to tell you. I am going to marry this prince tomorrow, as planned.' She held up a hand as Brica's mouth opened to protest. 'It is my duty as Ban Cré – you must understand that. We'll have to see something of him,' she repressed a shudder, 'though I'll make it as little as possible, you can be sure. The provisions for the feast are on hand? Good. Help me off with my shoes, and then go and tell the cooks to have it ready tomorrow eve. Come straight back – and don't speak to anyone, mind. I'll let the council know my decision in my own way.'

She sat down on the hearth-bench, and Brica bent to unlace the thongs of her leather boots. Linnet and Dercca were unrolling their packs in the guest alcove, behind a wicker screen.

Brica looked up at her mistress, but Rhiann's gaze was on the flames, trembling in the draught that came under the door. 'The Goddess has given him to me, Brica, and I'll use him for Her glory. And when he is no longer needed, then he can return from where he came!'

She said the last under her breath, for her own ears only, but she saw Brica cock her head.

Eremon had taken to watching the sunrise with Cù from a high, bare hump of rock that reared up just outside the Horse Gate, near the King's Hall.

From his perch that morning, wrapped in his cloak, he watched the chief druid leading the sun greeting outside the shrine with a great deal more grimness than usual, his face belying the soft, fine dawning of the day. Below Eremon's lookout, the dun burned with gossip. The princess of the Epidii, whom Eremon still had not seen, had apparently disappeared when told of the marriage.

Eremon could not understand her behaviour. His men had theories of their own, from Eremon's poor reputation in the bed-furs, to his prominent lack of beauty, but they quieted when he pointed out that if the bargain fell through, they would be cast out to wander Alba alone in the long dark. No, the Boar was looking on him kindly the day He brought them to these shores. Surely this chance would not slip through his fingers. She must come back, she must.

The Epidii had hunted again to stock up the larders for a

wedding feast, and the surrounding nobles of the royal clan had arrived from their duns in the hills. Eremon had been fitted for a new green tunic, and it was hastily being embroidered in gold thread by Talorc's wife. He also considered his jewellery stores, and picked a delicate silver necklace of his mother's as a wedding gift. A more lavish bride price was expected to come from his kin in time.

His kin. He fingered the other tusk from Conaire's boar, now tied around his upper arm, against his skin. Ah, he was playing a risky game, he knew that. But when someone like his uncle changed the rules, a man must adapt, or die.

At times the guilt of his deception pricked at him, but he had been trained to be ruthless as well as practical, and to limit his attachments to those he must use. And although his men came first, he also knew that with them, and his control over the Epidii warriors, he could keep to his end of the bargain. That would weigh against the lie, in the eyes of the gods.

He would be a strong war-leader for the Epidii. He would be all they needed.

This day, he and Conaire were called to break their fast with the council again, but the thick porridge stuck in Eremon's throat as much as it had on the last two mornings. Glances darted around the ring of benches in the King's Hall, from elder to elder, eyes catching each other as the cold light from the open door shone on their rings and furs. No one seemed to have anything left to say. Well, not in Eremon's hearing, anyway. Conaire and Eremon's eyes met, too, but Conaire just pursed his lips and shrugged, stretching his sore leg to the fire.

Then a shadow darkened the door, and a slight, black-haired servant was standing there, curtsying stiffly. She looked familiar, but Eremon couldn't place her.

'What is it, woman?' Gelert said irritably, his mouth full of bannock.

'Pardon, my lords, but the Lady Rhiann is here.'

There was an explosion of crumbs from Talorc, and mutters

from the others. To Eremon's further surprise, the servant shot one venomous look at him, but before he could wonder why, she turned, and a girl – no, a woman – was standing outlined in the cold sunlight spilling through the doorway.

Belen was on his feet in an instant, as were all the others, except Conaire.

The woman glided forward. She was dressed in a tunic of saffron, and her hair was unbound to her waist. Eremon could not see her properly until she walked into the pool of firelight by the hearth, and then he reeled, for the wide, crescent-shaped eyes, high forehead, and amber hair were those of the healer. This was his bride? Into the shocked silence, Eremon blurted, 'But you are a druid!'

The girl turned those arched eyes on him, and he saw some strong emotion there which chilled his blood. She swept him with a glance. 'No, I am of the Goddess. You do not have priestesses any more in Erin, do you?'

She had not addressed him with his title, and he felt an odd surge of anger.

Gelert stepped forward. 'Prince, this is the Lady Rhiann, daughter of Mairenn, who was sister of Brude.' He paused. 'Our Ban Cré.'

The girl bowed a graceful head, but when she straightened, there was a sardonic tilt to her smile. 'And you are Eremon, son of Ferdiad, King of Dalriada in Erin,' she recited. 'I apologize if I have inconvenienced you.'

With no more than that – no muttered excuses or embarrassed wringing of hands – she turned to the elders. 'The wedding feast will be ready as arranged.' Then she addressed Gelert, not hiding her distaste. 'The Lady Linnet is here to lead the wedding rites with you. We will be ready by noon tomorrow.'

Eremon's alarm was growing. During her healing of Conaire, he discovered her name but barely spoke with the girl, worried as he was for his brother. Now he racked his brains. Did he say something then to offend her? Impossible: they only ever talked of Conaire, and only in passing, for she left every time Eremon appeared at the door.

He was assuming that his bride's disappearance was a last attack of girlish nerves. But the remote face before him seemed to hold no fear, only contempt. Surely she welcomed the match? After all, he was comely, wealthy – what more could she want? Then he was struck by a new thought. What if she had bestowed her heart elsewhere? Perhaps she was one of those noble women who harboured dreams of marrying for love. Well, herders' daughters could do so, but not princesses.

He glanced at Conaire, confused. Politics he understood, but dealing with a woman like this was something else altogether. If they were to forge some sort of partnership, they were getting off on the wrong foot entirely. So he tried the only thing that occurred to him, and gave her his most encouraging smile. But she turned away before she caught the force of it, sweeping out into the morning.

'Prince,' said Gelert, 'when the sun is at its highest tomorrow, we will perform the rite. Bring your men to the forecourt before the shrine.' The elders followed the druid out until only Eremon and Conaire remained.

Conaire let out a whistle, kneading the healing scar on his thigh. 'Hawen's balls! The Boar certainly gave you a beauty, brother, but she never looked that way at me when I was in her sickbed! Let's hope your reputation in the furs holds up, for she'll be using those claws of hers on you if it doesn't.'

CHAPTER 14

By the middle of the next day, a merciful haze had settled over Rhiann, as a cloudbank from the west settled over the sun, plunging the crag into gloom.

She stood by her bed as the young noblewomen hummed around her like a swarm of bees, Linnet directing them with her firm voice.

Arms up, stiff as a corn-doll, and a fine linen shift floated over her head. Arms down, and sharp fingers pulled the embroidered sleeves to her wrists, and tied the gathering under her breasts. Arms up, and they eased the sleeveless undertunic over her shoulders; arms down, and it fell to the floor in a drift of green silk. Arms out, and they drew on the heavy, embroidered robe of crimson wool, pinning it on each shoulder. Arms in, and they flitted around her, tugging a bit of cloth here, settling a fold there.

Talorc's two daughters were hovering over her hair, braiding the lengths into fine plaits, weaving gold thread in among each braid. They chittered and breathed on her neck.

'That's my thread, Aiveen!'

'No, it's not, you gnat. You're taking too much hair!'

'Girls!' Linnet nudged one out of the way, and her soft fingers touched Rhiann's skin as she continued to weave. 'Breathe now, child.'

Rhiann nodded distantly, but she'd forgotten how to breathe. She didn't know what it felt like, what lungs were. She did not have a body, she was just a wisp of air, hardly chained to Thisworld any more.

This feeling was mostly due to the *saor* – the sacred herb

draught that freed her spirit from her body. She took it whenever she was acting as the Goddess in a rite. Normally, it brought warmth and light-headedness, as if, every time she tried to move, her body lagged behind for a moment. In some dim corner of her mind, though, she knew this was a different haze today; warm still, but heavy, an escape rather than freedom. But she did not care. If it dulled the fear, then that was all that mattered. She'd drunk a double draught of *saor*, just to be sure, though Linnet did not know that.

She comforted herself with the fact that this was a public rite, not a private joining. It was not Eremon mac Ferdiad wedding Rhiann of the Epidii; it was the war leader joining with the Land. She was bestowing sovereignty – however temporary – on him with her hand, until a king could be restored, and in return he had a sacred obligation to protect and serve her people in war.

She wondered if anyone had bothered to explain that part to him.

On the other side of the bedscreen, the girls' mothers rustled their dresses and gossiped by the fire, already shrill with the warmth of the mead. The highest ranking women were supposed to have a hand in her preparations, to bind them to the Mother. So far this had been perfunctory, sharp hands straightening a bit of cloth here and there, before they went back to their drinking. But when it came to her finishing finery, they crowded forward eagerly. She caught a glimpse of Aiveen with her mother, both faces bright with avarice.

A golden girdle, alight with garnets, went around Rhiann's narrow hips. Bronze arm-rings came next; snake-coiled on one wrist, deer-headed on the other. Her priestess ring shone on the third finger of her left hand; her others were left bare. Her braids were tipped with tinkling gold balls, which pulled at her scalp. At last, Brica put her priestess cloak around her shoulders and fastened it with the Epidii royal brooch, and then Linnet was before her with the matching royal torc to replace Rhiann's own. The eyes set in the mares' tossing heads were cold dewdrops of garnet, and as it clasped her neck, so Rhiann, her body reeling with the effects of the *saor*, felt as if she were sinking into the ground under all the weight of wool and linen, gold and bronze.

Perhaps she really would sink, she mused, and could rest at last as the dead rested, in the cold of the earth.

But a horn was blowing, and the seated women rose excitedly, their calls raucous to Rhiann's ears, scattering mead cups in their wake.

Linnet's gentle hand came to rest on Rhiann's shoulder.

Under a glowering sky she looks up at the prince's face, swimming above her like a pale moon through cloud, a green jewel blazing on his brow. Gelert's voice drones on.

The scene shifts and blurs, in and out of focus, and yet little things leap out in minute detail. The gnarled boles of age-darkened wood on the druid shrine. Light glancing off the boar that crests the prince's helmet. The damp wind lifting the braids at her neck. The rigid line of Linnet's mouth.

Beyond the murmuring of the crowd, the birds on the marsh cry, faintly. *I could fly there right now. I could be with them.*

A spot of rain falls, glistening on Gelert's balding scalp. He steps back, and the raindrop runs down into his beard. His eyes are slits; what lurks in them, she is beyond. Today he cannot touch her.

Linnet comes forward with the golden cup, and wraps Rhiann's chilled hands around it. Linnet blesses the prince with water from the sacred spring, while Rhiann stares at the clouds. One has billowed into the shape of an eagle's head. Or is it a goose?

How did I get here? This man . . . this man will take me . . . I am afraid.

The stabbing fear breaks through the *saor* for a moment as the prince accepts the sacred bread from Linnet's fingers. Then his sword is out, and he turns to her people, laying it across his hands. No! She pushes the pain away, not willing to come back into the shell of her body.

He is not marrying me. He is marrying the Goddess. The Goddess . . . I am the Goddess.

Yes . . . the cloak of numbness falls back into place, and she draws it tight. The fear recedes. She looks down into the cup of sovereignty in her hands. In it, there lies a pool of amber mead, like her hair. She must raise it to his lips now, so that he can drink and be one with her land, her people.

Don't look at him, though, as he sips, and fixes her with those green eyes. Don't look.

The Goddess. You are the Goddess.

Yes, he feels it too. He can look no longer: he knows that he does not join with Rhiann. And then it is over, and his eyes are hidden by his dark hair.

Linnet binds their hands together with a sash of deep red, a blood colour. His palms are damp. Linnet speaks of the Goddess and the consort, the defender of the land, ritually bound now with the bones of the land. And the people shower them with dried haws, for there are no flowers. No Beltaine flowers.

Goddess, he will take me. I am afraid.

'Please, my lord. Let me sing.'

Aedan's words were muffled, as Eremon tugged his helmet and circlet off and handed it to Finan.

'You'd better let him.' The older man winked at Eremon. 'He's got to show those fine threads off to everyone, after all.'

Now Rori was helping Eremon off with his mailshirt. As befits the new defender of the tribe, Eremon went to the ceremony in full war regalia, but he couldn't sit like that all night.

'And why did Aedan get *that*, while I got *this*.' Rori looked from Aedan's riotously embroidered tunic down to his own plain red one, which clashed with his hair.

The Erin men explained away their lack of feasting clothes by saying that their chests of personal belongings had been lost in the storm. The Epidii willingly furnished them with clothing for the wedding, although the quality had been a chance affair.

Aedan sniffed. 'Well, perhaps these people understand the true status of a bard. Second only to his lord, is that not right, sir?'

'In polite company, yes.' Eremon was curiously tired. Standing up there in front of the shrine, before all the people, he had suddenly become aware of what he was swearing to. A defender of their land – he had agreed to that with Gelert. But a consort for their Goddess? Just where did that come from? He was taken unawares, asked to make a lasting vow when, come a year, he would be leaving. But how could he have backed out then and there? So he drunk from the cup, and swore the oath to that older priestess – his bride's aunt – even though the girl herself would not even look at him.

Ah. He swore fealty to the Boar and to Manannán first, in Erin. He promised them he'd go back. This Goddess of the Epidii would just have to understand. He shrugged away an uneasy prickling that she might prove more demanding than he thought.

A bronze-rimmed cup of ale was thrust in his hand. 'And here's your first drink as a new husband.' Conaire grinned at him, took a gulp of his own ale. 'By the Boar, my leg was growling to stand so long! But this will take the pain away.'

The men were alone in the King's Hall, except for the servants turning the spits of boar and deer over the fire-pit, and rolling barrels of ale and mead into place against the outer walls. The feast would begin soon, but they had a few moments to themselves. Cù was pacing around the hearth, watching the sizzling fat spit into the fire, and squabbling with the old king's hounds.

'So can I sing, my lord?' Aedan was pleading now.

'Yes, yes. But choose your tales with care. That goes for all of you – hold your drink well, and keep your counsel.'

'Hold your own drink well, my brother!' Conaire nudged him. 'No going soft tonight, of all nights!'

112

'And fill up on boar,' Colum chuckled. 'You'll need your strength!'

Eremon forced a laugh, as the others let loose with a stream of sexual jests, while a servant refilled their cups. Tonight. He'd not forgotten that part.

A strange mixture of desire and apprehension stirred in him. Hawen, it had been a while without a woman. Unlike Conaire, he'd had more to think about since their arrival. And his new wife was comely, if thin for his taste. There was little enticing roundness about her hips or breasts, as far as he could see, but she certainly had a striking face, with its high cheekbones and generous mouth. And unusual hair.

As Finan launched into a ribald story about a wedding night in his youth, and Eremon's ale slid down his parched throat, he thought about that hair. An image flashed into his mind of pulling it down around his face, running his fingers through it. Hmm . . . now that thought was more interesting. His memory continued roving over her face, coming to rest at last on her eyes, and there the hot flush of desire abruptly faded.

Her eyes were striking, too, wide-set, tilted up at the edges. But they unnerved him. On the beach they held repulsion, in the King's Hall that morning, hostility. And during the ceremony – well, that was the most unsettling part of all. She stood there, but she wasn't *there*. Her eyes were not even cold; coldness requiring some emotion and presence. They were just blank.

He had seen plenty of druid rites in his time, and as the king's son, was often close to the brethren when they were communing with the gods. But he never expected that one day he would see that same unearthly light in the eyes of his bride. The touch of the Otherworld.

Still, she was a priestess, which must be something like a druid. And after going through all that joining-to-the-land thing, he had realized that this must be business to her as well as to him. He sighed. Politics were all very well, but in the

113

meantime, this betrothal could have been a pleasant inter-lude.

He had spent years trying to stop girls falling in love with him, because he did not want a wife. He was too busy roving Erin with Conaire, honing his military skills. With his looks and position, there had been no shortage of noblewomen making eyes at him, but he'd stuck to the safer options: regular tumbles with the dairymaids, the smith's daughter, and his mother's fine-fingered needlewoman. But this was altogether a different proposition. He must be careful with her. Especially tonight.

'So, to the health and fortune of our prince, a married man at last,' Conaire was saying, his cup lifted.

Eremon glanced around at the bright circle of faces, cups in the air, humming with the promise of the evening's delights – food, drink, and women. At least they were getting a feast out of it.

'To the prince!'

'The prince! *Slàinte mhór!*'

Rhiann knew it would be one of the longest nights of her life.

The *saor* had worn off now, and in its wake came a hollow sickness, and chills that brought a shiver to her skin. She desperately wished that she could take more, that she could return to the floating haze, and stave off the time when she would have to regard this hall and the people in it in the cold light of reality.

She glanced around the huge ring of benches, circling the hearth. Servants dashed back and forth, holding on high woven willow platters of boar-flesh, salmon with juniper, roast goose with blackberries, and baskets heaving with soft cheeses and honey-baked bread. Others mingled among the nobles with jugs of heather ale and pale mead. The calls for more ale! more mead! resounded from the roof-beams. The crowd was becoming louder, the jokes quickly bawdier. Normally she would be long gone to her bed . . . but tonight, tonight she would rather endure this than . . . *that.*

The bridal hut was waiting. With the houses always so full of guests, newly-weds were given their one night of total privacy. And she must go there, with *him*. The rite she had gone through today, to safeguard her people, it would have no meaning to them unless she disappeared into that hut with that man, and did not emerge until morning.

Her hand crept to her waist. The jewelled girdle was still there, but underneath her linen shift she had tied on her priestess pouch. She cupped it now through the soft wool of her dress, her fingers seeking security. For the people, she must go to that hut. But, just as no one knew what went on inside her head, no one would know what went on inside the hut.

Stop thinking.

She had exchanged barely any words with her new husband. He tried that boyish grin on her a few times, but it slid off her skin like a straw arrow glancing off mail. It may well work with the insipid, moon-eyed girls that seemed to find him attractive, but it wouldn't work with her.

Her other hand was gripping her mead cup so hard that the enamelled mounts were digging into her palm. She had no intention of being polite to him. She'd made the sacrifice, and that was enough. He married her for her position, and that was all that he would get. The council may be able to barter her away, but no one could control her mouth, her mind, her heart. They were hers alone.

One of the servant girls passed by again with the platter of boar-meat, and that great blond hulk from Erin paused to spear even more on to his knife. The prince was eating more sparingly, but she noticed his quick, nervous gulping of the mead.

Good. Get so drunk that you pass out. As her mind slid dangerously close again to what would happen after the feast, she resolutely brought it to bay. *Stay here, in the present. What comes after cannot be faced. It cannot be faced.*

At least she did not have to worry about Gelert. The druids

had blessed the feast and partaken of a sparse meal, and then left the hall to the warriors and their women.

On one side of her, she heard the prince and his brother talking about the Romans, speculating on what they might do. War talk, that was all they knew. Still, at least he had given up trying to speak with her.

'Take some more food, daughter.' Linnet, on her other side, squeezed her hand. 'You must eat after the *saor.*'

'I'm not hungry.'

A pause. 'You did well today. I was proud of you.'

'I did not have much choice.'

Linnet sighed, but she put a light hand on Rhiann's back, at the level of her heart. After a moment, a warmth began to tingle on Rhiann's skin, through the layer of the robe and the shift, growing into a pulsing glow of comforting heat that spread throughout her chest. And Rhiann remembered with a pang how Linnet had always been there, stroking her face, putting her healing hands on a scratched knee, a feverish cheek. It wasn't much. Right now, it brought tears dangerously close to the surface. But it was hers. It was all she had. She reached out and put her hand in Linnet's lap, and took another sip of mead.

The bards were tuning their harps near the door. One of the lesser bards had already been playing a series of wordless tunes throughout the feast, until it was time for the family lays to be recited and sung, to confirm the lineages and the new kin bonds. In effect, it was part of the marriage contract: telling the prince of Erin what he had got for his money.

Meron, the Epidii chief bard, told the story of Rhiann's own ancestor, Beli the Bold, who led his people out of the east, and crossed the great sea, fighting all manner of strange beasts to make landfall on Alba's fair shores. It was, of course, a favourite for the royal clan, many of whom knew it off by heart. Rhiann saw more than one old warrior's lips move in a silent echo of Meron's deep, melodious chant.

In the silent pause after Meron left the floor, when men were waking as if from a trance, blinking their drink-sodden eyes, a slight figure stepped out of the shadows into the cleared space beside the hearth.

It was the bard from Erin. He was so young, he must still be undergoing his training. And pretty, too, as she'd noted before, with his ripples of dark hair framing a heart-shaped face. He could almost be a woman, especially clean-shaven as he was today. She heard a muttered joke to this effect from somewhere to her left, smothered by a loud guffaw, and saw Conaire, the blond giant, pin the unfortunate joker to his seat with a glare.

The bard had borrowed a fine blue cloak to cover his tunic, and now he swept this back, somewhat theatrically, and paused, until a burst of talking and cries for more mead respectfully died down.

Bards – no matter their looks – were sacred. They were untouchable even on the battlefield. After all, they held a people's whole history in their heads – all the kinship lines, the battles, the marriages, the acts of kindness and outrage, the births and the feats of honour and glory. They could kill with words, by bringing stinging satire and shame down on a man's head, hounding him to his death. And they brought beauty, on the long nights when the cold winds prowled around, and all within were aching to see the sun again.

Someone hastily brought the young bard a stool, and he settled himself on it, tuning his harp, his fingers tracing over the strings lovingly. Rhiann's heart thawed just a little at this total absorption. This one did not wield a sword, at least. He was a maker of things, of beautiful songs, not a destroyer.

'I will sing,' he announced grandly, 'the lay of the Sons of Mil, the tale of my prince's most glorious ancestor, the first Eremon, who conquered Erin with his brothers, vanquishing the faery-people, the Túatha dé Danann. This you will see, is the line of his blood, the most noble line of our most noble island . . .'

And so on, so on . . . Rhiann took another sip of mead as the bard launched into his tale.

She had to admit that he had a fine, clear voice. The sons of

Mil, among whom numbered the famous bard Amergin, crossed from Iberia to Erin countless generations ago. Rhiann had never heard the story, and despite the fact it was about *his* ancestors, she gave herself up to the bardic rhythm of the voice, and the song of the harp, and drew some comfort from its beauty. People sat silent, relaxed if not always attentive, reaching their feet out to the fire, hands on full bellies, fingers curled around ale cups.

Then, looking around the room, Rhiann's eyes accidentally caught upon her new husband's hard profile. He had straightened on his bench, his eyes fixed on the bard. There was something about him of the stag sensing the air, an alertness that had not been there before. Curious.

She brought her attention back to the tale, where the bard Amergin's powerful words helped the brothers to vanquish the Túatha dé Danann, who retreated to their underground mounds. The sons of Mil then divided up Erin between them.

The bard continued proudly:

> *And so the warriors,*
> *The great warriors,*
> *The warriors-of-gold,*
> *Gathered about them ten thousand swords each*
> *And ten thousand spearmen.*
> *Five boars a night they feasted on*
> *And twenty gold arm-rings they gave away.*
> *But hark! Eremon mac Mil was the brightest*
> *And the fairest.*
> *And the gold in his hall,*
> *The gold on his walls,*
> *Shone out across the length of Erin.*

The bard's voice changed, and he paused to execute a difficult flourish on the harp.

Rhiann's glance now fell on the prince's hand where it rested on his knee. The firelight glinted off a jewelled ring, as he clenched his fist. Then, she saw him mutter something to

Conaire, who muttered something to another of their men, who slid away from the benches into the crowd beyond.

The bard's voice had hushed:

> *So began the strife*
> *The kin-strife*
> *The greatest kin-strife Erin has seen*
> *Brother on brother—*

Suddenly, his fingers fumbled, and his fine voice faltered. His eyes darted to the prince's face, and Rhiann, sitting so close, saw those sky-grey pools widen from the dreamy bardic trance into something more like . . . fear? Just then, the *gael* who had slipped away stumbled out into the hearth-space, clutching another man as if he was falling down drunk. The clutched man swore, and both careened into the bard, knocking him from his stool.

The room erupted into shouts of laughter. The prince waved for more ale, and servants dashed in, breaking up the edges of the crowd. Under cover of a burst of shouted jests at the supposed drunk man, who stumbled off outside, Rhiann saw some others from Erin rush in to help the bard up. By the time he dusted himself down and checked his harp, he'd lost the crowd's attention.

Some of the Epidii servants had pipes and drums, and they took the opportunity to launch into a raucous jig, and the feasters shouted for more mead, for they would rather talk and dance now, and grope their women.

The prince stood and nodded to her, his face grim, and then pushed his way through the crowd, his brother in his wake. Very curious. There was more to this man's lineage than he had spoken of, that was clear. Perhaps he was not as noble as his little bard was boasting!

'It is time to retire.' Linnet was brushing crumbs from her skirts.

'I'm staying.'

Linnet searched Rhiann's face. 'Then I will stay. I will see you to your marriage bed.' The line of her mouth hardened.

'No, go. You are tired.'

'I won't leave you here.'

Rhiann put her hand over Linnet's fingers, and looked in her eyes. 'It won't make any difference, aunt. Go. For once, heed me.'

Linnet held Rhiann's gaze, as all around them the music and the shouting and the jostling bodies swirled. 'I love you,' Linnet said.

'I, too.'

But if you go, I can hide from this fear that chokes me. Go. Please go.

CHAPTER 15

The moon outside was heavy and low, sinking to her bed. The King's Hall was hot now, packed to the brim with sweaty bodies, jostling their mead cups together. Another toast, and Eremon had to gulp from his cup for the third time in as many heart-beats.

Out of the corner of his eye, Conaire wove into view, his blond hair a blurred halo. Someone had spilled ale down Conaire's tunic, and there was a dark patch over his chest. A woman was hanging around his neck, her breasts pushing against her thin gown. Conaire was laughing and untangling her hands, trying to make his way through the crowd.

Eremon swayed back on his bench, desperate for air. By firelight and torchlight, people's faces swam in and out of focus, sheened with sweat, flushed with drink. Talorc was by the spits with a sick-looking Rori, forcing more mead down the young man's neck while the other men laughed.

Aedan was nowhere to be seen.

Foolish bard. He'd gone down on his knees outside and begged Eremon's forgiveness for singing that lay of the murdering sons of Mil, who turned, each on the other, and fought to the death, bringing Erin to its knees. The lay of that first Eremon, who killed his brothers for the throne of Erin. A tale too close to home.

Aedan got so carried away proving Eremon's lineage, boasting about him in front of these people, that he forgot the very reason they were here, and what they had to hide.

Kin-strife obviously runs in the family. Eremon swigged mead, and smiled. Ah, the bard was only doing what a bard did.

They existed to boast about their lords. Eremon was really only a little angry. After all, who here would make the connection? No reprimand had been required, anyway. Aedan's shame was punishment enough, and he had crawled off to be alone. Eremon would ask him to write a song about the wedding. That would keep him happy.

In front of him, Finan and Colum were crouched over a *brandubh* board in a cleared space; bets of rings and daggers were being passed furiously back and forth over their heads. The druids were long gone, as were most of the women.

Eremon shifted uncomfortably. His belt was too tight, for he had gorged himself on boar. But he was given the champion's portion, and could not refuse. He could not refuse the toasts of his new kin, either. *Ah! I should not get drunk, not now. It's not safe.* He peered at Conaire, willing him to come closer.

Something moved next to him. The girl. His bride. His wife. She had said nothing to him, but remained still and white-faced, rigid in her seat. The people and laughter and shouts, the drunken jests and spilled mead, eddied around her as if she were a pale rock in the middle of a dirty river. He looked at her. Her gaze was far away, locked on some point in the darkness of the roof. Why had she not gone to bed? She did not seem one for feasting like this.

In a sudden burst of bravado, he leaned into her, swaying slightly. 'I will retire if you wish, lady. It has been long enough?' With a great effort, his words came out clearly.

He sensed the way she froze, even though she did not move. Living skin became stone, just for a moment. Then she turned her head. 'No,' she said, and the word sounded bitten off, her voice harsh. 'It will never be long enough.' She turned away again.

He did not know what to say. His brain was stuffed with wool, and nothing, no thought, would emerge clearly enough from the tangle of the rest. He realized, vaguely, that she seemed upset. But why? Most maidens were eager for the marriage bed, few were wholly inexperienced. Or perhaps this one was. She could certainly freeze a man's balls at a hundred paces. He knew he must do something . . . must say something . . .

'Eremon!' Conaire's hand landed on Eremon's shoulder and he squatted awkwardly by his side, favouring his wounded leg.

'Where've you been?' He could hear his words were slurred now. He shook his head to clear it.

Under cover of the noise around them, Conaire leaned close to his ear, grinning. 'Where do you think? I've been in the stables tumbling the young lass who spilt her drink on me!'

'You're joking!'

'I'm not.' Conaire pushed sweaty tendrils of hair back from his face, and then deposited a piece of straw on the bench next to Eremon. 'She was very sorry for soaking me. *Very* sorry.'

Eremon laughed, then hiccupped. 'Brother – they're getting me drunk.'

'I noticed.'

'Couldn't say no, wouldn't be polite . . . to my new kin.' Conaire picked another piece of straw out of his tunic. 'Certainly not. I'm honoured you've made the sacrifice for us.'

'But it's not safe. The men . . .' He waved vaguely around the room.

'By the Boar, man! You deserve it.' Conaire settled his arm around Eremon's shoulders. 'Anyway, I'm here. I'll look after them all, don't worry.'

'You . . . sure?'

'As sure as the girl was sorry.'

'You're a good friend. *A good friend.*' Eremon patted Conaire's hand in emphasis.

'Now, my prince, save all that energy for your lady wife. I'll see you safe to bed, never fear.'

'Bed! Ah, bed. I shouldn't have drunk this much.'

'Don't worry, she won't be expecting a lot.'

'Hush, she'll hear.' Eremon hunched himself around Conaire in an attempt to shield his words.

'No, she won't. She's gone.'

Rhiann lay rigid, ears straining. The apple-wood fire threw off wafts of fragrant smoke, lacing the wattle walls of the hut with shadows.

The bed in which she lay was rawhide over a wooden frame, with a down-filled pallet, soft and springy. The linen sheets were cool on her bare legs, scented with imported lavender. The furs on top were the softest: otter and seal and beaver. No labour had been spared to make this bed a haven of beauty.

Her hand crept again to her waist, to the hard bulge of the priestess pouch. The young maidens who attended her had removed her outer dress, her undertunic, and her jewellery. One of them combed out her hair with a silver and bone comb, until it fell before her eyes in a silken sheet, copper in the firelight. They scented her skin with honeyed oils, giggling all the while. But she batted their fingers away from the lacing of the shift under her breasts, and with a glance at her forbidding face, they let her leave it on. They could think her modest; she did not care. She just wanted them to leave.

Now she lay there, in the half-dark, and did not know what to do.

I'm trapped.

Her breath came in shallow draughts, struggling to draw air into the heavy flesh that was her body. The detached part of her noted: *You are a noble woman. You are a priestess. You must know what to do.*

But she didn't. Her thoughts rolled around her head; one moment freezing into blankness, the next tumbling into fire. The moments crawled by, as moments do when they have been a source of dread for moons. She had avoided this moment, buried the knowledge that it was coming at all, and then, suddenly the time was here, now.

And she must face it. Hiding inside her mind no longer

worked, because it wasn't a case of minds now, of thoughts, memories, fears. It was about flesh, a man's flesh, his breath, his force.

She pressed the heels of her palms into her eyes. She could leave. But then every reason for marrying him would be meaningless, and her people would be no better off. It wasn't an answer, no matter how strongly it beckoned.

She must do the only thing she could do, and that was to use the iron-hard priestess discipline she had learned on the Sacred Isle, to wall herself up. The focus that was required for seeing, that she could use; the way of making sure that thoughts and feelings did not intrude. She could do that . . .

Outside, there was the sound of stumbling tread on the path, and men's voices.

And all the moments collided into one.

CHAPTER 16

Eremon was being jostled in a crowd of drunken men. Talorc pushed another cup of mead at him, spilling it down his tunic. 'More, have more. Consort of the Goddess . . . needs to be strong . . .'

'No . . . no more.' Eremon tried to catch himself from falling, as Talorc laughed and clapped him on the shoulder with one meaty hand.

Behind them, his men and many of the Epidii warriors were weaving along the paths between the houses, singing. A few stopped to bay at the moon, swimming through the racing clouds above, before breaking down into snuffles of laughter. Hounds barked in answer, and a woman's voice cursed the men for the noise they were making.

'I can walk,' Eremon slurred. 'Let me go.'

'Here we are. Here we are!' Talorc turned and called needlessly to the revelers.

Eremon leaned on the wall of the wedding hut. After coming out into the cold air, his bladder was bursting. The men swayed around him, still singing. Conaire took Eremon by the shoulders and said solemnly, 'May the tusk of the Boar stand up hard tonight.' His eyes twinkled in the moonlight, and the crowd shouted with laughter.

'Ha!' Talorc guffawed. 'And may the White Mare be warm and wet for her stallion, eh?' He pulled Eremon to him in a bear hug, his breath reeking of ale. 'Your seed is our seed, brother. All of you! Health to the house of Ferdiad!'

'The house of Ferdiad! *Slàinte!*'

As Talorc released him, his moustache scraped Eremon's

cheeks. 'Tonight, we add our strength to yours. Stand together, and we'll beat these dogs back to Rome, where they belong!'

'To Rome!' In a rumble of laughter and heavy tread, the men began to disperse. Conaire gave Eremon's shoulder a quick squeeze, and then he too was gone.

Gods. They are leaving, at last.

Abruptly, Eremon was alone on the path among the dark shapes of the houses. He fumbled in his trousers, and with great relief, passed his water as he leaned against the hut, his head pillowed on one forearm. When he finished, he raised his head, and the world shifted up and down disconcertingly.

Ah! I am drunk, then.

Well, what he had to do wasn't difficult. He knew he was good. That girl at his cousin's dun had said so . . . what was her name? That was two moons ago – two moons! With that thought, his body suddenly awoke with heat, a heat that suffused his loins and thrust his fuzzy mind impatiently aside. He took a deep breath, pulled the door cover up, and went in.

The hut was small, with the bed pallet to one side of a central fire. On the other side was a single bench. Among the bedclothes, there was a dark shape on the pillow; her hair. He could not see her face.

He stood by the bench and tried to pull his boots off, but swayed so dangerously that he sank down on to it, and tugged them off from there. His clumsy fingers fumbled over the brooch to unfasten his cloak, but he got it in the end. Then his belt, with his sword. Then the new tunic, the gold thread scratchy against his cheek, and then his trousers. They became tangled around his ankles, but by the time he got them off and straightened, he noticed how hard he already was. *Gods! Two moons!* Finally, he slid off his torc and finger-rings, leaving only the boar tusk around his arm – perhaps it would give him strength.

All the while, the girl lay silent, her face and body turned away.

She is shy. He sat down heavily on the bed, pulling the fur covers and the sheet back. The pallet dipped under his weight. All he could see was her white shift, and her hair spilling out over it. Her glorious hair. And then, with a shock, he recognized the pale pearl-sheen of skin. One shoulder, peeking out from the slashed neck of the shift.

His pulse leaped in his throat, and his breath caught. The heat in his loins ignited into an urgent flame. *Steady.*

Some part of him would normally be whispering to take it slow, not to scare her. But tonight, that Eremon had been drowned in a tide of drink and lust that had taken him by surprise. What did Conaire always say? *You're too serious. Have some fun.* Well, tonight he was doing that.

He put his hand out, to where the shift was rucked up a little against her hip, and moved it down to the lace edge. There, his fingers touched soft, warm skin. Living skin, the first life he had seen or felt in this cold beauty. The firm muscle of a white thigh.

There was no response. She seemed frozen. Frozen by shyness? Uncertainty? Well, he would make her certain; certain that she wanted him.

Slowly, so slowly, he slid his hand up inside the shift, up the thigh, to where the muscle gave way to the round swell of a hip. Gliding over that, he dipped down into the achingly velvet texture of her waist. His breath was coming so high and fast now that the dizziness had returned.

And then he felt it. The slightest quiver of her flesh. He knew he would be able to rouse her. Encouraged, he moved his body up to press against the length of hers, and grasped her by the shoulder.

Goddess of Light Lady of the Forests Giver of Life Bringer of Death She of the Three Faces Raven of War Mother of the Land Goddess of Light Lady of the Forests Giver of Life Bringer of Death She of the Three Faces Raven of War Mother of the Land Goddess of Light Lady of the Forests Giver of Life Bringer of Death She of the Three Faces Raven of War Mother of the Land Goddess of Light . . .

From far away, Rhiann was aware of him sitting in the bed.

It doesn't matter.

She felt the heat of his body as he moved closer.

It doesn't matter.

Then the alien hand touched her skin – and that is what broke her.

No! He will take; take what I do not choose to give!

The litany and the distance and the numbness slipped away. She tried desperately to grasp them, to hold them around her nakedness, but they were gone . . .

She is on the beach again. The sand crunches under her feet . . .

This time, the sudden shout behind is not just a shout. She scrabbles up the hillside . . . she is nearly free . . . and then an iron hand closes on her ankle.

Hands are everywhere then, wrenching her by the shoulders, throwing her to the boggy turf, so that sharp rocks bruise her breasts. More hands take her shoulders, more power than she has ever felt in her life, holding her down. Her cheek is pushed into a puddle of peat-stained water; the mud sucks at her scrabbling fingers. She opens her mouth to scream, gripped by panic, but the fist hits her. Stars explode behind her eyes, as she is wrenched over on to her back. There is a sound of cloth ripping. Her skin is suddenly cold. On her breasts, her belly. The hands on her shoulders have coarse, black hairs sprouting from them, the nails are dirty and torn. A man's guttural laugh comes from above those hands, and the weight of a bull lands across her body, extinguishing her breath. A black beard envelops her face; the reek of rotten fish clings to it, stifles her. A wet mouth, wet like a fish, grasps her lips, bites until she tastes blood. There are jeers from above. She cannot move cannot scream cannot think cannot breathe cannot feel cannot see . . . until iron hands push her knees apart, fingers digging into her skin. She tries to close her legs, but the bull-strength wrenches them open again, and she rails at her weakness. Helpless . . . helpless . . . Something rams into her, breaks into her body. But it is her *body . . . he cannot enter . . .*

She is impaled.

The invader plunges again and again and again . . . as the pain erupts, searing her insides. And in the dark of her own body he

129

*floods her with liquid shame, and she knows that, in answer, her
womb weeps blood . . .*

Between one breath and the next, the ice of Rhiann's mind
was shattered by the touch of the prince's fingers, and in its
place rage boiled over. With the strength of a cornered beast
she twisted, ripping open the waist-pouch, and in her hand
suddenly there was the steel of a dagger, firing off sparks of
light.

A dagger pressed into the soft skin at Eremon mac Ferdiad's
throat.

She felt the wildness pour from her eyes, as his face paled in
shock, and a single drop of blood welled around the knife tip.

He was helpless . . . helpless! She rejoiced at that, as her
heart sang in her ears, free of its constraints. Blood cascaded
through her veins, alive.

'If you ever,' she hissed, '*ever* lay hands on me again, I will
kill you.'

CHAPTER 17

The night was over. Crouched, shivering, on the bench she'd dragged to the open door, Rhiann watched the first streaks of dawn lighten the sky. She glanced down at the dagger in her stiff fingers, noting that, in the grey day, it was dull and lifeless. No sparks of fire flashed from it now.

Goddess, but her body was tired. The flood of rage had burned out just as quickly as it exploded, consuming the last dregs of her energy. Her mind, though, was strangely awake, the lassitude that had invaded it after the raid gone.

Something about drawing that dagger shattered it. Something about reliving the men on the beach, their touches . . . every agonizing heartbeat. In all this time, she had never let her mind replay that image, those feelings. All her night dreams ended with the shout behind her, when she clawed herself awake. And now this – a waking dream, a vision, brought on by the touch of the prince's hand.

She twisted to peer inside the hut, her eyes adjusting to the darkness. The prince was seated against the farthest wall, on the floor, as far from her as he could get. He stayed awake a long time in the night, after crawling from the bed and dressing himself. For hours she felt his eyes on her, as she crouched in her cloak by the door, but eventually the drink claimed him. Now his sleeping head was sunk on his breast, his legs splayed out.

She looked down at the dagger again, toying with the weight of it. She could plunge it into that vulnerable breast right now, if she wanted to. Then she sighed, and looked up at the sky. *And become like him?*

The pureness of feeling, the bright bloom of pain and rage and the unexpected, blessed triumph of that blade in her hand, pressed against his skin – all of it had fled with the grey light of day. For her, it was back to living by the mind. And the first rational thought that came was the realization that she'd drawn a weapon on her new husband, and shed his blood, though the nick was slight.

No one would understand her point of view; of course not. Though rape within marriage was condemned, he had not raped her. And no one knew what really happened on the beach, during the raid – not even Linnet. That was how well she buried it.

This man was her people's defender. Their hope. In that moment of her release, she had betrayed their trust. Part of her was appalled at what she'd done. Part of her could not help but feel satisfaction. *It was a moment of madness, that is all. I would not have killed him.*

She glanced back at him apprehensively. Would he declare her mad, then? Shame her before her tribe, repudiate her? Or say nothing, and beat her in the privacy of their bed-place? She realized with a shock that, in her self-absorption, she had taken no note of what kind of man Eremon of Erin truly was. She did not know if he was brutish. Or witless.

Stay calm. Think about this. She tapped the dagger on one finger.

He *had* stayed the night, as she had. After all, they married for sound reasons, and he had much to gain from this alliance, as did the Epidii. What happened was between them, for the moment. Yet would it stay that way? If he rejected her, she would be freed from the marriage, but her people would be weakened again. And the Romans were coming.

Now she heard a rustle of clothing, and she ducked her head, sliding the dagger out of sight under her thigh. It would not do to remind him of that too soon. In a moment, two booted feet entered her line of vision.

'Lady.' His voice was deep, though rough with drink and lack of sleep.

Taking a deep breath, she slowly raised her eyes, bracing herself for what she would see. His clothes were rumpled, but he held himself straight, his head high. The nick at his throat was a sliver of crusted blood. His fore-braids had come loose, and dark tendrils wound about his forehead. At last she could no longer avoid his eyes, and so, tensing, she met them. What would lay there? Disgust? Hatred?

What she saw was the last thing she expected, the last thing of all. His eyes were green and unflinching, and in them dwelt puzzlement, curiosity and . . . pity? 'Lady,' he said again. 'I behaved unspeakably last night, and I seek your deepest pardon.'

She was speechless.

'I have no excuse but that of mead, if you will take that as any excuse at all. Be assured that, in answer to your request, I will not lay a hand on you again.'

She opened her mouth, but no sound came out.

He was adjusting his scabbard on its chains, and peering out at the sky as if getting ready to leave. 'In view of the alliance between our two peoples, could we agree to keep my . . . indiscretion . . . to ourselves? Please trust that you have no cause to fear my attentions again.'

She nearly laughed with disbelief. But he had offered her the way out, so instead, she drew her cloak around her shoulders and nodded stiffly. 'I will not speak of it to anyone.' She wondered what else to add, and could think of nothing.

'Good.' He was brisk now. 'And our living arrangements are . . . ?'

'I am expected to move into the King's Hall. With you and your men.' At that, her voice caught a little, and he glanced at her keenly. Pity indeed! She put her chin up. 'However, I will keep my house as it is, for my healing and ritual duties, for which I need quiet, and space. I will spend most of my time there.'

'I see.'

A silence fell at last.

'Well, then,' he added, 'I have duties of my own to attend to. Lady . . .' He bowed to her gracefully, and then he was gone, the clasps on his belt clanking with each step.

She slumped on the bench, blowing out her breath. She had agreed to share a secret. With her husband. In other words – despite her wishes, in defiance of all her plans – a bond of sorts had been formed.

Between her and the prince of Dalriada.

The sling-stone whizzed through the icy air over the marshes, and fell harmlessly into a frost-fringed pool. The flock of black-striped geese rose with honking cries, before wheeling out over the Add, settling far to the north against the hills.

'Hawen's stinking balls!' Conaire slapped the leather sling against his good thigh.

'If you keep yelling like that, you'll scare them all away.' Eremon was crouched in the reeds, blowing on his chilled hands.

'Ah, I don't have your patience, brother. Give me a boar to run down any day!' Conaire squatted awkwardly on his haunches, still favouring his scarred leg, and rooted through his satchel.

Eremon worked the sling between his fingers, rolling the stone around. 'Patience . . . ah, yes, a great virtue of mine.'

He could not keep the bitterness from his voice, and Conaire glanced up, his hands around a flask of stiffened boar hide. 'Still proving elusive, is she?'

Eremon nodded, his fingers tracing the tiny scab on his throat, which he had explained away as a razor nick. He could not tell Conaire what really transpired in the bridal hut a week ago. He was too ashamed – not of his own behaviour, which was barely at fault, whatever he told the girl. But how could he admit that he'd not yet consummated the marriage? Or that a woman had drawn a knife on him; drawn blood? He could not bear the shame. And as for Talorc and the rest of the Epidii; he would instantly lose every grain of their hard-won respect. *And* he could say goodbye to any chance of leading them, of making his name, of returning to Erin in glory . . .

'I'm sure she'll come around soon.' Conaire shrugged. 'She must be shy, that's all.'

She's mad, that's all. Well, perhaps not mad. Something must have occurred in her past to make her like that – she had been sorely treated, that was plain. It was only this realization that had stayed his anger the morning after.

That sudden stab of pity had surprised him, as he looked down at her hunched on the bench. Until then, she'd been a forbidding figure, but in that one fleeting moment, she was just a frightened child. Then she thrust out that proud chin, and the moment was gone. But there was a mystery there, it was clear.

And what do you care for such mysteries? he chided himself. *What time do you have for such follies?* Rhiann of the Epidii was a riddle, best left unsolved. He forced a smile, his jaw tight. 'Let's just say that this alliance better prove its worth!'

'It is that bad?' Conaire took a sip of elderberry ale, and held the flask out for Eremon. 'Maybe you need some lessons in the bed-furs, brother!'

Eremon did not return the grin, and the twinkle in Conaire's eyes faded as he wiped his mouth. 'Come now! They are expecting an heir, and that is all you must give them. If it's like that, then grit your teeth once a week with her and think of Erin. Meanwhile, there are plenty of women willing to have some fun. That maid Garda says you are the talk of the dun – the fact that you have not partaken of their charms is driving the women even wilder for you. I say enjoy it.'

Eremon drank, his eyes far away. Then he came back to himself, his face relaxing into a proper smile. 'You're right, of course. And anyway, we have more important things to think about. Come.'

They continued down the path that ran between the tussocks of red moss, rimed with frost in the dawn shadows.

'I've decided to ask the council to call in levies from all the Epidii chieftains,' Eremon announced. 'We can house the extra warriors here at Dunadd.'

'But that's a standing warband – and not how things are done here, Eremon. Just like at home, each chieftain keeps his own retinue of men.'

Upright, they were in the full force of the bitter wind soughing across the marshes, and Eremon tucked his sling in his armpit and blew on his hands again. 'That is all well and good for cattle raiding, brother, but the Romans are an invading army! The Epidii will have to adapt – or die.'

'From what I understand, the council won't be happy to bring in warriors from the other clans. They've been concerned about a challenge to the kingship, remember.'

'And this is the best way to avoid such a challenge!' Eremon halted, scanning the reeds. 'Look! Are they swans?' For a few moments they searched for a path to the south, until they found one and set off, talking more quietly now.

'The best way to take control is to weaken the clan divisions,' Eremon pointed out. 'We bring the young warriors here, and work on making them loyal to me. They won't have a chance to get embroiled in any conspiracies. Not only will they be cut off from their own elders, but they'll all spy on each other, which saves me doing it.'

'As usual, you've thought this through.'

Eremon snorted. *And there's not much else to do on these long nights, when my wife lays with her back to me.* 'There's another reason,' he continued aloud. 'I have to meld them into some sort of coherent fighting force. That Greek treatise was clear: the Romans fight as one. We don't.'

Conaire sighed. 'I hear you, but what happened when we tried it in Erin? Everyone broke formation and scattered, but by the Boar we fought like devils! Who thinks of strategy when hungry for blood? For honour, a man fights alone.'

'Then we'll all die alone, too.'

Now it was Conaire's turn to halt in his tracks. 'There *are* swans! Quick.' He pulled Eremon down beside him. 'Steady now. Let's take it slow and sweet.'

'You don't need to tell me that, you great lumbering bear!'

They wound their slings around their hands, and began to creep along the path. Through a gap in the reeds, four white shapes sailed across a dark pool.

Eremon carefully loaded the sling with a ball from the pouch on his belt. Out of the corner of his mouth he whispered, 'How many women was Garda talking about?'

They returned to the gates of Dunadd at full morning, a swan slung across each back, fingers raw with cold, bellies growling. As they neared the King's Hall, Eremon caught the arm of one of a passing pair of servants.

'Girl!' Eremon untied the swan from his shoulders and shrugged it to the ground, gesturing to the girl and her companion. 'I want you to take both these birds to the Lady Rhiann. The feathers are a gift, tell her, from me. From me, do you understand?'

'Yes, lord.' The girls giggled, glancing covertly between the swansdown and Conaire.

As he and Conaire strode away, Eremon caught his brother's raised eyebrow, and in answer he shrugged. 'No harm in trying. She is a woman, after all.'

The festival of Samhain had arrived at last; the greatest of the four fire festivals, for it marked the dying of the old year and the renewal of the new.

For days beforehand, the herders drove great streams of cattle down from the summer pastures to gather on the fields about Dunadd. There they were penned, until the druids had made the choices of which would be kept for breeding, and which would be slaughtered. The air was filled with the sound of their lowing, and the rich smell of their dung.

It was not only cattle gathering in from the far glens. People, too, were coming, for all the tribe must participate in

Samhain. Now, the veil between the Otherworld and This-world grew thin, and it was a dangerous time: mortals could be drawn into the arms of the faery-people, the dead walked again among the living, shape-shifting beasts stalked the land.

Against this, the people must come together to be renewed by the Goddess, to commune with their ancestors and placate the forces that threatened to bring them into chaos.

On Samhain eve, Rhiann sat by her own fire in silence. This night she wore only one robe of undyed wool, and no ornaments beside a crown of rowan-berries. Her body felt lighter than it had at the betrothal, weighed down as it was then with gold and heavy wool. That had been an earthly rite, and as such needed the material things to bind her. Tonight, she must have as little as possible between her and the Otherworld.

'Mistress.' Brica was by her side, holding out an earthen cup of a dark liquid. The *saor*.

Rhiann drank deeply, fighting down the sickness in her belly. Samhain was the most sacred of nights, the start of the new year. The Goddess must be able to manifest, to calm Her people's fear at the coming of the long dark. But would this be the night when Rhiann was unmasked? When all would know that she no longer felt the Goddess within? That she could no longer see?

Rhiann sighed and rose, standing before the sacred figurines on their shelf. Then her fingers closed over one, the image of Ceridwen in her guise of Crone, the cauldron of rebirth in her hands. Tenderly, Rhiann placed the tiny figure in her waist pouch, under her robe, close to her skin.

Brica lifted the door cover and peered out, and Rhiann saw the triangle of black above her head, spangled with stars. Her escort would be here soon.

Now Brica came back to the hearth with the kettle in her hands, and she doused the last coals still glowing in the fire-pit. The house was plunged into blackness, and with the light went the old year. The new year would begin when Rhiann lit the great fire in the valley of ancestors, to the north, and the riders returned with flaming torches to ignite every hearth-fire at Dunadd.

There was the triple rap of a staff on the wall beside her door.

'Mother of the Land, rider of the White Mare. Your people need you to renew the fire. Come!'

Meron's voice soared to the cold stars above. From her position atop the old mound, Rhiann could see the black hole of the fire-pit yawning below, filled with the nine sacred woods, unlit. Although the moon was dark, and the crowd of hundreds silent, she could sense them on the plain around her, their breath rising in the frosted air.

The *saor* began to throb through her veins in time to the single drumbeat that accompanied Meron, and when his song ended, Gelert took up the chant to the dead, who this night walked in Thisworld as if alive.

By now, Rhiann was in the floating place where she saw little, and felt even less. Even so, a fleeting sorrow brushed her, light as a swallow wing, when she laid down a honey-cake for her foster-family in the feast of the dead. Yet that was all that came.

She sensed the Goddess presence on the fringes of her consciousness, just beyond her finger-tips. But the burning that used to envelop her was no more than a feeble warmth now that did little to thaw her heart. She hoped that the people could not see this; that to them she appeared as she used to, the priestess glamour swathing her like a cloak, making her taller, straighter, greater . . .

Linnet's touch came at her elbow. At her feet, two druids had kindled the need-fire, and were handing her a pitch-soaked brand. She held the torch in the fire until it burst into flame, and straightened, the sparks streaming away above her head.

And then, through her fear, words came, and the priestess

voice to carry them, more resonant than her own, more ancient.

'My people!' she cried. 'The land returns to My womb, there to be renewed. All will sleep the long sleep, but in My Darkness, old shall be made new again. As you shall be. Take this fire as a symbol of the light that will continue to glow, ready to flower once more when the sun returns. Fear not! For I am with you in all the turns of the days!'

From the flat valley bottom, Eremon watched the brand arc high in the air as Rhiann threw it into the great fire-pit. But he could not take his eyes off her, not even when the crowd parted to make way for the cloaked riders who, crying to the Mare, streamed back towards Dunadd with flaming torches.

It was the first time he had seen his new wife as Goddess, and when her voice changed as she made her proclamation, growing sonorous, deeper, the hairs on the back of his neck rose. Yet as the drums and pipes began, and figures began to dance around the roaring fire, he also saw that she was untouched by the crowd's release of tension, the renewal of laughter and talk. She remained unmoving atop the mound, and in her pale robe, her hair bleached by the starlight, she was a shard of ice: detached, unreachable, untouchable.

His heart chilled, he turned away.

There was mead and ale flowing now, and he drew a drink from the barrels, content to wrap himself in his cloak on the frosted slopes of the narrow valley that cupped the line of ancestor mounds. So much had happened in such a short time, that he took any opportunity he could to sit and think. It was, after all, the thing he did best.

The dancing had become wilder now, to chase away the restless Samhain spirits, and Eremon chuckled to see Conaire being pulled enthusiastically into the fray by the girl called Garda. She had been stalking his poor foster-brother for weeks now.

'My lord.'

He jumped and looked up. There, next to him, was another

girl. He'd certainly noticed her around the dun, mainly because of the way that her eyes always followed him. Round, blue eyes, they were, and she had a lush figure and thick, yellow hair. He smiled, not knowing her name.

'I am Aiveen, my lord, Talorc's daughter. I have been wishing to speak with you.'

A bold one, she was, then. No woman had yet dared to approach him, though tonight, for the first time, he was ready for them to do so. The mood of the dancing was infectious, and he had not forgotten Conaire's words on the marsh that day. He took a sip of mead, and then, impulsively, held the cup out to her. 'Then speak with me, daughter of Talorc.'

She sank down next to him and held her hands for the cup, drinking, holding his gaze while she did so. 'Are you enjoying our feast, my lord?'

'Most certainly. And more so now I have some company.'

She dimpled, lowered her eyes with false modesty and turned her cheek away. Ah, there it was. So the games begin. First the coyness, then the suggestive comments, and then her leg would brush his . . . All of a sudden, he reconsidered whether he could be bothered with the predictability of it all. *And it's an attitude like that, my lad, that will keep your balls blue for many moons to come.*

His eyes roved down her cheek, to where full breasts swelled against the neck of her gown. And then, in the light of the nearby fire, he noticed something. The hood of her cloak was fringed with feathers. Swan feathers.

He frowned. 'Where did you get those?' He flicked one with a finger.

For the first time, she looked uncertain. 'My mother received them as a gift for me. I thought . . .'

Abruptly, he laughed, raking his fingers through his hair. 'I see.'

So that's what Rhiann did with his gifts. On the far mound he could just see her, outlined against the fire, still and pale. So far away. Maybe there was no point in trying after all.

Aiveen's leg brushed his, and he decided to put Rhiann out of his mind. He leaned back, his elbows pillowed on the cold ground by his cloak, and smiled at the girl. 'The feathers become you very much.'

She dimpled once more, sure of him again. 'Thank you, my lord.'

'And no more of this "my lord"'. He brushed her cheek slowly with a finger. 'My name is Eremon. You may use it.'

'Thank you, Eremon.' She rolled his name around her tongue with obvious relish, and he felt an answering stab of warmth between his legs. She sipped the mead and gave it back to him. 'So, do you celebrate Samhain in the same way that we do?'

'Mostly.' He looked around at the dancing and the firepits, the small bands of musicians. 'But we don't have priestesses.'

A frown touched her brow at that; she would not want to be reminded of Rhiann. Cursing himself, he reached out and ran the back of his hand down her arm, and felt her answering quiver. Then she lay back on one elbow, near to the circle of his body. The movement made her breasts press even more tightly against the fine wool of the dress. When he raised his eyes to her face, her saw her knowing smile.

'And what do you do when the feast is over?' Her voice was low, throaty.

He knew that note well. This was proving much easier than he'd anticipated. A little too easy, if truth be told, but it made things simpler. If he did not have to win her, then she would expect nothing from him. 'We honour the gods with our bodies. What do you do?'

She laughed, throwing back her head to expose her white throat. Her teeth were pearly and even in the firelight. 'We, too, do this.'

'And how long until such – diversions – begin?'

She smiled and looked at him directly. 'The women have wondered about you. They said you would be difficult; that you must not like girls.'

'No one has tried.'

'Well, I am brave.'

'Yes, you are.' He stroked her hand again. 'And what will you say to these women now?'

'I will tell them that you don't like girls, of course.'

He laughed. At least she had some wit; it made things slightly more interesting. 'You did not answer my question.'

'And that was?'

'How long?'

She took the mead cup from him and rested it on the ground, then rose. In her eyes was triumph. Ah, yes. Being the first would matter to a girl like this. For a moment, he wondered about her father, but then put the thought out of his mind. He was a prince: it was an honour for her to find favour with him, and Talorc would be pleased at the connection.

'Eremon of Erin should wait for nothing.' Her hand was out, and she pulled him to his feet. 'Is that cloak of yours warm?'

He leaned in, his hands resting lightly on her waist. He could feel the curve of it, the burning of the skin through the cloth. 'The cloak is not so, but I am.'

As they left the firelight for the darkness of the valley slopes beyond, Eremon cast one look back over his shoulder. The lonely figure on the mound had not moved, and even in the midst of all that swirling, ruddy firelight and flickering heat, she was silver and still.

'Eremon.' The whisper came out of the dark. He turned and followed it.

CHAPTER 18
long dark, AD 79

T here was the taste of first snow in the air on the day they began the curing of meat for the coming season. It was heavy work, and bloody, too, but Rhiann relished the sheer physical effort of it.

She was supervising the women in the curing shed. One side was open to the slaughter yards, and the thin air was filled with the steam of cattle breath, the curses of men and the stumbling and pushing of beasts being driven in from the gates.

'Here, my lady.' One of the servants handed her a cloth to wipe her fingers, as she finished pressing a haunch of flesh into a pan of sea-salt.

She didn't really need to be here. She'd already blessed the cattle for slaughter, and the older women of the dun knew better than she how to cure the meat. But soon the snows would close in, and she would be trapped inside with little but sewing to do for many moons.

She stifled a sudden yawn, and saw the servants looking at her sidewise. The last thing she wanted was to give them more to talk about. The dark rings under her eyes and her exhaustion meant only one thing when one was new-wed. If only they knew the truth.

She barely saw her husband, in between gathering the last berries, skimming and curdling the last milk, and blessing the grain pits as they were sealed with their caps of clay. She ensured that the prince and his men had food, but often did not eat with them, excusing herself to attend the sick in her own house. Even if she did eat in the King's Hall, she and

Brica sat on the women's side of the central fire, keeping to themselves. It was only at night that he was near her, for they must share a bed in an alcove on the hall's upper gallery.

But – and she still could not believe it – he never touched her. He never even came close to touching her. After sitting late with his men, he pulled back the screen around their bedplace to find her hunched against the wall, and in return, when he lay down, he kept close to the pallet's edge. She could not even feel the warmth of his body.

At first she had lain there awake, rigid with tension, waiting for the hand on her shoulder once more, and not knowing what she would do when it came, for the hall was full of people now. Every night, she heard him shift and turn, and knew that he lay awake, too. But the touch never came. Subsequently, their shadowed eyes and short tempers triggered many knowing glances around the dun, and speculation about what was keeping them awake. It was an unbearable torture for Rhiann, but there was worse.

For now, she really had no choice but to admit to herself that Eremon of Dalriada had some honour after all.

Her eyes were gritty and weeping from the sharp, snow-tainted wind, and now she blinked to clear them. More glances came her way. *Dear Goddess.*

She dipped her fingers into one of the pickling barrels and touched them to her tongue. 'Maire,' she said to the servant standing by, 'add five more ladles of salt. And Anga, we need extra bulls smoked this year: one hundred altogether.'

Throwing down the cloth, she took up her cloak and walked to the gate that opened on to the main village path. Her nose was running, and her hands were beginning to ache from cold.

I'll get Brica to pour me a hot footbath.

Just then a sweet scent wafted over the blood and snow, as a jewelled Aiveen and her attendants hurried by. The reason for her haste was soon apparent, for Eremon and his men had entered at the gate. As the group passed her by on their way up the village path, Rhiann saw Conaire say something, and

Eremon reply with that sardonic half-smile, and Aiveen throw back her head, fingers pressed to her throat, her high, tinkling laughter carrying over the bustle of the village.

Rhiann grimaced. Honourable the prince may be, but possibly stupid, as well, if such a girl turned his head.

On the first day of snowfall, Eremon received a druid visit in the King's Hall.

'No, Rori, duck under, don't step back!' Eremon pushed himself away from the roof-post and grabbed Rori's sword arm.

The boy's opponent, Colum, rested his sword-tip on the floor, breathless and grinning, as the other pairs continued to spar in the cleared space to the side of the hearth, where the feasting benches had been pushed back. Conaire and Aedan were playing *fidchell* on the far side of the fire, beside a steaming cauldron of venison stew. Under their stools, Cù was tied up, sulking.

'Watch,' Eremon instructed Rori. 'This is the move that Colum made. I'll do it slowly. Now, show me again what you just did. You stepped back here and—' Eremon lunged in with his sword, and brought it up short, with the tip touching the vulnerable skin under Rori's armpit. 'See? You exposed your whole flank! Just because he changed his attack, doesn't mean you abandon that defence I taught you. Does it?'

Rori flushed to the roots of his red hair. 'No, sir.'

'Do this in battle and you'll be gutted like a fish.'

'Yes, sir.'

The doorway darkened, and Eremon glanced up to see Gelert standing there. He turned back to Rori. 'Now, do it again. Colum, swap with Fergus. I want to see the lad up against a different fighter.'

He left them and strode over to the druid, who was scanning the room with his sharp eyes, a mantle of bear-fur over his pale robes. 'You turn our King's Hall into a battleground,' Gelert observed.

Eremon wiped sweat from his face with his bunched-up

tunic and shoved it under his arm. They had all stripped bare to the waist to train close to the fire. 'And that is the reason you invited me within it. Will you have some ale?'

The druid waved his hand dismissively, but Eremon accepted a cup from one of the servant girls. He drank it dry, making no effort to put the tunic back on. Gelert eyed his sweat-streaked chest with visible disdain. 'Belen tells me that while I was away in the north, you badgered the council into supporting a strange plan of yours. Levies.'

Eremon handed the cup back to the girl. 'That's right.'

'This is a delicate matter, prince. We are trying to keep our throne, not invite rival clans to take up residence here.'

'I gave the council sound reasons, and that is why they agreed. If you wish me to be your war leader, then you must let me lead.'

'On the battlefield, yes, but—'

'Lord Druid, I am trying to build you a warband that will be strong enough to take on the Romans. We are not dealing with cattle-raiders any more. Things will need to change.'

Gelert's eyes flashed. 'You are dealing with tribal matters. You should have come to me; that was our . . . understanding.'

Slowly, Eremon rested the tip of his practice sword on the earth floor, leaning on the hilt with both hands. Though the druid did not move, a muscle twitched in his cheek.

'I *am* dealing with tribal matters, yes,' Eremon replied. 'But at such a time, war and politics are one and the same thing.' He let his eyes wander casually over the shields crowding the walls of the hall. 'It's strange but, in Erin, our druids confine their considerable powers to the spirit world. They leave the messy business of war to people like me.' He fixed Gelert with a cool stare. 'Am I to understand that things here are different? If so, I'll ask Belen and the rest of the council to explain it to me.'

Gelert regarded him for a long moment, his eyes veiled. 'The sea lanes will be open again in only a few moons.' The druid's voice was velvet. 'I must consult with you on where your father's dun lies, and how best to get our messenger there.'

Eremon bowed his head in acknowledgement. 'I will consider that nearer the time. But for now, there is much to do, and there will be more when the warriors arrive. So if you'll allow me to get back to my training . . .'

Gelert gripped his oak staff, his hands white over the owl's eyes. Then he turned for the door. 'Until leaf-bud, then, prince.'

Eremon watched him go, suddenly sensing Conaire beside him. 'Should you antagonize him so, brother?' Conaire asked.

'He needs to be reminded of his place. An understanding, ha! I will be no man's hound, to come at his call. Perhaps it is time for him to find out what he took on when he made me that offer.' Eremon threw his tunic down on the nearest bench. 'Come! Get your blade. I need to sweat this druid stink out of my skin!'

Rhiann hefted the heavy babe on her hip. 'Goddess, but he's a weight. He's fattening up nicely now!' She tickled the baby under the chin, and he giggled and butted his head into her shoulder.

'He is now, thanks to you, lady.' Aldera, the wife of Bran, the smith, smiled at her son indulgently. They were standing outside the door to Bran's house.

'Now, I still want you to give him the powder in mare's milk every day for one more moon. Brica, have you given Aldera the packet?'

'I have, mistress.' Brica was hovering over Rhiann with her cloak, eyeing the new crust of snowfall on the path.

Just then Rhiann caught sight of Gelert coming down through the Horse Gate from the King's Hall, his face thunderous. Behind him trailed some of the novices in training. As he drew level with them, he slowed his steps.

'Lord Druid.' Aldera bobbed a curtsy.

Gelert nodded at the women, and then his sharp glance took in Rhiann standing there with the baby. His eyes roved over her, resting so very deliberately on her belly. Rhiann just as deliberately kissed the soft hair on the baby's head.

She knew that Gelert missed little, and was no doubt marking her thinness and the worn creases of exhaustion. Yes, the pleased smirk that crossed his face as he kept walking left her in no doubt of that. He wanted to see if she was breeding. He wanted to see how much pain she was in.

Watching his departing back, the white hair straggling over his shoulders, she toyed with the thought of telling him exactly how she was, just to wipe that sly smile off his face. Showing him that his plans had not hurt her would give great satisfaction . . . but no. It would do neither she nor her tribe any good to unmask her relationship with the prince right now.

As she and Brica said their farewells and headed home, she was struck by the thought that if the marriage tie was severed, Gelert would seek to wed her to another man immediately. And that man would no doubt prove to be more demanding of his marriage rights than the prince of Erin.

That thought kicked her in the belly, and she froze. Brica halted too. 'Mistress?'

'I need to go for a walk.'

Brica looked up at the heavy clouds. 'It will be warmer by the fire.'

'I don't want warmth, I want air.'

Brica bit her lip. 'You must take care with your health, lady. This lack of sleep . . .' She trailed off, and Rhiann saw the anger in her sharp face. Brica still slept in her own bed. She, too, assumed that the prince was keeping Rhiann up of a night to satisfy his lusts.

'I am sleeping more now, and fresh air is as important as rest, as you well know – though delight in ignoring.' She said it lightly, as a jest, but Brica's mouth pursed.

The little woman put the pack of herbs on the ground and took off her cloak. 'At least put this on underneath your own. I've only to go a few steps.'

Rhiann complied, chastened. Brica tugged both cloaks

149

closed around her throat and pulled Rhiann's hood up. 'There.'

'Thank you, Brica.' The wind on Dunadd's crest would be fierce, coming in from the northern mountains, so she had to admit Brica was right.

She was having to admit all sorts of things about all sorts of people, she realized, as she walked away. And a cold face framed by dark hair flashed into her mind.

'Cù!' Eremon whistled, expecting to see the hound racing back through the Horse Gate at his call. But all he heard was a faint yip from the houses below the shrine. 'Fool dog!' he muttered, brushing the feathered snowflakes from his eyebrows, thinking of the warm fire behind him, and Conaire waiting with the *fidchell* board. But the hound was still young, not yet running with the king's pack, and Eremon didn't want him bothering anyone with his exuberance.

He followed the trail of yelps out of the gate and down between the houses, ducking along unfamiliar paths, slippery with frozen slush. Then, coming around the curve of a wall, he stumbled across a doorway, its hanging tied back. And this place he did know. He approached silently, almost fearfully, alarmed at the rumbles of Cù's growls coming from within.

It was his new wife's house. She was alone by her hearthplace, her back to the door, bent over. Both hands were clasping the end of a linen cloth that Cù was gripping and shaking madly, his tail a blur of grey, a growl punctuating each wrench of his head.

Gods! That was all Eremon needed. He raised a foot to step inside, to take Cù in hand, but then checked himself. For a most unexpected sound suddenly rang out. The princess was laughing.

Instantly, Eremon pressed back against the wall. Cù yipped once more, from the side of his clenched jaws, and pulled harder.

'You're a strong lad!' she chuckled, leaning back on her heels, tugging the cloth. 'But don't pull me over!' It was a

150

rich, throaty laugh, completely at odds with the coldness of her features, the thinness of her body, the way she always hunched into herself.

But the moment couldn't last; a breath before Cù himself noticed Eremon, she swung around, her face a white oval of shock and dawning embarrassment.

He took a step forward, drawing some dignity around him. She'd caught him spying! 'I'm sorry if the hound disturbed you, lady.'

Cù dropped the cloth and launched himself at Eremon, his paws landing against his chest and throwing him off balance. By the time Eremon disentangled himself, the girl had retreated to the other side of an oak workbench, set near the wall of healing potions. Her face was tilted, and he could just see the curve of her cheek, flaming a deep red.

He racked his brains for anything sensible to say. 'I – ah – as it happens, I needed to speak with you anyway.'

'Really?' She wrapped the chewed cloth around her fingers and grasped the handle of a steaming pot, pouring what smelled like hot beeswax into an earthen bowl. He thought he saw her hands tremble, just slightly.

'It's about these levies,' he said, stepping cautiously to her fireside. On the hearthstone, close to the coals, barley bannocks were toasting, and he sniffed.

'Levies?'

'Don't tell me the news has not gone around the whole dun.' He glanced at her, and she lifted her chin.

'I don't gossip with the other women.'

'Yes, I had noticed that.' He circled the hearth slowly, deliberately avoiding any sharp movements. Cù had by now flopped down by the fire. 'I'm calling in fifty warriors from each clan to be quartered here, and in the nearby duns. I'm going to train them as one warband.'

'Fifty each! But that's five hundred men!'

'Even that will be no more than a gnat bite on the hide of the Roman army, though it's a start. They will be here at Imbolc.'

'Imbolc? But the snows will only just be melting; the storms still fierce!'

On a low shelf near the door he passed a line of squat figurines, ochre-stained. Next to them, a collection of faded shells and dried anenomes. 'I'm going to clear the King's Hall and train them inside, in shifts. Any time we can, I'll train them outside. We'll need to drill the chariot teams as well . . .'

'You are going to train them outside?' Her voice was incredulous.

'Yes.' He reached out to touch the smooth back of a speckled cowrie shell. 'Armies may not march in the long dark, but we can certainly walk a few steps down to the river meadow.'

She was silent, and he turned, fighting down exasperation. 'As soon as the weather breaks, the Romans will be on the move again. Do you think they just came here to poke their heads over your border and wave their standards? We must be ready for them. It is the only way.' He had argued this very point with the council for a full day.

'You're right.' She was nodding. 'The Romans are here for more than that.'

He blinked, surprised. 'And how do you know this?'

'I am a priestess.'

'You have seen it?'

A pause. 'My aunt has seen it.'

'Well.' That was interesting. 'Let us speak of this soon. For now, I need you to think about how you'll distribute the men among the houses, and look to your provisions.'

A spoon clattered to the bench. 'I?'

'Yes, who else? You are to all intents the Queen of this dun, are you not? I've managed to decipher some of your admittedly strange kin system. And despite the unorthodox marriage that I find myself in . . .' At that, she lowered her eyes. 'Despite this, you are wife to the war leader. I must be able to rely on your support in that area.'

If in no other. He did not say the words, but the bitterness leaped to his throat, surprising him.

Her head reared, as if she heard him. 'I will organize which houses will take the men. We were already putting down extra provisions in case of siege or war, but I'll make sure to store more.'

Some small relief swept through him. She would co-operate, then. 'Good. And I think that we'll also need extra clothing.' He patted his leg, and Cù rose to heel. 'Thank you.'

His awkwardness had returned, but she was stirring her beeswax salve, staring resolutely into the bowl. 'Know that I put my people first. Always.'

As he left her, he wondered if he'd ever hear that laugh again. It would have warmed the hearthside, now that the snows closed in.

CHAPTER 19

The longest night of the dark was seen out with drums and yew boughs, and moon cakes of hazel and roasted acorns. And then, in the midst of a week of sleet storms, a clear day dawned.

Shaking out her riding trousers from the chest where they had lain musty for a moon or more, Rhiann piled on a wool shift and sheepskin tunic, and wound the thongs of her snow boots up her calves. She simply must get out of the King's Hall. It reeked of old sweat and unwashed male bodies and stew – she was heartily sick of mutton stew! Her eyes were strained and gritty from huddling over embroidery in the firelight, her fingers cramped and clumsy.

When Liath saw her riding cloak, she tossed her head and pawed the stable floor. 'Are you tired of this, too, my love?' Rhiann patted her nose. 'Too much soured barley and too little air. Let's stretch those legs of yours!'

Despite the clouds there had been little deep snow, and what was left was trampled into a muddy slush that made the going difficult. But Rhiann did not want to keep to the valley paths. She had something else to do. She took the southern trail, and then urged Liath away from it, up the slopes to the east, and into the forests.

There were many places sacred to the Old Ones there, slabs of rock with strange spirals carved on them, and an underground gateway to the Otherworld made of stones. And in a hidden fold of the land, there was a sacred pool, which a spring fed so slowly that the water was always clear and smooth.

Liath plunged gamely through the deeper drifts, her sturdy legs made for such going. Little moved among the ice-rimed branches and pale sunlight, but the robin's trill still sounded from a high branch, and more bird calls came, carrying far in the crisp air.

Rhiann tethered Liath on a rowan tree by the spring. Tattered scraps of cloth tied around the branches – last year's offerings – fluttered in the sighing wind that came down from the heights above. She spread out a hide on the banks of the pool and leaned over the water. The surface was unfrozen, and only a crust of ice frosted the moss.

From her pack she pulled a garland of dried marigolds, gathered in sunseason, and a copper arm-ring. It was Gaulish: she'd been careful to choose something that was not Roman. Lastly, she unstoppered a tiny vial of rose-scented oil. Dabbing it on her spirit-eye, she murmured, 'Elen, water guardian, I come annointed to your shrine. Hear my plea.' Then she cast the flowers on the water, and gently tossed the arm-ring into the deepest part of the pool. It spun, over and over, then faded from view.

Now Rhiann took a deep breath, closed her eyes, and tried to empty her mind. She'd deliberately not taken *saor* or any of the herbs of seeing. She wanted to find out if she could do this for herself, to gain some hint of what was in store for them when leaf-bud came.

She remembered the power that surged through her as she looked into the silver seeing bowl on the Sacred Isle . . . the pillar of light and heat that spilt into the top of her head and poured down her body, as if she stood under a waterfall of light. She ached for it again.

But to find it, she must breathe. And breathe.

Soon, the trickling of the spring out into its stream was dulled. The whoosh of Liath's breath softened into the keen breeze around her. All she could hear was her heartbeat, and the rasp of her breath, the rush of blood in her ears. 'Goddess of all, She of the Three Faces, Lady of the Forest. I plead for Your grace. Guide me today in love for Your people. Show me

155

what steps I must make upon the path back to You.' She opened her eyes and leaned out over the water, holding the steadiness of the heartbeat and the breath in her mind.

The surface of the spring shimmered with colour, and shifting shapes. Were there red cloaks there, swords, a ship? Her throat caught, as she leaned closer, closer, to the shining water . . .

Yes, yes . . . I see . . .

But at the last there was nothing: only her own face, the sun a nimbus around her hair, the branches of the rowan a mocking crown. She sank back on her heels, and bit her lip at the sharp flood of hurt.

It was a slow ride back, Liath stumbling now when before she had been so sure-footed. Rhiann was so sunk in her despair she did not notice the mare leave the path that led back down the slope. But suddenly she reined in, disoriented. 'Liath, where are we?'

The horse whinnied in reply, and shook her mane. Rhiann turned in her saddle in all directions, looking for a landmark. The melting snow and branches stretched out in all directions, but thankfully, without the obscuring leaves, she could just make out the top of a great rock slab that thrust out from the slope. She knew that; it was a lookout for the scouts. She had just come a little too far north, that was all. If she made for that and cut directly downhill she would hit the main track back to Dunadd.

Long after, she wondered at the compulsion that took her to the rock that day. If the sky had not been clear, or if she had ridden out later, or if Liath had not left the path, she would not have seen what she did.

First there was the scent of smoke. She pulled Liath up. There was movement at the base of the rock: it must be the lookouts, with their fire. She would pass by and see them, ask if they had any news to relay to the dun. Why, then, did she not call out? Why did she slip to the ground silently, and walk closer? Why?

Near the rock, she saw the horses. One of them was a big, black brute called Dòrn – the Fist.

The tribe's wedding gift to her new husband.

There was a fire under the shelf of rock, on the ground where no snow lay. Close to it, a deer-hide was spread, and a man and a woman were locked in an embrace, oblivious to the bite of the air, oblivious to Rhiann's pale form standing by a tree on the edge of the clearing. The woman, yellow hair spilling over the roan hide, was Aiveen. And the man's arms around her were Eremon's.

Stricken though she was, Rhiann could not make herself look away. She seemed to have lost all control over her eyes.

They lay bathed in the weak sun, close to the fire, moving together as sinuously as otters in a stream. Rhiann had never seen two people twine together in this way, like one being. Around the dun she witnessed rushed encounters against walls, in the stables or granaries. But as for the rest, it happened under cover of darkness, and the moans that came from people's beds always sounded painful to her.

She stared, burning with shame and fury, yet torn by an awful fascination. The kisses and caresses in the clearing grew more urgent, and she saw the girl's round breasts emerge from her tunic, saw them covered by Eremon's hands, shockingly brown against Aiveen's white skin.

A sickness stirred in Rhiann's belly, as the kisses became ever hungrier. And then Eremon pushed the girl back on the hide and edged her dress higher, and that part of the act Rhiann knew all too well. With the slapping of naked flesh, and the cries, sharp in the thin air, Rhiann's own newly-awakened memories rushed in. The same hoarse thrusting and grunting, the crying of her own voice in pain, the smell of old fish on the breath of the black-haired man . . .

Disgust roiled in her guts like curdled milk. She wanted to run before she was sick, before the dark memories came fully to life. Yet still she could not draw away. It was as if her feet had been frozen in place, imprisoned by the snow.

Aiveen whimpered and moaned again, and this time a deep

instinct told Rhiann that this cry was different to her own a year ago. It was low and throaty; not high and sharp. Not pain: pleasure. Rhiann's spirit was too naked and raw to deny it.

Abruptly, the old trauma faded into the pale-washed sky, and the scene before her leaped out in minute detail. Instead of the rough, red skin of her own attacker there was Eremon's strong, brown arms, glistening with sweat, Aiveen's hands spread protectively over tight muscles. Instead of coarse black hairs there was Eremon's tawny fuzz, glinting in the sun, and his dark braids falling into Aiveen's eyes.

The moans were growing louder and the thrusts faster now, and Rhiann felt her own breath coming shallow in her breast. And then at last, Eremon let loose a great wrenching cry and collapsed on to Aiveen's writhing body, and mercifully, it was over.

Rhiann's feet were released.

She stumbled back to Liath, heedless of the cracking twigs, a sob growing in the back of her throat. After flinging herself into the saddle, she wheeled the horse around, urging her off through the trees, away, away from the sickening scene behind her. But where the slope deepened, and Liath's hooves began to skid on loose mud, Rhiann suddenly pulled the mare up again, throwing herself to the ground, falling to her knees. And there she vomited in the snow, retching again and again, until all that was left was the spasm.

Shaking, she wiped her mouth, tipping back on her heels against Liath's leg. The mare leaned down and butted her with concern, and Rhiann twined fingers in the wind-knotted mane, her eyes unseeing.

The forest was silent around her.

All the birds had fled.

She rode back to Dunadd in a daze, now blind to the beauty of the day. The last sun was spilling through a rent in the clouds, slanting low over the ground, picking out each rock and tree branch with gold.

She saw none of it. The fury had cooled to dull anger, though she tried to hold on to its fire. In its place, ice ran in her veins. Eremon could do what he wanted. He had no tie to her. His taste was questionable, but then what more could she expect?

Yet all the while this monologue trailed on, against the backdrop of her mind . . . through her mind . . . tumbled images; visions of a clarity she had wished to see in the sacred pool. But they were not pictures of the man with black hair, and dirty nails. They were not the bunching of Eremon's back as he thrust, the white globes of Aiveen's breasts, yellow hair spread across the hide. They were images of a far more disturbing nature. And try as she might, she could not exorcise them from her mind.

Eremon's hands, caressing the girl as gently as he would still a filly. Eremon's fingers, running tenderly from Aiveen's waist along one flank. Eremon's lips, lighting on her shoulder, bare from its dress, as a butterfly lights on a flower.

Rhiann had felt such things with Drust on the Sacred Isle, when he painted her. But that was long ago.

Before the darkness came.

CHAPTER 20

At the rites of Imbolc the women offered to Brigid, goddess of leaf-bud, pouring pale streams of ewe's milk into the Add and burying kegs of the first butter deep in marsh pools.

And as the goddess heeded their call, and woke the land, the levies of men began arriving.

On a day weeping with sleet, Eremon lined the new arrivals up on the plain by the river, to see what this army of his was made of. There were young boys clutching their bows, their cheeks smooth, their eyes wide; there were thick-set warriors with scar-seamed hands, and cynical mouths; and finally a brace of chieftains' sons, with bright-checked cloaks and gold torcs, their chins jutting with pride. They watched Eremon – and each other – with hawk-eyes, and he knew why they had come. They were here to take his measure as much as he was theirs, to report back to their fathers what kind of man this *gael* was.

Eremon, too, had dressed in his best, bearing every arm-ring and brooch he possessed, his boar-crest helmet, and his bright shield. Fragarach was in his hand, the sleet-glare catching on its hilt as he spoke.

Balanced on Talorc's chariot pole, he explained in rousing terms why he had called them all in. He told them of the voraciousness of the invaders – and exaggerated their riches. He said that he would forge them into a hammer, which could fell the Romans with one blow. He told them they could become the strongest, most valiant, and most lauded tribe in Alba. That few generations had been given the chance to make such a name as they could make now; a name for the bards to sing of for ever.

And as the wind cut across the meadow like a knife-edge, and the melting flakes caught in shaggy, sheepskin cloaks and froze the mud on cowhide boots, he saw the light begin to kindle in the men's eyes. They nodded and grunted, and inside he permitted himself a sigh of relief. They would go along with him, then, and watch and wait. He had some little time to win them over.

Just then there was a shout from the river ford, and every head turned. Across the meadow, through the sleet, a careering chariot had appeared. Drawn by a pair of black horses, which seemed to fly through the whirling white, the chariot bumped and swayed dangerously on the rutted ground. The driver yipped and slapped the reins across the black beasts' backs, and they raced faster and closer, making no effort to slow as they neared the crowd, but swinging out in a wide arc. The wicker sides of the chariot and its iron wheels were painted scarlet, and against the grey sky and pale meadow it was a splash of blood on snow.

From his own height, Eremon watched this display with a frown. No one could bring a chariot over land in this weather. It must have been carried – carried! Whoever the owner was, he intended to make an impression.

The chariot executed a wild, sharp turn, but the warrior standing behind the driver kept his feet, and then the gathered levies were forced to scatter as the vehicle came to a skidding halt before Eremon, the horses rearing up in their traces.

With one lithe movement, the warrior leaped from the chariot, and stood looking around with challenging grey eyes. He was of an age with Eremon, taller, though with less breadth at the shoulder. His hair marked him from afar, for it was so fair as to be silver, and acted as a fine foil for the expensive, purple-dyed tunic. His torc was twisted gold and bronze, and his cloak was braided with the four stripes that

161

denoted a chieftain's son – though this was apparent enough in the set of his chin.

He raised his eyes to Eremon. 'Are you the son of Ferdiad?' Eremon stared him down. 'I am. And who are you?'

The man grinned, but topped by those glacial eyes, it was a baring of teeth. 'I am Lorn, son of Bettna. My father is Urben of the Dun of the Sun.' He shook his spear. 'I come to aid in my tribe's defence.'

'I thank you for joining us,' Eremon said.

'I thank *you* for joining us,' Lorn replied pointedly. 'Your sword arm will be valued in our fight against the Roman dogs.'

Out of the corner of his eye, Eremon watched the other chieftains' sons. He saw a mixed reaction. Some were absorbing Lorn's challenging tone, and turning bolder eyes up to Eremon. Others were regarding the new arrival with bristling wariness. He was reminded of the way dogs circle each other, their legs stiff and hackles up. Quite the normal greeting among young warriors, then. He relaxed.

'Your druids thought so when they made me war leader,' Eremon rejoined. He had given this young cock enough attention; he did not wish to lose those men whose hearts had begun to turn to his words. He surveyed the crowd.

'And make no mistake, it is my fight, as well as yours!' he cried. 'I am your brother-in-arms, and on the day I took the hand of the Ban Cré, I pledged myself to your service. There will be no "yours" and "mine". I will share the same food, and laugh through the same hardships and – if Manannán wills it – shed the same blood! We have one enemy only, and that is the Roman empire. Side by side, we can beat them into dust!'

Most of the men howled and cheered and spat curses at the Romans, and as they broke and filtered back through the village gate for the welcome feast, they were already jesting and cuffing each other. Lorn, though, strode with the sharpness of anger, and about him other chieftains' sons gathered closer, dark as crows.

'We must watch that one,' Conaire murmured at Eremon's shoulder.

'Yes.' Eremon's eyes followed the silver head until it disappeared among the houses. 'I feel he will not be cowed by words.'

'Good,' Conaire growled. 'Then he will have a chance to meet my fists.'

But Eremon needed to know more. 'Who is Lorn, the man with the fair hair?' he asked Rhiann the next day, as she left the dairy shed with a keg of butter in her arms.

She ducked her head, not meeting his eyes. 'Lorn? His clan is the most powerful after our own – when our own was powerful,' she amended.

'And this means . . . ?'

'It means that he was the strongest contender for the kingship, and his clan had high hopes of installing him so.'

In the weeks following, the plain below the dun echoed with the clamour of swords and hoarse shouts of men-at-arms. The Trade Path was alive with racing chariots; the air filled with whines and thuds as archers and spearmen practised on hide targets.

The hard work made hungry bellies, and Rhiann ordered a line of great pit-ovens to be dug, for baking whole pigs, and stone-lined water troughs for boiling joints of beef. Each woman's hearthstone was kept hot for bread baking, her cauldron full of barley porridge. The King's Hall stank of male sweat and rang with male voices. Only at night did the levies disappear to their host houses in the dun, the village, and surrounding farmsteads.

With so many weapons being oiled and mended and forged, and men walking about in clanking armour, Rhiann felt as if she were living in a war camp. When she closed her eyes she could still see the sun glinting off the spear-tips on the plain; and even in the quiet darkness of the dairy shed, her ears echoed from the din.

Yet her dreams were not of battle, or even of armed men. In

the night, a deeper part of her emerged, and the images that stalked her then were of an entirely different nature: Eremon and Aiveen in the woods, laying in the snow, devouring each other with a hungering need.

One night she jerked awake, still seeing Eremon's brown hand on the girl's white skin, still hearing the cries . . .

Snores and mutters drifted up from the main hall below. Next to her, she heard the deep, exhausted breathing of Eremon in his sleep. Her mind was instantly alert, as if it had been chewing over things for many hours, even while asleep. And with the perfect clarity that comes in those dark hours, she suddenly realized the message of her dreams.

How can he be the weapon in my hand, when I have no control over him? If I isolate myself, I lose my chance.

For Aiveen was not the only one enjoying his attentions. A few days before, Rhiann overheard Eremon and Conaire joking about the trysts they had enjoyed on their recent visit to one of the northern duns. And every time he lay with those women, they had his ear, and not she.

Well, I can't go as far as that.

No, not as far. But his words in her house came back to her, reminding her that she was wife to the war leader. Yes, there was a way forward; her mind pounced on it instantly and held on.

Perhaps, just perhaps, the Goddess had given her the sight that day in the forest after all. Rhiann asked for guidance at the sacred pool. In coming across that scene of lust, Eremon and Aiveen together, perhaps Rhiann had been given that guidance.

So she had lost her deeper spirit powers, and would be no breeding wife to him. But there was one other role to fulfil, perhaps the only role left to her now.

I can't fight with a sword. But I can use my mind.

Despite the war-light in their eyes that first day, the young nobles expected only to game and feast and hunt in this season. They grumbled at taking the field, for though fine weather broke through a little more day by day, at any moment the sun could be eclipsed by frozen storms that howled down the glen from the mountains, or blew in from the sea.

And at any opportunity that presented itself, Lorn's voice was the loudest. Eremon had been declared as war leader, and so never asked for opinions, but nevertheless Lorn disagreed about how many men to train as archers, and how many as swordsmen, and argued that the fighting techniques of Erin did not suit the longer Alban swords. Like a stinging gnat, he goaded the men without ever rebelling against Eremon openly.

Then, after one frustrating day, when Lorn's men ignored Eremon's commands and broke the formation he had been teaching them, Eremon's patience snapped. He would bring this to a head now, on the ground of his own choosing. Lorn was obviously not a man like Eremon – a man who would reason, or put the good of the tribe first. There would be no other way.

'Son of Urben!' Eremon growled, striding across the meadow. 'I ordered you to practise this formation; practise it until it becomes your second skin! If we were in battle, you would be dead now!' The silver head jerked up, for Eremon spoke as if to a boy.

Lorn's eyes flashed. 'If we were in battle, I would have ten enemy heads on my spear, and you none!' he boasted.

The lines of sparring men caught the scent of a brewing fight and instantly downed their weapons, racing closer.

'You teach us to fight like cowards!' Lorn cried, warming to his theme. He tossed his head boldly and stared down the men at the forefront of the audience. 'Use this stroke, turn this way, hold your shields like this! We are Epidii, and we fight like champions, from our hearts!' He thumped his chest. 'We charge, we dance, we fly! We don't tramp in lines, like mindless ants! Like Romans!'

Eremon rested the tip of his practice sword on the ground. 'I teach you to win!' he shouted for the benefit of the gathered men. 'Yes, our hearts are the fire in the forge – but Roman discipline is the tempering hammer. We can learn what they will throw against us; and turn it back on them! They fight as one beast: each man part of the leg, the claw, the jaws. We must move together as they do, if we are to defeat them!'

Eremon heard a murmuring at that, but in support or dissent, he could not tell. He rounded on Lorn. 'And you, son of Urben! I am in command here, no matter what exalted blood runs in your veins! And you will follow my orders or, by the gods, I will throw you out of this warband and send you home to your father with your tail between your legs!'

With a howl, Lorn threw his sword to one side and leaped on Eremon, bearing him to the ground. As he went face down in the freezing mud, Eremon was shot through with a bolt of pure elation, because at last he could let the fire burst free. Howling back, he threw Lorn off and jumped on his chest, landing a blow to his jaw. Around them, the other men erupted into a frenzy of cheering and yelling, and Eremon caught a glimpse of Conaire's wide arms holding them back, clearing a space for the two scuffling fighters.

That is, until three of Lorn's cronies broke free, piling on to Eremon's back where he sat astride Lorn, pummelling his face. The impact knocked the wind from him, and suddenly Eremon was at the bottom of a writhing mound of men, and Lorn's fist came out of nowhere and slammed into the side of his head.

Stars spun for a moment in darkness, and then from somewhere above there was an unearthly yell, greater than that of all the other men combined, and Conaire came storming into the fray like a bull on the rampage. Eremon heard the grunts as Conaire laid about him with his huge fists, and the press above him lightened as the men were dragged off one by one and felled with a hammer blow, until only Lorn remained, now pinning Eremon down.

Lorn was cut above one eye, and the blood dripped on to

Eremon's cheek. 'Yield!' Lorn screamed, fastening both hands around Eremon's throat. 'Son of the bitch of Erin!'

'Watch your tongue, puppy,' Eremon gasped, and then twisted to bring his knee up, ramming it into Lorn's groin. The Epidii youth howled again, this time in pain, and summoning a burst of strength, Eremon took the advantage and threw him off balance until they both fell sideways into the mud. There, Eremon wriggled one hand free, and swinging back his shoulder, punched his fist into Lorn's mouth. There was another spray of blood, and the hold on his arms slackened for a moment.

They both struggled to their feet. But Lorn had not finished, and he now bowed his legs and curved his arms in the grappling position of wrestlers. *So that's how he wants to play it!* Eremon took up his own stance, and for a fleeting moment they were still.

However, Eremon had one advantage that Lorn should have considered. From babyhood, his wrestling partner had been Conaire. And to win against Conaire's bulk, he'd had to train himself to focus on skill, and not brute strength.

So his eye detected the ripple of tension in Lorn's legs a split second before he jumped, and as the Epidii warrior crashed into his chest, Eremon let himself go slack. This turned the impact into a measured roll, and Eremon used Lorn's own momentum to flip them both over until Eremon was again astride Lorn's chest, pinning his arms with his knees.

'Now you yield,' he panted.

Lorn's eyes burned up at him, his fury tangible. For a long moment they held each other's gaze, and now it was Eremon's blood dripping on to Lorn's grazed cheekbone. Finally, Lorn dropped his eyes, and Eremon released him and got to his feet.

Trying not to wince, Eremon straightened and wiped some of the mud from his face, wriggling his jaw to check it was sound. He took a breath. 'Now, I want you all to try that formation again.'

Behind him, he heard Lorn struggle to his feet. 'No.'

Eremon turned. Blood was streaming from Lorn's brow, and his eye was turning a mottled purple. But his bearing was straight, his shoulders back. 'I won't stay here to be turned into a Roman!' He spat a glob of blood and saliva on to the ground. 'I am a prince of the Epidii, and I fight like my fathers did. Champion to champion! With battle lust and fury! Not in careful lines, weighing every move like a pack of muttering druids!'

Eremon stood and let the words wash over him. This would not be the last time that he would face these accusations. He could not conquer long-held views overnight. 'We need every strong arm that we have, son of Urben,' he said quietly. 'The Epidii needs us all united.'

Lorn wavered for a moment, before those pale eyes hardened. 'I serve my tribe well,' he bit out, 'by refusing to follow a *gael* and fight like a coward!' He whirled, striding across the field toward the palisade, his followers taking off after him without a backwards glance. The other men from Lorn's clan were confused, looking between his retreating back and Eremon, but then one by one, they, too, threw down their practice swords and trailed after their chief's son.

Soon after, Eremon heard the drumming of hooves on the southern causeway, and glimpsed the glitter of spears as Lorn and his men galloped out of Dunadd.

'Well,' Eremon said to Conaire. 'We are short fifty men. We'll have to call up more from the other clans.'

But as the last sun caught on that silver head, disappearing down the muddy road, Eremon sighed. *His courage would make him a fine leader. But there can be only one.*

CHAPTER 21

L ate that night, as Eremon brooded over the *fidchell* board, a scout arrived from one of the outlying posts, mud-flecked and breathless from riding. He bore ill news along with the scowl on his face.

The Romans were on the move.

Though the large camp remained, parties of soldiers were now marching across the Forth. And even worse, they were building what looked like permanent quarters. 'They are smaller than camps, my lord,' the scout reported, 'but made of wood, with palisades and ditches . . . the messenger was not exact.'

Once the scout had been fed and sent to rest, the hall fell eerily quiet: the men's laughter stilled; Conaire and Eremon's game forgotten; Rhiann and Brica silent over their sewing.

'Gods!' Eremon suddenly smacked his fist into his hand, and rose to pace the hearth. 'I won't sit here like some duck on the marsh, waiting for the Roman arrow! I must know what they intend – and when they will come for us.'

'Maybe we can strengthen the scout network,' Finan put in.

'We still won't see them coming until they are here.' Eremon strode the length of the hearth-place and back. 'We need more information. I must have more information!'

'We could raid these Venicones lands ourselves,' Conaire suggested. 'Capture a soldier and make him talk.'

Eremon raked back his hair. 'Romans don't venture out alone, brother. And we cannot walk straight into their lines.'

Silence fell. Then Rhiann's slim form stepped out from the dark shadows. 'What about *through* their lines?'

A host of male eyes turned up to her, surprise etched on twenty faces. Eremon knew his expression must be the most shocked of all: she never spoke to any of them freely, and certainly not about such matters.

Standing there primly, in her robe of green wool, hair unbound, she seemed very young. Then she looked directly at Eremon, and what he saw in her eyes was not youth, but calculation. 'You do not have the blue designs on your skin. You can pass as Britons from the south.'

Eremon saw the answering leap of interest in the faces of his men, and raised his hand to object.

'Yes,' Rhiann continued, thinking aloud. 'Your men can pass through the southern lands, as can I. You can be my escort.'

'And go where?' Eremon cut in. 'As wandering strangers, we will stand out as if the marks of the Albans grace our own faces. You are talking of a dangerous proposition, not an adventure!'

Her eyes sparked at him. 'I have a cousin of the Votadini, at the Dun of the Tree, on the east coast. I have not seen her for many years, but she would welcome a visit from me, I am sure. The Romans have already taken the Votadini lands; her people will know more of them and their disposition, their numbers . . .'

'It won't work.' Eremon knew he sounded curt. But she treated him with complete indifference for moons, and then here she was, poking her nose into war business. 'We come through their forward lines, from enemy territory – it won't work.' He turned his back, dismissing her.

'It *will* work,' she argued, pushing in front of him again. His men glanced at each other, their eyes wide. Then Rhiann took a half-burnt twig that had fallen from the firepit, and began scratching with it on the bare dirt before Eremon's feet. Amazed, he stared at her for a moment before dropping his gaze to the crude map taking shape in the firelight.

'We take a boat down this loch to the sea, then land here on the west coast, below the Clutha. From what we know, we will be south of the Roman line at that point. Then we travel up the river valleys, which run down from the high ground – here – coming upon my cousin's dun from the south. From the territories the Romans have already conquered.' She dropped the stick and brushed the charcoal from her hands, a challenge in her eyes. 'I will be a noblewoman from the lowlands, travelling north to visit my family. For Beltaine, perhaps; that would be a good excuse.' She looked around at them all. 'If we take a small escort, we can do it.'

Eremon was silent, determined not to get into a haggling match with his wife in front of his men. And yet, as he listened, he had to admit that it could work. It was daring . . . but just the sort of thing that would impress the Epidii. If he was successful, he would gain more power, and more status among the new levies. And sitting here doing nothing was just as risky – no, riskier. If only he had thought of it. He glanced at Conaire. An unspoken message passed between them.

'I think it is a good idea,' Conaire declared, as if trying to convince him. 'We know that the Romans passed through those lands quickly, so they must be at peace now. A small escort with – as you say, lady – no Alban markings, would attract little notice.'

'You are forgetting something.' Eremon folded his arms. 'Yes, the Romans passed through these lands quickly – but this means that these tribes are sympathetic to their rule. How else did the Eagles not meet with greater resistance?'

'That may be true,' Rhiann returned swiftly, 'but we won't know exactly what happened unless we go. Perhaps the Votadini did give in to save themselves. But my cousin is of the sisterhood, and she will support us, no matter what betrayals the men of her tribe have committed.'

Eremon was silent. What she said intrigued him, despite his misgivings.

'Don't you see?' Rhiann broke in again. 'This is the only way to get the information that you need. It is a perfect plan. I say you should be thanking me, not arguing with me!'

Eremon noticed Finan and Colum biting down smiles, and Conaire sported a distinctly amused turn to his mouth. Rori was looking from Eremon to Rhiann with shocked eyes.

'The chance of success is high, despite the danger, brother.' Conaire spoke seriously now. 'The Romans will take little notice of a few lightly armed men and one noblewoman.'

'Well,' Eremon said at last, allowing Conaire to convince him. 'We cannot sit here, waiting for the snare to tighten. We must take action, for the sake of the Epidii. I say we go.' He smiled magnanimously at Rhiann, but she just frowned, irritation written into every line of her body.

Good, he thought. *That will teach you exactly who leads this warband. My lady.*

'Rori, Colum, Fergus and Angus, you will come with us,' he added briskly. 'And Finan, you will stay here and continue the training in my stead. Whatever we discover on this journey, I want the men in some sort of fighting order before sunseason arrives. That is, if we even have that long.'

Rhiann may have won over her husband, but the council of elders reacted with horror at news of her plan. Tharan, the eldest, declared it madness, and even Talorc was unusually implacable in his refusal to let her go.

'Lady,' Belen said, 'our Ban Cré should not be riding around the mountains on some dangerous escapade! She should be here . . .' he trailed off, but Rhiann did not miss the glance at her belly.

Yes, the murmuring had already begun, for she had been wed for six moons now, and still no sign of a babe. Which gave her another reason to press for this journey, for news of the Romans would keep the council's attention away from her. For a time.

She dragged her gaze to Eremon, who now broke in smoothly to say that he and his men could accomplish the same goal without taking her, and in fact would prefer to not do so. At that, she had to bite down the urge to slap the smug smile from his face.

In the end, support came from the most unexpected quarter.

The meeting was in the shrine, for the day was fine, the air carrying a hint of the warmth to come. And lurking in the shadows of the pillars, it was Gelert who said they should go. 'It is as the Ban Cré said: the Romans will not touch her. They do not have enough men to keep peace themselves, but rely on winning local chieftains to their side, bribing them with wine and oil. When they feel secure, they move forward. For this reason, the prince and his lady wife will meet few Roman soldiers in the conquered lands. And her status will protect all of them among the tribes. She must go.'

'You – you support this escapade, Lord Druid?' Belen sounded amazed.

'Most certainly.' Gelert stepped forward, drawing himself up to his fullest height. The morning sun was dazzling on his white robe and hair. 'The Romans will roll forward until they slaughter our babes in their beds. We must do anything to prevent it.' His voice rose to the commanding pitch of druid pronouncements. 'The gods cry out for Roman blood! We must give it to them, or feel their wrath ourselves!'

This proclamation had no effect on Rhiann, but she saw the fear ripple over the faces of the elders.

'The gods wish us to let them go?' Talorc spoke gruffly, to hide his discomfort.

Gelert whirled, and opened his arms before the altar. The robe spread out into wings to either side, and the sun poured through the thin wool. 'They speak to me,' he hissed. 'They speak to me in the fire. They say that the journey will safeguard our tribe!' He spun back, and the robe fluttered out and then was still. 'The Ban Cré must do her duty, and the prince fulfil his oath. I have spoken.'

Gelert's words overrode the council's reluctance, and when the sun was high, the vote was cast to let the party go south.

As she left the shrine, Rhiann threw a look over her shoulder. Gelert was turning back to his altar. He paused and caught her eye; the curve of triumph in his crooked smile was unmistakable.

He had said nothing of their own safety.

CHAPTER 22
leaf-bud AD 80

F ar away, on the Orcades islands off Alba's northern tip, a
king sat brooding in darkness, alone. The wind blew
around his hall with a steady roar, as it had all through
the long dark, sweeping in from the north across the flat
plains around his dun.

He had a shaggy thatch of dark hair and black eyes, like all
men of the Orcades. But when his subjects were brought to
stand before him, they saw another kind of darkness in his
face, and the fire in his eyes burned with no warmth. He had
the girth of a bull, and around his shoulders he wore the pelt
of the great white bear that ranged the ice lands of the far
north.

This king was powerful, and held all of the islands and
many leagues of the mainland coast in his iron fist. However,
it was not enough.

It seemed to him as he sat there in his dark hall, lit only by
a single, sputtering torch and a smoky peat fire, that he was
not powerful at all. What he wanted was the warm vales of
the mainland, the tall forests and lush pastures, the rich
pickings of the trade routes.

He clenched the fist that rested in his lap, and stared into
the dirty glow of the fire. He – Maelchon, son of queens – had
to dangle here on the edge of the world, scrabbling for the
scraps to fall from the tables of the high and mighty tribes of
Alba, like a lowly, slavering hound. Take that Caledonii King,
Calgacus, arrogant upstart, lording it over them all, flashing
his jewels and his horses and his cattle . . .

Maelchon hitched up his belt as he shifted on his throne,

and then, suddenly, he smiled to himself. They were all in for a surprise. Soon, no king or anyone else would look at him with anything but fear and awe.

This thought brought the now-familiar surge of heat to his loins. Every time he gnawed on his plans, he could hardly keep still. But he had to wait, to put them in place with patience, so that nothing would go wrong. It was hard, so hard to hold himself back. It was not his nature.

Maelchon's excitement was pressing on his trousers now, and he knew he had to get up and move, before this need for slowness drove him mad. He could call for his wife, pitiful creature that she was, but useful for some things . . . or he could call for his druid, and go and see his broch tower.

He glanced at the dim light creeping under the musty door hanging, and beckoned to the guard waiting in the darkness behind his throne. Judging by the light, it appeared he had time for both. There was not much else to do in this accursed, blasted land.

Kelturan the druid came quickly, as always. He was a tall, thin man with a sallow face and sparse hair, and deep-set eyes that missed very little. He wielded his oak staff of rank, but it was an old stick from the days of his youth. No tree of that lineage grew on these islands – only stunted, hardy rowans that could cope with the endless wind. 'You will be wanting to start the work teams again, lord.'

Maelchon smiled, for the druid had read his mind, which was why he kept him by, and no other. 'I do. I have heard that the Caledonii King is considering his defence against the Roman invader. A change is on the wind, Kelturan. Unstable days may be coming.' He took a gulp of ale, regarding the chipped whalebone cup with distaste. Where were the gold goblets, the bronze-rimmed horns, the jewels? He knew well the answer to that: hoarded by men such as Calgacus, in their lowland duns.

'It would be better to be within stout stone walls,' Kelturan was saying, although he knew, as did Maelchon, that the islands had always been protection enough. 'I shall call the teams back tomorrow.'

'I want to go there now,' Maelchon said. He could see the druid thinking about the winds outside, but when he looked into the King's eyes, all protest died on his lips. As it should.

'Yes, my lord, but pray, let me get my cloak.'

'You will come with me now, Kelturan.'

'Yes, my lord.'

They emerged from the hall into the dank, stinking village, washed with a dull light that crept from behind heavy clouds. Maelchon was followed by two guards, although they were for show, not protection. Here, in his domain, he need fear no attack. His people were spineless. They bowed and scuttled away as he strode down between the scatter of rude houses to the beach.

There, rearing from the shore like a grim, grey crag was the skeleton of a broch, a round tower four times as high as an ordinary house, with immense walls as thick as a man is tall. Its shell was almost complete, except for one wide cleft, and as yet it was roofless. Within the cleft, the stairs and galleries that led from the ground to two upper levels could clearly be seen. Soon the timber for the floors would arrive from the mainland, the wood costing more than anything Maelchon had ever traded for. But it did not matter.

The broch's stout walls, its grim heights, spoke of Maelchon's power. They proclaimed that he was no provincial king to be ignored and scorned. And when his plan was complete, then he would have the gold and the goods to carve and clothe and furnish the broch with rich decorations, until it was a kingly dwelling to rival any in Alba. There he would sit in his majesty, and gather the princes of Alba, and dazzle them. And someday after he would cross over and take all the lands down to the Forth itself: Caledonii lands, Taexali lands, Vacomagi lands. And any bride he wished, of the highest blood.

His heart fed on these thoughts, gloating over them as if they were hoarded gold in a deep chamber of his house.

'Master?'

The druid's voice shook him out of this pleasant reverie, and Maelchon waved his hand. 'I will go up alone. Wait here.'

He started up the stairs of the broch, moving heavily but easily, for age had not as yet dimmed his vigour, and the feeling of these walls, of owning these walls, gave extra strength to his step. He came out on to a stone ledge, one of the cross slabs that formed a gallery, and looked over the unfinished walls, to the sea.

He gripped the rough stones and felt their strength, and savoured the knowledge of his dominion over them. He ordered that they be set just so, and they were. All things could be ordered, men most easily, but many other things as well. Even his druid could be controlled – a man of magic, supposedly. Ha! A true king had no time for druid power. For him there was only one kind of power – that over life and death.

He crossed to the landward side of the broch, and gazed down at the people in his village, going about their rude and pointless existence. And as always, anger at them grew within him.

They were good for few things, these island people, providing food and tribute, but little else. Their sheer baseness seethed within him. One day he would take his proper place among the nobility, and he would be lord of all those who thought they were greater than him.

Then it will be different, he thought. *Then I will do as I wish.*

CHAPTER 23

Rhiann watched Eremon's shoulders bunch again as he heaved over the side of the boat. The other men from Erin were similarly stricken, all except the big one, Conaire.

She stretched her feet out to the frame of the *curragh*. She, at least, was happy to be on the sea with no one to fuss over her, for she had left Brica behind, citing the woman's own safety as an excuse. It was good to feel free on the waves after the long, stifling moons indoors, and good to be away from Gelert's owl eyes, and the demands of the dun.

'Tell me more about this cousin of yours.' Pale, but endeavouring to look composed, Eremon moved up to sit by her in the bow.

They hadn't spoken since Eremon made his offering of spear-points and finger-rings to the sea-loch as they embarked, watched over by Gelert's impenetrable eyes and the dark gaze of the council.

'I don't have much to tell,' she replied. 'My father was of the Votadini, and Samana is a cousin on his side. Her father was of the Silures . . .'

'In the west of Britannia? I may have some kinship there myself.'

She turned to look at him. 'You have kinship on these shores?'

'Besides my new kinship with you?' As his mouth quirked in that crooked smile, she realized it was bitterness that lifted it, and never warmth. 'My mother was of the Silures. It was she who gave me my dark hair and skin.'

Rhiann glanced back to the mountains rearing from the water as they ploughed down the loch. 'Well,' she went on, not interested in his colouring, 'my cousin trained on the Sacred Isle. She is two years the elder, so I did not see much of her. She was rather . . . fiery . . . and did not enjoy the rituals as I did. As soon as she was initiated, she left. I have not seen her for nearly four years.'

Eremon frowned. 'Then this is not a close connection! How can you be sure that we can trust her?'

Rhiann was dismissive of his concern. 'She is a priestess. Her loyalty is to the sisterhood, and she is my kin. She wouldn't sell her tribe: it is the men of the Votadini who were likely seduced by Roman silver.'

'I hope you are right.' Eremon began to shift uncomfortably in his seat. 'Is there, by any chance, a treatment for this sea belly of mine?'

'Only time, I am afraid. You will get used to it.'

With a tight smile he rose and disappeared towards the back of the boat, and soon she heard him retching again. What a pity she did not bring any tansy tonic with her. It was most effective against sea sickness.

The Epidii boatmen landed them at a small village of fisherman's huts clustered around a rickety pier, both sheltered from sea-storms by a thrusting green headland.

The Damnonii tribesmen here were independent and fierce. Isolated on their windy coast, they looked to themselves, and not to any new Roman administration, and so were accepting enough of the strange arrivals. An exchange of bronze arm-rings bought Rhiann's party some scraggly horses, and enough bread, cheese and dried meat for a week.

Rhiann took the opportunity to treat the chieftain's son for his lingering cough, and this gained the welcome information that although movement had been restricted by the Roman commander's decree, there were too few soldiers to patrol every fold of the wild hills. Agricola had taken the bulk of his forces further north, anticipating fiercer resistance there.

'Our king just gave up, as soon as he saw their swords,' the old chief grumbled, picking his teeth with a sliver of deer bone. 'The inland clans are cowards.'

Rhiann accepted a cup of bilberry tea from the chieftain's wife, and stretched her damp boots to the smoky fire. While the two days at sea had been fine, the wind had now whipped itself into a squall that sucked rain from an encroaching bank of clouds. She heard it pattering on the thatch roof above.

Despite the chieftain's hefty belly and slow speech, Eremon's probing questions soon uncovered a raw hatred for the Romans, and for the Damnonii king who surrendered.

'In future, we ourselves may need allies to resist the Romans,' Eremon murmured, swilling the tea around in his cup.

The man's eyes gleamed. 'They bleed us dry with their demands for grain and meat. But we are many, scattered in the sea-bays. If the time was right, and the leader strong, our men would leap at the chance to win back their spoils.'

Later, as they saddled and packed their new horses, the chief pressed upon them the services of his best huntsman as a guide. 'He will help you to avoid the men of the Eagle,' he assured them. 'Until you enter Votadini lands, that is. Then ... may Manannán guide you.'

'We must give you something in return,' Rhiann put in.

The chieftain waved away her offer gruffly. 'My boy breathes easier than he has for moons. Use your gold in the fight against the invaders.'

She found herself catching Eremon's smile over the chieftain's shoulder.

Sleeping under the stars seemed a fine idea when Rhiann was cramped in the stale hall at Dunadd. But the reality was gnarled roots in the back, sore hips from hard ground, and a constant drizzle of rain leaking into the hide tent. Add to that the grating laughter of the men around the fire until late in the night, and Rhiann slept fitfully, if at all.

Luckily, the scraggly horses proved to be fleeter than they first appeared, and a few days munching the new grass of the valleys brought a lift to their step, so the party's progress was swift.

For the first two days they saw no people, following the Damnonii chieftain's guide up the hidden glens of oak and birch, hazed with the mist of new leaves. But one grey morning, the whistle of the huntsman floated down from a high ridge-top that he was scouting. Bidding his men halt, Eremon edged up through the yellow gorse to the rocks that guarded the pass, Rhiann creeping beside him.

Below, the hillside fell away in flint scree to a shining thread of river. To the south, the glen widened, and there she glimpsed the flash of crimson and steel and bronze.

Roman cloaks and shields.

Roman armour: bright and shining, sheathing every limb and torso and head.

Alban warriors fashioned their own shield designs and sword hilts, beaded quivers and spear-butts. They rejoiced in looking different, with hair braided this way, or a pelt tied that way, or a cloak woven with this border . . . yet all these Romans looked the same. From afar, they appeared as ants, separate but the same, acting with one will. Even their armour was in segments, moving as they moved.

And their will in this valley was apparent, for in the middle two timber buildings were taking form, side by side, long and straight. Around them, a high palisade was going up: Rhiann could hear the low of oxen hauling timber from the valley bottom, and the thunk of axes. The musty smell of fresh-cut wood floated up to her.

'They call them forts,' the Damnonii guide remarked, as he crouched in the lee of the rocks, an arrow nocked on his bowstring. 'Soldiers live there.'

'Is there another way we can go?' Eremon asked him.

'Yes. We must trek back a little, but there is another glen –

much narrower, and the scrub is thicker, so there will be no building. The climb out is hard, though.'

'No matter,' Eremon said shortly. 'It is plain that this way is blocked. Lady, come now.' He and the huntsman slid back down the slope to the men, but Rhiann stayed a moment, absorbing the sharp, authoritative movements of the soldiers below. They were so alien to the land.

She knew the Romans bribed their careless, absent gods with oils and gold, but they did not bless tree or river or spring, or propitiate the spirits of the laden beasts. She could sense the wound they made even now, the scar on the earth.

Heart-sick, she turned her back and left the valley behind, knowing that she could not leave the Romans behind so easily.

Late on the third day the guide left them to return to his people. By then, they had seen no more of Romans or forts, and so, when they came across a wide track that ran at the base of a low granite ridge, they decided to follow it a little way. There were no footprints marking the mud, and Eremon judged it safe until they could round the cliff and find some easier ground to climb.

But as they stepped from the trees, all of them caught in a ray of late sun breaking through the near-bare branches, Rhiann heard someone cry, 'Halt!'

Goddess, it was Latin! Rhiann knew some druid-taught scraps of the language, but had never heard it spoken by a Latin native.

A Roman.

They had been seen through the open woods; they were being pursued.

There came the sound of a horse's hooves, and the thudding of many feet in the mud. Rhiann froze.

'Fall back from her,' Eremon hissed to his men. 'Do not react. At any cost.'

Fall back from me? And then she realized that he was right. If the men leaped to defend her, the Romans would assume them hostile. She struggled to stay calm, feeling so vulnerable in the middle of the path by herself.

But the horse felt the tension in her legs and shied, tossing its head. And then she sensed Eremon beside her, taking the reins with a sure hand. She stared into his carefully mild face, gripped with a wave of panic that must have shown in her eyes. His own eyes burned, willing her to be strong, and then dropped as a mounted Roman soldier cantered up, his short sword drawn, his red cloak flying behind him.

'Pretend it's me,' Eremon muttered, just before the rider drew rein ten paces away.

What?

The rest of the Roman patrol marched around the bend, and drew up in formation, their hands on their swords. The sinking sun glanced off their helmets, the steel plates covering breast, shoulder, shin and forearm, the tips of their javelins. They were all hard lines: their swords plain but sharp, their bodies held in taut lines, their gaze cold.

The panic clawed its way up Rhiann's spine, threatening to break free.

The mounted soldier looked her up and down dismissively, and then weighed up her men behind. Hunting bows were strapped to the saddles, yet Eremon had ensured that not so much as a dagger tip was showing anywhere on their bodies, their swords buried deep in packs.

The alien eyes fixed on her again, glittering beneath a steel helmet. 'What is your business here?' the Roman snapped in the British tongue, which was near enough to her own for her to understand.

And the officer's tone, his harsh glance, did remind her of someone. Her eyes flicked to Eremon and back to that arrogant Roman face. Together, the voice and look were just enough to prod her into anger, dousing the fear. She relaxed her legs on the horse, and sat as straight and still as she could. *Pretend it's me.*

'What is the meaning of this!' Her voice echoed off the rock wall. 'We are a peaceful party. Let us pass!'

She held the officer's gaze for a long, silent moment, unable to breathe. Eremon had not moved, but she saw his fingers tighten on her mount's reins.

'Tribal movements are restricted by orders of the Governor. Who are you?'

'I am a princess of the Votadini, returning home after a year with my mother's people.'

'The Votadini, you say?'

'Yes. And we have been travelling hard, as you can see, and I'm tired, *and* wet. My father is the king's own brother, and will not be pleased to hear that you kept me. Now, let me pass!' She managed to get just the right mixture of imperiousness and rising hysteria into her voice.

The Roman's own stance had relaxed. He leaned back in his saddle, rested his sword across his thighs, and regarded her with impatience. 'Quiet, girl! Save your demands and your sharp tongue for your own people. You may find that things have changed in your absence – if I were you, I'd get home and stay there.'

The first blue shadow of dusk was now creeping over the track, and moving up the cliff. The officer glanced at it. He would not want to waste time – he would want to be safe within camp walls before long. She must help him to make up his mind.

Breaking Eremon's hold, she nudged the horse forward. 'And what is your name, soldier? I'll speak to my father about you and he'll speak to your commander! We are valued allies, as you well know, and I wonder what he'll have to say about you keeping me here after dark, not to mention your rudeness, and I—'

'Enough!' the officer rapped out. 'By Jupiter, be on your way, woman, and good luck to your father!' He jerked his arm and shouted an order in Latin, and the troop turned as one and began marching back down the track. The rider wheeled his horse smartly and took off after them.

The sun was suddenly eclipsed by the rocks, and the men from Erin were plunged into purple shadow. They all let out a collective breath. Eremon turned to Rhiann, his face tense with excitement. She could feel it too, the rush of relief singing through her veins, the skipping of her heart. Her knees, gripping the horse's back, started to tremble.

'You did well.' Eremon shook his head. 'I thought I had heard your worst, but apparently not.'

Before she could answer, Conaire crowded his horse close. 'What a performance, lady!' His teeth flashed in the gloomy light. 'You make a fine addition to this warband!'

She felt herself smiling back, stupidly, overcome with a warm glow of released tension.

'Did you see their armour?' Rori breathed, staring back down the path. 'It was like . . . like fish-scales!'

'I was watching what their spears were trained on, boy,' Colum retorted. 'Us!'

Their individual voices were lost in a babble of discussion, and Rhiann sat there in their midst, feeling strangely elated, almost giddy. She had done it – *she* had saved *them*! She was as strong as any man! Let them see her as a liability now!

And just then her vision narrowed, there was a ringing in her ears, and as she felt herself slipping sideways, the last thing she heard was Eremon's bark: 'Look to the lady!'

Then she fainted.

CHAPTER 24

Rhiann came to in a woodland clearing, and the first thing she saw was Eremon's face, the outline of his head blurred by the hazel catkins hanging down from the branches above. He was pressing a wet cloth to her forehead. 'Good, you're awake. I took the liberty of removing us to a safer place away from that path.'

She struggled to sit, and he put an arm behind and helped her to slide up the bole of the tree. 'Here.' He thrust a cup of water into her hands. 'Drink this.'

She obeyed, then closed her eyes and rested her head on the tree-trunk until another wave of dizziness passed. Her skull was sore at the back. 'Did I hit the ground?'

'No, I caught you.' Eremon sounded distinctly amused. 'But then your weight wrenched me off my horse, and between us your head collided with my chin. I'm sorry.'

She forced away the unpleasant image of being in a tangle of limbs on the ground with him, her skirt rucked up to her knees. 'I never faint.'

'You've never had to face Romans, either.'

'I've faced worse.'

He paused, and said drily, 'And you're welcome. It was my shoulder that broke the fall, you know.'

Hot shame surged up her cheeks. She had never been so womanly, so weak as to faint. 'Then thank you. I'll be ready to ride soon.'

'Are you sure?'

'I *am* the healer here.' She kept her eyes resolutely closed until she heard his feet crunching away on the dead twigs.

187

They were still half a day away from the Dun of the Tree when they reached the first of the settlements that clustered around it.

The houses were cleanly thatched and white-washed. All the land about was scored with furrows of new-plowed, rich earth, and there were pens holding a wealth of fine, fat cattle, which had not yet been driven to sunseason pastures. These enclosures grew ever more numerous the closer they came to their destination, and at last Eremon remarked, 'Your Votadini must be prospering.'

They saw the great dun long before they smelled its cookfires, for it crowned a hill that reared in a single hump from the plain like a basking seal on a beach. High above, the summit was encircled by ancient banks and a ridged timber palisade, with towers looking west over the fertile farmland, and east to the sea.

The track widened and began to spiral up the northern face of the crag, terminating before a pair of looming gatetowers. But the gate between was open, and guards leaned on their spears at ease. Nor were there many lookouts posted atop the walkway that ran the length of the palisade. These people clearly felt safe behind Roman lines.

Rhiann asked to send a message to her cousin. While they waited, she joined Eremon on the edge of the path where it fell away towards the plain. Here, the wind came straight off the sea, still bitter from the moons of cold.

'They have a fine position here,' Eremon remarked, patting his horse's neck. 'They must be able to see for leagues across the land.'

'It has always been a rich tribe. Yet it is prospering even more now.'

'The signs are not that these people resisted and were beaten into submission.'

'No.' Rhiann was thoughtful. 'We must be careful.'

'It is a little late to say that now.' Eremon grinned, and Rhiann felt the barest hint of her own smile in answer.

'Lady.' A slight, officious man was standing by. 'I am

Carnach. My mistress Samana is overcome with delight at the unexpected visit of her dearest cousin. She asks me to escort you to her home.'

As they walked through the hilltop village, there were more signs that it was thriving. The skeletons of new buildings reared everywhere; granaries mostly, and also storehouses of various sizes. Plainly, the Votadini were extending their trade networks.

But when they reached the centre of the village, Rhiann received the greatest shock. She had travelled to see her kin once, when she was very young, with her father. At that time, the heart of the hillfort was the King's Hall, bigger than that at Dunadd. Next to it was a wind-gnarled oak, planted generations before, which had given the dun its name.

Now, although the tree was still there, the hall was gone, and in its place was a half-finished, rectangular building that appeared to be a suite of rooms. Rhiann could only stand and gape. Although built of the same materials as the round-houses of her people, her eyes could not adjust to the straight walls and corners, and even more, the splash of red tiles that crowned its sloping roof.

Carnach ushered them into a large square room, painted with lurid pigments, floored with plaster, and furnished with delicate oak seats and tables. There were no feasting spits here, no shields and spears on the walls, no hides and furs, no cauldron over the fire. All was airy, and light glowed through square holes in the wall covered by a transparent material that Rhiann did not recognize. Later, she found it was the thinnest, oiled hide: she'd seen her first window.

Still in shock, she couldn't help but jump at the faint rustle at the inner door, before she swung around . . . and there beheld her cousin Samana again for the first time in four years.

She saw immediately that the girl's striking looks had ripened into a woman's full, rich beauty. Samana's hair, bound around her head, was a glossy crown as dark as raven feathers. Her eyes were jet, and drooped at the corners. On the Sacred Isle, this had given her a sulky and petulant cast. Now, even Rhiann could see the effect it had on a woman's face, especially matched with a fine-dyed saffron robe that warmed her skin to honey, and berry-stained lips. Rhiann sensed the male atmosphere in the room rising to heat.

'Cousin!' Samana swept across the room and grasped Rhiann's hand, kissing her on both cheeks. Rhiann was enveloped in a wave of scent, the sweet, ripe smell of apples. 'Sit, do sit!'

She settled them all on the array of strange chairs in the room, and clapped her hands for Carnach to bring them refreshments, before fixing Rhiann with her deep gaze. 'So, cousin, it has been many years. And now you have come so unexpectedly, and you bring me a fine catch of young men as a gift – men of Erin, your message said.' She smiled slowly around at the men in turn, pausing when she came to Eremon.

Rhiann eyed her steadily back. 'My message did not say that, Samana. Your priestess training still stands you in good stead, I see.'

'The Mother's gifts are powerful, and not easily forgotten, cousin.'

Carnach came in with a tray, and Samana directed him to hand each of them an empty bronze goblet, and rest a silver flagon on a three-legged oak table to one side. When the steward left again, Samana added, 'But come, introduce me to your companions. I like to know the names of those whom I entertain.' As she spoke she rose, taking up the flagon, and the sun spilling through the open door caught the rings on her fingers, and the gold bracelet encircling one slender arm.

'They are my guard,' said Rhiann, 'for we hear that the painted ones are no longer welcome among their southern brothers. Your people have new guests, it seems.'

'The Romans, you mean?'

'Of course.'

Samana was standing before Eremon now, smiling down at him. 'Always serious you are, cousin! We can talk of this later, but right now, I cannot serve one whose name I do not know.'

Rhiann gave in with great reluctance. 'Outside these walls he is my captain of the guard – but within he is my husband, Eremon, son of Ferdiad, of Dalriada.'

'A husband! How splendid!' Samana poured a stream of mead into Eremon's cup, and from where she was sitting, Rhiann sensed the leap of speculation between them. 'Why, then we are related!' Samana bent down to give Eremon the kin kiss of greeting, lingering over it a moment longer than was courteous.

As she filled Conaire's cup and moved on to the others, Rhiann caught the glance of boyish amusement that passed between Eremon and his foster-brother. She shifted in her chair.

As soon as Samana was seated again, Rhiann rested her cup on the small table and leaned forward. 'Cousin, what has happened here? Why are you living in this house? Where are the King and the council?'

Samana's brow darkened, but her voice remained light. 'So many questions are unseemly, Rhiann! I could also ask why you have come.'

'Lady,' Eremon put in smoothly, 'forgive our intrusion. We have had a long journey, and suffered from a great shock on the way. Perhaps we may answer each other's questions when we are more refreshed?'

Both Rhiann and Samana turned to stare at Eremon, Rhiann with growing anger, and Samana with, she could see, a much warmer sentiment.

'Well!' Samana's face was soft again, and the heavy-lidded look had returned. 'Your husband puts us to shame with his courtesy, Rhiann. There are guest quarters for you. Carnach can show you the way. When you have washed and rested, we will eat, and then we can find out all about each other.'

Rhiann and Eremon were given one small guest hut near to Samana's dwelling, and the rest of the men another. Eremon excused himself and went to join Conaire as soon as he put his pack down, so Rhiann enjoyed the customary foot-wash on her own. Yet there was also heavily watered wine, which she did not touch, and strange Roman oil lamps bathing the hut with light. After she unpacked the few goddess figurines she had brought, and lined them up above the bed, she felt much better.

Now she looked down at the serving woman sponging her feet. 'Tell me, where are the King and the council. Do you know?'

The woman's carefully inscrutable face registered nothing. 'Lady, the Romans came here and removed them. The Lady Samana is Queen now.'

'She rules here?'

The servant ducked her face and concentrated on her task. 'Yes, lady.'

Rhiann thought about asking more, but the woman would plainly say that she did not know anything, so she let it be. Better to hear the tale from her own cousin's mouth.

As the dusk deepened into night, the party followed a trail of torches back up the path to Samana's house. This time they were led to another room, golden in the glow of oil lamps flickering on painted walls. Samana had kept to the tribal way of seating guests on low benches, but used three-legged tables to hold the food.

This time they were served by a stream of servants carrying platters of silver and Roman redware, and bronze and glass flagons. The food was mostly Alban: sea bream steeped in honey and thyme, and roast goose with crab-apple, but there were also the Roman imports of olives and figs and a strange eastern bird that Samana called pheasant, and beef and oyster stew flavoured with a strong, fish-smelling sauce that Samana said was *garum*.

While they ate, Rhiann held her tongue, for to her the irony of coming all this way to learn how to defeat the Romans, and then eating their food, almost made her gag.

Samana kept the conversation to Eremon and his home on Erin, and Rhiann watched with interest as he dodged a few uncomfortable questions rather neatly. *So we all dance with our words tonight*, she thought, and sipped her mead.

Had she miscalculated this trip badly? Was Samana to be trusted? She thought back to their time on the Sacred Isle. Her cousin had always loved luxury – it was Samana's mother, the King's sister, who insisted that she join the order, while the girl herself always chafed under the priestesses' spartan rule.

Based on that memory, Rhiann could not really be surprised that Samana had become outwardly seduced by Roman goods. After all, so had most of the nobles of Britannia, and even those in Alba. But wanting Roman goods was a long way from wanting Roman rule.

She relaxed slightly. The King and his men must have given themselves up as hostages. Samana was probably making the best of the situation that she had been thrust into. After all, the girl had followed the actual teachings of the Sisters avidly, and displayed skill in seeing and magic, though her powers of healing were less developed. *She is a priestess, and that is her strongest alliance*, she thought. *If she was let down by men, as I was, then we make the best of our limited powers.*

Just as she was getting ready to ask the inevitable question, Eremon stepped in. Taking a considered sip of wine, he leaned back, outwardly relaxed. 'The meal was a triumph, lady. I have not partaken of so many Roman imports before.'

'I thank you. One must gain something in exchange when one is conquered.'

'Conquered?'

Samana looked sorrowful. 'It was a bad business, prince. After my father died some years ago, I was left in the care of my uncle, the King. We always had a strong trading network with our Roman contacts in Britannia, and Roman traders called here once a year. Well, when we had news that ten thousand Roman soldiers were bearing down on us – ten thousand, you understand – he decided that the protection of our people came first.' She shook her head. 'I, of course, was horrified. At least at first. I felt we should fight – but what is one woman's voice among so many men?' She took a sip of her wine. 'Before I knew it, messengers were going back and forth between the council and this Roman commander – this Agricola. Eventually, my uncle made a treaty.'

'But did your warriors not rise up at all?' Rhiann put in.

Samana sighed, turning to her. 'No, cousin. Perhaps you know already how little *some* men can be trusted.' She shot an apologetic look at Eremon, and then back to Rhiann. 'We already traded heavily in Roman goods. The Roman commander was not seeking to change our customs, our politics, our life at all really, in any way. They were just going to pass us by . . .'

'*Pass you by*?' Rhiann knew that she was glaring. 'Just where do you think all those soldiers were going, Samana? To a cattle fair?'

'As I said, Rhiann, the council decided that it was best for the people to make peace. That way we could preserve what we had, instead of seeing it go down in fire and blood.' She paused and wiped her eyes. 'Did you not hear what happened to the Selgovae? Their hillfort was bombarded with these *ballistae*, these iron bolts, and the people were slaughtered to a child. My uncle did not want this for us.'

'And where is the King now?' Eremon asked gently.

'Ah, well, that is the worst of it.' Samana sniffled. 'Agricola asked the King and his whole council to visit him – and took them hostage. The warriors here were baying for blood, as you can imagine. But if they make a move, the King will be executed. The lords have scattered to their duns and seem content to leave it be. They hope that when Agricola completes his campaign, the King will be returned.'

'Completes his campaign?' Rhiann's voice sounded harsh, but the false tears were going a little too far. She had never known Samana to cry.

'Yes, Rhiann – he will be driven back, or he will conquer.'

'And what of you?' Eremon was conciliatory.

Another great sigh. 'I've done the best that I can with what was left.'

194

Rhiann looked around at the oil lamps and ornate flagons with a raised eyebrow that she did not try to hide.

'I am the closest of the King's kin – there was no one left to take charge here, as the other lords have their own duns to attend to. Although I know little of ruling, I am keeping my dun safe and prosperous to await the King's return.'

'And this involves replacing the King's Hall with a Roman one?' Rhiann sipped her mead with great casualness.

The eye that Samana turned on her was not soft. 'Why, Rhiann! The King began this work before he was so cruelly taken. I cannot live in a half-finished building; nor did I want to waste the costly timber or tiles. The people understand.'

Rhiann thought about the signs of prosperity that she had seen among the Votadini. Yes, the people – those of the ruling class, at any rate – would understand all too well.

So, she did not believe that Samana was as grief-stricken about the situation as she made out. She loved the goods the treaty had brought her, and she was living here unmolested in her own house. And yet, the story itself made sense. Did vanity and greed equal treachery?

'Now.' Samana wiped her cheeks and smiled at Eremon. 'You must tell me why you have come.'

'It is a much shorter tale,' Eremon replied. 'We seek to find out more about the Romans, that is all. How many there are, where they are . . .'

'I take it, then, that you intend to resist?'

Rhiann opened her mouth to reply, seized with the urge not to tell Samana too much, but Eremon said quickly, 'Yes, we do.'

Samana smiled at him again, and reached out to touch his hand. 'I wish we had men of such determination here, cousin. Perhaps the result would have been much different.'

'Will you help us, then?'

She looked around at them all. 'I will tell you as much as I can, and may be able to get you more information. But please,' she put her hand to her forehead, 'not tonight.

Speaking of these matters has wounded me sorely. Will you excuse me?' She rose.

All the men jumped to their feet, although Rhiann stayed seated.

'No, please, enjoy your drink and food for as long as you like.'

She swayed slightly where she stood, and Eremon put out an arm to steady her. 'Let me see you to your quarters, lady. One fainting episode is enough this week.'

'Thank you, cousin.' She nodded at Rhiann. 'You are blessed by the Goddess in your choice of husband, Rhiann. Courtesy and strength: a rare combination.'

Rhiann smiled, but her face felt tight. Samana, leaning heavily on Eremon, disappeared through another inner door, the men watching her retreating curves with a great deal of attention.

When Eremon returned he was unusually jovial, his face flushed. Rhiann excused herself, too, and left them to their drinking. The glare of the torches around Samana's house blotted out the stars, and when she reached the darkness of her hut she stood in the doorway to let the moonlight bathe her.

This journey had taken an uncomfortable turn. Could she trust Samana? Could she even trust Eremon? How little she really knew him! Perhaps she had acted rashly in her desire to become involved in war. Perhaps she should have stayed with her herbs and her blessings and her embroidery. *Now, Rhiann*, she chided. *You have more courage than that. It is done now, and you will see it out.* Yet she would keep her wits about her, for she already sensed some powerful energies stalking this dun.

When Eremon at last came to bed, these undercurrents seemed to gather in greater force, until they were swirling around the small hut.

Eremon did not speak to her, which was not strange. Yet for as many hours as she lay awake, so did he, tossing and shifting about more than usual. Perhaps he felt it, too.

CHAPTER 25

Samana did not seek Rhiann out the next morning, pleading a headache. Instead, their entire party was offered a tour of the thriving Votadini port on the Forth. Here, a Roman merchant ship was docking, and they sat their horses and watched the rows of amphorae filled with olive oil and wine, fish sauce and figs, being unloaded on to Votadini carts. The harsh Latin tongue rang out as the dark-haired sailors carried the long, pointed jars of goods down to the pier.

Their voices reminded Rhiann of the soldiers they had seen building the fort, and she shuddered. Would this tongue one day be heard across her land? Would the songs of the bards be lost, and her people's own musical speech stilled? No! She would die before all that made them fine was destroyed.

That afternoon the men went hunting, and as Samana had still not surfaced, Rhiann decided to take things into her own hands. The obsequious steward looked put out at her unannounced arrival, but went to find his mistress, seating Rhiann in the reception room.

After a long while, Samana appeared, looking quite well and free of headaches. Her hair was unbound, and in her simpler blue robe and absence of jewellery, she looked much more like the girl that Rhiann had known on the Sacred Isle. She ordered nettle tea, and talked of inconsequential things until it was served and they were left alone.

Mindful that they needed Samana for her information, Rhiann could not ask all that was in her heart, for fear of pushing too much. Eremon would advise her to go softly.

'So, cousin.' Rhiann sipped her tea. 'It has been four years – and you look the better for it.'

Samana smiled graciously, then put her hand on Rhiann's arm, her smile disappearing in a frown of concern. 'I wish I could say the same for you, Rhiann. You look so thin and drawn. We heard about the Sacred Isle.'

Rhiann jerked her arm away involuntarily, then put her tea down. 'It was very difficult.'

Samana sighed. 'I think of the Sisters often.'

'Really? You were always aching to escape as soon as you could.'

That comment was unintentionally sharp, and Samana's dark eyes flashed. 'Too much praying and too little fun – you know it did not suit me in the end. And you were the golden child, after all, not me! The rest of us could only wait for your messages to come down from on high.' She smiled as if she were jesting, but her voice was tinged with something else. It reminded Rhiann of Samana's manner all those years ago. This dark, wild cousin had been a mystery to her even then.

'And are you having fun now?' Rhiann asked.

Samana trailed her elegant hands over the spout of a silver flagon. 'Yes, indeed, and I am not ashamed of it. I have beautiful things around me.' She fixed Rhiann with her dark eyes. 'And beautiful men in my bed. What more could I want?'

Rhiann blushed and looked away, and Samana laughed softly. 'Oh, Rhiann. I forgot that you have greater sensitivities about such things. And other priorities – after all, you must be far too busy in your role of Ban Cré to worry much about men.'

'Well, as you can see, I have been given a fine-looking man of my own, so little do I need to worry.' It nearly choked Rhiann to say the words.

'Ah, yes indeed. You are very lucky, cousin.' Samana paused. 'And he is a brave man, too.'

'Yes,' Rhiann agreed, not at all enthused about talking of Eremon. She wanted to come to the real reason she was here.

'I have to say it is admirable how you have been able to overcome your own grief at the King's fate so easily. The story you told last night was very touching.'

She held her breath, knowing it was impertinent – but anyone with two eyes could see that Samana had been acting. Anyone with two eyes and no bulge between their legs, that is.

To her surprise, Samana just laughed. 'Really, Rhiann,' she drawled, dropping the brittle politeness, 'let's be frank now.'

'That would be a new departure, Samana.'

'You've become rather droll since I saw you last! Life away from the island has spiced you up, then. Perhaps we shall get along after all.'

Rhiann picked up her tea again. 'What were you going to tell me?'

Samana dangled her cup between her fingers, at ease in her chair. 'You and I both were kin to kings whom we did not care for, who would bestow our hand in marriage to any smelly, hairy chieftain if he had enough cattle. Don't pretend to me that your uncle's death was a blow to your heart!'

Not in the way that you mean, anyway, Rhiann thought.

'So,' Samana went on, 'how can I pretend that I miss him, or that bunch of lecherous old men who would soon barter me away like a sack of barley? It was a blow, yes, but I've made the most of it. My people are still safe and have not been slaughtered in their beds. We have even more wealth pouring in. And here I sit, with more freedom than any princess in Alba. Don't tell me you don't envy that!'

Rhiann realized that envy of Samana's position had not crossed her mind. 'Freedom, Samana? When you have new masters now? How is this freedom?'

'Oh, come,' Samana said impatiently. 'The Romans do not interfere with my rule. If I were some hot-headed prince bursting with pride about my lineage and my ancestors and my precious cattle – well then, perhaps such a surrender would be hard to stomach. But you and I, Rhiann, know that we women have more sense in one finger than a man does in

199

his whole body. I did not choose it, but this suits me and my people well. Resisting now will mean their deaths, and the loss of everything we have!'

Rhiann was shaking her head. 'I *am* a woman, and I still don't understand, Samana. You are a priestess. The land is our Mother – you know this! How can you sit by and bear the blows of Roman tread on Her body, the tearing of Her flesh? How can you stand the rape of the trees, the sacrilege of the springs?'

Samana smiled. 'You were always more devout than me, Rhiann. The Goddess did not choose to bestow the powers on me that she did on you. I have my own talents, and I use them well. I honour Her in my own way.'

Rhiann caught the slight, sensuous movement of Samana's mouth, and had to look aside. She took a breath, tapping her fingers on her knee. 'Be that as it may . . . will you help us?'

Samana paused. 'Yes, of course, cousin. But what little I have to tell can wait until we are all together. No!' She stopped Rhiann's protest. 'I have allowed you to have your way, and now you will respect mine. Tomorrow night we will dine again, and talk further of these matters.'

'Tomorrow! Why won't you meet with us tonight?'

'I am still suffering from my headache, and will stay abed tonight. Besides, there are some administrative matters to attend to – I cannot go riding about the hills as you do!'

Rhiann regarded Samana's glowing face and bright eyes with scepticism. Still, she could not force her to do anything.

'To make it up to you, cousin, tomorrow I will have Carnach take you around our lands, showing you every little thing to do with Romans. Will that sweeten your disposition?'

'Do not talk to me like one of your brainless conquests, Samana.'

'My, how you have grown in wit, Rhiann.' Samana rose. 'I look forward to further discussions, but now you must leave me. I will see you tomorrow.'

Later that night, Rhiann sat on the bed in her hut, drawing an antler comb through the ends of her hair, watching the strands fall before the fire.

She had barely seen Eremon in two days, which normally would not concern her, but during their tour of the port he had been strangely distracted. Beneath his questions and jests, she sensed a deep disturbance.

Her comb stilled, as she was struck by a new thought. Now that he had seen what came of peace with the Romans, was Eremon regretting his oath to the Epidii? She suddenly realized, in truth, how tenuous his tie to her people was. He seemed a man of honour, but he would always put his position and his men first – of course he would!

What if he thought that he would have more to gain by joining the tribes who surrendered? Goddess! Desperate to take some control, Rhiann had not thought through the implications of putting herself in the hands of his men, who were, after all, still strangers.

Her mind turned over the hints about Eremon's past. If he was here to gain a name, as she sensed, then it did not matter to him how he won that name. And once he had won it, then of course he would be racing for home. Rhiann froze, unable to believe that she had not really considered this before. *Well, when he leaves, at least I will be free of him!* She need only pray that he remained as their defence against the Romans for as long as he was needed. What he did then was not a concern.

She heard a tiny movement now, and glanced up to see Eremon standing just inside the doorway. His stance was tense, and she thought his body quivered slightly, although it may just have been a breeze across the flames.

'I came only to get this.' He strode across the room and swept up his cloak from where it lay over his leather pack, then began to dig around, looking for something. 'The men and I are going back to the port. We're hoping to find out something from those Roman traders. I may not return until late.' His voice was strangely harsh, as if he could not breathe properly.

She rested the comb on the fur bedcover. 'Eremon, we must work subtly. Such a visit could be dangerous.'

He straightened, and she saw a stain of colour flush his face. His eyes were wild, the gaze far away. 'Don't question me! Outside these walls I may be your servant, but certainly not within.' He threw the cloak over his shoulders, tucked a dagger into his belt and was gone.

Well!

Rhiann rose and walked to the door after him, pulling back the cover and looking up at the sky. The clouds had all fled, and moonlight spilled down from the velvet darkness above.

But as she stood there, still smarting from Eremon's harsh words, she suddenly felt again the strange presence that had been pulling at the edges of her soul for the last day. With the other distractions of the port and her talk with Samana, she had successfully ignored it. But now, alone in the clear night, her full awareness rushed in.

There was some power at work here, whispering to her, taunting her. She sensed it within the pit of her belly, warm as it rose up the length of her body: a cloying warmth, slippery and mocking, yet with a chord of something primal. Closing her eyes, Rhiann held the doorpost and leaned out. And with her spirit-eye she glimpsed it; an energy, a vibration, snaking in streamers of fog, dark as dried blood, along the paths between the houses. It coiled into doorways and crept around corners, wreathing the feet of those few people walking by.

Although somehow Rhiann knew that the magic was not made for her, a sudden fear rose up from deep within, and with a silent cry she warded it away. *No! Be gone from me!*

The fingers of fog halted, and slunk away from her feet, and in their place a gust of icy wind blew up the village path, lifting the sweaty tendrils of hair from her face.

Rhiann shook herself free from the heavy warmth and breathed deeply. Whatever it was, it had gone, and would trouble her no more tonight. Magic could only gain entrance where someone had given it leave willingly. And she was not willing.

She remained at the doorway for hours, watching the stars sweep away the evil warmth in a flood of silver.

In the small room, all was golden heat and ruddy light. No breath of air crept past the fleece over the window, and the stillness was filled with liquid warmth, and the heavy scent of sweet, ripe apples.

Samana lay, her throat arched back, her hair a black fall of silk across the pillow. Sweat trickled over her breasts, and the man bowed his head to lick it from her skin, a deep groan escaping his throat. 'Again!' she cried, and he thrust deep within her, and she dug her nails into him fiercely, raking more welts among the tracery of red lines across his back. Their mouths met, tongues reaching for each other in animal hunger, and she raised her hips to plunge him deeper into her, grasping her white legs around his waist.

He wrenched her over then, and they tumbled, struggling and scratching, driven by the hot need of their bodies, yearning to go further to the wild places within. At last Samana pushed him back, her hair falling in a dark curtain about them, pausing for a moment to catch her breath.

His eyes were closed, his sweat-streaked chest heaving. She always left the lamp burning to let them see her beauty, to drive them mad with need of her, but this one did not want to look long at her. Oh, no. He wanted to lose himself. And to this she drove him, like the whip drives the slave, like the storm drives the waves before it.

So he bore her down again, hands hard on her shoulders as he found the warm, wet opening and entered anew, and she smiled to herself at his force and great strength. It always took her breath away, to feel the ridges of muscles tensing, hard as iron under her fingers, to know that she mastered a beast such as this.

She opened her legs wider, drawing him into the well inside her, drawing him into the centre of her power, clasping him with her legs so there was no escape. Then she raised her head and sunk her teeth into his shoulder, and his thrusts grew more frenzied, and he wound his fingers into her black hair and pulled her head back.

With a jerking, agonized cry, he reached his peak, and she followed, screeching like a wildcat into his shoulder. When it was over he collapsed on to her flushed breasts, legs tangled in the bedcovers, his body pinning her to the damp bed.

After a while, his breath stilled, and he slept.

Samana lay awake, triumph in her smile. For a while she watched the play of shadows on the walls around her, but then she closed her eyes and sent her awareness outside to seek the roiling and curling of her lustful spell as it snaked through the village.

She had always been able to see her magic working, and so now she hovered at doorways, listening in satisfaction to the animal cries of pleasure she drew from the people this night, and in even greater satisfaction to the cries of pain.

And then she saw the woman, a cold, still woman, outlined by the starlight in the doorway of her guesthouse. Samana laughed to herself as she saw that the spell had been warded there, and so lost its power.

And her body's hand drew a nail lightly across Eremon's sleeping back.

CHAPTER 26

Rhiann was gone before Eremon rose that morning. He asked one of the servants where she was, and discovered that she'd taken a horse to the beach. No one knew when she would be back.

He splashed his face with water from a pottery basin, and rubbed his bleary eyes. Gods! His head felt as if he had consumed the entire stock of Samana's wine, but he had only drunk two cups. His mind ached, intensely weary, but his body still thrummed with a heightened tension that he found almost uncomfortable. It was like an itch, making him feel jittery in his own skin.

He stretched his back and neck muscles, and sat down on the bed to comb his hair. What a surprise Rhiann's cousin had turned out to be! He smiled to himself. Only a madman could look at those curves and those sensual eyes and not want to bed her. Still, it wasn't like him to be swept away by such a feeling – although he was glad he had given in to her invitation.

By the Boar! Comparing Aiveen to her was like comparing a soft, fluffy kitten to a sleek wildcat. She had certainly given him a night to remember.

Suddenly restless, he rose and began searching through his pack. After such a night, his limbs should be heavy with the languor that follows the release of pent-up energy. But he could not sit still long enough to braid his hair! He found a fresh tunic and pulled it over his head, tugging his hair into submission with his fingers, stopping to detangle a few sweat-tied knots.

And then he realized that, far from seeing more of the Votadini lands this fine morning, or even talking with his men, there was only one thing that he wanted right now.

And that was to do it with her again.

It was much later than he thought, and when he got to the house where Conaire was staying, he found that his men had already gone.

'The Lady Samana sent her huntsman here quite early, lord,' the servant emptying the wash basins informed him. 'I hear he is taking them on a long ride to see one of the deserted Roman camps.'

'And why was I not woken?'

'The lady told us not to disturb you.'

'Did she now?'

'She also said that when you did wake, to tell you that you could break your fast with her.'

Well. There was only one thing for it, then. He found Samana standing by the window in her reception room, frowning over a wooden writing tablet. She wore her saffron robe again, and the sun filtered through the oiled paper, gleaming on her black hair and the gold rings on her fingers.

'Lady.' He bowed to her.

She smiled and swayed closer to him. 'Come now! There is no one here. Do you need to call me lady now?' She reached up and buried her free hand in his hair, drawing his lips down to hers. With her first touch, the burning that had driven all thoughts from his head the night before was ignited once more, and he forced her lips apart until their tongues met with the same devouring need.

When they broke apart, he was shaking at the strength of it, but had just enough presence of mind to turn away to the table. As he poured some ale he cursed himself roundly. He was no virginal boy, to react this way! He shook his head, for his mind was hazy, though every fibre of his body sang with lust. He took the ale in one draught and poured another, turning back to her.

Samana was sliding her eyes over him with frank admiration. Which made a change, he had to admit, from Rhiann's cold regard. Perhaps that was why his body was betraying him so soundly.

She offered him some bread and cheese from a platter, with deep speculation in those darkest of eyes. As he munched, he said, 'Why did you separate me from my men so neatly?'

Her smile widened as she put the platter back on the table. 'Ah, and a fine brain, too. I wanted to speak to you alone, of course.'

'You could have spoken last night.' Even saying the words brought a flood of warmth to his skin. *Now I am acting like a virginal boy!*

'I think we both had more pressing concerns last night.' She took a sliver of cheese from the platter and nibbled on it delicately.

'I am here to find out about the Romans. I need to be with my men to see what they see.'

'Oh, they won't see much.' She waved her hand. 'You will get your information by staying here. You must trust me.'

'You talk in riddles, lady. Speak plainly.'

Samana put the cheese back on the platter, and brushed off her hands. 'You know,' she said, 'I'm tired of having endless conversations in this room. It is a blustery day. Let us walk on the walls.'

The wind whipped Eremon's hair across his face, and slapped the tribal standard on its post above the palisade. Far off, the sea was a shining bowl of molten gold in the sun.

'You are proposing that I go with you right into a Roman army camp. Not a deserted one this time.' He leaned his back against the palisade, regarding Samana with wary surprise.

'You will be safe, I vouch for it.' Samana took his arm, the wind pressing her skirts about the outline of her legs. 'I have a contact high up in the administration. I must go and talk to him about the new taxes the Romans wish to levy. You can be my guard.'

207

'A "contact", Samana?'

She smiled thinly. 'Know your enemy is a basic tactic, is it not?' She tucked his hand in the crook of her elbow and pressed the length of her body up against his. 'Eremon, you know that the Romans have most of Britannia, and they are not going away, I promise you. You have not seen them, but I have! They are incredible soldiers, and they have not been removed from any of the lands they've taken over. As they will not be removed from our lands.'

'We can stop them advancing.'

'Then we will be at war for ever! For they will be here for ever, make no mistake about that.'

He pulled her away from him, and looked down searchingly into her upturned face. In the sunlight, her dark eyes were sheened with gold. A flame-hued silk wrap set off the colour of her stained lips. 'So you say that we should give in as your king did, Samana, is that it?'

'No! I would never say that. What I say is this: make friends with the Romans, as I have. You have some influence to convince the northern tribes to make a treaty with them.'

'A treaty! I did not come here to be a Roman pawn!'

'You don't understand! Alba is different from the rest of Britannia, mountainous and hard to control. All we have to do is give in – temporarily. Agricola will not station many men here; he'll just claim the whole island to please his god-king in Rome, and then turn his back on us.'

'How do you know all this?'

'My friend told me.'

'Samana, I know enough to understand that when the Romans take your lands, you are no longer free. I do not want to be part of an alien empire – no man of Erin would.'

'Extraordinary threats require extraordinary decisions, Eremon.' Samana tossed her head. 'Men! They think only of honour, not of practicalities. All we have to do is *appear* to give in. They will not have the inclination to build roads in Alba, or construct great towns – they hate it here. So we just go along with them, until they do not care about us any more, and then we take Alba back!' Her smile was triumphant.

Eremon removed her hand from his arm. The ripe smell of her and the press of her breasts was making it hard to think. It was a strange and unexpected power that she wielded over him. 'It is a large gamble to take.'

'You are being too cautious!' She strode to the palisade, before turning to look up at him pleadingly. 'You came here to find information, and now I give you the chance to hear it from Roman lips! Who else could help you to do this? You will be safe as my guard, I swear it. If what you find convinces you to make a treaty, as we have, then that is well. If not, you have lost nothing, but gained much.'

He looked deep into her eyes, trying to see if she was lying, attempting to kick his normally sharp instincts back into action, pulling them away from the power of her body.

'It is a daring thing to do,' she purred now. 'What a name it will win you; what renown!'

It was as if she read his mind. How could she know what he hungered for, even more than he hungered for her body? *Renown.*

He turned the treaty idea over in his mind. He had no intention of speaking with any Romans in any Roman camp, of course, but . . . the Epidii warriors were not yet quite ready to face the invaders in battle. Some sort of false treaty might just keep Dunadd safe until he had his own army up to full strength. Then he shook his head. No, that was madness. He only wanted information, for now.

'Why take me, Samana? I am a stranger. If you wish for a treaty so much, then take one of your northern princes.' He folded his arms over his chest, as a gust of wind flapped the edges of his cloak.

Samana snorted delicately. 'Our princes are not leaders! Their bulls and their lands are their pride, and in this matter their hearts would rule their heads. You though,' and she put her hand up to his cheek, 'you have a great mind, a king's mind. And there is one more thing.'

'What is that?'

She dropped her hand. 'If we fight, the Romans will win, make no mistake. How long will your own land stand free then, Eremon? They will turn their greedy eyes on Erin, and by then she will be alone.'

He faced the west, and blew out his held breath. 'If the Epidii found out that I met with Romans, I would be killed as a traitor.'

'No one will know until after the fact, and then they will be too pleased at what you have to tell them, and too admiring of your bravery.'

'And what of Rhiann?'

'Just tell her what you intend to do and why.' She was dismissive. 'You are her husband, after all. Or does the great prince need his wife's leave?'

Stung, Eremon said gruffly, 'No, of course not.' He paused, chewing his lip. Conaire always said that he was too cautious, and perhaps he was, at times, right. Maybe the wildness of Samana's bed had loosened something in him, for he found himself saying, 'I will go as your guard, but only to seek information. I make no promises about any treaty. And you will stay with me at all times.'

'Do you not trust me?'

'I do not trust them.'

After returning from the beach, Rhiann sat on the bed and listened to Eremon in silence, her fingers splayed over the drying salt-stains on her cloak. She let him fill the space with explanations and excuses, but behind it all she could still sense the taint of Samana's magic, clinging to his words, and the stink of stale sweat and male seed that he had brought back to their bed last night.

So this is the way it would be.

At last she spoke, her throat thick with disgust. 'Why risk yourself by going alone?'

'Because I am meant to be her escort, and one man will attract no attention. And there is something else.'

'Yes?' She began to unwind the wool wrap from her neck.

'I know very well what you think of this escapade, but weighed up against what I can gain, I consider it worth the risk. *For me.* My decisions risk my men all the time, and you cannot know what it costs me. For once, I'll make a move that affects only me.'

'You will not be swayed from this, will you? Even though we need you at Dunadd, and you risk the safety of the Epidii with such a rash action?' *An action based on lust, not reason!* she cried in her mind. But she could not say that to him; he would think her jealous.

He looked down, tapping his finger on the carved back of a chair by the hearth. 'What I do, I do for the Epidii.'

'No.' She raised her chin at him. 'You do it for yourself – you may as well be honest about it!'

Guilt flared in his face for one moment, then he mastered it and drew himself straighter. 'What I will tell you, is that on this I will stand firm, no matter what you or even Conaire say to me.'

She shrugged and turned to the wall, determined not to argue, though her chest burned. 'Then I won't try. But I think you make a mistake.'

'Then it is my mistake.'

Eremon did not expect Rhiann to say farewell, but as he leaned down from his horse to grasp Conaire's hand at the gateway, his eyes darted around of their own accord.

He did concede that the expedition seemed foolhardy. He was not even entirely sure what he would gain. This was disquieting, for he was used to being sure of himself. But since their arrival at Samana's dun, everything had taken on a more charged air; everything felt different. Rhiann was ever more remote, while his body's thirst was being slaked by Samana. It was a heady and disturbing combination.

All of his life his feelings had been absolute, his plans laid well in advance – until his uncle turned on him, disrupting the flow of his destiny for ever. So perhaps, now, he should just give himself up to the shifting course of life in this strange, wild country.

He glanced at Samana, as she sat neatly on her horse in the bright morning sun, resplendent in a green cloak that showed off the shine of her hair. She did not look as if she were undertaking a dangerous sortie into an enemy camp. Distrust flickered for a moment.

But they are not her enemy.

Conaire was regarding him with shadowed eyes. 'For the last time, I fear for you on this quest of yours.'

Eremon's horse shifted impatiently and he stilled him, forcing a smile. 'Are you questioning my swordsmanship?'

'Never,' said Conaire. 'But I have been by your side through everything. Only I know your weaknesses in battle, and how to cover them.'

'My friend, we are going into a camp of five thousand Romans. If it comes to a pitched battle, even you could not save me. But do not worry: I will keep nice and quiet, and look stupid.'

They had replayed this conversation many times over the past two days, and so although Conaire's face darkened, he did not say anything more. Eremon put his hand on his foster-brother's shoulder. 'I gave in to your demand that I take our men with me, as close to the camp as is safe. Now you'll give in to mine. I need you to stay and look after Rhiann. I trust only you to keep her safe, and if needed, to return her to her people.'

'I will stake my life on that. I trust Rhiann, Eremon.' As he said this, Conaire glanced at Samana.

Eremon fought down a surge of anger. It was fine for Conaire to question Eremon's choice of woman – his foster-brother had his pick. He was not tied to such a marriage.

He wheeled his horse around. 'I will see you in a week.'

'Watch your back, brother!' Conaire called after him.

For all the way down the dun path, Eremon sensed Conaire's eyes on him, warmer on his shoulders than the morning sun. Yet as the riders rounded the ridge and were lost from sight in the fields, he felt the severing.

He did not look back.

CHAPTER 27

The Roman camp was three days by horse to the north-west, where the River Forth spilled out into its great inlet. For most of that way they crossed flat farmland, dark-furrowed under a clear sky. Eremon found it difficult to travel in the open at ease, and almost wished for a heavy rainstorm to sweep in, obscuring the colours of their cloaks, hiding them with a curtain of grey drizzle. But it was not to be; leaf-bud had bloomed early, and the farmers hurried to sow their new crops under a pale sun, and high, scudding clouds.

Of the two Roman patrols they did meet, neither challenged them once they saw Samana. He found this even more unsettling than the piercing black eyes raking him over from head to foot. But now it was too late to turn back.

'I have been puzzling over something,' Eremon remarked to Samana on the second day, as they rode side by side along the edge of a field.

'Yes?'

'Why did the Romans advance so quickly, and then stop as suddenly?'

There was a fraction of hesitation. 'I can tell you that easily,' Samana replied, 'for it was common talk among the soldiers. Last leaf-fall, their emperor – this Vespasian – died. He was close to Agricola, and he had authorized the advance. His son, Titus, has succeeded him, and it seems he has more pressing concerns than Alba. He ordered Agricola to halt the advance. That is all I know.'

'Well, it solves the riddle for me. I would have wished,

though, that something more serious had stayed Agricola's hand – illness, perhaps, or problems in the south.'

'Ah, I have heard no rumours of any such difficulties.'

'Then long may Titus be occupied elsewhere.'

Eremon had no intention of taking his men closer than necessary, and despite Rori's protests, he bid them stay and camp in a hidden glen, high in the hill range that rose south of the Forth. Then he and Samana carried on, setting up their leather lean-to that night in a thick copse of hazel trees above a stream ford.

Faintly, the whinnies of horses carried over the night air, and he could detect a distant hum of voices. They were so close now, so close.

It was then that the fear rose, and he wondered if he had indeed made a mistake.

'So your prim little son-in-law has gone back to Rome?' The moon had long since sunk to her bed, yet even after her ride through the night Samana was awake, poring over Agricola's maps, a cup of wine in her hand.

'Tacitus has taken my assurances of support to Titus.'

'And what will your plans be then?'

'Nothing, until he confirms my orders to advance. For now, there is much to do to consolidate my new frontier in your lands.' Agricola leaned back in his camp chair, stretching his neck muscles. 'I have no doubt you can read maps well enough by now, Samana. Yet still I see no results. The surrender of the Taexali and Vacomagi kings has not been forthcoming.'

She sipped her wine, looking out at him from underneath her brows. 'I will get you results soon. I need more time.'

'I thought that a woman in your position would know more about your northern neighbours. Could it be that your much-vaunted status is not all it seems, my dark witch?'

She hated that word! Putting down the goblet, Samana took his hand and slipped it inside her gown, so he could feel a nipple standing up hard against his palm. 'Why, my lord, it seems I give you more than just information. Be patient for the one, as you do not need to be patient for the other!'

Agricola said nothing, but reached out with his other hand and grasped the wine cup, moving it so it could not spill on to the maps. Samana kept the smile on her face. Curse this Roman! He was unlike any man she had ever met – his mind was of equal strength to his loins. She would need all her considerable talents to deal with him. Happily, despite his worn face and grey hair, she did not have to pretend her moans with him. Power was desirable; the face it wore did not need to be.

She sat down on his lap, wriggling a little to settle herself. 'As it happens, my lord, I do have a present for you.'

Agricola raised one eyebrow. Samana was toying with the brooch fastening his cloak, wetting her painted lips with her tongue. 'I have heard it said in the camp that you are looking over the sea to Erin.'

'Perhaps.'

'Would you be pleased with a prince of that land, then, to smooth your way?'

Agricola looked down at her fingers, moving over his chest. 'Are you asking whether I would be interested in a coward? A man who would sell his people for his own ends?'

She was silent, smiling, knowing him.

'Such a man would be welcome, indeed.'

At that she laughed. She had more in common with these people every day.

'But your men, whatever their faults, are not cowards, Samana. Why would he entreat with me? And where did you find him?'

'He has married into the Epidii in the north, through my cousin. So, as yet, he does not have a deep loyalty to Alba . . .'

'You must be a good match, then.'

Samana ignored that. 'He has influence through his wife, and I understand it is growing. He is a man of stature and strategy. If you show him your might, I feel sure that he will

216

convince the rest of the tribes to make treaty with you, as I have done for the Votadini.'

Agricola looked at her with speculation. 'And will he also send the Epidii king and his nobles to their deaths, my pretty? Does he know of your own manipulations?' She avoided his eyes, and he laughed. 'Well, then, what do you get out of it?'

'I want a Roman land, that is all. Roads, and peace . . .'

'Yes, and riches, I understand well. And if it comes to war, perhaps a certain prince of Erin to rule the defeated, with you as queen?'

Samana looked up, her eyes deliberately wide and shocked. 'Oh, no, my lord! I would wish to stay with you – you must know that!'

'I have a wife. You would give up your status, such as it is, to follow me around as a camp whore?'

She controlled her flash of temper before he saw it, and instead stroked the skin beneath his ear. When she spoke, her voice was husky, as he liked it. 'If the tribes make treaty with you, all of Britannia will be under your control. You won't need to be on the march any more. I will live wherever you wish.'

He considered for a moment, softly scratching his stubbled chin. 'You have this traitor tucked away hereabout, I am sure.'

'He is camped alone with me, very close now.'

'Well, bring him, then.' He started to move her away from him.

'You don't wish me to go, surely,' she purred. 'I have not received any reward yet.'

He looked at her thoughtfully, but unfortunately not with desire. Then he did push her away, setting her firmly on her feet, and went to where his personal belongings were stacked in their leather packs. He rummaged through them, then tossed something small and bright to her.

'I have a meeting, late though it is, and must go. There is food, there, near my bed. Bring your prince to me tomorrow night. The fewer the men who see him, the better.' And then he was gone.

Samana looked down: nestled in her palm was a ring, the ring of a priestess, engraved with the three faces of the Mother. And then she noticed that it was encrusted with something dark. *Blood*. She tried to laugh at his cleverness, but suddenly she did not want to eat. She left the ring there when she went.

It was near dawn when Samana slipped back under the lean-to cover, next to Eremon's sleeping form. Immediately, her arms were gripped by his hard fingers, and his body rose over hers in the dark.

'Where in Hawen's name have you been, lady?'

His voice was harsh, without any of the desire that she had become accustomed to. 'You're hurting my arms!'

'I'll hurt more than that if you don't explain yourself now!'

'I will! Let me go!' He released her and she sank back down, breathing hard. 'I rode to one of the camp outposts, to let them know that I was coming with you tomorrow.'

'They know you well enough for you to just walk out of the dark?'

'I am a woman, Eremon. They would hardly shoot at me, all on my own. Anyway, as Queen of their closest allies, they have given me a seal to show.'

'And they did not think it strange that you come, with no escort, in the middle of the night? It hardly ranks as an official visit, does it? If you can do that, they will wonder why you bring me at all!'

She sighed. The closer she came to the truth, the better he would be pacified. 'If you must know, I have a friendship with one of the camp clerks, and I have in fact visited on many occasions. In the night.'

He did not answer, and she propped herself on one elbow, pressing her breast against his arm. The boar tusk dug into her skin. 'Don't play shocked with me, Eremon. I'm sure you enjoy the favours of many women, so why can I not do so with many men?'

He snorted. 'Because they are Romans, Samana!'

'Romans have as much between their legs as you do!' She nestled her head into his chest, but he remained rigid, and did not take her in his arms, 'It was a short-lived thing, many moons ago. I gained much knowledge that was of use to my people.'

He still did not answer.

'Eremon!' She was exasperated. 'How is this any different from you wedding my cousin? You do this for your own reasons – you bed her to gain something! How is this different?'

After a long while he sighed, and his body relaxed a little. 'When you put it like that, it is little different. Except that the Romans are the enemy.'

'You see them that way. But I have chosen not to fight, remember.'

'You are a dangerous woman, Samana.'

She smiled in the dark, and her hand crept down towards his *bracae*, cupping him through the thin wool. The vestiges of her magic would have faded by now, but it had bought her time enough to ensure that his body was bonded to hers, and his mind less sure of itself.

Its power over him had surprised even her, for magic could only intensify existing desires. And when she cast her spell she'd no idea that such a wealth of passion lay untapped in a man such as this. The prince of Erin had obviously not found what he needed on the shores of Alba yet.

This thought made her smile even more as she sought out his lips to claim them.

CHAPTER 28

Conaire did not see Rhiann on the first day of Eremon's departure, though as he came back into the dun near dusk, breathless after a beach ride, he was seized with a sudden impulse to seek her out.

Even more surprising was the pity that drove him; a feeling that arose when he noticed her distress after learning of Eremon's plan. He'd never anticipated feeling anything at all for his brother's bride, and she certainly was not an object of pity for anyone else. But from the time that she proposed this mad southern journey, his interest in her had increased.

She seemed to think like a man, which was a new idea to Conaire, but intriguing. She and Eremon did not like each other, obviously, although Conaire failed to see why. She was sharp-tongued, and did not throw herself around like Aiveen and Garda. But so what? The way she handled the council and then that Roman patrol had sealed her worth so far as he was concerned. Eremon should forget about seeing her as a woman – for she obviously did not encourage that – and just treat her as a comrade. There were plenty of other girls about to lay with.

He sighed as he dismounted and handed the horse to the stable-boy. For all Eremon's undoubted talents, he knew very little about women. Take Samana. As much as Conaire would bed her in a moment, something about the Votadini Queen made him uneasy. It was not herself, for she looked to be a wild one in the furs, and that was a pleasant thought. No, it was the change he had seen in Eremon.

Conaire had enjoyed his share of women, but had never

been in thrall to a particular one. And had this hold of hers affected Eremon's judgement? Conaire's thought felt horribly disloyal, but as he strode along the dun path in the fading light, he was overwhelmed by a flood of frustration. He and Eremon had never been parted this way, certainly not when either of them was going into danger.

He realized that his footsteps had taken him right up to Rhiann's door. He stared at the cover, and when he heard movement inside, acted without thinking, and entered.

Rhiann was shaking moisture from her skirts and handing her damp cloak to a servant. She seemed tired, and he blurted out, 'I am curious how you got so wet on a fine day, lady.'

She glanced up in surprise, and then a look of wariness settled on her face. 'The woods are still damp.' She waved at the basket set down near the door. 'I have been collecting plants. There are different medicines here than at home.'

Conaire rocked on his feet, not sure what to say, but she broke the silence. 'They are gone, then?'

'Yes, this morning.'

She nodded, and he could see now that she was unusually pale. 'Good evening, then.' She turned away to the bed.

'Ah . . .' he began, just stopping himself from catching her arm. Then he knew he could not say anything of Eremon, not now. There was pain there in her face, and it was clear to see if you were looking.

He struggled to choose his words, which he was not accustomed to doing. 'I never gave you thanks, lady, for saving me and my leg.' He grinned and patted his scarred thigh, and was gratified to see colour rush back to her cheeks.

'Your own body did most of the work but . . . thank you.'

'I seek your help again, if I may.'

The wariness returned to her eyes. 'How?'

'Well . . .' He ran his hand through his hair. 'I am terrible at waiting. If it is acceptable, perhaps we could eat together?'

He trailed off, knowing she would refuse, but to his surprise she hesitated, and then shrugged. 'Yes, why not? Maybe it will help time to pass.'

He grinned again, conscious that she looked less anxious and more . . . approachable. But then, he only ever saw her around Eremon.

They ate together that night, eschewing the Roman chairs for benches. When the food was brought in, Conaire was surprised to see good, honest fare piled on the platters – roast pig and sorrel leaves, sea-beet and salmon. The wine had been replaced with ale.

Rhiann was watching him, with a small smile that might almost be called mischievous. 'I told the cook to give us food from home. Nothing Roman!'

He laughed. 'I was getting a bellyache from those spices. And the wine! The aches are worse than with ale.'

'Assuming you drink so much,' she returned lightly.

Conaire never expected to talk with Rhiann, of all people, in the way that he spoke to Eremon, but soon he almost forgot that she was a royal lady, and his brother's wife. Conaire only bedded women, never conversed with them, and having one without the other was fascinating.

The next day she invited him to join her again, and the evening after. He found that he was able to make her laugh a little, even though the dark circles about her eyes showed her real state of mind. Soon he found himself suggesting that he accompany her gathering expeditions.

So they rode, and talked, and ate.

And they waited.

The harsh challenge rang out from the gloom above. Instinctively, Eremon's hand went to his sword, but then he remembered he had left it with Conaire. He only had one spear, as would befit a lady's escort among allies.

Samana stepped forward, leading her horse and firing off a sentence in rapid Latin. A torch flared on high, and peering up, Eremon could see two Roman soldiers standing on an earth bank, the flame bouncing off polished leather armour and javelin tips, and the timber palisade behind. To get this far, he and Samana had already passed through two outposts, and been funnelled between a strange arrangement of other banks to reach the camp gate.

Now his attention was claimed by the scrape of the gate being dragged open, and as Samana ushered him inside the camp, he remarked, 'They know you well.'

'I told you, I have had much to do with this camp.' Samana stopped, and moved closer. 'Trust me, my love,' she breathed softly into his ear. But fear had sharpened Eremon's senses, and her honeyed kiss did little to allay his unease.

After releasing the horses to one of the soldiers, Samana led him towards the glow of torches, across a cleared space of crushed heather and stamped-down turf. And here Eremon had to stop, for his feet would not move.

Hundreds and hundreds of leather tents were set out in orderly rows that stretched away into the gloom, and fire glowed in pits before each one, shining off stacks of hide shields and spears and helmets. Torches wove serpents of light among the pathways, aflicker with the shadows of many men. To one side, horses nickered on their lines, and behind them the oxen teams shifted and stamped. Further off, in the darkness, he could just make out another bank and palisade.

'The tent spaces are marked out for the troops in the same way for each camp,' Samana whispered. 'The position of the officers and units are known by all, so that in the event of attack every soldier knows where to go! Isn't it marvellous?'

Eremon heard the note of awe in her voice, and followed behind her more slowly.

She led him on through groups of soldiers milling about, ducking in and out of tent flaps, stirring pots over banked fires. From every dizzying direction came sudden shouts of laughter and the clanking of weapons and harness. There appeared to be close to ten men in each tent, making for the whole camp . . . no, he did not wish to know the numbers. Never had he seen so many warriors in one place.

Samana came out on to a wide path that led straight to what appeared to be the centre of the camp. There, he saw a larger tent, flying a standard from its apex: the emblem of the

Eagles. Eremon's stomach tightened when the firelight caught the banner, and he wondered, with rising alarm, just who they were going to see.

The formidable guards at the tent's entrance lowered their spears when they saw Samana. Eremon balked then, his instincts flaring, but it was too late. He must not draw attention to himself. He looked down as he followed her inside, avoiding their eyes.

A three-legged brazier bathed the interior with light. Eremon caught a glimpse of a low bed and leather satchels stacked up in neat piles, before his attention was claimed by the man who rose from a stool by a high table. Three other men with him turned to the door.

The first man only came up to Eremon's nose, and his hairline was receding, but he carried authority in every line of hooked nose and strong, shaven chin. Eremon recognized that he was staring at another hardened warrior. Dark eyes bored into his own from a few paces away, as if the man sought to read Eremon's mind before he spoke.

'You are a prince of Erin, yet you have married into the tribes of Alba.' The man spoke in accented but clear British.

Samana had tricked him! Eremon glanced at her, eyes widening, but she was at the table, staring intently at one of the scrolls. What a fool he had been! Yet despite the shock, the contempt in the man's face made his own pride surge. 'And you are of the Roman kind,' he replied, lifting his chin, 'yet you seek to take a country not your own.'

The man smiled, and said something to Samana in Latin. She swept forward to introduce them, avoiding Eremon's eyes. 'This is Eremon mac Ferdiad of Dalriada in Erin. And—'

The man broke in, taking instant command. 'And I am Gnaeus Julius Agricola, Governor of Britannia.'

Icy fear drenched Eremon, as the man added, 'Forgive my rudeness. I have been on the march for so long now that I have forgotten how to entertain distinguished guests.'

Eremon quickly recovered. 'I did not know I would meet

with you, Gnaeus Julius Agricola. Your deeds are known to us even in Erin.'

Agricola raised his eyebrows. 'That is praise indeed.'

'The refugees that came to our shores did not think so.'

When Agricola spoke, his voice was still pleasant, though his gaze was not. 'Ah, yes. When one is new come to a position, one must make a name.' He took up a silver jug and poured wine into a cup. 'You are a young prince, I am sure you understand that. Perhaps you are even in the process of making your name, too?' He looked up and smiled, then handed the cup to Eremon. 'But enough of that – wait.' And he turned back to his men and continued his discussion, leaving Eremon standing where he was.

Eremon's face suffused with heat, and he didn't know what he wanted to do first; wipe that smile from Agricola's face or take Samana by the arms and shake her. Eventually the officers saluted and left, each one staring curiously at him as they passed.

Agricola went to the door of the tent and called in his guard. 'I had a bed prepared for you,' he told Eremon, then looked at Samana with the hint of a smile. 'And you, lady. Or would you rather they were one and the same?'

Eremon put the cup on the table and stepped to Samana's side. 'We will stay together. But what do you intend? Is it a ransom you wish from my people?'

'You mistake us!' Agricola shook his head. 'I only wish to talk. I have something to show you. You would like to see our camp in the light of day, would you not?'

Eremon stared him down. 'Of course.'

'Then so be it. Enjoy our hospitality. I will send for you.'

Eremon and Samana were shown to a tent as spacious as Agricola's own, and as soon as they were alone, Eremon did grasp Samana's shoulders, his fury boiling over. 'What in Hawen's name do you think you are doing?'

She stayed pliant between his hands. 'It was the only way to get you here. He wants to speak to you of a treaty, as I said.'

'You did not tell me I would be meeting with the

commander of Britannia's entire army. Nor that you would tell him who I am! Do you want me killed?'

She was breathing hard. 'No! And this is the only way to keep you alive! Don't you see? You have no choice! You must ally with him. He is the power in this land.'

The red fog of rage in Eremon was abruptly doused by cold reality, and he stopped the torrent of angry words from spilling from his lips. Samana was in league with Agricola. If Eremon angered her, she could have him executed.

And just like that, he was back in control – the haze that had invaded his mind ever since they set foot in Samana's dun fell away. It was like the coming of sunrise after a long dream, but a cold sunrise at that. He breathed in deeply, and as he let out the breath, he felt his mind clear, and then his heart. Now there was no confusion or indecision to grapple with; only the reality of bitterness and shame. But at least they were true.

'Hear what he has to say, Eremon. See the might of the Romans. You are not witless, which is why I brought you here!'

He released her shoulders. 'He wants my support for a treaty, is that it?'

'Yes.' She was rubbing her arms, her expression wary.

'What will you do if I say no?'

She reached out and put her hand over his heart. 'I have not been entirely honest with you.'

He snorted. 'This I know.'

'I had to get you here first, to make you hear what he had to say. But now, I can tell you the rest of my plan.'

'What is it?'

'Regardless of the tribes, regardless of any treaty that he makes or does not make with others in Alba, I want you to agree to personally support Agricola.'

'You are telling me to turn traitor to the Epidii?'

'What loyalty do you have to them? They are nothing to you! You must think only of yourself.'

226

Eremon sat down heavily on the camp bed, his eyes roving around the tent; at the claw-footed table, the elegant wine jug, the carved oil lamp, the platter of figs. Everything in it was foreign to his eyes.

'Like you, I think the tribes will fight,' Samana was saying. 'And the Romans will win. But as I said before, they will not stay. There will be need for new rulers. Rulers like us.'

His head jerked up, and she came to kneel by him. 'Think, Eremon! More land, more power than you could ever dream of. All for the sake of lip service to the Romans!'

'My only desire is to return to my own lands. I had no thought for taking more.'

'Well, start thinking!' Her face was alight. 'What a formidable team we would make together!'

'And what of Rhiann?'

'What of her? For this is also your choice. I have no intention of being caught up in a fight with the Romans – I have already made my decision. Yet Rhiann will choose with her heart, soft fool that she is.'

To Eremon, this sounded utterly unlike the Rhiann he knew, but Samana caught his hand and pressed it to her cheek. 'Eremon, Eremon! I, too, am a princess. I can also give you the help you need. My people are powerful. And you enjoy me in bed, do you not?'

'Of course, but I could not do that to her.'

'She was forced into this marriage, you told me. She will be happy to let you go, and return to her blessings and her horse and her . . . *peasants.*'

The scorn in her voice surprised him. 'You hate her!'

She seemed to recover herself and rose, smoothing down her skirt. 'She is inconsequential to me. But you are another matter.' When she looked down at him, her mouth was soft, her eyes as wide as when they lay in the bed furs. 'We were meant to be together, you and I. We can forge a kingdom that spans Alba and Erin. Think of that!'

'But if I say no?'

The softness was extinguished with a shrug. 'Then go back to Rhiann, back to your dry marriage bed – and to a future that guarantees a Roman spear through your heart.'

CHAPTER 29

Although at first Rhiann was furious to hear that Conaire was her guard, as if she were a fragile child, within days something unexpected happened. She began to feel grateful for his presence.

The strain of the last few moons, of constantly being on her guard with Eremon, had worn her down. Conaire's jests, though often forced, somehow managed to slide in under her broken defences. And although she knew it slumbered within him, for she had seen the scars, there was no hint of the violent warrior in his open face and blue eyes.

Without him, she would have gone mad with frustration, though she did not let him see that. Never had she been so trapped. The cage of her marriage was one thing, although she had come to some peace about that. But this waiting, not knowing if she were in danger . . . All this for a man – for the same man!

Every hour the urge came upon her to take her horse and race for home. And yet, though she railed at her weakness, she could not give up on Eremon quite yet. Even if she went back to Dunadd, she would still be bonded to him, and the council would not back her in the face of Eremon's warband. After seeing the way he trained the warriors, she knew how important he would be if it came to war with the Romans.

That is, if he stayed on their side.

Surely he would not betray them, as Samana had obviously done? For now that she could reflect, it was plain to Rhiann that her cousin was in league with Rome.

Rhiann had not mentioned her suspicions to Eremon

before he left. He would think it jealousy talking, which it was not. After all, they were married in name only. Liaisons outside such unions were the rule, not the exception.

No, she was only angry that he had left her behind. Her frustration only stemmed from this enforced waiting. These were the only things that ate at her, she was sure.

The soldier led Eremon through the camp, which was just beginning to stir. The smoke from new-lit cookfires puffed into the chill air, and all around he heard the harsh sound of the invaders' language, so different from the musical flow of his own.

A good league away from the gates, the heather slopes of a hill flowed up on to a stony ridge, high above a flat river plain. The spears of two guards at the base of the hill glinted in the dawn, announcing their presence, as they moved into position on either side of Eremon and escorted him up a steep track. Above, a figure was outlined against the greying sky. He felt like a prisoner being marched before his captors, and with a shock he realized that was exactly what he was. Agricola would never let him go if he refused him.

'I trust you had a comfortable night,' said Agricola, when Eremon reached him.

The camp was spread out below them now, and though shrouded in dawn mist, Eremon could just glimpse its layout. He marvelled that the Romans would build something like this as a temporary halting place. It was more substantial than many of his own people's homes. He turned back to Agricola, conscious that he was about to give the performance of his life.

'I did, thank you. Your hospitality was not as bad as I have heard.'

Agricola smiled. He looked fresh, considering his age. Being in the field obviously agreed with him, and he looked out over his camp with relish. 'I wanted to show you two things, man of Erin. One is this camp: see how strong it is, and how many men lie within it. See how well-armoured they are, how perfectly controlled, like one beast, rather than many.'

'I see that.'

'Good. Then I wish you to tell what you see to these Albans, these painted men. We are many, and we are strong beyond their imagining. And my intention is to make all Alba Roman. Be very clear on that. We have done it in the south, and we will do it here.'

'I shall tell them.'

'If they resist, they have no chance. Their people will die or be enslaved. Yet if they make peace, they will become part of the greatest empire the world has ever known!' Agricola swept his arm out. 'They will have roads, baths, heating, running water, temples. They will have access to the goods of the world – spices, jewels, exotic cloth. All will be orderly. All will be peaceful. Their clan raids and petty squabbling will be but a memory.'

Eremon tried not to let his feelings show, but Agricola sensed the curl of his mouth and turned to him. 'I know you people have this fixation on freedom. But what is freedom? Fighting and warring incessantly? Starving to death during a hard season?'

'Freedom is ruling yourselves.'

'But peace is true freedom. And that is what we bring, son of Ferdiad. We bring peace. Peace to raise crops, to raise children. We have found the best way to live, and we want to share it with the world!'

Eremon forced his face to relax. 'The peoples of this island find this concept difficult, Agricola, as you know. Fortunately, I think differently.'

'Yes, so Samana has told me – a man with a cool head, not a fire in his belly like so many of these fool Britons. They do not understand what is best for them. They are like children, playing at war. They need a strong guiding hand – that is what Rome was made for.'

Eremon's belly was, in fact, on fire. But Samana was right about one thing. He did have a cool head on his shoulders, especially when it was a matter of life and death. His heart nearly thrust through his chest with each beat, but he kept his mouth still.

Agricola cocked his head at him. 'So will you agree to be my messenger, to convince the tribes to make a treaty?'

Relief began to course through Eremon's body. It appeared that he might escape lightly after all. 'Yes, I will tell them of your intentions, and of your might. But I am not a prince of their own. There are many different tribes. I cannot promise they will acquiesce to you.'

'I realize that. But no matter, I have come prepared for a fight. I will crush them anyway.'

Eremon clenched his hands, desperate to throw himself on this man and rid the world of such ruthlessness. But he knew there were more Romans to replace him; many more. And the guards could stop him before he completed the deed.

Why die for the Albans anyway? he thought. *I just need to get home to Erin.*

Agricola took his arm and looked up searchingly into his face. 'Now that I see you are a reasonable man, there is the second thing.'

He dropped his hand and gestured for Eremon to fall into step with him. They picked their way between dark outcrops of granite, until the land again fell away. Gazing out, Eremon could see lower hills and ridges that rose to a haze of purple mountains.

Agricola pointed. 'Erin is westwards, is it not?'

Eremon's heart sank again. 'Yes.'

'I am considering it as my next conquest.'

The sinking lurched into nausea.

'Your arrival has made me think,' Agricola went on. 'It is easier for us to make peace if we have a ruler of the land to smooth our way. In exchange for offering no resistance, he gets to keep, and in fact increase, his power.'

'Client kingship,' Eremon remarked. His voice, thankfully, was steady.

'Yes. It suits us, and it suits him. It seems fortune has

232

brought you to me at this time, does it not, Eremon of Dalriada?'

'You are proposing that I become your client king.'

Agricola nodded. 'With my forces, you can gain as much of Erin as you wish. And we will accomplish it far quicker than you could with Albans by your side.'

'And in return?'

'Your followers keep the peace for us, and we don't have so many troublesome uprisings to deal with. It saves me men, but I get the same result: all Erin and Alba for Rome.'

Eremon stared at that far horizon, where his land, his Erin, lay nestled out of sight. Dark fingers of cloud were now creeping up from the wall of mountains. The clear skies would not last.

Agricola put a hand on his shoulder. 'This may have come as a shock, I understand. I understand also that you barbarian princes hold your concept of "honour" highly indeed. But what is honour? Saving lives and stock and land, surely? Think about it. You have until dawn tomorrow to answer.' He dropped his hand and strode back towards the camp.

Eremon noticed that the guards who had followed them immediately moved in closer. Towards the western edge of the ridge, more guards were stationed, cutting off all thoughts of escape. He watched Agricola's retreating back, conscious that the Roman toyed with him. For if he refused, he would be killed or imprisoned. And the former was much more likely.

It was only when he turned back to his home that he realized, with dawning horror, that part of him was wavering over Agricola's offer. *I could go back now*, this voice in his heart whispered. *I could kill my uncle and release my people!*

Then from somewhere deeper, a darker thought arose. *I could increase my kingdom, its splendour, its might . . . High King of all Erin, I could be . . .*

Appalled at the turn of his own mind, he spun on his heel, and saw the flash of red from Agricola's cloak as he re-appeared in the camp below.

By the Boar, what would he do? It could all be over now; he could have all that he wanted. But what did he want?

Samana was lounging on Agricola's bed when the commander returned.

'This does not help your case with your prince, Samana.' Agricola handed his cloak to a slave. 'I gather he does not know about your other exploits. What if he sees you here?'

Samana picked at the grapes on a platter by the bed. 'He won't. I have left guards outside, and at our tent.'

'Still, I am relying on his feelings for you to guarantee his loyalty, as you know. Do not endanger that.'

Samana licked juice from her chin. 'Do not keep him here long, then. One of your men may talk.'

'He will give me his answer tomorrow. If it is yes, then he will stay. If no . . . he won't be leaving!'

'Do you think he will do it, my lord?'

'He appeared strongly tempted, and acquiescent. You say he does not have the powers for guile?'

'No, he prides himself far too much on his honesty. None of the peoples of these islands have such powers.'

'Except you.'

'Except me.' She slipped off the bed and came to link her arms around his neck. 'I must be a Roman babe that was exchanged in its cradle. Which is why you must take me with you, wherever you go.'

'And what will your man think of that?'

'I can tie him to you until he sails for Erin in your name. Then he will be in too deep. He is hardly going to give up what he has won there and come back to chase after me.'

'You are too modest, Samana.'

She shrugged.

'So, you do not care for him at all, then,' Agricola said. 'This is all just to please me.'

She pouted. 'Of course! But if you do not want me, then I will go with him. Only as a second choice, you understand.'

'Ah, yes, you still need a man to warm your bed.'

'I need to rule more than I need that.' She kissed the corner of his mouth. 'You can at least give me that, my love, if you turn out to be so cruel as to reject me. Set me up as a client queen.'

'You already are.'

'I mean of all Alba. Once you get rid of those coarse northern tribes.'

He untangled her arms. 'I will not promise you anything, because then you won't try so hard.' He cupped her breast and stroked the nipple through the fine wool. 'Talking of my empire always inflames me, and I missed you last night.' He pushed her to her knees. 'There are troop inspections this morning. I don't have long.'

Eremon stayed on the ridge-top until the sun had long been eclipsed by the brooding bank of cloud creeping in from the west. Outwardly he was still, but inside the fires were raging, and as the hours crawled by, the shame he felt for even thinking of joining Agricola burned brighter.

The voices warred within him. What was best for Erin? What was best for his men? What was best for him? And, though he did not like to admit it, one face kept shimmering in his mind – a fine-boned face framed by amber hair. She did not want him as a man. But she needed him as a leader. Could he do that to her? He pushed the image away, replacing it with a fall of raven hair and the scent of apples. The other choice, as Samana said.

Surely, though, a choice between two women was not as important as the other issues. As his men. As his country. As his pride.

His guards grew bored, and soon squatted down nearby to throw bone pieces on the ground in some sort of game. He heard them talking and laughing together, and dimly realized that he understood their speech. He turned to look at them directly. Both had dark hair, but instead of Latin eyes, theirs were grey. Then he remembered that the Romans had been in Britannia for more than thirty years now.

One soldier saw him looking and nudged the other. There was no kinship in their hostile regard. These men were born of Roman sires, and though they spoke British, their blood was a source of shame for them, not pride. 'Stuck in a bit of a hole are we, then?' one of them jeered.

The other laughed. 'Our commander has you right where he wants you, to be sure!'

Eremon turned his back.

'You puny, savage kings think you lord it over all of us,' the first guard muttered, loud enough for him to hear. 'But our commander will take everything from you, princeling. He's already got your woman, eh?'

The other man snorted with laughter. 'Everyone in camp has had that witch!'

Eremon's heart chilled, and he remembered the strange glances between Agricola and Samana. The way the other guards looked at her.

'Our prefect Marcellus says she does some interesting things with that tongue of hers,' the first continued. 'You know that one, prince? Or does she keep it for her real men?'

Eremon spun around, fixing them with a cold glare. 'Speak no more of the woman, or when I wield a sword again I'll take it to your throat.'

'I'd like to see you try!' the first man spat. 'There'll be no more of these petty raids of yours, no fine duels. Our army will march right over your rabble, and we won't stop until Alba is ours, so the commander says. Just wait and see, prince. Wait and see.'

By the fifth night Rhiann's doubts had become unbearable. She paced her hut in the firelight, hair unbound and uncombed, frustration tearing at her. She could not sleep, nor eat. Was Eremon betraying them, betraying her, even now? Were Romans marching at this moment, on their way to capture her? It seemed impossible in the daylight hours, but at night, her fears grew as distorted as the flickering shadows on the walls.

Suddenly, she stopped pacing, her eye falling on her medicine bag. Of course! She waited here like a blind woman, when she had something that would surely bring her the information she needed.

Then she resumed pacing. No, it was too dangerous, far more dangerous than a simple seeing, when the priestess stayed in her body. This trance would involve leaving the confines of her earthly form.

Linnet would be unhappy that she had any spores of the rye fungus in her possession, the spores that could release the spirit from the flesh. It was reserved for the very rarest druid and priestess trances, for aside from being painful to use, many spirits did not return to their own bodies, and were lost in the Otherworld.

She paused again at the line of goddess figurines, their faces in shadow. A flare of firelight caught Ceridwen's eyes. Were they . . . pitying? Nay, disapproving, surely.

But it was the only way! Only the spores could ensure her a seeing, now that her powers were so weakened. She stopped again. It could be unpredictable, but anything would be better than this waiting.

There was only a trickle of water left in her wash basin, but she did not want to go creeping about the dun in the dark for more. It would have to do. She stirred up the fire, setting the shadows to leaping and dancing, and unfolded the tiny curl of birch bark, buried in the secret pocket of the pack. She took a few pinches of the dried powder and mixed it in a cup with the water. Then, before swallowing it, she sat cross-legged on the floor, breathing in the priestess way, right down to the feet, then right out to the top of the head, striving to still the trembling, to centre her heart energy.

The centring was important, to ensure the soul did not sever its cord with the body; to ensure she was not lost in the terror of hallucinations, or led astray by glittering dreams dangled before her by fey spirits.

When she could clearly sense the column of soul-light running the length of her body and into the earth, anchoring her, she at last swallowed the liquid in the cup and then rose to lay on the bed, staring into the fire.

She did not know how long it was before the flames began to flicker with more than just the draught.

First her spirit began to contract from the edges of her body, growing smaller and smaller as the dark walls around her loomed larger, undulating like kelp in the sea. She lost the feeling in her toes and fingers, yet there was a terrible burning in her tongue.

Then, when her spirit had shrunk to a tiny pinprick, it began to rush down a dark tunnel, faster and faster, the walls of the tunnel spiralling and flashing with spears of light. The wild music of the Otherworld called to her . . . *Come to us! Come! Be free! Let go!*

But she resisted the pleas and the unbearable pull, remembering she was a priestess, remembering what she had been taught: slow the rush by breathing *through* the cord, see it tied still to her body, see it still anchored to the heart energy of the earth, see its silver light pulse and strengthen with each breath . . .

Yes . . . the cord is rooted, unbreakable . . . I can return . . . I will return . . . and the tunnel opened out into light, and she retained a last flicker of awareness that behind her in a shadowed room, her body was in spasms on the bed, jerking with rigid limbs, pouring with sweat . . .

Normally a scene resolved itself to her spirit-eye gradually, as she floated between space and time, focusing on what she wanted to see. But now there was a sudden lurch, and the light turned from golden warmth to cold day, and in the light two figures stood. The figures grew clearer as she drifted closer.

It was Eremon, and another man with a large nose and a shaven face – a Roman. They stood under a clouded sky, talking, but it was hard to see if their faces showed anger, or friendship. She was drawn closer. Ah, now she could see Eremon's face. He was smiling.

Tied to the pinprick spirit by the cord, her body registered a jolt of some emotion, and then she was following Eremon, floating helplessly as the air shimmered around him, turning to night.

He emerged out of darkness into a pool of warm firelight: the inside of a tent. And Samana was there, drawing a comb through her black hair and smiling as they ate together. No! Rhiann tried to pull herself back, but she could not. Something in her wanted to see, something would not let her go.

There were bands of coloured light around Eremon now, and anger swirled there, battering against Rhiann's spirit senses. What did it mean?

Then he was bearing Samana down to the bed, wrenching her robes to one side, exposing a lush landscape of honey-coloured skin. An urgent feeling of sickness was starting to creep into the edges of Rhiann's consciousness, from her body far away.

Pained, she watched Eremon enter Samana, saw the burning of his eyes as he slapped her across the face, and heard Samana's cries of ecstasy. How could she? Eremon's hand left a white mark on Samana's face, but her cousin's eyes were glittering with excitement.

Mercifully, something in Rhiann let her go then, and with another sudden lurch she was back inside her body, on the bed, the room spinning around her. She lay dazed, staring at the leaping flames of the fire, the entire surface of her skin a burning agony of sharp, stabbing pains, and then she rolled on to the floor and vomited violently into the wash basin.

For an eternity she retched, over and over, until the spasms passed enough for her to wipe her face and crawl weakly back on to the bed. Some nausea was normal from the spores, but she was frightened at the ferocity of her reaction.

She lay there until the room stopped spinning, and some feeling returned to her limbs.

The images that she had seen were tumbling through her mind. She tried to concentrate on the first scene and to forget the second. Eremon had been smiling, as if he gave some sort of respect to this Roman. Was this proof? Should she flee?

Her mind gnawed on itself, endlessly spinning, until at last dawn crept through the chinks under the roof.

That day, Conaire found her crouched in the shelter of the rocky spur below the walls of the hillfort. It was a private place, hidden in the oak trees, and she had taken to going there, watching the western road.

'We will know soon,' she said, when she saw Conaire. He sat down beneath the trees, and after searching her face, patted her awkwardly on the shoulder, a gesture that would have been unthinkable a week before. But then, they had been thrust together here in a way that would have been impossible at home.

'He will return, Rhiann,' he said, using her name for the first time. 'No one is as true as Eremon. He has seen too much betrayal himself to be false.'

Rhiann glanced at him sidewise, noting the bitter quirk of Conaire's mouth at the mention of betrayal. And she wondered again what that bitterness meant when it marred Eremon's own smile. 'But what are his true ties here, Conaire? What are yours? I am not ignorant; I know he only wants to make a name here, just as I know if I ask you why, you won't tell me. But what if the best way is through Rome?'

Conaire shook his head, leaning back against the oak behind him. 'He married you. He made kin ties with your tribe. He vowed to support your people. He will not go back on these vows, Rhiann. Not the Eremon I know.'

She could not believe that. 'Conaire, do you know much about druid practices?'

Her question obviously surprised him. 'No, and I don't want to know!' He grinned. 'I only want to know about the Otherworld in song, in tales, and when I eventually go there myself!'

She did not return the smile. 'But you know about the sight, don't you?'

'I know what it is, yes.'

She drew absently in the dirt with one finger. 'Last night I did a kind of seeing. And I saw Eremon, and a Roman. They were talking and smiling, like friends.' She looked up at him. 'Like allies.'

'But you may have been wrong. Sometimes seeings aren't true.'

'Mine usually are.'

'You could not hear what they said—'

'He was smiling, Conaire.'

Conaire thought, the stirring leaves flickering shadows across his face. 'Could you see his eyes, closely?'

'Well, no, but—'

'There, then!' He sounded relieved. 'Only I could tell if Eremon was lying, and only if I saw his eyes.'

'Lying?'

'Rhiann, what if they have pressured him to do something he does not want to do? He might have to appear to go along with them. I'm sure you have done it, many times, as he has. He is very good at it.

Rhiann frowned, clasping her knees. 'It does not seem the most likely explanation.'

'It does if you know Eremon. And trust him.' He touched her arm. 'Do you trust me, Rhiann?'

She looked into his startling blue eyes. 'You make it hard not to.'

'Then wait a few more days before you do anything.'

'If you believe in him so much, then why aren't you riding off to save him?'

'Did he appear to be in danger?'

An image of Eremon and Samana on the bed flashed into Rhiann's mind, and she hunched into her arms. 'No, not directly.'

'Then I say this. He told me to wait here, and I won't disobey him – that is how we both stay alive. He will find a way to come back, and if he can't, I could not help him anyway. He would want me to save you.'

She stared at him in disbelief. *Why? Eremon does not care about me.*

'He will come back, Rhiann,' Conaire said firmly, closing his eyes, resting his head against the rough bark. 'To us.'

CHAPTER 30

E remon started awake. By the Boar, he hadn't meant to fall asleep again! He wanted only to wait until Samana was deep in slumber, not join her there himself.

He sat up, carefully disentangling his limbs from hers. But she only murmured and rolled over, her breathing even and slow. He knew just by the feel of the air creeping under the tent walls that it was close to dawn. His intention had been to wake long before this. He cursed himself, and edged closer to the table by the bed, to where his discarded clothes lay in an untidy pile on the floor.

But as he quietly slipped on his tunic and trousers, and began pulling on his boots, his eye fell on the half-eaten platter of food on the table. The wick from the oil lamp was glowing, near drowned, but its faint light outlined Samana's meat dagger, sticking out of the roast duck.

Smiling, he grabbed the knife and thrust it down the side of his boot. Then he looked over at Samana. 'You always were too sure of yourself, my lady,' he whispered, and slowly got to his feet. It was time to extricate himself from this mess.

He emerged into a thick mist, lit to a lurid glow by the last, sputtering torches on stakes around the tent. Peering around, he jumped when a figure materialized out of the fog; a soldier muffled in a woollen cloak. Agricola had obviously posted a guard. Well, Eremon expected as much. At the man's challenge, he thought frantically, and then managed to make it known that he wanted the waste pit. It was the only thing that he could think of, and at least it would get him away from Samana.

As they walked between the tents he could hear the soldiers stirring within, and the scrape of spoons on cookpots, and he pulled his own cloak closer about him to shut out the dank air. He had little time.

The waste pit was a long trench dug on the edge of camp, screened from the tents by a length of coarse sacking. Eremon disappeared around the screen ... and the soldier followed. Without thinking, Eremon twisted and struck, the meat dagger burying itself in the man's throat to the hilt, only a gasp of air escaping to raise the alarm. With distaste, Eremon then rolled the body into the reeking cesspit, out of sight until dawn, at least.

Wiping the blood down his tunic, he skirted the pit edges and slipped between the stakes of the screen on the other side. Now there was only a broad, cleared lane between him and the lines of tethered oxen, and behind them, the palisade, disappearing into the mist. The sky was already lightening to grey, but Eremon was sure that, in his brown cloak, in the heavy fog and half-dark, he would be very hard to detect, even if someone was looking for him. Which they would not be. Yet.

He stood for a moment considering the bank and palisade. Fortunately, Roman camps were built to keep enemies out, not in. It was not too high on this side. He blew out his breath. 'If I fall, I fall,' he murmured to himself. 'A Roman sword in the gut is better than turning traitor.'

But despite these words, he closed his eyes, fingers on the boar tusk, and prayed fervently to the Boar and to Manannán, and even to Rhiann's Goddess.

To help the Epidii, and eventually Erin, he pleaded, he must get out of here alive.

Didius sat his horse as one of his assistants buckled his saddle-pack. While the beast shifted and stamped beneath him, he rubbed his chapped hands mournfully. This northern climate played havoc with his circulation as well as his bowels; he had been plagued with the flux ever since they left the more civilized lands in the south. If you could call them civilized.

He threw a longing glance back over his shoulder to the camp gate, which had just scraped shut behind him. Today he must go and mark out a new watchtower for Agricola's frontier, but it was ten miles away, and so he had to set out before dawn. As if this land was not cold and dank enough in broad daylight.

He sighed. He couldn't see anything in this cursed mist anyway. Even the nearby trees were just ghostly skeletons of branch and trunk. If the weather didn't lift, then his uncomfortable journey would be wasted, and he'd have to return to Agricola with his task incomplete. The thought of his commander's hard gaze made him shudder, and the shudder turned into a hacking cough that made his jowls wobble.

Blasted cold!

And that wasn't all. He peered into the trees again. Though the entire territory had given them no trouble, and the natives had surrendered, still Didius laboured with a sick fear in his belly, as if he'd swallowed lead. What if they ran into some of those blue-painted savages from the north? The centurions delighted in telling him stories about what these barbarians did to prisoners. Internal organs played a large part in their descriptions. Ah, to be tucked up safe in his own home.

And so, while the two soldier-assistants led his horse along the line of the camp walls, he began his morning ritual of longing for Gaul: for the grapes ripening slowly on the vines, the rich scent of new-turned earth, the sun-warmed red tiles over whitewashed walls. Most of all, he ached for his house. Though modest, it was his pride and joy, with its cunningly heated floors for winter and cooling vents for summer. His greatest love was reserved for the central fountain that diverted streams through the sleeping rooms so that occupants had fresh water on hand at all times. Automatically!

He sighed. A feat of engineering it was, worthy of his

talents. Much more interesting than designing forts and walls and roads in this freezing place at the end of the earth. But to please his ageing soldier father, and win honour for his family, he had no choice but to join up. He sighed again. Perhaps soon he'd be transferred somewhere warmer. Africa perhaps . . . or Macedonia . . .

Which was when his reverie was interrupted by the single most terrifying thing he had ever seen in his life: a tall, cloaked figure that suddenly rose up from the ditch outside the walls like an avenging wraith and shot towards the nearest of Didius's two guards. The next few moments seemed to slow down to hours.

Didius's mouth dropped open in surprise, but when he heard the unmistakable sound of a blade sinking into flesh, and the pained grunt of the guard, his surprise melted into a shocked gasp.

'You there!' The other soldier ducked under the horse's neck, but when the cloaked man let his victim's body fall to the ground, a short sword was already in his hand. Now that the man was closer, Didius could discern his barbaric long hair and checked trousers. It was that savage! The one all the officers were talking about! He'd escaped!

Didius tried to draw breath to scream, but all that came out was a squeak, as, in a blur of ringing steel and harsh breath the other guard was run through, dropping to the muddy ground with a thud.

And then the savage was looking at the horse, and then up, up into Didius's own face, and all sound died on his lips, frozen there by utter terror. In the half-light, the man's eyes glinted with the same coldness as his stolen blade. Didius saw death there.

Suddenly there was a commotion at the gate behind them, and the shouts of soldiers from inside the camp. The whites of the man's eyes flashed as he glanced behind him, and before Didius could do anything he vaulted on to the horse's back behind the saddle, his hard legs gripping Didius's own.

Didius twisted, gagging with terror, hearing the gate being

wrenched back, the snatches of alarm in his own language. And then something hard slammed into the back of his head, and he slipped into the merciful dark.

As the horse raced through the mist, Eremon concentrated on maintaining his speed as well as his balance. If he fell, he would be dead. And he did not have much of a lead. Hopefully, though, it would take time to mount a pursuit. With any luck, it was just enough of a surprise that they would do nothing until they told Agricola.

Luckily, these Roman beasts were big, and he'd judged that this one was large enough and fresh enough to carry two for a short while.

He kept a grip on the Roman slumped unconscious before him. Strange, that sudden, but undeniable compulsion to knock the man out and take him, rather than dumping him on the ground. It was an impulse from the gods. But why? Obviously, the man's information would be useful. And perhaps he would also buy back the trust of the Epidii after this escapade.

Perhaps he would make up for Eremon's doubt on the hilltop.

They were reaching the edge of the open fields now and approaching the forest. Even in the mist, Eremon had his bearings. He would have to slow down in the trees, but there was no other way. Then, just before they reached the dark mass of the woods, he felt a pattering of drops on his face. He glanced up. It was raining, and judging by the sound, it was settling to be hard rain, and long.

Eremon was pleased, for it would wash away his tracks. Samana knew where he left his men, but he did not think she would come out in this weather, not unless Agricola dragged her.

His lip curled, and now that he was on the run, he released the fury that had been simmering within him since yesterday. *Fool! You were nothing but a rutting bull. Now you find your cow was being mounted by a good many besides you.*

He'd kept it all damped down, as he was watched by the soldiers on the hilltop, as he ate and lay with Samana – though he had worked some of the rage out between her thighs. But now, beneath his wet clothes, his chest burned. Did Samana bewitch him after all? She must have done, for the hate he now felt was as strong as the lust had been. His skin crawled again with the memory of her ensnaring, slippery magic, and he shivered to be free of it.

Through the rain and mist, day could barely be seen, and time seemed not to move as he forded streams and kept to the high paths. But eventually he reached the mouth of the glen where his men camped, and Colum and Fergus stepped out before him.

'We must go!' he gasped out. 'Leave everything but your swords!'

The men knew better than to ask questions now, though they all eyed the Roman, still slumped in the saddle. Eremon felt him stirring, and grabbing him by the hair, he turned his face, intending to get him to ride behind. But the Roman's eyes rolled white with terror, before they faded and closed once more.

With a few curt commands, Eremon had him tied over the horse's rump more securely, and in moments they left the valley through its higher entrance, coming out on to the top of the ridgeway where they could run unhindered for a good way.

Rori galloped alongside Eremon as they went, obviously burning with questions, but after one look at his prince's face he kept his silence.

They flew through that day and night, heading south, keeping to the ridges and glens, only stopping to rest the horses. There did not appear to be any pursuit, but Eremon drove them on relentlessly. 'We have to get back to Conaire and Rhiann before Samana can send word home. Then we must fly for Dunadd!'

CHAPTER 31

By the seventh day, Rhiann and Conaire had dropped all pretence of engaging in other activities. They simply waited, looking out from the spur at the dun's base.

The sun was low when Conaire suddenly sat up a little straighter, shading his eyes. Rhiann was curled up next to him, making up for the sleep she had missed these last nights. A single rider was making his way along the track that ran between the fields. As he came closer he reined into a trot, and Conaire recognized Rori's red hair.

'Rhiann!' Conaire hissed, jolting her full awake. He stood and waved at Rori from the shadow of the trees, calling out in their own dialect. Rori started, but seeing it was Conaire, quickly nudged his horse off the path and into the lee of the rocks. He was plainly exhausted; wet and covered in dirt, and the horse was lathered, rolling its eyes. 'Eremon has sent me to get you,' he gasped out.

Rhiann bent down for their water flask, and Rori gratefully took a few deep gulps. 'He went to the Roman camp alone, and there met some sort of treachery – he will not say what. But two days ago he escaped, and we have ridden through the night to outrun pursuit.'

'You are being followed?' Conaire was holding the horse's bridle.

'We have seen no one, but Eremon said we must return here ahead of the Lady Samana or her messengers. That is all he said.'

'Where is he?' Conaire asked.

'He and the men are in hiding a day's ride away, to the

south-west. Agricola is north. When we left the camp, Eremon thought it better to head due south, until he reached that range of big hills we passed on the way here.' Tired though he was, Rori puffed out his chest. 'I begged to come for you. Eremon was afraid that he would have a price on his head, but I am fast, and good at not being noticed!'

Conaire clapped Rori on the shoulder. 'So you are, my boy!' He turned to Rhiann. 'We must leave immediately. We'll go straight to the stables and get our horses. Is there anything that you need from the lodge?'

Rhiann shook her head. She'd taken to bringing her medicine bag with her in case she saw anything she wanted to gather, and kept her figurines and other personal totems in her pack, close by, to ease her heart. And Conaire kept his and Eremon's swords with him, too.

When they entered the gates, the Votadini guards barely gave them a glance. Rhiann and Conaire were now a common sight to them, and in Samana's absence they had not been given any orders that the Epidii Queen and her escort were any danger to them.

Rhiann, Rori and Conaire feigned relaxation until they had walked their horses out of sight of the walls. Then, mounting up, Rori took them off the main path into the range of hills to the south.

They reached Eremon by the next dawn, stiff and cold and aching from riding. In the blue shadows of a grove of tall birches, Rhiann was unable to discern one man from another, until she made out Eremon by Conaire's horse, talking softly but urgently. At the sound of his voice, all Rhiann's memories of fear, her sleepless nights, her burning vision . . . rose up in one surge of anger, choking her.

Now he was standing by her leg, looking up. She stared straight between her horse's ears, and then suddenly urged it forward until she was level with Conaire. 'Are we going home?'

The other men fell silent around them in the cold shadows.

'Yes, lady.' Conaire's voice had resumed its distant, respectful air. 'At all speed.'

'Good,' she replied. 'You will ride with me, then?'

Eremon was in the saddle again, and he walked his horse to Conaire. Rhiann could just glimpse a dark mound slung over his stallion's rump. 'Yes, brother, please look out for the lady. Make sure she does not fall behind.'

'I can ride as well as you,' Rhiann retorted. Eremon did not answer her.

They rode far west before turning north, as Eremon explained that Agricola's men were massed near the outfall of the Forth on the east coast. And at each brief stop, the Roman captive, for that is what Eremon's burden turned out to be, was propped against a tree.

Rhiann began to take him food and water, as something about the pitiful fear in his dark eyes stirred her, despite the fact that he was the enemy. Or perhaps it was because kindness to the Roman seemed to irritate Eremon, and she was still too angry to even look at *him*.

The druids had taught her some scraps of Latin, for talking with foreign traders, and so she was able to glean the captive's name and station.

And the fact, important to her, that he was not a fighter but some kind of builder.

Until her anger had run its first course, she avoided all talk with the men, wrapping herself in her cloak away from their whispered debates. But after two days, she needed the facts of what had happened, for her own peace. As they climbed in pairs up a high, twisting glen, she slowed her horse to keep pace with the prince.

He glanced at her. 'Does this mean you will hear what I have to say at last?'

She nodded.

'Then hear this.' He looked away, his voice subdued. 'It was Agricola himself in the camp, Rhiann.'

So that was the man in her seeing! 'What happened, Eremon? I deserve to know.'

He sighed, and hunched his shoulders. He was exhausted, but she hardened her heart against him, thinking of her own sleepless nights.

'He wanted me to get the tribes to agree to a treaty. And . . . he also offered to make me a client king, to send me home to Erin with a Roman legion at my back.' He said the last words in a rush.

Rhiann gasped, and when he did not speak, stared at him more keenly. 'So, the decision was difficult, then. But why refuse? I gather you did, else why escape?'

'Of course I refused!' he snapped, but for a brief moment, she saw guilt in his face. 'He had me in a trap,' he went on more softly. 'If I told him what I really thought, he would have killed me. He gave me one day to decide, but I escaped before I had to give an answer. I think he assumed I would agree.'

That fitted with her seeing, and what Conaire said. But there was, of course, something missing. 'What of Samana in all this?'

To her satisfaction she saw his face set like stone. 'She was in league with Agricola all along. She had no intention of ever trying to win free of him.'

Then why did Eremon still lay with her!

As if reading Rhiann's thoughts, he added, 'I had to keep my real intentions from Samana. So I was . . . normal . . . with her, too.' He shifted and cleared his throat. 'Rhiann, have you not wondered why we have, as yet, seen so few patrols? Or why there were so few on our trip here?'

She shook her head.

'We are still in Votadini territory, that's why.' He was bitter. 'Agricola is so sure of them, that he does not feel the need to patrol their lands. He's using this peace to start the building of a line of forts across the land between your Clutha and Forth. From his base in the east, his grasping fingers are already reaching west. It won't be long before he cuts off the southern tribes. Then he will turn his face to us.'

'And you believe that Samana herself is behind this alliance, and not her king?'

Eremon's mouth twisted. 'Oh, yes.' He wrapped the reins around his fingers. 'I admit I was wrong, Rhiann, in many things. And . . . I'm sorry.' He seemed to want to say more, but instead compressed his lips and pulled up his horse so she could enter the pass alone.

Stunned, she was blind to the broad sweep of valley that opened up before her. The great Eremon, apologizing? Humbling himself, to her? And Conaire's words came back to her, describing an Eremon she had never seen. *The best of brothers, the best of friends* . . .

She watched her horse's hooves striking the stony path below, lost in thought. But for the first time in days, something cold and strained in her began to soften.

In fact, there was no pursuit. Far behind, Agricola dismissed the interlude to his men.

'He can do nothing,' he said, when his commanders had been roused from their beds that morning. 'We will be at war soon. The next time we meet the prince of Erin he will be on the end of my sword!'

'What of Didius?' one asked.

Agricola shrugged. 'He was witless enough to get caught. We will tell his family he died in battle – only his death could win *him* honour, anyway.'

Samana, though, was not so calm, storming and stamping and cursing. 'Give me men now, and we can overtake them!' she begged Agricola. 'Or send your fastest messenger to my dun so I can have them taken! And my cousin too!'

Agricola shook his head. 'He is not worth the trouble to me, Samana. I have lost four men, I will not risk more on some race across the country. You will have to accept that this bird slipped your net, lady.'

Samana's eyes burned with black fire. 'No! I will not accept that. I never lose!'

Agricola grabbed her wrist in an iron grip. 'You are still

mine, Samana. Since when am I the second prize? We are going to win, so you will not need your prince in any case.'

Breathing heavily, Samana's eyes focused back on him. 'Of course, my lord,' she said, controlling herself. 'But I am going home. I must check that nothing came to harm while the barbarians were there.'

Agricola released her arm. That was the Samana he knew – the way she said 'nothing' rather than 'no one'.

Her deep disregard for people always impressed him.

CHAPTER 32

On a clear morning, the looming edge of the Highlands rose starkly from the broad Clutha plain. Eremon had been keeping the river to their left, but not following it too closely. If Agricola was building forts across the isthmus, then there must be troops around here somewhere – and the river provided a good artery for supply.

So far they had been fortunate. After leaving the high ground to the east, they kept to the woods that clustered in the dips and folds of the open plain, and the alder scrub that fringed the river narrows. The sudden warmth had unfurled the leaves, and the trees offered better cover now than on their trip east.

But Eremon still kept a tight watch. They had crossed into Damnonii territory now, and the people here had been subdued by the sword before their kings surrendered, so there was a greater chance of meeting soldiers.

Soon the river widened into a slow-moving swathe of green water, and turned away from its northern path to seek the sea in the west. In a saddle of woodland between two ridges, Rhiann again sought out Eremon. 'There are few paths over the mountains. One that I know of will bring us to the Loch of the Waters and down to Dunadd. To get there we must bear away from the Clutha, north, until we reach a great loch as large as a sea.'

They were edging down the slope of the River Elm, which ran into the Clutha, when they heard faint screams on the wind, and saw a thick plume of smoke erupting from the valley bottom.

'Slowly!' Eremon cautioned, and when they'd tethered their horses in a clump of birches, he and Conaire crept away to investigate. By now the screams had turned to sobs, and the smoke was spreading in a dark stain over the clear sky.

Rhiann realized that her palms were sweating, and she wiped them on her dress, gritting her teeth as another shriek rent the air. When Eremon and Conaire reappeared, their eyes were bright with a steel light Rhiann had not seen before.

'Fergus.' Eremon was curt. 'Take the Roman into the trees and let him pass water or whatever else he wants to do. But make sure that gag is tight, and keep your sword at his side.'

After Fergus had shoved his charge away around a stand of dead oaks, Conaire spat on the ground. 'There are strange soldiers raiding a farmstead. Big men, in rough uniforms. They are not Albans.'

'Are they . . . hurting people?' Rhiann's voice came out faint, too faint.

'Yes,' Eremon answered, but his eyes were fell, not seeing her. 'It is too late to save them. But not too late to teach these wolves some manners!'

'Eremon!' Rhiann blurted. 'We cannot put ourselves in danger!'

He did not seem to hear her. His hand went to Fragarach's hilt, his mouth tense with excitement. 'How my blade longs to drink of Roman blood!'

'My blade, also,' Conaire added, and in the fierceness of his face Rhiann could no longer see the gentle person who had befriended her. All the men were instantly charged with energy.

'We have the element of surprise,' Eremon was saying. 'They are only ten on foot; we are six, mounted. We can storm them from the higher ground here, down into the valley. I don't want anyone to stop and fight. Our swords are longer and we have the weight of the horses. Cut down as many as you can and keep going.' He shaded his eyes. 'A little way east we saw tracks leading to a ford. Cross that and it's clear to the hills. We'll regroup there, on the other side.'

Colum slapped his sword and grinned. 'At last, some real fighting to do!'

'Eremon,' Rhiann spoke quietly. 'What about me?'

He seemed to focus on her then, and his battle light faltered.

'Lord,' Rori put in, 'I long to whip these Roman dogs, too. But if you wish, I could circle around with the lady and cross the ford.'

Eremon's face cleared. 'Rori, you are a brave and resourceful man.' Somewhat contradicting these fine words, Rori blushed. 'But wait until you hear our attack,' Eremon added. 'We won't let any get near you.'

With one look around at the men, Rhiann knew that nothing she could say would divert them. Eremon's movements were quickened with an energy and sureness he had not shown for days, and the priestess in her understood that he needed to do this. To purge himself, perhaps, of what had gone before.

Fergus returned with the Roman, Didius, and Eremon ordered the men to tie him over Rori's horse. When that was done, Rhiann struck out with Rori along the base of the ridge, stopping herself from looking back.

Eremon's breath stirred the blades of grass before his face. He was on his belly behind the trees that fringed the settlement, checking his count of the soldiers again.

They were armoured differently from the patrol they had seen ten days before, and had the fair look of the northern sea-peoples, rather than Latins. Samana told him that Agricola had auxiliaries from other parts of the Empire with him. Perhaps these were Bavarians.

A rutted cart path ran down from the ridge between two round-houses, their roofs alight in sheets of crackling flame. Through the smoke, three soldiers were loading sacks of grain on to a cart, and four were driving a handful of bony cattle out of the one rickety pen. The other three were engaged in less productive pursuits; Eremon saw one pulling himself off the still body of a woman, her skin white against the red clay path; the other two were taking their turns with a girl-child, who lay splayed in the gateway. The bodies of the menfolk lay about the burning houses. As Eremon tensed to rise, torn by a desire to save the child, the last man rolled off her, fumbling with his tunic, and then reached down to cut her throat.

Eremon crept back to his mounted men in the shadow of the trees, and grimly slid on to his horse. Jerking his head, he got them into formation behind him, and slowly and silently unsheathed his sword, raising it above his head.

They could just hear the shouts of the soldiers, hear the cartwheels rumbling. They would be grouped now, close together. Eremon took a deep breath and slashed the sword down, kicking hard.

The horse burst out of the trees like an arrow from the string. Conaire was racing on the path by his side, and Eremon heard the grate of his sword leaving its scabbard, and then they were both yelling the war cry of Dalriada.

'The Boar! The Boar!'

They rounded a bend in the track in a hail of mud. The soldiers were frozen to the spot, staring up with wide eyes. They had only a moment to drop their sacks and try to draw their weapons, but it was too late.

Eremon's attackers careened into them like a driving fist, trampling some beneath the flailing hooves. In the confusion, Eremon's horse reared, and he found himself staring down into the wild bearded face of one of the soldiers, his short sword aiming for the stallion's belly, a snarl of spittle on his lips.

It seemed to Eremon then that the man's features shifted into the sneering mask of Agricola himself, and with one great yell he gripped both hands around Fragarach, slashing crossways, and the man's throat erupted in a spray of bright blood. The heavy body dropped between the horse's hooves, just as another man came screaming at him from behind, his sword over his head. Eremon had little time to wrench his horse around, tangled as it was in the fallen man, but Conaire had just dispatched a soldier with his initial drive, and now he pivoted in his saddle and thrust out desperately, and his sword-tip slashed across the second man's arm, opening it to the bone.

With a scream of pain, the soldier stumbled, his iron helmet slipping, and Eremon, his horse freed, swept his blade down across the back of his unprotected skull. Bone cracked, and the man dropped. Panting, Eremon caught Conaire's eye, before they kicked the horses onwards.

Ahead, he saw Colum struggling with a man who sought to pull him from his mount, but with a fierce cry Angus was suddenly there, his blade dripping blood, and he drove it into the man's neck beneath his helmet guard. Fergus was already riding hard ahead, and Eremon paused only long enough to see Colum and Angus leap away, with Conaire in front, before Eremon, too, urged his mount from the farmstead, along the riverbank.

As he went he glanced back over his shoulder, counting swiftly. Eight men lay without moving, some at the back of the cart, two at the head of the oxen team, and the rest tangled among the bodies of those they themselves had killed. The other two were alive but too badly wounded to ride, crawling in agony on the path.

Catching his breath, Eremon kicked the horse along the bank and across the ford, water spraying up all around him, blood pounding in his veins, Fragarach singing in his hand.

Rhiann's throat ached.

From the far side of the ridge, snatches of ringing swords and cries came on the wind. She knew that sound well; far too well. She knotted her fingers in the horse's rough mane, her head low on her breast as if she could shut out the sounds.

She was so sunk in memory that she hardly noticed when

the cries stopped, until Rori's urgent voice penetrated her haze. 'Hurry, my lady!'

She looked up. They were at the ford, and Rori had almost crossed over. Shallow foam swirled around his stallion's legs, as he anxiously scanned the path on the far bank. 'I can hear my lord just ahead. Hurry!'

She nudged her horse through the overhanging willows and into the rushing water. But as her mare crunched across the gravel and lurched up the bank, as Rori's face registered relief, there was a high whine, and a javelin thudded into a deep cart rut not two paces from Rhiann's shoulder, its shaft vibrating. She jerked, crying out in shock, and her horse shied.

She heard Rori curse, as his mount, laden with the Roman's weight, leaped away from the riverbank in terror, and glimpsed him struggling to haul it back. Ducking low over her rearing horse's neck, Rhiann tried to urge it forward, and with relief recognized Eremon's voice, faintly. 'Fly! As fast as you can! All of you!'

From behind Rhiann now came the dreaded shout in Latin, and the splashing of many feet over the ford. She glanced under her elbow, and saw a red cloak, and the sun glancing off armour, and men pouring from the trees they had just left.

Terror gripped her heart in a fist, and she kicked the horse again, but although it at last burst into a gallop she was so far behind . . .

The thorn-scrub that fringed the track tore at her hair, and all she could see was a jumble of branches and confused slices of sun and shadow. Another javelin whizzed by, and her horse screamed, stumbling in its stride. It was hit!

Now a set of hooves sounded behind her, closing in, and she knew it would be the mounted commander of the Roman troop, like the one she had argued with so many days ago, the one with hard eyes.

'Eremon! Eremon!' The whipping branches dragged at her braids until hair fell into her eyes, and she could not see him.

The javelins had stopped falling, but the galloping hooves behind were louder, as her horse slowed and began to limp.

Then a hard arm gripped her waist, dragging her to another saddle, and she fought instinctively, clawing at the face above with her nails.

'By the Boar, woman, let me be!' She stared up into Eremon's eyes, for once alight with fear. 'Now lie flat!' He pushed her face down, and she flung her arms around his stallion's neck, nose buried in horse sweat and mud. She felt the muscles in the beast's forelegs bunch as Eremon wheeled him, and the shifting of Eremon's thighs against her back. And the clash of blades rang in her ear.

The mounted man behind screamed a curse in British this time, and then all Rhiann could hear were grunts and hard breathing, and she felt each blow of the Roman's sword on Fragarach shake Eremon's body.

There was a quick, thrusting movement, another curse, and the fall of something heavy to the ground.

Eremon wheeled the horse again and kicked it hard. 'Ya!' he yelled, slapping the reins, which just missed Rhiann's nose. Then the cascade of hooves began again, and she saw the earth rushing past beneath.

Eremon's breath was rasping in her ears, but to her it sounded as sweet as music.

After Eremon unhorsed the centurion, the path was quickly swallowed in a defile that led up into the lower reaches of the hills. Perhaps Agricola was regarding that as a natural barrier, for although Eremon did not let them slow until they had cleared the pass to the great Loch of the Beacon, they neither saw nor heard any more of the invaders.

The mountains crowding the loch rose steeply from the black waters below, leaving only a narrow stony path. Above them, the peak of the Beacon snagged the clouds, drawing them in a dark cloak about its shoulders. The riders clattered beneath a misted waterfall, and in the dusk, turned west into a high, clouded glen where Eremon at last let them halt.

For the first time he loosened his hold on Rhiann, and she slid to the wet carpet of moss and ferns, too tired to speak. After a while, there was the bloom of fire among the dark trees, and a shadow crossed it as Eremon came with his warmed cloak for her shoulders. 'Here, this is for you.'

'No, you'll need it.' As Rhiann said this, her teeth chattered.

Eremon squatted down next to her. 'It is shock; it happens to all of us the first few times. Look! You're shivering.' He wrapped the cloak around her, and it enveloped her shoulders with a comforting weight.

'Thank you.' She held his eyes. 'Thank you.'

He knew of what she spoke, and looked down at the cup he carried, before holding it out to her. 'I would have done the same for any man here. That's what happens when you join my warband.'

'You don't need a woman here.' She took the cup and sipped the mead, feeling warmth coming back into her limbs. 'I should never have fallen back like that . . . it was foolish.'

He brushed dried mud from his thighs. 'Our attack on the men raiding that farmstead . . . it wounded you, and that is why you faltered.'

She said nothing. In the fading light, she could see that his right arm was drenched in blood to the elbow, and there were spatters of something else on his tunic that she did not want to identify. Pressed against him as she had been, it would be smeared on her own skin. She swallowed hard.

'I heard tell in the dun that you witnessed a raid that killed your foster-family,' Eremon ventured.

She wanted to deny it; did not wish this tender part of her to be exposed. Yet he had saved her life. 'Yes,' she whispered. 'I saw it all.'

He nodded once, sharply. 'War is my business. Yet I am sorry that my attack on those soldiers grieved you so.'

She sighed. 'You were defending my people, I know that. Yet still I react badly to such scenes.' The wedding night flashed into her mind. Was he thinking of this, too? 'I'm sorry I was careless.'

'No, *my* guard was down – that was even more foolish. I should have made sure you were already across.'

'No, the fault was mine. I endangered us all.'

A flare of firelight caught the shadow of his crooked smile. 'Perhaps that's enough guilt for one night, for both of us.'

'No, no, it's not enough.' She took a breath, for her next words were difficult to say. 'I miscalculated, Eremon. I assumed where Samana's true loyalties would lie, but I was as wrong as I could be. We should never have come, and it was all my doing.'

His eyebrows rose, and she hunched deeper into his cloak. 'I will never tell you what to do in such matters again.'

He straightened, and a hand came down on her shoulder in a friendly pat. 'If I thought that the truth, I wouldn't take you anywhere. Now sleep; we stay until morning.'

She watched his retreating back, mystified.

CHAPTER 33

In his dark northern hall, Maelchon received the craftsman Gelur. Kelturan's orders to resume work on the broch
had been passed on. Gelur was the foremost wood-worker
of the kingdom, and also skilled with shaping stone, so he
had been set as the master over the construction.

Gelur was tall for the islands, with hair so black it was
nearly blue, but his skin was marked all over by the scars of
the pox he'd had as a child. 'My lord,' he began, twisting his
hands before him. Maelchon watched him with satisfaction,
letting the fear grow.

'What do you want, wood-man?'

'My lord, it is impossible for me to start the building again
so soon. The men must finish the sowing, and take the boats
to sea, or we'll starve.'

He did not say that his family's fortunes rested on the
carving and building that he did for the rich men of the
mainland, or that he had an important commission to fulfil
before sunseason. Maelchon knew this, though, for Kelturan
had many ears and eyes.

He leaned forward on his throne. The chair had been
carved in his grandsire's time, and both arms were in the
shape of sinuous otters, curling in underwater spirals, their
eyes set with amber.

'You are getting above your station, Gelur,' he warned.
'You will start work now. There is an end to it.' He turned
away to a table set by his side, where stood, as always, the
great ale cup.

Gelur did not move, did not bow and scrape and leave, as

264

was expected. He remained where he was. 'I must disagree, my lord.'

Maelchon glanced up in surprise. He admired such courage, even when misplaced. It would not be enough to save the man, of course, yet he did need him for a while longer.

So Maelchon sat considering, tapping his fingers on the otters' eyes. 'I will think on this,' he finally said. 'But you will abide by my decision.'

Gelur hesitated for a moment, then bowed swiftly. But as he neared the door, Maelchon suddenly spoke. 'One more thing, wood-man. Remember to give my blessing to your beautiful wife, and your new babe. A son, wasn't it?' He smiled.

Now fear did alight on Gelur's face. 'Yes, my lord. I will, my lord.'

When he had gone, Maelchon let the smile die, and stared at the wall, his eyes burning.

That night, he dined with his wife. As usual, she sat as far from him as she could, shrinking her slight body into a protective crouch.

He watched her over his wine cup. She was young and sickly, with skin the paleness of a drowned thing, and hair lank as seaweed. The bones of her face showed through her skin, giving it a pointed look he found unpleasant. He did not visit her much at night, for she was weak, and he could not risk a kin strife yet, poor prize though she was. From a lowly branch of the Caereni – not even a princess of the royal blood!

Of course, soon he would be able to choose any bride he wanted, from the highest houses in the land. Any maiden . . . anywhere. No one would refuse him! A memory of red-gold hair flashed into his mind. No one would refuse him *this time*.

As always, the reminder of that day, the exact shade of that hair, brought the surge of fire to his groin . . . the pressure. So he scraped back his chair and smiled at his wife, and at that smile she froze, like a thin, pale hare caught outside its burrow.

Maelchon had dismissed his servants, and Kelturan was early in his bed, as usual. So, alone, he rose and came around the table to where his wife sat. Her eyes darted wildly about her, but there was no escape. She whimpered.

Yes, that is good.

'Are you going to fight me, my dear? For you know well what I want.' He stroked her cheek with a gnarled thumb, and wound his fingers in her hair, pulling her head back sharply so she was forced to look into his face. Yes, there was fear in her eyes, but hatred, too.

Ah, hatred is good; even better. Small and weak though she was, there was a spark in this girl, a spark that came from this hatred he had nurtured in her.

Suddenly he wrenched her out of her seat with his great, bear arms and threw her on to the table among the half-eaten food and spilled ale. His wrists were so thick that one of them could easily hold her down while the other exposed himself and tore away her tunic and shift.

She was struggling now, as he hoped she would, and the flailing fists and scratches only inflamed him further. He continued to hold her, prolonging the moment, as his member stretched out and hardened, red and pulsing in the firelight.

Then he could wait no more, and he rammed into her, his heart devouring her grunt of pain. The feeling of her slight bones beneath him, the knowledge that he could crush her as easily as a bird, brought a tide of dark anger that stoked the lust. And as always, the blurred memories came in a rush.

The glow of that hair against dark heather slopes; sea-light in blue eyes; a mouth that taunted with promise.

The memories deepened the anger, and fired the rage, until the lust and need to destroy merged into a glorious whole, and he lost control of his thrusting in a wild roar and spasm and wrench of his thighs, the images now sparks behind his eyes.

When he withdrew, panting, she did not move to cover herself, but lay there, her thighs smeared with blood from wounds that never seemed to heal. She was not a real woman, just a stunted mockery of one.

He yanked up his trousers and threw himself into his chair, hardly noticing her scuttle away.

For a brief moment, staring into the fire, he enjoyed the sweat drying on his neck, his ragged breathing and pounding heart. But this relief would not last long, he well knew.

As always, the return of the hunger, the need for ascendance, would prod him and prick him and torture him.

Until he did what he must do. Until he had everything he deserved.

CHAPTER 34

I nside the lower gate of Dunadd, all eyes were on the squat man in the torn cloak, being untied from a Roman horse.

Although the captive was soon propped upright, he only came to Rhiann's shoulder, and so the village children immediately got over their fright and crowded close. The man tried to remain aloof and proud, but as he could not stare over anyone's head, the effect was diluted.

As he watched the tall, fierce men throwing questions at Eremon, as he listened to the skirling of an unknown language, Rhiann saw the aloofness falter, until only sheer fright remained. His dark eyes grew wide, and in them was reflected a white circle of leering faces.

To make matters worse for him, it was the turning of leaf-bud, when the druids said the days and nights were of equal length, and so time for the yearly horse fair. With the barley seed now sown, people had come from the furthest Epidii lands, the mountains and far islands, to trade for breeding mares and stud stallions, and to offer last year's colts for chariot teams. They also came to give their tributes of furs and wool, in exchange for grain and iron, dyes and herbs, and to gather news and arrange betrothals. The numbers within the village had swelled, and the river plain was covered with horse pens and tents, some crowned by banners of outlying clans.

The normal trickle of people passing in and out of Dunadd's gate had become a flood, all eager to partake of anything curious or exotic.

Dirty hands reached out to finger Didius's cloak, his

smooth-shaven skin and close-cropped hair. People laughed and pushed closer, until the whites of the Roman's eyes showed, rolling like those of a frightened horse.

This terror only grew greater when Eremon gestured to Fergus to prod his charge along through the village and up to the King's Hall, Rhiann and the other men following. The children scampered alongside them, and soon began to jeer at Didius, using the terms that their fathers had been spitting into the fire for many a moon.

'Invading scum!'

'Murdering dog!'

And then a clod of mud came flying through the air and hit Didius behind the ear. He stumbled, and Fergus and Angus laughed, pushing him on before them. Rhiann whirled on the children fiercely. 'Cran! Begone with you now! Such behaviour is beneath you.'

The boy fled with his playmates; a last stone clattering defiantly against the nearest house wall.

Rhiann turned to see Eremon standing with one hand resting on his sword, watching her. 'Why do you care for this Roman?' he asked, frowning.

Rhiann hesitated, for she didn't know herself why she pitied the man. 'He is not like the others. He's a builder, not a soldier. And I know what it feels like to be so alone.'

At the amused twist of Eremon's mouth, she snapped, 'Why do you keep him then? Why not kill him and be done with it!'

His smile faded. 'I may still do so. But I am hoping that in time he can furnish us with some information. He does not look the stoic type.'

'War is one thing; cruelty another, Eremon.'

'And I know why I am here, lady, and what I have to do. You would do well to remember that, too.'

Despite his hard words, as soon as they reached the King's Hall, Eremon unbound Didius. But he also ordered Bran the smith to forge a set of leg chains, and though his arms would be free, the Roman was to remain securely hobbled.

*

In the last light of day, Rhiann plucked a handful of woodruff from the base of a spreading oak by the river, and rested her palm on her back, gasping. When Eremon wrenched her from her horse, muscles had torn, and the hard ride home had bruised her thighs so much she was still limping three days later. But there would be no rest.

When she had returned to her house, it was to find Brica fending off a steady stream of women from the outlying duns clamouring for the medicines that were not available in their mountain homes.

With the sudden trip south, Rhiann had not yet replenished any of her stocks after the long dark, and the returning sun would be bringing many of the brief-blooming plants into flower. She had allowed herself the hottest comfrey bath she could stand, for her aching muscles, and donned clean clothes before taking up her digging stick and nettle bag.

For two days she made herself scarce downriver, in the woods close to the bay, glad for the chance to think. She needed to consider all that had happened on their journey – and most especially what she had learned about Eremon of Dalriada.

Now she spotted a rare patch of candle-flower, and was just straightening with the fragile leaves in one hand and the woodruff in another, when something whizzed past her cheek and thunked into the tree behind her.

It was an arrow, fletched with white ptarmigan feathers.

As Rhiann jumped back in shock, the crushed flowers falling to the ground, someone yelled, 'Goddess Mother-of-All!' and a slight figure came bounding through the undergrowth, bow in hand.

'I did not see you!' the figure squeaked. 'Forgive me, lady! Forgive me!'

Her hand to her leaping heart, Rhiann sank back against the trunk. 'You nearly killed me!'

The woman, for the voice was female though the appearance not, flung out a frightened hand. 'I did not mean to hurt you! I was just practising! Oh, don't have me beaten!'

This was such an odd thing to say that Rhiann's shock fell from her, and she straightened, taking a proper look at her assailant for the first time. The woman was close to Rhiann's age, but there the similarity seemed to end. She was small, and dressed in male clothes – worn buckskin *bracae* and a rough, faded tunic of indeterminate hue, which was too big for her wiry frame. Over her shoulder a quiver was slung, full of the same white-fletched barbs, one slim arm sported a stone wrist-guard for the bow-string, and at her waist hung a dagger that almost reached her thigh.

Her hair was carelessly braided and wound back under an old leather helmet, so that only a few fair strands curled about her cheeks. Beneath that, a heart-shaped face peeped out, cupped by a determined, pointed chin. The whole was smudged with mud, the grime only making her wide-set blue eyes stand out more. Despite being the strangest-looking individual that Rhiann had ever seen, something about the woman seemed familiar.

'Who are you?' The sharpness had left Rhiann's tone, because the baggy clothes and jaunty helmet looked so comical. She had never been introduced to anyone in quite such a manner.

The woman tried to sketch a bow, but it was plain that she had never executed one before. 'My name is Caitlin, my lady. I come from Fethach's steading in the southern mountains.' She thought for a moment, and then added, for want of any other title, 'I am a great archer among my people.'

The twitch of Rhiann's mouth threatened to break into a smile. 'I have no doubt of that, but I would see such skill used against an enemy, rather than my own self.'

The woman puffed out her chest, gesturing with her bow. 'And so it has been, lady. I even killed a man of the Eagle.' When her tunic fell back from her inner arm, Rhiann noticed a large blue bruise marking the fair skin.

'A Roman?' Now Rhiann was truly intrigued.

Caitlin nodded. 'I was hunting a wolf pack, and saw a

271

patrol, which had, unfortunately for them, strayed too far up our glen.' She grinned. 'They went home with one less man.'

'You hunt wolves as *well*?'

Caitlin's teeth were white against her grimy cheeks. 'A wolfskin was the only fur I was missing from my stores. That's why we've come to Dunadd – it's the first year that I have anything to trade.'

So the girl had never been here before. Then why did Rhiann feel that she knew her? Rhiann shrugged to herself. 'And do you like it here?' she asked, reaching down gingerly to her bag.

'Oh, yes.' Caitlin glanced over her shoulder, though no one was in sight. 'But my family does not know my *real* reason for coming. The news reached us at last that the *gael* war leader is creating an army to fight Romans. I have come to lay my bow at his feet.' She said this in such a solemn manner that Rhiann swallowed her smile. Though she was not dressed as one of warrior blood, the girl handled her chosen weapon with confidence. What she said about her skill may well be true.

'I happen to know that the war leader needs as many good fighters as he can get,' Rhiann assured her. 'If you are as good as you boast, he will find a place for you.' She slung her bag over her shoulder, and smiled. 'Well, Caitlin of Fethach's steading, I hope your trading here is fruitful. Perhaps I will see you again, under less dangerous circumstances. I am Rhiann . . .' She hesitated for a moment about giving her other titles. After enjoying some small friendship with Conaire, she was beginning to see how such things kept her alone. 'I am Dunadd's healer,' was all she added.

Caitlin's eyes widened, and she looked down. 'I am in the archery contest tomorrow, lady. If anyone wishes to see me shoot, tell them to come. And to bet on me.' The grin flashed up again from under the downcast eyes.

Rhiann laughed. 'I have no doubt that you will make a name for yourself here. Perhaps I will even see you win.'

CHAPTER 35

'Agricola! What is this?' Belen and most of the other council members jumped to their feet, shouting angrily.

From the shadows of the King's Hall, Eremon glimpsed Gelert's pale head jerk to attention, and felt the prick of his eyes on his skin.

'It is as I say, my lords,' Eremon replied. 'I met with Agricola himself.'

'Is this treachery?' Tharan stamped his staff, half-rising from his bench, his bear cloak quivering.

'No,' Eremon said, but could not help the slight hesitation. He swiftly explained what had happened.

'You were a guest of this Roman leader for two days?' Tharan thundered then. 'And we are meant to trust you?'

'I was a prisoner,' Eremon corrected.

'By the Mare!' Spluttering on ale, Talorc heaved himself to his feet, turning on them fiercely. 'How sorely we treat our prince! He escaped from a Roman camp of five thousand men! What a deed! And you doubt his words?'

This set up a muttering and shuffling of feet.

'True,' Belen put in. 'And he did return.'

'Aye! To betray us!' someone called from behind the crowded benches.

'Lords!' Eremon tapped his sword on his feet. 'I understand your doubts. But hear me now. Agricola did ask me to betray you.'

At this there was such an explosion of curses that Eremon had to hold up his hand. 'But!' he cried. 'I did not agree! He offered to make me a client king in Erin. My escape was my refusal – and I killed three of his men to emphasize the point!' He thrust his sword into the earth floor impatiently. 'I *have* proven myself to you. I threw his offer back in his face, when it would have meant gaining more power than I have ever dreamed of ! But I will give you more!'

The hall fell silent, and Eremon continued more quietly. 'A message has come from the Damnonii. Agricola is building a line of forts across their territory, and this line has nearly reached the sea! So what I will do is this: take the levies and join with our Damnonii brothers to attack the newest fort, the western fort . . . and destroy it, utterly! Will you take that as my proof ?'

There was one startled pause, before the hall erupted in another roar, this time of approval.

'I will take that as proof !' Talorc cried.

'Aye!' said another man. 'Bring us back Roman heads on your spears, and we'll all believe you!'

'We should not be sending our men into danger!' Tharan protested, as two of the older warriors backed him up. But the younger men, those of hotter blood, soon shouted the dissenters down, and in the end they were drowned out.

When, at long last, the hall emptied, ale cups littering the floor, Eremon slumped down on a bench, exhausted. For a moment, he put his aching head in his hands. Gods, but would there be no rest for him? No . . . he could afford none.

The idea for this attack had taken shape on the way home from Samana's dun; the Damnonii message only gave him the target. He had guessed how news of his meeting with Agricola would be received by the Epidii. And although a new expedition was the last thing that he felt like mounting, it was important. Important for so many reasons.

The lower step of the gallery ladder creaked, and he jumped. 'There is no end to the surprises in you, prince.' Eremon looked up into Gelert's yellow eyes. 'You have not turned out at all as I expected. I offered my services as adviser, but you reject them.'

Eremon was too weary to spar. 'I never agreed to being your servant, druid, only that of your people.'

The old man sported his usual bloodless smile, but the edges were tight, his lips a thin line. 'And that involves meeting with our enemy?'

'You heard what happened, along with everyone else. I did what I judged to be correct at the time, and did not need to consult you! I have my own mind.'

The druid glided to the door, then paused with one gnarled hand on the post, his bowed back to Eremon. 'So I see, prince. So I see.'

The news of the planned expedition reached Rhiann as, of all things, gossip.

On a day as warm as sunseason, she and Brica were in the camp, at the tent of an old woman who always supplied Rhiann with the finest heather honey. As they left her baskets full of sealed clay pots, they stopped to browse at a table spread with bolts of cloth and embroidered braids and tassels. Two of the dun women were there, fingering some lengths of soft, checked wool, and from their unguarded chatter Rhiann learned the welcome news that Aiveen had been married off to a chieftain of the Creones while they were away.

'This stuff is too fine,' one then said, laying down the cloth. 'I'll need the felted wool for a new cloak for my man. He'll be sleeping out in Goddess knows what weather on this raid of theirs.'

Rhiann's ears pricked up at that. 'Raid?' she echoed.

'Yes, lady,' the second woman answered, suddenly noticing Rhiann. 'The raid in Damnonii lands. On a dun of the new invaders, my man said. The prince has ordered it. Aldera says she's hardly seen Bran, he's at his forge day and night, making weapons . . .'

Rhiann whirled and thrust her basket at Brica. 'Take these back to the house.'

'Yes, lady,' Brica answered, as Rhiann hurried off.

After much searching, she eventually found Eremon at the

back of a large crowd on the edge of the training field. He was perched on the pole of an unharnessed chariot, shading his eyes as he watched the archery contest. Conaire was standing nearby, peering over people's heads. As Rhiann reached Eremon's side, there was the thud of an arrow into a target, and a great shout from the crowd.

'You are taking the warband to raid a fort?' She was breathless from haste, but Eremon merely glanced down at her, his face distracted.

'Yes.'

'Why did you not tell me?'

Now there was an even greater shout, and Eremon's attention jerked back to the field. Conaire was grinning. 'By the Boar, the little one's done it again!' He shook his head.

'It does not concern you, that's why,' Eremon replied to her. 'I go to fight this time, not to hide and skulk as a lady's escort.'

'You are in a charming mood today.' The words were meant to stay in her head, but somehow had dropped from her lips.

He looked down again, and this time his eyes glinted with amusement. 'I apologize.'

She ignored the sarcasm. 'Eremon, why put yourselves in danger again so soon? We only just escaped with our lives as it was!'

He wiped sweat from his forehead with the back of his hand. 'Then now is the time to strike, when Agricola least expects it. I know the southern lands now, and I've seen how they build. The Damnonii know where Agricola's latest fort is taking shape. It is time to put this warband to the test. Ah!' He broke off, as Conaire turned and thumped his arm.

'She's won!' Conaire crowed. 'That's one arm-ring you owe me, brother. You were fooled by that girl's size, but she's strong. A score of hits *in a row*. Have you ever seen the like?' He disappeared into the crowd, which was now surging around the victor. Rhiann had already guessed who they were talking about. Caitlin's skill had been no boast.

She addressed Eremon again, determined not to be distracted. 'You are not making this personal, I hope.' When he blinked at her, she held his gaze boldly. 'Endangering these men because of guilt. About the choice Agricola gave you.'

That stung him, she could see. 'Ever the priestess,' he answered. 'But no, there you are wrong. It is not out of guilt. Why should I feel guilty? I came back, after all.' He held her gaze just as long, clear-eyed. It was she who dropped her eyes.

'Rhiann.' He was exasperated now. 'I don't understand you. You suggested the trip south in the first place. You played your own part in it, and well, I might add. Just what do you think I am training these men for? Not just for defence. For *attack*. We must make Agricola realize that, even though the Votadini surrendered without a whimper, if he comes this side of the mountains, he will receive a different reception!'

She prodded the chariot wheel with her toe. How could she tell him that she worried for them all? For Conaire, with his lamentable jests and impudent grin, and little, shy Rori, who could hardly speak a word to her, yet had jumped to protect her.

'Ah,' Eremon said from above. 'You're just worried that you'll miss something, that's it, isn't it? That you'll be left out. You can't stand it.'

Her mouth dropped open. The presumption! It did not deserve an answer. She swallowed her enraged reply, and whirled on her heel to stalk away.

'Rhiann, I'm sorry. Wait.'

She stopped, but did not turn. 'What?'

'I need your help with our Roman – he seems to trust you. I want you to ask him about the design of the forts. His information may help us.'

She paused. 'I'll do my best. But you must treat him well.'

'I'll try,' came the unsatisfactory answer.

Eremon watched the stiffness of Rhiann's retreating back with some amusement. In fact, it was not so much stiff as

277

straight. He had to admit that he admired the way she held herself. She had the finest carriage he had seen on a woman, a product of her training, no doubt. There had been little else to recommend her up until the trip south, but that was a start.

Of course, then, there was the courage she showed when confronted by that Roman patrol. And she had apologized about Samana, which had shocked him ... He shook his head, shifting his stance on the chariot pole. She was also good at her probing, but about the reasons for his planned attack, she was entirely wrong.

What drove him to this was not guilt. The guilt had been spent when he ran down those raiding auxiliaries, and splattered a man's brains on his tunic. That had been enough. No, what drove him now was nothing less than fear.

He glanced up at the clear sky, and felt a light wind, carrying the first real warmth, lift his hair. Soon, very soon, the threat of leaf-bud storms would be over. The sea lanes would open. The Epidii would send a messenger to his people, and find out the truth – if a passing trader did not deliver it first. And, by the Boar, he must have a strong victory to lay at their feet before that happened. He must prove his worth beyond any doubt.

He sighed again, the weight of it pressing so heavily on his breast. Still, at least this was one stress he could share with Conaire. His eyes sought out his foster-brother's towering form, making its way back to him.

'I think you should grab that archer for our warband,' Conaire remarked. 'That's real skill there, that is.'

Eremon smiled. 'And her being a woman has no doubt escaped you, then?'

Conaire snorted. 'Woman! It's hard to tell under all that dirt. And anyway, you came down here to see if there were any good fighters among the mountain people. She's the best archer we've seen. You'd be mad to let her go, female or not.'

'All right! All right!' Eremon leaped down from the chariot.

'Now, walk back with me. We must speak of our attack plan, for, by the Boar, it will have to be one of the best-laid of my life.'

CHAPTER 36

Didius was retrieved from his pallet in the shadows of the King's Hall and taken outside for his interrogation. Rhiann told Eremon it was because the rushes were being cleared out and replaced with fresh ones, but in fact, she wanted to draw an audience in the hope that this would prevent any violence being done to him.

A bench was brought out for her to the Horse Gate, and a stool for Didius. Eremon stood on one side of him, his arms crossed, and Conaire stood at his most glowering on the other side, one hand resting on his sword.

Eremon's men were gathered close, and many of the nobles and their servants from the upper tiers had joined them. Even Talorc had dragged himself from his morning meal, chewing on a mutton bone.

Rhiann smiled at Didius. The little Roman was clean now, at any rate, and the black bruises around his eyes from the rough ride home were fading to green. His Epidii tunic came past his knees, and the sleeves were so long he looked as if he had no hands. But he refused to wear trousers, and his ankles were mottled with cold above the skin boots. He glanced up at Eremon apprehensively.

'Do not fear,' Rhiann said in her halting Latin. 'We need information. No one will harm you.'

Didius regarded her warily. 'Information?'

'Yes.' She smiled. 'We have given you food, and a bed. There will be no harm, I promise.'

The Roman's eyes strayed up to Eremon again. The depth

of fear in them was almost painful to see. Plainly, Didius had not recovered from his first meeting with the prince.

'He won't hurt you,' she hastened to add. 'I give my word. We need to know about the . . .' she sought for the word, 'the forts.'

Didius's eyes jerked wider with alarm. 'You want me to betray my people?'

Rhiann considered how to answer this, and then realized she could not. After all, she would refuse if it were her. There was no way to trick him. She shrugged helplessly. 'I need you to answer this. It will keep you safe.'

Didius shook his head, his chins quivering, and Eremon's dark brows drew together. Then Rhiann thought of one tack to use. 'We need only to destroy the buildings. Tell me how many men there are, and their . . . positions . . . and they will be safer.'

She doubted the real truth of that, after seeing the look on Eremon's face before attacking those soldiers. But she was caught in this, just as Didius was. If it saved her own people . . . her friends . . . then a half-truth was a small price to pay. Wasn't it?

But her heart sank when she saw the Roman's face harden into refusal. Eremon once said that Didius was a coward. Perhaps he had more backbone than they had supposed.

'No,' Didius said, lifting his chin. 'Just kill me. You are barbarians. You care for nothing. You—'

But there he broke off, for Eremon drew his sword with one sweep, grasped the Roman's hair and wrenched his head back until his stubbled throat was exposed. Rhiann went to cry out, but bit her tongue.

'Rhiann.' Eremon's voice was mild. 'Tell him that if he does not give us the information we need, I will cut his fingers off one by one.'

'You would not!'

His eyes flickered her way. 'Tell him.'

'He said he'd rather die.'

'That can easily be arranged. But lingering pain is more persuasive. Tell him.'

'Release him first.'

Eremon let Didius go and stepped back. With more speed than anyone would have expected, looking at him, the little man wasted no time coughing or rubbing his throat, but immediately threw himself off the bench. The leg chains tautened, and he fell down at Rhiann's feet, grasping the hem of her dress and pressing his face into it. 'Mercy!' he cried to her, his shoulders shaking. 'Lady . . . mercy! Give me protection!'

Eremon jumped forward at the sudden movement, and his face was now close to Rhiann's own, his sword a breath away from the Roman's neck.

Rhiann glared at Eremon, then took a breath. 'My lord,' she said with calm formality, as if she did not have one man snivelling into her robe and another with drawn sword at her knee, 'I ask a boon of you.'

The shadows of the gate deepened Eremon's frown. 'What boon?'

'As my husband, I must crave it of you. Will you give your word to grant it?'

Eremon suddenly seemed to remember his audience, which was gaping at the little scene, and he straightened and sheathed his sword. But his gaze held a silent warning to her. A warning she ignored.

What could he do but agree? Generosity was valued in kings – or princes – above all things. He nodded at her stiffly.

'Then,' she said, 'I ask you to give me this Roman for my own household. As a servant.'

There was a collective gasp. 'If I have more time, if I show him mercy, I can win his trust,' she added swiftly. Eremon's eyes bored into her, burning with the things he so obviously wanted to say, but could not. She thanked the Goddess for the foresight to arrange this in public.

At last Eremon bowed. 'As you wish, lady. May he serve you well.' He looked around, addressing the crowd. 'We know where the fort is, and we have seen them building. With or without this man's aid, we will burn it to the ground!' He glanced down at Didius, his mouth curling. 'At least tell him that!' Then he flung his cloak over his shoulder and stalked away. Conaire raised one eyebrow in Rhiann's direction before following him.

Rhiann stayed there without moving, straight-backed, until the murmuring crowd dispersed. Didius was still face down at her feet.

'It's safe,' she said in her own language, touching his shoulder. When he looked up, she saw that his face was not as crumpled or tear-stained as the shaking shoulders had led her to expect. Instead, his eyes were bright as they darted around.

'You are mine now,' she said slowly in Latin, and shrugged, smiling. 'If you serve me, I can keep you safe. You can learn our words. Then we can speak.'

He nodded, the colour flushing back into his cheeks.

It was as she turned to lead him, hobbling, towards her own house, that she became aware of a slight figure hovering near her elbow. 'Lady?'

It was Caitlin, her helmet under her arm. She was pale beneath the grime, and Rhiann's practised eye fell on a dark bruise along her jaw that had not been there before. This girl, for she could not help but think of her as a girl, was being hard treated. 'Congratulations on your win.'

Despite her previous bravado, Caitlin darted wide eyes towards Didius, then along to the King's Hall, where Eremon and Conaire had gone. 'I did not know that the prince was your husband, lady,' she said in a hushed voice. 'All the camp is talking of him: his sword, the warband he is gathering.' She took a deep breath, steeling herself. 'Do you think that he will let me join?'

Rhiann glanced at the bruise again. 'You know that you will need to leave your home and live here. What about your family?'

Caitlin's blue eyes slid down. 'They're not really my

family,' she confessed. 'But they won't like it, all the same, because my hunting keeps them in meat. My furs bring them wealth. That is why I come to you now. You seemed . . . kind.' She smiled shyly, and something about the set of her mouth caught Rhiann's attention. Again, that sense of familiarity nagged at her.

She patted the girl's arm. 'My husband demanded levies from the other clans, so he can certainly demand that your family release such a talented archer into his care. For the cause.' She held Caitlin's eyes. 'You will have your wish.'

Some understanding passed between them of what they truly spoke, and Caitlin propped her helmet back on her head with a relieved air.

Rhiann avoided asking Eremon anything until she judged that he had cooled down after their altercation. Yet though he ignored Rhiann herself, he readily agreed to her request, and took Caitlin's solemn and over-elaborate vow of allegiance with some veiled amusement.

As they both left the hall, Rhiann sensed Caitlin's glowing excitement begin to dim. Looking again at those bruises and the shadow of fear in Caitlin's eyes, Rhiann decided to set aside her gathering expedition and accompany the girl to the river camp to tell Fethach of her decision.

Among his scruffy, bickering, black-haired clan, Caitlin's colouring blazed out like bronze against dull iron. It was as she said, Rhiann thought, watching a glowering Fethach thrust Caitlin's small pack at her – there was no possibility in the Mother's name that Caitlin shared any blood with these people. So how had she come to belong to them?

Caitlin turned away from the jumbled tents and scratching hounds without so much as a backwards glance. It may have seemed heartless, especially as Fethach's wife set up an obligatory wailing and show of tears, but Rhiann, watching Caitlin closely, thought she could guess what sort of home life the girl had enjoyed.

She brought up the subject of parentage as they returned to the King's Hall. Caitlin waved her hand. 'Warriors did battle in our valley with Damnonii raiders. After it was over, Fethach's wife found me, a babe, caught under one of the dead man's bodies. She took me in.'

'That's all you know?' As Caitlin walked, Rhiann was admiring the feline grace that would suddenly suffuse the girl's movements when she was unaware; the grace of a hunter, a bowman. No, she was surely not made to live out her life hidden away in the mountains. She had the stamp of something else upon her; Rhiann's senses fairly hummed with it.

'Fethach's half-wit sister also said once that my blanket was of fine blue wool. And there was a shell necklace – but I broke it when I was small.' Caitlin smiled. 'I'm of warrior blood, I am. I've always known that. And now, at last, I'll have the chance to prove it!'

Eremon tested the spear-tip on his finger, and smiled as a drop of blood welled up on his skin.

'The best we can make in the time,' Bran said gruffly, wiping soot from his face with his hand.

'You have outdone my expectations,' Eremon replied, surveying the pale shafts of new spears with satisfaction, the piles of studded shield bosses, ready to go to the woodworker's shed, the mounds of arrowheads.

As Eremon left the smithy, taking the spear to test its balance, there came a trumpet call at the gate. A party of men on horses was riding under the tower, and Eremon saw silver hair flowing from beneath a helm of iron.

Lorn dismounted and strode up to him. 'We received the news of your planned attack.' The young warrior's gaze was distant, fixed at some point over Eremon's shoulder. 'My father requested that I come to lend you the aid of my arms, and those of my clansmen.'

To keep an eye on me, more like, Eremon thought. He knew that the Dun of the Sun bred good fighters. But would the extra strength be worth the disruption? Lorn's rivalry with

Eremon would make him a weak link, and this warband must act as one man.

'I would be honoured to accept your aid,' he replied carefully. What could he say? Lorn's father was one of the most powerful Epidii nobles. It was likely that only fear of reprisals from Eremon's kin had prevented him from yet mounting a direct challenge for the King's Hall.

Lorn looked directly at Eremon now, disdain in his pale eyes. 'When do we leave?'

'In four days. Tonight, I will brief the chieftains' sons on the plan.'

'Then I will be there.' Lorn nodded at his men, and they followed him up the village path to the houses of his kin.

Eremon watched him go. He knew why old Urben had sent Lorn here. A man would soon lose power if he kept to his dun, away from the centre of tribal defences. Urben did not want Eremon winning any glory that was not shared by his son.

As Eremon returned to the hall, he chewed on his lip, trying to weigh up the risks. Lorn was impulsive and fiery, and chafed at following Eremon's lead. Yet he commanded many good fighters. And what of his father's men, his father's might?

At last Eremon sighed, for there was only one answer. He could not refuse Lorn's aid: it would shame Urben's whole clan, and antagonize the council. Such a rift between two men would soon widen to a tribal divide.

Suddenly, Agricola's face swam into Eremon's mind, the mouth curved with customary contempt. *He* would be pleased by such a rift, for that is how the Romans won power.

'And so you will not have it,' Eremon muttered, and, lifting the spear, drove it into the ground at the door of the hall.

Full of misgivings, Rhiann stood on the palisade above the cheering crowds at Dunadd's gate. The horse fair was over, but all of the visitors had stayed to see the spectacle of the warband's departure.

Eremon was taking 200 of the best-trained warriors, and though the day was heavy under cloud, still the mailshirts shone, and helmets and spear-tips glittered, newly burnished, as lines of men marched out of the gate across the causeway, shouting war songs.

All of the fear of the Romans had been focused here this day, and in defiance, had emerged as fighting spirit. The energy of the milling crowd grew and swelled behind the wedge of marching men, pushing, thrusting, like the arm that sends the blade home.

Linnet heard her niece's sigh. 'It will be well, daughter,' she murmured, her eyes on the men filing past below.

Rhiann folded her arms. 'I still don't understand why he needs to do this. It's too dangerous.' Far off, at the head of the lines, she glimpsed Eremon's dark hair flowing from beneath his boar-crest helmet.

'Something drives him,' Linnet replied. 'He seeks to make his name, and soon. You understand this, surely?'

Rhiann dropped her arms. 'And when did you become such a defender of my husband, aunt?' she teased, pursing her lips. 'Can I not use your ear to complain about him? Is this not what wives do?'

Linnet smiled serenely. 'I think it sits hard on you to remain behind. Perhaps your journeying has made your heart restless!' She reached out, as she often did, and tucked Rhiann's hair behind her ear.

'That's what *he* said!' Rhiann grumbled. But then she felt Linnet's hand freeze, and her eyes fixed on something below them.

'Who is that woman?'

Rhiann followed her gaze. Below them, a familiar figure in buckskins was waving up at her madly. Before she left, Rhiann had managed to get Caitlin into a bath, with heated water and soapwort, to scour off the years of dirt ground into her skin. The wooden tub behind Rhiann's bed-screen had to be emptied twice, much to Brica's disgust, before the water ran clear.

Now, with her helmet under her arm, her clean hair tumbling down her back, the girl's features stood out. 'That is Caitlin,' Rhiann answered, waving back. 'An archer, from a small steading in the far south. She came here to join Eremon's warband. She is exceptionally skilled, I hear.'

Linnet's face had drained of colour. 'Where, exactly, is she from?'

Rhiann thought hard. 'She told me that her home is hard under the Maiden's Hill, near the Loch of the Beacon.' Puzzled, she looked down at Caitlin, now striding happily away with the foot warriors, and back to Linnet. 'Do you know her? I feel that I do, more so now that we've scraped off that dirt. But she's never been here before. There is some question over her parentage . . .'

'Question?'

'A mystery.' She attempted a smile, alarmed at Linnet's pallor. 'Actually, everything about her is a mystery! You'll like her, she—'

But there she broke off, for Linnet abruptly turned away, pulling her hood around her face, though the day was warm enough. 'I must go.'

Rhiann's priestess ears picked up the control that Linnet was exerting over her voice. 'Aunt, what is it?'

She reached out a hand, but Linnet edged away, her face hidden by the folds of the hood. 'Leave me be. I must go.'

Rhiann frowned, as Linnet pushed through the cheering people on the palisade and disappeared down the stairs to the ground. Baffled, she turned back to the warband, but Caitlin's small figure was now lost in the ranks of marchers, and only the battle trumpets floated back on the wind.

CHAPTER 37

T he stone had been digging into Eremon's ribs for hours. But he had other things on his mind, so he only shifted on his belly so that the stone began to dig in somewhere else. 'There, do you see?' He kept his voice to a murmur.

The Damnonii chieftain, lying next to him on the ground, shifted his aged bulk more uncomfortably. 'Yes, I see.'

They lay among the trees at the crest of a low hill. Across a stream that fed into the River Clutha, a ridge rose in terraces of oak and elm. Crowning the bare ridge-top, the half-built palisade of the fort stood out against the sky like teeth in an antler comb. Men and oxen crawled up and down a narrow path, hauling logs from the woods below.

'Every day is the same,' Conaire put in. 'As soon as it is light, they go to the river bottoms for timber. It will be finished within a day or so.'

Eremon flashed a grin at the Damnonii chieftain. 'We have you to thank for getting us here, Kelan, before their defences were complete.'

The old man licked sweat from his lip. 'I told you when we met that my people seek revenge. When the eagle-men began this fort, so close to our villages, we could stand no more.' He shook his shaggy head. 'The people still needed a prince's call to act. A call our own princes would never give, now that they have been bought with Roman silver.'

'Cowards!' This was muttered by a younger warrior lying next to the chieftain, a battered helmet pulled down so far that only his dark eyes glittered from beneath it.

'Peace, nephew,' the chief replied. 'Save your fire for when you lead the men in my name. Make me proud.'

'We will all be proud,' Eremon assured him. 'Agricola's boot seeks to crush us. But we will only hack it off at the ankle, again and again, until he seeks no more.'

They wriggled on their bellies away from the hilltop and out of sight, before rejoining the other men. To avoid detection, the warband had been broken into many groups, which now lay hidden among the trees.

'So,' Eremon said, when the leaders of each troop were gathered around his map, scratched into the hardened river mud, 'I have watched as long as I dared, but we must act now, before they finish their walls.'

'Do we have the numbers?' Finan asked, leaning on his sword.

Eremon nodded. 'We match their numbers, since Kelan here managed to gather so many Damnonii men. Now, is everyone clear on the plan? This is our last chance to speak.'

As he said this, his eye fell on Lorn, whose cheeks darkened with a betraying flush. Eremon had not given him the command of any wing, yet he attended such meetings as if he had. 'I don't understand why we need this trickery,' Lorn declared. 'If our numbers are even, then our charge will be enough!'

Eremon breathed out silently. 'I'm not arguing this again. You are going to follow my plan to its last detail, or you don't join the raid.'

Lorn's chin jutted out. 'I command my own men, and you cannot stop me from joining the fight.'

'Yet I command the warband, so you follow my orders. You and your men look to Kelan's nephew, understand?'

In answer, Lorn clapped his helmet on his head. 'I will see you at the gates.'

Later, Conaire and Eremon lay hidden in a thorn thicket on higher ground far behind the fort. 'You take a chance with that Epidii cub,' Conaire remarked, fingering the tips of his throwing spears.

Eremon hefted his boar shield, craning to see through the branches. 'I know, brother. But I seek to keep the peace after this raid, and I've tried to give him the most harmless of roles.'

Conaire snorted. 'Harmless, him? As harmless as a trapped wolf, he is. Those jaws can still snap.'

Eremon's eyes followed the distant figures digging the fort ditch. 'So long as they snap at the Romans, and not at me.'

'My lady!' Brica hurried into the stable, her hands tucked in her cloak. She stopped before Rhiann, the shuffling of her feet betraying her distress.

'What is the matter, Brica?' Rhiann ducked under Liath's neck and waded through the straw to the stall gate.

The little woman took a deep breath. 'My lady, I know that I should not be speaking with you here. But – I must.'

'Yes, Brica. Slow down now. What is wrong?'

Brica shook her head, and wisps of black hair escaped her head scarf. 'When you were forced to take *him*, I held my tongue, I did. I vowed to serve you, and you are She. But all the men . . . so many men! Blood-letters, killers . . . they reek of it!'

The woman had spoken of little but the forced marriage these last moons, but Rhiann had no idea she was so deeply affected. 'Yes, I know,' Rhiann said gently, resting the horse-comb on the paling. 'But we must make of it what we can, and–'

'No!' Brica was trembling now, and Rhiann suddenly realized it was not with fear, but fury. 'I cannot! And now the prince of Erin has brought this murderer . . . this child killer . . . here. A Roman! And he is in my house!'

Ah. Rhiann nodded. 'I know this must be of concern to you, but really, he is harmless. He is not even a warrior.'

'No!' Brica dropped her eyes. 'No! I cannot be near these men any more. This prince. For nearly two years I have served you, but the Mother would not ask this of me now, I know it!'

'Then what are you saying?'

Brica seemed to gather herself. 'I must return to the Sacred Isle, mistress. I have been thinking of it for some time, and now I . . . know . . . that I can serve you no longer.'

'I see.' Rhiann looked at the woman more keenly. 'Brica, I would never keep you here against your will. You have served me well.'

'Thank you, lady.' Brica spoke stiffly now. 'A trading party leaves tonight. I can go with them as far as Caereni territory. There, I have kin who will take me home to the Sacred Isle.'

Rhiann nodded. 'Then go, with my blessing. I would give you gifts to take to the Sisters, to Nerida and Setana. Will you carry them?'

'Yes, lady.'

Rhiann was thoughtful as she walked back to her house, but she could not pretend that she would miss Brica. The woman treated Rhiann as if she was the Goddess herself, rather than a person. This often made living with her less than comfortable.

Rhiann sighed. She would need a new maid then, someone young this time, perhaps. Rhiann had offered Caitlin a bed in her home when she returned from the raid, realizing that she had no kin, and a household consisting of one Roman and a half-wild woman warrior would test even the stoutest heart. She needed someone with courage. Who would complement such a group?

And then she had it. Of course – Eithne! The daughter of the fisher family.

The women of the dun would expect her to choose someone of a higher rank, perhaps, as a maid and companion; one of the craftsmen's daughters – the bronze-smith or the master-carpenter. But Eithne was quick and clever, and not as serious as Brica. Yes, she would be a fine choice.

Her mind made up, Rhiann turned back to the stable. She would take Liath and go to ask Eithne herself right now. It was a fine afternoon for a ride. And soon, she really must visit Linnet. There had been no explanation of her sudden departure, nor had she returned to Dunadd.

That it was to do with Caitlin was obvious. But what it could be was as much a mystery as the girl herself.

'By the great Mars, what is that?' The auxiliary raised himself in his saddle for a better view, peering past the oxen teams lumbering up from the river.

His companion pulled his horse's head shy as a pair of unburdened oxen, tossing their horns, squeezed past a loaded team. 'It's a herd of cattle, sir. A large herd!'

'Those cursed Damnonii said they'd given up all their surplus cattle!'

The second man nudged his horse to the edge of the path. 'They're driving carts, too, sir. Barley, no doubt, or rye.'

'They said they had none of that left, either!' The first man, the decurion, frowned. 'We need that food. How many warriors guard it?'

'They are ranged around the herd . . . but at least thirty.'

'Thirty! They are not supposed to travel in such groups.' The decurion turned his horse. 'Pull half the century off guard, and half the diggers, and get them down here after me. I want those cattle!'

'Who speaks for you!' The decurion, barking out his demand in British, reined in just where firm ground gave way to mire. The cattle were plunging through the mud, lowing and milling around in great confusion, and the native warriors had worked their horses and carts around to the other side of the herd when they saw the infantry troop advance.

One of the natives wheeled his restive horse. 'I do!' he cried over the bawling cattle.

'These beasts are the tribute that we demanded, and were not paid,' the Roman continued. 'Drive them to the fort, now.'

The native smiled, his dark eyes glittering with defiance. 'If you want them, Roman dog, then come and take them!' From somewhere near his saddle he pulled a naked blade and swung it high, letting loose an ear-splitting war-cry that was taken up by his men.

With a sharp command, the decurion ordered his men forward, and they marched around the edges of the milling herd, pulling up in lines, shields overlapping, javelins poised for launch . . .

Then the cattle themselves seemed to rear up with slicing blades, as scores of wild-eyed savages with blue tattoos burst from the cover of the herd, shrugging off hide cloaks to free their deadly swords.

'Hold!' the decurion cried, as the screaming horde hit the lines of shields with the impact of a fist. 'Hold!'

By the time the rest of Eremon's warband came hurtling down on foot from the higher ground, another hundred of the Romans in ditch and on rampart had downed tools and run to defend their stricken brothers on the plain.

Even as he raced, legs pumping, sword heavy in hand, Eremon's cool head registered the hail of arrows from his archers, arcing in from two sides of the fort, and his heart swelled so much that the war cry burst from his throat: 'The Boar! The Boar!'

His lines held their wedge, driving right at the gate, and didn't splinter into wild disorder. Taken by surprise, those defenders who were left could only turn and fight on the spot.

Eremon struck down two soldiers in his initial rush, but the Romans were now outnumbered three to one, fighting in knots before the gate and stumbling in the ditches, and in only a few breaths he could pause to look down on the river plain.

What he saw struck him like a blade to the chest. The Romans below were supposed to be chasing the cattle party, lured to follow them away from the fort by a false retreat. This would engage most of the soldiers, giving Eremon a chance to defeat those who guarded the fort. But instead, the sun flashed on swords among the milling cattle, and from afar he could just hear the war cry of the Epidii.

And now, faced with such fierce fighters, all of the Romans were retreating, streaming back towards the fort. Towards Eremon's men.

'Gods, you dog, Lorn!' he cried. But there was no more time, for the retreating Romans were now pouring up from the river path, shouting commands to re-form as they realized that their fort was under attack. Suddenly, the odds had switched, and they came at Eremon's men like a hammer blow.

Cursing Lorn with every slice and thrust of his sword, Eremon's mind raced to find a way out. Around him, Epidii and Damnonii warriors both fell under the onslaught of the returning soldiers, who worked in unison to pin Eremon's men against the palisade.

The tip of a blade burned a trail across Eremon's arm, but as he turned to defend with his shield, Conaire had already despatched the attacker. Then there were two more coming at him, and his sword glanced desperately off tightly overlapping shields, before he threw himself into a roll and thrust upwards. One man screamed and fell as his groin artery was slashed, his blood drenching Eremon's eyes, blinding him, while the other tripped over the tangle of limbs. Conaire stabbed him before he could rise, and pulled Eremon to his feet.

'We must retreat!' Conaire cried.

'Retreat where?' Eremon spat the blood from his mouth. The Romans had them tightly surrounded, their backs to the ditch.

But suddenly more cries came of, 'The Mare!' and Alban warriors from the plain were flinging themselves from the cover of the trees in all directions, and the Romans were pinned now between the two wings of Eremon's forces. Sensing victory, the fragile discipline of Eremon's band disintegrated, and they threw themselves against the Roman shield wall with renewed vigour.

In the middle of the wild fighting, Eremon had to leap back from the hooves of a Roman horse, rearing above him. On its back, Lorn whooped and spun his sword.

Eremon looked straight up into his eyes, as the fighting swirled on past them. 'You were supposed to draw the soldiers off *before* circling around!'

Lorn wiped blood from his cheek with one shoulder, as the horse shied. 'Run away? Urben's son does not run! I am an Alban, and I fight!'

'You could have killed us all!' Eremon stormed. 'Because of you, the Romans went into retreat, back here to me, pinning us against the fort! Do you realize what you did?'

Lorn's pale eyes were on fire, and his face dripped sweat. 'Yes,' he cried, surveying the slaughter around him. 'I brought us victory!'

And then he was gone, and above the last knot of fighting Romans, Eremon saw his silver hair flying.

Agricola received the news of the raid while inspecting his troops.

Samana was lounging on a seat at the edge of the field, sheltered from the sun beneath a parasol – a Greek invention she had quite taken to. But as the messenger leaned close to talk to Agricola on his horse, and she saw the shock flicker in his eyes, she sat up.

Later, as the details were dissected by his officers in the command tent, Agricola maintained a stony reserve. It was not until he and Samana were alone that he let his feelings show at all.

'Gods and all in heaven!' He paced back and forth, striking the hilt of his dagger into his palm.

Samana had never seen him lose his composure. 'The prince of Erin will have led it,' she remarked. 'You know it – they must have scouted the land when they returned home. You should have chased them when you had the chance. I begged you to—'

Agricola whirled on her. In the light of the brazier, his dark eyes blazed. 'I would thank you to keep your mouth closed, lady!'

As the answering spark leapt to Samana's throat, she bit down on it. Seeing the look in his eyes, who knew what he might do to her?

Agricola turned his back and went to the tent flap. From behind, his shoulders were taut with anger.

Samana waited a moment, and then said in her throatiest tone, 'You must raid north again now, my lord, and put down Eremon and his rebels. If not, he will do it again.'

He said nothing for a long moment; only his harsh breathing filled the tent. And then slowly his shoulders relaxed to their normal level. 'No.'

'No?' She was incredulous.

When he faced her, he was composed, although the line of his mouth remained grim. 'I have orders to consolidate this frontier, and that is what I will do. Personal revenge does not come into it.'

'I cannot believe this!'

He held her eyes. 'That is how I lead, Samana. Not with emotion; with clarity. I have no intention of being drawn into a hide-and-seek game with your Erin prince. At the moment, I do not have the hold on the lands that I need. In the mountains, his men can pick mine off one by one.'

She tried to swallow down her fire. 'Then at least allow me to put greater pressure on my northern . . . contact. More goods will assure his co-operation; we may need to keep a closer eye on unfolding events.'

His gaze was hooded. 'Use any means you wish. When the Emperor gives me leave to move north again, we will already have weakened them from within. Then, there will be only one way to proceed.'

'Which way?' She knew the answer, but loved to hear him say the words.

The coldness in his eyes was Otherworldly. 'I will goad them, and taunt them, until I bring them all to bay in a place of my own choosing.'

The danger in his voice thrilled her, and she put down her wine goblet and joined him, pressing up against his hard chest. 'And then?' she murmured, breathless.

'And then we will crush them.'

CHAPTER 38

W hen Rhiann trotted into Linnet's yard, her aunt's maid Dercca was walking to the hut with a bucket of water. The dying sun cast long shadows across the earth, touching the mossed walls with gold.

'Lady Rhiann!' Dercca jerked in surprise, and water sloshed over her dress. She put the bucket down, tutting to herself as she pulled the clinging wool away from her legs.

'Good evening to you, Dercca.' Rhiann swung herself from Liath's back. 'Is my aunt here? I have heard nothing from her.'

'Yes, lady.' Dercca took up the bucket again without meeting Rhiann's eyes. 'She is at the sacred spring. Perhaps you would like some honey cakes?'

This last was said in a rush, and as Rhiann tied Liath's reins loosely to the fence, she glanced over her shoulder at Dercca. Now that she thought about it, the woman's reaction to her arrival had been rather strong for a frequent visitor.

'You could always tempt me with your honey cakes, Dercca, but I'm afraid I really do need to speak with her now.' She stared hard at the maid. 'Is everything all right?'

'Oh yes, lady!' Dercca smiled brightly, but her cheeks were stained.

'Then I'll let you get on with your duties.'

Shrugging to herself, Rhiann took the path that led up from Linnet's dwelling to the sacred spring. Rhiann made no effort to hide her approach, but when she reached the spring, Linnet was seated on its stone-built rim, staring into the water, as if she had not heard her. Was she seeing?

But no, for as Rhiann paused at the circle of birch trees, Linnet started and looked up.

Rhiann fell back a step, struck by her aunt's haggard appearance. Beneath her tightly-wound braids, Linnet's eyes were dark and huge in a white, drained face. There were smudges of shadow under her lashes.

'Daughter!' The colour flushed back into Linnet's cheeks, and she rose. 'What are you doing here?'

'I've come to see you! Did you not get my messages? I sent two!'

Linnet blinked, as if awakening. 'Oh, I . . . yes, I did.'

'So why did you not come? Or return my message?'

Linnet looked down into the water. 'I've been so busy, that is all.'

Rhiann sat down on the edge of the pool, its lip built of smooth river pebbles. What was wrong?

'Have you heard any news of the raiding party?' Linnet reached over to pick a stray leaf from the water, but her hands trembled.

'Nothing yet. Have you seen anything?'

'Alas, no.' Linnet edged around the pool, collecting up the flowers she had scattered during her rite.

'Is that all you have to say?' Rhiann rose too, striding around the spring to take Linnet's hand. 'You're shaking! What's happened?'

And at last Rhiann saw something clearly in Linnet's face. One flash, very subtle.

It was fear.

'Aunt, you are worrying me! I ask you again – what has happened?'

Linnet sighed, and pulled her hand away. 'Rhiann, this girl of yours . . . this Caitlin. When she was . . . found . . . did she have any tokens to identify her?'

'Well, she was wrapped in a blue blanket, I think she said, and had a necklace of shells, though they are long gone.'

Paleness washed over Linnet's face, and the sudden flare of pain in her eyes hit Rhiann in the belly. 'You know who she is, don't you, aunt? It's in her face. I've been thinking it over, and it seems she has the look of our house. Is she distant kin to us?'

With a gasp, Linnet turned and wrapped her arms around herself in the same way that Rhiann often did.

Rhiann's blood began to surge. There was so much pain here; it filled the clearing as the spring filled the pool, throbbing in the air. There was more, obviously, much more, to Caitlin's mystery than the curiosity of shared kin. Linnet was shocked, torn, fearful.

Why?

There could be only one reason. For one wild moment, Rhiann wondered whether she should just flee from this place, and leave Linnet to her secrets. No one needed to know about Caitlin. What did it matter?

It matters to me.

'Aunt,' she said in the priestess voice, the commanding voice that she had never used on Linnet, 'tell me whose child she is!'

Linnet's shoulders vibrated with one spasm of emotion, and the flowers fell to the ground, crushed. Then she put her head up, and turned, surrender in her face. 'She is mine.'

The world lurched, and Rhiann clutched the lip of the pool. 'No!'

Linnet said nothing, holding her eyes, and so Rhiann knew it was true.

'I thought she was dead!' Linnet cried out.

Rhiann shook her head as if to clear it. '*You* have a child? You had a *baby*, and I never knew? You kept this from me?'

'I thought she was dead,' Linnet repeated in a whisper, and her hand crept to her mouth.

Rhiann was still shaking her head. 'Of course! She looks like me; why did I not see it?'

Linnet jerked as if struck.

'Dear Goddess! She is of the king's line!' Rhiann could not suppress the wave of hurt that welled up. *Then she could have married, not me. I wasn't the only one after all!*

301

Linnet buried her face in her hands, her shoulders shaking. And at last her distress penetrated Rhiann's own shock, and with that, she felt the chasm yawn again. 'Aunt,' she said, terror suddenly stabbing through the hurt, 'Aunt . . . there is more, isn't there?'

Linnet slowly raised her face. It was ravaged by tears, and the fear that Rhiann had seen earlier was there, no longer subtle, but naked and raw. 'Rhiann, she is even closer kin to you . . . than that.' Her brow crumpled with pain, willing Rhiann to understand.

And Rhiann did.

The dawning of it sparked across the space between them. If before the shock had been a blow, now it was a spear thrust. *Her father.* Linnet and her own father.

'No!' With one moan, Rhiann turned, stumbling blindly, feeling Linnet's hands grasping for her.

'You must understand!'

'Understand?' Rhiann whirled to face her, and all the shock and pain coalesced into one burning font of rage. 'You said you loved my mother! But instead you betrayed her!'

Linnet recoiled. 'No, no! Listen to me!'

'I won't! Everything you ever told me was a lie! A lie!' Rhiann's heart was in her throat, choking her. 'And when did this happen? When did you lay with him? Is she older than me? Younger?'

'She is older by six moons.'

'So you did take him from my mother!'

'No!' Linnet took a deep, shaking breath. 'She did not love him, Rhiann, though she had to marry him for the alliance. I did not betray her heart; I never would. You cannot know of the love your mother and I held for each other—'

'No, I cannot! I cannot because I never had a sister. Although now, apparently, I do!' Rhiann's voice cracked, and tears welled over. She wiped them away impatiently. 'How *could* you, of all people?'

Linnet's jaw was tight with pain, and she grasped Rhiann by both arms. 'Daughter, please! When your father came here from the Votadini I fell in love with him. I fought my feelings for so long . . . and then, once, I was weak. It was foolish, but it never would have happened if she had loved him, too. Don't you see? She had everything I wanted: a home, a man . . .'

Rhiann shrugged her shoulders free. 'But you rejected all of that – the chains of the hearth – for your faith!'

Linnet's smile was bitter. 'No, Rhiann. I fled to my faith when I lost it all. The baby, the man, and your mother.'

'But you hated the thought of being a wife, a mother. *Goddess*! I envied you. I envied you this place, this peace, the lack of ties and obligations. You betrayed me, you made me hate it too!'

'I never made you hate that world, Rhiann. And if I did not betray your mother, then I did not betray you.'

'It's all just words! I don't know you any more!'

'I'm the same as I was. Rhiann!' Linnet's voice softened, and her eyes filled again. 'It was my pain, and my loss. It cut me deeply, more than you will ever know. Have a care for that! What have you really lost?'

What have I lost? The words echoed around Rhiann's skull. 'Everything,' she whispered, rubbing her hands over her face. 'I must go.'

'But it's getting dark. Stay and talk with me!'

'Not now – I cannot!' Rhiann caught up her cloak from the pool and strode to the edge of the clearing.

'Rhiann.'

She paused, and then turned. Linnet's still form was outlined in gold; the last rays of the sun picked out the tears on her face. 'When she returns, send her to me. Tell her who she is, and send her.'

Rhiann nodded once, coldly. 'She has a right to know.'

The journey home passed in a blur of dark shadows under the trees, and flares of moonlight on her hands, tight in Liath's mane. Darkness and light, shifting, confusing her.

The scrap of peace she had won had now been torn away. She no longer had a mother, for that mother, whom she'd trusted with all her heart, had lied. All along, the woman she worshipped, the woman she followed on unsteady, baby legs had been someone else. She betrayed Rhiann's real mother, seduced her father . . . and worse, the worst thing of all, kept the secret from Rhiann, whom she was supposed to love like a daughter. The hurt was sickening; it burned.

And yet behind it all, something else throbbed, too. Rhiann now had the closest of kin, a real sister. And not only a sister, but one who carried the king's blood, and so could provide their heir.

Shadow and moon, darkness and light, betrayal and truth.

By the time she reached Dunadd's gates, the moon had sunk behind the hills. She stumbled up the pathway towards her house, her heart as heavy as the blackness around her, now stabbed only with the cold light of stars.

CHAPTER 39

Eremon sent a messenger to tell the council of his success, and asked him to seek out Rhiann to give her the news.

She was deeply relieved to hear that there had been so few losses, and that her friends were safe. But beneath that, her fear and pain surged anew. For Caitlin would be coming home.

No word had come from Linnet, and no one in Dunadd knew that anything had changed. And yet for Rhiann, everything was different. She spent the days after the confrontation in a cold haze from which she could not awaken.

Until on a day of soft sun, Eithne arrived with her belongings in a pack, and Rhiann was forced to emerge from her darkness to take the girl in hand.

Rhiann had already warned Eithne about Didius, and she was relieved to see the girl display curiosity when she first saw him, rather than fear. And after all, Didius was so despondent, merely sitting and staring at Rhiann's walls, that he couldn't appear frightening to anyone.

'Eithne, I have one very important duty for you,' Rhiann said, when Eithne had deposited her meagre belongings on a shelf. She led the girl to Didius's pallet by the fire. Rhiann smiled at the Roman, and received a wary look in return. 'Eithne,' she said, pointing at the girl. Didius barely nodded.

'Now, Eithne, I need you to start teaching Didius our language. I don't know how long he will stay here, but we will never be able to make any use of him unless he can speak – and I think his time here will be easier for him, as well.'

Eithne's black eyes widened, and darted to the Roman's face.

Rhiann smiled. 'The other rule here is that you can say what is on your mind. Will this duty I speak of distress you?'

'Oh, no, lady. If it will help the tribe, I would be honoured.' She raised her chin proudly.

'Good. It is a very important task, as I said, and we all must do our part.'

'But lady, why do you want to make his time easier? He is the enemy!'

Rhiann chose her words carefully. 'His people are our enemies, that is true. But compassion is part of the way of the Goddess, Eithne, and so lives in this household. All people are Her children – even Romans, though they seem not to know it. I would defend myself against any Roman trying to harm me, or those I loved. But Didius will not do so, I sense it strongly. And the Source is about balance – perhaps something will come of our compassion for him, something good. Do you understand?'

Eithne smiled shyly. 'A little, lady.'

'Then let me be more plain. His information may aid us, but I will not allow him to be tortured. If we – you and I – can win his trust, then we accomplish what we need without cruelty. Now do you understand?'

Eithne's smile broadened. 'Oh, yes, lady! I will do my best.'

'I'm sure you will. Just point at things and tell him the words. He is a man of some expertise among his people – he will learn quickly.' Rhiann looked down at Didius kindly. 'Eithne will help you to speak,' she said in his own language.

As Didius scowled, she squatted down. 'You must learn words so we can speak.' She gave him her most engaging smile. Surely he would see the wisdom of being able to communicate with her properly? At last he nodded.

Rhiann stood up, sighing. 'Now,' she said to Eithne. 'Go to

the well and fetch us some water. Then you can start teaching him.'

Eithne took up the earthen pot by the fire. But only a few moments after leaving she came running back in. 'Lady, lady!' she cried. 'The warband is back!'

Catching up her cloak, Rhiann hastened with Eithne down to the village gate. They could just see the horsemen in the front ranks coming over the causeway, and a bright flash of red along the flanks of their mounts.

By the time they pushed their way up the stairs to the gate tower, Eremon was riding past underneath, formidable with his boar helm and shield. But the sun also picked out the gleam of steel on his thighs, for before him he held a Roman helmet, with its wide neck-guard and bronze-tipped cheek flaps. And strapped to his saddle was a Roman shield, square and red-painted, with an eagle emblem outlined in yellow.

At this sight, the people broke out into ragged cheers, which only increased as Conaire followed, riding slowly under the shadow of the gate towers and back out into the sun.

Next to Conaire, surprisingly, rode Caitlin, straining to hold up a standard that the Romans used, a banner on a tasselled pole. Even from where Rhiann stood, she noticed that Conaire's eyes were for once not drinking in the crowd's adulation, but fixed on her cousin, no, her *sister*: the gleam of her hair, the fierce glow in her eyes, the graceful line of her shoulders.

But when Conaire caught sight of Rhiann above, he paused to wink at her, and grinned.

As dusk crept over the marshes, Eremon, attended by the druids, offered the Roman spoils to a deep, still pool beside the river. Beneath the blast of the war trumpets, he dedicated the shining helmets and swords to Manannán, in gratitude for the warband's success.

And when night fell, so one of the greatest feasts of the year began, on the plain between the roasting pits and the pier.

The sky was so deep and clear with stars that it brought the touch of frost, but no one noticed the cold.

Only Rhiann was unable to lose herself in the sheer relief and triumph that ran through the veins of every other man, woman and child. For generations the Romans had loomed as a dark threat on the horizon, the monsters with which mothers threatened errant children, the stuff of nightmares. Now, the Epidii had won a victory against these people. They were not monsters after all, they were only men, and could be killed.

The warriors of the attack party glowed as if new-come from a furnace. The tale of every sword stroke was told and retold to wide-eyed groups of admirers, and the bards rushed from fighter to fighter, composing snatches of songs and poems on the spot to immortalize each deed. Two groups of horn and pipe-players competed with each other, and already ragged lines of people danced in the space between two roaring bonfires.

Rhiann glimpsed Caitlin laughing, surrounded by young men, though Conaire's golden head hovered closest, and his great shoulders were being put to good effect, keeping the other admirers at a distance.

Eremon sat at the centre of the benches that had been brought from the King's Hall, as toast after toast was made to him by Talorc and Belen and a score of others. Tonight was his night, and as Rhiann sipped her mead on the edge of the firelight, she listened to the tales being boasted of around her, gleaning that the battle had been won with sound strategy as well as strength. Eremon was a good war leader, then, perhaps a great one. The Epidii men near her were certainly speaking of him with awe: it seemed he had well and truly won them over with this one daring attack of his.

A cheer went up, and the crowd parted to let through the servants bearing the first roast boar on its litter. The beast was paraded around one of the fires to cries and wild drumming, before being set down at the centre for the carving. Declan oversaw this, for each portion must be allotted to the proper person, from the chief druid to the clan elders to the king's cousins. The haunch was reserved for the tribe's champion, but just as the druid was directing a server to take it to Eremon on a bronze platter, there was a disturbance, and raised voices.

Rhiann pushed closer to see who spoke. It was Lorn, standing before the boar. 'The champion's portion is due to me!' he was crying. 'It was I and my men who brought us victory!'

He turned on Eremon with a flourish, and the Erin prince's face darkened as he slowly got to his feet. 'That is a lie.' Eremon's voice was calm, but raised to carry to the suddenly hushed crowd. 'The attack succeeded under my orders. Orders that you ignored, endangering us all.'

'You name me a liar?' Lorn howled. 'You tarnish my honour, and that of my clan! I demand that you retract it. *I demand that you retract it now!*' He drew his sword in one sweep.

'What is the meaning of this?' Talorc growled, elbowing his way between the two men. He rounded on Lorn. 'We have heard the bards; the tale is clear! Withdraw your challenge.'

'I will not!' Lorn's eyes flashed. 'He excluded me from command because I would not rely on trickery rather than the courage of the Epidii! *I* brought us victory, and still he seeks the glory! The champion's portion is mine!'

'And what do you say to this, prince?' Talorc addressed Eremon now, and Rhiann could see that the old warrior's eyes held a message, a warning. 'Do you retract your accusation? If so, all is well and we will eat.'

Eremon's face was taut in the firelight. 'Again, I say he lies. He disobeyed me, and would have been our death. I protect no such man.' Despite the words, his voice held resignation, not anger.

Around Rhiann there were gasps, and the movement of people drawing back, the benches now abandoned. 'Rori,' Eremon's voice was calm. 'Get my sword and shield, and quickly now.' Rhiann found herself only a pace away as

Conaire grasped his foster-brother's arm, his face close. 'Eremon,' she heard Conaire murmur, 'this cub fights well.'

Eremon's eyes were cold. 'I have seen that for myself.'

'But Eremon . . . he hates you. He will not fight to disarm; he will fight to kill.'

'I know this.'

'Then do not be careful.'

'No?' Eremon cocked his head at Conaire, his grim mouth lifting.

'Be angry.'

Eremon nodded, holding Conaire's gaze, as Rori raced back, breathless, sword in hand.

Lorn was circling one of the fires now, like a pacing wolf, but as soon as he saw that Eremon was armed he sprang forward, and those around the Erin prince could only scatter, falling back to the edges of the crowd. Rhiann realized that she was clenching Conaire's arm, the nails digging into his skin.

With a war cry Lorn leaped on to one of the abandoned benches to launch himself at Eremon, and the prince dodged to one side, the swords colliding with a clash. Around they skirled, first one falling back and then another, the blades glowing like brands in the firelight, the crowd stumbling over each other to escape.

Rhiann did not know the art of sword fighting, but still she sensed the gulf between the two men; Lorn thrusting and slashing wildly, rage palpable in every limb, compared to the tightness of Eremon's body, the holding of thought followed by the careful stroke.

'No,' she heard Conaire mutter, 'let it go, let it go!'

And then Lorn leaped to the benches again and Eremon followed, beating the Epidii prince back in a flurry of thrusts, until suddenly Eremon slipped on a puddle of spilled mead and went down to the ground with a thud, limbs flailing.

The people let out a great cry as Lorn flew from the bench to press his advantage, and under Rhiann's fingers, Conaire's arm tensed. She strained to see, but could only glimpse Lorn's back and Eremon's legs splayed on the ground. There was the clash of steel and a harsh grunt of pain.

Whose pain, *whose pain?*

Then Eremon seemed to twist, and suddenly Lorn was falling back, pinned against the bench, and Eremon was on his feet again. In the firelight, Rhiann could see the torn tunic over his arm, dark with blood, and how the tightness in his face had been lost in flushed cheeks and glittering eyes.

He glanced down at the blood, the whites of his eyes livid in the firelight, and then something seemed to give, and he let loose one wild, unearthly yell and bore down on Lorn, shield high, blade flying. Lorn returned the thrusts desperately, the light in his own face faltering at the unexpected rage of the onslaught, but, forced to throw every grain of attention to defence, his awareness wavered.

The edge of the bench caught his leg, and he stumbled. It was only a moment, but it was enough. With shocking suddeness, it was over, Eremon's sword at his throat.

And in the silence, Rhiann saw the trembling of the blade, as Eremon fought to regain control.

There was no cry of triumph from the assembled people, no cheering or excitement: only the harsh panting of the fighters. 'You see, son of Urben,' Eremon gasped out at last, 'you need both ice and fire to win.'

With a grim mouth, Lorn pushed Eremon's blade away with his palm, sparing no glance as he sheathed his sword and left. The crowd cleaved before the darkness in his face, sensing, somehow, that this was no real victory. For such a division was dangerous at this time, and Lorn was a respected fighter, his father a renowned chieftain.

The feast resumed, but the chatter and music was muted now. Rhiann watched Eremon chew the boar haunch with grim eyes, and now men did not look at him, but huddled in groups, talking among themselves.

Later, by her own hearth, Rhiann scrutinized the wound on his upper arm. She'd had a time convincing him to let her see it at all, for he would not move from the fires until he had drunk deep with the nobles, seeking to quiet their unrest. Now she could see why his tunic was drenched in blood; it was a deep slash, though clean.

'You were not surprised when Lorn challenged you.' She put down the moss pad and took up a bone needle threaded with flax.

'No.' Eremon flinched at the first piercing, but held his arm still. 'He told me on our journey home that he would do it. He was just looking for an excuse.'

'The people were not happy when you won; nor would they have been happy if Lorn had won.'

'I know.' Eremon shook his head. 'This breach has weakened us, yet I had no choice. If I gave in, I may as well have handed the leadership to him tonight.'

She concentrated on her sewing, holding the flesh together so the underlying skin would bind.

'Rhiann,' Eremon suddenly said. 'I do not wish to talk of painful things. I wish to tell you of the fort attack. I thought you'd like to know that the training has paid off – paid off a hundred times and more!' His breath caught as she worked on the deepest part of the wound. 'Your warriors fought with valour and discipline. The way they held to my orders . . . we stormed the gate and would have easily taken the fort if . . . well, if not for Lorn. I can forge them into something strong, I know that now. Agricola will find more than a disorganized rabble if he comes west.'

Was he asking for her approval? Surely not. 'I still think it was foolhardy,' she said cautiously, laying down the needle and wiping blood away. 'But as you said, it has paid off.'

'Difficult to draw compliments from, aren't you?'

'You hardly need more from me! After this night, I'm surprised you can get your head through the door.'

He chuckled, then winced again as she began to wind a bandage around his arm. 'Well, if that is the case, I need only come to you.'

She sighed. The tension of the last days and the stress of the fight had worn down her patience. 'You know you did well,

Eremon. There are hundreds of people here to tell you so. I'm glad that you had success. I feel safer for it. Are you happy now?'

Eremon turned his head to stare at her. Above the smeared dirt on his cheeks, his eyes were sharp. 'Something has befallen you while I was gone. Something has disturbed you.'

She bit her lip, tying off the ends of the bandage. He was going to find out about Caitlin very soon; they all would. Should she tell him now? And then anger surged in her. She hated that he could discern her emotions, hated that he did not let her be.

'I must sleep now, Eremon.' She rose and cleared away the bronze bowl, the needle, and bandages. 'I will stay here tonight, for the hall will be noisy with men.'

When he thanked her and left, his gaze lingering on her face, she let out a breath she did not realize she held.

He sees clearly for a man. Too clearly of me.

Deep in sleep, Rhiann nevertheless sensed the movement of the door cover. Raising herself on her elbow and peering through the bed-screen, she saw Caitlin's slight form outlined against the fire, unpinning her cloak. Rhiann drew on a robe and padded out.

Caitlin glanced up from the hearth-bench in surprise. 'Rhiann! We had no chance to talk after the fight – wasn't it exciting? Of course, I knew Eremon would win after seeing him in the raid. Even though I was in the woods with the archers, you could see his sword from a league away ... I mean Lorn is a fine fighter too, but Eremon just *had* to win ...'

Rhiann stared down at Caitlin's glowing face, at the gilded tracery of Linnet's bones, of her own bones. And for that moment, her anger at Linnet fell away. She perched on her chair, and watched Caitlin pull her boots off with an easy air that was fast becoming as familiar to Rhiann as the way that Eithne tilted her head when she was grinding grain.

And Rhiann was suddenly swept by a much softer – and

stranger – feeling than that which had consumed her on the ride home from Linnet's house.

Sister.

'Caitlin,' she said, stopping the chatter, looking into the girl's shining eyes, 'I have something to tell you . . .'

CHAPTER 40

Rhiann never found out what happened when Linnet and Caitlin met. At first light, hardly able to contain herself, Caitlin threw on her clothes, although she had barely slept.

'Do you think I should wear something else?' she asked Rhiann anxiously, dragging a comb through her hair. Rhiann poured blackberry tea and thrust a cup at Caitlin. Her own hands were shaking, but Caitlin was too beside herself to notice.

Rhiann spoke as calmly as she could. 'She won't care, Caitlin.'

'Are you sure? She's a great priestess, you said. What if she finds me coarse?'

'She's not like that.' Tears welled up dangerously in Rhiann's throat, and she swallowed them. 'She is very gentle. She will be proud to have you as . . . a daughter.'

'I hope so!' Caitlin slurped the tea, then put the cup on the hearth-bench. 'Oh, I'm so nervous! Won't you come?'

Rhiann shook her head. 'This is between you and she.'

'But did she not tell you anything else?'

Rhiann hesitated. She had not told Caitlin that she and Linnet argued. She had not told Caitlin who fathered her. Linnet could reap that particular sowing herself. Why spoil what was, to Caitlin, such an unexpected and joyous occasion? 'Again, only that she thought you dead all these years. It's better for you to gain the details from her yourself.' *And because I did not stay to find out any more.*

Now Rhiann brushed Caitlin's nervous fingers aside,

unwound the single lumpy plait, and started braiding again. 'I will leave it to Linnet to tell the council.' Rhiann's usually nimble fingers were also dulled this day, but she managed to get the hair into a serviceable braid before winding it around Caitlin's head and securing it with bone pins.

'Oh, should I wear the jewelled pin you gave me?' Caitlin fretted, hopping from foot to foot.

Rhiann grasped her by the shoulders and gave her a little shake. 'No! She will love you as you are.' Her breath caught on the last words.

'Oh, Rhiann! We are cousins!' Caitlin threw her arms around Rhiann's waist and hugged her. Rhiann instantly stiffened, for no one beside Linnet had touched her like that; not since she left the Sisters on the Sacred Isle. But Caitlin had already let her go, and was hastily thrusting bits of clothing into her leather pack.

In a flurry of nervous chatter she disappeared into the pale dawn, her belt buckle jingling. Rhiann was left alone at her door to watch the sun come up. A curlew called its plaintive cry, far out on the marsh, as the golden light washed over the reeds.

She will be proud to have you as a daughter.

Rhiann put her face in her hands. And the tightness that she had carried inside since she saw Linnet melted, and so began to hurt.

Linnet returned to the dun two days later, with Caitlin by her side. Rhiann saw them enter the gate when she herself was returning from the river, but she could not face Linnet, not yet, and so she turned aside.

She was far downstream, collecting comfrey from the damp soil beneath the willows, when she heard hooves on the Trade Path. Out of the corner of her eye, she glimpsed Dòrn's distinctive black coat. She froze, one hand wrapped around the fleshy leaves, the other holding her herb-knife. Eremon had announced that he was riding to Crianan that morning. Perhaps if she bent low enough, he would not see her.

But the hooves slowed and stopped, and there was the thud of boots to the ground. 'We should just hand you over to the river sprites and be done with it,' Eremon said. 'You spend all your time up to your ankles in mud.'

She straightened, watching him warily, and pulled her feet one by one out of the mire until she could reach her net bag. 'I gather you've heard, then?'

'Yes, we all have.' Eremon looped the reins over a dead alder and perched on a broken stump, cradling his bandaged arm. 'Linnet called what council members there were in the dun together, and told them. You must be happy.' The last statement seemed like a question.

Rhiann squatted, wiping mud from the leaves as she laid them out. 'I found out while you were away . . . it was a great shock.'

'A shock, yes, but surely a pleasant one?'

'Of course, a pleasant one!' She willed him to go away and leave her be.

'So.' He sounded satisfied. 'This is what was bothering you the other night.'

She frowned up at him. 'What are you talking about? Caitlin is my kin . . . I am proud she is my kin.' That, at least, was true, and she was able to say it emphatically.

But Eremon was chewing on his lip, his eyes boring into her. 'Forgive me if I misunderstand, but if she is Linnet's daughter, then does she not have the same status as you, when it comes to carrying the king's blood? Apart from you being Ban Cré, I mean.'

'Yes,' she said through gritted teeth, packing the leaves in the bag. What did he care for their kin laws? And why was he here?

'But you are not jealous, of course. That someone else now has that rank?'

'Jealous!' She shook her head, laughing with soft bitterness. 'Ah, if only you knew how many nights I have lain awake, wishing there was a woman to share that burden with me. How little I wanted it at all! How glad I would have been to be

317

born someone else's niece!' She shook her head again, and got to her feet. 'You are not as perceptive as you pretend to be, prince.'

'Yet something has hurt you.'

'And what business is it of yours, exactly?'

He did not answer her, but simply held her eyes: she could almost hear his mind working.

Annoyed, she picked her bag up and took to a boggy path that ran away into the reeds. She knew he would not follow, for he had his new boots on, which she herself had sewn. Unfortunately, her exit was less dignified than she wished, as mud squelched loudly between her toes.

'Rhiann.' She glanced over her shoulder. He was leaning against the tree trunk now. 'Jealous of her position; perhaps not. But you fear something.'

'Fear!' She turned, heedless of the picture she would present. 'You presume too much, trying to see into my heart!'

He shrugged. 'And yet, you don't hesitate to do the same to me. Why is it right for you, and not for me?'

Her mind raced for an answer, but he used the stump to mount Dòrn, and crossed his hands on the reins. 'You know, whatever you fear, it is better to face it than to hide here in a bog. I credit you with more courage than that.' With a polite nod he urged the horse back to the Trade Path.

She watched him go, breathing hard. For despite not wanting to hear it from him, what he said struck her to the core. She was hiding; it was true. She glanced towards Dunadd.

I am angry with Linnet, but . . . fear? What do I fear?

Rhiann waited until dark had fallen before she returned. She put her head in at the stables and saw, with relief, that Linnet's horse Whin was gone. But even before she gained the sanctuary of her own house, the whispers reached her from the women gossiping at their doors, babes slung on their hips.

Linnet had acknowledged Caitlin as her own, but did not

name the father. The people assumed that the girl was gotten by a man at the Beltaine fires, or in some other mysterious priestess ritual. And it would also be expected that a priestess in retreat would send the child away for fostering, so Linnet's lie was covered there as well. Only Rhiann knew that she'd wanted to hide the baby because of its parentage.

Rhiann was glad to find her house deserted. Eithne would be up at the hall cooking for Eremon's men, and she'd probably taken Didius with her. But as Rhiann hung up her cloak, she heard racing footsteps outside.

'Rhiann!' Caitlin threw herself into Rhiann's arms. 'Oh, Rhiann, I have so wanted to talk with you these last days! It has been like a dream!'

'Hush, now. Take some breaths!'

Caitlin flung herself down on the hearth-bench, clasping her fingers between her knees. 'Linnet – I can't think of her as my mother – was so glad to see me, Rhiann. She cried!'

Rhiann's heart clenched. 'Did she?' She sat down. 'And you, too, I imagine.'

'No – I was too excited!'

'And do you like her?'

'Oh, yes!' Then Caitlin frowned. 'But she is a very great lady. I don't know what to say to her yet.'

'She is gentle, as I said.'

'Gentle, yes, but strong, too. She is so like you, Rhiann.'

Rhiann's throat closed over. 'It has been said before.'

'And she told me how losing me was all an accident. She was sending me to the Votadini for training as a noble lady, because she had kin there, but her servant must have been killed in that raid, and I was taken. She searched for me for such a long time, until eventually she had to accept that I was dead.' Caitlin shook her head. 'And all along I was growing up there, not far from the path. Fethach's wife obviously would not give me up.' She looked over at Rhiann with pain on her brow. 'Why, Rhiann? Fethach's wife never seemed to want me, not after I grew from a babe to a girl. Why did she not return me? How could she do that?'

'Some people do not do what is right, Caitlin. They think only of themselves.'

Caitlin sighed and yawned, obviously exhausted from the high emotion. 'And so we came here, and she told all the men who I was. They stared at me in the full light of day, Rhiann, and that nice druid, Declan, declared the story true. The elders were shocked. But then they started looking at me differently!'

'So they might. Did Linnet explain your position here?'

Caitlin nodded, reaching for a bannock on the hearth-stone. 'But I didn't really listen; I don't care, much. Belonging to someone – to anyone – is all that ever mattered to me.' As she bit into the bread, she glanced at Rhiann with alarm. 'That's not ungrateful, is it, Rhiann?'

'No,' Rhiann assured her. 'We think alike, you and I.'

'That is because we are cousins,' Caitlin mumbled through her mouthful, then swallowed and leaned across to take Rhiann's hand. 'This must be a shock for you, too, Rhiann. You know I won't take your place anywhere, though. I couldn't.'

The blood beat on Rhiann's ears. 'We don't need such words between us, cousin.'

Sister.

The word trembled in the air between them. But Rhiann knew the truth would strike Caitlin's heart with guilt and confusion, and Rhiann could not dampen Caitlin's joy at finding her family. Perhaps in time . . .

There was, of course, one other thing. 'Caitlin.' She paused to choose her words carefully. 'Did Linnet explain everything about your position? You and I carry the king's bloodline, but only I can be Ban Cré because of my priestess training.'

Caitlin nodded. 'Of course! And thank the Goddess for that, for I have no desire to deal with the Otherworld, Rhiann!'

Rhiann smiled tightly. 'But the blood brings something else, Caitlin. Another obligation.' She steeled herself. 'One of us must bear the next king.'

Caitlin's face did not darken, but lit up with pride. 'I understand, Rhiann, though I have pinched myself over it for two whole days! I cannot believe it!'

Rhiann was stunned. 'You are happy about this?'

'Who would not be! *I* could bear a king! A strong son to come after me . . . a babe to train in bow and sword . . . to see off to war in pride . . .' At the incredulous expression on Rhiann's face, she stopped short. 'Don't worry, Rhiann. You can be sure that I'll pick a man worthy to sire a king. I may have been brought up as a commoner, but I understand this. He'll have to fight for me, and well.' She grinned.

Rhiann rested her chin in her hand, and watched Caitlin devour the bannock, hiding a smile. She wondered if she would ever understand this child-woman, who saw life so differently from her. She hoped not. Understanding would tame her, and Rhiann wanted her to remain just the way she was.

Sister.

CHAPTER 41

I *t is better to face your fear than to hide.*
You are so like her, Rhiann.
Some people think only of themselves.
All these words – Caitlin's, Eremon's and her own –
pounded on Rhiann's mind from dawn to dusk, as she made
her way around the dun to prepare for the Beltaine rites.

Beltaine marked the start of the season of fertility, the
growth season, when all was renewed and that which was old
was left behind. And Rhiann knew that, as Beltaine came, she
must resolve this with Linnet. The breach between them
ached like an infected sore, an echo of the agony she felt
when such harsh words, such rage, had sundered her from
the Sisters on the Sacred Isle. It could not happen again . . .
no! She could not bear it.

The quickening of the earth, the warm smell of the
sprouting grain, the house, which for once was filled with the
laughter of Caitlin and Eithne . . . all of it passed her by
because of the darkness that lay over her.

She decided to wait until her anger cooled, for she
remembered some of the things she had said to Linnet with
shame. But as time went on, the betrayal did not fade – it
only grew greater.

She took to riding further afield on her own, willing the
peace and beauty of the dawning sunseason to soothe her,
nudging Liath into long races along the field strips, which left
both of them sweaty and breathless. But nothing helped.

The other thing I share with Linnet is stubbornness. Rhiann
pulled Liath up at the shoulder of the hills that encircled

Dunadd, and sat watching the haze of cookfires rising lazily on the high breeze. She sighed. In truth, that fault was hers alone. Linnet was not stubborn.

Then why has she not come?

After all I said to her? Why would she?

And underneath, a deeper child-voice still cried with a wordless anguish Rhiann could not understand: *I need her. Go to her.*

'I cannot!' She nudged Liath into a steep run, hooves and mud flying.

The next day Rhiann and Eithne went to Crìanan to see Eithne's family, for the baby brother had been suffering from a troublesome, lingering cough. After treating him with a coltsfoot brew, Rhiann took up her gathering bag and left Eithne with her mother.

Eithne's family lived near the place of the otters, a hidden bay silent with dark rocks, the water thick and smooth with kelp. The tide was out, and Rhiann wandered over the exposed rocks, picking the strands of purple and brown weed, for they made a fine dye.

When she reached a sliver of pale beach she stood, eyes half-closed, letting the sun's reflection on the waves shatter into sparks.

'Rhiann.'

At that familiar voice, she whirled.

Linnet stood behind her, eyes shadowed with the water's darkness. 'I came to Dunadd for you. Caitlin told me you were here.'

At the sight of those beloved eyes, something twisted within Rhiann. Seeing that regal form standing so straight, the calm purity of Linnet's face . . . Goddess, Rhiann wanted to run to her, to bury herself in those arms, so much. But the depth of the wanting brought forth another, stronger impulse: to push her away, to keep such a love at bay for the hurt it could inflict. With a catch in her breath, Rhiann stumbled away.

'Rhiann!' Linnet's cry was roughened with grief. 'Speak to me! I have suffered enough!'

Rhiann halted, her throat closing. *'You've* suffered! High on your mountain, doing as you will, taking whom you will, and then disposing of the evidence because it would shame you? You've suffered?'

Why did these words spill from her mouth? Why was the font as white-hot, as overflowing as that day at Linnet's spring? Time had healed nothing ... time would heal nothing. 'Just leave me alone!' she gasped out, and went as if to go.

'No!' Linnet's cry this time was arresting. The pain of it trembled in the air. *'I will not lose a daughter again!'*

Rhiann reeled, as with that cry, all the suppressed betrayal of the last two years came rushing through the breach in her defences. 'But we have lost each other!' She turned, brushing scalding tears from her eyes. 'You say you love me, and yet you have kept so much from me! You hide things from me!'

Linnet watched her with tight eyes, her hands helpless by her sides.

The pain was growing now, an immense upwelling that threatened to break free of Rhiann's body. She felt the burning consume her ... and all reason at last slip away. 'I've seen it in your eyes, the deep things you will not share with me! Like Caitlin, like my father! And why did you not stop my marriage? What held you back? Why did you let them sell me? Why did you not protect me?'

'Rhiann—'

'No!' Rhiann's mouth twisted, holding back tears. 'You were not there when I needed you most! When Gelert stabbed me with his hate ... when the council sold me off like a brood mare ... when that prince came to my bed ... when those men took me—' She gasped, slapping her hand to her mouth; her treacherous mouth.

Linnet's eyes grew huge. *'What?'* She strode forward, grasping Rhiann's arms. 'What did you say?'

Rhiann had lost the power of speech, her muscles rigid

under Linnet's hands, trying to hold the pain in. They stared into each other's eyes, both naked, at last, soul to soul. And in that moment, all barriers between their senses melted, and the knowledge passed from Rhiann to Linnet as easily as a sigh . . .

Rhiann saw the storm descend as a dark veil over Linnet's eyes. 'No.' The denial was a moan. 'No! No!'

The moan turned to a shriek, but Rhiann, caught in the crystal web of pain they both shared, knew the denial had no power. Saying it did not take the truth away. Rhiann had tried, had tried it a thousand times.

And the twist of that futility wrenched her own tongue loose. 'Yes!' The relief of it coursed through her. *Let it consume me then . . . burn me to ashes . . . then I will be free . . .* 'Those raiders did not just kill, they took my body. They lanced me, tore me, bled me. They marked me with their nails and teeth. They took me . . . and left nothing . . .'

Linnet jerked in horror, and her face looked human no longer. 'My little girl . . .' The words came out in a whisper.

'No,' Rhiann said bleakly. 'No more. There is no little girl.'

Then she felt Linnet's body sag, and they sank to the sands, Linnet clasping Rhiann to her breast. But her aunt's arms held no tenderness now, only the bloody fierceness born of anger, of guilt, of grief as wild as a long dark storm.

She pressed Rhiann into her as if she would take her inside her own body, holding her in the womb as she had never held her in life.

And so the storm broke over both of them, bearing them down on the wet sand, and their tears became one river, and it carried them away.

CHAPTER 42

Rhiann opened her eyes to see blue wool against her cheek, and sand between her fingers. Her head was in Linnet's lap, her body chilled by the rising dampness of the sand. Her aunt held her softly now, singing low in her throat. Hands smoothed the hair at Rhiann's brow.

Linnet felt Rhiann stir. 'The Goddess blinded me.' Her voice was quiet, drained of all emotion. 'She must have blinded me, for I did not know.'

Rhiann pushed herself to her haunches. 'I never told you.'

Linnet nodded. 'You felt that if you did not speak it, did not share it . . . it would all go away.' She put her arm around Rhiann and tucked her head into her shoulder. 'Oh, child! Was I so busy with my visions and my thoughts of the future . . . all our futures . . . that I failed to see what was happening under my very nose? With the person who was dearest to my heart? You are right. I failed you.'

Rhiann remembered the nights that Linnet sat, nursing her through the grief over the raid, forcing draughts down her throat, stroking her hands. 'No, aunt. Without you, I would not have come back from the doorway to the Otherworld. When I wanted to die, to leave this place, you brought me back.'

'To what? To be married off to someone when you . . . when you had been through all that?' Linnet shifted restlessly. 'Now I know why you resisted so much, why you were hurting.' She sighed. 'Oh, Rhiann, I was blinded. Forgive me. Forgive me.'

Now that Linnet spoke the words Rhiann had so often

wanted to hear, she realized she did not need them. She was quiet for a moment. 'Did anyone know about Caitlin?'

'Only Dercca.'

'And when you lost her?'

'No one knew. No one ever knew.'

Rhiann sat straighter. 'Caitlin said that we are very alike, you and I. We both have the strength to hide our innermost pain. The greater the pain, perhaps the better we hide it. How could you know, really, what had happened to me, when you were up against someone as strong as yourself?'

Linnet's eyes roved over Rhiann's face. 'You are wise, daughter. But I feel that in this, perhaps we both were wrong.' She brushed sand from Rhiann's cheek.

'Aunt, I still don't understand why you hid Caitlin. If my mother did not love my father, then surely you could both lay with whom you wished?'

'Such things perhaps do not concern the herders in their huts, Rhiann. But we were dealing with dynasties. My concerns were the concerns of my brother, the King, and his alliance with the Votadini through your father. Such things require control. Not uncontrolled lusts of the flesh, but controlled marriages. Controlled births. I could not have a baby by your father before the Ban Cré did. It would have cast grave doubts on her fertility.'

'But you could have rid yourself of the baby, if you wished. You had the knowledge.'

'Yes. But I did not know if I would ever have a baby to anyone else and I . . . When she was inside me, I heard her, Rhiann. I heard her soul, the music of her soul. And I could not do it.' She rushed on. 'I secreted myself away. As a priestess, it was easy to find excuses, even for your mother. I bore the babe, and by that time your mother was pregnant with you. I could not shame her, Rhiann. She would have known whose child it was. I thought that if I sent Caitlin away for a few years, just a few years, then your mother would have a gaggle of children. And it would matter less; so I could bring Caitlin back.' Her throat moved as she swallowed.

'But she disappeared, and I could get no news of her. A few moons later I lost your mother.' She bowed her head. 'You were all that kept me going.'

Rhiann put her hand on Linnet's back, palm over where her heart was, and just held it there. Purged of her own grief, she could at last feel Linnet's anguish. And she knew that it had been great, burning with bitterness and guilt. 'I understand, aunt. I am sorry for the words I said.'

'You said nothing that I have not said to myself a thousand times and more. Yet I buried the memories in another life . . . another time. That is why I kept my silence.'

'I know.' Rhiann smiled wearily. 'But the gap between us just kept getting deeper. When you told me of Caitlin I felt it all slip away . . . I was so scared.'

'You feared she would take your place in my heart.'

Rhiann caught her breath. 'Yes.' It was so simple after all, but this truth had escaped her. That is why the betrayal cut so deep, and would not heal. That is why the anger burned and would not cool. Eremon was right. It was fear all along; and she had been blind to it.

Linnet grabbed her hand and kissed it. 'No one could take your place. You will never know the love that I bear for you, just as I will never know how much your mother loved me. Perhaps if I had trusted it, trusted her enough to tell her, she would have accepted the babe.'

'As I should have trusted my secret with you,' Rhiann said softly.

'Yes. I wonder sometimes if we bring any knowledge with us from our other lives. We seem to make the same mistakes over and over.' Linnet let her breath out. 'But at least we can change some of them. Now that I know all, you must be released from this marriage. I thought you were just shy about the bedding . . . I cannot leave you with the prince now.'

Rhiann flinched. 'Aunt, I must tell you something. He has never bedded me. I . . . asked him to leave me alone. He has done so.'

Linnet gasped. 'Can it be true?'

'It is strange, but true. And – I hardly thought I would ever say this – I want to stay. If he is to help our people, then I must be involved in his campaigns against the Romans.' At Linnet's frown, Rhiann rushed on. 'It is a marriage in name only; I could not hope for more! And I am not the only female of the blood now. Caitlin is more amenable to mating than I. She will bear our heir.'

The concern in Linnet's eyes lingered, though she said only, 'That is good for the tribe.'

'Yes.' Rhiann got to her feet, and held out her hand to help Linnet up. 'And aunt, despite my fears, know that I grow to love Caitlin. She is unlike anyone else I have ever met.'

Caitlin's grin suddenly flashed into Rhiann's mind, and alongside the bone-deep exhaustion, she sensed the lift of hope, a light that for so long had been shrouded by her darkness.

'Yes,' she said again. 'For all that we have lost, we have gained her.'

Beltaine: the festival of fire and renewal. Even the air smelled of fertility, heavy with the scents of damp earth, woodsmoke, and flowers. Rhiann drew in a deep lungful, loving the way that as dusk fell, the dampness released the captured warmth of the day's sun.

Only six moons had passed since Samhain, when she stood on this same mound in the valley of the ancestors, the cairn stones sparkling with ice under the silver moon. Then, she had been so cold and frightened. And alone.

Now, there was laughter and music, and the Beltaine fire's warmth caressed her bare arms. There was rosy light in the sky; the promise of the fair nights to come on the way to the longest day. Her head was no longer crowned with rowan-berries, but with thorn blossom, which hung in the valley thickets in garlands of cream.

Now, when she looked down to the faces ranged below her, upturned and shining in the firelight, she saw friends. Caitlin, laughing, as Conaire pulled the flower chains in her hair. Eithne, her black eyes huge and round, her hands clasped before her in delight, as Rori tried but failed to catch her eye. Aedan, dreamy, his face full of the stories he was weaving. And Eremon, breaking into his slow, crooked smile when she caught his eye.

She felt a touch on her arm; it was Linnet. Rhiann was pleased to see how much of the strain of the last year had smoothed from Linnet's brow. She supposed that the same must apply to her.

Under cover of a burst of Meron's singing, leading the bards, Linnet squeezed her hand. 'How beautiful you look tonight, daughter,' she murmured. 'The bloom has come back to your cheeks, as it comes to the land.'

'I was with the maidens at dawn, and washed in the dew of may,' Rhiann answered, smiling. Yet she knew it was more than that, for after Eithne braided her hair with gold thread and touched her lips with *ruam* dye, she took the bronze mirror from its place at the bottom of her carved chest, and looked at herself for the first time in one full wheel of the sun.

The face that looked back was sad, but no longer haunted. It was the Rhiann she remembered, with fuller cheeks and rounded lips, a nose that, while still long, fitted her face and gave it refinement. The shadows were gone from under her eyes. Their depths still held grief, but there was also a light, which had been missing before.

On the valley floor, scores of cattle were being driven between the purifying bonfires, as Gelert sacrificed a new lamb and offered its blood to the four corners of the earth, to ensure a good harvest. One of the druids then recited the marriage laws, as the betrothed couples leaped over the low flames on the bonfire's edge, their hands clasped, before stepping up to Rhiann for the Mother's blessing. She touched their foreheads with a paste made of water and earth and ash, and called on Rhiannon to give them many children.

By the time she finished this task, the *saor* had taken full effect, and unlike at Samhain, this time she felt its freedom sound a clear note, vibrating deep in her flesh. She was wrapped in its warmth, and her spirit floated dreamily, wafting with the scents of roast deer and the sacred Beltaine moon cakes, baked over the need-fire.

This was no festival for the dead, as Samhain had been. The host of silvery ghosts were gone – this was a night for the living, for fecundity, and richness, for fire and laughter, for the warm glow of gold and bronze jewellery, the bright cascade of cloaks and wraps and flowers. And the light of hope that Rhiann had felt on the beach with Linnet still clung to her, its roots tiny, but clasping the earth. It would grow.

Now Meron was singing a song of the goddess, the Mother, and as his voice soared to the stars Rhiann looked out over the heads of the throng, and beheld a shimmering thread of light reaching up from each person.

The threads met and mingled in the air, and the whole web rippled, just like the strange coloured lights in the far northern sky. Then Rhiann knew what it was – love, made visible to her bodily eyes by the *saor*.

Meron sang:

> *She gives us our breath*
> *Her tears the streams*
> *In Her womb we grow strong*
> *Love is Her song.*

With these words, the golden web swelled into a wave, and it rushed towards the mound and broke over Rhiann. She felt the lifting in her heart, and the sensation of her whole body swelling, growing. The crowd burst into song with Meron, all the myriad voices yearning for the Mother.

And Rhiann felt just the merest touch in her soul, the presence of the Greater One, the rich, heavy, rounded feeling in her limbs, which made her skin glow with light. For that moment, a joy sprang up in her heart, the joy of the stag running through the forest, the salmon leaping the falls, the

331

eagle crying in the high air. For that time out of time, she held the energy for her people.

She caught her breath, desperate not to fail.

But she held on long enough for the wave to wash outwards again, enveloping the people in gold. The Goddess may not speak to Rhiann any more, but the people would know She was with them that night.

How long Rhiann channelled wave after golden wave, she never knew. The singing went on, full-throated, until people had no more to give. And yet they were still held in it, cradled for that moment as one. At last Meron's voice fell away, and pipes started up again, wild and free, and people broke from their reverie to dance their joy.

As the energy left her, Rhiann slumped, but Linnet was there, holding her. 'Well done, child!'

Through the dizziness Rhiann saw Eithne holding out a cup of mead, and she sank down on the carved chair behind her, sipping it until the daze passed.

Linnet leaned over her with a smile in her eyes. 'Go now,' she urged, pointing to where Caitlin, Conaire and Eremon stood at the bottom of the mound, among the swirling dancers. 'They are waiting for you, child. Tonight is for friendship, for fun.'

Eithne's bright face and shining eyes swam in Rhiann's vision. The *saor* vibrated through her. 'But what about you?' She turned her face up to Linnet.

'I will enjoy watching you young people from here. Now, go!'

The impulse to surrender rose strong in Rhiann, merging joyously with the *saor*. The relief of her confession to Linnet still sang through every cell in her body, loosening it from the frigidity of grief. And after the work this night she was both spent and elated.

'Rhiann!' Caitlin was calling.

Eremon was remembering back six moons, to quite a different festival. Then, he had lain on the frozen ground

332

with Aiveen. Now, there was Conaire and Caitlin, laughing, silly with mead, pushing each other off balance until Conaire gave in and tumbled down the hill.

Eithne was perched demurely on the grass eating her Beltaine cake, but she had one hand to her mouth, stifling giggles. Rori was close by her side. Further off, Eremon glimpsed Aedan dancing in a circle, the firelight warming his dark hair to copper; and there lounged crusty old Finan and Colum by the mead barrels, and Angus and Fergus jostling each other to take deermeat from the spits. And Rhiann.

The place next to him, this time, was warmed by Rhiann.

He looked at her sidewise, hardly believing that this was the same woman who stood so cold here last Samhain, a pillar of moonlit ice in undyed robe, pale and remote. Now, she was crowned with blossom, and her dress was the colour of new leaves, her cloak scarlet, embroidered with gold.

'Rhiann, you must dance!' Conaire was pulling at her hand, and Caitlin grasped her other hand, and together they hauled Rhiann to her feet, ignoring her protests. The next instant the three of them were whirling in a dance of their own invention at the base of the slope.

Through the haze of his own mead-soaked mind, Eremon's senses jolted. He had never seen her dance. Conaire held her hands now, and spun her around while Caitlin clapped with glee and shrieked, the horns and pipes between the fires leaping faster and higher. And for one moment, framed in the firelight, Rhiann threw her head back and looked up at Conaire, and she laughed. The mead and the fire had brought a rosy flush to her face, her amber hair blazed, and her eyes shone, their light clear at last.

As her dress clung to her skin, Eremon suddenly noticed, with a kind of shock, how much fuller and rounder she had grown. He had not looked at her properly for so many moons. But there it was. The strained, starved look of her had softened.

Into beauty.

She whirled free of the dance then, and came up to collapse

breathless on the ground by his side, while Conaire and Caitlin danced on, using ever more ridiculous gestures until they were both helpless with laughter.

'Lady.' Rori leaned over to refill Rhiann's mead-cup, and she thanked him and downed it.

'You drink like a man,' Eremon teased her.

She cocked her head at him. 'And that's the only thing I'll ever do like a *man.*'

Now that Eremon could see her close up, there was a glazed look in her eyes. She had been drinking a lot, and did she not take some herb mixture before these rites? He smiled to himself. Surely Rhiann was not drunk!

He threw his own mead back and swallowed, raising one eyebrow. She struggled to sit up, boldly grabbed the jug and poured another cup for them both. 'You think you can better me in anything, prince of Erin, but you're wrong!'

He stifled a smile. 'Fighting words! I must take you along on my next raid.'

Conaire and Caitlin raced up the slope, and Conaire threw himself down on the earth with a great sigh, both of them breathless. 'Oh, Rhiann!' Caitlin's cheeks were glowing as she sat down. 'Beltaine was never this much fun in the mountains!'

'And the best is yet to come,' Conaire offered, his eyes half-lidded, staring at Caitlin's mouth.

She returned his look haughtily. 'If you're talking about honouring the Goddess on the ground with *you*, Conaire mac Lugaid, then think again.' She put her nose in the air. 'I outrank you now.'

There was a startled silence, and then Eremon snorted with laughter, and Caitlin's mouth twitched at the bewilderment on Conaire's face.

'That's a first, brother – a girl turned *you* down,' Eremon said.

'And not before time,' Rhiann put in. They all turned to her in surprise.

'Well said, cousin!' Caitlin rejoined. 'I think you men of Erin make far too much of yourselves. Don't they, Rhiann?'

Rhiann threw Eremon a satisfied look. 'They certainly do.'

'Well, brother.' Conaire addressed Eremon. 'I think if these ladies continue to talk so when they are together, we must part them.' He clasped Caitlin's hand and jumped to his feet again, pulling her up with him. Her tiny wrist disappeared into his huge fist. 'There's more dancing to be had.'

Caitlin was laughing. 'No more, I'm exhausted!'

'Then food – the boar smells delicious.'

'Well . . .' She had to bend her head back to look up at him.

'Come on, I'll get a piece of the belly just for you.' He drew her with him down to level ground, until they both disappeared into the milling crowd.

'Lady?' Eithne said timidly. 'Do you need me? I must eat as well.' She spoke to Rhiann, but her blackberry eyes were on Rori.

'No, no!' Rhiann waved her hand. 'You go and have fun, Eithne.'

When they had gone, Eremon leaned back on his uninjured arm. He could just see the top of Conaire's head near the cookfires, towering over everyone. 'It seems your cousin has captured my brother's heart.'

Rhiann followed his gaze. 'Goddess! Nothing but a passing fancy for him. But if he hurts her – I will kill him.' She spoke gravely, and then hiccupped.

Eremon glanced at her sharply as she sank on to her back, her arms out. He tried not to look at the swell that her breasts made through the thin fabric of her dress. He tried not to notice the cries coming from the darkness behind them – cries that were not those of wild animals.

All over the valley, on the edges of the firelight, couples were slipping away to the dark places beyond, to honour the gods on the fertile earth. Just as he had done with Aiveen . . . although that was more about frustrated lust than honouring.

'Oh . . .' Rhiann sighed.

'What is it?' He leaned over her . . . saw the flames gilding her cheek . . . blazing in her rich hair . . .

'Oh . . . I feel sick.'

CHAPTER 43

Rhiann blinked her eyes open, squinting in the bright light of a new fire. She put out her hand and felt the bed furs. She was home. But the room was spinning.

A dark shape crossed her vision. 'Drink this.' There came Eremon's voice, the feel of his arm behind her head, and then the sweet coolness of water as he held a cup to her lips.

She gulped. 'What . . . ?'

'Don't speak. The sickness will pass.' Dimly, she heard the amusement in his voice. 'I think you got most of it out of you on the grass. You'll feel better soon.'

She sank back on the feather pillow. But the room did not stop shifting, and it got worse when she closed her eyes. 'Thank you. But go now . . .' She struggled to string the words together. 'You will miss the fires . . .' She nearly said, *Aiveen will be there*, but then she remembered that Aiveen was married now, and wasn't she far away in her dun?

'Sleep now.' His voice was gentle, gentler than he had ever spoken to her. 'I'll go in a moment.'

As she slipped away, down into the whirling darkness, she thought she heard him say, 'You did well tonight.'

Freed, her soul floated aimlessly, watching the stars spinning together. Far off, one pulsed and swelled, growing brighter by the moment as it drew near. It was a ball of light; golden and rose-red and fiery, and in it pictures swirled.

It was her beautiful dream . . . the *saor* making it more vivid than ever before. And as the power filled her, as she held the cauldron of the Source in the valley, the man by her side, she understood for the first time just how much she wanted that power. She wanted it with a desperate thirst, with a hunger. She would wield it for good . . . but she wanted it for her own. The power would make her truly special, shining, unique, so the dark memories could never hurt her again . . .

'Rhiann?' The voice was a dash of cold water, shocking her awake. 'Are you all right?'

She blinked again, and the room swam into focus. The fire was so low as to be almost ashes, and early daylight washed the inside of the house with grey. The Beltaine wreaths of hawthorn were dark against the rafters.

'You cried out,' Eremon said, beside the bed. 'Are you in pain?'

She struggled to sit up a little against the wall. Immediately, her head started to pound. Eremon still wore his clothes from the previous night, and he smelled of woodsmoke. Steam drifted up from a boiling pan in the coals, and a half-eaten moon cake lay on the hearthstone.

'What – what did I cry out?'

He sat down gently on the end of the bed, his face still in shadow. 'Something about the men of the Eagle, and a cauldron, and a sword. You said "Turn to me".'

She winced, and immediately he got up and went to the fire to pour her nettle tea. She didn't know that he'd ever noticed what she drank in the morning; perhaps Eithne laid it out the night before. She could just see the girl, bundled up in her blankets on her bed.

Eremon followed her eyes. 'She's exhausted,' he whispered, handing her the tea. 'I think they must have all seen the dawn in – Caitlin has not even returned. Yet your little Eithne has more fire than I would have given her credit for. I practically had to tie her down to stop her fussing over you.' He gave a tired smile.

She cradled the cup, drawing comfort from its warmth. 'You stayed here all night? But then you missed the celebrations!'

'Like you, I had done enough celebrating.' He shrugged.

'Besides, it's not often that I get to sit all alone for hours with my thoughts before a nice fire. That was a rare treat, I can assure you.'

She could understand that. He was always surrounded by people.

He scratched the stubble on his chin. 'Now, what was all this crying about? The men of the Eagle – a dream about Romans?'

She glanced down into her tea. 'It is nothing.'

'No.' He was gazing at her sombrely. 'After seeing – no, *feeling* – what you did last night, then it is far from "nothing". You have a gift, I see that now. If this gift will aid us in our fight, then we must use it.'

She did not speak.

'Rhiann. I respect that gift. I will never laugh at it, or dismiss it, I promise.'

She sighed. How could she tell him? She herself did not really know what it all meant. Except that in her hidden heart, she had always wanted the man in her dream to be one person . . . Drust.

Maybe she could just tell Eremon some of it. So she did. But when she came to the part about the sword-wielder, she left out the bond between she and him – the recognition of souls. Eremon would never understand that. Besides, she did not want him inserting himself into her dreams when that place would be filled by another, she hoped, one day.

Eremon listened to her carefully, his head down. And when she finished, he did not say anything for a long time. Then he asked: 'You are sure that these people you defended were all the people of Alba? All of them?'

'Yes.' The speaking made her head pound, and she massaged her temple.

'I must go, and think on this.' Eremon rose, his eyes far away. But his mouth was tense with that excitement she'd seen when they attacked the Roman raiding party. He strode swiftly to the door to get his cloak.

'Eremon, thank you for looking after me . . .' she called, but he barely acknowledged her before lifting the door cover.

Well! She stared after him, hoping that he did not think her foolish. But he had promised not to.

Now her head was throbbing from thinking, so she put the cup down beside the bed and snuggled back into the warm hollow.

She stayed in her house that day, doing as little as possible. It was a heavy, wet afternoon that matched her body's lethargy. Eithne was quiet as well, and could do little but grind barley. But the grating of the quern hurt both of their heads, so instead they sat and spun wool listlessly as the rain drummed on the thatch.

Rhiann's head was still tender the day after. But leaf-bud was the time of fevers, and there was no rest for a healer.

The call soon came to attend the chief's daughter at the Dun of the Cliff, for she was with child again, and suffering from chills and sweats. Rhiann and Eithne saddled their horses – Eithne on the pony that Rhiann had given her for her nameday – and in grey mist and rain they crossed the marsh and climbed the valley to the Dun of the Cliff, perched high on its rocks watching the sea pass.

The chief's daughter turned out to be suffering more from marital irritation than fever. After dosing her with tansy, treating her child's boils and lice, and listening to a long and wearisome tale about how the woman's husband had taken up with her cousin in the next dun, Rhiann patted her hand and got up to leave.

When she and Eithne emerged from the chief's house, the heavy cloud had broken up, and sunshine and showers were chasing themselves in from the west. The dun looked out over the wide blue expanse of the sound towards the Isle of Deer, and the whole sweep of island, loch, and sea was spread out like an embroidered blanket below, clear of the morning's mist.

Faintly, the sound of hoofbeats came on the wind: a fast

horseman was climbing the southern road to the dun. Soon the thudding grew louder, and they turned. It was Eremon on Dòrn, Cù loping by his side.

'So you are here.' He swung himself down awkwardly, kneading his arm.

Rhiann took in his rain-wet cloak and muddy boots. 'You shouldn't be galloping like that until the wound has knitted. What's wrong? Is someone sick?'

'Nothing's wrong. I've come for your advice.' That was Eremon, never one to waste time on courtesies unless he had to.

'You raced all the way here for my *advice*?'

He flicked wet hair out of his eyes. They were glittering green, reflecting the sun on the sea. 'I couldn't wait. I was passing the shrine, when Declan sought me out. It appears that he left the Beltaine celebrations to meditate there all night with the seeing bowl ... and was sent the most extraordinary vision. You must tell me what it means!'

Now Rhiann recognized the glitter in his eyes. She glanced at Eithne. 'There is a patch of lovage just down there, do you see it? Go and gather some new leaves to take home.'

Eithne nodded, and with a swift look at Eremon, untied a pack from her saddle and took it off to the cliff edge.

'Now,' Rhiann folded her arms, 'tell me what druid words could have made you ride all this way!'

Eremon turned his sea-eyes on her. 'He saw a god holding a torc of Erin gold; a god with a boar's crest. It was about *me*, I know it! But then the god shifted and became the lord Manannán. Declan says he knows him well!'

'Manannán?'

'Yes.' He flicked the ends of the reins across his palm. 'He is the patron god of Erin, too. But there was a goddess there, as well – his wife. You call her Rhiannon; you were named after her. She is patron of *your* people.'

'Yes.' It came out as a whisper.

'Declan saw people, thousands of people, covering the land. Then he heard Manannán say: "My son, brother of my

341

sons. Will you give your sword to Me?" And Rhiannon rose, and she said: "My son, brother of my daughters. Will you wield your sword for Me?"'

Rhiann's breath came short, for the tale was heavy with the power of true vision. She felt the air around her crackle with it. 'And then?'

'And then . . . he woke, and knew no more.' Eremon's eyes were alight. 'But, Rhiann! The god of my people, and the goddess of yours! Asking for my sword to protect all of the brothers and sisters. You see, don't you? After your dream, it all makes sense!'

Rhiann bit her lip, watching him. His face glowed with power, and the sun blazed on the copper threads in his dark hair. He looked more than a prince. He looked, undeniably, like a king. A king who could inspire a following.

She knew what was alive in his face; knew it in the depth of her bones. Just across the strait, the Eye of Manannàn swirled, sucking in any boat that came near – and that was how this vision felt to her spirit senses. The fabric of Thisworld was being pulled into a maelstrom, and nothing was going to be the same again.

'Your dream and this vision, they mean the same thing, you know it.' He was earnest, staring deep into her. 'I am meant to bring together the people to defend Alba against this Roman.' He paused. 'All the people of this land. All the people of Alba as *one*.'

'Yes.' She breathed the word in surrender. She had held the cauldron in her dream, so she knew what it meant. She had tasted the power; it had sung in *her* blood. And, as if awoken, it surged through her now, just as she remembered it.

'I knew you would see it!' He clapped Dòrn's neck, and the stallion whinnied. 'So I have spent the day thinking it out. Is there one king above all others in Alba? Someone who is the most powerful, who holds the most land and warriors?'

She felt the blood drain from her face. 'Yes,' she whispered.

'And his name? Where is he?'

She tried to speak, but her mouth had gone dry. 'Calgacus,'

she managed. 'His name means the Sword – he is a great fighter. His dun is on the great north-east bay of Alba.'

'And how long will it take to send a message to him, and receive a reply?'

She licked her lips. 'The Great Glen is the quickest passage, for it splits Alba in two, and is the only way to cross the mountains to the east coast. A chain of lochs lies at its base, so a man can travel by boat and horse, and be there and back in around fifteen days.'

'Good.' Not noticing her disquiet, Eremon pulled himself into the saddle with his good arm. 'Then, my lady, I will send my message with Aedan as soon as I can. And then I must be ready to pay a visit to this Calgacus. For a council of war!' He yanked the reins and wheeled, whistling for Cù, and the hooves churned the mud as he raced away, until the sound was lost in the cry of the gulls.

Shaking, Rhiann leaned back on Liath's steady flank.

Calgacus *was* the strongest king of Alba . . . and father of a man she had not seen for seven years – Drust, the tattoo artist, the dreamer.

Drust, whose long, fine fingers had smoothed her skin, and awakened the fires that burned long before a raider ever laid his hands on her. Fires that were now cold ash.

And then she began to tremble, as the pattern of the Goddess was made clear. Wearing Rhiannon's face, She had come to place Eremon's feet on his chosen path. Yet in doing so, She would reunite Rhiann with Drust – for Rhiann had no intention of being left behind when Eremon went north.

Is Drust the man in my dream, Mother? Is that why you take me there? Am I worthy of him?

Somehow, perhaps she and Drust were wrapped in Eremon's fate, for it was plain to her now that the Erin prince must play a vital role in delivering Alba, not just saving the Epidii. Of course, Eremon was not in *her* dream, but it would take all of their efforts to accomplish such a task, and perhaps her own vision only showed the part that involved those close to her.

As she and Eithne crossed the marshes below Dunadd in the lengthening shadows, she told herself again that the man in the dream must indeed be Drust. He was the only man she had ever touched; the only one to be gentle and refined and noble. The only one to open the door to her desires. But she was not the girl Drust first met. Would he still feel for her, still want her?

Despite her fears, like the sun glimpsed through cloud, she suddenly sensed an echo of that desire: how it felt when her blood flowed hot and free, before the darkness came to twist and deform it.

Could a miracle happen? Could Drust awaken that in her again?

CHAPTER 44

Eremon chafed at having to seek the council's approval once more, but the power of Declan's vision turned many minds towards him, and Eremon's fine words easily inflamed those who were undecided. And the success of his raid still carried him high in the hearts of the Epidii warriors, who trained with ever greater fervour on the river plain.

The raid had lit a fire in them that could not be put out now, and they fought and yelled, tussled and cursed, and ached to confront the Romans once more.

'And this visit I pay is one step towards that glorious day,' Eremon told them, from his customary perch on the chariot pole. 'For with an alliance of all Alba's tribes, we can beat them back to Britannia!'

It took most of another two days for Aedan's pride at being chosen as messenger to conquer his fears of the northern tribes, but eventually, trembling and stiff in a new tunic and cloak, he was despatched with gifts, ten warriors, and his harp. Eremon knew that, despite his youth, Aedan would speak to Calgacus with words of beauty – and he wanted this king to know he was a prince, not some cattle-raider seeking blood-lust.

After that, Eremon wasted no time, and was everywhere at once, from dawn to dusk, training men, visiting the nobles, and strengthening the territorial defences, especially to the east. Scouts were continually going to and from the King's Hall, as he briefed them about where he wanted watching posts, and how many, and who the scouts would report to in his absence.

Again, Eremon was leaving Finan in charge, although the old warrior did grumble this time, for the glory of Calgacus's dun was being talked about among the men. But he knew his duty, and the Epidii elders respected him now that he'd bonded with them over many ale-soaked tales.

Eremon took Rhiann's news that she was going with him with no flicker of resistance, merely grunting, 'Good,' before turning away to speak to one of his scouts.

So she and Eithne collected blankets and hide tents, and baked hard bread that would not spoil. Caitlin was under their feet all the time near the fire, steaming ash rods for a new set of arrows, and boiling glue for fletching – until Rhiann put her foot down over the pungent smell of birch tar, and Caitlin was removed to the King's Hall.

Then Rhiann rode to see Linnet. 'You will remember that Tiernan's wife birthed her other babies early, won't you, aunt? And that Neesa's second son has twisted legs: they need massaging with this salve every day.'

'I remember it all, child.' Linnet was feeding her goats, and she put down the bucket of slops, her eyes twinkling. 'I have been doing this a long time, you know.'

'Forgive me!' Rhiann shook her head, and scraped some of the mud from her boots against Linnet's fence. 'I feel as if my head is stuffed with hazelnuts, all rattling around!'

Linnet wiped her hands on her skirt. 'Don't worry, I will look after everything for you. It is too great a chance to miss. The great Calgacus came here as a young prince, long ago – we thought he would offer for your mother. But then he became king of his own people, and could not be tied to us.' She sighed. 'His totem is the eagle, and he has the look of that bird, very fine.'

'Why, aunt, you sound like a blushing girl! I'm interested in his mind, not his face.'

Linnet laughed, and came to lean on the fence. 'He has a

fine mind, too. He will see what both you and Eremon see, Rhiann. He will see the sense of unity among our people.'

'I hope so. The tribes have never joined before. But then, we have not faced this kind of threat before. Together, we will be stronger.'

'Yes, but whether the warriors will see that, who knows? Women are better at discerning the patterns, for we are the weavers.'

Rhiann sighed. 'I will do what I can, anyway, for the dreams tell me that I must.' She frowned. 'You will not mind moving down to Dunadd, will you, aunt? I know I ask a lot of you . . .'

'Of course not – especially since I won't have to share the dun with Gelert.'

'Why? Where is he going?'

Linnet's eyebrows rose. 'Don't you know? Dercca's sister told her that he is going with you.'

When Rhiann reported this to Eremon, he only shrugged. 'Yes, I know. He said that he needs to speak with the northern druids on our behalf. And it would look better for us; the war leader is supposed to have the full support of the chief druid. So long as he keeps out of my way, I don't care. He can't do us any harm.'

Privately, Rhiann thought that Gelert was anything but harmless. She had noticed, of late, that he was acting strangely. But he had stopped looking at her belly, and instead would hunch over into himself when he saw her. Perhaps, at last, he had turned his mind to other things.

Seventeen days after leaving, with the tension of waiting running high, Aedan returned, travel-worn, but with a new firmness in his face. 'He received me,' he announced to Eremon in the King's Hall.

'Well, and then what?' Eremon demanded.

'I gave him your message in your exact words . . . and a few of my own, of course.' Aedan blushed, then drew himself up with great self-importance, throwing his mud-flecked cloak over his shoulder. 'And this is his answer: Calgacus, son of

Lierna, the Sword, King of the Caledonii, the Bronze Eagle, sends his greetings to Eremon, son of Ferdiad, prince of Dalriada, war leader of the Epidii, consort of the Ban Cré.'

Eremon raised one eyebrow.

'Greetings, sword-brother,' Aedan went on. 'I would be honoured to entertain the slayer of Romans and destroyer of forts at the Dun of the Waves. We have matters of mutual interest to discuss. Come in one moon, and celebrate the longest day with us.' Aedan's stance relaxed. 'That is all, lord. He fed and watered us well, and gave us fresh horses, and bid me seek you out with all speed.'

Eremon was smiling now. 'So!' he cried to his men. 'We leave in two weeks!'

The hushed murmur of the river carried clearly through the night air. Inside the storehouse, the smell of new-turned wood mingled with the sharp scent of dyed wool. A shaft of moonlight caught the gleam of gold and bronze.

But Gelert had not come here to gloat over the Epidii riches. In the dark, his lip curled. Such worldly wealth meant little to him; it was nothing compared to the power of the spirit – or the power over men's hearts, which made them do what you wished; made them turn to you in all things. That was what he wanted, and the brute strength of a warrior, the gilded words of a *prince*, were not going to stand in the way. He, Gelert, would command this world just as he commanded the Otherworld. And if one vessel had proved faulty, it was time to seek another.

Now he heard the jingle of a horse bridle, and glided, wraith-like, to the doorway. Under the old oak by the river, a dark shape moved. There was the soft thud of feet landing on moss, and then the shape slipped into the shadows of the storehouse walls.

'You came then,' Gelert murmured.

The man jerked, for the druid had been still. 'I have no wish to labour under the son of Erin's yoke.' He pitched his voice low, but he could not hide the bitter tone. Gelert smiled to himself.

'Lord Druid, as you ordered, my men are hidden in the hazel wood outside Crìanan. What do you want from me?'

'I need a man of courage, to act as my messenger, my herald.' Gelert paused. 'To go to Erin.'

The hiss of breath was like a sword unsheathed. 'Erin?'

'The prince is not all he seems; I need to know his true position. The knowledge will give us power. Power over him.'

The shadow leaned forward eagerly. 'And you need me to gain this power?'

Gelert smirked. They were so easy to manipulate, these swordsmen! But then, next time, he wanted a king who truly was a brute with a sword. He would not make the same mistake again.

'It is a delicate – and possibly dangerous – mission. I need a man with the stoutest of hearts, and the most silver of tongues. A man who has no love for the prince of Erin.'

'Then you have found your man. I can stay here no longer and watch our people turn to the foreigner – my bile curdles day by day. Charge me with this, and I will not disappoint you!'

Gelert drew out the moment, then said, 'So be it.'

The man's shoulders relaxed. 'What are your orders?'

'There is a boat waiting below the Dun of the Spears. The boatman knows the sea-lanes. Land in the northernmost part of Erin, and seek out news of the prince's kin. But do not put yourselves in danger. If all is as he says, then present this to his father's druid.' He handed the man a short stave of ash, on which he had carved the sacred druid symbols. The man took it and tucked it carefully into his belt.

'And if it is not?'

'Then keep your heads down, and use the gifts I have left in the boat to buy as much news as you can. When you return, make all speed to join us at the dun of Calgacus the Sword. Tell no one you are leaving, and speak to no one when you return. Unless you die . . .' he lingered over the word, 'I want the message from your own lips – or I will call down the curses of all the gods on your family. Do you understand?'

The man's breathing came fast and harsh. 'Yes.' He bowed his head, returned to his horse and levered himself into the saddle. 'I will bring you what you seek.'

Gelert folded his hands in his robe, satisfied. Now he knew he had judged this man well.

As the rider left the shadow of the great oak and started down the Trade Path, the moon swam out from behind a cloud, bleaching his hair to a cascade of silver.

Rhiann decided she could not risk taking Didius on the journey, for fear of what the Caledonii would do with a Roman in their midst. The only time she had seen him smile was when he was learning something new, so she brought him to Bran's house.

The smith, a towering man with brawny shoulders, looked down at the Roman. 'You wish me to guard him for you?'

Rhiann smiled and shook her head. 'I wish you to take him as your guest. He works with his hands and his mind – you may use them both.'

Under his brows, singed by the forge to stubble, Bran's blue eyes were speculative. 'A Roman as an apprentice?' His large, blistered hand, with ash-rimed nails, landed on Didius's shoulder and ground the bones together. 'He doesn't have much muscle. How useful will he be?'

Didius flinched, but held his gaze bravely. 'I can show you how to make water flow uphill.' His accent covered the musical language of Alba in a heavy coating of harsher sounds, but he was understandable. Eithne had done well. 'I can show you how to drain waste from your house.'

Bran's eyebrows rose, then he smiled. 'Perhaps you will be useful, then, Roman. But I am charged by the Ban Cré for your safety. Do not shame me by trying to escape.'

'I will not,' Didius replied, but he was looking at Rhiann.

'Do you need me to go over anything again?' Eremon stood by Dòrn beneath Dunadd's gate tower.

Finan shook his head. 'No, my prince. It is all perfectly clear.'

'And the scouts are all along the mountains to south and east?'

'Yes, they're in place.'

Eremon scanned the party around him with a practised eye. Rhiann was checking her pack once more with Eithne, as Aedan deferentially held her bridle, his harp cradled in one arm. The bard had regained his strength after his recent journey, and although he'd balked at returning the same way so soon, he declared that he had no intention of missing the meeting between two great men.

Caitlin and Rori, both mounted up, were scrutinizing one of Caitlin's new arrows. Fergus and Angus chuckled together as they took leave of three maidens who wept and held on to their bridles.

There was a detachment of Epidii warriors, and an equal one of Eremon's own men – ten of each. Just behind him, Conaire sat easily in his saddle, and from his spear swung their new standards: a bristled boar crest on its strip of leather, and the plaited tail-hair of a mare.

In the shadows beneath the tower, Gelert and two other druids sat atop grey horses. Druids almost always walked on such journeys, but Eremon had asked Gelert to ride so they could reach Calgacus quickly. Surprisingly, Gelert agreed, his yellow eyes glinting with some emotion that Eremon had neither the time nor inclination to decipher. The druid would be under Eremon's own gaze from now on, anyway. He would have no chance to make mischief.

But just as Eremon swung himself into the saddle, some instinct made him check. He looked out at the crowd who had gathered for their farewell, shading his eyes. 'And watch that young buck Lorn,' he murmured down at Finan. 'Where is he, anyway? I saw him at Dunadd only two days ago . . . I thought he'd be here cheering, happy to see the back of me!'

Finan also scanned the crowd. 'I haven't seen him. Perhaps he's gone to lick his wounds at home.'

'Well, watch him all the same. He is a problem I have not yet laid to rest.' He touched Finan's shoulder. 'Farewell, old friend. Look for us in one moon.'

Finan stood back as Eremon nodded at Conaire, and the standard swung through the clear air, the polished spear-tip flashing.

The crowd let out a great cheer, as the horses moved through the gate into the sunshine beyond.

CHAPTER 45

sunseason, AD 80

After the steep-sided lochs and wild crags of the Great Glen, the Caledonii lands flowed over the eastern plain like the soft folds of a cloak: fertile, heavy with furrows, the barley high and ripening to gold. The homesteads were so numerous that the smoke from their fires hazed the air with blue mist.

Calgacus had inherited his kingship through his mother, a Ban Cré. She died before Rhiann was born, but her name was known and greatly respected, still, by the sisterhood. A powerful priestess had given birth to a powerful king. It was as it should be.

Unfortunately, their arrival was heralded by a sudden rainstorm that swept down from the western heights in drifting sheets. They pulled up their hoods and hunched over their horses, and were so absorbed in shielding their faces from the rain that they nearly ran into a great stone, which reared up out of the drizzle beside the track.

Rhiann and Eremon, at the front, halted their horses. Scored into the granite was a carving, the height of a man. It was an enormous eagle: its noble head to the west, its eye bold, its beak sharp. But that was not all. The lines of the carving had been filled with molten bronze, and the curves of the great bird's wings and talons shone through the grey rain, glowing with power.

Conaire, coming up behind, let out a soft whistle.

'Calgacus's totem is the eagle, is it not?' Eremon asked.

Rhiann nodded, staring at the carving.

'Then this king must have some fine artists. I have never seen such quality.'

Rhiann's mouth had gone dry, and she swallowed with difficulty. Something rapped, faintly, far at the back of her memory. This carving bore a recognizable stamp.

'Calgacus the Sword is rich, and powerful.' They were the first words Gelert had spoken for the entire journey, stooped over his grey pony, face shadowed in his hood. 'He is no man to treat lightly. You may find you've met your match at last, prince.'

Eremon glanced back at Gelert with distaste. 'This I hope, druid. Perhaps then he will understand the necessity of an alliance.'

'Perhaps. But even your gilded tongue may not be enough to persuade this king.'

With a sharp movement, Eremon nudged his horse on, and Rhiann followed, shielding her view of the stone with her hood, her mind already slipping past Gelert's words.

The carving *was* familiar; there was no doubt. Her hands trembled on the reins.

Soon they reached a sweeping bay, and here Calgacus's stronghold reared up out of the rain, crouched on a headland between a swift river and the sea. From the heights on which it stood, it bellowed out his power and influence over the plain and the port at its feet, clustered with boats.

As Dunadd was impressive to anyone from a small homestead, so the Dun of the Waves was as impressive again. A massive ditch had been delved, shouldered by sweeping banked walls three times the height of a mounted man. The bank was then crowned by a timber palisade and walkway, and lookout towers reared from the breastwork every thirty paces. The oaken gate, the width of four chariots, was flanked by two sturdy gatetowers. Over it all, banners flew, embroidered with the eagle totem, and the posts they hung from were capped with gold so they shone bright in the sun.

Inside was the familiar jumble of squat roundhouses and

ramshackle sheds, but everything seemed larger and noisier and more frenzied than at Dunadd. The air of prosperity was tangible. Wooden walkways kept feet free of the mud. House walls were bright with colour, and hung with banners and trophy skulls. The thatch roofs were new and golden.

Once they dismounted and were ushered up the main pathway, Rhiann could see that many of the house posts were carved in the same beautiful designs as the stone they had seen. Unconsciously, her hand went to her belly. She could almost feel the tattoos on her skin burning through the thin cloth. The same hands that drew the designs on her skin carved the stone, and the doorposts. Drust's stamp was everywhere she looked. But where was he?

Despite being weary from the ride, after they were shown to the guest lodges, Eremon took his men to look at the defences of the dun in the fading light. When he and Caitlin returned to Rhiann at their lodge to get ready for the welcoming feast, the room was soft with the light of rush lamps and torches.

As Eithne took their cloaks to dry by the fire, and began to cluck at Caitlin about the state of her hair, Eremon reached the screen that hid the main sleeping alcove from the rest of the room. There, he stopped.

Rhiann was sitting on the fur-covered bed holding her mirror before her. In place of wet clothes and bedraggled braids, she wore a gown of green wool edged with yellow flowers, and her hair was piled high in intricate whorls, and gilded with jewelled pins. The gold drew the firelight to her royal torc, clasping her slender neck, and the great brooch of the Epidii glittered on her priestess cloak.

He had never seen her shining so brightly, and to his immense surprise, his body responded. For a moment, he found himself wishing that things were different between them, that he could walk up to her now and take her hand, and see her eyes alight on him with desire. And later, to bury his hands in that glorious hair and tumble it down around his face in the dark, as she called his name . . .

'We must look our best.' Her voice broke in upon his thoughts, as she gestured down at herself, laying the mirror on the bed. 'They must respect me as a Ban Cré, and then they will respect you.'

A flash of anger instantly extinguished Eremon's desire. *I can gain my own respect!*

'I laid out your clothes.' Rhiann waved at the other side of the bed. 'I picked your blue tunic.'

As he changed, he watched out of the corner of his eye as she applied a stain to her lips from a small vial. Her hands were shaking.

And this was all to impress a gathering of old men?

There was a rap on the doorpost, and Conaire and the other men piled in. When Caitlin rose from Eithne's braiding, Rhiann drew a leaf-green cloak over the girl's borrowed dress and declared that she would make the Epidii proud. At that, Caitlin pulled a face and stuck out her tongue at Conaire, who laughed.

But Eremon saw the way his foster-brother's eyes followed Caitlin's shiny, plaited head as they left the house, and he sighed. At least Conaire had some chance of seeing his look returned.

The massive carved timber doors of Calgacus's house swung open to reveal an immense room, clustered with benches, its roof soaring to the apex, far above.

'This king has some fine craftsmen,' Eremon observed again to Rhiann, as they waited in line to be greeted with the other nobles. He was admiring the carvings on the inner posts that held up the upper gallery. Rhiann followed his eyes, and then looked away quickly, a flush staining her cheeks.

What *was* the matter with her?

Eremon's attention was claimed by a tall man before the central fire, crowned only with a mane of hair the exact shade of the great eagle's plumage. His face, too, bore the noble stamp of that bird, with a strong, hooked nose, and far-seeing golden eyes beneath straight, fair brows. Eremon noted with approval that the King's body was well muscled and upright. Though there were furrows beside his eyes, and grey at his temples, he had obviously kept to his warrior life, and not given in to the softness of age.

'The Lady Rhiann, Ban Cré of the Epidii, and Eremon mac Ferdiad of Dalriada of Erin,' a steward announced to the room, and ushered them forward to his lord.

Eremon glanced at Rhiann. She was smiling politely at Calgacus, but her eyes were darting around the room, as if she were looking for someone.

Calgacus gave her the kiss of greeting on both cheeks. 'I remember your mother,' he said. 'She was a great beauty. And you are her image, my lady.'

'Thank you,' Rhiann replied, bowing her head. 'So I have been told. It is an honour to meet you, my lord. I understand your mother was also a woman of great ability. The Sisters still speak of her.'

Calgacus smiled and turned to Eremon, looking at him with a speculation that was not unkind. 'You interest me very much, man of Erin: why you are here, and why you wish to fight with us. I look forward to speaking with you about these things.'

'As do I, my lord,' Eremon answered. 'We have much to say to one another.' He returned that long, appraising look, green eyes holding gold. And he suddenly realized that no matter how things went, he would value this man as an enemy or friend alike. He knew, in the instant leap of energy between them, that their fates were somehow bound together.

Then Calgacus smiled, seeming to come to the same conclusion. 'Relax tonight, but tomorrow I will send for you. I am still waiting for my nobles to come in from their duns, so we cannot meet in council for a few more days. But I would like to hear your news myself first.'

Eremon bowed his head, before they were led to one of the benches around the walls and seated.

Though he was soon deep in conversation with the warrior to one side, Eremon remained conscious of Rhiann beside him. Her beauty, which shone this night as on no other, had left him with an awareness of her every gesture. He even caught her honeyed scent when he moved his head to take a draught of ale.

So he noticed when she suddenly tensed, and without breaking off his conversation, he followed her gaze. A young man had entered the house, and was standing with Calgacus in the centre of the room. He was close to the King's height, and their faces shadowed each other, though his hair was darker. He moved his hands expressively as he spoke, head held high and bright eyes restlessly scanning the room. His clothes were very fine, finer even than those of Calgacus himself, and coloured with a multitude of hues. Jewellery glittered and shone from every limb, setting off the gold lights in his hair.

Eremon glanced again at Rhiann. Her face had drained of colour, and she had a look in her eyes that he had never seen before. Fear, and something else. Suppressed excitement . . . tension. No, it could not be what he thought it was. Not desire!

His stomach turned. Before he could stop himself, he leaned into her ear and said, 'Who is that man?'

She jumped, drawing away. 'That is Drust, the son of Calgacus.' She reached for her cup of mead.

Eremon's companion stopped talking when it was clear that Eremon was paying him no attention, and turned to the man on his other side, insulted. Eremon knew he should get back to his discussion . . . but the words leaped out of his mouth nonetheless. 'And you know this man?'

Rhiann took a sip of mead, and spoke reluctantly, it seemed. 'Yes.'

'I thought you had never been here.'

'He came to the Sacred Isle when I was young.' She turned her head, and the tiny gold balls on a jewelled hairclip rang softly. 'Remember our lineage laws, Eremon. You should concentrate your diplomatic efforts on Calgacus's heirs – his sisters' sons. That man means nothing to you.'

Not to him perhaps, but Eremon remembered Rhiann's fingers dabbing the berry stain on to her mouth. He fought the desire to question her more, and she turned away.

She did not seem to be looking at the golden man any more.

CHAPTER 46

Once hunger had been sated, but before heads were too dulled with ale, Calgacus rose from his bench to retire. 'Tomorrow I will begin to consider the issues of this council,' he announced. 'We will need clear heads to share our ideas.'

'Or our misgivings,' the warrior next to Rhiann muttered.

With a sinking heart, she realized how hard it would be for the warrior-nobles to come to some agreement. The ability to act with one will was not bred into them as into the peoples of the Middle Sea: the Romans, and before them, the Greeks.

But that was even more reason why they could not fall under the Roman yoke! Her people would wither and die, like caged hawks. And the land would die, too. With no one to sing to it, to guard the gates to the Otherworld, to commune with the sacred spirits of tree and spring, the land would become a barren place, bereft of its soul. The Mother would be ground under heavy Roman tread, and the air would stink of temple fires to Roman gods. Sightless statues would stare out across the mountains.

She could not allow that!

She looked up. Eremon was standing before her, offering his arm so that she could rise. Once on her feet, a lightness in her head told her that nerves had made her drink more than usual, and when she stumbled, Eremon looked at her keenly.

She wished he would stop paying her so much attention! But she knew why – he had seen her looking at Drust. Men, even when they did not care for a woman, were as jealous as fighting stags.

As if saying his name in her mind drew her, she found herself gazing at Calgacus's son. What a fine man he had grown into! He was at the centre of a crowd, and she watched covertly, as he threw back his head to laugh, exposing the tendons in his throat. His teeth were white, and his eyes flashed as he held the circle around him in thrall. A few steps more, and she was close enough to hear the laugh, as it rang out over the heads of the people around him, cleaving the bustle of talk. That laugh rooted Rhiann to the spot.

In a whirl the years seemed to fall away, and the one fragile place within her that held memories of passion, of burning touches in the night and stolen kisses, leaped into flame. Her breathing quickened, and hidden behind Eremon in the crowd, her hand pressed her belly once more, as if she could feel the tattoo designs taking shape there all over again.

She had edged closer to Drust in the press of bodies, and from the corner of an eye she watched as he sketched a story in the air for his audience. He had fine, graceful hands, with no sword calluses, only the honest grit of stone-dust beneath his nails, the thickening of skin on fingers that held a chisel, an awl. This man created; he did not kill or maim.

Suddenly, Eremon turned to introduce her to someone, and she struggled to regain her poise. But even with her back turned, she could still feel the golden heat emanating from Drust.

Soon she would speak to him. Somewhere quiet, so she could see if he remembered her. Surely he remembered her!

Later that night she lay beside Eremon in the narrow bed. His broad back was towards her, as it always was, and in the last light of the fire, she could see its darker shadow against the plastered wall.

For once she felt, acutely, the great gulf that lay in that single hand-breadth between them.

It must be the memories of Drust that had given her this new awareness. She could just feel the heat coming from

Eremon's body, but it did not draw her closer as had happened with Drust all that time ago.

Seven years ago . . .

Those memories were all of heat and flame, whereas with Eremon there had only ever been the chill of fallow land; the coldness of rain. She turned over to her belly, restless.

Something happened as she stood in Calgacus's hall that night. A door she had thought closed burst open; feelings she had thought destroyed by the raid now lanced her anew. Yet, how could she feel any of this after those men? Was that part of her not dead and buried now?

She turned over again, trying not to wake Eremon.

Ever since the day on the beach with Linnet, everything had changed. The tears had washed something away; or woken it. The wound between her and Linnet was healing. The dream of glory had revealed its purpose, with its promise that she would regain her access to the Source, and take up a role to save her people. And Caitlin . . . Caitlin drew her into life, with her laughter. All these things had given her hope.

So perhaps other things were melting too, now, like the leaf-bud flood, when streams were released from the ice peaks to cascade down the mountains. The thought was immensely frightening, for once started, where would it stop? She glanced at Eremon's sleeping back. Floods destroyed things, too.

She put a hand behind her head. The day she rode Liath back from Eithne's house after the birth, she had reached out her hand, longing to be drawn into the Otherworld. Longing for something else. Well, the Goddess had heeded her call, although not in the way that Rhiann had foreseen. She yearned for change, and it had been forced upon her, with this marriage, with Caitlin, and now, with meeting Drust once more.

You have two choices, her practical voice asserted. *You can blind yourself to it, and retreat again. Or you can let the flood take you. What will it be?* The throb of excitement in her belly

362

beckoned. It pulled her, called to her. She closed her eyes, and just slipped into the stream, to see how it felt.

And as she did, every limb was enveloped by the memory of a time before pain ever stalked her. Seven years ago . . . Goddess! How innocent that girl with Drust seemed! The memories were of touch and smell as much as sight . . .

Drust when she first saw him, his hands drawing tales in the air . . .

His hot breath on her fingers, when he kissed her hand in greeting. . .

And later . . .

. . . there had been warmth all around, and firelight gilding her skin. She lay naked on a bed, sheened with sweat. Drust's face glowed above her, his eyes closed, his hands poised.

She looked up at him, her body quivering, almost straining towards those hands. She could feel the heat from his palms, burning a trail from her neck over her breasts. But he did not touch her, did not part the sweet folds between her thighs to find her core, that lay, throbbing, aching for his fingers.

A tide of longing rushed over her as her eyes devoured the fine lines of his face, the long eyelashes. And then to his hands, with their long fingers, stained with the dye of the woad. They looked so soft. If only she could feel how soft they were . . .

She squirmed, and he opened his eyes and smiled at her. 'Ah, my beauty.' His voice was velvet, like the tines of the stags in leaf-fall. 'What art I can create, with you as my inspiration.'

She smiled. No man had ever spoken to her this way. No one had ever looked at her this way. Men in the dun were rough and red-faced, with gravelled voices. But this man was soft and refined and clever and beautiful.

And then, bliss, as he touched his finger to the hollow at the base of her throat. She closed her eyes and listened to his voice, as he glided his finger in spirals and whorls, down over her breasts and slowly around each nipple, then over the ridges of her ribs and on to the swell of her belly.

He traced the design he would create with a finger, telling her of the sinuous curves of the river that ran through the heart of her homeland, and how those same lines would run on her body. In delicate strokes he drew the deer of her islands and mountains, and then, right on the greatest curve of her belly, the horse. For the Epidii. He traced the lines that joined the places of power, where the Old Ones built their stone gates, and the springs marked doorways to the Other-world, and finally, the sacred symbol that showed the male and female halves of the Source; two spears guarding a crescent moon. All of them would mark her, brand her, tie her to the land, channel its power into her body so that she could be Ban Cré, the Mother of the Land . . .

The tattoos took ten nights.

Ten nights of lying there motionless under Drust's softly moving hands, of sharp pinpricks from the bone needle, pinpricks that rode the unbearable line between pleasure and pain so that he often had to lay down the needle and hold her until the shivering ceased.

For a week her world shrunk to tiny, focused senses: the glow of firelit walls, the butterfly touches of his hands, the forest smell of the woad steeping in pots on the fire. There was no sound except their breathing. No feeling except the needle, and the brushing fingers.

And then, on the last night, he laid down the needle. The skin on the front of her body was tender and swollen, but she hardly felt it. All she knew was his eyes.

He kissed her then, over and over, murmuring words of love, words of beauty, words of desire. He was glorious . . .

Rhiann lay next to Eremon's cold back and stared at the roof.

After the tattooing, Drust left the island. He did not return for her, but she had been so young, and soon she became ever more drawn into her priestess training. She did not forget the nights of flame and soft fingers, but gradually, the memory receded until it was like a pleasant dream.

At times she caught herself thinking of him, and when she did, the deep knowledge came that one day they would meet again, when she was older. And then, perhaps, she would ask for him to be her husband. In the dark, now, her mouth curved with its customary bitterness. Many things had intervened in *that* plan.

But then she thought of her golden dream, and the face of the beloved, always hidden. And she asked herself the question she had asked a hundred times and more. Could Drust be the man in the dream? No man had ever awakened such feelings, so it must be him.

And if he had done it once, then perhaps Drust could awaken her a second time! Perhaps he could bring those feelings back, so that she felt innocent and untouched again. Perhaps he could sweep away the stink of the raiders' coarse hands, the searing pain of them invading her body.

A shudder went through her. As much as the fire, the desire, beckoned, she was afraid to find out. She didn't want to open up to anyone ever again.

For what if she did, and inside she was just cold: cold ashes in a dead fire? What if she was unable to rouse or satisfy a man?

What if she was not a real woman at all, and he found out?

CHAPTER 47

The next day, Eremon received an invitation from Calgacus to ride out with him to his coastal defences. Eremon thought they would speak alone, and instructed Conaire and his men to join a hunting party, but to his disappointment, he and the King were accompanied by some of the more glowering of Calgacus's nobles.

The vast inlet that split the eastern coast was shaped like an arrowhead, with the dun right at the point. Offshore, in the head of the arrow, an enormous peninsula formed a narrow strait, guarded on each side by heavily-manned duns that oversaw all sea traffic on its way to the Dun of the Waves.

As they rode around the shore dun, Eremon looked suitably impressed, and asked many questions, which Calgacus's nobles fell over themselves to answer. He could almost see what was going on in their minds. *We are invincible. We don't need you, foreigner. We will fight our own battles.* Yet Calgacus himself said little, and every time Eremon turned his way, he saw those gold-flecked eyes on him; penetrating and far-seeing.

As they left the gate in the dun wall for the curving beach beyond, Calgacus called Eremon up to ride beside him. After a while, the King abruptly said, 'Do you race on beaches in Erin?'

Eremon was surprised. 'Yes, my lord.'

Without warning, the great man flashed Eremon a challenge, and drove his heels into his mount's flanks, a big bay with fire in his eye. The horse sprang forward, and in a heartbeat Eremon had Dòrn beside him, until both stallions were racing neck and neck, their hooves pounding on the wet sand. The wind sang in Eremon's ears, and he nearly laughed.

When they pulled up at the rock headland that blocked the beach, panting, Calgacus's eyes were fiercely bright. He glanced back, to see his more portly nobles trotting sedately along behind. For a moment, they were alone.

The horses shook their heads and snorted, their sides heaving. The sun was hot above this day, a bright glare on the sands, and Eremon massaged his scar, strained by the ride. Rhiann would not be pleased.

'So now I know you have a good seat,' Calgacus remarked. 'Yet there are many other mysteries about you.'

'Yes?'

'You come here to trade, and yet instead you take up arms against the invaders.' The eyes were eagle-sharp now. 'You walk into, and out of a Roman camp. You attack a fort. You seek me out as an ally. Why?'

Eremon's mouth went dry, and he remembered clearly the day he had to defend himself to Gelert. The first day he had to lie. And watching now the directness of the King's gaze, Eremon felt a deep pang of regret that he would have to lie to such a man as this. A man whose respect, he suddenly realized, he desperately wanted.

By the Boar, I wish the day would come where I never had to lie again, he thought bleakly. But Calgacus was waiting, so Eremon took a deep breath. 'It is simple. When I met Agricola, he was looking over the sea to Erin. My land is no safer than yours. I may have come to trade, but I did not count on the Romans. I am only doing what you yourself would do. Will do, I hope.'

Calgacus weighed that up, fingering the eagle talon around his neck. Then he smiled. 'You presume to know my mind! You are a great judge of men, for one so young.'

'I had little chance to be young, my lord.' He had not meant to say *that*.

But Calgacus did not laugh at him. 'When you are marked for the throne, there is little time for boyish games. That is why it is the King's prerogative to have a little fun when he wishes.' The light of the wild ride flickered in his face. 'You should remember that.'

The pang of the lie returned. 'I will do so, my lord.'

Calgacus was measuring again. 'I like you, prince of Erin. You have great strength in your face. You have proven your courage, your foresight. Unlike *them*.' He threw an impatient glance over his shoulder at his nobles. 'They only care for their furs and gold, and their Roman wine and oil. They see Roman coin in one hand, and not the dagger concealed in the other. You, though, I feel, had to fight for your birthright, as did I. There was more than one possible heir to my uncle's throne, and I had to win it with a sword, not with flattery. And I do not intend to lose it through the seduction of wealth, or power.' He patted the sword at his side. 'Here lies power.' Then he laid his hand on his chest. 'And here. I trust only my own heart, and that is how I keep my throne. We speak the same language, do we not?'

Eremon's breath caught. Did this mean that Calgacus would support him? 'We do, lord,' he replied. 'Except that you have someone else to trust, now. For I tell you on my father's honour, that the Romans will come for your lands. Only by standing together can we defeat them.'

'Perhaps. I believe in their danger, as my nobles do not. But I do not think that they will come north.' Calgacus looked over his shoulder again. 'Know also that there are many kings in Alba. And we have never, in living memory, acted together.'

'The world changes,' Eremon said shortly. 'We change too, or we fall to Roman swords like grain to the scythe.'

At that Calgacus smiled. 'Perhaps you should have been a poet, prince. If you use such gilded words with my chieftains, and the other kings, you may get your wish. Do you fight as well as you speak?'

'Yes.'

'Good. A king should be truthful above all. If you can fulfil any boast, then the bards will sing of you for generations.'

Hot sun beat on Rhiann's brow as she left the lodge of the Caledonii Ban Cré, an old aunt of the King. The priestess was bent and lined, with swollen joints, yet her eyes had sparked with vigour as she and Rhiann spoke of the coming celebration for the longest day. The second turning of the year was fast approaching now; the night sky held its grey until morning, and the sun hardly seemed to sink before rising again.

Seeking a breeze, Rhiann crossed the stableyard and there spied the stairs to the upper walkway. But when she came out on top of the palisade, who should be standing before her but Drust.

He was holding court where there was a view of the sea. The group of attendants around him was unremarkable: sons of some of the lesser nobles, and their wives and unmarried daughters.

Drust was explaining something he had seen when visiting his mother's kin in the south. '. . . and the Romans make their symbols on stone, not flesh and wood as we do,' he was saying. 'That is why I carved the eagle stones for my father.'

'What do the Romans carve?' one of the girls asked prettily. She was looking at Drust with intensity, but he seemed oblivious to her. His face was alight with some passion. Rhiann's cheeks grew even warmer.

'Mostly names,' Drust said, dismissively. 'But imagine seeing my designs on stones all over Alba!' He swept his hand out to the horizon. 'They would last for ever! They could be set up at all points of the land, as the Romans do with their milestones, and then everyone would see our power!'

He paused, and Rhiann took the opportunity to speak, as the audience fell into impressed silence. 'My lord Drust.'

Drust swung to face her. 'Lady Rhiann!'

Her belly flipped over. He did remember her!

'I have been hoping to speak with you,' he said.

She was rooted to the spot, speechless. It was not the greeting she had expected. He spoke as if they were friends, and had just seen each other days ago. She sought for something to say, but in one smooth movement he took her arm and turned her away from the others. She noticed the sullen looks from the women left behind. This would not do!

'I have been watching you,' Drust murmured. 'I am glad you sought me out.'

In her sleeveless linen tunic, Drust's touch burned Rhiann's bare skin more than the sun above. Then she remembered who she was, and removed his hand from her arm. 'It is good to see you again, my lord.'

He flashed a look she could not decipher. 'And I you – but I am sure you do not wish to speak with me like this.' He gestured at the little group, all straining to hear what they were saying. 'Can we meet somewhere more private?' His face was tilted down, and now he looked up at her from under his eyelashes; a look her body remembered.

This was ridiculous! He had not spoken to her with the proper degree of respect for either her rank or their unfamiliarity. And she could not arrange some secret assignation; it was beneath her. Yet . . . Goddess . . . she *had* to meet him. She had slipped into the stream, she had already let it take hold of her.

What if someone sees me? She dismissed that thought as soon as it came. She was no Roman woman, forbidden to speak to a man not her husband.

So in a quirk of impulsiveness, before she could back down, she answered: 'Yes. I will meet with you.'

'There is another feast tonight.' He was eager now. 'It is outside the walls, on the plain. Come back inside the dun and go to the eastern stables, after my father has declared the toasts. We will talk there.'

Rhiann wavered. To steal away, and meet him at night! But his eyes were on her mouth, as he said, softly, urgently, 'I must talk with you. Please come.'

And suddenly she was in the hut on the Sacred Isle, with the firelight on the walls and his hands tracing the curved lines over her belly. He had looked at her then with the same urgency. So she found herself nodding, and turned away, her damp hands clenched by her sides. *I will only talk!* she told herself fiercely. *I just want to see the man he has become.*

For how else would she know if he was the one in her dream? She did not stop to think if she wanted him to be. The beloved was here in Thisworld, somewhere. He was here to take her from her loneliness.

To help her to be something great.

The feast was under a pale sky, its swollen moon a bronze shield hung to catch the last light. Beneath the sparks of bonfires, Calgacus toasted his ties with the Epidii. But he did not speak of the Roman threat.

Watching him, Eremon realized that until he, Eremon, spoke before all the Caledonii nobles, Calgacus would not show his hand. After all, what did Eremon mean to him? Calgacus had powerful men to placate: men with kin bonds to hold warriors to them, men who, massed together, could take his throne.

Who was Eremon to him?

And yet, even so, Calgacus kept Eremon close, giving him the best cut of boar and the best ale, and introducing him to all the influential men who had arrived that day. He jested with him, and told him of his lands and his peoples with pride.

Eremon could see that the pride came not from boasting of wealth, but from the King's knowledge that in his twenty-year reign he had built his people into the foremost tribe of Alba, until every soul, from the lowliest cattle herder to the King himself, felt strong and secure and prosperous.

To this, Eremon listened with envy. He realized that, absorbed as he was with losing his father's hall, and the fighting and scheming, he had long ago stopped thinking about what kind of king *he* would be.

Like this one, he thought now, as Calgacus held court before a fire.

Imagine having the peace to build, to forge a people into something united and strong and safe. To wrap power around them all as a man enfolds his children, so they can watch their barley grow fat in the fields, their cattle multiply, and their babies sleeping safe in their beds.

That would be a good life's work. He sighed. His own father had felt it necessary to war incessantly with his neighbours over some slight or another. Even the seeds of Donn's betrayal had been sown between the brothers long before.

Standing there, a prince with no lands, Eremon promised himself fiercely that he would keep fighting, not for his own glory, but so he could give his people of Dalriada a king like Calgacus.

A snatch of Aedan's voice drifted up with the spiralling sparks, and Eremon turned his head to hear better. Nearby, the bard was keeping a sizeable group entertained with his new song about the attack on the Roman fort. Seeing the eyes of the listeners wide and shining in the firelight, Eremon smiled to himself.

Well, perhaps he could bask in a little glory.

Just then he caught sight of Conaire with Caitlin across the crowd, and realized that he had not spoken to Rhiann all evening, or even found out what she did that day. Now, she was just here a moment ago . . .

His eyes scanned the crowd near Calgacus, where he'd last seen her standing. But she was gone. Perhaps she was getting something to eat. He wandered around the fires, peering at every woman that passed, seeing if it was her.

Many women looked back, but none of them were Rhiann.

Something made him glance up to the walls of the dun, then, and he glimpsed a figure disappearing through the gate. From the grace of her walk he knew who it was, and without thinking, he found himself following her.

Soon the men would meet in council, he told himself. He really should see if Rhiann had any other news to add to what he already knew. Women found out all sorts of interesting things from other women . . .

But when he entered the gates, she was not on the torch-lit path up to the guest lodges. Turning around, he just caught sight of her vanishing into the maze of tracks that led towards the worksheds and stables. He knew there were no houses there, because he had toured the walls with Conaire only that morning.

Something in his chest thumped, and his mind began to race.

Why is she going there?

Perhaps she is visiting a friend.

But she has never been here before.

Perhaps she goes to check on Liath.

Liath is in the western stables; I took her there myself.

He realized, belatedly, that he was being ridiculous. So instead of giving in to the urge to pursue her, he forced his steps back out of the gate and down towards the fires on the plain.

But despite his determination to put Rhiann out of his mind, when he got there, he began to look for someone else in the crowd.

And as he suspected, Calgacus's son was nowhere to be seen.

Rhiann made her way down the darkened path to the stables. *I feel like a maid on the way to meet her stableboy!* She shook her head, but beneath the wry smile, her belly churned.

It was all very well to lie and think about this in the night. It was disturbing enough to see Drust in daylight. But this was something else entirely. She could not quite believe she was doing it.

And yet, recklessness, which she rarely felt or ever surrendered to, was thrumming in her blood. She'd seen Eremon with Aiveen and Samana, and caught snippets of Conaire's tales about his conquests. She had not missed Rori making eyes at Eithne, nor was she blind to the growing feelings between Caitlin and Conaire. *Everyone else is doing this, why can't I?*

Despite these brave thoughts, she still half-hoped that Drust was not there. And when she got to the darkened stable and heard only the snuffling of horse breath, she shook with a sigh of relief. So that was that, then.

'Lady.' The voice slid out of the night, and a shape moved within the shadows of the walls.

The blood leaped in her veins. 'Prince, I am not accustomed to meeting men in stables.' She thought she should remind him of who she was.

He laughed softly, a purring sound. 'Would a moonlit walk on the walls suit you better?'

'Yes,' she managed to get out, and he took her arm and led her up to the walkway once more. The moon had now paled from bronze to silver, and the plain below was glowing with fires, like bright coals in a darkened hearth.

Drust turned to her, and the warm breeze ruffled the hair at his brow. Her fingers remembered the exact thickness and weight of that hair, and ached to bury themselves in it again. When he shifted closer, his shoulders caught on the wool of his tunic.

'I noticed you the first night, at the feast,' he was saying.

She dragged her attention to his mouth, trying to listen to his words.

His lips softened. 'You are the most beautiful woman here, by far.'

His words, which she had longed to hear, sounded thinner than she remembered. She hardly heard them. Instead she found herself musing on how that mouth would feel on hers . . .

'I had heard much of your beauty, of course, and longed to see it for myself. I love beautiful things.'

She looked into his eyes, startled. 'But it has only been seven years. Have I changed so much?'

A frown touched his brow, and then it cleared. 'Why, you have only grown in beauty, my lady.'

But Rhiann's heart was sinking. 'You do not remember me.'

She saw him searching for words, but before he could speak the lie, she cut him off. 'You came to the Sacred Isle. We spent a week together.' She wanted to say, *You painted me, you caressed me* . . . But of course, he was a tattoo artist: he painted many girls. And how many did he touch in that way?

Foolish woman! Stung, she turned away, rubbing the pebbled skin on her bare arms.

'Rhiann.' His breath brushed her ear. 'Forgive me. I do remember. It has been a long time.'

When she did not answer, he moved around in front of her, gently taking her arms. 'Rhiann! When I left, you were going to be dedicated to the Goddess. I did not think of you that way because I was leaving, and you were going to be out of reach.'

She searched his eyes, wanting to believe him. Suddenly, he smiled in that boyish way of his, which tugged at her heart just as it had before, and ran his hands down her arms to her fingers, before pulling away. His touch left flame in its wake. 'What does it matter now, anyway? You *are* the most beautiful woman here. We can walk and speak of the old days, surely?' He waved carelessly. 'All this talk of war and Romans bores me.'

An image of Eremon's face, lit up with the fire of his dream, flashed across Rhiann's mind. She felt herself go stiff. 'I am here because of the Romans.'

He shrugged. 'That is for my father and your husband to debate. They can frown and mutter like two old men. In the meantime, we can make the most of the fine weather. I have many stone carvings to show you.'

He reached out to flick a braid from her shoulder, and in doing so, touched her neck. All protest at his words died on her lips. In this moment, she did not care that he had not remembered her. It *had* been a long time. And everyone else managed to live and laugh while going about the business of war, even Eremon. Why not her?

Her wiser side was hammering out a warning in her mind, but she ignored it. Dear Goddess, she was standing here with a handsome man under a full moon. If she was ever going to kiss someone, it should be now. And if she could just get it over with, perhaps then she would start to feel normal. Like other women.

Sensing the indecision in her body, the touch of Drust's fingers changed. His thumb began to make soft circles on her skin, and gradually his hand moved around her neck until he cupped the back of her head.

It was not her mind hammering now, but her heart, and the throbbing warmth she had last felt seven years ago was a hot flood, loosening her thighs. Drust smiled, his pupils huge and dark in the moonlight. She closed her eyes.

His lips were cool and dry, not warm as she had expected. But then she felt the muscles of his chest brush her breasts, and that burned. He pressed even closer, his tongue parted her lips . . .

. . . and then she felt the hardness between his legs.

A wave of fear washed over her. She pulled back, feet tangling, both hands pressing against his chest, as if warding him away.

'Lord Drust?' The brisk voice came from the gate tower, schooled into that blandness that servants perfect. Rhiann swung away, hiding her face.

'Yes?' Drust was breathing hard, and he ran his fingers through his hair.

'Your father asks for you.'

'I will come.'

Drust cursed under his breath, but looked at Rhiann with a smile. 'Duty calls. Perhaps we can continue our reminiscing another time? After the hunt tomorrow, I ride south to visit one of the nobles who is too ill to attend the council. I will be back the day after.' He brushed her lips with one finger, regretfully. 'Meet with me again.'

Rhiann could not think straight, could only look down at her feet, but Drust took that as agreement, and left her there with a sure smile.

When he had gone, she took a shuddering breath, leaning against the palisade. Tears of shame pricked her eyes, as she remembered how she pulled away. Perhaps she was too damaged after all, even to enjoy a man's kiss. Perhaps she would never be a real woman.

She glanced down at the fires, and saw the shapes of the people moving around them, heard the snatches of wild music. Down there was warmth and cheer and laughter. And here she was, alone again. Despairing, she made her way back down to the main path, and thought about curling up in her cold bed.

No. No more.

The warm light beckoned through the open gates. She would go back to the fires, and have a cup of mead, and smile at Conaire's bad jests, and listen to Aedan's sweet voice. And she would sit with her shoulder touching Caitlin's, and talk to Eremon of the council.

That is what she would do.

CHAPTER 48

In a fine dawn heavy with dew, the nobles set off for their hunt the next morning along a wooded path that wound up a glen north of the dun. Eremon rode with Conaire at the rear of the party, behind Drust.

'Brother.' Conaire kept his voice low. 'I found out what you wanted to know.'

'Yes?' Eremon stared at the back of that dark gold head in front.

'The King's son paints the tattoos, on women mainly. At their first moon bleeding. The tattoos are sacred in some way.'

Eremon gripped his spear harder. 'Go on.'

'Although he is the King's son, when artists show their talent early, they are taken for some kind of druid training. It is probably the best thing he could do, since he cannot be King.'

And I imagine that hurts, Eremon thought.

He did not see anything sacred in this man. Indeed, looking at him now, riding out on a carefully brushed stallion, dressed in bright clothes, he seemed nothing more than a strutting capercaille, all shiny plumage and strident cries.

When Drust reappeared at the fire last night he stood by his father's side, but Eremon watched closely, and saw him paying far more attention to the pretty women there than to what Calgacus was saying. Shortly after, Rhiann also appeared. When she sat down on a bench next to Caitlin, he noticed how flushed her cheeks were.

Now, the memory made him feel sick all over again.

He could not understand Rhiann's interest. She did not suffer fools – how could she not see what was so apparent to him? Then he thought of Samana, and how he had been blinded by her.

But that was because of the demands of my body.

Abruptly, he yanked the horse up. Did this mean that Rhiann had succumbed to Drust? No, surely not! It was impossible. But was it? Here he was thinking she did not want any man . . . when perhaps it was just that she did not want him.

His sinking heart suddenly made the connection. Rhiann said that she met Drust on the Sacred Isle. And there, he must have painted her when she had her first bleeding. That meant that this man had seen her naked, and put his hands on her breasts, her belly. Perhaps he had even raised passion in her, when all Eremon had gained was her dislike.

He kicked Dòrn, and the stallion broke into a trot. When he drew level with Conaire again, his foster-brother glanced at him from the corner of his eye. But Conaire knew that set of his mouth, and let him be.

Not long after, the hounds brought the boar to bay in a shadowed hazel thicket. The nobles sat their mounts a safe distance away, breathless from the chase, as two Caledonii princes advanced on it with their spears raised.

The beast was enormous, with spittle running from its gaping mouth, which was framed by curving tusks, stained and yellow. Its tiny black eyes were full of rage. Eremon wished he had been the one to bring it down so that he could sink a spear into something. Then he became aware that Drust had nudged his horse up next to him.

'Prince,' Drust said in greeting. Eremon nodded, watching the boar and the figures advancing on it.

'I hope you are enjoying your stay with the Epidii,' Drust continued, brushing dried mud from the gilded harness of his horse.

'My marriage has brought me much joy, yes.'

'Ah, your wife. She is most beautiful. I have spoken with her. You are a very lucky man.'

'I think so.' Eremon breathed through his nose, striving for calm. *You have done more than speak with her!*

Drust paused. 'My father said that you met with Agricola himself. That he offered you allegiance.'

'An offer I refused.'

'But did you not think of joining him, even for a moment? I mean . . . it must have been a difficult decision for you.'

What was this? Calgacus's son, intrigued by Romans? And if so, how dangerous to betray this to Eremon! But then Eremon realized that this man had never had to learn the art of politics, born as he was with all the trappings of a prince, but no threat to those who desired the throne.

One of the Caledonii princes launched his spear, and it pierced the boar's eye. The flame of animal rage faded to the black of death. Eremon turned his horse to return to the dun, and Drust kept pace with him.

'Difficult?' Eremon said at last. 'On the contrary: I would not wish to be a Roman slave.' He finally looked Drust in the eyes – which soon fell under Eremon's stare. 'I value my freedom as much as I value my wife.'

All of the Caledonii nobles had arrived, and at last Eremon had a chance to put his case forward. For the first time in days, Gelert emerged from his deliberations with his brethren, and appeared at the council with Calgacus's chief druid, a tall, stooped man with grey hair and dark, piercing eyes.

Before a ring of full benches in Calgacus's hall, Eremon told what he knew of the Roman advance. But as he spoke, he saw with leaden heart that the rows of faces remained unmoved. The objections, when they came, were familiar.

'The Romans own the south and have for generations,' one gruff warrior said. 'They don't come north.'

'I've seen tents in vast rows, like sprouting barley,' Eremon replied, sweeping his hands out. 'I've seen swords and spears for all those men in all those tents. Agricola has assembled an army the likes of which you have never seen. Did you not hear what I said? He wants Alba.'

Another noble shrugged, his torc clanking on his shoulder brooches. 'What he says and what he does are different things. Of course he'll boast to you – he knew you would spread his words. Words meant to quash our courage.'

Eremon bit his lip in frustration. 'He has already come farther north than ever before. You know that.'

'This is true,' another man put in. 'But we have the strength to resist him. The mountains are our first defence, and our warriors the next. Look to your own lands, and we'll look to ours.'

'Have you ever seen twenty thousand men in one place?' Eremon rapped. 'When you have, you will know that no mountains can stop them. They will pour over your plain like a great sea-wave.'

'They won't stay,' the first man stated flatly.

It was as if they could not hear him.

'I saw the forts he is building,' Eremon said, striving for patience. 'Some are as enormous as his camps. This Roman won't retreat south in the long dark, as before. He builds permanent bases. They are staying.'

There was a shifting of feet, and a murmuring that swelled like a rising stream. Louder it grew, and from snatches, Eremon knew that he was already losing their attention. Then Calgacus raised his hand.

'I have gained my own information,' he declared, leaning forward in his high carved chair. His cloak was edged with otter fur, and on his head he wore a gold circlet. 'The Roman leader did advance rapidly, but then stopped. So far, he meets my expectations.'

Eremon turned to Calgacus. 'Your information is correct, lord, but I have spoken with someone close to Agricola. This person told me that the only reason the advance halted was because the emperor died. The new emperor, Titus, is busy in the east, and Agricola has orders to stay where he is. But it is only a matter of time. When Titus secures his borders, his attention will return to us. I am sure of it.'

The King's golden eyes looked long at Eremon. 'Then we are relying on your word only.'

Eremon raised his chin. 'Yes.' *And your own brains!* he wanted to cry. How could people be so blind to what was obvious to him? And yet, deep in Calgacus's eyes, there was a hint of regret. Perhaps he did see.

'My King.' The stooped druid broke in then. 'We have sacrificed a lamb and read its entrails. We have studied the pattern of birds flying from the south. The man speaks what he knows, but the gods know more. They are not alarmed.'

Stung, Eremon glanced at Gelert. Yellow eyes were fixed on him, sharp and hard. The druid had obviously not been spending his time pleading Eremon's case.

'What are you asking of us, prince?' the gruff man demanded.

'I think we must pool our strength now, while we have the breathing space. If we forge an alliance of tribes, then we can train our warriors as one. It is the only way to create an army to match his.'

Several of the nobles snorted.

'What you ask is impossible,' someone said. 'We don't fight like this. Our warriors are the best and bravest in Alba. We are strong enough alone. An alliance!' He shook his shaggy head. 'Just the excuse to let those cursed Decantae and Vacomagi overrun our lands.'

'If we don't ally, then Agricola will pick us off one by one. That is how the Romans work!' Eremon let his frustration show in his voice, and Calgacus stood up.

'We will debate your news among ourselves, prince of Erin, and give you our answer in two days.'

Eremon kept an impassive face, but inside he was heartsick. He caught Gelert as he was returning to his quarters. 'Why did you not convince the Caledonii druids that my plan had merit?'

Gelert spread his hands in a gesture of helplessness. 'I tried, but as he said, the Otherworld signs did not comply.'

'But you know how important this is!'

Gelert looked down his nose at him. 'You have done an able job of strengthening our warband. And yet, so far, your success has rested on reckless attacks that endanger our men, and not on defending our lands. Perhaps you should keep to the role that we charged you with, prince, and leave the rest to those who know better.'

Eremon watched his retreating back with gritted teeth.

And then he realized that the druid had never supported him publicly. Gelert had not opposed the attack on the fort ... yet neither did he support it. It was Declan who convinced the council to let him come to Calgacus. Eremon had taken Gelert's silence as a sign that the druid would stay out of military affairs. But suddenly he wondered at the hint of triumph in those yellow eyes, and when he would find out what it portended.

The shores of the Western Sea were lashed by strong winds, even in sunseason. Agricola liked Samana's hair down from its braids, but the breeze whipped the black strands across her eyes, and made it hard to see. She brushed it from her face.

From the saddle, she could see the soldiers marching out the Damnonii tribesmen and throwing them to their knees on the ground. Screaming women were dragged by their hair, children by any limb that came to hand. Behind the red rows of shields, the burning houses billowed clouds of black smoke into the blue sky.

Samana swallowed and looked away, out to sea. She loved the thrill of plotting, of wielding power over people's lives, of dreaming when she would be Queen of all Alba. But to see these plans turn into action, and then to see these actions *in person* was an unnecessary and vile imposition. She glanced at Agricola angrily, but he was not watching the destruction of the village, either.

From their vantage point on the edge of the headland, the

sea beckoned to her. Erin was just over that horizon somewhere, the place *he* had come from. The man who kept disturbing her dreams.

She had never cast any spell that ensnared her own self, and yet this must be why, despite trying to hate him, she could not. Or was it because he'd thwarted her, and the ceaseless burning of her rage bound them even though moons had passed? For she could find no hiding place from the memory of his lips, his smooth muscles under her hands. Curse him!

'Soon you will see the reason for our journey!' Agricola smiled at her, raising his voice over the crashing of the surf on the rocks below.

She swallowed her thoughts and admired her nails, affecting boredom. 'So the slaughter of these rebels was not the reason?'

'Not entirely. But finding the standards of my missing regiments here was an unexpected bonus. It seems these dogs were part of the raid on my fort.'

The horse beneath her shifted, and Samana patted it gingerly. 'What are we waiting here for, then?'

'Watch!' Agricola urged.

Off the rocks, something caught her eye. White wings, moving on the sunlit sea. Birds? But then the wings became sails, and rounding the point to their south glided a flotilla of ships, double-sailed, the oars rippling like the legs of some exotic insect.

Samana clapped her hands. 'Boats!'

'Ships,' Agricola corrected. 'The front lines of my new fleet.'

They watched the pointed prows nose into the bay, where the pall of smoke now hung heavy over the destroyed village.

'Do you want to see them?' Agricola's eyes were fierce with pleasure.

'Oh, yes!'

A tour of the command ship soon made Samana forget the scenes taking place onshore. Her own people built *curraghs* and traders, but nothing so lean and quick and fine as these ships – or so deadly. Her eyes devoured the catapults lined up on the deck; the attack towers from which soldiers could leap to shore.

'The keels are sheathed in bronze,' Agricola added. 'For ramming.'

Yet the most exciting thing was how many soldiers each ship could hold. 'You can discharge soldiers anywhere along the Alba coast!' Samana marvelled.

'And quickly,' Agricola remarked, inspecting the troop lists with the ship's commander.

'Then what holds you back?'

Agricola dismissed his officer and came to join her at the stern. 'I am not ready for a full-scale invasion, not yet.'

'You're all caution,' she mocked. 'Our warriors have no thought for it. If they could command such a fleet, they would fling it against every town on the coast of Alba!'

'Which is why I will win and they will lose.'

'But there is a time for action, or have you forgotten?'

He did not reply as they were rowed back to the shore. Then, once they were alone on the sands, his hand gripped her wrist. 'And are you having second thoughts about allying yourself to me, Samana? Would your hot-headed Erin prince be less cautious?'

Samana forced the flush from her cheeks. 'Don't be ridiculous.'

But as she followed him up the beach, her eyes strayed to the west again, until she bit her lip and forced her gaze away. If the cursed prince died, would his voice leave her mind?

'Sir.' One of Agricola's centurions strode up to them. 'We obtained the required information.'

'And?'

'The raid was organized by the Erin exile, as you thought. He brought his men from the north and allied with the tribal chieftain. That is all the man knows; he was not part of it.'

'Good. You can dispose of him now.'

'Yes, sir.'

Agricola resumed his pace, but this time Samana could not

hold her tongue. She ran up beside him, pulling on his arm. 'By sea, you are not far from Dunadd, my lord. *Dunadd.* You could catch the fox in his den.'

Agricola stopped and looked down at her, frowning. 'It is heavily defended, so you have said. Nor is it directly on the coast.'

'No, but very close. And you would have the element of surprise.'

He scratched his chin, which meant that he was thinking. She held her breath. *I will rid you from my heart, prince!*

'A sea attack on a well-defended fort would be too dangerous.'

'But you could capture Eremon in his bed!'

'I will not risk my troops for one man, Samana. You forget my words about revenge. But . . .'

She was poised on her toes, pressing against him. *Say yes!*

Agricola thought out aloud. 'I need to test my new crews. Something quick and small would do, with no protracted fighting.' He came back to himself, nodding. 'A warning for our prince. Yes – that could be just the thing.'

She smiled, and rubbed her breasts up against his arm, slowly. 'Are your inspections over for the day?'

His eyes darkened with desire. 'Most certainly. And I expect you to be very grateful for my indulgence.'

Later, as they lay in his camp bed among rumpled blankets, she said: 'You will take me with you, won't you?' She rolled over and rested her chin on his ribs.

'Who says I plan to join this expedition?'

She stroked the hair on his chest. 'I do not believe you are as patient as you appear.'

He laughed softly. 'In my heart, no. But in my mind, yes. One of my most trusted officers will lead this raid. When *I* set foot on the soil of these Highlands, I aim to do it with twenty thousand men at my back. And no intention of retreat.'

CHAPTER 49

When Drust returned from his trip to the south, he asked Rhiann to ride out with him in his chariot. Eremon was stamping about the guest lodge like an angry bear, and after one look at his taut mouth and hard eyes, Rhiann sent a message back accepting Drust's offer.

She did, however, ask Caitlin to ride alongside on her mare, so that Rhiann had the opportunity to see more of Drust without being betrayed by her body.

For ever since the kiss, her skin had come alive. When Eremon touched her accidentally in bed, she jumped, and he looked at her long and hard before she dropped her eyes. She felt she didn't fit her bones any more; she was restless, even as her mind floated far away in dreams.

Their ride took them through a land that was coming into the full ripeness of sunseason. The barley drooped its golden heads in the heat, and clouds of bees hovered over the meadows. The oaks along the river cast pools of shadow across their burning faces.

Drust took them on a tour of his carved stones, which had been set up at many points on the main trackways between the Caledonii duns. Rhiann and Caitlin murmured appropriately at the scenes of hunting and war, and the symbols of leaping salmon and fighting stags. Many of the stones bore the sign of the eagle, of course, although none in bronze like the stone they had first seen.

'They are the same symbols I paint on skin, do you see?' Drust's chariot horses were a matched pair of roans, and they tossed their heads gaily as they trotted on, ringing the tiny bells on their enamelled harness. The chariot bumped on the uneven ground, and Rhiann was thrown against Drust's arm. He grinned, and holding the reins with one hand, curved his free arm around her waist.

Rhiann glanced at Caitlin, but she was absorbed in racing around an old stump ahead, shooting her new arrows into the gnarled trunk from every direction.

'I have travelled far in the south, seeking out Roman milestones to study stone carving, and even meeting some of their carvers.'

Rhiann looked up at Drust in surprise. 'You have been to Roman lands?'

The chariot bumped again, and Drust released her and grasped the reins with both hands. 'Of course! That is not forbidden, is it?'

Rhiann's eyes rested on the tattoos curling over Drust's soft cheeks. He was marked as one of the barbarians of the north. It must not have been easy to gain safe access to Roman towns.

'I am much better than they,' he added. 'They carve numbers and dead people's names . . . and gods' faces. But they all look the same.'

'I hope you will not carve our gods' faces,' she said. 'They can only be rendered in living wood.'

'Yes, oh high priestess,' he intoned, smiling. He pulled the chariot up and waved at Caitlin, who had now dismounted to pull her arrows from the tree. 'And here is a fine place to eat.'

They spread out a deer hide by the river, and Caitlin tethered her horse and unslung her quiver before bounding up with a flushed face. 'Isn't it wonderful, cousin! I have never been to such a fertile land!'

'Of course not,' Drust answered. 'You are from the mountains.'

'Dunadd is also on a plain,' Rhiann put in, suddenly feeling defensive. 'Our valleys may not be as good as yours for grain, but we raise fine sheep and cattle.'

But Drust seemed bored by that, too.

There was smoked beef and bread and soft cheese, and wine and a strange kind of nut – a walnut, Drust said. Everything was served on Roman plates and in Roman cups. 'Look at the workmanship.' Drust held up a silver goblet set with carnelians. 'And the Samian pottery. See – they carve in clay!'

'You sound as if you admire the Romans,' Rhiann remarked.

'Taste this wine, lady.' He rolled it around on his tongue. The sun picked out the gold sheen in his brown eyes. 'How can you not admire a civilization that produces this!'

'You do not act like your father's son.'

Drust picked a shard of nut flesh from his teeth with his meat-dagger. 'I must find my own place in the world. Yes, we must defend ourselves from Roman expansion. But in the meantime, why can't we enjoy what they have to offer?'

Caitlin's grin had faded to a glower. 'Eremon says that if we take Roman wealth, we as good as invite them into our lands.'

Drust laughed at her, and patted her hand. 'Let's leave such heavy matters to our leaders, little lady, and enjoy the day.'

Caitlin's scowl deepened. 'I'm going to cross the river to see what lays there,' she said, jumping up.

When she left, Drust's attention shifted to Rhiann once more. 'Do you remember the sunseason we met?' He flashed that disarming grin. 'Lying in the sun, just like this, on the warm sand?' He covered her hand with his own, stroking her skin.

Rhiann nodded. 'Did you ever think of me?' She despised herself for asking, hated the girlish sound of the words.

'Of course,' he replied. 'And now that I see you once more, I don't know why I did not ride back to you with my arms full of marriage gifts!' He drew her hand to his mouth. 'But alas,' his eyes were on hers, 'you are married already. And you will not be here long.'

She understood the question in his eyes, though she did not know the answer. Her body was responding to his touch with the same hunger as before, for that door could not be shut so quickly. But her heart was heavy. What had she expected? That love would strike her down like a bolt from the sky?

When they returned to the dun, preparations were underway for the longest day feast. Drust handed Rhiann down from the chariot in the yard before the stables. As he busied himself unhitching his team, Caitlin whispered, 'An old friend of yours he may be, but I do not like this prince.'

Before Rhiann could answer, Drust was before them. Caitlin thanked him stiffly and left, her head high.

When they were alone, Drust bowed over Rhiann's hand to say farewell, turning her palm up to brush it with his lips. 'Tonight, many will be honouring the gods in the fields.' He looked from under his lashes, the promise in his eyes. 'Perhaps we will have our time again then, Rhiann.'

From the walls above, Conaire and Eremon watched the little party come through the gates and dismount. When Eremon glanced at his brother's face, it was shadowed with the same feeling that tore at his own heart.

'He rode out with Caitlin,' Conaire muttered.

'He rode out with *Rhiann*,' Eremon said.

'He's nothing but a strutting cock. Caitlin would not be fooled by him.'

Eremon wished that he could say the same about Rhiann, but so far, that had not been the case. He knew fear and desperation could make someone act out of character. But why would Rhiann be afraid or desperate?

It was as he was halfway down the stairs that he caught sight of Gelert leaving the dun through the northern gate, in the company of a messenger that had arrived on horseback a short time before. Eremon watched the white-robed figure for a moment, his senses suddenly alerted.

'Hurry up!' Conaire called impatiently. 'I'm going to Caitlin right now, and I'm going to find out every word the cock said.'

Eremon glanced at the druid's back again. Should he follow him? Then he jumped the last few steps with irritation. First Rhiann, and now Gelert! Did he have nothing better to do than skulk around after mysterious priests?

'On second thoughts,' Conaire amended, seeing Rori and Angus coming their way with their hunting spears. 'Let's forget about women and chase some boar instead. We have many hours of light left, after all.'

Eremon's shoulders relaxed. 'That's a fine idea, brother! The further I am from here, the better.'

Rhiann hardly knew how Drust managed to draw her away from the fires that night. But after the burning of the sacred sun herbs, and the crowd's wild, joyful scattering of the ashes on the fields, as her voice grew hoarse from chanting and her feet sore from dancing, the *saor* and mead entwined into a warm haze that took over her senses.

And as the people danced between the barley rows, suddenly Drust was there behind her, his arms twirling her away from the path. Laughing, she stumbled against him, and abruptly all grew dark and quiet, as the dancers and musicians with their torches carried on without them.

It was not much then to sit on his cloak and catch her breath, not much to stretch out under the purple sky to look for the first scattered stars, his arm beneath her . . .

. . . and when his lips first found hers, and she tasted his tongue, sweet with mead, she tensed only a moment before being swept away by the rising column of heat in her body.

Now, a stray flare of firelight carved shadows over his face, and her fingers traced over the fine cheekbones, as she breathed deeply of the mingled scents of warm earth, the crushed herbs on her hands, and his sweat.

She buried her fingers in his hair, as she had longed to do, and it flowed between them like wild honey, and as she did, his fingers covered one breast, stroking her through the fine linen, and then eased down over her hip. She closed her eyes, torn at once with fear and longing.

But he still knew exactly how to touch her, and the languorous stroking of her legs merged somehow with the *saor*, sending her deeper into the daze that had engulfed her all those years ago. Suddenly she realized his hand had eased up under her shift, and was burning a trail across her naked skin.

Her eyes flew open, her breath catching.

'Hush,' he murmured. 'My beautiful Rhiann. My precious one.'

The words flowed into her thirsty heart, as he drew her shift higher, exposing her belly and the lower curve of her breasts. Shy, burying her head in the angle of his neck, she was suddenly glad that she had filled out, that she had a roundness to her now.

His breath sharpened, and she could feel the thud of his heart against her skin. 'My most beautiful design . . .'

He eased his arm from under her, and suddenly his lips were tracing fire over her belly, following the blue designs he had painted there with his own hand. His mouth moved higher, higher . . . over her ribs, leaving butterfly kisses in its wake, until he reached her breasts.

Her breath came short and fast.

And an image flashed into her mind; a man's hand, black-haired, on the whiteness of her breast . . .

She pushed the image away, concentrated on Drust . . . Drust's mouth, Drust's fine, smooth hands. Drust! His mouth enclosed her, and she buried her hands in that honey hair and drew him closer. It would be all right!

He kissed his way up her body again until he reached her neck, and then his weight came down on her. 'Rhiann,' he groaned.

A man's weight, crushing her, the cold tip of the knife at her throat . . .

She made herself unfreeze, with sheer will, forced the blood back into her skin. He did not notice, as, murmuring all the time, he began showering her breasts and belly with kisses once more.

She bit her lip. *It is Drust!*

But then she felt him fumbling with his trousers, felt him move up the length of her, felt the thing that was somehow soft and hard at the same time pressing into her thigh, the sword that would be sheathed in her body.

A man's weight, crushing her . . .

'Rhiann!' Drust groaned again. 'I need you!'

The cold tip of the knife at her throat . . .

'No!' The cry burst from her, shocking them both, and she was pushing her hands against his chest. 'I can't . . .'

He looked down at her, blinking as if waking. 'What?'

She pushed harder. 'I can't do this . . . I am sorry.'

He rolled off her, breathing hard. 'What do you mean, you can't!'

'Don't ask me!' She pulled her shift down, flushed with mortification.

'Lady.' He leaned forward to kiss her. 'Don't play shy with me. I thought you were all grown up.'

She wriggled away from his lips. 'I mean no!'

He froze and pulled back, and this time his eyes were burning with anger. 'Of all the . . . you promised!'

'I promised nothing!'

With a quick, impatient movement, he pulled up his trousers as he got to his haunches, the barley heads scratching against his shoulders.

Rhiann sat up, pulling her cloak around her. 'Drust, I am sorry.' She touched his arm. 'It is just – quick – for me. It has been a long time.'

His muscles were tense under her fingers. 'You are a beautiful woman. You cannot play with my feelings.'

'I didn't mean to.'

He let out a shuddering breath, his face turned away. 'My control is not great, so do not tempt me any more than you already have. Go.'

Her face aflame, Rhiann left him.

A warm breeze blew along the furrows, lifting her hair, and

the soft cries of man and woman all around taunted her. She put her head down and made for the shadows by the river, where she could nurse her shame in peace.

CHAPTER 50

Eremon's frustration about the Caledonii deliberations was eating at him unbearably the next day. And to make matters far worse, Rhiann had disappeared during the dancing at the feast, and then came to bed late, smelling of ash and earth and river mud.

Gods!

There was nothing for it but to hunt once more, driving his men further and harder until they were all sweat-soaked and exhausted. A clear shot through a buck's eye did little to lighten his mood, neither did Conaire breaking open a flask of Epidii ale to toast the kill. As the afternoon faded, Eremon's temper darkened with the sky.

When they returned to the dun, Eremon managed to gain a brief audience with the King in his hall, as his nobles left.

'Nothing has been decided,' Calgacus told him, laying aside his ceremonial sword.

'But lord, you are the King! You must see what I see!'

Calgacus regarded him sombrely. 'I am more convinced than my men, and less convinced than you. No!' He held up his hand when Eremon opened his mouth. 'I have heard your excellent arguments. But we are well defended, and further north than you. We feel secure – for the moment.'

'Then why did you agree to meet with me?'

'I wanted to see what kind of man you are. The situation may change, and if it does, then we have been able to take each other's measure. We can move swiftly then.'

'Not swiftly enough, I fear.' Eremon tried to rein in his frustration.

'Prince, I told you that I had to fight for my throne, but I not only faced rivals from my own tribe. When the old king died, our neighbours seized the moment and raided us from two directions. It took everything in me to restore order, and win our land and cattle back.'

'Such a victory would have consolidated your position.'

'True, but I have reigned for many more years now, and the stronger we get, the hungrier our neighbours become to gain our hard-won riches. Envy stalks my borders.'

'What has this to do with the Romans?'

'My nobles fear that an alliance could give the other tribes the advantage they have been waiting for. Alliances require trust between the parties, and that means letting down our defences.'

'So your men think that – what do *you* think?'

Calgacus stroked his chin. 'My head tells me they are right. But my heart whispers that it would like to believe you, prince of Erin. That we could join together as something glorious and strong, strong enough to drive the Romans out of these islands altogether. Out of Alba, out of Britannia.' He smiled wryly. 'Perhaps these are just the fancies of an old man. Perhaps you tempt me with all your youth and boldness.'

'Bold I may be, but I assure you that I am rational rather than impetuous. Just ask my brother.'

'Nevertheless, it is too soon to do as you ask.'

Eremon's head came up. 'Meaning that in future, despite your reservations, you may well support me?'

'If circumstances change, then I am open to it.'

Calgacus's words soothed him momentarily, but that night, in the King's Hall, Eremon noted how the nobles avoided him, and the dark mood of the afternoon returned with greater force. As the hours wore on, he drank, and he sat alone, and he brooded.

He was doing all this thinking and fighting for them, these tribes of Alba, and how did they repay him? His wife dallied with an idiot, his druid schemed, and these rich, well-fed men smirked at him and threw his help back in his face. He should just leave them all to the Romans and find support for his own cause in Erin elsewhere.

He gulped the rest of his ale and wiped his mouth, then held the cup out to a passing serving girl for refilling. Just then there was a waft of honey scent before his face, and Rhiann sank down next to him on the bench. He shifted to make more room for her.

'I heard from Conaire that the nobles are not very open to your suggestions.'

'You could say that.'

'What we ask is unusual, Eremon. They need time to adjust to the idea.' She brushed her hair back from her shoulders. It was long and loose tonight, except for one braid at each temple, finished with blue beads. It made her look very young and vulnerable.

He took a deep draught of ale, and when he saw her frown, he took another. 'I don't think time will change anything,' he muttered. 'I have a druid that's undermining me at every step, and a—' He just stopped himself from saying, *And a wife that flaunts herself with another man.*

Her gaze sharpened. 'What of Gelert?'

'Nothing . . . really. It's just that he didn't even attempt to gain the support of Calgacus's druid.'

'I hope you were not expecting much of him. He's afraid of you, you must know that.'

'Afraid of what? He looks after his realm and I mine.'

'No, he wishes to control all realms. I think he hoped to control you, too, and because he cannot, that makes him angry. You're getting too popular.'

He squinted at her, for in the firelight she was already blurred around the edges. Here he was, all sweaty and greasy with meat, and she just looked fresh and pretty. 'Thank you for telling me all this now. I could have left him behind.'

Her mouth pursed. 'I don't think he would have listened, and besides, I'd rather have him here under our noses than getting up to Goddess knows what at Dunadd.'

She was right, but that just made him more annoyed. And why was it that the only conversations they ever had were all so *rational*. Look at Conaire and Caitlin over there, giggling like a couple of fools . . .

'And where is the handsome Drust, then?' he snapped.

Rhiann's cheeks flushed. 'You're drunk.'

'Trying.'

'Well, at least he doesn't bark at me like I'm some sort of—'

'Wife?' He raised his eyebrows.

Rhiann's flush deepened, and her eyes sparked. '*You* can talk!' she whispered furiously. 'Your conquests would fill the King's Hall and more!'

'I don't remember taking a vow to be chaste all my life!'

She looked as if he'd slapped her, which is what he wanted to do but . . . gods . . . he'd never hurt her . . . It was too late, she was on her feet, and there were tears in her eyes . . . tears!

'Rhiann, wait!'

But she was gone, and people were looking, and he couldn't run after her. 'Girl!' When the servant came to him, he took the whole pitcher of ale from her.

And gave her the cup in return.

Outside, Rhiann's feet pounded the pathway in time to the litany in her head. Of all the rude, belligerent, hypocritical . . . beasts!

Of course, she should be back in the hall using her charm and position to sway the nobles, persuade them . . . but doing anything for the prince of Erin right now galled her.

She realized that her feet had taken her to the door of Drust's workshed, where faint lamplight edged out from under the cover. There she stopped, taking some deep breaths. Perhaps she should try to smooth things over with Drust, instead. Perhaps he would just smile again and be easy . . .

Eremon's last words still rang in her bruised heart. *I did not take a vow to be chaste.*

No, he did not; she was the damaged one. Yet perhaps if

Drust could be patient, he and she might try again. If he loved her just a little . . .

She lifted the cover and slipped silently under it. Inside, workbenches were scattered with awls and chisels and half-finished carvings, and the tarred scent of wood shavings hung in the air. A seal-oil lamp was burning in the corner. She walked closer to the lamp, to a pile of fur-covered straw there.

They did not even hear her.

It was no surprise, really.

Drust was groaning, his broad, smooth back thrusting forwards, and the girl, face hidden, wrapped her white legs around his waist.

It was no surprise. None of it.

Rhiann watched them blankly, until hysteria bubbled up from deep within her, and whistled out through her teeth. At the sound, Drust started and turned, and the girl's wide eyes shone up underneath him. He did not leap to his feet, flustered. He did not look ashamed or abashed. If there was anything in his face, it was only the briefest touch of regret. And in his eyes, a shrug.

Rhiann turned and left them. She could have bitten her tongue out – that, or lash herself with it until she bled. How foolish could any one woman be! And she, of all people! She, who had taken more care of her heart than all the careless Aiveens and Gardas put together, only to throw it at some feckless man, just because once, long ago, he made her feel like a woman. She buried her face in her hands.

This time, a cold bed really was the only option. As she lay there in the lodge, she thought back to the memories of firelight on skin that she had held in her heart for so long. He could not take those from her; no one could. But what about the other dream of the sword-wielder? If her hopes of Drust had been dashed, did that mean that, all along, the dream had been no more than fancy?

At some point in the night, Eremon finished the second jug

of ale. He vaguely remembered challenging some braying young idiot to a duel, but when he stumbled outside, and the air hit him, everything went dark.

The next thing he knew, a pair of thick, strong arms were around him. 'I've got him,' Conaire's voice muttered from somewhere above.

'What can I do?' That was Caitlin, worried.

'Nothing, I will look after him. Just you go back and make light of it to that young buck.'

'I could carry his sword—'

'No! Leave us alone!'

There was a pause. 'I was just trying to help.' Now Caitlin sounded angry. 'You don't need to shout at me!'

Conaire's breath whooshed in Eremon's ear.

Like a horse, Eremon thought dreamily. *It's Dòrn, he wants his feed . . .*

'Sweeting,' Conaire said more gently, 'I look after Eremon. You know that.'

'Hmph!' Caitlin's feet thudded away.

Eremon hiccupped. 'You've done it now, brother . . .' He tried to stand, but his legs buckled under him, refusing to obey.

'Easy there.' There was a jerk, and then the world turned upside down, as Conaire tossed him over his shoulder. They jigged along, and just when Eremon was feeling very sick, Conaire laid him down on some hay.

'Where . . . are we?'

'A stable. You don't need women fussing over you. And you'll probably be sick on someone. Rhiann wouldn't appreciate that.'

Rhiann . . .

Eremon remembered her pretty hair, the tears sparkling in the firelight. 'Brother, I'm in trouble.'

'What trouble?'

Eremon wrenched his eyes open, tried to focus on Conaire, but all he could see was a blurred halo.

He closed his eyes, gave in. 'I'm in love,' he slurred. 'With my wife.'

The entire Epidii party came to the King's Hall to hear what Calgacus and his nobles had decided.

Only Rhiann was absent. Eremon had not seen her that morning. He awoke in the stable with a pounding head, but a dunk in cold water and an oatcake fried in bacon fat had gone some way to restoring his normal alertness.

She probably sees Drust again, he thought, studying the nobles' faces on the benches around him. And why wouldn't she, when he made such a fool of himself? Thank the gods he had not spoken that last admission to *her*. He shuddered. It was just the drink. It had to be.

Trying hard to put the image of Drust and Rhiann out of his mind, his eyes roved over the walls behind the benches. Gelert was there, his enigmatic smile broader than usual. Conaire, Rori and the others kept to the shadows by the door, Caitlin with them.

Like the warrior-king he was, Calgacus did not waste time. 'Eremon mac Ferdiad, will you rise so you can hear our judgement?'

Eremon obliged, standing in the pool of daylight that fell through the open doorway. He'd belted on Fragarach, and donned his best tunic and gold circlet. He would look every inch a king. When they refused him.

Calgacus rose too, which surprised Eremon. The act denoted a certain equality between them, which judging by the dark looks and mutters, did not sit well with the King's men. His heart lightened.

'My chieftains have considered the plan put before them, prince of Erin.'

Calgacus locked glances with him, and for a moment it was as if he and Eremon were the only two in the room. But the gold-flecked eyes held regret once more. Eremon's heart sank back in his breast.

'They do not feel that the danger is sufficient to warrant the alliance you advise,' Calgacus added.

Even though Eremon had expected it, the disappointment was still crushing.

'We will ward our borders well, as we have always done, and monitor the Romans' movements.' The formal tone softened. 'I know this is not what you wanted to hear.'

Eremon took a deep breath so that his voice would carry to every man there. 'You make a serious mistake; possibly a fatal one. But know this,' he turned slowly, fixing every chieftain there with a piercing gaze, 'I will still make every effort to secure the co-operation of the other tribes. They may see things differently.'

Calgacus bowed his head, accepting. He didn't seem angered by the bold words. *What an ally you would make!* Eremon thought fiercely, and his disappointment swelled.

'And on whose authority will you do this?' The challenge rang throughout the hall, and every head turned towards the speaker.

Gelert stepped forward, his oak staff of office held high, so the daylight glittered on the jet eyes of the owl. Such was Eremon's surprise, that he could think of no immediate reply.

'You speak as if you are a man of substance, to make this claim,' the druid said. 'A man with many swords sworn to you, a man who could gain the backing of all the tribes of Alba.'

Eremon narrowed his eyes. 'What do you speak of, Lord Druid? I am this man.'

Gelert's lip curled. 'Are you?' he said softly, and clicked his fingers. The light from the doorway was shadowed as a tall warrior ducked his head to enter.

The man straightened to face Eremon boldly.

It was Lorn.

CHAPTER 51

There was a mutter from the direction of Eremon's men, and he was conscious that Conaire had taken a place behind his shoulder.

'Who is this man?' Calgacus demanded.

'I am Lorn of the Epidii, my lord. My father is Urben of the Dun of the Sun.'

'And why do you disturb my council?'

Without taking his eyes from Eremon, Lorn gestured at Gelert. 'I come at the bidding of the Chief Druid. I have news of the prince of Erin, which concerns you.'

A dreadful suspicion was thickening in Eremon's belly. Lorn had not been there the day they left Dunadd. Where had he been?

'A week ago I returned from Erin,' Lorn announced.

The blow took Eremon's breath away. Yet he realized, dimly, that he had not moved one muscle, and there had been no sound from his men, not even an indrawn breath from Conaire. In that moment, he was proud of them.

Calgacus frowned. 'What you have to say is between you and your war leader. We will finish our council, and then you can deal with your tribal business.'

'No!' Gelert cried. He took a step forward, his eyes blazing, and then swung his staff so it pointed at Eremon. 'This man has lied to us all! He is not who he says he is!'

Eremon's heart thudded erratically. Hawen's balls! He clenched his fists, as all eyes turned to him.

'Of what does he speak?' Calgacus demanded. 'Are you not the son of Ferdiad, king of Dalriada?'

Eremon raised his chin. 'Yes, I am.' The breath hissed through his teeth.

'No longer,' Gelert retorted. He faced Lorn. 'Tell them what you found.'

Lorn smiled. 'The prince's father is dead, and his uncle ran him out of Erin with only the clothes he was in, and his twenty renegades. He is no longer the heir. He has no kin, no swords sworn to him, no home. He is an exile.'

That word again! It rang to the rafters. Eremon felt the hard gaze of the Caledonii nobles pierce him, he smelled the stink of Gelert's poison, he heard the triumph in Lorn's voice.

They were all against him. He had gambled, and lost.

Perversely, it was at that very point that a wave of calm rolled over him. All the fear of being found out could now be released. Secrets were heavy things: now that his were laid bare, he could put the weight down. Sweet relief coursed through him, and he stood straighter, his hand on his scabbard. He would make his father proud.

'Is this true?' he heard Calgacus ask, from far away.

Eremon turned to look at the King. He was the only man here who deserved an explanation. 'It is true.'

This time the gasp from the audience was audible, and Eremon saw that Lorn was thrown, the smile in his eyes fading, his brows drawing together. *Did he expect me to lie?*

'I *am* the heir,' he declared. 'My uncle acknowledged it, and laid his sword across his hands to me. But on my father's death, he broke his oath. Those men he could not buy, he cowed into submission. My followers and I held out against a warband of one hundred, but were eventually driven to the shore. There, we escaped. To Alba.'

Calgacus waved to quiet his men, for the muttering was growing louder.

But it was Lorn who spoke first. 'You admit this?'

Eremon locked eyes with him. 'Yes.'

One of the Caledonii chieftains interrupted. 'My lord! This exile lied to us. We did well not to listen to him.'

Eremon rounded on the man. 'I did not lie. Nor did I lie to

this druid.' Glancing at Gelert, he allowed the contempt to drip from his words.

'Do not listen to him, lord,' Gelert began, and a host of other voices joined him.

But as the din grew in volume, Calgacus finally roared, 'Quiet!' The lash of his voice was impressive, and had the desired effect. 'I wish to hear the prince of Erin speak. And the next person to say *anything*,' he glared at Gelert, Lorn, and at his own men, 'will have to fight with me, hand to hand. Now sit down, all of you.'

In a moment Eremon was alone in the middle of the floor again, but this time the hostility in the room was palpable.

'I did not lie,' he said again. 'The druid asked me if I could help the Epidii against the Romans, and this is what I agreed to. And so far, I am fulfilling my bargain.' He swept them all with proud eyes, and his voice grew louder. 'Yes, I am exiled, and yes, my uncle is King. And no, I do not have more than a score of men sworn to me. But I tell you this: I have studied how the Romans fight. I met with Agricola himself, and saw how they move and camp and think. Under my leadership, we destroyed a Roman fort. I am as valuable to you as I ever was when you thought me a landed prince – more so, for I have something to prove, something to win!' He speared Calgacus with his eyes, his head high. 'If the Epidii break the alliance with me, then others in Alba would welcome a leader such as I. Mark me.'

Lastly he looked at Lorn. 'Mark also that this man who accuses me, who sought to bring me low, is the fiercest warrior of the Epidii.'

Lorn's eyes widened.

'The druid forged this breach between us, but in doing so, has played right into Roman hands.' He appealed directly to Lorn. 'We are brothers-in-arms. If we cannot hold a tribe together, then how can we hold Alba? How can we resist the Romans? You saw them, you fought beside me. You know I'm right.'

Lorn broke his gaze and put his head down, shaking it.

There was silence, but of what kind, Eremon could not tell. Then Calgacus was by his side. 'Prince, how old are you?'

'Twenty-one years, my lord.'

'So at such an age, when faced with the vilest of betrayals, the loss of a father, and one hundred warriors to your score, you made your escape with your men's lives intact?'

Eremon's heart leaped at the light in the King's eye. 'Yes.'

'You then crossed a sea with nothing, but managed to win an alliance within a moon. You attacked the invaders and won. You crossed Alba to challenge us, the strongest of tribes, and faced down a council of hard men, using bold words to turn our hearts. Not once, but twice.'

Eremon smiled. 'Yes.'

'And do you plan to seek your throne, prince?'

'On my father's honour, my lord. And I will win it back.'

'I can well believe it.' The King's mouth lifted in a private smile, and he turned to face his men. Before he spoke, he reached out and put a hand on Eremon's shoulder.

'My council has made its decision for the tribe, and I must abide by it. But I say this to you all: here stands the most courageous and resourceful of men. As he says, he is even more valuable as an ally because of who he is and what he has done, not in spite of it. From now on, let it be known that he has my personal support.'

There was a strangled cry from Gelert. 'But this man gained his alliance falsely! He has no men, no army!'

Calgacus's disdain for the druid was clear. 'Then we admire his bravery all the more; to take so little and turn it into so much! Such a man makes a true king: you should thank Manannán for bringing him to you.'

Gelert's eyes blazed with a wild rage. 'We gave him our Ban Cré, made him the father of our royal heir!'

'His blood is noble enough. But then, there is the matter of the Lady Rhiann.' Calgacus faced Eremon. 'Her honour must be maintained.'

Eremon nodded. 'The year-marriage can be broken when we return to Dunadd.'

'It is well.'

Gelert's mouth dropped open. The hatred in his eyes scalded Eremon's skin, and then without another word he gathered his cloak around him and swept from the hall. Lorn followed him, hesitantly, it seemed, and glanced back at Eremon once.

The Caledonii nobles stood stiffly, unsure how to react to Eremon in the light of their King's pronouncement. Eremon's men swirled around him, but behind them, Eremon could see the eagle eyes of Calgacus, regarding him with pleasure. *Well done, my son*, they seemed to say.

Eremon had never heard those words from his father.

For the first time since he left Erin, the hard knot of betrayal around his heart began to ease.

Rhiann had sought refuge from her humiliation over Drust in the house of the Caledonii Ban Cré. She was there, showing the old priestess a new wound herb she had gained from the traders, when Caitlin's flying feet found her.

'Rhiann, I've been looking everywhere for you!' Caitlin's chest was heaving as she struggled to draw breath. 'I ran the length of the walls and back!'

'What is it?'

Caitlin glanced at the other priestess, hesitating. The old woman's instincts were keenly honed; with twinkling eyes she excused herself, suddenly remembering a prior engagement.

Caitlin hopped from foot to foot with impatience, as the woman gathered a wool shawl around her and took up her medicine bag. As soon as the door flap fell back into place, Caitlin drew Rhiann to the hearth-bench, the words spilling from her mouth, relating everything that had transpired at the council.

'Oh, Rhiann, you should have seen him!' Caitlin's face was glowing. 'And Calgacus stood up by Eremon, and Gelert was chased from the hall!'

Rhiann listened, the rosemary leaves crushed in her fist, until at last Caitlin faltered.

'Goddess!' Caitlin's glow faded. 'I was not thinking, Rhiann, I'm sorry. He lied to you, I know. This must hurt you.'

Rhiann stared at the wall, the pungent herb smarting her eyes. All along she knew he was hiding something, that he was not all he seemed. Yet, as his successes grew, she had ceased to think on it.

Caitlin's small, white hand covered her own. 'Rhiann, if only you could have heard what he actually said – you would not be as upset, I know it. I'll tell you what I remember.' And she repeated Eremon's speech, nearly word for word. 'He means to do the best for us all. He was forced into an impossible situation, but he faced it with courage. That counts for something, Rhiann, doesn't it?'

Rhiann glanced at her, saw the hopeful look. 'I – I just need some time to think on this.'

'Of course you do! But,' Caitlin bit her lip, 'it doesn't need to change everything. You know that Eremon is the war leader we need. And now he has the personal support of Calgacus.' At Rhiann's silence, she rushed on. 'However, I know that does not change how you feel. And Rhiann, as a warrior, I follow him, but my loyalty is with you. If you want to cast him out, then I will support you.'

Caitlin could win a smile from a stone.

Eventually, after many reassurances, Rhiann convinced Caitlin to leave her there so that she could think. And how did she really feel?

She brushed the rosemary needles from her fingers, swallowing the lump of anger. The liar! Gaining her hand when he was a landless, friendless nobody! If the truth had been known at the start, she never would have been forced to marry him. And then he had dared to criticize her, last night, for not being what he expected!

It was then that her thoughts roamed to Drust, and the bitterness of the little scene in his workshed rose up once more. Her hopes there had been extinguished, but where did that leave her? If she did reject Eremon, would the council just marry her to someone else? Or, if Caitlin married, would they leave her alone? Perhaps, after all, she could join Linnet on the mountain.

Perhaps.

Think! She must think, and quickly.

She emerged from the lodge, expecting to see a crowd of people staring at her. But everyone was going about their business as usual. As she reached the yard before the gate tower, a party on horses was leaving the dun: Gelert, his druids, and some of the Epidii warriors. The Chief Druid must be going home, after his humiliation. She peered at each warrior in turn, but could not discern Lorn among them.

Rhiann paused, twisting her hair around her finger. She knew she would be receiving another visitor soon, but not what she would say to him. So she took herself up the stairs to the walkway, on the stretch that faced the sea. It did not make her harder to find, but at least the breeze on the sunlit water braced her spirits, and gave her courage.

Sure enough, it was not long.

There was a cough behind her. 'Lady,' Eremon said formally, 'I assume you have heard my news.'

She did not turn her head, but merely nodded. His presence so close beside her made the anger and hurt surge up anew, and all the reasoned arguments retreat.

'You can see why I could not tell you.' He leaned on the palisade next to her. 'I truly believe that I can do the best for your people. But I needed the chance to prove myself; to show you who I really was, regardless of my kin.'

At her continued silence, he straightened, and from the corner of her eye she saw him put his hand on his sword. 'I have come now to agree to the severing of our betrothal, which we can finalize at Dunadd.'

She snorted with exasperation and turned, folding her arms, and he stepped back in surprise. 'Eremon.' She struggled to keep her voice level. 'Caitlin told me every single thing that you said in council. And it was true – every word.'

Eremon's eyebrows rose, and for once, he looked unsure.

'You *are* valuable, and you *have* proven yourself. Calgacus backs you. With you by my side, I can also do the best for my people. I like what we've built.' She paused. 'For these reasons, I want the marriage to stand.'

He gasped, and tried to speak, but she held up a finger to stop him. 'But Eremon, I am so angry with you that I could tear your eyes out right now! If you say one more word, that's what I'll do. Now leave me alone and don't speak to me until we get home. Understand?'

He nodded, but his eyes were shining.

The deck beneath Samana's feet heaved in the heavy swell. She clung to the mast, exhilarated at the lash of the wind on her cheeks, the drifts of spume catching in her hair. Craning, she could see only islands and dark hills and crashing surf on the rocks, for the sails of the fleet had been lost among the twisting straits.

'Can we not go closer?' she begged Agricola over her shoulder.

'No.' He stood, hands behind his back, rocking easily with the motion of the ship. 'I am not here officially, Samana, remember.'

'But we can't see anything!'

Agricola smiled. 'Then use your imagination, my witch. The burning will be the signal, soon enough.'

But the sun had to sink two hand-spans before she saw the smoke at last rise against the sky, clouding it as blood clouds clear water.

CHAPTER 52

E remon was saddling Dòrn in Calgacus's stables, preparing to leave, when he heard the shuffling of feet. At the look on Conaire's face beside him, he swung around. It was Lorn.

The Epidii warrior was ill at ease, but kept his head high, his eyes fixed on the stable wall. 'I did not return to Dunadd with the druid.'

Eremon regarded him gravely. 'I see.'

'Lugh knows I have tried my best, prince of Erin, but I cannot defeat you. Perhaps the gods have sent you a different fate. The way you faced those men down . . .' He looked at Eremon, puzzled. 'It was not the response I expected.'

'I will always act so.'

Lorn let his breath out. 'Urben's son will be the servant of no druid, only of his own gods. And they seem to favour you, so I will listen.' He eyed Eremon warily. 'I do not like you, prince, but I am loyal to my people. What you said . . . about bonding the Epidii together, the people of Alba together . . . it felt like truth. A bard's truth.'

'And you are far-seeing to sense that,' Eremon said. 'I need you by my side.'

'I have courage too, prince, and boldness. But know that my oath to you only lasts as long as the Roman threat. After we win . . . who knows?'

'I will take my chances. Will you ride back with us?'

Lorn nodded.

'Conaire is my second-in-command in all things,' Eremon added. 'Your loyalty to him will not be displaced either.'

Lorn met Conaire's eyes, but when he spoke, it was to Eremon. 'I won't always agree with you.'

'Nor would I want you to!' Eremon grinned at Conaire. 'You don't accept my every word as law, do you, brother?'

Conaire stretched his massive shoulders, holding Lorn's eyes. 'No. But I obey your direct orders.'

Lorn nodded again. An understanding passed between them.

When he had gone, Eremon and Conaire led their horses out into the sunlight.

'Brother,' Conaire remarked, 'let's get home now before any more surprises come our way. The Epidii cub, giving you allegiance! Hawen save us!'

Eremon smiled. 'Some have been good surprises, though. Now I have Calgacus's personal support, a united tribe – and I still have a wife, just!'

Conaire's grin faded. 'Eremon, what you said that night in the stable . . . about Rhiann.'

'I don't want to speak of it. It was the ale talking, that is all.' Eremon buried his head in Dòrn's flank, tightening his saddle.

But he felt Conaire's eyes on his back.

Calgacus gave them a formal leave-taking, but on the day of departure was also there to see them off at the gate. He had come from his hunting hounds, and his faded tunic was marked with muddy paw prints, his hair tangled. But it was as if a golden light shone out from him over all others.

'Farewell, prince of Erin.' The King reached up to Eremon on his horse, and the two men clasped wrists.

'I thank you for your support,' Eremon answered.

'That you have. If you are ever in need, then call on me. And I would be grateful if you'd keep me informed of all developments.'

'Of course.'

They smiled into each other's eyes, and Calgacus lowered

his voice. 'I look forward to the time we take ale together again. Time to ride, time to talk.'

'I, too.'

'Well met, my son.'

Calgacus watched them pass out through the tall gates of the Dun of the Waves, his hand raised. A lone bard sang their farewell from the battlements above, and a line of warrior-guards saluted with their spears.

Up ahead, Rhiann and Caitlin rode beside Conaire with his standard. As ordered, Eremon had left Rhiann alone, but his eyes now followed the graceful line of her back. Though she was in love with Drust, she had not rejected Eremon as husband. The reasons were political, but still he had not lost her entirely.

He sighed, the pain stabbing anew, just when he least expected it, and with one last glance at Calgacus he brought up the rear of the party.

'My lord!' Aedan dropped back beside him, his grey eyes dancing. 'I have written a song about your meeting with the King, and your triumph over the druid. Will you hear it?'

Eremon smiled his assent, and settled back in his saddle.

Dunadd called them home.

They smelled the smoke from a league away.

'What . . . ?' Eremon drew rein and shaded his eyes against the low sun, gazing down the last rise in the track before it curved around the hills to Dunadd.

Rhiann stopped too, patting Liath's neck. The mare's head drooped, and even Caitlin and Conaire's jesting had long since fallen away into exhausted silence. Soon Rhiann would be home again; in her own little house, her own comfortable bed . . .

'By the Boar!' A string of curses rent the air, and Eremon wheeled to face them. 'Lorn, take your men and escort the women back to the dun. If there is any sign of danger, then retreat with them into the hills until we know more. The rest of you, ride with me, as fast as you can.'

413

'What is wrong?' Rhiann cried. 'What do you mean by "danger"?'

Eremon's eyes were chilled. 'Crìanan is burning.'

CHAPTER 53

Arutted cart track led off the main path, angling towards the sea. As he galloped down it, Eremon strained to see across the marshes, and to his relief realized then that Dunadd itself was safe. The banner of the White Mare still flew from the King's Hall.

Crìanan was another matter. When they thundered up the ridge to the port, a ruin of smoking houses met their eyes. The piers had been burned to the waterline, and the corpses of wrecked boats lay forlornly on the tidal sands. The sound of women's wailing filled the air.

Across the dark bay, the palisade of the Dun of the Hazels was scorched and splintered, and smoke obscured its high crag. There, too, lay boats, half out of the water on the rocks, skeletons of blackened frames and broken masts.

Eremon leaped to the ground and grabbed the shoulders of a man hauling a crumbling roof-post from the collapsed walls of a house. 'Who did this?'

The man's eyes were soot-rimmed and heavy with grief. 'The red invaders.'

'When?'

'A week ago. We dared not return until now.'

Eremon released him, his throat closing over with rage.

Finan met him outside the gates to Dunadd. 'It was unexpected, my lord.'

Eremon looked up at the sturdy gate timbers, the rock walls of the crag. 'Tell me.'

'Five ships, with many oars. They ran in on a westerly from the Isle of Deer, so swift that the defenders at the dun only had time to launch a handful of boats. But they were soon rammed and sunk.'

'And then?'

'The Romans bombarded the dun and the port with iron bolts and fireballs.' Finan was pale. 'My lord, they did all that from the ships, from the water!'

Eremon closed his eyes. 'Casualties?'

'Around a hundred. The fishing fleet was out, thank the gods. But after the bombardment, soldiers landed, striking down all who had not fled, then leaping back aboard their ships. They left as swiftly as they came.'

Eremon let his breath out. 'If Dunadd was ignored, then it was not a concerted attack.'

'No?'

'No. It was a warning.'

Sick with dread, Rhiann scanned the milling crowd at Dunadd from Liath's back, but could not see Linnet. She leaped down and pushed through the jostling bodies, then ran up the path through the Moon Gate. And there Linnet met her, and they threw themselves into each other's arms.

'I didn't know if you were alive!' Rhiann cried.

'Inside here we were safe.' Linnet's eyes were shadowed with grief. 'The poor souls at Crìanan were not.'

'Dear Goddess! And what of Eithne's family?'

'They are well. Only Crìanan and the Dun of the Hazels were attacked.'

'I'll get my medicine bag, then. Take me to the injured right away.'

'Daughter.' Linnet's voice was bleak. 'They left none injured.'

Eremon sent Lorn back to his father's dun, with orders to mobilize the southern chieftains into a stronger chain of defence. The scouting posts on southern and western flanks were increased in size and number, but most importantly, all the cliff-top duns near the sea were furnished with beacons, to signal each other and Dunadd of seaborn threats.

Eremon would not be caught out again. Agricola had a fleet, even though he did not come to destroy Dunadd.

He came to teach me a lesson, Eremon thought. *One that I have no intention of learning.*

And then it struck him that if Agricola had ships on the west coast, he likely had a sea presence in the east as well. And Calgacus's people lived by the sea.

He called for a messenger. 'Deliver our news to Calgacus the Sword. Give it only to the King, in person, using my name as passage.'

As he watched the messenger ride away from the gates, he wondered if the Caledonii nobles would consider this a 'development'.

For days, Eremon supervised the levies in the clearing of the destroyed buildings and piers. Linnet and Rhiann had the sorrowful task of attending to the funeral rites of the people who died, and purifying the site so that it could be built on again when the mourning period was over.

So it was some time before people turned their attention to what had transpired at Calgacus's dun.

'Gelert rode in with a great rage in his face,' Linnet told Rhiann on the beach, as they gave the last scatterings of ash and flowers to the sea. 'He did not explain what happened, just gathered his belongings and told his brethren he was going away.'

'Away where?'

'To wander Alba, to commune with his gods, retreat into the forests: I do not know.'

Gelert's sudden departure was a relief, but when the first shock of the attack had receded, and the rebuilding began, Eremon knew it was time to carry the full truth of his background to the council himself.

Lorn came from the south to speak for him, far more eloquently than Eremon would ever have expected from the brash young warrior, and Rhiann gave her support, showing little of the anger that still dwelt in her eyes whenever she looked at him.

Declan the seer, who was now acting Chief Druid, was calmer and more practical than his master, and had never understood Gelert's hatred of the prince. He listened carefully, his fingers interlaced at his chin, and then rose to report that he read the signs in the flight of the birds, in the entrails of a trapped hare, in the falling of bones across the diviner's hide.

And the gods were clear: the Epidii needed the prince of Erin now more than ever.

For the fear of the Romans, which receded after the fort raid, had now returned in full. The people could not face being vulnerable again, leaderless, no matter what the prince had said or done. He was a strong war leader, he had trained many men, strengthened their defences – and perhaps most of all, he now had the support of Calgacus the Sword.

Of all the Epidii, Talorc and Belen would not meet Eremon's eyes, which grieved him. But he knew that Belen was a practical man, and would accept what was best for the tribe. And as for Talorc, Eremon's daring gamble had appealed to a warrior like Calgacus, and eventually, no doubt, when his heart had cooled, would have the same effect on Brude's cousin. Only Tharan voiced dissension.

'Crìanan never would have happened if you had not launched that needless fort attack,' he raged.

'The council itself agreed to it,' Eremon replied coolly.

Tharan glowered beneath thick white eyebrows. 'The Roman chief did this to get at you personally, prince. Instead of bringing us safety, you put us in danger!'

'There may be some truth to that. But I guarantee that Agricola has also raided the east coast. He is testing us. And because of *my* levies, the strength that he saw here at Dunadd may make his step falter.'

'Bah!' Tharan shook his shaggy head. 'Your tongue is gilded, and too much for me.'

But he did not speak out again.

It was some days before Rhiann retrieved Didius from Bran's house. As she approached, she noticed that a strange arrangement of earth channels had been dug around it, filled with dark sludge that seemed to flow down the slope to the outer walls of the dun. On the upslope side, one of Bran's daughters was emptying a pot of cooking water into a shallow pit.

It seemed that Didius had kept his promise to Bran.

Now she found him in the forge with the smith, plunging a new adze head into the water barrel. As the steam hissed and cleared, the Roman's face emerged, blackened with soot and sweat. His tunic sleeves had been torn off to fit the length of his arms, and his upper lip was covered with a scraggly moustache. He looked happy.

'Aye, he's been a good apprentice,' Bran confirmed, laying down his hammer. 'Once the children stopped shrieking, they've quite taken to him. He tells them stories; he can speak properly now, all right.'

'Indeed?' Rhiann raised her eyebrows at Didius, who smiled shyly. 'Well, then,' she said. 'Bran, I want you to remove his leg chains.'

'Are you sure the prince would allow it?'

'I will answer to the prince. Now take up your chisel.'

Didius did not speak as they returned to her house, but his eyes remained so fixed on her face that he stumbled over a sack of wool outside the weaver's shed.

Rhiann caught his arm and steadied him. 'Working suits you better than captivity, does it not?'

He nodded.

'I know you are a builder,' she continued. 'I freed you because I want you to help rebuild our port.' She watched him carefully, wondering if he would refuse.

He thought for a moment, and then his brow cleared. 'I will do as you wish, lady.'

'You have no objections to undoing the work of your own people?' Her voice roughened with pain, and he coloured.

'I do not love the slaughter of women and children. But do not ask me to strengthen Dunadd. Do not ask that of me.'

'Why not?'

'I cannot betray my commander. I will help you to build houses, or forge tools – but not create weapons or defences.'

She regarded him thoughtfully. 'You furnish us with no information. Nor can we access your skills for our own ends. So what is the reason to keep you here, son of Rome?'

'Do you mean to send me back?' His face lit up with hope.

'Alas, no. You know too much of us.'

'Then what will become of me?'

Rhiann's answer seemed to rise up from a deep part of her. 'One day, our two peoples will meet on a great battlefield.' As she said it, she knew it was truth, and smiled at him sadly. 'Perhaps then you can return to them again.'

'You have always been kind to me, lady. You saved my life.' Didius pushed his chest out, but his cheeks flamed brighter. 'Being your personal guard would not be a betrayal of my people.'

Rhiann looked down at the short, round figure, the stumpy legs, the belly pouching over his belt. 'I am honoured, Didius. But you must take an oath that you will not abuse the freedom, and seek to escape.'

'I swear it on my father's good name, and on my own honour.'

'Then so be it. I hope never to need your services, but it would ease me to know that you are by my side.'

The Roman's dark eyes shone with pride.

Eremon's reaction, however, was more prosaic. 'Then he will have to defend you with his fists, for he cannot carry a weapon.'

'He will not harm any of us.'

'I doubt that applies to me.' On the rocks above the beach at Crìanan, he and Rhiann watched alder piles being driven into the silt.

'If he proves himself, in time can I furnish him with a spear?'

'Perhaps. But why is this important to you?'

Rhiann was caught off guard. 'I don't know. But there is something about him . . .'

'Well, he obviously does not have the courage to attempt an escape, or to take his own life. So what use he will be to you, I can't imagine.'

From the walls of the Dun of the Tree, Samana watched the Roman ships gliding out of the harbour, their oars stabbing the air.

They were bearing north, up the eastern coast. She did not know what Agricola's plans were for them. He dealt with the Venicones leaders himself now – after she had put in all the work to bring about their surrender!

She looked out across the field-strips below, golden rivers of barley flowing in the afternoon sun. Soon the harvest would begin, the granaries would fill . . . and Roman traders would come to lay silks at her feet, and unseal jars of wine for her to taste. Normally she gloated over such things, but today she did not care much for what went on in her own lands. Her heart was in the west, and it chafed her to know how close she had been.

To *him*, the man to whom her own spell had bound her . . .

Goddess curse all magic, curse the Romans . . . and above all curse him!

Restless, she paced the length of the walls and back. Her sight was not as strong and clear as Rhiann's. From here, she could not discern what Eremon did or said; how he moved and ate and slept.

She could only hold up her memories to the late sunlight, one by one, examining them and wondering if he was happy.

And if he was not, when she would have the opportunity to sway him to her side again.

And if he would not be swayed, when she could have him killed, so that he would leave her heart at peace once more.

421

CHAPTER 54

A moon after the attack, the last house at Crianan was nearly finished. Dangling his legs over a roof beam, far from the ground, Didius looked out over the heads of the busy thatchers, over the lines of oxen hauling timber, over the pits where clay was being mixed, to where the red marsh stretched away under a hot sun.

Beyond the reedbeds, buzzing with midges, the southern hills rose. He twisted on his perch. To the east, more hills; to the north, the valley . . . and then mountains, marching in craggy rows from horizon to horizon.

Out there in all that wilderness, things lurked. Wolves, and bears . . . and wild-eyed savages with blue tattoos and long, sharp swords. He shuddered. Jupiter forgive him, but he was too afraid to chance an escape.

What if something caught him, and ate him? What if another warrior found him, and there was no Rhiann to stop him being tortured?

His face flushed with shame, as it always did when he had this debate with himself. But he just could not do it.

Right now, he could almost see the answering sneer on Agricola's face. *He* would have broken free as soon as he was captured. But no – he would never have *been* captured. The commander would have fought with Eremon to the death, that or raised the alarm in the camp.

Ah, and that was the heart of the matter. For even if he did survive an escape, he could not go back. Agricola and his officers knew what he had done, how weak he had been. He would be dismissed, in disgrace, and it would tarnish his family name for ever. His ageing father would not look him in the eye; his mother would weep ... better, surely, that they thought him dead.

He caught one of the younger thatchers glaring at him, and he busied himself knocking a wooden peg into the rafter.

It was a miracle they let him up here at all, a miracle the workers on the site had not murdered him, right here where his own people had caused such misery. After all, each house had been built over a sacred pit filled with the bones of the dead. And they could easily have been *his* bones, for what more fitting offering could there be? But though the men looked long at him, they let him be. They might stare at him, but no one would raise a fist. And all because of the Lady Rhiann.

A woman's control over such men was not the only thing that had surprised him.

At first, when he was captured, he had existed in a fog of pain and misery, hardly daring to look around him, conscious only of all those harsh voices speaking that tongue-twisting language.

All he remembered were hard eyes, like those of the prince, fixed on him, and the clanking of bright swords, like the prince's. The gruel they gave him was tasteless, their houses dark and smelly, their men barbarically hairy. They had no fountains, no heating, no lamps beyond stinking seal-oil and torches.

But after the kindness shown to him by the lady, he began to awaken from the fog. With the help of the little maid, he started to distinguish words. And it was then that he stopped seeing them as grunting animals, for at last he could make some sense of what went on around him.

The skills of the big smith impressed him; he possessed all the metallurgical knowledge of the civilized world. But it was in artistic flourish that these people outdid his own. They decorated everything, from scabbards and cauldrons to belt buckles and hairpins. Even horses displayed showy fittings of rare coral and enamel. The handle of a ladle might be laboured over for days, just to get the sweep of a swan's neck right.

These things were amazing enough on their own, but it was nothing to the understanding that came when he gained a better grasp of the language.

Everyone in the dun was treated well, and none went hungry or cold. Women seemed to be making decisions on their own, and transacting business. He stood by and watched a druid – those monsters that Julius Caesar wrote about – deal out calm justice according to a set of laws so complicated that Didius lost track of what was going on in moments.

At the edges of fires, he sat and was swept away by their music, wilder and less refined than the lyre tunes of his homeland, but filled with passion and soaring beauty. He struggled to follow their story-tellers, but was rewarded with tales of such poignancy and mystery that tears were wrung from his eyes.

Yet the greatest surprise occurred only a few days before. In taking a message to Rhiann, he happened upon the prince debating some decision or another with his warriors. Didius expected him to threaten the men into submission with that sword of his, or perhaps challenge one of them to a fight, like snapping dogs.

Instead, he was astonished to see him listen gravely to each speaker in turn, ask measured questions, and deliver a verdict that, judging by the faces, managed to satisfy all combined.

Perhaps he is civilized, Didius thought, until the prince's eyes sought and found him in the crowd, searing his skin. Didius put his head down and hastily moved on. Perhaps not.

Rhiann, of course, was another matter. Now Didius paused to wipe sweat from his face, his eyes moistening. As a newcomer, he seemed to contract every illness that passed through the dun. He soon lost count of how many nights he laboured with a hacking cough or streaming nose, aching to the bone.

But his memories of those nights were not of pain. They

were the softness of the lady's hands as she sponged the fever from his face, or held his head to gulp down those horrid potions of hers. They were the lilt of her voice, as she sang over him, deep in the night, and the scent of her hair as she leaned down to check his breath.

She was as skilled as any doctor he had come across. And she cared for him as she cared for her own.

No, life here was not so bad, now that he was near her.

The traders had returned with the sun and calm seas. The river was thick with punts being poled up and down from the port, and the storehouse doors were flung wide to the breezes. The hides and furs, grain and horses left on their journeys north, south and east, and in exchange, the goods of other lands flowed in: tin, silver, jet, glass, rare dyes and cloth, pins and brooches, cups and bowls.

And one day a swarthy trader brought more than amber from the northern sea: he brought the news that a moon past, the Roman fleet attacked two of the southern Caledonii ports, putting the inhabitants to the sword. As to what would be done about it, Eremon had to wait another week for a message from Calgacus himself. This contained both encouraging and frustrating news.

The frustration was that Calgacus's nobles would not take reciprocal action, beyond closing their ports and moving the people inland.

The encouragement was that Calgacus himself did not believe it was an isolated attack, and was taking it upon himself to call a full council of all the tribes of Alba.

'It will take many moons to convince the leaders even to come,' the messenger repeated. 'Also, there is word that the Romans are already retreating south of the Forth again to their forts in preparation for the long dark. For these reasons, the King has named next Beltaine as the time for the council.'

Eremon gripped his sword harder. 'So far away! Yet better than nothing. Tell him we will be there.'

*

While many were rebuilding the port, all the other hands had been busy on the land; the men cutting the barley, the women tying it into sheaves. The threshing floors rang with the thudding of feet, the air was thick with floating chaff. Others laboured to bring in the wild harvest of cherries and brambles and hazelnuts.

And once the fields had been cleared, and fires lit on the golden stubble, the festival of Lughnasa began: a time of rest after the harvest, a time for drinking and music and good cheer. But the feasts that ran late into the warm nights, the dancing in the fields, the breaking of the first new bread; all of these had a subdued air this year. Many were still in mourning for loved ones lost; others scented danger on the wind.

Rhiann had her own escape, for she must sprinkle the fields with offerings of mead and milk, to thank the Goddess for Her fertility. She liked to do this alone, walking the furrows of an evening, when the sky was the colour of a dove's wing, and the earth breathed out the perfume of the sun.

One dusk, she stood long by one of the ancestor stones, looking across the stubble and river to the hills beyond, where women picked the heather flowers, now coming into full bloom. Soon, the bracken would die, the leaves would turn, and the earth would enter the dark half of the year, the womb half.

Suddenly, her ears caught the soft crunch of feet in the stubble behind her. 'You have lived too long among us,' she said over her shoulder. 'I heard you coming.'

'Oh, Rhiann!' The feet began to run, and then Caitlin's arms came around Rhiann's waist and whirled her.

Rhiann laughed and disentangled herself. 'What brings you here, barging into me like a badly-behaved wolf cub?'

In the fading light, Caitlin's eyes were dancing. 'I have some news!'

'It does not involve a certain warrior of Erin, does it?'

'Oh, how did you know? Honestly, I can never surprise you!'

It was not much of a surprise. A few nights before, Caitlin, in a cart drawn by mares with red-threaded manes, had borne the corn doll aloft around the last harvested field, and then, as harvest queen, led the dancing – with Conaire as her partner.

It was then that Rhiann had seen, though Caitlin still jested with Conaire, she no longer pushed him away. And her eyes held the same light as his, when she gazed at him across the flames.

Now Caitlin clapped her hands. 'He has asked to marry me! He loves me!'

Rhiann kissed her, smiling. 'Of course he does! And do you love him?'

'I think I always did. But I waited, to be sure. He did not seem very constant.'

'But he has proven himself now? You are sure?'

'Oh, yes.' Caitlin's eyes softened as she gazed out across the heather. 'Sometimes you look in someone's eyes and you just *know*.'

Rhiann wished that were true for everyone. 'It is clear how much he cares for you,' she offered. 'I don't think he's ever waited so long for anyone.'

'And that is why I made him wait! If he were playing, he would have lost interest when I did not fall into his bed!'

Rhiann smiled. Caitlin had her full share of female wisdom. 'So you will be joining the happy couples next Beltaine, then? I will rejoice in giving you the blessing of the Goddess.'

'Oh, no!' Caitlin's face held consternation. 'No, once I've made up my mind I can't wait that long.'

'You wish to marry at Samhain? It is a dark time of year for a wedding.'

'You got married, then, didn't you?'

'Well, yes, but that was different. It was a matter of state, not love.'

Caitlin's chin jutted out. 'This is too, is it not? I carry the king's blood, and Conaire is a chieftain's son. We are strengthening the ties between Erin and the Epidii.'

'But don't you wish to be married under the sun, like other brides? With flowers and light . . .'

'Rhiann.' Caitlin's dreamy smile was back. 'If he is by my side, I care nothing for flowers. He brings the sun; he is the light.'

At Crìanan, Eremon took the news with far more discomfort than he could show.

'She is beautiful, and will make you a fine wife.' He clapped a glowing Conaire on the shoulder. 'For a while there, I did not think you would wear her down!'

Conaire grinned. 'For a while there, neither did I! For one so small, she has a will the size of a bear.'

'It does seem to run in the family.'

A shadow crossed Conaire's face. 'Will the council agree, though, Eremon? With her riding around the borders beside me, I forget her real status. Won't they make her marry an Alban prince?'

'They will do no such thing,' Eremon assured him. 'We have proven ourselves, and I have gained much of the control that I need. I won't let them refuse you.'

But Conaire still looked worried.

'They usually marry their princesses to foreign men,' Eremon reminded him. 'You are a chieftain's son, do not forget. This strengthens their ties with us yet again.'

Conaire chewed over that, and then sighed. 'You know, brother . . . I did not expect this. I have never wanted any woman beyond one night! I know you don't approve, for one day we will leave. But there has never been another, not like this. I will not live without her.' He raised his chin, and his eyes held a look that Eremon had only ever seen on the battlefield.

A jest sprang to Eremon's lips, and then he realized the solemn tone for what it was. When a man spoke from the deepest part of his soul, the listener must give the moment its due. He bowed his head, his heart suddenly sore. For an answering part of him wanted that, too – to feel that. Few things would be as great.

When Conaire left, Eremon leaned on the half-built pier, digging his heel into the damp sand. It was one thing marrying for expediency, as he had done. It was another marrying for love. The way the bloodlines ran in this strange country, the Epidii would not give Caitlin up to Erin. And how could Eremon ever do without Conaire by his side?

It was easy to become embroiled in what was happening here with the Romans, but Eremon had never forgotten his ultimate goal. Kingship over his father's lands was all he had been bred for, all he had thought about his whole life.

It was all that kept him going when they crouched behind that barricade on the beach, arrows falling around them; when they sailed away from Erin's shores, burning with rage and hurt. And if Eremon could just bring the Epidii through the Roman threat intact, he'd have an army at his disposal, ready to land in Erin and take his own dun back.

In all of that, there was no place for love . . . and certainly not with a woman who felt nothing in return.

Rhiann.

He kicked the piling on which he was leaning, and Cù yelped and bounded around him, expecting a game. But Eremon had no heart for that.

There was no place for love.

'You!' he barked at one of the workers, stripping off his tunic. 'Help me to haul this post up. Now!'

CHAPTER 55
leaf-fall AD 80

The harvest was barely in when the weather suddenly turned. The wind grew sharper as it blew down from the hills, tugging at the golden leaves of alder and willow along the river, and after a clear night of stars, the first frost covered the ground.

On a day of cloud and stinging rain, Rhiann mysteriously banned Caitlin from her house. Caitlin spent the morning playing *fidchell* with Aedan, but she was too intrigued about what Rhiann was doing to bother concentrating. Aedan won easily, which stunned him so much he did not speak for the rest of the afternoon.

When Eithne came to get her, her black eyes sparkling, Caitlin leaped up and was down the path at a run.

She ducked under the door cover of Rhiann's house, straightened, and gasped.

'Your dowry,' said Rhiann, half-embarrassed, and Caitlin's eyes widened.

Stacked on the floor were nests of woven baskets, wooden bowls, bronze cauldrons, and a set of ornate fire dogs. On the bed, piles of bedlinens, furs and tanned hides spilled over wall hangings and bright rugs. On top, a fine linen undershift was spread, and a dress of the softest blue wool, edged with white mink.

Before Caitlin could speak, Rhiann handed her a wooden chest bound with bronze. Inside was a delicate golden torc, the two arms deer heads set with eyes of amethyst. There were also hair pins, and shoulder brooches of bronze and silver in the shape of wolf and salmon and eagle – all the symbols that Caitlin loved.

She shook her head, her eyes bright. 'How can I accept these? I cannot, I have never—'

Rhiann turned away, straightening the bedlinens. 'Hush! I am your closest kin here at Dunadd, and in the absence of father and uncles I must furnish your dowry, for I represent the clan.'

Suddenly Caitlin's arms wrapped around her, and she buried her head into Rhiann's shoulder. 'Thank you, oh, thank you!'

Rhiann looked down at the small, fair head, and her own arms came out to gather Caitlin close. 'There, there,' she said, patting Caitlin's back. 'This is a time for happiness, not tears.'

Caitlin pulled back and wiped her face, leaving a dirty streak. 'I am happy! That is why I cry!' She laughed, shaking her head. 'It is just that I did not expect such a thing!'

'If these men from Erin insist on taking royal brides from Alba, then they must not be disappointed!'

Caitlin smiled shyly, and stroked the head of one of the brooches. 'I do not think he will be disappointed,' she said, in a low voice.

Rhiann turned away, knowing that he would not.

Two husbands of Erin, yet two very different stories.

Conaire and Caitlin's marriage took place at dusk on Samhain eve, before the fires were extinguished and Rhiann's ride to the mound in the valley began.

The ceremony, not being the symbolic union of the Ban Cré with the war leader, did not need to be public, and only Linnet officiated. So it was that the couple's hands were tied with the red sash before the sacred fire of hawthorn, with only Eremon's men, Talorc and Belen, and Eithne and Rhiann in attendance.

Throughout the simple ceremony, Caitlin remained calm and glowing in her new gown, while Conaire was all fingers and toes. But when Linnet finally called on the Mother of All to bless the union, Conaire lifted Caitlin off her feet with one arm to kiss her, and his face softened into a look of such tenderness that Rhiann's breath caught in her throat and she had to look away.

Of anyone she knew, Caitlin deserved love most of all. But that did not stop the jealous ache in Rhiann's breast. For who would not wish for that?

As she turned her head, her eyes fell on Eremon. He was pale tonight, but the unusual fairness of his skin brought out the crimson of his tunic, and deepened the green of his eyes. He wore all his jewellery tonight, which on many men would appear gaudy, but to her surprise it only enhanced his straightness and the breadth of his shoulders. Draped with the gold and jewels of the civilized, what was raw in him only stood out more starkly.

She raised her gaze to his face, and her heart gave a thump. The pain there was as finely drawn as Conaire's tenderness had been. Flushing, she looked down at her feet. She knew that she had glimpsed something private.

Something she was not meant to see.

Later, under a clear, frosted sky, Rhiann found herself pushed close against Eremon around the bonfire as they watched the dancing. And she realized, suddenly, that they had not spoken properly for moons.

At first she'd been so angry about his lie, but by the time she forgot to be angry, he was deeply involved in the rebuilding of Crìanan and the strengthening of their tribal boundaries, and often away from the dun. She had been busy with the storing of grain, the preserving of the berries and roots, the meat and cheese and honey. At night, she was too exhausted to sit with his men in the hall, and more often than not she left him to sleep in her own house.

'You never dance,' she said now, as they watched Caitlin and Conaire leading the whirling couples. 'Could it be that the shining prince of Erin lacks one skill?'

432

She said it lightly, with a smile in her voice. But he barely turned his head. 'No one has ever asked me.'

She searched his hard profile, black against the fire. 'Well, then, dance with me.'

A pause. 'I do not need to be pitied.'

'Don't be silly!' she retorted, stung. When he did not answer, she snapped, 'Don't dance with me, then!'

'As you will.' He folded his arms.

They stood for some time in silence, as the music swirled around them, and then, with an impatient movement, Eremon turned. 'Come then, and dance.' He sounded angry, and his grip on her arm was hard as he pulled her into the mass of twirling bodies and stamping feet.

The musicians were just ending one dance, and she and Eremon stood for a moment facing each other. His face was flushed, but Rhiann recognized the challenge there, and when the next song started, she raised her chin and held his eyes, as they circled each other to a slow drumbeat. He was surprisingly graceful, although since he rode and fought and spoke with grace, it should not have come as the surprise it did.

Now the beats quickened, and Rhiann had to hold her skirts up with both hands to free her feet for the intricate steps. But she did not look down, and as Eremon danced faster, nor did he. Her blood pounded from the exertion, but that was nothing to the lurch of her belly when he took her around the waist to turn her. He did not laugh down at her, like the other men. His mouth was a grim line scoring his face, and his arms were iron bands, bruising her skin.

Her hands came up against his chest, and she could smell the sweat on him, the scent of his hair . . .

Then someone grabbed her hand, and someone else took Eremon's hand, and they were all spinning in a great, linked circle around the bonfire. When the circle broke up again, Rhiann had lost him in the crowd. With trembling legs, she pushed her way to the mead barrels, trying to catch her breath. No wonder he never danced!

But it was long before her heart calmed, and when she at last sought the bed in her own house, still sleep was elusive. Every time she closed her eyes, flashes of memory crossed her mind.

Last Beltaine, when he lay at ease on the mound in the firelight and smiled at her. When he held her head and gave her water. When he looked down at her with such gentleness in his face . . .

Mother! Do not venture down that path, Rhiann. Only pain waits there.

And he had not been gentle tonight. In fact, he'd looked on her with nothing less than dislike. The journey to Calgacus had changed him. Perhaps he felt more secure in his position now, and no longer needed her. Perhaps he knew all about Drust, and thought her foolish.

But the look of pain on his face as he watched Conaire and Caitlin came back to her, and she lay and wondered far into the night.

Cù shivered, and curled closer around Eremon's thighs. His master's hand came down and gently stroked his head. 'I'm sorry, boy. I try your patience at times.'

At the sound of Eremon's voice, Cù raised his head and licked his hand. Eremon shifted so that he could wrap his cloak around both of them. It was ridiculous to be here in a workshed at this time of year, with no fire. But the coldness was somehow comforting; it helped to scour out his heart, to numb it.

He leaned back on the straw, watching the starlight through a crumbling gap in the wall under the eaves. Samhain. The long dark was nearly upon them. He'd dealt with the attack on Crìanan as well as he could. He had done as much as possible to ward their borders. The training was continuing under Finan's care. The tribal meeting would go ahead.

So, there was little for him to do for many moons.

And that prospect yawned before him like a black pit. As his responsibilities had lessened, so the feelings that he had successfully buried since their journey north were surfacing. Gods! When he saw the way Conaire and Caitlin looked at each other ... . that stab of despair had taken him by surprise. For Rhiann would never turn such eyes on him.

How could his heart be so treacherous? He had never asked for these feelings, never wanted them. A hundred other women were yielding and pliant and warm – and interested in him. Yet out of them all, he had to feel this way for *her*!

And when he tried to freeze her out, tried desperately to maintain the distance between them, what did she do? She taunted him, using her fine eyes in the firelight, pressing her soft body up against him in the crowd ...

She did not even care for him, so why did she do it? She loved Drust, for some unknown reason, and had never shown Eremon even a grain of affection. He must be mad to feel this way. And yet . . . gods! Nothing he thought or said to himself made any difference. He could wrench at his heart, stamp on it, curse it, squeeze it, and tear it until it bled. But it would not surrender. It was the first thing in his life he had been unable to conquer.

Cù heard the harshness of his breathing and whimpered, and Eremon buried himself deeper in his cloak, turning his head to look at the hound.

'I can't stay here through the long dark,' he whispered. 'I'll ride out as often as I can, stay in the other duns. You'd like that, wouldn't you? We can keep moving. Perhaps it will be better then.'

At the word 'ride' the hound's ears pricked up.

Eremon sighed. Maybe that was all he needed.

Women. Hard riding. Cold.

Silence.

CHAPTER 56
long dark AD 80

From that day on, as the light took on a steely edge, and the wind tore the leaves from the trees, Rhiann realized that Eremon's presence was growing increasingly scarce.

After much urging, Conaire and Caitlin accepted the offer of a honey-moon. As marriages were traditionally made in sunseason, the couple would be cloistered away in a hut for one moon, with liberal supplies of honey mead. Even though it was now grey and cold, the newly-weds took over one of the guest lodges in the village, and were installed there in a shower of innuendo and scented rose-hips.

So it was that Eremon left to ride the border defences without Conaire's customary companionship. He returned on a day that Rhiann was attending a birth in a nearby dun. By the time she came back, he had gathered some supplies and gone again.

'I don't like it,' she heard Finan mutter to Colum one night in the King's Hall.

'The Romans are all tucked away,' Colum replied, yawning. 'Likely he's just restless. He's a young lad; we forget that, eh?'

'He has not been himself. If you can't see it, you're more stupid than I thought.'

When Conaire and Caitlin eventually emerged from their lodge, they both floated around in such a daze that Rhiann had to turn away from the light in their eyes. She knew what brought such love to their faces, what consumed them through the endless dark. And the fear that she would never have it was a wound on her soul.

Life in the village below tumbled on towards the longest

night, but high in the King's Hall the atmosphere for Rhiann was as barren as the landscape, slowly freezing day by day.

Once she managed to be in the dun at the same time as Eremon, and she heard him arguing with Conaire in the stables.

'I'm not happy about you patrolling the lands on your own,' Conaire was grumbling.

'Well, come with me, then!' Eremon tossed back. There was a silence, and then Eremon's chuckle. 'I didn't think so. You stay and enjoy yourself with your new wife. I can see in your face how hard it would be to tear you away.'

'You don't need to be out there.' Conaire sounded ashamed, and angry. 'That's why I let you be. You are doing it for your own strange reasons.'

'Someone must keep an eye on the Romans. Let the men enjoy their food and fires, for next year we may not have them to enjoy at all.'

'Just promise me you'll stay well within our borders. Don't do anything reckless.'

'And since when have you known me to act like that?'

'Never. But a blind man can see you're not yourself.'

There was the clanking of harness being tightened. When Eremon spoke, it was the harshest that Rhiann had ever heard him talk to Conaire. 'I did not come back to be questioned. I will let you know where I am.'

After the feast on the longest night, the druids held a ceremony to call the sun back from the south. Rhiann and Linnet conducted their own at the sacred spring above Linnet's house, on a day so cold that the rime on the branches cracked and fell in showers of ice, and they must gather close to the need-fire, lit to show the sun its path home.

Yet as they chanted the long dark prayer, Rhiann felt, faintly, the throb of the Mother pulsing up through her feet. It did not envelop her as it used to do, but its touch did more to warm her than any fire.

437

Afterwards, Dercca was waiting in the house with hot, spiced mead, and while Linnet spun, Rhiann at last unburdened herself about Drust, for the pain and humiliation had faded enough for her to speak of it.

Linnet listened to the whole tale, saying nothing, but her eyes were deep with shadowed thoughts. 'It is well that you saw Drust for what he is,' she said at last.

'But I was so foolish!'

'No!' Linnet shook her head. 'You loved a memory, and that can be one of the most powerful forms of love. In memory, all faults are stripped away, and all that is left is a reflection of your own divine; perfection, a dream.'

'Well, I soon woke up,' Rhiann muttered, prodding the burning logs with an iron poker.

'That matters little. You felt love, passion, desire. These are as important to life in Thisworld as bread and meat.'

Rhiann swallowed, suddenly realizing that she could not speak of what happened in Drust's arms – how she had failed. The shame of that ran too deep. She had never been able to tell Linnet that she was no longer a true priestess. How could she tell her that she was not a true woman, either?

'And what of Eremon?' Linnet busied herself with the wool in her lap.

Rhiann sighed. 'Who can tell?'

'Do you not know your own heart?'

'I admire him . . . we have become friends. But beyond that he makes me feel confused and annoyed. That is all I can say.'

'And do you know his regard for you?'

'It became like a friend; no, more like a brother to a sister, I think. But even that is no longer. He looks at me with such coldness now.'

'Why?'

'Because he despises me for dallying with Drust! Because I was so horrid to him! Because he will return home one day . . .'

'And have you spoken to him?'

Rhiann snorted delicately. 'He is hardly ever here: his

438

feelings are plain.' She looked up, forcing a smile. 'Aunt, do not confuse me any more by asking such questions. Now, give me another spindle and tell me a tale of some warmer land. This night will be long.'

As Rhiann entered the Dunadd stables the next day, she surprised Eremon, who was leading Dòrn out. Cù was at his heels, and came immediately to Rhiann, his feathery tail wagging.

'Oh!' Rhiann stopped, as her belly gave a peculiar lurch. 'Are you leaving already? When did you come back?'

'Yesterday.' Eremon's trousers, tied tight around the ankle for riding, were crusted with mud up to the knees, and his face was wind-bitten, flushed across his high cheekbones. His braids had been left uncombed for days, and dark wisps, torn free by the wind, curled about his forehead.

'And . . . will you not stay for some days?' She attempted a smile. 'I know your men miss you.'

He looked down his nose at her, and his eyes were glacial. 'Do they now? But life goes on unhindered, otherwise?'

She fell back a step at the lash of his voice. 'Well, of course. But is your place not here?'

'There is little for me to do here now. And since I am here only to serve your people, I should be out among them, don't you think?'

She let out her breath, ruffling Cù's head between both hands. Eremon was spoiling for a fight; he had the same look in his eyes as on the night they danced. Plainly, he did not wish to be near her at all.

'Whatever you think is best,' she answered, her heart sinking. Without a word he led Dòrn past her, and whistled for Cù. The dog gave one backwards look at Rhiann, then scampered after his master.

Rhiann stood frozen for a moment, until she was suddenly seized with an urge to call Eremon back, to draw him to the fire and give him a cup of ale, to let him warm himself, take off his boots. She cast about for the words that would draw that crooked smile to his face; something to take the chill out of his eyes.

At the last moment she nearly did cry out; it sprang to her lips, and her feet came to life under her. But by the time she reached the gates Eremon had already kicked Dòrn up into a gallop, and now was only a dark speck against the pale hill-slopes, crusted with new snow.

She gazed after him, feeling strangely empty.

Next time she would make a better effort to reach him. There must be something she could say to bring him back.

The forest was hushed.

Cù's pawprints embroidered the ground all around, as he raced first one way and then the other. But Eremon hardly noticed the hound's playful yapping. He was all but blind to the tracery of black branches above, the glimpses of white-capped hills, the crunching of Dòrn's hooves beneath. All he could see were Rhiann's eyes: the sheen of them like sun on clear water, the faint veins throbbing at her temples.

He gripped his reins harder. The time away had healed nothing, but just made it worse. The women at the southern duns, their soft hands stroking him, their hair trailing over his bare chest in strands of black or gold or red – they had not quenched the fire, but stoked it. They were just bodies in his bed, because on every one of them he transposed finer features: a long nose, tip-tilted eyes, high cheekbones.

There were no fiery depths in those women to be explored, no dry jests to be deciphered, no smile lifting so wryly at the corners. They were not maddening or changeable or elusive. They were just available.

There was a moment when he cried out his ecstasy, that the pain was burned away. But all it took was one glimpse of her in a stableyard, and every shred of that peace was destroyed all over again.

He came out on top of a ridge and reined in, whistling for Cù. The hound burst out of a mass of tangled hawthorns and raced up, panting. Ahead to the south, the snowy peaks were lost in dark banks of storm.

Beyond, lay the newly-conquered territory of the Romans.

Eremon chewed the scar on his lip. The trips from dun to dun, the long nights of mead with the chieftains, the deer roasting over open fires at scouting posts – all of these served a purpose. He had strengthened more ties with more people than ever before.

But it wasn't helping *him*. He must push himself to his limits, if he was ever to exorcise Rhiann from his heart. Only in great cold and weariness might he find peace.

He looked down at Cù. 'We must go further, little brother. Come.'

He nudged Dòrn over the ridge and down the other side.

'Lady, I think you should come.'

Eithne was standing at the door of Rhiann's house, strangely pale.

'What is it?'

Eithne opened her mouth and closed it, and something cold gripped Rhiann's heart.

'Come where?' she cried, flinging on her cloak. 'The gate, the hall, where?'

Eithne just pointed down to the gate, and Rhiann was flying, her feet crunching on the snow.

When she got there, guards were crowding around something at the steps of the gate tower. She frantically pushed through the wall of burly shoulders. 'Get out of my way!'

The men fell back, until she was at the centre of the circle. She looked down, and her breath froze in her throat.

It was Cù, matted, lean and rangy, shivering as he stared up at her with mournful eyes.

Alone.

CHAPTER 57

'There is no time to lose!' Conaire was throwing random pieces of clothing and weapons – two daggers, a sling, slingshot – into a leather pack beside his bed. 'Get someone to prepare my horse!'

'We must move swiftly,' Rhiann agreed. 'But I just need a little time to make sure we have enough clothing and food – it is madness to rush out at this time of year—'

'We?' Conaire stared at her wildly. 'What we?' He looked from Rhiann to Caitlin, who was standing by the bed, her hand at her mouth. 'No one is coming with me. I'm going alone. *I* did this to him, *I* should have been by his side—' His voice cracked.

Rhiann had expected the cold mask of a warrior, but that was not what she saw. Instead, someone stricken to the core looked out of Conaire's eyes. The anguish was so raw she had to look away, realizing that it was mirrored in her own body. That was why her hands were trembling so. *Goddess! Take control, Rhiann. If he can't, you must.*

'My love.' Caitlin placed a tiny hand on his huge shoulder. 'Of course we will all come. We don't know what has happened to him. It is safer this way.'

'No!' Conaire whirled on her. 'I'm not losing you, too. I let him down and it is for me to find him!'

Rhiann took a step closer. 'Conaire, I understand. But if he is in trouble, you will need warriors. And if he is hurt,' she swallowed, 'then you'll need me, too.'

'And I'm not letting you go anywhere without me!' Caitlin put in, suddenly fierce. As Conaire tried to argue, she stamped her foot. 'No, and no! If you try to leave me here, son of Lugaid, then by the Goddess, I'll follow you and . . . and if I get lost then it *will* be your fault!'

There was an exasperated sob from Conaire, and Caitlin ran into his arms. Over her sister's head, Rhiann saw that his eyes were wet.

Of course, not a single one of Eremon's men would stay behind in the dun. After the initial shock had worn off, Conaire took charge, adding ten Epidii warriors to the already substantial band. He also sought out two of the best trackers.

Rhiann gathered every salve or brew to help wounds and fevers, plus rolls of linen bandages. Of course, perhaps he had just fallen from his horse. But her healer's instinct told her what to take, even while her conscious mind tried to shut out the possibilities. It would not be a mere sprained ankle; she sensed it.

Within a day they were ready to go. Cù seemed to know what they were doing, and paced back and forth from the gate to the yard as they saddled up, whining. But despite his desperation to get back to Eremon, Rhiann left him with Aedan, since with the recent gap in the snows they could easily follow Eremon's tracks.

Luckily, Eremon had wandered up the slopes to the east without going near another dun, where his prints would have become lost. For two days they followed him, up and down ridges and hollows where no one else rode during the moons of the long dark. Although more snow had fallen, Dòrn's hoof-prints were still clear.

Rhiann looked down at them from Liath's back as they passed, sick in her belly. *He* had come this way not so long before. Tired, perhaps, alone, angry.

But alive. Breathing.

At last they stood on a mountain spur that marked the edge of the settled Epidii lands. The actual borders were further to the south, but the Romans had been roving those lands from their new forts, and many southern people had abandoned their farmsteads to seek the protection of the northern chieftains. Yet Eremon's tracks went down the ridge and led up a wide glen, a fine, wavering thread against the snow.

Conaire straightened from peering at the ground, holding his bridle. 'Why, by the gods, did he go south? There are no more duns, no steadings, even. Why?'

Rhiann thought about the look she had seen lurking in Eremon's eyes that last day, and suddenly recognized what it was: despair. But what could she say to Conaire? She had been the last person to see Eremon. Was it something *she* said or did that had propelled him to seek this danger? She cleared her throat. 'We all know that he has been . . . restless. Perhaps he felt he had more to prove.'

Conaire kicked at a drift of snow. 'Well, when I find him, the first thing I'll do is throttle him.'

In another two days they were at the border, where the Highlands ended and the Lowlands began that led to the Clutha. Still Eremon's tracks continued. They found his camps, saw his pacings. They even saw faint, older signs of Roman patrols. But Eremon did not stop and turn back.

'It is likely that since the snows the Romans have bedded down,' Conaire said one night, as they huddled in their leather lean-to, swathed in sheepskins. He looked over at Rhiann and Caitlin. 'I do not want you to come any further, but short of tying you up, there is little I can do.' He smiled wearily. 'In the absence of Eremon, I act for him. I don't suppose you'll do as your lords and husbands command, will you?'

As one, Rhiann and Caitlin shook their heads.

Conaire sighed. 'I did not think so.'

Their goal, when they reached it, was a shock. As they moved south, Conaire sent the trackers ahead, since they were best at staying hidden. And so it was that one of them came scrambling back down a narrow glen, to where the others had made a fireless camp. The day was dark with cloud, and flakes of snow were being driven against the rocks above by icy blasts of wind.

'I've found something,' the tracker reported breathlessly.

Rhiann ducked out from the lean-to. 'What?'

'Just below the ridgeline he stopped. He dismounted . . . he was not taking care.' The man began to draw in the air. 'Roman feet sweep up from the trees, here. There was a scuffle, the ground is marked with foot and hoof prints.' He paused, glancing at Rhiann. 'There are traces of blood.'

A chill swept over Rhiann.

'And what else?' Conaire's voice was hoarse.

'The Roman tracks and the horse continue south-east. I followed the trail as far as I dared without coming out into the open. There is more blood, but not a lot, along the way.'

Conaire sighed. 'Then they have him alive, though wounded.'

The trackers were sent to seek the destination of the patrol, but no amount of pleading on anyone's part broke Conaire's determination to stay where they were. 'We're not moving until I know for sure that every last Roman is tucked up in bed.'

That afternoon one of the trackers returned. 'There is a new fort, in the middle of a pass. The patrol has gone there. No one is out on foot now. No one has left there since they arrived with the prince.'

Rhiann stood among the bare trees, snowflakes catching in the wisps of hair that escaped her sheepskin hood. The pass below was a blanket of white, broken only by the dark tussocks of frost-blasted sedge. In the middle, the Roman fort reared up defiantly, yet was dwarfed by the immensity of the encircling hills.

From where she stood, Rhiann could just make out the snow-filled ditch that surrounded it, echoing the dark line of timber palisade and gate tower. Behind the gate, two long, thatched buildings crouched.

'It is no more than thirty paces along each side.' Conaire was beside her, and behind, Caitlin struggled through the snow-drifts towards them, barely visible in a white wolfskin

445

cape. 'Surely it only holds four score soldiers! We must storm it now – who knows what they are doing to him!'

His voice cracked again, and Rhiann looked up, noting the dark circles under his eyes. She put a hand on his arm. 'Perhaps brute force is not the way, Conaire. Do not endanger Eremon's life through rash acts.'

Anger flooded Conaire's face; the first time he had ever looked at her that way. He was indeed suffering. 'If you mean trying more trickery, well, that has its place. Eremon himself takes that path – don't I know it! But Eremon is not here!'

His face twisted, and Caitlin cut in smoothly, her hand on Conaire's other arm. 'I cannot use the fire arrows, for he is within. But the odds are with us, if we have the surprise.'

Rhiann nodded, pointing at the sky. 'And it may be that the land itself will help us.'

To the south the clouds were so low and dark that the peaks had disappeared, and flurries of snow rippled down their flanks, like racing horses. It was a storm wall, advancing towards them – and towards the fort.

Conaire turned to Rhiann. 'I know we can do it, although we are at a disadvantage, with that ditch and rampart. But in the storm, we can get close without being seen, and if Manannán blesses us, the Romans are all by their fires, assuming no one else will be out in such weather. We can do it!'

'But you'll need a distraction,' Rhiann said. 'I can provide it.'

At this Conaire frowned. 'What do you mean? Eremon would skin me alive if he knew I had put you in danger.'

'You are not putting me in danger – I am! Surely I can use my trickery, as you call it, for some good thing.' She stared at the fort, lost in thought.

'Rhiann has the right to fight in her own way,' Caitlin put in.

Conaire sighed. 'Hawen's balls! What chance do I have between the two of you?'

Then Rhiann was struck by an idea so daring that fear rose

446

cold in her throat. She whirled to face them both. 'What if I could get the gate *open*?'

On the gate tower, a young soldier shrugged deeper into his cloak, shivering. Blasted, forsaken, barbarian land!

It was always raining, and as soon as the rain stopped, it snowed. Snowed! He was from the Hispanic lowlands, and snow was alien to him.

A burst of laughter sounded faintly from one of the two barracks below. *They* were all in the warmth, gaming and eating and drinking. But as he was the youngest, the centurion always gave him the worst watches. Mars save *him* if the commander ever found out that one man had been left to watch alone.

He peered out into the bank of whirling snow. What was the point of standing guard on a day like this anyway? He couldn't see further than a few paces away from the gate. And anyway, they'd been patrolling northwards for the last few moons, and seen nothing of the natives.

It was as Agricola said. The barbarians had fled, terrified by the might of the Roman army.

He jiggled from foot to foot. The only exception was the itinerant they caught a few days before. He was in rough clothes, and although he wore none of those barbaric gold rings, there was a fine one in his pack. And his horse was fine, too. The centurion decided he must be a thief on the run, and the man confirmed this with the few bits of information they'd beaten out of him. A thief might be an outcast, and an outcast would turn traitor easily.

The centurion thought that such an unusual catch might furnish those higher up with some good information, and so tomorrow he was being sent south in the wake of the army, back towards the nice, snug winter quarters that everyone *else* had been given. If the commander was pleased with them after that, perhaps they'd get an extra ration of beer. Or some warmer socks.

Suddenly the soldier blinked and tensed, instantly alert.

Below him in the snow, a figure stumbled. He brought his spear to bear with both hands. 'Who goes there!' he barked in his own language.

A faint cry came back; a high, clear voice.

A woman's voice.

CHAPTER 58

The wind drove stinging snow in under Rhiann's hood, and the ground was like iron, the cold seeping up through her boots. Ahead loomed the dark gate tower, and faintly she made out the shape of a soldier standing on it. When she recognized the outline of his spear, she suddenly felt desperately alone, and vulnerable. Would he attack?

At every step she tensed, waiting to hear that high whine, feel the impact in her chest. Her palms inside the sheepskin mittens were slick with sweat, and her heart nearly drowned out the storm itself. But perhaps he could not aim true in this snow . . . yes, surely. And somewhere, not far behind, the men crept with their swords. Somewhere, Caitlin crouched with an arrow on her bow-string.

The only thing that kept Rhiann's feet moving was the knowledge that Eremon was in there, hurt and despairing. She had to do this for him.

That thought gave her courage, and she warded away the fear and drew her scattered thoughts deeper in, calming them with sheer will, centring her power in the middle of her breast. Beyond the cold, and the screaming wind, she tried to feel the heartbeat of the land.

Somewhere, deep underneath her, it was there. She'd not told Conaire that she didn't *know* if she could do this, if she could reach the Source. If not, she was the only one in immediate danger. But she just had to pray that, if not for her, the Mother would help Eremon.

Breathe . . . breathe . . . there . . . feel it, wait for it . . . there! The throb came once, twice, three times.

Now she drew it slowly up her legs, desperately hoping that she would not lose the thread, letting it pulse in waves of warmth.

You are the tree, came Linnet's voice in her mind. *Your roots reach down to the Source. The Source is light. Draw it up through your roots, your legs, and hold it . . . here . . . in your heart. First, let it fill your chest as if it is a pool of light, and the Source the spring. When the pool is full, draw it higher. Then, let it fill the centre of your throat, and finally let it rise to the spirit-eye on your brow. Now you can feel using the Source, you can speak using the Source, you can see using the Source.*

Within the grainy ice and white wind, Rhiann burned.

The man shouted another challenge, and she walked forward. The Source enveloped her with its heat.

I am cold, weary, stumbling, she projected towards him. *I am alone.* He would not hear the words, for they would fall straight into his heart. He would only feel them.

The man did not raise his spear to throw.

Despite the snow, Rhiann nudged her hood back, so her unbound hair fell free. *I am young. I am beautiful. By far the most beautiful thing you have ever seen. I am a goddess, come to bring you warmth in the endless cold.*

The man was still, but did not cry out for his comrades.

She closed her eyes to see with her spirit-eye, and realized that he was young, very young. And transfixed. A glowing ball of light surrounded him, as it did all people. In it, his emotions swirled in bands of red and blue and violet. She was not strong enough to penetrate that. But she could sense it.

With her own spirit, she grazed the edge of his light-body. And something reached out for her, urgently.

Desire.

'Help me!' she cried, raising her hand. She spoke halting Latin; perhaps he would think her from their allied tribes. But into his heart she radiated something else. *You are weary, too. You are lonely, and frustrated. It is long since you felt a woman's skin. Here, this is the taste, the touch, the smell . . . remember . . .*

He had come forward, was gripping the edge of the palisade. 'Why are you out here, alone?'

She was close enough now to look up at him, and she knew that what fading light there was would fall on her upturned face. She barely felt the snowflakes on her skin. His dark eyes gazed down at her from beneath his helmet. Her other senses felt his breathing catch, and grow faster.

Now that she was closer, she could loop her own web of light around him, snare him in it, bombard his heart from all directions with a cascade of senses: honey lips, white breast, skin-scent, fingers of fire, breath-murmur . . .

It was like the magic she felt at Samana's dun. But in that moment, Rhiann's was stronger, for it was fuelled by all the love of those men about her, for Eremon. Though they would never know it, right now, the love of Eremon's men for their prince fed the Source as it flowed through her.

'Please help me,' she pleaded. 'My family was attacked by the northerners and I fled. I'm lost, and cold.'

I am harmless. I am alone. I am a woman.

His body-light flared with a last burst of defiance. 'You should seek your own people, girl. This is no place for you.'

'I'll die in the storm if I go. Please.'

If I stand close, you will smell the perfume of my skin. I am a barbarian woman. My appetites are strong.

She saw him glance nervously over his shoulder.

They will never know. They left you here, cold and alone. You will show them. You are a man. I need a man to save me. I will be grateful.

Luckily, he was young and inexperienced, and hadn't lain with a woman for many moons. Magic could not sway someone's mind, it could only whisper to the urges already there, stirring up coals to fire. It plucked at weaknesses.

She held her breath, saw the energy in him wavering. As it did, she put all her effort into drawing the Source up in one last fountain of white-hot light, and whirled it at him. The weak resistance shattered, and she nearly cried aloud with the rush of power that flooded her.

451

He swore, softly, and disappeared. And then there was the creaking of the bars on the gate.

A black gap opened, and wood scraped over icy stones. 'Come on then, girl,' the youth murmured. 'And be quick about it.'

Rhiann had to put her shoulder into the gap, for he would not open it wide. And as she did, she locked her eyes with his and held them, spellbound, smiling with all the promise she could muster . . .

. . . just long enough to throw her whole weight against the gate, so it was wrenched from his hands. And before he could wake himself enough to leap on her, a line of wraiths rose up from the snow-filled ditch, where before there had been no men at all, and flew at him on padded feet.

She felt the nightmares of Alban giants and monsters rise up and paralyse the boy's voice. And a moment later, as Rhiann ducked, something whizzed past her ear. The boy's body fell like a stone, a white-fletched arrow protruding from his throat. Without breaking stride, Conaire stepped over the body and was inside, the other men following silently but swiftly.

Rhiann slumped against the gate, and watched the boy's blood pool on the icy ground, the snowflakes falling on his upturned cheeks.

Mother. The power had receded in a rush, leaving her trembling. *Mother, forgive me.* She had brought death. She, a Goddess-daughter, who revered life. And yet, as she had joined this fight, so she must partake of its bitterness, as well as its triumphs. Eremon would tell her that she had no choice. But the least she could do for this boy was to accept that she did have a choice, and had taken it, and blame no one but herself for what it brought.

She reached down and closed the boy's sightless eyes, and left a finger's caress on his lips as she heard Caitlin's slight steps in the snow behind her.

'The kin bids you farewell,' she whispered, her tears falling into his mouth, 'the tribe bids you farewell, the world bids you farewell. Go in safety.'

Eremon lay in the darkness, wrapped in pain. The pain centred around his chest, where the beating had been worst. Every breath, every expansion of his ribs, was agony. At least he'd stopped feeling his broken fingers. Here, in this end of the barracks, it was freezing, and his hands were bound behind him, cutting off the circulation.

Curled in a corner, he shut his swollen eyes and tried to extinguish the images in his mind: the brightness of their helmets against the snow; the jeering faces; the hatred in those dark, alien eyes.

It was not like battle, where he locked eyes with an opponent, consumed with the thrill of pitting himself against an equal. For a moment out of time, only two existed, sharing heartbeats, sharing breath, sharing blood.

But to be tied up like some animal, arms pulled back so the fists can penetrate deeper; to watch a sword-hilt come down on his fingers, helpless and exposed . . .

A whimper escaped his tightly-closed mouth, and he was flooded with shame. *I am a leader. I have courage. I will die with courage.*

He did not know why he was not already dead. They must want to send him to the main camps: any information from the north would be valuable. A shuddering now took hold of his limbs, and he bit his lip to stop himself crying out.

I will find a way to kill myself.

It is the best I can do for Alba.

Conaire clustered the men under the darkness of the gate tower. Within the storm, the day had become no more than a dark, featureless stew of grey cloud, but Conaire's heart beat clear and slow now, his mind sharpened with a grim resolve.

The open space inside the rampart held two long buildings. One was dark, and seemed lifeless. From the other, the nearest one, firelight spilled from a row of small windows. Every now and then a faint roar of laughter sounded.

'Colum,' Conaire whispered. 'Take five men and surround the door of that building.' He indicated the dark barracks. 'When you hear our attack, go in with caution. If you meet resistance, deal with it. If you do not, and Eremon is there, leave two to guard him and the rest come back and join us.'

Colum took his picked men, and they crept around the rampart wall. Through the whirling snow, Conaire saw the dark shapes edging into position.

'We have the best odds we'll ever see,' he murmured to those remaining. 'We're outnumbered, but I'm betting they feel safe inside their walls, and won't have weapons to hand. We must take three down each.' He paused. 'Agricola will know it was us if they remember our unpainted faces. Leave none alive.'

He eased his sword free, the sound masked by the high keening of the wind, and slipped across the space between gate and barrack block, his men following, ducking as they went beneath the windows.

In a moment they were all outside the door, spread along each wall. There, sheltered from the wind, the sound of talking and laughing swelled. Peering at the door closely, Conaire saw that it was flimsy – not designed to keep out anything, except wind.

With tight lips and a jerk of his head, Conaire got his swiftest, heaviest fighters into a tight wedge behind him, as only the first handful would have the element of surprise, and they must clear a space for the others to swing. With a quick prayer to the Boar, he tensed back a few steps, adjusted his shoulder.

And ran.

Like a charging bull, he burst through the door as if it were brushwood. By the light of fire and lamp, he glimpsed scores of men, lined up on the benches and floor, gaming, drinking. While the surprise was still dawning on their faces, Conaire, his sword held two-handed, swept it across the nearest men like a scythe.

Screaming, his warriors charged in after him, laying about them in great circles of blade. Arms and heads were hewn from living bodies; in moments the floor was slippery with blood.

Conaire saw the men at the edges scrambling for their weapons in the farther reaches of the barracks, and with a roar he cleaved the crowd, cutting a swathe through those who were ill-prepared, striving to reach those who sought for arms.

Some had their swords up by the time he barrelled into them, but he was unstoppable. Fergus and Angus were tight up behind him: as Conaire drove the wedge, so they had time to swing. He felt the sting of Roman blades on his arms, but they were just glancing pinpricks. His own sword bore them down like a storm wave.

In his head, a litany thrummed. Eremon. Eremon. Eremon.

The litany brought the fire to his limbs, the strength to his legs . . . and at last it burst from his lips, as he felt the blood-lust bloom in his chest. The men took up his cry, until among the curses of the Romans and cries of pain, one name rang to the rafters.

'Eremon!'

As if waking from a dream, Eremon stirred. There was a noise . . . something familiar, out there in the howls of wind. He raised his head, though it rang with dizziness.

Manannán.

His name. Someone called his name.

Was it the gods, come to claim him at last? Had he passed over to the Otherworld? But no: he opened one swollen eye. It was nearly dark now, but a last drift of light caught on the nubbled plaster of the wall before him. He was not dead.

'Conaire?' he managed to croak, through cracked lips. The sound faded away in the room. Gritting his teeth against the pain, he edged himself up the wall, his hands still bound behind him. He took a deep breath. 'Conaire!' he cried, louder now, hardly knowing why he called, for Conaire was far away.

Though the sound was mewling to his ears, like an injured cub, in an instant the doorway was filled with the dark shadows of men. He tensed, but had no arms free to raise in defence.

'My lord,' someone said. It was a language he knew. Words that made sense, at last.

'Boar's balls, get your knife,' someone else said, and arms came around him, cutting his bonds. The blood rushed back to the ends of his fingers, bringing agony.

He fainted.

At the edge of the slaughter, Conaire paused and risked a glance back. His men were fighting in knots all over the room. In the first charge, perhaps a score of Romans had died, reducing the odds to two to one. But in such a confined space, with the Roman order in tatters, the men taken unawares, the odds had become, in truth, even.

The strength of the Romans lay in their discipline, so Eremon always said. Hand to hand, like this, armourless, unprepared, they had only their brute fighting skills to save them. And Conaire's men were taller, heavier. In this they could triumph.

The Roman soldiers that had not been killed were backed up against the walls, led by someone who seemed to be their commander, but the Erin men were hacking their way through their defences. The room was deep in bodies, the floor awash with blood. Fergus was just pulling his sword free of a downed man, and with a yell, threw himself back into what remained of the fray. Angus must still be fighting in the shadows.

But it was only a matter of time, now, and they could do without Conaire at last. So he hurried back through the splintered door, and across to the other building. Two soldiers lay dead just inside the doorway, and voices echoed from a small room at the far end.

Conaire plunged through the inner door, to be faced with the sight of Eremon laid out on the floor. He knelt down, pushing Colum to one side. 'Alive?'

'Yes.'

Conaire gathered Eremon in his arms. Though only half-conscious, Eremon moaned in pain. 'Gods!' Conaire cried. 'Rhiann's not far. Find his horse and pack and follow me. I want him out of here, now!'

CHAPTER 59

Mercifully, Eremon missed most of the journey home.

He remembered snowflakes falling on his face, and shivering beneath blankets before a tiny fire, which swelled and shrank, as he tried to look at it through half-open eyes. He remembered wafts of Rhiann's honey scent, and the thudding of her heart against his ear. He remembered water being squeezed between his cracked lips, and then warm broth.

And her voice swam in and out of his mind.

'I'm giving him as much as I can . . . it will make him sleep. It's the only way for us to travel fast, he'll be in too much pain otherwise . . . No, we can carry him on the horse . . . it's only the fingers broken . . .'

And so it went on for an endless time: the lurching of the horse beneath him, and the stabs of fiery pain; the cold that crept in under his furs, clawing at his skin; the wind scouring his face. He burned, and then he shivered.

'Thank the gods for snow,' came Conaire's voice, from far away. 'Our loop would not throw them off long otherwise.' A rough hand cupped his shoulder.

And sometimes, when the lurching stopped, there would be singing, very soft and close to his ear.

Rhiann sat by the sickbed in her house, gazing down at Eremon's face. The men had just laid him in the furs, and she had given him an extra dose of the sleeping flower, so she could examine his injuries.

It had been hard to do by firelight on the journey home, although she saw from the grotesque swelling that the Romans had broken three fingers on his left hand. Luckily the breaks were clean, and she splinted them while he was unconscious. He had two black eyes, but no damage to the eyeballs. Mainly, she had concentrated on breaking the fever, and getting some food and water into him.

'Rhiann,' Caitlin said now, 'tell me what to do and I'll do it. I'll hold him up for you, hold him down for you, whatever you ask.'

'No,' Conaire broke in. 'I'm staying by his side. I'll do it.'

'I will treat him alone.' Rhiann's own voice sounded so strange to her ears, strained and cold.

'But we can help!' Caitlin protested.

'Mistress,' Eithne moved to Rhiann's side, 'the brew will be ready soon. I can bring it for you.'

'No!' Rhiann turned on them. Three pairs of eyes widened. '*I will treat him alone! Now leave me!*'

Astonishingly, they did, seeing in her face, perhaps, a glimpse of the anguish in her heart. When they were gone, she let out a shuddering breath. For the first time in days, the healer self began to recede. She'd had to be strong, to get him home.

Until now.

She peeled back the furs, and eased his tunic up over the planes of his belly, over his ribs, up to his chest. And then she looked down, and gasped.

The entire surface of his skin was webbed with red welts. And beneath them, mottling his ribs and abdomen, were wide swathes of purple and green bruises. Of the kind not only made by fists, but also by feet.

Her fingers jerked free of the fine linen, and her eyes sought his face, the pale oval blurred by her tears.

In sleep, his mouth was a soft curve. His hair flopped over one injured eye, the lashes long and black against his cheeks. Perfect.

And yet below, ruin.

*

Eremon's fingers had been well-splinted, and though Rhiann's prodding of the bruising detected a cracked rib, no internal organs were damaged. The hunger and thirst and beating had weakened him, bringing on the fever, but it was a slight illness, and soon burned itself out.

On regaining consciousness, the first thing Eremon asked about was his men. Conaire looked down at him with sorrow in his eyes. 'Angus and Diarmuid did not make it, brother. Three of the Epidii warriors also died.'

Eremon turned his head away at that, and did not speak for a long time. Caitlin pulled fiercely at the lacing on her sleeve, while Rhiann went to tend the fire. Conaire sat heavily on the covers without saying anything.

'I was foolish.' Eremon's face was pale. 'I knew I should go back but . . . I saw only the danger to me. Curse it! Curse *me*!'

Conaire shook his head. 'We dealt the Romans an incredible blow, brother. Like any of us, Angus and Diarmuid would be honoured to die for this cause. They feast with the gods now; the bards will sing their names.'

'We all ache to kill the invaders, Eremon.' Caitlin rested her hand on Conaire's shoulder. 'I was with Angus and the others, I heard them speak. They were where they wanted to be.'

But Eremon's eyes remained bleak, and no amount of Rhiann's strengthening draughts seemed to bring the colour to his cheeks.

It was at this time that Didius, who had been staying with Bran, returned to speak to Rhiann. He crept inside the door and stood as far away from the sickbed as possible. But Eremon, the hollows in his cheeks dark with shadow, caught sight of him.

'Son of Rome,' he croaked. Didius froze. 'Your countrymen offered me the same hospitality as we did you.'

'I know,' Didius replied, watching Eremon warily.

'Then we are even, are we not? We have shared the pain. So stop scuttling around me as if I will eat you. You perform a good service for my wife.'

Didius nodded, surprised.

Eremon's eyes seemed to look beyond the Roman then, into the shadows on the wall. 'Your governor seeks all Alba, and he is the kind of man never to rest until he has something. Is this not right?'

Now Didius glanced at Rhiann, confused, and back to Eremon. 'This is right.'

'The deaths of countless men won't stop him, will they? So the death of one foolish, weak man will gain nothing . . . will mean nothing to him. Will it?' The dark wells of Eremon's eyes sought no answer from Didius, but Rhiann went forward to the bed.

'No, Eremon, it won't,' she said softly. 'Only to us.'

Eremon drew a shuddering breath then, as if a battle had been fought. From that day forward his recovery was swift, as youth and strength reasserted themselves in knitting bones and warm cheeks. Youth and strength; and perhaps duty. Certainly duty.

It was only then, at last, when Eremon was out of danger, and needed little of her care, that Rhiann's own feelings about the whole matter were able to surface. And they surprised even her.

The first evening came when they were alone. Conaire and Caitlin, reassured about Eremon's recovery, had gone, and Rori had called in to take Eithne for a walk, as the snows had thawed, and the days were fast growing clearer.

For the first time, Eremon was well enough to sit up by the fire in a new rush-backed chair that Didius had made for Rhiann. As she plumped the cushions behind him to ease the pain in his ribs, Eremon said, 'I heard what you did at the Roman fort.'

She turned to adjust the cauldron chain, lowering it closer to the fire, not sure how to answer.

He raised his voice. 'You must have relished the chance to prove yourself against them.'

She glanced back at him. His smile was tinged with that familiar bitterness, his eyes, circled by fading bruises, were shielded. She remembered the last time she had seen him in the stableyard, and how that bitterness lashed out at her. And look where that led!

Instantly, all the anger she suppressed while acting the healer rose up in full. First she nearly scared herself to death outside the fort, then she went without sleep for days, cold and exhausted – and all for him! And now those green eyes of his were prodding her again, and his voice held that same sarcastic edge, still! Something in her snapped. 'Unlike you, I don't care about *proving* myself! You should be ashamed for putting me through all this!'

'Sorry to inconvenience you.'

'Eremon, don't be stupid, and stop feeling sorry for yourself! You ride around without a thought for anyone else, get yourself captured and beaten, and then I'm supposed to put you back together! And after everything, you dare to look at me like *that!*'

His face was hard and white. 'I was not thinking only of myself . . . not at all!'

'Oh, really?' Rhiann put her hands on her hips. 'So when you scared the life out of Conaire and the others, it was all to benefit them, I suppose! And what about me? *I've* never been so terrified in my life – and it was all fear for *you*, foolish man!'

There was a startled silence. 'Imagine that,' Eremon said faintly.

'I'm more surprised than you, believe me!' She stirred the fire up fiercely, then flung herself down on the hearth-bench. 'I don't know what to make of it!'

This time she heard an intake of breath, and she glared at him, before realizing, suddenly, what she'd said.

Smoothly, simply, Eremon leaned forward with his good hand and took her own, so confidently that it brooked no denial. And with that one gesture, all the words, the currency of the past year, were suddenly and simply redundant.

She waited for the unconscious flinching of her body, but the touch of his fingers just felt . . . natural. Their hands fitted together as if they had been forged as links in a chain.

Frozen, she stared into the fire, as the house held its breath around her.

'Rhiann,' Eremon said softly, after what seemed like an age.

She raised her eyes. And when she saw what lay in his, naked there, she did flinch. But still he leaned closer, and she found she was watching his full, curved mouth, was enveloped in his musk scent, her heart skipping.

I cannot be what he wants me to be. I will let him down. I do not want to let him down.

As his face drew near, as his eyes held hers, reaching deep into her breast . . . she looked away, pulling back in her seat, breaking the hold of his hand. 'Eremon I . . . cannot.' She dared not look at him again, for the shame was burning too bright in her face. Yet it was better that he did not begin to care for her; better for them both.

At her words, he had stilled, and now he slowly sat back in the rush seat. 'I see.'

'Let us not change what we have,' she begged, her voice low.

He said nothing more for a long time, and then he asked, abruptly: 'Surely I am now well enough to sit with Conaire in the hall?'

She nodded, and he rose and drew on his cloak with one hand, keeping the other arm close to his injured chest. When he had gone, she curled up in the rush chair, laying her cheek on one arm. Why couldn't everything stay as it was?

She pressed her fingers to her lips, smelling where his scent lingered. And she remembered her own words to Linnet only a moon before. *One day he will be going home.*

If the thought of losing him to the Otherworld had brought such pain, then she knew what would come when he took sail again for Erin. No, she must ward her heart well.

He was her war leader, her partner, and friend. And that he would stay.

CHAPTER 60

T he next day was Imbolc, and the gift of ewe's milk to the river soon brought the return of weak sun and a flush of green to the bare trees. But the fair weather brought more than buds: the southern wanderers had come back to the marshes in clouds of whirring wings.

Though he had been ordered not to swing a sling, Eremon could stalk, and a day of fowling gave him and Conaire an excuse for air and exercise. They had little chance of a catch, anyway, for Cù was splashing in the pools and snuffling among the reeds, following one trail and then breaking off to lurch the other way.

He knows how I feel, Eremon mused, watching the hound's indecision, and his warring thoughts clamoured once more. He should not have tried to kiss her. But, by the gods, her eyes had flashed with that rare fire, and the light was in her hair . . .

His breath caught, and he stumbled over a tussock of sedge. 'Quiet,' Conaire muttered, scanning the reedbeds.

Eremon squatted down beside him, but could not keep his mind on the hunt.

At first she had been afraid for him – and she let him take her hand! Yet then she pulled away. Was it that she did not care enough? That struck a note of pain, and yet he could have sworn that he saw something deep in her eyes, a flame that mirrored the fire in his heart . . .

Was it something else, then? Something about her past? He stared out over the marsh, his eyes unseeing.

One thing only he knew: it had taken him so long to win

her trust, to turn hatred and fear into friendship, that he would do nothing – *nothing* – to risk even that. If she only cared a little, if she only let him near her sometimes, then it was still more than he had ever had from her, or wanted from anyone else.

So he would not scare her again. Nor would he let that bitter anger grow in him once more. Apart from driving her away, it had made him do something so foolish that men died. For loyal Angus and Diarmuid, he would be stronger.

His heart lifted a little. She had given him a small sign of hope, after all, so it was easier to keep the bitterness at bay. Where there was that kind of opening, more could grow, in time.

As if reading his thoughts, Conaire spoke up. 'You should have seen Rhiann when she heard of your capture, brother. I've never witnessed her so upset.' He was fiddling intently with the sling.

Eremon smiled. 'I know. She told me herself.'

'Really?' Conaire raised his face, and grinned. 'Well!' He nudged Eremon's arm with his shoulder. 'Perhaps she's looked past your ugly face, at last!'

Eremon pushed back hard enough to edge Conaire off balance, and he fell on his haunches. Cù, coming up behind, yipped and barrelled into Conaire with great excitement. 'Get off, dog!' The pair disappeared into a jumbled mass of grey fur and flailing arms.

By the time Conaire extricated himself, Eremon was far ahead, sauntering along the trackway. 'Hurry up!' he called over his shoulder. 'I've got my heart set on a nice roast duck, and you must shoot for both of us!'

As the earth woke from its slumber, so Rhiann's blessing of flock and herd began, before the stock was released to the higher pastures. And after the long, fair nights of the previous sunseason, the women of the dun began to bear another kind of fruit, keeping her busy bringing babes into the world – a task to ease any heart.

And behind the rhythm of sowing and planting, the rites for fishing and lambing and birthing, Beltaine drew closer. And with it, the preparations for their journey north to the tribal council that Calgacus had called.

Far up the valley of the ancestors, past the crooked standing stones, Rhiann sought for Linnet at her favourite copse of hazel and oak, a reliable source of sorrel and other herbs coming into full leaf.

'You used to say my eyes were the colour of bluebells,' Rhiann said, coming up behind Linnet in a dell of the flowers, their cups touched by the gold of dawn.

Her aunt straightened, herb-knife gleaming in her hand, breath misting the air. 'They haven't changed. I can still see you sitting here with your little, fat hands, squishing blue flowers against your nose.'

Rhiann laughed. 'Aunt!'

Linnet stored the cut sorrel in the bag over her shoulder. 'Is it time for you to leave already? I was on my way to see you today.'

'Tomorrow we leave, but I needed some peace away from the preparations. It seems I just get back and unpack and off we go again.'

Linnet smiled. 'One thing about your prince: he is not in one place long enough to become stale. Here, sit by me. Dercca warmed the mead.'

Seated beneath a spreading hazel, Rhiann took a sip and handed the flask back to Linnet.

'Rhiann.' At the note in Linnet's voice, Rhiann looked up. Linnet's brow was shadowed. 'Last night, I stood under the sky with the moonstone beneath my tongue. I sought a vision . . . of your journey.'

'And?'

Linnet shook her head. 'The visions made no sense. But afterwards I thought long on what I had seen. And the knowledge that came was . . . that there can be no clear visions. The fates are in flux, more so than ever before. As if all our paths are suspended.'

'That is little to go on.'

Linnet shrugged. 'I know. But the flux stems not from the Source, not from the Goddess. Something . . . some choice . . . needs to be made before the paths become clear again.'

'Whose choice?'

'Again, I do not know. But there is something else. The one thing I could discern in the visions was darkness, a thread of darkness.'

Rhiann watched the sun through the leaves. 'Well, the Romans are our darkness.'

'No, no, this was not the Romans.'

Rhiann stared at her. 'Do you wish me not to go?'

Linnet shook her head, perplexed. 'No, you must go, for on the journey, I feel the choice, whatever it is, will be made. A way forward will be found. And yet at the same time, there is danger, and you must take great care.'

Rhiann took Linnet's hand. 'Aunt, all around us is danger. If we sit here and do nothing, we are in danger. If we move, we are in danger.'

'I know.'

'You worry for me, but I am discovering that being Ban Cré is not just about blessings; it is about protection. We have been thrust into change, and I don't know yet what my role should be. But I have to find out.'

Linnet forced a smile. 'Then perhaps this journey will show you.' She stroked Rhiann's hair. 'If only you could stay my little, fat-cheeked girl, right here in this bluebell wood.'

'Many times I have wished the same.'

'And now? Things are better for you?'

Rhiann looked away, suddenly shy. At such questions, the warmth of Eremon's hand came back to her so vividly. 'Yes . . . better.' She bit her lip. 'But look to Caitlin and Conaire to be breeding soon. They will be fruitful, I know it, and we . . . Eremon still respects my wishes.' She looked down, shamed, for this was only the second time she had told Linnet of the true state of her marriage bed.

Linnet's hand came to rest on her arm. 'I am glad. I just

wish both my girls to be happy – even though their paths may be different.'

Once Rhiann had gone, Linnet stayed by the hazel for a long while, her eyes closed, seeking the comfort of the tree's life source.

For she had not told Rhiann that the choice centred on her alone. And that it must come from her own deepest desires. Any other influence, from Linnet or anyone else, would twist and warp its power.

The darkness was another matter. If Linnet could discern where it came from and whom it would strike, she would speak out. But Rhiann was right. Darkness was all around them, in many guises. Who could say what this instinct meant?

She remembered the visions that came to her in Rhiann's childhood. The man in the boat had been real, the blood on the sands . . . undeniably real. But the sea closing over her head, the great battlefield, littered with bodies . . . as the first had come true, would these come true as well?

She rubbed her face. Sometimes being blind and deaf to the Otherworld was easier, for there were then no tantalizing hints to bring anticipation or concern. After all, human powers gave only a glimpse of the Source; the sight was not always clear or timely.

Then she sighed. She always asked Rhiann to trust, and now so must she. Only this time she must trust Rhiann herself, this sad, changeable daughter of hers. When the choice came, Rhiann would know what to do. Had the Sisters not said she was the most gifted, before the darkness came?

Of course, Linnet was well aware that after the raid Rhiann had lost her way with the Goddess. But the raid itself must be part of the Mother's loom, the pattern of fate.

Rhiann's footsteps were weaving her life's path, and somehow, the thread was looping, drawing her back.

CHAPTER 61

In the spattering of rain and gusting wind, the pyre proved difficult to light. Maelchon stood by impatiently, wrapped in his bear cloak, his dark eye on the smith crouching at the pyre's base.

The flame wavered and disappeared once more, and the smith glanced up fearfully.

'Hurry, man,' Maelchon growled.

With shaking hands, the smith tried again, touching dried twigs to the coals in his firepot, then sheltering the tiny flame from the wind with his bulky shoulder. At last it caught, and he blew on it until it reached the dribbles of pitch beneath the body, where it burst into life.

The King nodded at the old wisewoman, who clutched her thread-bare cloak as she strained to sprinkle the head of the body with sacred water. But Kelturan the druid had become shrunken before he died, and the woman could not quite reach across the branches to his wasted face.

Maelchon snorted to himself. Peasants!

It was Kelturan's own fault. The old man got rid of the other druids on the islands, and sundered his bonds with those on the mainland. What did he expect Maelchon to do for him? There was no one competent left to officiate at such a ceremony.

Sighing, Maelchon inclined his head towards Gelur the craftsman. It was only the slightest movement, but Gelur quickly limped forward to help the woman, hunching his pock-marked face away from the King's gaze.

Maelchon watched him, satisfied. That obstinate pride of a

year ago had been nicely quelled. With Gelur's family now 'guests' of the King, the craftsman worked ceaselessly on Maelchon's building projects with no word of complaint. Yes, everything was proceeding as planned.

Beneath his robe, Maelchon stroked his hands together, as he did when more pleasant thoughts arose. By the time of *his* own passing, he would be a rich king, the richest in all of Alba, with twenty druids to sing him on his way, and ten stallions to slaughter, and slave girls to lie by his side, and a jewelled helm . . . He smiled to himself, and the old woman, watching him with nervous, rheumy eyes, rushed to the end of the rites.

Back in his hall, he pondered the message he had received only that morning. The messenger, now resting in the guest lodge, had come from a surprising source. *Calgacus*.

That proud, boastful, arrogant king, who thought himself above all other men in Alba.

Maelchon gulped his ale, then sat, tapping his hands on his otter throne. The message was an invitation, to discuss the Roman threat. So Calgacus had got it into his head to bring the tribes together, to get himself declared war leader, had he? He must think the other kings witless indeed! If they loosened his reins, he'd just trample all over them. There would be no escape from his greedy maw then.

Still.

It might be prudent to go to this council, to see where the other kings sat on the issue. Maelchon might even be able to turn such an opportunity to his advantage: whisper in a few ears, sow dissent. If the other kings felt threatened, they would be easy to play against each other.

It would be painful, of course, to see everything that Calgacus had, which he, Maelchon, did not. The fat-marbled beef would stick in his throat, the fine mead would curdle in his gut. But the advantages outweighed such trifles. He needed to know what was happening in the heart of the tribes, if he was going to survive, and such offers, such meetings, came rarely.

'Get the Caledonii messenger,' he ordered his steward. 'And send for my wife, too.'

When Calgacus's man had been dispatched with a carefully-worded acceptance, Maelchon caught sight of his queen hovering in the darkness by the door. 'Come here, girl.'

She crept forward into the torchlight, her head down.

'Stand up straight – you are a queen! Though I suppose no one could mistake you for such.'

The girl raised her pale face, and her eyes burned. Maelchon smiled. When the spark came, it was so much more diverting than that pitiful surrender. 'I have been invited to a council of all the tribes, at the Dun of the Waves. You will come with me.'

The girl dropped her chin again. She was probably terrified at the thought. Well, what good was that?

'You must reflect well on me. Get your women to make you new dresses. I'll find you some suitable jewels, arm-rings, brooches. And do something with your hair . . . you look like one of the fishermen's sluts.'

'Yes, my lord. When do we leave, my lord?'

'In a week. You'd best be ready, or I'll leave you here.'

Still averting her face, she scuttled out.

Maelchon shifted on his throne. For a moment there, that hatred in her eyes had stirred him. It was the only time he could ever rouse to her, but of late she had become irritatingly subservient. Calm, even.

Yes, the southern trip presented a timely opportunity. He might be able to sell her to some other king. Or, if her kin was there, he could have her declared barren in public and get his bride price back.

All to make way for when he would have his pick of the Alban princesses. No tribe would turn him down then. No scornful island cattle-lord who was not even a *king* . . . The surge of anger, of burning bitterness, poured into his belly. His breathing quickened.

After all these years, that memory of red-gold hair – and the hatred that fed it – could quicken his loins far easier than any real, physical woman.

He lurched to his feet and groped for his bear cloak. Among these dark, northern peoples, so strong in the Old Blood, he had discovered a wench with red hair living across the bay. With her, he found something that could slake his thirst, for a little while.

For a little while only.

CHAPTER 62
leaf-bud AD 81

T he sea-wind swirling around the Dun of the Waves still
held the bitterness of the long dark in its wings.

Wrapped in her riding cloak, Rhiann gave the eagle
stone no more than a glance as they passed, and was pleased
to note that this time, there was no trembling and no
churning in her belly. Her heart was free of Drust, then. She
glanced at the back of Eremon's dark head. If she could do it
once, she could do it again.

Under dark clouds, the bright banners of the tribes on the
plain glowed like blooms in shadowed woods. Tents and
shelters were thrown together in a jumble of oiled linen and
leather, ropes and poles, and there were lines of painted
chariots drawn up in rows, and carts full of hides and furs and
bolts of wool. Hounds barked, children dodged among the
tents, shrieking, and faintly, there came the clink of a smith's
hammer and the shouts of men drinking and gaming. The
scattered peoples of Alba rarely gathered together, and this
was too good an opportunity to miss: trading would take
place, fosterings and betrothals would be transacted, and
complaints heard by the druid judges.

As a mark of Calgacus's regard, Eremon was given the same
central lodge as before. The two married couples took beds,
and Eithne and Didius had pallets by the fire. The rest of
Eremon's men were happy to set up their tents on the plain,
for the smell of roasting meat, and the faint sound of pipes
and cheers were already floating up from the encampment.

They had arrived when the sun was high, and there was time enough for Caitlin and Rhiann to take a turn on the walls while Eremon settled his men in the camp. Didius shadowed them, a few steps behind, while they wandered the length of the battlements to the stretch that faced the sea.

After much pleading from Rhiann that Didius must be able to defend himself at the tribal council, Eremon relented and allowed the Roman to carry a small dagger, reasoning that no warrior worth his sword would ever let such a weapon under his defences. Rhiann then gave Didius the most ornate sheath that she could find in the storehouses, and a helmet with a crest in the shape of a stallion.

Didius strode along behind them now, his hand resting on the dagger sheath, his eyes darting from beneath the brow guard of the helmet as if he expected an attack on Rhiann at any moment.

'I do love it here!' Caitlin threw her arms out to each side and leaned over the palisade. 'The sea is so flat and you can look out so far ... like you can fly away!' She glanced at Rhiann, her face clouding. 'Not that I don't love Dunadd,' she amended hastily. 'The view of the island is beautiful, too.'

Rhiann laughed. 'You are allowed to love more than one place at a time, cousin.' She cocked her head back at Didius. 'And what do you think of this fine stronghold?'

Didius remained grave. 'It is very fine indeed. Although a different angle of gate approach would put attackers at a greater disadvantage.'

'Don't let Calgacus hear you speak so, Didius.' Rhiann winked at Caitlin. 'You would find it hard to stay silent before him.'

'He'll have you working on the gate before you know it,' Caitlin added, a smile hovering at the corner of her mouth.

But Didius was looking behind them, his eyes widening and Rhiann heard a musical voice speak her name, low, breathy. Just as she remembered it. She turned.

Drust was dressed soberly for once, in a dark blue tunic and ochre-dyed trousers, his skin burnished by the sun and wind, until he was all dusk and gold and copper. He still looked beautiful. But her heart did not cry out this time, nor did her breathing quicken. The last time she saw that face, it was wet from some other woman's kisses. Those broad shoulders were being grasped by long, feminine fingers. Now, his nearness did not make her feel warm and trembling, but sick, and cold. As she stood there, face to face with nothing but illusion, the last of him slipped from her heart.

'Rhiann, do not look like that.' His hand closed over her arm.

Caitlin tactfully drew a few steps away, taking Didius with her.

Rhiann lowered her voice. 'Do you mind taking your hand off me?'

Drust's brown eyes bored into her. 'Yes, I mind.'

She made to pull away, impatiently, but he only gripped her hand. 'I know we did not part well. But I missed you when you left. I was foolish.'

Rhiann smiled sweetly. 'No, *I* was foolish. Let us leave it at that.'

'I don't wish to leave it.'

She took a breath. 'Drust, let me go, *now*!'

In answer, he tried to pull her closer, and that was when she smelled the ale on his breath. The feasting on the plain had begun that morning, and in the camp, there would be as many willing women as casks of ale.

'I mean it!' She dug her nails into his palm, and it was only then that he released her. Out of the corner of her eye, she saw Didius press forward, his hand quivering over his dagger.

When Drust became aware of the Roman's approach he fell back, barking a laugh. 'Strange little guard dog you have there, lady.'

'I did not think I would need one here.'

'No.' Drust smoothed down his tunic. 'We'll speak later, then.'

'If you have something to say when you're sober.'

Flushing, Drust pushed past them and made for the stairs, and Didius turned and watched him, his hackles up.

Rhiann stood for a long moment, watching the space where Drust had disappeared. And deep inside, she sighed. The golden dream of the man must have been false after all. She had to let it die, for good.

The feast that night in the encampment was a rowdy affair, as would be expected with so many men-at-arms together in one place.

'I am still waiting for some of the distant chieftains to arrive,' Calgacus yelled over the pipes, as he and Eremon stood by one of the spits of roast deer. 'Even Maelchon is coming from as far as the Orcades.' He waved a half-eaten duck wing in a northerly direction.

Eremon swallowed his deer meat. 'The Orcades islands?'

'Yes. People know little about him. He does not trade much with the rest of us, and yet by all accounts he has a powerful warband.'

'And do you think we will gain the support we need from the other kings?'

Calgacus shrugged. 'Once blazing, we burn bright, prince. But we are slow to light, as you have seen.' He took a bite and chewed it. 'There were two more sea raids, on Taexali villages.'

'*What*?' Eremon stared at him. 'Then surely the kings will see sense!'

Calgacus shook his head, swallowing. 'I don't know. Raids we are familiar with: tribes raid us; we raid them back. But no one has ever even faced the thought of an invading army.'

'You don't sound hopeful, then.'

Calgacus smiled. 'Our last council was full of surprises, prince. This one will no doubt prove to be the same.'

Eremon grinned back. 'Don't remind me.'

'And in what state is your alliance with the Epidii now?'

'Strong, in view of the attack on our port. Although . . .'

Eremon glanced away, embarrassed. 'In the long dark I paid another visit to a Roman fort – an unwilling visit this time.'

'This I had not heard!'

Eremon hesitated, and then squared his shoulders. 'I made a mistake. I was alone when I was captured. My men then destroyed the garrison.'

The King's eyebrows rose. 'The judgement of the best king can falter. But mistake or no, you have an uncanny ability to dally with these Romans and escape unscathed. My trust in you was not misplaced – you must tell me the full story.'

For a brief moment, Eremon thought about mentioning Rhiann's part in that episode. But although Calgacus was the son of a priestess, Eremon doubted that he would respect a man who had to be rescued by his wife.

As if this omission conjured her into being, Calgacus suddenly exclaimed, 'Lady Rhiann!'

Rhiann gave the King the kiss of greeting. As this was an informal feast, she had not worn her royal jewels, and her hair was unbraided, just as it had been that awful night when they were last here. Eremon could not let a scene like *that* happen again, especially not with Drust around. The thought that she would see the King's son tonight, and the wondering about what she felt for him, had been pricking at Eremon's heart for hours.

And here she was, smiling up at him. Immediately, it struck him that this was a real smile, which reached her eyes. A smile for him alone. Some of the tension unwound from his shoulders.

Calgacus excused himself, and Eremon made a show of looking over Rhiann's shoulder. 'And where is the redoubtable Didius? Fighting off wolves? Bears?'

Rhiann wrinkled her nose at him. 'I let him go to bed, if you must know. He seems ill.'

'Really? What a pity.'

'Do your men know what a waspish tongue you have?'

Eremon grinned. 'I save it all for you.'

'Hmm.' She beckoned to a servant holding a pitcher of

mead, who handed her a cup and filled it. 'For your information, he did protect me today.'

Eremon noted how she tilted her face away, and his grin faded. 'What do you mean?'

A faint sigh. 'Drust had been drinking ale, and he tried to speak with me. I pulled away and he wouldn't let me go.'

'Oh.' Eremon watched her warily. 'So?'

She glanced up, her smile wry. 'So . . . my Didius postured with his dagger, and sent Drust into retreat! I told you the Roman would help me.'

'He should not have touched you.' Eremon was not speaking of Didius.

Rhiann held his eyes. 'No,' she said softly. 'I didn't want him to.'

A man barrelled into them then, as a fight broke out on the fringes of the group. Rhiann fell off balance, and Eremon caught her, then shouldered their way clear. 'Come,' he said, taking her hand. 'Conaire and Caitlin will be nuzzling somewhere more peaceful, no doubt.'

But when they found their friends, and places were made on logs by the fire, Eremon did not release Rhiann's hand.

And as Aedan sang of the thrice-born Etain, fairest maid to ever walk in Erin, Rhiann hardly noticed Drust join his father, or who he spoke to. She let herself become lost in the sparks of the bonfire, the voices soaring to the stars, and the warm nest of fingers enclosing her hand.

For now, these were enough.

When the house emptied the next morning, and only Eithne was there, pinning up Rhiann's hair, Didius crept from his bedclothes to stand before her. 'Lady,' he whispered.

Rhiann peered at him from under Eithne's arms. Dark circles shadowed his eyes, as if he'd spent a sleepless night.

'Yes, Didius? Are you not feeling better?'

The Roman opened his mouth, but no sound came out. Then he took a shaking breath. 'That man . . . on the walls . . . yesterday. Can he harm you?'

'What are you talking about?'

Didius ducked his head and fidgeted with his dagger. 'Are you . . . close to him?'

Rhiann put up her hand to still Eithne's fingers. 'No.'

As the Roman's stance relaxed with relief, a sudden suspicion entered Rhiann's mind. 'Didius.' Her voice was stern. 'What do you know about Drust?'

Didius's chin dropped lower, and he would not meet her eyes. She leaned forward and took his hand. 'Tell me.'

'I have seen him.' It was no more than a whisper.

Rhiann caught her breath. 'Seen him where?'

Didius looked up then, anguish in his eyes. 'Don't make me choose. I just don't want him to hurt you.'

She turned his palm up, and put her hand over it. 'Didius, if you don't tell me, then he could hurt me very much. Now, have you met him in a town before?'

Didius shook his head miserably, and Rhiann's heart jumped. *'Didius, did you see him with the army?'*

The Roman hesitated, and then nodded, his shoulders slumping. 'Yes. Enough times to remember him. He met with Agricola in the camp.'

Rhiann gasped. 'He is a traitor?' She jumped to her feet, scattering hair pins everywhere.

Eithne gulped. 'Lady . . . ?'

'I must tell Eremon.' Rhiann threw her cloak around her shoulders, but before she left she stood before Didius. 'We owe you great thanks, Didius. Such a man could prove our undoing.'

Didius's lip trembled. 'I betrayed my people, for you. What he had to say to Agricola may have helped us. I will never forgive myself.'

Rhiann took him gently by the shoulders. 'Nevertheless, you have won our gratitude for ever.'

But Didius turned his face to the wall and would not speak.

The men had gone hunting, but Eremon had to return early when Dòrn stepped on a twisted root and bruised his leg. Watching out for him from the walls, Rhiann hurried to the stableyard and, as he dismounted, murmured her news.

Eremon swore and thrust Dòrn's reins at the horse-boy, drawing Rhiann into one of the empty stalls. 'The treacherous little worm. Wait until I get my hands on him!'

'Eremon, calm down. You cannot shame Calgacus before all these kings by breaking his peace and fighting with his son. They will see it as Didius's word against his, after all.'

Eremon swore again, scraping his hair back with both hands. Then suddenly, his eyes gleamed. 'I know what I'll do.'

'What?'

'Why, simply give him the chance to tell his father himself.'

'And if he won't?'

'Then I'm not breaking the peace, am I? He is a traitor, and will be treated as such.'

Eremon's moment presented itself almost immediately. More and more fights were breaking out in the camp, and so, on the first clear day after the rain, Calgacus ordered a contest of sports to keep the warriors out of trouble. There would be foot and chariot races, spear throwing, archery, *fidchell* and *brandubh* matches – and sword duels.

'What are you going to do?' Rhiann hurried to keep pace with Eremon's strides as they crossed the wet grass of the sporting field, a wide meadow along the river.

'Just wait and see.'

'Eremon, I am part of this! Now tell me!'

He stopped and took her arms. 'Rhiann.' He swallowed. 'Did Drust . . . shame you?'

The blood rushed to her cheeks. 'Yes.'

'Then we both have a score to settle. But let me do it my way. You always talk of balance: well, some balance needs to be restored with this Caledonii princeling.'

'You're not going to challenge him, Eremon! He is no warrior, and Calgacus knows you know that!'

Eremon's face was stone. 'He is of the warrior class, which means he's been taught how to fight. It's time he showed that his sword is more than just decoration. Come!'

CHAPTER 63

Eremon paused as a glittering rain of spears arced through the air, the sun catching on their tips. Beyond them, he could hear the galloping thud of arrows into targets long before the archers were visible over the heads of the crowd.

Conaire was clapping and whooping at Caitlin, who had just taken her last shot against an opponent twice her size. Caitlin was leaning on her bow, looking proud and rather abashed, as the other warrior squared up to shoot.

Conaire caught sight of Eremon and Rhiann, and grinned. 'She's going to win me a fine leather belt – I've already bet on it.'

'Brother, I need you to come with me.'

'Wait a moment . . .' Caitlin's opponent released his arrow, and it struck the wool-stuffed target at the edge, far from Caitlin's white barb. 'Yes!' Conaire yelled, as the watching crowd erupted into cheers. 'Yes, she did it!'

'Conaire.' Eremon tried again. 'I need your support.'

'What? I can't go anywhere; Caitlin has another round coming soon.'

'Both of you must come – it won't take long. I think you'll find this interesting.'

Caitlin ran up, her bow in one hand, and threw herself into Conaire's arms. Then she hugged Rhiann. 'Did you see? I won!'

'Of course!' Rhiann squeezed her hand. 'But we need you both to come to the dueling ground now.'

Caitlin's eyes lit up. 'Oh, Eremon, are you going to enter the ring? Who are you challenging?'

Rhiann and Eremon exchanged a look.

'What's going on?' Conaire asked, glancing from one to the other.

'I'll tell you on the way,' Eremon replied. 'Come, let us get this over with.'

Sword fights were by far the most exciting diversion of the day, and it was here, beside a ring of oak stakes, that Calgacus and the other kings sat, watching a sparring pair of warriors from the Taexali tribe. The clash of swords and shouted war-taunts pierced the chatter of the ladies in the audience, and the cries of their men setting bets.

'I need you also,' Eremon muttered to Rhiann, as they approached.

'Me?' Rhiann looked up at him. 'Why me?'

'Because Drust is a coward. He'll need some incentive to accept my challenge. Shame will do it.'

Rhiann searched his face. 'I understand.'

'I knew you would.'

'Prince!' Calgacus waved them over to the benches. 'You've missed some fine swordsmanship. Are you going to join us?'

Eremon bowed. 'No, my lord. I wish to fight.'

'Excellent! We will be pleased to see the skills of one already named the bane of the Romans.' He glanced around at the other kings pointedly.

'Actually, I thought it high time for a challenge between the Epidii and the Caledonii,' Eremon remarked.

'Indeed!' Calgacus looked pleased. 'Then I shall have to call for my champion.'

'I have already chosen my opponent, with your leave.'

Calgacus was surprised. 'By all means, if he accepts.'

Eremon swivelled on his heel, towards where Drust sat near the back, a jewelled mead cup in his hand. The King's son was dressed in gaudy clothes again, his hair carefully oiled and braided, his fingers flashing gems.

He was staring at Rhiann, suddenly alert, and she returned his interest with a level look.

Eremon raised his voice over the chatter. 'Then I challenge Drust, son of Calgacus, to a duel. As two princes, we should be well matched.'

There was a ripple of whispering, and all the blood drained from Drust's face. His eyes darted over his shoulder, only to fall on Conaire, who had moved up to block his way. Then they flickered to Eremon, and finally to Rhiann, where they came to rest. There was a question on his face; or it might have been an accusation.

Rhiann replied with as challenging a stare as she could muster, raising one derisive eyebrow. In answer, the colour rushed back into Drust's cheeks, and he rose to his feet.

Through all this Calgacus said nothing. He would know that his son was no match for Eremon. But he could hardly admit it; he, the great Calgacus the Sword. Rhiann dared a glance at the King, and saw the grim set of his mouth.

'Of course,' Eremon added, 'I am aware of your *special* position, prince. If you are not able, perhaps your father can call for his champion after all.'

It verged on insolent, and there was another flurry of whispers. Some people, no doubt, would know that the prince of Erin's wife had been involved with the King's son.

Drust's cheeks darkened to crimson. 'I accept.'

Two pied bull-hides were staked out on the duelling ground, side by side. Across them, Eremon and Drust faced each other, the sunlight glancing off their swords and painted shields. Whoever drove the other off the hides would be declared winner.

Like Eremon, Drust had shed his fine clothes and was now bare-chested, his checked *bracae* tied tight around the ankle. Comparing them, Rhiann could see that though Drust had the greater height, Eremon's arms and chest bore the sharp muscle growth of a practised swordsman, and his stance was more sure. The boar tusk around his arm gleamed fiercely.

She resolutely tried to keep her mind on the fight, but it was difficult, seeing them there like that. One of these men she had caressed, stroking his smooth skin. The other slept beside her night after night, and she had only touched his bruises. But she realized now which one drew her eyes, and she glanced away, twisting the braid on her sleeve.

Conaire noticed. 'Don't worry.' He stifled a yawn. 'It won't take long.'

'No one is a match for Eremon,' Caitlin added gravely, 'except Conaire.'

Rhiann bit back a smile. 'Yes, I know.'

By now, the news had raced around the encampment, and men broke off their own games to crowd around the two princes. But at last Calgacus raised his hand, and the combatants stepped to the centre of the hides and raised their swords.

Beneath his helmet, Drust's eyes were narrowed. 'I know why you challenge me, prince,' he muttered.

'Really?' Eremon shifted his weight on his feet, testing his balance.

Drust smiled. 'And I just want you to know she's not worth it: a scrawny, pale thing like that can't satisfy a real man.'

Eremon compressed his lips, and relaxed his hold on his sword. He would not allow himself to be goaded. One of Calgacus's cousins now came forward, and began reciting the rules for the benefit of the swelling crowd.

Under cover of the man's voice, Eremon murmured, 'As you say, prince. But in fact, I call you out because we know you are a Roman spy.'

Drust turned white, as if a foam wave had rushed over his face. 'Liar!'

'I have the proof; someone who saw you with Agricola.'

'I'll have you shamed for such an insult!'

Eremon ignored that. 'Now, you have two choices. If you win, you confess to your father, and submit to his justice. If I win, I tell him, here and now.'

Drust said nothing, but his breathing was harsh. He raised his sword. Then they heard the call: 'By Taranis!'

It was the signal to begin.

Swift as a hawk plunge, Drust's sword swept down, and Eremon blocked it with a fierce thrust of his shield, tilted so that it caught Drust's wrist. It was an aggressive move that he had perfected with Conaire, which left the opponent's flank exposed. And sure enough, with a thrill of satisfaction Eremon saw Drust drop back and swivel on his heel to defend. As he did, Eremon brought his own sword up for a thrust, which Drust had to catch at an awkward angle.

Eremon leaped for the advantage, his blood instantly alight. With Lorn, he'd had no time for tactics, and as Conaire pointed out, must match fire with fire. Though Drust was no equal opponent, Eremon still wanted a quick, decisive victory, which showed off his own skills, and left no room for foolish errors.

So with Drust still off balance, he began to rain sword blows down on his shield so fast and so hard that the Caledonii prince had no chance to get his sword up again. With every ringing blow, Eremon advanced, relentlessly, and Drust had no option but to retreat, closer to the edge of the hide.

Eremon had practised blows such as these with Conaire. The awesome strength in his brother's arm called forth an answering strength in his own, but it was the rhythm that was key. His whole torso twisted in a steady beat that gave both speed and power to his arm. His sword was a blur as it glanced off Drust's shield, again and again, one blow flowing into another so swiftly that Drust could find no faltering gap to exploit.

It was never going to be an even contest. Eremon deliberately drove Drust backwards towards one of the stakes that held the hide, and between one breath and the next Drust was forced to dodge the stake, and in so doing stumbled off the hide, skidding on the wet grass.

The crowd broke into cheering, but it was tinged with disappointment, for it had been too easy.

'I win then,' Eremon panted, his sword-tip pointing at Drust's chest.

'Wait!' the Caledonii prince hissed, his eyes burning. 'You cannot shame my father here, before these men. You have it wrong: I can explain it to him.'

Eremon hesitated, but glancing up, he saw the darkness in the King's face, and his heart twisted within him. 'You have until the end of the games.'

The prince slowly backed away, and without looking at his father, disappeared into the crowd.

Rhiann understood that Eremon gave Drust that time out of respect for Calgacus. And yet she felt uneasy about the wisdom of letting the prince return to the dun alone. Since no one would miss her, she decided to follow him herself, slipping away as Conaire brought Eremon water and Caitlin a cloth to wipe the sweat from his face.

But just as Rhiann approached the dun, a large party of mounted warriors forced their way past. And that was when she felt it: a dark shimmering in the air, and a pressure, like a storm growing.

Her stomach turned, and she peered around. Hordes of people were streaming in and out of the gate, many now cursing as the warriors' horses neighed and shied. On the far side of the crowd, she glimpsed a black-haired man dismounting, and the pale sheen of white bear-fur over his thick shoulders. But then the shifting mass of people swallowed him up, and Rhiann was nudged along inside the gate.

After pulling free of the press of bodies, she hurried to Drust's workshed. He was not there. She waited until the steward that looked after the King's Hall returned from the storehouses, and asked if Drust had returned. He had not. When she insisted, he took her to Drust's empty bedplace. She then searched the stables and other worksheds, but could find no trace of him.

Cursing, she raced back down to the field, seeking for Eremon.

Drust had vanished.

After dusk that day, as Eremon delivered his unwelcome news to Calgacus, he wished that the King had the time to grieve in peace. But all the tribal leaders had now arrived, and the welcome feast must go ahead.

Calgacus and Eremon were alone in the King's meeting room, a screened alcove off the second floor gallery. The King sat heavily in his carved chair, the straight line of his shoulders for once broken.

'He went straight from the dueling ground to the port,' Eremon said. 'He must have planned it moons ago, secreting clothes and jewels with someone in the village, who organized a boat to stand by. He must have done it in preparation for such a day.'

Calgacus shook his head, still stunned.

'I am sorry, my lord,' Eremon added, for the third time. 'I challenged him to force his hand, to give him the opportunity to tell you himself. It may have redeemed him.'

'If he had not run, then I may have doubted your information, prince. But – gods!' Calgacus struck the arm of the chair. 'He confirms his guilt with his own actions. *My son* . . . a Roman traitor!'

Eremon's heart ached, but he kept his silence.

After a long while, Calgacus sighed. 'He was always the first down the pier when the Roman traders came in. The first to sport the latest jewellery, or cup, or bowl . . .' He gazed around the room in despair, for among the woven wall hangings and bronze of spear and shield there gleamed the red glaze of Roman pots on claw-foot tables; the glitter of glass goblets and silver wine jugs. 'He was always asking leave to travel south, to learn the stone carving. I should have seen it myself!'

'A man should not have to doubt his own son,' Eremon said quietly.

Calgacus sat up straighter, and got slowly to his feet. 'Son?'

His eyes were bleak. 'I have no son. I will never speak of him again, and we will tell no one of what happened here today.'

As they reached the woven screen, Calgacus put a hand on Eremon's shoulder. 'Though it grieves me sorely, and though I hated he who brought me this news, if only for a moment, you did the right thing. If my real son had even a grain of your honour in his soul, prince, then this would never have happened.'

The words 'my real son' echoed in Eremon's mind. He looked up into the King's eyes. 'It is not a role I was happy to play.'

'Nevertheless, if he had been here longer, he may have had useful information to impart. As it stands, perhaps his Roman reception will be colder than he hoped, for what can he say? That we meet in council, that is all. If this causes Agricola to fear, it is well. One day he will find the truth on the ends of our swords.'

This halted Eremon. 'Am I to understand that you will speak in favour of an alliance tomorrow, then?'

Calgacus gave a grim smile. 'I have placated my nobles enough. The betrayal of my son is a sign that I must rid Alba of the Roman poison. I will overrule my chieftains, and take my chances with their mistrust. Yet I fear it will not be long before our friend Agricola makes his move, anyway, and we are proven right.'

CHAPTER 64

The feast that night in the hall was subdued. The Caledonii did not know about their prince's flight yet, but they always took their mood from that of their shining King, and this night he was sunken and silent, and shining no longer.

Rhiann stayed close by Eremon's side. They spoke little, sad as they were for Calgacus, but she was comforted by Eremon's leg pressing against hers on the benches, as they shared meat from the same platter, and mead from the same cup, and jested with Conaire and Caitlin. Whenever Eremon leaned in close, she caught the musk scent of him, and for the first time, she found that comforting, too.

Although it had been traumatic for the King, Rhiann was relieved at the turn of events. Drust's betrayal had severed any last feeling she had for him, and for all of them, it was better that he was discovered now, before he could pass on sensitive information to the Romans.

She sighed and scanned the faces around her, lit by the hearth-fire, banked high against the clear cold of the night. Men murmured to each other behind their cups, their eyes darting one to the other, sharp as ravens, firelight glinting on heavy rings. How could Calgacus be assured of allegiance from any of these men? The Romans had been a trading force to the south for generations. People in Alba were used to gaining from them, rather than fighting them. How in Thisworld would Eremon convince the kings to join?

And that was when she froze, for among the faces flushed with drink and heat, swathed in smoke, a dark pair of eyes was fixed on her. They glittered, and yet somehow sucked the light around them into twin voids of blackness.

The eyes belonged to a broad man with a coarse black beard and tangled mane of hair. His heavy, slack cheeks were ruddy, as if wind-scoured, and his swooping nose was thick-veined from ale.

Among the restless throng of people, he alone was still.

Again, as at the gate, she felt the storm pressure beating on her spirit-eye, and for a moment, caught by those eyes, something tugged at her memory. Eremon sensed the tensing of her thigh, her shallow breath, and laid his hand over hers. 'You've gone pale, lady. What ails you?'

Rhiann ducked her head. 'Don't look right now, Eremon, but there is a man over there, with black hair and eyes, watching me. Do you know who he is?'

Eremon gazed idly around the room, and then back to her. 'Calgacus pointed him out to me. It is Maelchon, King of the Orcades islands.'

Maelchon. Rhiann mouthed the name, but could not place it.

'You are very beautiful,' Eremon murmured, 'but I'll be damned if I'll let some king stare at you like that, no matter how powerful.' He slipped his arm around her waist, returning the man's bold look, and Rhiann found herself sinking into his side, so close she felt his heart beat against her arm. And the pressure on her faded a little.

It was only when Eremon said, 'He's leaving,' that she dared to look over again. And when she did, she caught the back of Maelchon's black head moving through the crowd, and behind him, a slight, hunched girl with brown hair who shot a glance at Rhiann of equal intensity, before following the King.

'Why are they doing that?' Eremon asked.

'I don't know,' Rhiann replied. But she felt the darkness in the room drain away.

At the sinking of the moon, when all that lay above were the

491

cold pinpricks of stars, Maelchon prowled. A wind-storm had blown up during the feast, and now, as he paced high on the palisade, it clawed at his bear cloak, whipping his tangled hair before his eyes.

In his own home, such restlessness, such denial, could be quickly assuaged. But here, there were no maids under his control, to take at his will.

Seeing the Epidii queen tonight had shocked him; it was wholly unexpected. Yet the sudden shock made the fire that had only smouldered in him for three years burst into searing flame; a flame that sucked the breath from his lungs.

Her hair was just the same, but the new maturity in her bones, the shadowed eyes, the hint of woman breast under her dress, only made her more maddening, more alluring than her girl-self had been.

And seeing that Erin cub pawing her, his head close to that hair . . . it made the meat stick in Maelchon's throat, and his hands tremble, itching to close themselves around the prince's neck, to wrench the life away, to wipe that scornful smile from his perfect face.

And the girl had been given to *him*.

The hair had been taunting him throughout the feast, for as she dipped her head it flowed in a drape of copper and gold over her shoulders, catching the light . . . bringing back every bitter moment. He had seen that same sheen in the sun, against the heather of the Sacred Isle. Yet the memory of that time was inflamed by more than her beauty; far more.

A marriage with you is out of the question, the foster-father had said. *The Epidii have high hopes for a foreign alliance.*

But the man's piercing eyes, the shared glances with wife and nobles in the great hall on the island, had belied his words.

You are nothing, their eyes said. *A petty king from a poor land; coarse and ill-gotten. You are beneath us. You are nothing.*

Far from the sentries, as the wind tore at the trees below, Maelchon gripped the palisade and a moan escaped his throat, forced past rigid muscles by the rage that roared within.

The arrow flew wide, missing the trunk and driving deep into the mud beneath the oaks, yet Eremon let fly another and another, wrenching the barbs from the quiver across his back so swiftly that he was soon out of breath.

When the quiver was empty, he stood, panting, and realized that he had a hunt through the undergrowth ahead of him, and really, it hadn't made him feel much better.

'I'm glad my wife can aim properly, at least.'

Eremon turned to find Conaire leaning against a nearby birch tree, his thick arms folded.

'It has been some years since I took up a bow, brother.' Eremon waved it ruefully. 'Yet I needed to shoot at something, and could not find you to go hunting with.'

With so many men to fit into Calgacus's hall, only the kings themselves had been invited to the first council. The kings, and Eremon.

'That bad, was it?' Conaire picked up a discarded arrow and wended his way through the bushes, handing it to Eremon.

'That bad. Only the new Taexali king – a young buck with hot blood – Calgacus, and myself support an alliance. The others refuse, even after we set out our case; even after I was told that the Damnonii villages, including Kelan's on the coast, were pillaged by Agricola after our raid.' Again, Eremon swallowed down the anger and pain that accompanied that particular piece of information, for after the Roman attack on Crìanan, he had been too lost in darkness over Rhiann to remember to check how the Damnonii fared. Well, now he knew, and he cursed himself for it. 'And there was more, brother, and still they do not see!' He struck the tree trunk with his palm.

Conaire was rooting around under a tangle of hawthorns for more arrows. 'More?'

'The Romans are fast building a new line of forts across the land between Forth and Tay: Venicones lands. Apparently, the Venicones have surrendered, just like the Votadini.'

Conaire straightened, an arrow in his hand, his tilted mouth now grim. 'And what do the kings say to that?'

'That the Venicones are no more than traitors, which is why Agricola has established a border there – but so long as we are less inviting, he won't come further.'

'Ah.'

Eremon spied an arrow sticking out of the deep loam beneath another tree, and wrenched it free. 'It's not a border, it's a frontier, can't they see that? It's not to keep us out, it's a place of strength from which to launch an attack!'

'What was the reaction, then?'

'Well, let me see if I remember one king correctly.' Eremon folded his arms, the mud-flecked arrow sticking out from his clenched fist. '"*This is our land, not yours, prince, and we do things our way. Our mountains keep us safe, and I'm not spending my men's lives protecting someone else's rich, fat lowlands!*" He glanced at Calgacus as he said that – I'm surprised the King didn't call for his sword right then and there!' Eremon threw the arrow down with the bow. 'And what galls me, brother, is that all the while we sit here and bicker, Agricola is out there, somewhere. He's waiting for the signal from his emperor to move north, and he will get it. Soon, he will get it!'

On a rolling, windblown ridge above the Earn plain, Agricola sat his horse and watched the oxen hauling the last load of timber from the river below. On his right flank, atop a rise of cropped turf and heather, his latest watchtower was taking shape. The ditch and rampart were in place, and the timber breastwork complete. His soldiers now only needed to finish the tower itself, with its lookout platform and beacon.

Against the purple heath, the granite scree and clouded sky, it did seem vulnerable, but Agricola had not listened to the officers who said he must retreat south into safer lands. If the legions left now, the tribes would think them cowed and weak, and would be encouraged to exploit that weakness.

494

In any case, the attack by the Erin prince on his western fort only succeeded because it was half-built, and the men unprepared. And as for the other fort, well. He snorted. Carelessness had done the barbarians' work for them. The gate showed no signs of having been forced, it was open – *open* – with one watchman dead of an arrow wound. How that had happened, Agricola could not guess. He did not know if this was also the work of the Erin prince, but his heart suspected it.

He sighed in exasperation. One thing he must not do, was attribute every setback to Eremon of Erin. That would only signal the start of a dangerous obsession. Samana was already a shade too interested in the happenings among the Epidii, which was natural, he supposed, after she had been so thwarted. But he had a nation to subdue, not one man.

There was a scrabbling behind him, and one of the Venicones cattle-lords – he hesitated to call them chieftains – topped the rise on a stocky hill pony. 'My lord.' The man was breathless, although it was the pony who had done the walking, not the man.

'What is it?'

'They have done well to keep it secret, but we have had word that the other tribal kings are meeting at the Dun of the Waves.' The man pushed his chest out, so that it was nearly level with his paunch.

Agricola's horse flicked its tail and stamped. 'I know.'

The warrior's mouth dropped open. 'How – how did you know?'

Agricola glanced at him derisively. 'Did you think you are our only allies in the north? I have other informants.'

'Are you going to attack?' The cattle-lord sounded eager to get his hands on those rich Caledonii lands.

'No. My informant also tells me that this dun is very well guarded, and that this king, Calgacus, will have notice of our fleet entering his waters long before we are close enough to strike his dun. We would find an ambush waiting.'

The warrior fell silent, and Agricola pursed his lips. These people were tiresome, and the sooner they were under the Roman yoke, the better. They had no idea how to conquer a land. Launch a village raid, perhaps, or steal a few cattle – but never take over a whole territory, from sea to sea. When that territory was split by snow-scoured mountains and impenetrable bogs, its coast slashed by sea-loch after sea-loch, one could not embark on some blind, grappling assault.

Like the barbarians' *fidchell* game, the plan must be put in place tiny piece by tiny piece. Every move had to be considered carefully, and weighed up for consequences. When the emperor Titus released the army units he had recalled, Agricola would have twenty thousand pieces to command, to move across this mountain-checked board. And then he would make no mistakes.

He glanced over his shoulder, to the east, and the sea. He knew that the two fort attacks galled his officers, and that the men ached to be let loose on the Albans. But in truth, his hands were still tied.

After his succession, Titus had drawn some of Agricola's forces back to Rome, to fight on the German and eastern frontiers. Though Agricola was loyal to the Flavian dynasty, and supported Titus's father, Vespasian, to the throne, he secretly chafed at this hiatus in his advance. He hoped it would not last long.

Still, the only reason he had moved so quickly to start with was the surrender of the Votadini, and now the Venicones. The latter had provided a large peninsula between Forth and Tay, which he could protect with this new line of forts. This gave him rich land from which to extract supplies for his men, good harbours for his fleet, and an abundance of timber for forts. All safely tucked away from the wilder land to the north.

The game was slow. But after those fort raids, the next move would be his. He sensed it, deep in his heart.

Soon, very soon, he would have leave to advance.

CHAPTER 65

Ducking out of a sudden rain-shower, her hood pulled around her cheeks, Rhiann did not see the slight figure of Maelchon's wife hurrying out from the granary door, a covered basket in her hands. Before Rhiann could catch herself, the two collided.

'Oh, I am sorry,' Rhiann gasped, holding the other's arms for balance, trying to remember her name. She found she did not know it, for the girl was not memorable; small and brown and timid. Yet Rhiann was immediately arrested by the look that flashed over the Orcades queen's face before the mask of civility came down. It struck Rhiann in her breast, like a physical blow: hatred, almost violent hatred, with a searing undercurrent of pain.

Rhiann suddenly remembered that she had seen that same look on this girl's face at the feast. She dismissed it then, but now ... Rhiann struggled to find something to say, but Maelchon's queen squirmed free, all dignity forgotten, and slipped away.

'Wait!' Rhiann hurried after her. She could not imagine why this girl would hate her, but she must pursue an answer. Eremon said that her husband was very powerful, and such undercurrents and their source could affect the prospects of an alliance.

When she reached the corner of the granary, the girl had disappeared among the twisting pathways, rapidly turning to mire under spattering rain. Rhiann paused there, the water trickling down her cheeks, her mind racing. She must speak to her. Eremon would agree that at this time, all such occurrences should be explored. There was too much at stake.

The next day she tried to find the girl again, but it proved harder than she had supposed. 'Where may I find your queen?' Rhiann asked the maidservant in the Orcades lodge.

'We heard there is a sacred spring in the hills over the river, lady. I think she is there, with the healing waters.'

Rhiann walked away, thoughtful. Well, the men would stay in council all day. She may as well pay a visit to the shrine herself, and perhaps meet the lady in question on the way.

Didius was still sunk in misery, and would not respond to her jests with even a hint of a smile, so she and Caitlin went alone. The leaf-bud rains had swelled the river, and the yellow water plucked at their horse's legs as they crossed the ford. Deep in the woods on the other side, Rhiann couldn't see far ahead, but she could feel the voice of the spring calling to her; a tugging of the Source from within the earth.

When the call grew stronger, Rhiann pulled Liath up in a grove of ash trees and slipped to the ground. 'I would like to go on alone,' she said to Caitlin, drawing a pouch from her saddle-pack. If Maelchon's wife was there, she might not speak before anyone else.

'With all these rough men about, Rhiann, that may not be safe,' Caitlin replied, frowning.

'It is just up that little glen, there, see? I won't be long.' Rhiann could not resist teasing her. 'I will scream loudly if anything happens.'

Caitlin rolled her eyes, and slid to the ground. 'If you are doing anything Otherworldly, cousin, then I'll keep my distance. But I'll watch with an arrow on the string, nevertheless!'

On a blanket of moss and slick, brown leaves, Rhiann walked as the Sisters trained her to do, eyes closed, completely silent, while the soles of her feet sensed the path. The stream from the spring leaped among the rocks beside her, but a deeper note rang behind its joyous chatter. *Come, sister,* it seemed to say. *I welcome you!*

As the glen narrowed and steepened, she opened her eyes, and there the pool lay, formed in a bowl of rock, fringed by trees that fluttered with scraps of offering cloths. But she was not alone – and nor was Maelchon's queen.

The girl stood, her slight frame enveloped in the arms of her guard, her head on his chest. She was weeping, her thin shoulders shaking, and as Rhiann watched, the man stroked her hair tenderly and murmured in her ear.

Just at that moment he saw Rhiann, and stiffened, and the girl, feeling the movement, raised her head. Rhiann had seen that pinched face transfigured by hatred; now terror leaped into it. 'You!' she gasped.

Rhiann instinctively raised her hand as if warding off a blow. 'I am sorry. I did not know that anyone was here . . .'

But the girl rushed to Rhiann's side and fastened on to her arm, her face streaked with tears. In the light of the open clearing, Rhiann realized she was no more than fourteen years old.

'Do not tell him what you have seen! Oh, please do not tell him!' she cried.

'Your husband? Why would I tell him anything?'

Yet the wild fear did not leave the Queen's face, and Rhiann was struck with pity. She touched her fingers where they gripped her dress. 'I said I will not tell him,' she repeated.

Some of the tautness left the girl then, and she stepped away from Rhiann, wrapping her arms around her thin body, her tears overflowing once more.

Rhiann felt helpless in the face of such pain. 'What has happened?' she asked, holding out her hand. 'How can I help you? What can I do?'

'Nothing!' The girl cowered. 'You have already done so much! No one can help me, except Rawden here, and only when we can steal away. When *he* is away.'

Rhiann recognized the fear and loathing in her voice, and tried another tack. 'What is your name, lady?'

The girl sniffed, catching her breath. 'Dala.'

'I am Rhiann.'

'I know who you are.' The words were sharp.

'Why do you hate me so?' Rhiann asked, not knowing what else to say. 'I have never met you, but believe me, I will do anything I can to help.'

'If you don't speak, she may tell *him* about us,' the guard broke in, his voice sullen.

Dala buried her face in her hands. 'Your hair really is the colour he described.' Her voice was muffled. 'And your face. So beautiful, he has said, over and over again. Not like me . . .'

Rhiann shook her head. Had they confused her with someone else? 'But I have not met the King!'

'Yes, you have!' Dala raised her face. 'He saw you on the Sacred Isle, when he was looking for a wife, three years ago. He asked your family there for your hand, and was refused outright. It tortures him still!'

Rhiann frowned. Many people came to Kell's broch on the island. Vaguely, she remembered a stranger from the far north who stayed with her foster-father for some days. The man had ridden past her as she walked with Talen and Marda in the hills, but as she was living with the Sisters by then, she never took a meal with him, and did not note his name or features. He left abruptly, she did remember that. And that Kell spoke harshly of him after he had gone. But no one ever told her he had wanted her, or that he had been refused.

Dear Goddess! But how could this matter to anyone so many years later? And why was Dala so torn? It could not be jealousy, for she hated the man, obviously.

'Yes, yes, you refused him,' the girl babbled on. 'And so in the end he took me instead!' She burst into a fresh bout of sobbing.

This girl has been driven mad, Rhiann thought. She could feel the fragile sanity of her, like an eggshell around a storm of pain.

When the wild sobs had quietened, Rhiann touched Dala's shoulder. 'You must trust me. I do not understand what I have done to you, for I was young, and was never even presented to your husband. But . . . he hurts you?'

'In every way you can imagine.' Dala's voice was despairing. 'In your refusal, you condemned me to a life of terrible pain, but it does not end there! Even now the image of you inflames him, and he . . . he . . . uses me so terribly, imagining it is you.' She clenched her hands, her nails digging into her palms.

Sickness rose sharp on Rhiann's tongue. 'By law your husband cannot treat you like this. Where is your family, your clan?'

Dala shook her head mutely, tears falling on the tarnished brooch that fastened her cloak. 'I am of the Caereni. My father is dead. And the rest of them . . . they are too afraid of my husband to protest. They were well rewarded for giving me to him.'

'Then why does no one in the Orcades help you?' Now Rhiann's voice shook with anger. The girl looked up at the fierce tone. 'What about the druids, Dala? The council? The priestesses? His nobles? Someone must stand up to him; a king cannot rule this way!'

'He does,' the girl whispered. 'He controls everyone. He banished all the druids and priestesses except one, Kelturan, though he is now dead. The nobles have been driven out or killed, one by one. He rules alone, with only his warband to support his violence. And they are trained to loyalty when young; he has built their strength over many years.'

Rhiann squeezed Dala's shoulder, and released her, drawing herself up. 'It was well that we met, for I will let no woman be treated this way, especially not when I am the unknowing cause of your pain.'

A flash of hope lit through the distrust on the girl's face.

'I am the Ban Cré of the Epidii, and I will do all I can to help you. From this day you are under my protection. Yet I ask you one thing only. You must stay with him and act as if nothing has happened until the end of the council. It is only a day or two more. Then . . . trust me.'

Dala, her cheeks hot and streaked with drying tears, looked at Rhiann for a long time. 'I don't know why, but I do trust you,' she said at last. 'I hated you for so long, because you caused my pain. But perhaps you will save me, too. Perhaps this is the way it should be.'

Rhiann smiled. 'You are wise beyond your years. It is balance, a sign that the hand of the Mother is in this.' She gestured to the dark pool of water. 'And we were drawn together by Her spring, do you see? Let us now make our offerings, and then you should return. Wait for me to act.'

Rhiann sought out Eremon as soon as she returned, for he was in their lodge, shaving in a bronze basin. She quickly told him what had happened.

'That is a strange story,' he offered, laying down his knife and splashing the stubble from his face.

Then he stood up, flicking water over her, and she frowned and handed him a linen towel. 'It is a terrible story.' She was still angry.

'This Maelchon has stayed silent so far, but Calgacus said he is very powerful.' Eremon's voice was muffled as he rubbed his hair with the towel. 'He holds territory on the north coast as well, I hear.'

'I know he is powerful,' Rhiann snapped. 'But I am not leaving that child to be tortured by him!'

Eremon began to rub down his bare arms and chest, and Rhiann flushed and fixed her eyes on the door hanging. It was embroidered with a golden eagle in full flight.

'Rhiann, I agree the story is sad, and the part about you . . . very disturbing. The sooner we are away from here, the better. But Maelchon would make a formidable ally. And the prospects of an alliance with the other kings, based on what I'm hearing, are not good.'

'I knew you would say that!' Rhiann was furious. 'It does not matter that he rapes her and hurts her, and kills people! He has power, and that is all that matters, is that it?'

'No, that is not it.' He looked more closely at Rhiann. 'I'm just saying not to overreact. He is obviously not a good man

. . . he is a disturbed man. But he may still prove a valuable ally. You will not endanger that, will you?'

Rhiann put her chin up. 'What he does to her is wrong, by our laws. In my position I have a responsibility to do something about that. But I will wait until the end of the council.'

Eremon's brows drew together, but she held his gaze defiantly. At last he sighed, throwing down the towel to take up a fresh tunic. 'Then that is the best I can ask.'

At the feast in the camp that night, Rhiann shrugged deeper into her cloak, her eyes on two men wrestling in the firelight. All around her people were laughing, calling out encouragement or abuse, lamenting their betting losses. The smell of roast boar and burning peat were close in the air, and she found herself drifting to the edge of the crowd, to where the dark woods hovered, dampness creeping from their skirts.

And when she felt the pressure of eyes on her back, she knew what she would find when she turned. She could ignore Maelchon, but she was far too angry for that. He bullied everyone around him, yet she would not be cowed.

So she did wheel around, raising her eyes to his, her shoulders straight. The aura about him now was like a roiling thundercloud. She glared, unafraid, and suddenly he smiled, raising his mead-cup to her. His teeth glinted.

By his side stood Dala. She glanced at Rhiann, shivered and lowered her eyes, then followed her husband as he disappeared into the crowd.

CHAPTER 66

The deliberations continued for another day, but it was clear that the kings had fallen into two factions. The smaller, consisting of Calgacus, the Taexali and Vacomagi kings, and Eremon himself, continued to push for co-operation.

The arguments went back and forth for hours, and just when a few of the chieftains were at last wavering, unsure, the King of the Orcades finally lumbered to his feet.

Eremon had watched him at both feasts, and seen his black head close in with the most vociferous opponents of the alliance, including the Creones King, he who had told Eremon to keep his nose out of their business.

'I have listened carefully.' Maelchon stroked his beard, his hand on his sword. 'And it is plain that the danger to us in the north is slight. The danger from the *Romans*, that is.' He paused, looking around at his northern neighbours. 'Far more dangerous are the ambitions of those southerners who seek to rule over the rest of us.'

He did not glance at Calgacus when he said this, but sitting next to the Caledonii King, Eremon felt his arm tense.

Garnat, the Taexali King, leaped to his feet. 'That is an insult!'

The Creones King also rose. 'Is it? It seems to us that you are over-eager to appoint a war leader who will *control our men*! And what will he do with that control? Turn it on us, that's what!'

'Liar!' one of Garnat's chieftains cried.

The council erupted into a baying pack of shouting men, each trying to be heard over the other.

Eremon waded into the fray, desperately trying to calm the men down, knowing that a rift could be born that would be impossible to heal.

It was right at that moment that the smell assailed him – the stink of untanned hides, and unwashed skin. The air in the hall was split by the rap of a staff on the floor, and the kings stopped arguing, and fell silent. Heads turned towards the door, and then the crowd of men fell back.

First Eremon saw the shock of matted, white hair, and then the burning of yellow eyes. It was Gelert, his robe dirty and torn, covered by a raw wolfskin. His arms were thin, the skin of his face drawn tight across the bones, his legs scratched as if by branches. Around the end of the owl staff a cluster of tiny skulls were tied, which rattled as he shuffled towards Eremon.

He stopped, and pointed the staff at the prince. 'And here I find the devil, still speaking lies in our midst!'

Declan, who had been listening to the council along with the other druids, hurried forward. 'Master?' he whispered, incredulous. 'Where have you been?'

Gelert turned to him. 'I've been to the stars, brother! I've been to the bowels of the earth. I've broken down the doors of the Otherworld. I've burned in the fire!'

The kings began to glance around at each other, the fear plain on their faces.

'And do you know what they tell me?' Gelert boomed. 'That *he*,' he pointed at Eremon again, 'has been sent by the lords of the underworld, to twist and capture us, to weaken us, to speak his lies to us. He seeks our blood for his own ends, and will sell us to the invaders . . .'

Eremon snorted. 'This is ridiculous!'

'Brother.' Calgacus's chief druid, the tall, stooped man, glided forward. 'You are worn, and have travelled far, it is clear. Come with me now, and we will speak of what you have seen.'

The staff thudded on the floor once more. 'If you let him into your mind, he will turn your thoughts to his own ends!' Gelert cried. 'He ever seeks his own glory, not our safety; he will bow his head to no one but his own foreign god. You must banish him now, before you succumb!'

Calgacus and his men stayed frozen to the spot. This was druid business, and no warrior could lay hands on a member of the brotherhood and live.

'You have been living hard, master,' Declan murmured. 'Come and rest now.' Gelert looked as if he might argue, and then seemed to realize where he was, and pulled his composure around him before striding from the hall. As he went, those burning eyes seared Eremon's skin.

There was an audible outrush of breath from the chieftains and kings. Eremon found his legs trembling, for the strength of Gelert's hatred had been tangible.

'He speaks mad words,' Calgacus said, staring after the druid. 'We will give him no more thought.'

'What he says may have truth in it.' Maelchon at last stepped forward, his bulk filling the hearth-space.

Eremon swung to face him. '*What*?'

'All of us here are loyal to Alba, except one.' Maelchon bared his teeth at Eremon in what passed for a smile. 'A foreigner, who came to seek his own glory, as the druid said, not to protect us. And even worse, this is a man who, if we believe him, met this Agricola, vanquished a Roman regiment – *and then walked free from a Roman fort.*'

Eremon caught his breath. How had he known that? And yet, Eremon did not tell his men to keep it secret. If he knew Aedan, the tale had already been taken up by a host of bards who would spread it throughout Alba.

'And exactly how did he do this?' Maelchon looked around at the other kings. 'He has had a little too much to do with Romans, so far as I can see. How could he walk free unscathed . . . unless he has closer ties with them than we suspect?'

Eremon's hand went to his sword. 'That is an evil insult.' He kept his voice low, but Calgacus rose to stand beside him. 'Peace,' he growled at them both. 'I will have no fight in my hall. The prince of Erin is loyal to Alba, and a sworn enemy of the Romans. He is my ally, and has my full backing.'

Maelchon looked as if he would say more, but he evidently did not want to speak out openly against Calgacus. He preferred to stir other men to do that for him.

Calgacus continued mildly. 'And in answer to the debate in progress before we were interrupted . . . it does not matter who is appointed war leader, only that our forces are combined for greatest strength. No one is seeking anyone else's lands. I wish only to keep my own free.'

He could say it over and over, but Eremon saw, in the eyes of the most recalcitrant chieftains, that they did not believe him. Not before, and certainly not now.

The Caledonii Ban Cré tottered to the fire to refill the cup. The herbs would help to strengthen the druid's mind and body, as he lay tossing feverishly. It was plain that he had been living wild in the forest for moons now, eating little.

She looked down at him, her senses confused and repelled by the emanations of the man, of something more than darkness. There was a void, as if the Source in him had been cut off.

The sooner he was gone, the better. It would not be long: his physical hurts were slight, and the scratches would soon heal. One good sleep and some broth and the druids would take him back, thank the goddess.

There was a tap at the door. 'Yes?' she called.

A man came into the lodge and straightened. He was slight and stocky, with tangled black hair. 'My master wishes to know of the druid. Is he well enough to receive a visitor?'

'He's sleeping.'

'But he will not lie abed with sickness for long?'

The old priestess squinted at the man. 'And why are you asking me all these questions? What do you want?'

The man hesitated. 'My master is a powerful king. He wishes to speak with the Epidii druid.'

'And why? What business is it of his?'

The man scowled. 'He does not answer to you, old woman. Tonight he will come, and you will tell no one of it.'

The priestess drew her old bones up to resist him, but they ached, and after a moment she shrugged and turned away. Kings, druids. What did it matter to her?

The two men stretched their feet out to the brazier in the King's room, for the evening wind had grown sharp, swinging to the north, driving a squall in from the sea. As the lamplight ducked and leapt, they were silent, each deep in their thoughts, twirling their mead cups.

There was a light tap on the carved screen, and a steward announced the Lady Rhiann. Calgacus rose and bowed, taking her damp cloak, urging her into his empty chair.

'You had success?' She searched Eremon's face, but he only stared moodily into the brazier coals.

'No,' he said. 'Maelchon stirred up the fear of the northerners that an alliance will lead to their subjugation by Calgacus. They will not agree, not now.'

Rhiann sighed. 'We feared this, yet what else can we do?'

Eremon rested his cup on the three-legged table beside him. 'There is something.' He glanced at the King, who nodded. 'Calgacus tells me that not all the tribes were represented at the council. The Caereni and their allies from the western coast chose not to attend.'

Rhiann nodded. 'That is not surprising. People from the east travel to the Sacred Isle, but as for the mainland, the tribes there are isolated by the central mountains, and have always kept to themselves. We do not even know their true numbers.'

'Exactly,' Calgacus agreed. 'Which is why we need to find out. I would guess that they feel no threat from these Romans, and so took my summons lightly. We must make them see differently, and quickly, before the dissenting kings from this council return home.'

Eremon leaned forward, his hands on his knees. 'The King will give us a boat, to sail north and then west around Alba, on a diplomatic mission in his name. Then we get there before the other kings have a chance to spread the false rumours of that slippery druid, and this trouble-maker Maelchon.'

'Druid?'

Eremon threw a look at her. 'I'll tell you everything later. But the King and I feel that it might be best if we leave now. Because of your connection, among other things, Maelchon has fixed his baleful eye on me. I do not wish to damage Calgacus's efforts with the other kings. What do you think?'

As he spoke, Rhiann realized that her hands were trembling, her tongue dry against the roof of her mouth. The Caereni lands were so close to the Sacred Isle; to the Sisters. She had gone nowhere near the island since the raid; since she stormed away, determined never to go back, never to face the shame that she had not done enough . . .

Now she took a deep breath, seeking calm. They weren't going to the Sacred Isle. 'It is a fine idea,' she said at last. 'When do we leave?'

'In two days, before the kings scatter to their homelands. Calgacus is ordering a boat to be made ready.'

'Then I have something else to do first.' She turned to Calgacus. 'Maelchon's wife has sought my aid, for he is mistreating her. Her kin will not act to protect her, but I must, as a member of the sisterhood. It is our duty to offer protection to all women.'

Calgacus's brows knitted together. 'His wife? What does she accuse him of?'

'I would prefer to keep that private, for her sake. But your own Ban Cré and I have talked with her at length, and her guard also offers proof. I am invoking the law to release her from the marriage.'

Calgacus sighed. 'Then this will inflame him even further.'

The lamplight drew the flecks of gold from his eyes. 'I cannot ask you not to act, under the circumstances, but you are sure this warrants such drastic action?'

'Yes.' Rhiann's voice was flat. 'I am sure.'

'What do you wish to do, then?'

'I am going to confront him now.'

Eremon jumped to his feet, his mead forgotten. 'You're not going near him without me!'

She smiled. 'Well, of course not. But I must talk to him alone, with only Dala and the old priestess. I will not shame the girl before other men. You can wait outside.'

'No.' Eremon was firm. 'I will stay by your side, with my sword to hand.'

'Eremon, Dala will not speak before you. If you surround the house, there is nothing Maelchon can do, and he knows it.'

Eremon tried to argue, but Calgacus raised his hand. 'The Ban Cré is right,' he said. 'This is women's business. Remember that I grew up at the knee of a priestess; I know when to let them be.'

'Then perhaps you could teach that to my husband,' Rhiann retorted. But as they left, she turned to Eremon. 'You can stand just inside the door, then, but not too close.'

Maelchon tried to push aside the fog of rage that clouded his mind.

The red-haired vixen dared to stand here and accuse him. Accuse *him*! In front of his mouse of a wife, and that doddering old healer – and of course, in the background, that cur from Erin. All of them, joining forces against him, like they always did. He shook his head, and focused the force of his attention on the Epidii Ban Cré.

She did not look away or tremble with fear. Her blue eyes were clear, and they burned with anger. Great gods, that fire and hate aroused him more than anything he had ever experienced in his life. He longed to lay hands on her creamy

510

skin, to shake her until her anger burned all the brighter, and he could conquer it with his body . . .

'I said, what do you answer to these charges?'

He caught his thoughts, froze them. 'That they are unfounded. She is my wife, and under my control.'

'And there you are wrong,' the vixen snapped. 'She has her own rights, under the laws of the Mother, as the druid judges will confirm. She cannot be beaten or . . . taken . . . in that way. We have a witness from your own lands who will attest to her injuries. I myself have also examined her.'

Maelchon glared at his wife. She was half-hidden behind the Ban Cré, her head down – as it would be. Behind, the firelight glanced off the sword of the Erin prince, but his face was in shadow. Maelchon had no doubt that there were other swordsmen outside the house – they were all in thrall to the Epidii Queen and her husband, and would do what they said.

He puts his hands on her, he takes her when I cannot. The red fog swirled and beat on his temples.

'Now, we can debate this before the druids and Calgacus and the other kings, in council, or you can agree to release your wife, here.'

'You have no power to order me like this!' he growled.

She smiled. 'Oh, I do. I understand you have no druids or priestesses in your islands, so you may have forgotten how the laws are applied in civilized lands. Here, what you do is wrong, as all would agree. We can win your wife's freedom with force if you wish.'

Maelchon glanced at the prince behind her. The man was quick, and by all accounts deadly with that sword, and he, Maelchon, did not have his own blade to hand. He had been caught unawares in his lodge, without even his own guards to hand.

Gods! In the end, what did he care for his pathetic wife, anyway? He wanted to get rid of her, and they had given him the way. 'Bah! She is nothing to me – she is worthless. You can take her.'

'And her dowry?'

His lip curled. 'Pitiful though it was, she can have it. I'll send it to the Caereni when I return home.'

'Good.'

He watched with beating blood as his wife crept to her bedplace and took her few personal belongings: a shale bracelet, a broken antler comb, an old bronze mirror. And then she scuttled out the door, the old priestess hobbling after.

The Epidii Ban Cré turned on her heel and left him without a word, as if he were beneath her notice, and only the prince dared to glare at him before following.

Maelchon stood for an endless time in the centre of the house, as the rage erupted and boiled over inside, drenching his body in a flood of sweat, though he moved not a muscle. *If I can't have her, then, by Taranis and the Dagda and dark Arawn himself, the Erin cub will not.*

And the way had already opened before him.

CHAPTER 67

Calgacus spent the last days of council feasting the kings even more lavishly, mending what bonds had been weakened, trying to create bonds when there were none.

The time would come, he explained to Eremon, when there would be no choice but to fight. And then, it must be Calgacus those kings ran to in their fear. He must rebuild any bridges that had been weakened by Maelchon.

The Orcades King himself left immediately after his confrontation with Rhiann, not even taking his leave of Calgacus – although the Caledonii King was grateful for this.

'After knowing his treatment of his wife and people, I don't wish to look in his face again,' Calgacus said to Eremon, as they stood on the walls of the dun and watched Maelchon and his followers ride away.

'Is there nothing we can do to find out more of him?' Eremon asked.

Calgacus pursed his lips. 'He patrols his sea-lanes well, and guests are not welcome. Yet I will think on it.' He sighed as the Creones King also rode out close behind Maelchon, his back stiff, his eyes covered by his helm. 'So you taste the bitter cup of a king, Eremon. Men's anger, men's distrust, men seeking to bring you down.'

Eremon glanced at him, and noticed for the first time the deep furrows that ran from that hawk nose to a decidedly grim mouth. The council and his son's treachery had taken a great toll on the King; Eremon remembered suddenly that he was not a young man.

'But there are other things too, lord,' he murmured now. 'The respect of those who ... who look up to you. Pride, admiration ...' He fixed his gaze on his own hands, clenched on the palisade. 'Where you lead, there are those true of heart and mind who will follow. Believe it. Alba needs you.'

The King's hand came down on his shoulder. 'I once said you were a poet, prince. As you bend hearts to war with your talk, so you can bend mine to hope. Don't listen to my old man's weariness now; your youth and fire will lead us too, as mine did me.' Eremon looked up to see that the grimness had lifted from the King's face. 'My uncle, a great king, said something to me once that I have always remembered: Be true to yourself and your path will always lay straight as a new spear, no matter how twisted and beset by troubles it seems to others.'

Eremon smiled. 'That is sound advice.'

'It is. And I have also learnt that as a king, you walk that path alone. It used to seem a harsh choice when I was young, but only alone can you hear the deep music of your heart, and then it will guide you more truly.'

Eremon thought for a moment. 'So something I see as a burden is also a source of strength.'

'Yes, it is the making of a great king.' Calgacus grinned. 'And there is always time for mead, and tales; never forget that, Eremon! The love of your brother and your men ... and your wife ... will always be waiting when you return.' Something deep in the King's eyes twinkled at mention of Rhiann, and despite the solemn words, Eremon felt himself flush.

On the morning of their own departure, Calgacus asked to take his leave of Eremon and Rhiann in private, in his hall. When they entered, Calgacus was sitting on his throne, his gold circlet in his hair, his jewelled sword across his knee.

Eremon glanced down at his own plain tunic and trousers. 'I fear we have not dressed for such a formal leave-taking, lord.'

Calgacus smiled, rising to his feet to kiss Rhiann. 'I am dressed in state because I have a matter of state to address.'

He beckoned to two servants standing against the walls, and they came to him. One held the great, jewelled mead cup that was passed around at every formal feast, to join honoured guests together as kin. The other held an intricately carved box made of cedar, a fragrant and costly wood from the other side of the Middle Sea, in the desert lands.

Eremon and Rhiann exchanged glances.

A third servant, a girl, glided forward with a pitcher of mead, and filled the jewelled cup as the King held it in two hands. Calgacus fixed them both with his golden eyes. 'I come to offer you a formal alliance with the Caledonii.'

Eremon heard Rhiann gasp. A formal alliance! Up until now, Calgacus had spoken only of his personal support. This was something entirely different.

'I hereby bond my people to you as brothers and sisters against our common enemy – Rome. We will share our forces, our intelligence, our ideas. And perhaps, our blood.' Calgacus held Eremon's eyes as he said this. 'What is your answer?'

Eremon cleared his throat. 'I cannot accept on behalf of the Epidii, in the absence of the council. But I can, and do accept gladly, on behalf of my men and my own people. We will be as brothers, bonded by oaths that cannot be broken.'

Calgacus smiled. 'Then pledge with me now, that we will fight together, to do all we can to rid Alba of these invaders. Wherever that may take us, to whatever battlefield.' He raised the cup and sipped from it, then handed it to Eremon.

'I pledge myself and my own forces and, the gods willing, those of the Epidii to fight with you, wherever it may take us.' Eremon sipped and passed the cup to Rhiann.

'And I pledge my support to both the Epidii and Caledonii as Ban Cré,' Rhiann added softly, 'in the defence of my land.' She took a sip of the golden mead, and the servant took the cup from her.

Now Calgacus reached to the cedar box and lifted the lid.

515

Eremon caught his breath, expecting to see the glint of gold or bronze; the shine of gems.

But instead, there on a finely-embroidered cushion lay a stone. It was a disk of polished, dark granite, the size of an apple, though flat, perforated by a hole through which an ochre-stained leather thong was threaded.

Calgacus lifted the stone by its thong, so it swung in the light, turning around and around. They could just see the lines of carving on both its surfaces.

'I had this made for you by my best stone carver – my best carver *now*,' he amended, and for a moment, his mouth tightened. 'It is not of iron or bronze, for they rust. It is not of gold, for gold is soft. It is of stone: hard, unbending, true and unchanging. It will not perish, or lose its lustre.' He looked directly at Eremon. 'It represents my bond to you, for that will be eternal, and never falter.'

Eremon's throat seemed to close over, and he swallowed.

'Look closer,' Calgacus said. On one side of the disk there was the familiar carving of the eagle, its head noble, its eye sharp. And on the other was the most beautiful carving of a boar that Eremon had ever seen. The fierceness of its crest had been caught in stone, its bunching muscles flowed like a song.

Around the edges ran lines of symbols sacred to the druid kind.

'My personal totem, and yours,' Calgacus explained, 'joined together on a message stone. This declares to all who see it that we are allied in soul, for ever.'

Eremon's voice came out as a croak. 'What does the writing say?'

Calgacus turned to Rhiann, and she also cleared her throat before speaking. 'It says: Calgacus of the Caledonii, son of Lierna, pledges allegiance and brotherhood to Eremon, son of Ferdiad, of Dalriada.'

Calgacus smiled. 'No untruth can ever be written down this way, so no man will ever be able to dispute that you speak in my name.'

Eremon took the stone from Calgacus, and slowly, reverently, placed the leather loop over his head. When it was settled, the boar stone lay on his breast, below his torc. 'I thank you, lord. I have no gift in return, but that of my own oath.' Eremon clasped the King's arm, wrist to wrist, and looked in to the gold-flecked eyes. 'Yet I tell you now: it is as eternal as this stone.'

Calgacus furnished Eremon and Rhiann with a large *curragh*, for they were to stay close to inland waters, and the hide boats were the most versatile craft, able to navigate river and loch as well as sea if need be.

Yet it could only hold twenty, so she and Eremon decided to send Eithne and a still-silent Didius back to Dunadd with Declan, Rori, Aedan, and the horses. The Epidii warriors would be their escort.

Rhiann insisted, however, that they take Dala and her guard, Rawden on the voyage, for even though Maelchon had gone, she wanted to keep a close eye on the fragile young girl.

Though only the Epidii party knew in advance of their leaving, on the day of departure the pier was swarming with people. Rhiann stood in the bow of the boat, her eyes narrowed against the sharp glint of sun on the sea, watching the crew hoisting barrels of water and food and storing them between the ribs of the hide hull.

The captain, a wiry, salt-swept man, was bustling up and down the pier with vexation because one of his crew had suddenly been taken ill. But a man loading the stores immediately volunteered in his stead, and after scrutinizing his height, the captain took him on, relieved at the presentation of an easy solution.

When all were aboard, the oars lifted and dipped, and the boat slid away over the mirrored water, the clear sky above captured in its smooth net. Rhiann cast only one glance back, with great relief, for she wanted to be free of the disturbing emanations from the dun, which had been plucking at her senses for days.

But then . . . her gaze was caught and held by burning, yellow eyes, fringed by straggling hair. Gelert, standing alone among the sea-grass, on the slope above the pier. Across the stretch of water between boat and land, she felt a faint last groping of his will. Yet, though the distance widened by the moment, his mouth quirked in that way that she knew so well: calculation, and a hint of . . . triumph?

Icy dread pierced Rhiann's belly, and she turned, seeking Eremon, close behind her. 'Rhiann,' he said, biting his lip. 'In the rush, I forgot to tell you that he was still here, being cared for by the druids. I'm sorry.'

He must have recognized the surge of fear in her face, for now he took her hand, rubbing her fingers. 'No, Rhiann, he cannot hurt us here. For we are gone, and he is left behind. Look!'

'His reach knows no bounds,' she answered, her voice high and strained.

Eremon smiled reassurance and moved to block her view of the pier, speaking of calm things until he was called away to the captain.

But though the day remained fine, Rhiann had to wrap her cloak close against the chill that invaded her, until the Dun of the Waves fell far behind and was lost against the shore.

They made good time under sail, with a blustery south wind skirting them along Alba's coast. The captain hugged the high cliffs closely, never straying too far from land, and when the water ran out after three days, he put in to the slivers of beach that edged the rocks and hauled barrels up and down the steep cliff face.

It was when they rounded the first cape and began heading west, that the brisk wind died, slowing their advance. Rhiann mostly sat with Dala and Caitlin in the bow, where the men had erected a small shelter from the sun. For a few days the water was as still and green as Roman glass, and they were forced to travel solely under oar, the sail furled and tied away.

Yet despite the unseasonal calm, Rhiann's unease grew, rather than faded.

Dala, too, became restless, as soon as they reached the strait between the Orcades islands and the mainland. She withdrew into herself, her head sunk into the hood of her cloak, and did not respond to Rhiann's gentle ministrations. Only when Rawden came did she look up, and then only to hold him and weep.

The scars were yet so fresh, Rhiann thought with pity, and one day she left the two lovers together and went aft to speak to Eremon. He had taken a place next to Conaire at the oars, and Caitlin was endeavouring to goad them into a race.

Standing by the mast, Rhiann watched Eremon, noting that, as usual, he knew how to win over the handful of boatmen that Calgacus had provided. His broad back strained, as he encouraged the others to pick up their speed, and Rhiann saw the sidelong looks he received, the dawning respect on salt-rimed faces.

All except one man – tall and, black-haired with a pock-marked face – the man the captain had taken on as they left. He never smiled or spoke, but hunched his thin frame over the oar, avoiding the other men's eyes.

Rhiann turned back to Eremon, putting the dour man out of her mind. Eremon did not seem to share her unease. Indeed, although he was initially downcast at the failure of the alliance, the further they sailed from the Dun of the Waves the lighter he became.

Has this to do with me? Rhiann doused the idea as soon as it came. She truly had no say over Eremon's happiness – and even if she did, what had happiness to do with life when it was duty and threat that called to them both?

Now Eremon caught sight of Rhiann, and joined her by the mast. He had stripped off his tunic to row, and she saw the beginnings of sunburn across his shoulders. 'I shall have to put an elder salve on that.' She touched the flushed skin.

He grinned, his eyes still dancing from the race. 'And *I* shall enjoy it,' he murmured, looking up at her from under his lashes.

Though he jested, the light in his eye caught at her throat, and she pushed him away playfully. 'You should have been a sailor after all! You're like a boy on his first trip around the bay.'

'Oh, no! I only like it when the weather is calm. I still remember our arrival – I thought the Albans must be mad to go out in boats.'

'And now do you think us mad?'

He cocked his head. 'Most certainly! But it's that potion you gave me that really helped. I have not felt sick for a moment.'

She smiled, but plucked at a splinter on the mast, distracted. What could she say? That she had a feeling? It was not much to go on. And yet, he did say he trusted her intuition. 'I have been feeling very strange, Eremon. I don't know what, but something is wrong around us.'

The laughter in his eyes died. 'Wrong?' He looked up at the sky, blue and clear from horizon to horizon, and then at the captain, picking the remains of the morning's meal from his teeth.

'Captain,' Eremon called, 'are the weather portents good?'

The man shrugged one shoulder, but a frown touched his brow. 'Such calm conditions do not bode well, as it happens, prince. Such a lack of wind, such unusual heat, usually mean one thing.' He pointed to the open ocean in the west. 'A storm may be building, far out at sea. But we will see it grow, with enough time to retreat to shore.'

'There!' Eremon smiled at Rhiann. 'You sense a storm, that is all. Though my belly won't like it, we can go ashore. We will be safe.'

Rhiann shrugged unhappily. 'Perhaps you are right. I just wanted you to be wary.'

He nodded, and put his hand over hers on the mast.

'Always tell me everything you feel, Rhiann. I will always take you seriously.'

She forced a smile. 'I know.'

Suddenly he glanced away, hot blood rising to his cheeks.

He was like a boy with her now, she thought, wondering. So different from before. But then she corrected herself. *He has been different for many moons now. It is I who keep us apart.*

Later she sat by Dala as she slept, gazing out over the smooth, dark waters ahead of them. All looked well: the gentle swells that lifted the bow, the gulls crying and wheeling above. The ridge of the mainland cliffs was broken now, with shattered rocks falling into the sea, and bright green shelves of turf, and every now and then, curls of sand and ragged bays, which offered refuge from the sea.

Perhaps it *was* just a storm she sensed. But as she thought back to Gelert's smile, she didn't think so.

At night they slept ashore in tiny scraps of cove, though they saw few people or trails of smoke, for the lands on the far north coast were wild, and few dared to scratch a living from the rain-lashed soil.

And then finally, on the sixth morning of calm, they pushed out the boat and rowed clear of the enclosing cliffs, and saw a faint smear of ochre in the sky, far on the western horizon. As they came out into the full force of the swell, the smooth wave hollows became broken, chopping against the hull, edged with foam.

The captain spat over the side, and rubbed his chin. 'There she is.' He squinted in all directions. 'We are fast approaching the great cape, and there are no landing places on its tip,' he explained to Eremon. The men at the oars cocked their heads, listening. 'Yet I think we can clear it in time, and reach the bay on the other side.'

'Are you sure?' Eremon peered into the sky. 'We are in your hands.'

The captain hesitated, then broke into a gap-toothed grin.

'I'm sure, if your men and mine row as fast as Arawn's hounds can fly!'

Eremon looked up at the cliffs sliding by. With the return of the wind, his senses were sharpened to the threat that Rhiann had felt.

Well, he had been trained from birth to deal with unexpected dangers. Taking after him, his men were prepared for almost anything, and Calgacus's rowers could handle a boat. Together, he was confident they would be safe.

Gods. Pray that I do not bring bad luck to sea trips.

CHAPTER 68

'It seems our captain misjudged his weather.' It was a few hours later, and now Eremon held one of the ropes, his other arm steadying Rhiann. Under the hull, the sea heaved restlessly, and the dark cloud ahead reared up like a wave itself, growing far more rapidly, the captain spluttered, than he expected.

And then, abruptly, the cloud eclipsed the late sun, thickening the air to murk, yellowing the light. Stray gusts of wind tugged the rigging under Eremon's hand, as he released Rhiann and turned to the captain. 'Now what do we do?'

The man's face was sheened with nervous sweat, and he wiped his forehead with one arm. 'The swell has pushed us too close to the cliffs here.' He pointed at the rocks lurking at the base of the cape; dark teeth glistening with spume. 'We must turn back immediately, and make for the last cove.'

They wheeled, and rowed back east again for what seemed an age, time lost in the sulphurous gloom, the wind rising to a soft, ghostly moan. Now hanging over the bow in the deepening dark, Eremon's face had lost its boyishness. 'I thought your Goddess looked after you!' he muttered, as Rhiann joined him, pulling the wind-whipped hair from her eyes.

'Her will is never clear,' she said.

'Then I will put my faith in earthly power – my hands and those of my men. That is all that will save us.' He turned away, barking orders to lash down the loose packs and barrels, and Rhiann crept back into the shelter, where Dala was crouching, her eyes wide and unseeing. Next to her, a

523

prone Caitlin caught Rhiann's eye and smiled weakly. She had a mountain soul, and even Rhiann's tansy tonic had done little to help her through the past few hours.

'The storm comes for me,' Dala whispered now. 'I knew I would escape him, I knew it.'

'We will be safe.' Rhiann pushed away her own fear and laid a hand on Dala's head. It was damp with sweat. 'We are close to the landing place now, child. Do not worry.'

'No, no, I will die.' Dala spoke in a monotone. 'It is coming closer now – the end of my pain. I run to meet it, to be free.'

Rhiann shivered at the energy of the seeing coming from the slight body next to her. The girl had the power! She took Dala's freezing hands and chafed them between her own. 'No, child, come back now. Run to life, not death.'

But Dala only looked through her, her eyes vacant. 'You will live, sister. You and your love.'

Rhiann met Caitlin's eyes, now wide and bright with fear, and just then a shuddering sequence of waves hit the boat, outriders of the storm whipped up in the open ocean days before. Still holding Dala's cold fingers, Rhiann closed her eyes, as they were all three tossed against the walls of the shelter in a squall of wind, and she fell to her knees.

Mother, deliver us.

Further back, the rowers fought to hold their seats in the face of the freak waves, lashed into a growing frenzy by the rapidly rising wind. Eremon pulled at his oar until the sweat broke out on his brow, casting desperate glances over his shoulder for a glimpse of the bay that signalled safety.

By Hawen's balls, I am never again setting foot on a boat!

Yet as he looked back again, the fear of the waves and the wind lurched into sudden anger, as one man struggled to his feet and abandoned his oar. The man, the tall one with pitted skin, stumbled and fell into the hull, as another wave struck the boat, and Eremon threw his own oar aside and started towards him, his fists clenched.

But the sharp scolding died in his throat when the man

looked up from his crouch, for in the bruised light of the storm, his lips were drawn into a terrible rictus of despair. Pain billowed out from him and struck Eremon's chest, filling the boat as blood fills a wound.

Then a scream split the air; Eremon now jerked towards the unearthly sound and saw Dala standing by the shelter, her arm reaching out to the pock-marked man while Rhiann held her. And when Eremon's eyes traced back along the line of Dala's fingers, the shock struck him.

For the man was on his feet now with a sword in his hands, and he scrambled up on to the railing of the boat.

Is he going to kill himself? Eremon thought wildly.

But the man looked instead into Eremon's eyes, and tears stood on his cheeks. 'Forgive me,' he cried.

And with that, he launched himself like a diving gull, his sword pointing down beneath him, his whole weight driving it into the toughened hide hull of the *curragh*.

CHAPTER 69

'No!' Eremon threw himself in a great leap towards
the man, over the benches, arms out. But he was
too late. As he fell face down in the hull, seawater spurted
through a wide hole, drenching his face.

Then he was on his feet, fingers seeking for the traitor, but
he was lithe as a weasel, and before anyone could stop him,
he flung himself over the side into the black waters below.

Eremon realized only then that the waves had pushed
them around the headland at last, but they'd strayed too
close to the pitted rocks at its base and were tossed now in a
flume of boiling foam, knocking him to his knees.

There was another agonized shriek. Eremon looked up to
see Dala's lover leaning desperately over the bow, but there
was no sign of Maelchon's Queen. When Rhiann's scream
came again, the guard too was gone, leaping after his love.
Eremon's body tensed to follow, until a restraining hand
clamped on to his arm. 'I won't let you, brother,' Conaire
warned, pointing at the seething waters below.

The captain was frantically ordering the men to the oars on
the landward side, and in their panic, the rowers wrenched
the boat away from the rocks in only a few strokes. In the
maelstrom of pale surf and dark water, no heads surfaced. It
would be death indeed for any to venture there.

Despairing, Eremon looked down at the hole made by the
sword. The force of the traitor's leap had opened a long rent,
and they had little time, as the freezing water was already

ankle deep. Some of the men now abandoned rowing and began bailing with any container that came to hand.

'Can we make it to shore?' Eremon cried to the captain, over the rising wind.

'I think so!' the man choked out, pointing past the rocks. Through the gloom, Eremon could see a pale blur of sand, and hear the pounding of surf. 'We can swim, prince, but can you?'

'Most of us can,' Eremon answered. 'Yet empty out the barrels, anything that may float. We don't have long!'

He splashed through the water to the bow, where Rhiann crouched, her arms wrapped around her body. Eremon knelt and cupped her wet face, as Caitlin hovered over her, holding back tears.

'I tried to hold her, but she fled from me.' Rhiann's eyes were wide, torn with grief, and Eremon pressed her face into his shoulder.

'It was not your fault, my love.' He brushed damp hair back from her cheeks. 'Can you swim?' *I cannot lose her . . . I will not lose her . . .*

'Yes,' she whispered. 'I learned on the island . . . I can do it.'

'Good girl.' Relief coursed through him.

Conaire reached them now, and enfolded Caitlin in his arms. They murmured together, and Conaire turned, his face stricken. 'Caitlin cannot swim, brother.'

Rhiann gasped and struggled to her feet, as Eremon raked the hull with desperate eyes. 'Those food barrels are empty now. Tie her to one – you can keep her afloat, I know you can.'

The fear in Conaire's face tore at Eremon, but then he saw him grasp at Eremon's suggestion, and gain control.

The seawater was now up to their knees, but the men still rowed, trying to edge the boat closer to the beach, past the rearing cliffs that gazed down without mercy. The growing waves aided them, pounding on their seaward side, the wind flinging foam up over the stern.

Eremon took one of the barrels from Conaire and brought

it to Rhiann where she stood, clasping Caitlin's hands. 'Hold on to this when you go in,' he said, tying a length of the rigging around the barrel. 'Don't let go, whatever you do.' He touched her face, as Conaire took hold of Caitlin in his arms.

The sound of surf on the shore was louder now, but the boat was foundering, the water from the rent dragging it low enough for the sea to begin pouring over the sides. There was no more time.

And then they were in the water, and all fears were shattered by freezing, breath-wrenching cold, and the shock of the suffocating water, grasping for their lungs. Then the heaving of the current took hold, and there was desperate pushing up to air, and frantic kicks away from the boat as it fell out from beneath them.

Eremon came up spluttering, twisting around and around, peering frantically at the splashing figures surrounding him.

Rhiann! his heart called.

Rhiann's first thought was, *I am cold*. Her second was, *Why am I in Eremon's arms?*

Yet an instant later, memory rushed in, and she opened her eyes to a dawn as grey as her heart.

She shivered, remembering the sea sucking at her, and the seething waves pounding her down, filling her nose and eyes with stinging water . . . the striving for sweet air, before Eremon dragged her up on to a shelf of sand. She remembered struggling to her feet, as Conaire followed with Caitlin in his arms, and holding her sister to her heart, fiercely, until she knew that she breathed, and would live.

And then none of them could do more than collapse on the shingle, flung up like driftwood, utterly spent. Later, they crawled under a rock overhang, shivering through the night as the storm lashed the bay, and the winds drove the sea far up on the sand.

Now that storm too was exhausted, and in the dripping silence, Rhiann was left only with the memory of the other sister, who had not survived the sea. Dala.

Tears started to her eyes, melting the salt crusting her eyelashes, and Eremon stirred as he heard her breathing grow ragged, and his arms around her tightened. She felt the familiar urge to pull away from him, but the need to surrender to his warmth, his safety, was stronger.

'Rhiann?'

She tilted her head up. 'I am well, Eremon.'

'Thank the gods.' His voice rumbled against her ear, and she fought the surrendering, the sleepiness, and struggled to sit up.

'Eremon, the men . . .'

Though she knew they lived, in the shadow of the overhang her eyes again sought for the twin gold heads of Caitlin and Conaire, wrapped together, and Colum's grey hair, and Fergus's bright eyes. They were safe, but Eremon would know better than she that damp clothes and cold were dangers unto themselves, and in a moment he had roused everyone to their feet.

They took stock of what had been saved, but it was not much. Most of the food had been emptied out of the barrels, and their weapons and other supplies were gone, except for two bows, the strings unfit for hunting until they dried. And to the Alban men's amazement, Eremon had saved his sword, despite its weight. 'It was my father's sword,' he stated bluntly. 'I had no intention of leaving it at the bottom of the sea.'

Warmth was the most important need, and Eremon sent Caitlin and the men to search for any wood that had escaped the rain, while he and Conaire began to break up the barrels. As they did, he glanced at Rhiann, sitting silently on the sand near the water. He told her to rest, and for once, she had obeyed him.

But when he saw her wipe her eyes, and bow her head, he left Conaire and came up behind her. 'Eremon,' she said, though she did not turn. 'The feeling I had was real. I knew there was something wrong with that man. Why did I not see?'

Her voice broke, and he laid a hand on her shoulder. 'How could you? It was not your fault.'

'But I should have known!' she cried, looking back at him. 'Now I do know, but it is too late, for Dala and Rawden!'

Tendrils of hair were plastered to her face, and he brushed them away. 'What do you know?'

She turned back to the sea. 'The pock-marked man came from Maelchon. He wanted to kill us . . . because I shamed him . . . because of his obsession . . .' She picked at a strand of seaweed. 'That man had a burden of pain laid on him, I could feel it from the start!'

'It was the act of a desperate soul,' Eremon agreed, remembering the man's last words. 'He didn't want to do it, Rhiann, but Maelchon must have had a very strong hold on him.'

'And Eremon, what about Gelert? He *knew* this was coming. He must have discovered we were leaving and told Maelchon. He tried to kill us as surely as if he wielded the sword himself.'

Eremon's mouth tightened. 'When we return, it will be time to challenge this druid openly.'

Rhiann sighed. 'Yet we have no proof.'

'Nothing but the evidence of our own eyes!'

'We wouldn't have that if his plan had succeeded.' She shuddered. 'Yet I still don't understand why Maelchon's man waited so long into the journey to act. Because of that, we did live.'

Eremon squatted down. 'Maelchon would not want any evidence of us, our deaths, to be attached to him. My guess is that our man had instructions to wait until we were as far from the Orcades as possible. Perhaps the storm changed his plans, perhaps he thought he'd take his chances before we were safe ashore.' He considered the wild despair in the man's eyes. 'I don't think he was acting rationally, Rhiann, and there Maelchon miscalculated. Fear is not the best way to control people.'

'Well, it controlled Dala. She almost leaped from my arms when the wave knocked her free. I think . . . I think she was too hurt to want to live.'

'Then it wasn't your fault.'

Just then Caitlin appeared, picking her way over the rocks that bordered the next bay. Her small face was grim beneath her tangled braids. 'We found Dala,' she said, her eyes on Rhiann. 'And her man.'

With a cry, Rhiann leaped up and hurried away over the rocks.

Eremon stopped Caitlin from following. 'Let her go,' he said. 'She needs to grieve alone.'

'We found the traitor, too,' Caitlin muttered. 'Further along. The storm washed everything in.'

Eremon brushed sand from his fingers. 'He will have a burial the same as the others. They were all victims of the same man.'

The Caledonii captain knew where they had landed. 'If we cross this cape, we will come across more settlements along the western coast,' he said that night, around a feeble fire made of barrel staves. The rain had stopped, though the wind was still high, and clouds crowded the sky.

'Perhaps we can pick up a vessel going south to Dunadd,' Rhiann added.

Eremon looked at her across the fire. Conducting the burials that afternoon seemed to have calmed her, the ritual restoring strength of body and spirit. The shadow of grief lurked in her eyes, but acceptance was growing there, too. *Good*, he thought. *I need her in her full power if we are to get safely home.*

'The people here are isolated,' she was explaining to Caitlin, 'so the blood of the Old Ones runs more truly than elsewhere, and members of the sisterhood are revered as we are not in all parts of Alba. Perhaps it will not be long before we find help.'

Though they were still weak and hungry, Eremon got

everyone moving at first light the next day, as faint sun crept through rents in the heavy cloud. He wanted to be back within stout walls soon, and at Dunadd soon after.

Two days of hiking among the barren glens brought them to the Western Sea, and a long sand beach, its dune grasses bent double in the harsh winds. But still they could find no game among the treeless hills behind it, their roots sunk deep in peat, the seams of their gnarled rocks running endlessly with water.

After a sparse meal of limpets, scraped from the shore, they rolled in their damp cloaks in the dunes, huddling close to the dying fire.

'Tomorrow we must leave the coast so we can find meat,' Eremon said to Rhiann, as they lay, each wrapped in their own cloak. 'I cannot let the men get weaker. We may have to defend ourselves soon, and we have no weapons but my own.'

'You will not be in danger with me here.' Rhiann turned over to her back.

'How can you be so sure?'

Before she could answer, there was a cry from Fergus, who had been posted as first watch. All of the men leaped to their feet.

Straining into the darkness, Eremon could not take in what he saw: a circle of small men emerging from the cloak of night, as if they grew from the dark rocks around them, or crept out of hiding from the earth herself. Their clothes seemed to shift and change, patterned in colours of wet sand, seaweed, lichen. Their eyes glowed like those of wolves in the light of the fire.

Then one of the figures came forward, pushing Fergus before him.

'He shot an arrow into the sand, my lord,' Fergus gasped out. 'When I went to investigate the noise he got behind me. He has a spear at my back. I am sorry, I was exhausted, I—'

'Hush!' said Eremon sharply. 'It is too late for that now.' He raised his own sword so that the light glinted from its surface, unmistakable to their attackers. 'If you harm this man you will feel the bite of my sword, I promise you!' he shouted.

The man holding Fergus said something harshly that Eremon could barely understand; he seemed to be using a strange dialect. But Eremon made out the word *gael*, and then he realized, to his horror, that these people had seen him and his men in the daylight. They knew they did not have the tattoos of the Albans. This made them strangers, raiders. A dangerous position to be in on this isolated coast, with no weapons but his own.

He sensed Rhiann by his side. 'If this is the only time you listen to me, do it now,' she said softly. 'Do not interfere, or we may all die. Each of those men will have an arrow on the string.'

Before Eremon could stop her, she walked towards the man who had spoken, saying something sharply in the same dialect. Eremon made out the words 'Ban Cré' and 'Epidii'.

The man answered her, less boldly now, but still pressing his spear to Fergus's back. Then Rhiann stopped, and drew herself up, and flung out a hand. When she spoke, her tone was compelling, as it had been when she spoke the litany for the drowned Dala and Rawden, and in the dancing shadows of the flames, her outline seemed to tremble and grow somehow taller, straighter, brighter, as she pulled the priestess glamour around her, just like at Beltaine. Her hair was a nimbus of flame around her head . . . or was it just the light?

With her words the other small men came to life, stirring and muttering, and the one who had spoken called out to them, harsh as a gull, falling back and releasing Fergus.

As Fergus stumbled back to Eremon, the leader of the newcomers slowly approached Rhiann with his spear laid over his hands, and knelt and placed it at her feet. He remained there, his head bent in apparent submission.

Eremon's breath whistled out through his teeth. The attack had only taken a matter of moments, but his body was vibrating from the rush of danger. He watched Rhiann put a hand on the man's head and say something, more softly now, before he again got to his feet.

Eremon could see that he only reached Rhiann's shoulder, and his hair and eyes gleamed black in the firelight. He was dressed in checked trousers and a sleeveless tunic of that shifting, lichen hue, but despite the night wind, wore no cloak. The answer was slung across his back: a skin quiver, its ornate beading and ochre-dyed arrows, and the polished stone wrist-guard a signal that these people valued the bow highly indeed. A cloak or sleeves might hinder the drawing of the string. Only a band of spotted seal-fur around an upper arm, and a necklace of shells, differentiated him from his men.

Eremon walked slowly to Rhiann, his eyes on the man, who looked back at him frankly, even proudly, though he had to tilt his head up to do so.

'Remind me to let you walk into danger more often,' Eremon murmured to Rhiann.

'Eremon.' Rhiann gestured towards the leader. 'This is Nectan, son of Gede, a headman of the Caereni. They are one of the Western tribes we came to meet. He wants to know why I have brought *gaels* into his territory.'

Now that he was closer, Eremon could see the silver running through his attacker's dark hair, and realized that the man's height and litheness belied the wrinkles by his eyes; seams of amusement, and the squinting that comes from sea-wind and sun. 'Then you'd best tell him who I am.'

After the introductions were complete, Nectan directed a torrent of questions at Rhiann that Eremon could barely follow. Rhiann answered him patiently, and soon he seemed to be satisfied, looking Eremon up and down with an air of speculation, before joining his own men. There, they began to talk among themselves in a cascade of musical voices.

'Why can't I understand him?' Eremon wondered.

'These people use many of the old words. That is why you can understand part of it, but not all of it. He will be able to speak with you, though, when he chooses.'

'So what did you say to him that made him surrender?'

Rhiann smiled wryly. 'He did not surrender. He paid homage to a Ban Cré. Here the worship of the Goddess is stronger than the worship of the sword gods. I spoke sacred words to him. Then he truly believed.'

'And what did you tell him about me and my men?'

'That you were my bonded man, here to help me—'

'Bonded man?'

'Their meaning for "husband" is slightly different.' She put her hand on his arm. 'Eremon, this is all old lore. All that matters is this is the help we needed. They will take us to their village, and then I will ask them for help to get us home. They respect me, but are wary of you, so you are in my hands in this. There is nothing more to be done.'

He saw the truth of it, and nodded. 'I will be on my best behaviour. Especially if they give us food; my belly growls like a bear.'

CHAPTER 70

Nectan came back to Rhiann and instructed that they follow, so long as the 'man with the sword' stayed by his side. The rest of his men fanned out to surround the little group, and in this way they were led back into the dunes until they came out on to a narrow trackway that ran south.

The clouds had been blown away by the last of the high winds, and the moon now sailed in the dark sky, sheening the surface of a shallow loch by their path. They splashed through a stream trickling over the sands, before climbing higher ground once more, reaching Nectan's settlement before the moon had sunk halfway to the horizon.

There a strange sight awaited them. Among the dunes, a scattering of small, pointed roofs rose above the sand, like the helmets of a buried army. Nectan stopped outside a passageway that led into the dune towards one of the roofs. 'Come, we will eat,' he said. 'Then, we will talk.'

Eremon looked up at the tiny cone of thatch poking out of the sand, and down to the narrow doorway. 'All of us? Surely there are too many to fit in this house?'

'No.' Rhiann's voice smiled in the darkness. 'Among these people, not all is as it seems.'

They walked down a passage roofed with massive lintel-stones, and then Eremon discovered what Rhiann meant, as they emerged into an enormous house that had been built snugly into a great pit in the dune.

Firelight from the central hearth warmed the outer stone walls, but there was also an inner ring of pillars that held up a flat, corbelled roof. In the centre, where the stone ceiling ended, an opening was capped by the thatched roof they had seen from outside. It was hard to believe such a house could not be seen from above, and yet was safe from the wild winds and rain of the Western Sea.

Eremon turned eyes full of new respect on Nectan, who was watching him, a glint of amusement in his own. 'Son of Gede, this is an extremely fine house. I have seen none so cunning, even in my own lands.'

Nectan beamed and clapped Eremon on the back, gesturing for him and his men to sit around the hearth. Rhiann he led to his wife, who bowed and kissed her hand fervently, seating her and Caitlin on embroidered cushions nearest to the fire.

Rich smells of leftover mutton and carrageen stew were still curling from the iron cauldron, but as the family had already eaten there was not enough to feed unexpected guests. But Nectan's wife sent her numerous children scurrying to the other houses, and soon they returned bearing gifts of porridge and bread and new cheese; enough to bring strength back to their limbs.

They fell to eating, ravenous. Nectan went to a barrel in a storage alcove and returned with a wooden jug of ale, which was just as quickly consumed.

As he ate and drank, Eremon saw the little man gazing at his golden torc; those alert, dark eyes made him uneasy. Rhiann ate more slowly, murmuring all the while to Nectan's wife, and then to Nectan, who came and sat near her. Soon Rhiann shook her head, her voice raised as if she were striving to explain something. Then Nectan frowned, his mouth stubborn. Caitlin was worried, looking from one to the other.

Rhiann glanced over at Eremon. 'I told him why we have come – that war with the Romans is near.'

'What does he say?'

'That the Goddess smiles on us. All the Caereni and Carnonacae leaders are travelling to the Sacred Isle, over the sea.' A shadow of pain crossed her face. 'In less than a week it is Beltaine – a most sacred Beltaine to the island people, for in the moon cycle it only comes around once every eighteen years.'

'Then it *is* a god-given opportunity!'

'Yes.' She stared at him, unseeing.

'Cousin.' Caitlin put a tiny hand on Rhiann's arm. 'What is wrong?'

But Rhiann did not answer, and Eremon could see her struggling with some strong emotion.

'I wish to speak with the Ban Cré alone,' he said. Nectan bowed his head, signalling to his wife to get sheepskin cloaks for them both.

Outside, they walked in silence on top of the dunes, where the sinking moon turned the sand to bronze.

'Landing there before these kings with only the cloak on my back is not the most auspicious of entrances.' Eremon ran his fingers through his salt-tangled hair. 'Yet, by the Boar, it is too good an opportunity to miss!'

Rhiann said nothing, watching the gleam of light on the sea. Then Eremon took her elbow, and felt the shiver that went through her.

'You are distressed,' he said. 'It is because we must return to the island that was your home, isn't it? Where the raiders came.'

'I cannot go back. I cannot!'

'Rhiann, I know the memories run deep, but it seems we must go.' He drew her closer. 'I will keep you safe there, when the dreams come.'

Though the wind was not bitter, another shudder wracked her. 'You don't understand! I said to Eldest Sister, Nerida, that I would never go back, that I could never look on those faces again! And if I go, I cannot hide . . . from *them*.' She bowed her head. 'You do not understand.'

One knotted braid fell across her face, and he tucked it behind her ear. 'What do you want to do then? We can walk south, though it will be hard. But I will do this – my men will do this – if you wish it.'

She sighed and raised her face. 'No, you cannot do that,

Eremon. Calgacus has charged us with his trust, and in one visit you may be able to win thousands of men to your side. It would be great folly not to go . . . yet I will stay with the boats, and hide my face away.'

They slept that night in an alcove of Nectan's house, on a bed of moss and dried bracken covered by seal-skins.

Deep in dreams of a lonely coastline, Eremon heard a plaintive cry, a gull wheeling in the air above him. But the cry tailed off to a whimper, and the dream-Eremon realized that something was wrong; a gull did not cry like that.

Suddenly he was awake, and when he heard the whimper again he realized it was Rhiann, curled up with her face turned to the wall. He laid a gentle hand on her shoulder. 'Rhiann?' She gave a great, shuddering sigh, and then he felt her body tense as she woke fully. 'Hush,' he said in her ear, 'Hush, it is me. Is it the dream?'

She nodded, struggling for breath, and he drew her rigid body into the curve of his own. 'That was long ago, Rhiann. You are safe now.'

As if the soft words released something in her, her body was rocked by spasms, and she burrowed her face into her arms. And all the while Eremon held her, murmuring nonsense words, words to calm and gentle her.

Yet beneath his pain at her distress, he could not repress a guilty stab of elation. *She has never let me hold her like this*!

Rhiann was too exhausted to hold the tears back. The shipwreck . . . being so close to the Sacred Isle . . . suddenly finding she would stand on that familiar soil again . . . all had torn a breach in her heart, through which pain could pour.

And with the clarity of utter despair, she knew now that the sundering from the Sisters was the most acute of all those griefs in her life. She had hidden it well, but now they called her. They called her home.

The anguish rose, twisting her mouth as she tried to swallow it, wracking her body from feet to head. Dimly, she was aware of Eremon's soft voice, and though she did not know what he said, somehow the meaning of safety, and loving, and belonging came to her. And the pain was realizing that this was what she had missed these last years.

At last, when the tears were no more than salt tracks on her cheeks, Eremon spoke. 'How long were you on the Sacred Isle, Rhiann?'

'Thirteen years,' she whispered.

'Tell me about those years, then. Surely there were happy times, too?'

She sighed. *Mother, I made my peace with You. Why have You brought me back? Have I not suffered enough?*

'The pain of my mother's death was strong,' Eremon murmured now, his breath on her ear. 'But I remember her eyes . . . and her smell . . . like honey and milk. The way her hand felt when she stroked my head. I think boys are meant to forget these things. But she was the only softness in my life. I have never forgotten.'

Surprised, Rhiann thought of Drust, and how she had loved his tales, his refinement. How she had always hated the warriors, the rough men with swords.

'You are safe,' Eremon whispered again. 'Tell me what you remember.'

And with those words she was winging over the choppy seas under moonlight, to a low island of rock and turf, once so dear to her heart. The wind-lashed coast, the scattered lochs, the rocks, wet with rain, all passed through her mind.

It was she who needed to remember, not Eremon who needed to hear. It was like the sea rushing up the sands, sweeping her relentlessly to a place that held precious things: a memory of belonging, a memory of the Goddess-light, the Sisters.

She longed to surrender to this, just for one night. It would be like returning to a time before pain.

'I will tell you something, then,' she said at last, her eyes open in the darkness. 'I will tell you of the day I became a woman.'

CHAPTER 71

Eremon was to remember that telling his whole life, for he entered into it with her, saw and felt everything as she laid it out before him. Another Rhiann walked through that tale, a Rhiann he once thought he would never reach; a soft Rhiann that laughed and cried and loved.

It was a gift he never forgot, a memory that ever after took him back to that night, when he did not know if they would be alive in a year.

Alive, or free.

He closed his eyes, breathed the sea scent of her hair, and listened, as he had listened to the tale-tellers during long nights on Erin . . .

'A girl's first moon bleeding is a powerful time,' Rhiann said, 'for she can now give life, the most sacred gift. She becomes ruled by the Mother's tides: it is her deep connection to the Goddess in Her earthly form.

'I was twelve when my time came. In the maidens' hut, the Sisters doused coals with water and wild thyme, and as the sweat dripped from my skin, so my child-life washed away with it. Then in a rowan cup they gave me the dreaming herbs, the *saor*, that would let me feel one with the Mother, that would awaken the deep memories of my birth in Her womb.

'At full dark, two of my Sisters came to lead me into the woods, but I could not see their faces. In a daze I walked, and they led me to a glade that I did not know, and turned to me. Then I saw them.

'Inside their hoods were two wooden masks, painted white. One had the full moon on the brow, wound about the edges with barley-heads. She was the Mother. The other had a waning moon, and on her mask were bare winter twigs, with scarlet hawthorn berries. The Crone. So I was the Maiden, and my other two aspects, that I would wear one day in turn, had led me forward.

'"Daughter," the Crone said. "You must stay here until dawn. Let the Mother bathe you in Her light, and hold you to Her breast. Let your blood run freely into the earth."

'They bade me remove my shift, and laid me down in the middle of the glade, on a patch of soft leaves. Then they left me, the scent of wood-flowers all around. I stared up at the sky, and the stars began to spin as the herbs took hold, until at last I heard a heartbeat.

'The heartbeat swelled until I was somehow inside it, and it thrummed on my skin in waves and hollows. I lay like this for a long time, for hours, as my blood drained from between my legs into the soil, binding us, marking Her with my journey.

'After an age, it seemed, I opened my eyes again. It was then that I saw the Stag.

'His crown of antlers brushed against the branches above him, as he came, picking his way among last-year's leaves. The velvet was hanging in strips from the antler tines, and they brushed my face as he leaned down and breathed on me, a sweet smell of berries.

'Then he looked into my face, and I saw eyes that had something of the forest, the stag, and something of the man in them. He looked at me with desire, though I did not really understand yet what that was.

'I closed my eyes as he breathed on me again, and when I opened them I held in my arms a man, but above my head I could see the spread of antlers outlined against the moon. I remember a rush of great joy, and then there was nothing . . .

'Another age later, perhaps, I began to feel different . . . as if my whole body was swelling and pulsing in time with the heartbeat, growing round and full like the waxing moon. It seemed that I grew bigger, until I could see out over the tops of the trees, and then swelled even more, until I could see over many lands, and across the seas between them. Finally, only the arch of the starlit heavens stretched over me, and when I looked down at my belly, huge with child, I saw I was clothed with forests and seas.

'From between my legs the blood still flowed, but it was blood no longer. Now it was all the waters of the earth, tumbling out from me to form rivers and springs, and deep lakes. And after the waters subsided, so the pains came, wrenching me from within, making me bear down, though I was not feared, and the pain was not more than I could bear.

'And so from inside me came pouring a torrent of animals; birds flying, fish leaping, and the other creatures of the land, wriggling, and hopping, crawling and slithering, running and lumbering and jumping. I saw people, too, and they were running with the fleet creatures of the forest, but were soon lost in the outpouring of life from within me.

'The outpouring was ecstasy; it was joy and fulfillment as one, for I *was* the Mother, and had birthed Love.

'When I was at last spent, I lay down again, shrinking until I was once more just Rhiann in the forest glade. I fell asleep, knowing I was safe, for she was Mother of All. And I was Her.

'When I next awoke – and I have never before or since woken so fresh – sunlight was pouring through leaves, bathing me as I lay curled like a baby in the womb. I did not move for a long while, wondering if the night had been real, or if I had dreamed it all. And then I opened my hand.

'Clasped within it was a piece of velvet from the tines of the Stag.'

Eremon started, not knowing how much time had passed since Rhiann stopped speaking. Her voice put him in a trance, and he had been floating between the worlds, as she floated between them that magical night.

He shifted, and she sighed. She was not asleep, then.

He lay silent, knowing that what she told him was a great

mystery, and that the telling showed immense trust in him. He was afraid, at first, to break the spell.

'Who was the stag, Rhiann?' he whispered at last. 'Was he real?'

Her voice was dreamy. 'He was the God, the Great God, the first god; in his true role as consort to the Goddess. His seed makes Her the Mother. His strength holds Her so She can let the life flow.' She paused, twisting her head. 'You understand? For that one moment out of time, I *became* the Goddess. He came as the God, to join with me.'

'But was he truly there?'

'What is "truly"? You will see something like it at Beltaine. A priestess will act as the Goddess. A man will be the Stag, the God. Her consort.'

'We do not have such a rite at Beltaine.'

'The Britons to the south do not have it either, nor the Gauls over the sea. It is the mark of the Old Ones, the time when there was only one god and goddess, when deer were life, before we knew how to grow grain.'

Eremon felt sleep starting to claim him now, and he yawned. 'Did it help?' He drew her closer, into his warmth. 'Did it help you to tell me?'

Rhiann was silent for a moment. 'The pain is still there, Eremon. But some of the darkness has fallen away. I . . . I thank you.'

'Then every time the dark returns, tell me something else. Tell me of every happy time you had. I will listen, always.'

In answer she clasped his fingers on her waist, and with that he slipped away to sleep.

Soon he was dreaming of running through the forest, and antlers brushed the leaves above his head.

CHAPTER 72

During the long day it took to cross to the Sacred Isle, Rhiann noted that Eremon wasted no time, engaging Nectan in deep conversation in the bow of the headman's *curragh*.

There was more than enough room for them all in the small boat, for after recovering their strength, the men from Calgacus's dun had set off overland to return home, and only the Erin men and Caitlin now accompanied them.

When Rhiann approached the bow with cups of water, Eremon appeared well pleased. 'It seems I have gained Nectan's understanding. He knows of Calgacus, and he pledges that he and his men will fight! Their skills with the bow will be much valued, and I can see already what fine trackers and scouts they will make, for they have a knack of moving without being seen – as we know to our own initial regret!'

'May the other chieftains see as clearly as he.'

They made landfall near dusk on a sloping beach, by a village huddled at the mouth of a shallow stream. Turf slopes rose up all around, hiding the rocky bones of the island that outcropped to the west. The sands were littered with hundreds of *curraghs*, and wood-built traders were tied to the pier.

'Nectan says he has close kin here in the village,' Rhiann said, as Eremon helped her out of the boat, holding up her cloak. 'We will all bed here tonight, and tomorrow he will take you to the other side of the island, where the broch of the chief lies. And the Stones.' She darted a nervous glance at the headland that reared from the end of the beach.

'Are you sure?' Eremon shaded his eyes from the last sun spilling through a cleft in the hills. 'I hate the thought of you being alone.'

'I will stay with you, Rhiann!' Caitlin piped up, splashing free of the shallows, her boots in one hand.

Rhiann forced a smile. 'No, cousin. I would not stop you from seeing the Stones, or the Beltaine rite. You will never see such a gathering anywhere else.'

But Conaire, standing nearby, was not happy with any of it. 'Is it a good idea to place ourselves so whole-heartedly in their hands, here or at the broch? We don't know these people.' He eyed a bundle being carried up the beach; Nectan's spears, the sharp tips wrapped in cloth.

'We use no weapons here,' Nectan said, appearing suddenly behind them. 'It is the Sacred Isle, the Mother's Isle. The spears are for hunting only. No one will harm you: I give you my word.'

Conaire's suspicions were plain on his face, but later, in the house of Nectan's cousin, a platter of fresh fish and plentiful ale helped to allay his fears.

Rhiann's presence caused great excitement, but as soon as she had eaten she excused herself and retired to the guest bedplace, a platform behind a deer-hide hanging. She did not want to take part in the drinking and tales around the fire. She wanted only to be far away from here.

But sleep eluded her. Somewhere, only a few leagues away, there were houses filled with the clean scent of herbs, and the soft music of women's voices. There, in the Stones, the Source was drawn so close to the earth that the very soil vibrated with it.

But she had renounced it all with a few words of pain and rage. *Why could I not save them? Why could you not?*

Did they think of her? Did they miss her, as she missed them? She had heard no word from them these last years, so perhaps they had truly forgotten her. There was no going back from the words she had spoken.

Surely no going back.

*

Rhiann was lying on her pallet in a doze, the banter and laughter of those around the fire a bright thread weaving through her dreams. And then, suddenly, she woke, sensing a rapping on the brushwood door. She sat up, her heart already pounding.

A rush of wind swirled in as the door opened and closed, and the voices around the fire faded away. Rhiann struggled out of the furs to her knees, peering through a gap in the hide cover.

In the doorway, outlined by falling moonlight, was a woman. Nothing could be seen of her save a glimmer of pale face, for she was swathed in a dark blue cloak, its hood drawn up over her hair.

The wife of Nectan's cousin rose to her feet. 'Welcome to our house, Lady Sister,' she said. 'Come and join us, if you wish.'

The priestess shook her head, but took a step fully into the room.

'I have not come for your food or ale,' she said in a melodic voice, 'though blessings be upon them. Where is my Sister? For she knows why I have come.'

As the people glanced at each other, not knowing what to say, Rhiann stepped out from the bed-place, her own cloak thrown over her shift, her eyes on the figure at the door. As she stared at the priestess, she sensed a strong tug of familiarity, although all she could see was the gleam of dark eyes. 'Fola?' Her voice sounded wavering to her ears, with none of the power that she was trained to project.

In answer, the priestess put back her hood, uncovering dark, curled braids crowning a solid face, broad and smooth and mild as milk. Yet the sloe-black eyes twinkled with suppressed excitement, as if the composure required in the presence of people tried her hard. It was indeed Fola; Rhiann's closest friend during her priestess training on the island.

'I am here to call you home, Sister,' she said aloud, as

another sense flowed into Rhiann's mind. *Did you really think that we would let you go, now that you have come back*?

Rhiann's mouth went dry. Of course they would know she was here! How foolish to even think that she could hide! 'If you wish to speak to me . . . Sister . . . we will go outside.'

Fola bowed her head and turned through the doorway again. Rhiann caught a glimpse of Eremon's frown as she crossed the room, and then she was out in the night, and the moonlight flickered and leaped from between high, racing clouds.

'These last years have treated you well, Rhiann,' Fola said, her smile now let out into the night air. 'You are a regal woman; a queen.'

Rhiann shook her head, not knowing what to say, as the wind blew hair across her face. Fola had always known exactly what she was thinking, and they had spoken mind to mind from childhood, not with words, but with feelings and pictures. Yet no one had crossed that threshold since she left.

'I asked to come,' Fola added. 'I wanted to be the first to see you.'

Betraying tears pricked at Rhiann's eyes, and she held her hair and turned away, knuckles tight against her neck. 'I was forced to sail here. I will stay in the village, until we can leave.'

Fola moved to stand in front of her. 'That won't do, Rhiann. Come with me. Come home with me.'

'But I turned my back and left you!' Rhiann cried. 'How can you act as if nothing has happened! My life, such as it was, ended here three years ago. I am different now. They do not want to see this Rhiann. I am not fit to walk among the Stones again.'

Pity shone now in Fola's eyes. 'There you are wrong. You are our Sister. You must know that nothing can change that. *You* cannot change that – however hard you try.'

Rhiann could not answer.

'The Mother brought you here,' Fola said. 'Why did She do this? To cause you pain? To hurt you?'

'She hurts if She chooses. She brings pain and death. You, of all people, know why I left.'

Fola shook her head. 'And if you had stayed, you would have learned more than this.' Her soft voice bared a hint of impatience. 'She brought you because it is time to come home. You know this.'

Rhiann drew a deep breath. 'It seems that everyone is sure of this except me. Do I not have a choice?'

'Of course! If you ask me to, I will walk away and leave you here tonight. But before I do, I have a message from Nerida. Will you hear it?'

At the sound of that name, Rhiann was flooded with shame . . . and yearning.

'She said this: tell our Sister that I know her heart is sore, that she feels she failed us, that we failed her. This may be true, but there are other, truer things; deeper than betrayal, deeper than shame. Love, forgiveness, faith. Ask her to heed the call, if only for one last time.'

Stricken, Rhiann stared over Fola's shoulder, at the shattered moonlight on the wind-blown waves, the dark shadows of boats on the sand, their masts creaking.

'That is the message,' said Fola. 'Though I have one of my own.'

Rhiann brought her gaze back to Fola's face, and saw the entreaty there.

'Please come with me, Rhiann. We have missed you so. Just come for one night, that is all. If you wish to leave then, no one will stop you.'

'But there is too much pain there for me,' Rhiann whispered.

'Then how will it be healed? You know the lore. Running away does not heal such pain; facing it does. With those you love. And who love you.'

Rhiann felt herself wavering. So many nights she had dreamed of singing in the Stones, and sharing barley cakes around a dawn fire. Each time she had woken with tears on her face.

Little seal, came Fola in her mind. *Exile yourself no more. We want you back. You want to come. Who is punishing whom?*

Rhiann hesitated. Could she really go back to the bleakness of her heart without them, now she was so close? Surely the melting, which began with Eremon, made that choice unbearable. She reached out and clasped Fola's hand, and with the warm fingers in her own there was no turning back, though a great fear leaped into her heart. 'I will come.'

'Then you are not so far gone as I feared,' Fola returned, with a grin.

Eremon, however, was not happy about Rhiann leaving alone in the middle of the night.

'As you can see, there are only two horses,' Rhiann said to him, fastening the straps of her pack to one of the saddles. After hugging Rhiann hard enough to squeeze the breath from her lungs, Caitlin had retreated inside with Conaire. She, at least, did not question Rhiann's actions.

'But why not wait until morning?' Eremon held her bridle, his face in darkness.

'The weather is clear, and it is not far.' Rhiann looked up at him. 'I know I have not explained it well, Eremon, but this is . . . a hard thing I do. They are calling me, and I must go. I must go now, before my fear stops me again.'

In the moon-shadow of the walls, Eremon leaned in and pressed his lips against hers for a moment, softly. 'We will be at the broch soon. Come to me when you can. I need you.'

'I will.' She was surprised at the kiss. 'I will come, soon. But first I have things I must do.'

He helped her on to the horse, and stood back, as she followed Fola up the path that led into the dark of the hills behind. At the last, she looked back, but he was swallowed by the shadows of the houses, and she could only press her finger to her lips in the chill night air.

CHAPTER 73

Crossing the island in the dark was easy for Rhiann; she knew every one of the hundred tiny lochs that sprinkled the peat-cloaked plain, and every ridge and rock outcrop, from the rolling hills of the north to the mountains rearing in the south. Fola could not contain her questions about Rhiann's life and marriage and unexpected arrival, but though Rhiann answered, her heart was full of scents and sights that were at once so familiar, yet now so foreign.

By the time they smelled the sea again, the moon was swollen, close to the horizon. *A full moon on Beltaine*, Rhiann thought, and suddenly shivered, before shaking it away. *We will attend the rite, we will talk with the leaders, then we will be gone . . .*

But she could not lay to rest the foreboding that there was more waiting for them than this.

She saw the path of silver glittering far out in the Loch of the Seals first, and then a glimpse of torch and firelight among the priestess lodges, crouched in the lee of a headland. Fola halted her horse.

'The Stones,' whispered Rhiann, coming alongside, trepidation deepening to fear. 'I can still feel the Stones . . .'

Fola twisted in her saddle. 'Did you think you would not? Once you have been trained to hear, to feel, it never goes away. They welcome you, as we do.'

And Rhiann remembered again the lore as she had been taught it, so many years ago.

This island is not about what you can see. It is about what you can feel. Rivers of power run beneath the land, and where they meet, the gateways stand: the sentinels.

A track skirted the lodges, rising to the headland and the black fingers that reared up from its crown. 'Do you want to go and see them?' Fola asked. 'I don't mind waiting for a moment.'

Rhiann nodded and nudged the horse up the short, sandy path. And then, there they were, reaching up like a circle of dancers, in supplication to a starred sky. Built by the Old Ones so long ago that their birth was lost to memory, they were in the form of a great cross, with spreading arms, and a circle at the centre.

The night had grown colder now, close to dawn, and in the stillness the only sound was Rhiann's breath, rasping in and out in a cloud of mist.

Here, at these Stones, the lives of the Sisters were about tending, and propitiating with rite and offering. They kept the balance of the Source as well as they could. But the Mother's creatures still died for no reason. She glanced north, to where the broch lay out of sight over the hills. Her loved ones still died.

Why?

There was no answer from the Stones. She knew what they would say, though, for many times she had asked the same question of the elder Sisters, a question that grew more and more urgent after the raid. And the answer was always the same, until she wanted to hear it no more.

There is a pattern in the cloth of Thisworld that we cannot glimpse. Each act is a thread in that pattern, even when it brings grief and pain. The Mother weaves for all her children, but we only see the nearest threads. One day, though, we will see it entire, and then we will weep tears of joy, not pain.

She turned the horse to nose its way back down the path to the main track, her heart leaden within her. She knew this lore well, but she had lost the faith. Would the Sisters see that she had lost it? In this most holy place, her lack of trust, her sundering from the Goddess, would feel like a blight to those who had trained here all their lives, untouched by the outside world.

Then she straightened her shoulders. This was who she was – all of it; broken and blighted and damaged. Perhaps she was not even fit to cross the doorway any more. But it was time to try.

She and Fola rode down into the sheltered dell where wizened rowans and hawthorn murmured together, and the little cluster of stone houses huddled like old women before a winter's fire.

Fola took the horses away, and Rhiann stood alone with her thoughts for a moment in the yard before Nerida's lodge. Her heart was hammering now, and she breathed deeply to quiet it, gathering her warmth there in the way she had been taught. *The way I was taught here.*

Then Fola was back, taking her hand, drawing her inside.

The air in the room was close, as if the fire had been burning high all night. The flames lit the unadorned walls, the sparse benches, the narrow bed with its faded wool blanket. Nothing would suggest that a great priestess lived here, yet everything was just as Rhiann had last seen it – when she hurled those bitter words at one she had loved with all her heart.

And there she was, Nerida, alone in her rush chair before the fire. She had aged in only three years. She sat lower in her chair, though straight, and her grey braids had faded to snow-white. Yet her blue eyes were still clear and unfilmed, and beneath their pure gaze, words failed Rhiann.

The awkwardness only lasted a moment. For in that gaze there was no shade of recrimination. None at all. And then Eldest Sister reached out her hand.

Before she knew she had done it, Rhiann threw herself at Nerida's feet, her face pressed into the soft, wrinkled palm. Nerida neither moved nor spoke, as the thaw took hold of Rhiann's heart, the ice crumbling, and three years of being alone were released in a flood of salt-tears: three years of an aloneness so complete that she ached with it from the moment she arose to the moment she fell asleep.

In the midst of it all she realized she had buried her face in Eldest Sister's lap, her knees cold on the stone floor, and the old hand was stroking her hair. Where it moved, she was bathed in warmth, like the glow of sun on her head, and the warmth seemed to draw the poison from her heart.

It was not so hard, after all, Rhiann heard then in her mind. *You are very stubborn, but that is not so ill. You will need it, that strength.*

Rhiann looked up, wiping her face. *Could you always speak to me like this? Even then?*

It was as if Nerida held the deepness of the night sky in her eyes: sapphire pools lit with the sparks of ancient wisdom. Yet Rhiann felt a very human smile in her heart. *You are not the only one who has grown these last years.*

And Nerida spoke, and her voice was wind across the sea-grass.

'So you come at last then, child, to lay down your burden in the same place you took it up.'

CHAPTER 74

Rhiann opened her eyes to a lattice of low, worn roof beams and a rough plaster wall: a sight she thought for ever lost to her. She pushed herself up on her elbows, and slowly blinked. Her eyelids were swollen, and she was bone-tired, and yet energy sang through her heart.

Generations of girls had stared at that ceiling, wondering, if they were new-arrived, what would befall them. And later, reliving the wonder of their first rites: fertile Beltaine, the heady joy of Lughnasa, the scent of bonfires at Samhain.

Her own memories welled up then, and she sank back on the pillow. The horse races with Fola over the plain; dancing on the beach at dawn.

And then, in slipped an image of Rhiann and Elavra, her foster-mother, shelling beans on the doorstep of the broch. For once the memory lingered, and she did not push it away. She let it flower ... the salt on the air, the faint bleats of sheep, and Marda and Talen's laughter as they played on the pale beach until late in the night.

The images started to rush headlong through her mind, one after the other, and just as the time of blood and pain grew closer, Fola's laughter rang out on the other side of the bed-screen.

'Wake up, sleepy! It is only two days until Beltaine and we have much to do; you've missed the sun's greeting already! Hurry!'

In the clear sun the cluster of white lodges, yellowed by the salt air, looked smaller to Rhiann's eyes. But the faces that crowded around her were the same: old friends asking questions and exclaiming at the change in her, while new girls peered at her curiously.

Rhiann looked around. 'Where is Brica?' she asked Fola. 'I expected to see her.'

'Brica? Ah, yes. She went back to her own people, Sister, on the north coast. She did not wish to serve us here any more.' Fola shrugged. 'You will see her at Beltaine – the whole island will be there!'

Nerida was seated on a bench against her lodge, soaking the early sun into her old bones. Next to her was Setana, the second eldest and the sisterhood's clearest channel for the Mother. The people of the broch thought Setana touched in the head, for she said odd things, and laughed when others were silent. But these were part of her gift: to be so open she must stand with one foot in the Otherworld and one foot in this. It was reflected in her features: wild, fey eyes shone from a child-like face, broad-cheeked and rosy with sun.

Both Sisters had spent their whole lives serving the Goddess on this very island. Many festivals had wheeled under their aegis, many babes had been born into their steady hands, many a soul had found comfort in their ministrations during their last hours in Thisworld. They were part of the very soil, as strongly rooted here as the Stones themselves. And as the others dispersed to their duties, the activity swirled around Nerida and Setana as if they were twin rocks in the middle of a rushing torrent.

Rhiann's return, though momentous to her, had to be put aside this day, for with Beltaine so near there was much to do. But this is how she would have it anyway: she was still exploring this new openness, and after her unburdening wanted only to immerse herself in the rhythms of her old home.

Following Fola to the dairy, she paused to glance up at the Stones crowning the headland above, their surface, made of a strange rock, glittering in the sun. Already the Otherworld energies were being gathered there by the earth singers, who, with their chants, drew the Source up from the river of power beneath.

Behind the ordinary scenes of the lodges, of goats being milked and grain being ground, a pressure was growing in the air. Rhiann could sense it swirling around her, and in the churning of the milk and pressing of cheese, she felt it increasing, until it beat on her temples like blood throbbing on a hot day.

The older priestesses did not break from their duties, only exchanged knowing glances.

But the maidens looked sidewise at each other, and wondered who would be picked to lay with the Stag at the Beltaine fires.

Eremon had never seen one of the famous brochs of the north. As he and his men climbed the track to the massive stone tower, perched on a ridge above a shining sea-loch, he marvelled that such a dwelling had been built here, at the edge of Alba.

Yet of course, he was interested in this broch for more reasons than how it was built. He pulled up his borrowed horse as they reached the gate to the broch wall, and gazed down a narrow glen to the sea, where a glimpse of shingle shone through the encroaching tide.

This was where Rhiann's nightmare began. This was where she saw her family slaughtered.

This day, the sun sparkled on the water, bathing the hill that rose above the broch, patterned in heather and moss, and catching the thatched roofs of the village that spilled down the slope below it. But despite the fairness of the day, he was swept by a feeling of utter desolation. For in truth, it was here that he had lost Rhiann. If she had not been so torn by what happened, perhaps her hatred of warriors would not have stood between them at the beginning, and soured what could have turned into something else.

When he ducked in under the massive lintel, and climbed the stairs to the first floor hall, he was still blinded by the afterglow of the sun. But when his eyes cleared, he was faced with perhaps a score of men seated on hearth benches, already deep in their ale. They wore checked cloaks, and the pelts of different beasts, and their ornaments were shell and shale and copper.

As one they stopped speaking among themselves. Eremon watched the black eyes fall on his shining sword and the gold torcs that his men still wore, for they clasped the neck tightly, and no sea could wrench them free. Yes ... despite their faded, salt-stained clothes, they still had enough presence to make a man think. And Nectan's message would have presented them well. So he hoped.

Nectan stepped to his side. 'Lords,' he said, 'this is Eremon mac Ferdiad of Erin.'

Eremon bowed his head, and the kings of the western tribes nodded.

'You are welcome,' one of the men said, rising. He was only a few years older than Eremon, but stocky, with wind-blown cheeks and a drooping black moustache. A cape of seal-skin covered his shoulders. 'I am Brethan, the chief here, now that Kell and his kin are gone. Nectan says that you are the bonded man of Rhiann, foster-daughter of Kell and Elavra.'

Eremon nodded.

'You come from Calgacus the Sword,' another man remarked.

'Yes. I am war leader of the Epidii now. The Epidii and the Caledonii have become allies against the invaders – the Romans.' As he spoke, Eremon pulled the boar stone from his neck and held it up to the light. 'Here is the token of Calgacus himself.'

Brethan beckoned, and a young druid, hovering in the shadows, came forward, scrutinizing the symbols before nodding his assent. 'It is as he says.'

There was a general murmuring, but already Eremon could sense, from the slowness of their voices, that it would take a lot for these men to be galvanized into hot words and deeds.

'I think you have much to tell us,' Brethan said now. 'But

the kings arrived only this morn, and we must deal with our own business first. Later, we will hear your plea.'

Setana rapped her staff on Nerida's doorpost and entered without waiting for an answer. Nerida sat at her fireside, as she liked to do alone after the sun greeting, drinking her morning brew of honeysuckle for the aching bones and chills of age. In the fire, she saw many things.

'I must speak to our girl Rhiann,' Setana declared.

Nerida looked up, blinking. 'Why?'

Setana smiled and clapped her hands. 'Because *She* wants her, Sister.'

Nerida shook her head, and rested the ash cup on the hearth-stone. 'She asks much of us, Sister, and much of Rhiann. She is fragile still.'

'Yes!' Setana whispered. 'Oh, yes! But a man has softened her heart.'

Nerida let out a breath she did not know she held. 'And yet the pain stands in her way; I can sense it.'

Setana smiled, as if they did not speak of such weighty matters. 'Foolish woman! Do you not trust the Mother yourself? The pain is the strength, if she surrenders.'

Nerida sighed, and glanced down at her age-gnarled hands, remembering the bitterness in Rhiann's eyes after the raid. 'Her will is strong, Sister. Once before I asked her to understand, and I all but lost her.'

Setana laughed, the sound echoing on the bare walls, and she brushed Nerida's face with her hand. 'You worry too much, old woman.'

'Old! We are nearly of an age, you and I!'

Setana threw her wrap around her shoulders, as she strode from the room. 'You still worry too much. Trust!'

In the hall, Eremon charted another course through the blindness of men.

'Why should we care for the Roman invaders?' a chieftain

rumbled, eyeing a basket of new-baked bread being carried in. 'We are safe, on our islands.'

'No one in the islands will be safe if Agricola takes Alba and Erin. He has a fleet; he can be on your doorstep within days.'

'Then we will draw into the mountains,' another king said.

Eremon leaned back on his bench, holding their dark eyes. 'In western Britannia, Agricola went up into the mountains, which are nearly as harsh as yours. And he hunted down every last man, woman and child of the Ordovices. In the *long dark*. Your mountains will not keep you safe. Nor will your seas. Do you wish to know why?'

'Why?' Brethan asked, frowning, his hands clenched on his knees.

'Because at the council, one man spoke out against myself and Calgacus at every opportunity. Is he sympathetic to Roman rule? Does he want to rule over you himself? For he then tried to kill me and the Ban Cré by sinking our boat. This man is known to you all; he has power in the northern seas.'

'What man?'

'Maelchon of the Orcades.'

'We wish to speak with you, child.'

Rhiann was startled, so absorbed had she been in the play of an otter against the bronze dusk on the loch, its tracks a ripple across the tide-race.

Nerida was leaning on an ash staff, Setana grasping her arm; they had climbed the headland to the north of the Stones just to find her. The reflections from the loch caught at the many wrinkles seaming their cheeks.

'You are well, our daughter?' It was Nerida who spoke.

Rhiann hesitated, and bowed her head. 'I thought I would never come back, that I never could, because you would not have me. Now I feel like . . . a child again.'

'But you are not a child any more.'

Rhiann's head jerked up.

'Daughter, daughter, do not look like that!' Nerida smiled,

yet sadness crept at the edge of her mouth. 'You were not cast out, nor could you ever be. But you have responsibilities now, as a child does not. Though I would give you more time for these feelings of . . . childishness . . . the Goddess cannot give us this time. I vowed to follow the Mother, and that is what I must do. As must you.'

Why can I not sink into the joy, after so much pain? Rhiann thought, with a stab of anger.

As if she heard her, Nerida looked deeply into Rhiann's eyes. 'Listen to me, and trust me, even if you never trust me again. We've come to ask you to take up your duty. A child cannot be a vessel for the Goddess. Only a woman can do that.'

Rhiann's shock chilled into dread. *A vessel for the Goddess.*

'We understand your pain, as we understand the joy you felt last night. But life is neither all pain nor all joy, Rhiann. It is both.'

Rhiann thrust out her chin. 'You wish me to go back to the pain, then, after all I have been through?'

'Some of this pain you chose yourself,' Setana broke in, her eyes seeking to be gentle. 'Do not forget that, child. You chose to leave, and you chose to stay away.'

'But I have chosen differently now!' Rhiann cried, her fear rising. 'I want to stay here with you! Let me do that, please!'

Setana closed a hand over Rhiann's own. The grip was strong, yet not to hurt. 'No,' she said quietly. 'The world has need of you. I have felt it. We all serve the Mother in different ways. Your home is not on these shores.'

The women glanced at each other then, and Rhiann knew that worse was to come.

Setana released her hand, and Nerida straightened her shoulders. 'The Goddess has chosen you to perform the Beltaine rite.'

'*What?*'

'The Mother has chosen you to do this for the people.'

Rhiann glanced back and forth between them wildly. 'No!'

'I promise you – I *promise* you – Rhiann, that in the joining with the land, with the God and Goddess in the rite, there will be joy again.' Nerida smiled reassurance, yet the sadness had now reached her eyes.

Rhiann shielded her heart with her arms, as if warding away the sharp grief. Just as she found some peace, so it was taken away. Even here, she could not find refuge; even here among those who were supposed to love her. Despair rose cold in her throat.

And that was when she felt the touch of Setana in her mind. *No, daughter, it is not like that*! She stepped forward and took hold of Rhiann's elbows, raising her bowed face with one finger. Her grey eyes no longer shone with feyness, but glittered with tears.

Nerida moved up to stand next to her. 'The world is changing, child, and the sisterhood must change with it. In the times to come people will need a different kind of priestess; a priestess that does not live in seclusion, as Linnet does, as we do. For the message we heard is this: show women that the Mother lives in them by working side by side, sharing their joys, their pains, their birth pangs. Teach them that they *are* the Goddess, by living that ourselves.'

Setana nodded. 'To do this you need to live, Rhiann. Hurt, fear, love fully. Show the people that the Goddess is not something apart, but the warp to their weft threads, so closely bound up with their souls they cannot be separated.'

Setana stopped, breathing heavily, and Nerida put a gentle hand on Rhiann's shoulder. 'You must start this now by trusting us, and surrendering to love, for this will root you in the land. The Beltaine rite will be a doorway for you. You must leap, with only faith as your wings, but we are here to tell you that you will land in safety.'

Rhiann trembled, gripped by their words, for they fell into her heart as truth, as rain on to parched soil.

But still she fought, for she had steeled herself well against these very things for so many years now. She didn't want to become part of the weave of men and women and children; she didn't want to risk loss. She could not be a true priestess, and she certainly was not a true wife. How could she be a mother, an aunt, a grandmother?

She stood now at the lip of a chasm, and knew that Nerida and Setana asked her not to step into life, but into a void. Step, she might then, out of duty – for she knew duty well. But trust again? That she could never do.

Later, when Nerida and Setana left her, when darkness had devoured the loch and the hills and night crept into her bones, she remained on the headland, unable to return to the fires. The warmth of companionship below beckoned, but there would be no true belonging now, for no one knew what Nerida's order meant to her.

A man, a vessel for the God, would join with her, as a vessel for the Goddess. He would come in his guise of Stag, the Great Consort, and in the merging of the two halves of self, male and female, the perfect balance would be struck, and the Source would flower. The energy would bloom, expanding outwards to the people, the creatures, and the earth, charging all with life.

It was the most wonderful act that she could perform; the greatest of honours. Yet despite her training, a deep part of her cried, *Eremon*!

She had hardly thought of him, so taken was she with the sights and sounds of her return. But she thought of him now, watching her join with another man in the circle, his hair falling about his face like dark fire, his green eyes blazing with hurt. He would not understand, she was sure.

And how could she herself bear it?

No one bar Linnet knew what truly happened to her in the raid. No one knew how her powers had failed her so many times since. What if the Goddess did not come to her in the rite? Then she would be conscious . . . she would feel every thrust, every touch of the man's fingers.

And the Sisters would know . . . they would all know at last that she was a priestess no longer.

CHAPTER 75

'Urgh!' Conaire dunked his head into a barrel of cold water behind their lodge. 'My skull has broken in two!'

Eremon wiped down his own face with his hands, squinting into the morning sun that sliced between the village houses.

The feasting had gone on well into the night. By the time it ended, more than one chieftain had draped his arm drunkenly around Eremon, regaling him with tales of a sword he once owned just like Eremon's, or recounting long-ago trips to Erin in his youth. The Alban and Erin men boasted at the top of their voices about which peoples made the better ale, who had the strongest fighters, and later – after Caitlin had gone to bed – who possessed the most beautiful women.

Eremon thought he could recognize quite a few of the Caereni women on first sight, just from the lewd descriptions that had been shouted in his ear. 'The pain may well be worth it, brother. I think I managed to turn their hearts at last.'

Conaire flung his hair back, splattering water over Eremon. 'Well, it took long enough! When they ignored all your dire warnings of marching Romans, I thought we had lost them.'

'So did I.' Eremon retreated into the shadow of the lodge wall, the sun too much for his aching eyes. 'And the thing that changed their minds was Maelchon.'

Conaire grinned. 'Of course, you don't actually *know* that Maelchon is in league with the Romans.'

Eremon's answering smile was grim. 'No, but he tried to kill us, and I don't care how I stop him. He is a threat to Alba's peace, I know that, and if these kings join me out of fear of Maelchon, then I accomplish both aims at once. He sails west here often, Nectan said. He'll find a different reception next time, I hope.'

They went back inside the lodge, where Caitlin was still rolled up in the furs, deep asleep. Conaire gazed at her for a moment, a smile curving his mouth, before he scooped some barley porridge from the cauldron into a bowl. 'I still find it curious that they were more angry about the attack on Rhiann than anything else.'

Eremon sat down on the bench to pull on his boots. 'It is as Rhiann said: they revere the Goddess here above all gods. And I don't care how I galvanize them, so long as I do. With some well-placed questions I was able to gauge their numbers, and these people, though scattered, are great. We *must* make them join us.'

Conaire took a spoonful of porridge. 'What did Nectan say to you when you left?'

Eremon shrugged. 'That they greatly fear a joining of Maelchon and the Romans, and so are open to my plea – but they do not trust a man of Erin to lead.'

'No wonder Fergus looked fit to burst! So where does that leave us?'

'I don't know yet.' Eremon sighed. 'Nectan disappeared then, and later I saw him with Brethan's druid.'

He glanced out into the bright sun. Waiting on Nectan's word was not the only thing on his mind.

I have heard nothing from Rhiann. Perhaps now that she is here, she will never wish to leave.

A day later, and Beltaine was here at last. In defiance of Rhiann's cold fear, a bright sun sailed clear of the early clouds, warming the rocks of the peat hills as she rode across them in the dawn, touching the little lochs with copper, brushing each water reed with gold.

Now she stood on the beach below Kell's broch, listening to Eremon's footsteps crunching over the shingle behind her, and with each step, so the beauty of the day seemed to recede.

'I would recognize you from afar, even without your message,' he said over her shoulder. 'But why did you ride straight here, and not come to me at the broch?'

She turned to him, unclasping her fingers. 'I ... I just needed to see it again. The place where it all happened.'

She glanced down the narrow strip of sand, and then back up the glen to the village, where gulls wheeled, crying, and comforting smoke – the cooking kind – curled lazily into the clear air. It was all so serene, and yet she could not look at it without seeing another kind of smoke behind her eyes, the raging, black cloud that screamed out danger and death.

Where the waves hissed over tumbling shells, red boats landed, and Kell's blood ran in the clear water. And behind her, where the slope steepened, a man's hand closed on her ankle ...

Eremon moved to her side. 'I am sorry, Rhiann. I wish I could take the memories away from you.'

She shivered. 'I know you do.'

When he looked away, she glanced at him sidewise. He seemed to be avoiding her eyes, and she detected something that disturbed him; something other than concern for her. 'Has your reception by the kings not gone well?'

He poked at a half-buried shell with one foot. 'I think I may be getting somewhere, at last, though they won't give me my answer until the day after Beltaine.'

'I am pleased. Nectan believes in you, and though he commands few men, they are hardy fighters, and the best archers on the coast. And he is held in high regard for his insight. Winning him was well done.'

'And you? Are you enjoying your reunion?'

'Yes.' The stilted words sounded so brittle between them.

Because ... all she wanted to do was cry, *Eremon, I'm so sorry. I do not wish to do this! It is not me laying with a man. Not me!* But how could she tell him about the rite, which would

566

begin at dusk? He would never understand. He would hate her, because it would hurt him . . .

Out of the corner of her eye, she saw the breeze draw a dark tendril of hair over his cheek. The tiny movement ached in her heart, for she wanted to reach out and tuck it back . . .

She bit her lip. She could just cope with doing this, for herself. She knew about these rites, what they meant – and did not mean. But he would not know. What if she told him right now?

'Eremon,' she said. But he would try to stop her, and the Sisters would be angry, and she would have let everyone down.

He swung to face her, a question in his eyes.

'I . . . ah . . . must be getting back soon,' she finished, blinking tears away. 'I have to fast for the Beltaine rite.'

'Are you participating in this rite, then?' The ridges of his cheekbones flushed.

'Yes, with the other Sisters.'

'Rhiann.' He took her hand, but kept his eyes on their entwined fingers. 'You know what you mean to me, don't you?'

'Oh, Eremon, don't, please!' Guilt washed over her, and she pulled her hand free.

No, he would not understand; he would think the rite barbaric – he might even walk away and not come back.

Eremon's arms dropped, and a mask fell over his eyes. 'I will see you tonight then, Rhiann.'

His feet crunched away, and she rubbed her stinging eyes. Here, on this beach, all the tears began. Perhaps here they would end, too. For if she lost what she had with Eremon, fragile though it was, she would never cry again.

There would be nothing left within her to weep.

CHAPTER 76

The hand slid up Samana's arm, and she shrugged it away and turned back to the camp bed. 'You're a fool!'
'How dare you talk to me like that!'

She whirled on her heel, and fixed the man with a glare. Among the shadows of the Roman tent, the lamp picked out his golden hair and the sheen on his eyes. But they held no charms for her now . . . if they ever did. 'I *dare* because I gave you many luxuries in exchange for information. And look what you do!'

Drust strode to the bed. 'I had no choice! How could I know the Epidii Queen and that Erin cur would have a Roman traitor with them? I *had* to run.'

At the mention of both Eremon and Rhiann, Samana's rage nearly choked her. 'I see more than you think, prince; that your loins and your pride rule your head. If you'd kept your trousers on and your sword skills honed you may have been able to help us. As it is, you're useless to me!'

His fingers closed on her wrist, and his eyes burned. 'You whore.'

He was angry!

'You still don't understand, do you?' she spat. 'You're in my control! I *am* Agricola's whore, and you happen to be in his camp!' She took a deep breath, calming herself. 'But not for long.'

Drust released her, and now fear leaped into his fine face. 'What do you mean?'

She rubbed her wrist. 'What use are you to us now? You're an exile, so no good as a hostage. And you can give us no information. When you ran from the Erin prince, you sealed your own fate.'

'Is Agricola . . . going to send me away?' Drust clenched his fists.

She sat on the bed and took up her wine cup. 'Why would he do that, prince?' She smiled up at him.

The fear turned to terror, and Drust sank to his knees before her. 'Lady!' He pressed her hand to his lips. 'I've pleased you before and I'll do it again. Keep me by you, and I'll do anything you say!' His desperate eyes did not raise even a hint of warmth in her.

She turned her face away. 'I can do nothing for you.'

Agricola glanced up at the sky, pleased to see that it would be a fine day. The line of forts and watchtowers along the Gask ridge were coming along well, but a bout of good weather would hasten their completion.

His horse shifted impatiently beneath him, and he patted its neck. He, too, was getting hot under his heavy parade armour. 'I thought I gave the order to bring him out!' he barked to the tribune standing at his ankle.

'So you did, sir. I'll just . . .'

But then there was a stirring of the soldiers around the open gate, and the massed standards of the cohorts waved and dipped against the ramparts. A murmuring began that soon gathered force, spreading among the men as they parted to let the man through. From Agricola's vantage point, he could see what the soldiers nearest to him were craning to glimpse, and he smiled.

The centurions had done a good job: the Caledonii cur was weighed down with so many spoils of war that he could hardly walk. A garish, checked tunic was topped by a cloak with an ornate fringe that dragged on the ground, taken from the Votadini king, Agricola vaguely remembered. This was pinned with a cartload of brooches, and his arms, tied before him, were encased by rings and gold torcs to the shoulder, the better to keep his neck bare. His hair had been limed into those barbaric peaks, the savage tattoos drawn over in ink.

As the captive stumbled through their midst, prodded along by two soldiers with javelins, the murmuring of the other men grew louder, until it became a chant that was taken up by the steady beat of swords on shields, accompanied by the harsh blast of trumpets.

'*Galli! Galli!*'

Agricola's smile broadened. Yes, to the legion, this man was not only Alba, but all the barbarian peoples that dared to stand against Rome, with their pride and arrogance, greed and folly. And he sensed that his men's frustration and enmity, which had, as yet, found little outlet, was being released now.

So the Caledonii traitor had been useful for something, at the last.

Agricola glanced at Samana, seated under her parasol to the side of the field. She feigned boredom, but he saw the glint of her black eyes, fixed on the swordsman waiting before the block.

Now the captive fell on his knees before the executioner, the gold and bronze on him flashing in the sun, and the men's chanting grew louder, as the trumpets were joined in their cacophony by the horns, curving through the clear air.

Agricola raised his hand, and watched the sword rise. The headsman eyed his commander sidelong, arms poised. Agricola drew the moment out, waiting until the chanting grew into one great shout, the beating of swords like peals of thunder, the horns like the shrieks of beasts.

Yes, this man is Alba. And like him, it too will fall.

He brought his hand down, and the sword descended with it.

Rhiann stood at the lodge door and gazed at the rising moon. Faintly, sounds carried on the still evening: girlish giggles, the clatter of pans from the kitchen sheds, the faint vibration of the Sisters chanting.

How many times had she stood here on an evening such as this, filled with excitement for the coming rites?

Then, such festivals meant something different. She had stifled her own giggles, as the novices wove flowers into each other's braids, while a priestess lectured them sternly on the proper decorum. Then would come the solemn beat of the drums, and her heart stirring at the sight of her Sisters snaking to the Stones in long lines, blue-hooded, their feet in perfect time.

She remembered feeling so close to the Goddess that she could surely reach out a hand, up to the heavens, and touch Her face. When divine words of love seemed to be part of the night air, breathed by the wind. Above all, she remembered being part of something greater than herself.

And here she stood tonight, and she had never felt so alone.

Everything in her cried to run away, far away, so that she would never have to see that look of repudiation on Eremon's face, or feel the disappointment of those she loved, when they saw her fail.

'Dearest.' Fola's voice startled her. 'It is time for the *saor*.'

Her friend stood behind her, an earthen cup in her hands, and by her side were the four maidens who had attended Rhiann all afternoon, dressed in white, may blossom pale in their hair.

All that time, Rhiann kept her thoughts desperately guarded, as they bathed her and rubbed her with sweet oils. She was silent as they sang, painting her palms and feet with woad, her nails with berry juice, combing her hair with silver. Nor did she join their chants to the Goddess, the pleas to bless Her Maiden, as they pulled the robe of soft, bleached linen over her shoulders and bound it with a girdle of sea-grass.

Perhaps they just thought her silence a sign of nerves, but now Fola squeezed her hand. 'Trust,' she said, smiling. 'Trust Nerida, and Setana. Trust the Mother.'

Rhiann looked deep into Fola's dark eyes, and saw a gleam of pity there. Perhaps Fola did know, after all.

Beltaine was a time of life, when the earth was growing ready to fruit and flower, to give of its power, so that the creatures of Thisworld could live.

So why, then, did Rhiann feel as if she walked the death path this night?

Before her, Nerida stepped, so graceful and upright, even in age, a flowering branch of hawthorn held before her. A garland of honeysuckle crowned Rhiann's head, and as the sun-warmth was released from its blooms, the perfume became heady, dizzying her as it merged with the *saor*.

To each side, and ranged behind, came her Sisters. Now, Rhiann could clearly see the ties of light that bound them, just as she did last Beltaine, at Dunadd. But did the golden light touch *her*, weave itself around her? She could not tell. She did not think so. She stumbled, her feet tangling with fear and the herbs, and arms reached out to steady her, with no break in the singing. She glanced to one side, and saw Fola's eyes within her blue hood.

As the host wound up the path, the singing grew and swelled, as the Sisters sang of the Goddess as Maiden, young and fresh and fruitful. Rhiann was not a maiden. But Nerida had picked her ... there was something they wanted from her, something they believed could call the Source into full being tonight. But what? She felt so dry, so withered with loss. What was left in her to bloom?

It was then that she saw the Stones rearing black against a bonfire, the dark figures leaping before it, and her composure deserted her in one great flood that loosened her knees to water.

For all the dancers at the fire were men, tall against the flames, broad-chested, their hair flowing down over their shoulders. The women of the broch and the chief's wives, in contrast, had formed a ring of linked hands around the stone circle. The men wielded the fire of life; the women guarded the gateway.

But which man would it be? Who was the Chosen One?

As Nerida came closer to the bonfire she stopped, and as one, the great flowing river of priestesses halted too, the singing dying away. Nerida stepped forward, the blossoming thorn held high. 'The Goddess-daughters are here, with our gift: a Maiden to birth Her light for the land. Who is worthy of this gift?'

At her words, a druid in a white robe emerged from the crowd of men. He held a torch, and its sparks streamed away to the stars. 'The God-sons are here, with a consort for the Maiden: a Stag to call forth Her light for the land. We name him worthy of this gift.'

Nerida turned and held out a hand to Rhiann, and Rhiann took it. *Courage, child*, the old priestess said in her mind. *We love you. And so does She.*

As Nerida led her up the avenue of stones to the inner circle, Rhiann was floating so far from her body that she hardly noticed another Sister fall into step with them: Setana. All the people had now fallen silent, and there was only the crackling and spitting of the great fire, and their soft footsteps on the turf. The eyes of the circle of women flashed in the firelight . . . but beyond them the Stones themselves seemed to sway before Rhiann's shifting gaze, as if they had once been truly supplicants, bending and twirling in an endless dance . . . and then she saw other figures between them, where no human walked.

Flashes of light, like darting swallows made of fire . . . gliding wraiths with wings of smoke . . . gnarled faces that seemed to rise from the glittering surface of the Stones, singing of times long past, when the people knew only deer and fish and rock and wood, when the Old Woman in the Earth ruled them all, and no man was struck down by sword or spear . . .

All these things Rhiann sensed with the *saor*, until the count of the years became dizzying, and she must wrench herself away to be here, in her time, stepping at last into the sacred space at the heart of the Stones.

And as she did, the throbbing of the Source hit her like a wave; a deep booming, a thrumming of power. Like the breathy hum of a bone pipe, it was, yet the vibration was coming not from one small hole, but from the very ether around her. And she walked through it as if it were honey, thick and yielding, flowing into the space behind each step.

The vortex of power swirled around the centre of the circle, where the greatest stone stood, alone, rearing high above her head. Here, Nerida and Setana drew Rhiann's robe from her shoulders, and on a cloak of soft skins, in the shadow of the great stone, they laid her down.

Then, their hands on her heart and belly, they began to sing, and their voices flowed at the same pitch of the throbbing, so that Rhiann felt the two women become joined with the swirling, the humming. And channelled by their hands, the Source entered her.

The rush flooded through her body as the spring tide floods the sands. She was swelling, floating, sinking into the earth as she rose towards the heavens.

There was a drumbeat from far off, a shout from male throats: 'He is come! He is come!'

She sensed Nerida and Setana rise to their feet. The night was cool, but her naked skin now glowed with heat where their hands had been. They had called, and the vessel had filled. It was then that they left her.

And there was time for one last caress from her heart. *Eremon. Forgive me.*

Blinded by the firelight, peering through the smoke, Eremon could not see where Rhiann was. All the blue-hooded priestesses looked the same, and walked the same. From the other side of the fire, he glimpsed a blur of a woman in white, being led away, but he did not know, or care, who she was.

Rhiann! his heart cried out to her. Where was she?

He knew how important this ceremony was. He understood that all of them must play their parts, that the Otherworld must be held in balance, so that life in Thisworld did not descend into chaos.

But despite the power that was already surging through them all, a power that could be wielded to keep them safe . . . he just wanted Rhiann. He wanted to take her in his arms, and leave this place, and be alone, somewhere warm and safe, somewhere that he could tell her all that lay in his heart, whether she would hear it or not. Somewhere that all could be made right between them.

Here he stood, and the fates of thousands of people, of this land Alba, of his own land, Erin, swirled in the charged air, their futures in the balance. But through the mind-haze, the effects of the drink the men had shared, all he could think about was her, and his heart clenched that they should be so parted.

Her eyes . . . her hair . . . her lips.

Tiny things, focused things, far from the wider world of war, of conquest.

Her breath . . . her scent . . . her smile.

He knew what the Beltaine rites meant. He knew that the forces would be let loose tonight, and in the frenzy, many a man and woman would be drawn to lay together. The thought made him sick. Would some coarse northerner take her here, on the earth? Would he see her from afar, joined with another? Could he reach her before that happened? *No!* The pain of it lanced him.

And then the first drumbeat struck.

Another rang out, and another, and the primal chord reached through his scattered thoughts, and plucked a string deep in his loins that he did not even know he possessed. A string that vibrated with the air, with the power of old urges, deep desires that were not spoken. Nectan told him the drink would call it: a summons that could not be denied.

'He is come! He is come!' he heard the men around him cry, full-throated.

And Eremon stepped forward, slowly, and with the movement, the antlers bound to his head swung from side to side.

CHAPTER 77

When Rhiann sensed the male steps breach the circle, she closed her eyes tightly. If she did not look, then it would not matter who the man was. She could leave her body, lose herself in the stars, and not even know it was happening.

But all of a sudden, the women burst into song. The voices rang out from all around her, as the drumming from the male fire increased in tempo. The song was not the sweet, soaring melody of the priestesses giving homage to the Goddess.

This was a song from the Old Ones, the Old Time, when, so it was said, people ran in the forest with the fleet deer, living by hunting alone. Then, the deer must be called by the Mother of the Tribe, to sacrifice themselves so that people may live. And the Stag must be called, to take the Mother, to make her fruitful.

The chanting was a summons, low and sibilant, throbbing in time with the primitive, galloping drum. It panted, rising and falling in the rhythm of a heartbeat, in the surging of birth, in the thrusting of desire. Adrift with the *saor*, Rhiann's body could not help but respond, for the music reached down into the forgotten part of her that still, somewhere, ran in the forest.

The footsteps grew closer now, softer, padding. A fringe of deerskin brushed her fingers, and she smelled the earthiness of the hide cloak as the man leaned closer, and sensed the heat of naked skin close to her own.

The leap of faith.
Setana told me to jump.

To surrender the vessel to Her, with all my heart.
I will do it.
I can do it.
Surrender! Let go, Rhiann . . .

But she could not. For suddenly, the beat within was drenched in a flood of cold terror. It froze her, pinning her down, and she knew that she would fail again, the fire within no more than ashes . . .

She heard the rustle of the cloak, discarded by her side, and then – oh, Goddess! – the warmth of a man's naked body covered her own, smooth and hard, the shoulder muscles slipping under her fingers. He was gentle . . . somehow unwilling, in the way he touched her thighs, and pressed them apart. His head was turned away into her shoulder, for she felt his hair brush her skin.

But unwilling or no, his heart thudded against her in time with the drumming, his breath quickening, and she knew that the power of the God-Stag had taken him, was driving him to the surrender she should be reaching herself.

Should, but could not.

At the moment she felt his hardness at the gateway to her body, seeking, pushing, her panicked soul scrabbled as far away as possible, taking refuge in her head, just as she had on the day of the raid. And that was when three years of bitter desolation rose to claim her, and she could not stop the sob from escaping her lips.

'Lady?'

The voice was low, breathy. Her eyes flew open against her will. Above her, she saw the sweep of antlers against the stone. And below them . . . green eyes, blinking in the firelight, as if they had been closed.

As the shock of it crashed down upon her, she saw the same shock mirrored in his face.

Eremon.

Eremon was the Stag.

It was then, as their eyes met, that something leaped

between them, bearing all the fear and pain away to a dark, forgotten place.

Without thinking, without fearing, Rhiann drew him down, hungering for those lips more than she had ever hungered for anything in her life. Every smile that had touched them, every gentle word of love, of friendship, of honour, of laughter . . . she tasted them all. It was beyond the sweetness of honey. And as their lips met, his body slipped inside her own, the gate opening for him as easily as a sigh.

Dizzy with the feel of him, the smell of him, the taste of him, the *saor* running in her veins, Rhiann sensed their bodies moving together in the beat that came from without them, around them, within them. It was everywhere, that song, and in the joy, at last, came the surrender.

Rhiann felt the energy fill her, the glow rising, expanding, swelling.

It was the Presence. The Goddess had come.

In the spaces between the stars, Rhiann and Eremon floated, their souls drifting close, watching the bodies in the circle below. To Rhiann's spirit-eye, the bodies seemed made of stars themselves, and within lay the divine energy of God and Goddess, as vast as the whole sky.

Then Rhiann looked at Eremon, and his soul appeared as a flame, ever burning but not consuming, and though he bore no man's face, she knew it was him. She would know the flame anywhere: she had always known it.

At that moment, her dream flared into life around them, a living image made of fire and stars.

She saw the valley, and the thronged souls of all the people. She saw herself with the cauldron, the glow of power from within now laid bare, so bright she could not look at it even with her spirit-eye. She heard the Eagles cry, and saw the man defy them, the Sword of Truth held on high.

Turn to me, she cried, as she always did. *I need you!*

And at long last, heeding her call, the call of lifetimes, the man turned, and his face was Eremon's, looking back at them from the vision. Now the dream-Rhiann held out the cauldron, and poured the grace of the Mother over him, and he shook his head and laughed as if it were a shower of water.

With that, they were both back in their bodies on the ground, the crescendo building; nearly at its height. Though they had reclaimed their forms of flesh and blood, Rhiann and Eremon knew only that their twin flames were burning and surging, and around them was the glimmer of the greater forms still gracing their bodies. They strained to join, deeper, faster, hungry for life.

And it happened: the flames fused and flared into one wave of perfect, white light, and in the midst of the flare, Rhiann felt Eremon's joy cascading over her. 'You!' she cried. 'It is you!'

Then the wave broke, and they were both borne up, as it fountained from the earth under their bodies, a twisting spire of light, the pure Source, arcing from the centre of the circle to the heavens, showering the people with life.

And shouts were wrung from Rhiann and Eremon as they had never shouted in life – purely, and with open heart.

As they lay, hearts thundering, the awareness of deerskin and damp grass and singing only gradually returned.

But all they felt were the stars, still close around them like a cloak, and they knew it was well done.

CHAPTER 78

An age later, Eremon and Rhiann came to themselves, still pressed together. Trembling, Rhiann opened her eyes, seeing the white cloud of stars strewn across the dark sky above Eremon's shoulder; feeling his heart pounding against her, his breath rasping in her ear.

But for all these human sounds, she could still see the glimmer of light around their bodies, and feel a last, soft caress as the Goddess left her.

She looked up into Eremon's eyes, and he into hers. 'You,' she could only say again, and in answer he touched his lips to hers, and in the wake of the urgency and hunger, there was tenderness.

The moment did not last. A crowd of people swept into the circle to raise them up and pull tunics and cloaks around their nakedness, while they stumbled, still dazed with the *saor*. Disoriented by the din, the beating of drums, the skirling of the pipes, the massed voices who shouted and cried, they were torn apart, and after their longed-for joining it was agony.

Rhiann cried out, but no one heard her.

Eremon grasped for Rhiann, to speak of what had befallen them, to touch her for a moment, but he was being pressed and jostled on all sides by the warriors.

Then he was thrust, roughly, out of the circle, and he heard a voice – was it Nectan's? – yelling in his ear. 'It is not over yet, Stag! You make the sacrifice now, to prove yourself the Consort above all others. Run, and catch Her! To the cliffs!'

He was pushed again, and he fell, but in a moment he was up. The antlers were unwieldy, scraping on the stones, and feminine fingers clutched at his arms and reached between his legs, hoping for a touch of the fertility that had burst from him this night. Some grasped his legs and feet, seeking to hold him back. Faces loomed up around him, laughing, wild with the night, swimming together as the *saor* blurred his senses.

He struggled to shake off the cloying hands, and then he heard Nectan's clear laugh. 'Away, away with the Stag!' The press around him lightened, and he glimpsed Conaire and Fergus and Colum, laughing as they pulled his captors from him. And he forgot that he was the God, and had a role to play. He only wanted Rhiann. He cried her name, but the sound was taken from him in the din of voices.

Then far, far away, it seemed, he saw her hair shining, and the moon under the clouds over the sea. He must reach her. The thought gave him strength, and he took another breath, and was free and away, with the night air cold in his lungs.

Behind him Nectan cried again, 'Run fast for us, our God!'

Over rocks and slippery turf he flew, sensing the bunching of muscles in foreleg and flank, the deep stirring of forest blood, the power in striking hooves. He raced down onto a spit of shingle where a stream ran, then up, up on to the headland, towards the moonpath on the sea. And there, at the very edge of the cliff he halted, panting, for Rhiann stood, a group of priestesses around her. He did not pause to wonder how she had got there so quickly, for the *saor* made time move and change, and he had been delayed longer than he realized.

Gasping, he sank down on one knee.

When Rhiann felt the Mother come into her again, it was a different sensation from the circle, as if her soul had merely moved aside, yet lingered still within the confines of her body. She could see the glow around her hands, and feel the greater presence within, but when she looked at Eremon, all she could see was his own soul-flame. There was no sign of the God. Was something wrong?

Uncertainty lurched in her, and shadows gathered, but then she heard the whisper in her heart. *Peace, little one*, it seemed to say. *But be ready, be ready for him!*

The moon was bright above Rhiann now, yet to Eremon her face was in shadow.

As he sought desperately for her eyes, wanting to speak with her, hands grabbed him from behind and pressed him face down on the ground.

He knew a moment of fear as his wrists were tied with a rope, but then he made himself relax. It was all part of the rite; Nectan had explained it. The hands turned him upright again, forcing him on to his knees.

When Rhiann spoke, it was not with her own voice. 'Are you the one worthy to become my Consort?' she asked. Her voice was deep, ancient, resounding with power.

'I am, lady,' he answered, struck with awe by the Goddess light around her.

Rhiann put out a hand and rested it on his head, between the antlers. 'And as my Consort, will you vow to uphold the Laws of the Mother? To revere the things She has made?'

'I will, lady.'

'Will you use your sword for justice, and not for greed?'

'I will.'

'Will you be the first to go cold, the first to hunger, the first to take up arms to defend my people?'

'I will.'

'And as the King Stag, will you sacrifice yourself for the land? Will you give your blood to keep it safe?'

He took a deep breath, closing his eyes. 'I will.'

Then he felt another touch on his head, grasping his hair, pulling his head back until his throat was exposed.

There was the cold touch of a stone knife on his skin.

Floating, detached, Rhiann watched the crowd of priestesses

part, and the little figure come forward to take hold of Eremon's hair. Through the last vestiges of the *saor*, she struggled to see who it was, for it suddenly seemed important.

And then her drifting soul registered puzzlement. It was Brica! Why was she here? Why had she not come to greet Rhiann?

The lurch of unease returned in full.

She saw Eremon's throat, long and white in the moonlight against Brica's rough dress, as she pressed his head back into her chest. She saw Brica raise the black blade of stone that was used for this symbolic sacrifice. And suddenly it all came flooding in, as the hand was raised, as the knife flashed down.

The knowledge that she loved Eremon. And that he would die.

It was time for the choice that Linnet had seen.

Save him! came the cry in her soul, in her mind, shocking her back into her body. The *saor* fell from her like a cloak flung to the ground, and without thinking she threw herself at Brica and the knife.

She crashed into the cold hand that clasped the blade, but was not quick enough, though the knife sunk itself into Eremon's shoulder instead of his vulnerable throat. He cried out in pain, falling sidewise, the blood already pouring over Rhiann's cloak.

Brica had been knocked over backwards with Rhiann on top of her, and Rhiann found herself staring into her black eyes, shining under the moon. There was a snarl on Brica's lips, and Rhiann took in the fanatic gleam in her eye, the burning hatred.

'You wanted this lady!' Brica whispered fiercely, and it was as if the icy blade had sunk into Rhiann's own heart. 'I do it for you!'

'No!' Rhiann cried in horror. 'Oh, no! I do not want this!'

Abruptly, the gleam faded, and now fear leaped into Brica's face, as the priestesses came to life around them, crying out in anger and confusion, taking hold of them both. But as Brica was drawn to her feet, Rhiann saw her glance darting wildly from side to side, and when the woman wrenched herself free of the arms that bound her, Rhiann heard herself crying again, 'No!'

It was too late. With a wild shriek, Brica pulled free and ran for the edge of the headland, before throwing herself off into blackness.

And Rhiann knew no more.

When she woke, it was to see Nerida's face hovering over her. Behind, the night sky was still scattered with stars. People murmured all around.

'Eremon! Where's Eremon?'

'He is well.' Nerida spoke soothingly. 'Though the wound is deep, it is not in a dangerous place. But he is weakened, and the druids have taken him to their lodge in the broch.'

'The lodge! No . . . no! He should be here, with me . . . I will nurse him!'

'Hush.' Nerida took Rhiann in her arms. 'He shed sacred blood. The druids will care for him well.'

Rhiann struggled to sit up, but her head was swamped with dizziness.

'There, now,' Nerida murmured. 'The shock was too great for you. The fasting, the *saor* . . . stay and rest for a moment. We are bringing a litter.'

Rhiann sank back down, and all of a sudden the events of the night flooded back to her, and she began to shiver uncontrollably. 'B-Brica?'

Nerida paused. 'She is dead, on the rocks.' She shook her head sadly. 'I do not understand. She asked to wield the knife, and I allowed it because I thought she had a bond to you.'

'She – she wanted to kill him.'

'Yet we have had no true sacrifice for generations. Setana spoke to her family – two days ago Brica began to say that as the danger of the Romans is great, the sacrifice should be real. They did not take her seriously. I fear she lost her mind.'

'No.' A wave of shudders wracked Rhiann. 'It was me. I fed the hate . . . when I was forced to wed Eremon. She drank it in, and in her twisted mind it grew. She must have discovered who the Stag would be. *My hate* nearly killed him!'

Nerida brushed her hair back. 'No, child. For was it not your love that saved him? The bond with him gave you strength, otherwise you would have been too late.'

'Oh, Goddess . . . I nearly lost him! How many people must die because of me!' Suddenly, she knew she would be sick. Nerida held her shoulders as she rolled to one side and retched, and then someone was there with a cool cloth soaked in seawater, and they wiped her face.

'Hush, child.' Nerida rocked her. 'You speak words of pain, but they are not real, not true. I am proud of you, not ashamed.'

But Rhiann was swiftly falling again, into a blackness that came upon her in the aftermath of the shivering, the retching.

At the last, she heard Nerida say, 'You chose well, daughter. We knew you would.'

CHAPTER 79

Rhiann slept the next day away, so heavily that she did not dream. She woke to soft singing by her bed.

It was Fola.

Rhiann opened one eye, blinking, and saw from the light against the wall that the day was far advanced. There was an aching, a soreness between her legs. She shut her eyes again, tightly, so that Fola would not know she was awake.

Dear Goddess. He had joined with her. A man had invaded her again.

No . . . no, not invaded. It did not feel like that at all. She remembered the way she drew Eremon into her, the hunger that consumed her limbs. How could this be the same body that once threatened to kill Eremon for touching her? How could that feeling of degradation exist alongside the yearning?

Perhaps it was because Eremon was the soulmate, the sword-wielder.

The dream had not died after all. It lived in them.

Before she could swallow it, a sob forced its way from her throat, and then another. In a heartbeat, Fola was there, gathering Rhiann in her arms. 'There, there,' she murmured. 'Cry it out, Sister. It will help.'

She did not know how long Fola held her, as the release of the tears claimed her body, or how long, afterwards, they sat silent, as they had often done in this room.

But the shadows had moved far up the wall, and the sun-warmth had faded to the cool of dusk, when there was a hesitant tap on the door-post and Caitlin was filling the room

587

with her smile.

White gull feathers were tucked into her braids, and beneath her torc, she had strung herself a necklace of purple shells. Her buckskin trousers and scarlet tunic were startling after the priestess robes that had surrounded Rhiann for days.

Now Caitlin flew to her and hugged her tightly. 'Cousin, we have been so worried! Every time I asked, they said you were sleeping!'

With a faint smile, Fola moved to the chair to take up her spinning again.

Rhiann lay back on the pillow. 'After such rites, the body needs that sleep. Do not worry; I look worse than I feel.'

Relief flooded Caitlin's face, and she took Rhiann's hand. 'I tried to get close to you last night, but when I saw the Sisters all around, I thought you would want me to follow Eremon.'

At the mere mention of his name, Rhiann's fingers tightened. 'How is he? No one will tell me anything except that he is well.'

Caitlin's brow wrinkled. 'And I can say little else. I followed his litter back to the broch, along with Conaire and the men. But the druids took him into their lodge, and Nectan and his men set up guard at the door, barring everyone from entering. The kings have come, but even they would not be admitted. Conaire was on the verge of breaking down the door to get to him, but without laying hands on Nectan, he could not.'

'Why will they not let anyone see him?'

Caitlin shrugged. 'Both Conaire and I slept outside the door – the druids have been stepping over us all morning! They say he is resting, that the wound is clean and not too deep. They ask us to respect their wishes. What can we do without offending every warrior in that broch?'

Rhiann slid her legs out of the bed and pulled her shift straight. 'Then I am going.'

Caitlin glanced at Fola, who quickly put down her spinning. 'Oh no, my girl! You are to stay abed. Nerida has ordered it.'

Rhiann was tugging her dress over her head. 'No one can order me in this.' Her face came free, and she blew strands of hair from her mouth and looked at Fola. 'I love him! He has waited two years to hear me say it, and I'm not making him wait longer. After all the talking and dreaming we did in this very room . . . will you stand in my way?'

Caitlin clapped her hands together and put them to her mouth, her eyes shining.

Fola was grinning at Rhiann. 'Now that you put it like that, how could I stand in the way of anything?' She shrugged. 'Nerida knows well how stubborn you are. She will not punish me for your rebellion.'

Fola quietly saddled the most placid of the Sisters' mares, and led it to the edge of the settlement, where the path wound up out of the dell through the hawthorns. Caitlin and Rhiann managed to slip from the house, undetected by Nerida or any of the older priestesses, and when Caitlin led Rhiann away on the mare, no one came rushing out to stop her.

Or perhaps they expected her to do this after all.

When Caitlin tied the mare up outside the druid lodge, Conaire hastened to help Rhiann to the ground. 'Rhiann! We have all been worried about you!'

Rhiann gave his waist a squeeze, smiling over his shoulder at Colum and Fergus. 'I am quite well, as you can see – just a little wobbly on my feet. I want to speak to Eremon.'

Conaire frowned and shook his head. 'They are guarding him like a pack of wolves.' He threw a glance over his shoulder, to where Nectan stood before the door with a spear, flanked by two of his men. 'I knew we should not have trusted that one.'

'Peace, Conaire. I will talk to Nectan alone.'

When Rhiann approached the door of the lodge, Nectan looked up at her with a touch of defiance, gripping his spear.

'Am I not to be allowed to enter, either?' She spoke his own dialect, smiling.

'No women can enter, lady.'

'But I need to see him! If not, then tell me why.'

Nectan jerked his head at his men, and they relaxed their stiff pose and moved to one side, out of earshot.

'Lady,' Nectan said respectfully. 'This is a matter for the druids, for the God. For all of us. Your man came for an alliance, and an alliance he will have – if he chooses. But the moment hangs in the balance. The moment must not be disturbed.'

Rhiann stared at him, a suspicion suddenly entering her mind. 'Nectan, do you know why Eremon was chosen to be the Stag? A stranger, a foreigner?'

Nectan's grin was proud. 'I did it. The kings were beginning to be convinced, but they did not wish to heed the call of a *gael*. We only follow our own. I spoke with Brethan's druid. The druids have seen the signs . . . they know the Source is disturbed, that danger is near. They saw that the Goddess brought your man to our shores, in the eighteenth year. He, who has shed Roman blood, and had his own blood shed by Romans. He, the bonded man of a Ban Cré. Who else could be the Stag? She had called him. And if he became our God for this night, then perhaps the kings would heed him.'

Rhiann nodded. Of course! Now, her mind free of the *saor*, she could see it all. 'Nectan.' She bowed her head. 'You are wise beyond imagining. We have much to thank you for, if what you say is true. But will they follow him? Have they told you so?'

'That depends.'

'On what?'

'On what he says when they give him the choice.'

In the druid lodge, Eremon lay curled up against the wall, on a bed of soft skins. His shoulder throbbed only faintly, for it had been cleaned and packed with herbs, and the druid healer gave him a draught of something that took the pain away.

It was not his bodily hurts that kept him huddled as far from the chanting druids as possible. It was his spirit that was utterly overwhelmed, and not just from the power he felt in the stone circle.

No. It was the moment when Rhiann chose him, when *she* pulled his mouth down to hers, that would be burned on his memory for ever. Nothing would ever come close to that sweetness ... to the feel of her wanting him so hungrily. Nothing.

If he could have died right there and then, if he could have slipped from his body, and taken her to the Otherworld, leaving everything, he would have done so. Right at that moment, life became as pure as it would ever be.

'Prince.' It was Brethan's druid. 'I would speak with you.'

Painfully, Eremon turned, shifting his body higher against the pillow.

The young druid's eyes were cavernous, burning with excitement. Over his shoulder, other druids kept up that sibilant chanting, and every now and then, one would throw a handful of something on the fire that caught at the back of Eremon's throat.

'You know why we chose you to be the Stag.'

Eremon nodded dizzily. 'Nectan told me.' He coughed, and the druid handed him a cup of water, and waited while he sipped it.

Taking it from him, the druid sat on the edge of the bed pallet. 'And our choice was right. The flowering of the Source was the most powerful we have known for many, many years. You did well.'

Eremon's mind was on Rhiann. 'I am glad. Now, if you'll just get me my cloak so I can go to my wife ...'

But the druid was shaking his head. 'No, there is more.' He leaned forward, almost hungrily. 'When the island woman took the knife to you, she shed your blood. Instead of the symbolic sacrifice, *your blood truly ran from the sacred knife, into the earth.*'

'Don't remind me.'

'Prince, you must understand. *You* have given the blood

sacrifice – the first Stag to do so for generations. It has bonded you to us; the Goddess has claimed you.'

At those words, something crept coldly into Eremon's belly, and he remembered the day he first stepped ashore at Crìanan, and how he sensed that something waited for him.

'Because She demanded your blood, which none of us looked for or planned, you have gone far beyond the Beltaine rite. But you are not yet wholly ours – you walk the path between the worlds. It is too dangerous for any but a druid to come near. We cannot even celebrate the Beltaine feast until the doorway is safely closed once more.'

Eremon shivered at the druid's tone, and then his mind caught on something. 'Yet? You said, "You are not *yet* wholly ours." What do you mean?'

The druid bowed his head. 'I come to give you your choice. We can draw you fully back to your body, and release you to return to your world unchanged. But know that if you do this, the kings will not heed your call.'

'Or?'

'Or we give you up to Her, and make you truly ours – our war leader, the Consort of our Goddess, the King Stag for as long as your lifeblood flows.'

'I wish I knew what you were talking about.'

At that, the druid smiled. 'We must brand you, prince, brand you as one of our own. I speak of tattoos, for the lines of power will bond you to the Mother, and to us. A few steps away, twenty kings and chieftains are poised to bend their knees to you, to offer up their swords. But they will only give you their allegiance, if you give Her yours.'

As the meaning of his words finally penetrated Eremon's mind, the fear in his belly overflowed. By the Boar! 'I . . . I need to speak with my brother.'

'No one can see you.'

'I demand it! I have made commitments to my own people, oaths that I must take into account. Would you have me break faith with them?'

The druid hesitated. 'He can speak with you, if he does not get too close.'

'Then will you let me rise and walk with him outside? I can hardly breathe in here.'

The druid's brow darkened. 'No. It is dangerous for my people. You must make your choice here, alone. To go further, or to pull back. It is a choice you make in your heart.'

Eremon managed to get all the druids to leave, except Brethan's, who said he must ward the door. But he withdrew far enough away for Conaire and Eremon to speak alone.

Conaire sat on a stool a few paces from the bed, listening to all Eremon had to say. Afterwards, he was silent, his chin resting on his hands, his blue eyes far away.

'What does this mean for us?' Eremon asked, hoarsely. 'I am my father's heir. My home is in Erin; I gave my people an oath to serve them.'

'Yet does it break an oath to them, to take another here?'

'I don't know!'

'But you gave your oath to the Epidii.'

'I know but . . . that was different. The Epidii *said* that it was a marriage to the land, to the Goddess, but I did not feel it at the time. This feels real.'

Conaire sighed. 'Eremon, the only way to regain your throne is to make alliances here. Only then can we return you to your rightful place.'

'We did not count on the Romans intervening in *that* plan.'

'No, but they have. As have . . . many other things.'

At the wistfulness of the tone, Eremon glanced at him. 'What do you mean?'

It was only when Conaire lifted his eyes that Eremon saw the suppressed excitement; a glow that had not been there before. 'Caitlin is to have a babe.'

Eremon was speechless.

'Brother!' Conaire's excitement flared. 'He could be a king! The next King of the Epidii!'

Eremon looked long at him. 'So,' he said. 'You have your own bonds here now; you have taken your own oaths.'

Perhaps Conaire fancied that he heard disappointment in Eremon's voice, for he raised his chin. 'Yes. I did not come looking for Caitlin, but I found her anyway. My path led me somewhere I was not expecting.'

'As has mine.'

'As has yours.'

They were silent, each turning over their own thoughts.

'You know,' Conaire offered, with his disarming grin, 'Erin is not far away. Perhaps we shall found a clan that spans both sides of the sea! My son may be King here, yours in Erin! Aedan said as much to you when you wed Rhiann.'

'Yes, he did.'

'Eremon.' Conaire leaned forward, his hands on his knees. 'We were led here, and I say we take the gifts we are given. If you lead the Albans, it does not mean you stop leading us! You protect those in Erin by what you do here, for we all share a common enemy.'

At his simple words, Eremon's heart at last lightened. 'Now I know why I have kept you by my side all these years.'

Conaire grinned again, and looked sidelong at him. 'Rhiann came to you.'

Eremon tensed. 'Where is she?'

'She spoke to Nectan, and then she went away. She must know of the druid's proposal. But they would not let her in to see you.'

Strangely, though he yearned for her, this knowledge brought Eremon a wave of relief.

Much had passed between them in the stone circle. What if she did not feel the same about it as he did?

CHAPTER 80

Rhiann could neither eat nor sleep, sew nor grind nor cook. Her fingers would not obey her mind, for her thoughts bubbled and roiled in her head like the surface of one of Fola's stews.

She knew only that Eremon had agreed to the tattoos. So, he had chosen them.

But her? Had he chosen her?

At last, Caitlin came for her in the grey dawn. 'He has emerged!' she cried from the doorway of the dairy, catching Rhiann around the waist. 'And the kings are making ready to swear their oaths. The Beltaine feast will go ahead!'

Rhiann disentangled herself. 'Well, what does he look like? Is he well? Did he speak?'

Caitlin shook her head, smiling. 'You can answer all those questions yourself. He walks on the beach below the broch. And he wishes to speak with you.'

Rhiann's mouth went dry. 'Now?'

'Yes, now! Honestly, Rhiann, anyone would think you two had never met. He's nervous, you're nervous – what's the matter with you both? Hurry!'

From the doorway of the Eldest Sister's lodge, Nerida and Setana watched Rhiann ride away under a heavy sky, the wind whipping her hair from her hood. They could see that her face glowed, yet her eyes were shadowed with apprehension.

'So, as we longed for, the rite has brought healing,' Nerida murmured, folding her aching hands in her robe.

Setana cocked her head as if listening. 'It is . . . part . . . of the healing. The time for her to learn the rest of it is not now.'

'But when?'

Setana closed her eyes. 'It came to me in a dream. The time for her true healing is not ours to pick. We can only help her along the path. She will be sorely tried . . . and then she herself will choose the time and place, for it is she who must come back to the Goddess of her own desire. I see . . . war . . . swords and spears, and men crying out. I see . . . a babe. And . . . a grave, a strange stone.' She opened her eyes. 'That is all.'

Nerida turned back to her fire. 'Your warnings are grim, Sister. But however she makes her way back, I will be content.' She sighed. 'Though I fancy we will not be here to see it.'

'Not in Thisworld, Sister,' Setana agreed, spreading her hands to the flames. 'But we will know. We will see.'

When Rhiann saw the broch rearing from its ridge against cold clouds, and smelled the smoke of the feasting fires, swept her way by the wind, her heart grew heavy.

It was all very well that *she* opened up in the circle, and surrendered. But what about Eremon? He had loved her once, she knew that, but did he still, after she pushed him away so well? Was what she saw during the rite just a product of the *saor*, the drums, the night? Especially since he had now been offered two powerful alliances of his own: Calgacus and the Caereni. Perhaps he did not need her any more.

Around and around it went, and the closer they got, the more sick she began to feel.

After dismounting, she and Caitlin skirted the broch wall and made their way down the glen to the sea-loch.

'There.' Caitlin stopped and grasped her arm, pointing. Right at the end of the narrow stretch of beach, Rhiann could just make out a figure watching the waves, which were rolling in on the skirts of a squall. 'He said that he'd had enough of walls and smoke and chanting to last him a lifetime, and he wanted to get as far away as possible.'

'Well, he certainly did,' Rhiann said. 'I'll have more than enough time to decide what I want to say, with that walk.'

Caitlin regarded her quizzically. 'Say? If I were you, I'd just kiss him – he looks as though he needs it!' And with a flick of the feathers in her braids, she was gone.

Rhiann was left alone where the turf met the sand. She dallied there for some time, despite the chill of the salt-laden wind, the threatening sky. But behind her, up the valley, the noise from the broch was growing. There was music, shouts and drums. Soon, they would want him back. Soon, he must stand in the hall and be a prince again. Everyone would want to speak to him.

There was little time.

She took a breath, squared her shoulders, and set off. There was only one thing to say, after all.

CHAPTER 81

Eremon watched the swell rushing up the rocks, his eyes unfocused. The spume rose up in a salty cloud, which drifted over him where he stood.

And to this land I am now bound.

Across the inlet, smooth cliffs of turf reared, glowing with sea-pinks, alight with gulls riding the high winds. And he marvelled, as his eyes followed the birds, that when he first saw Alba he had ever thought it barren, and cold, and forbidding.

Just like Rhiann.

He had not thought this for a long time. In all their journeying, he had come to love the broad sweep of the glens guarded by grim mountains, and the moors with their swathes of bronze sedge. It was a harsh land, but it called to something deep in him, something wild that did not wish to be tamed. It was not a soft, yielding place, yet all the more exhilarating for that.

A worthy mistress, for the son of a king.

He stretched a little to one side, and then the other. His bandaged shoulder still ached, and his belly and chest stung from the bone needles of the druid artists. The skin was swollen, and he would not be able to see the design clearly for some days. But Nectan had told him of the stag, and the eagle, and the boar that they carved into his skin; the curving lines that drew the power of the Mother to his body, just as Her power ran in those lines beneath the land.

Rhiann possessed those same curves on her belly, and her

598

breasts, although in the darkness of the stone circle he had not seen them clearly. At the thought, his body groaned.

Rhiann. She would be here soon. And what would he say?

Would she remember what happened in the circle, or was she just swept away by the *saor*; the power of the Goddess in her? Had she felt anything for him as a man?

He did not think, after opening to her like that, that he could ever go back to the way things were. If she did not want him as a man, then he must leave the Epidii. He had many allies now, and many places of refuge. Yet the thought of being sundered from her sickened him.

There was the softest pad of feet on the shingle behind him.

She was here.

Rhiann knew that he must have heard her steps, although he did not turn. Her courage quailed, and she faltered.

But no.

He had risked his heart many times before, with her. And she knew now that only in trusting had she been able to leap into the void. Her trust of Nerida and Setana opened the door to the Goddess-light. She must find more now.

She was one step away from him, close enough to see the faintest quivering across his shoulders. His hair lifted in the wind, the tendrils damp from sea spray. That was all she could see. And still he did not turn.

The hardest thing, for her, would be to reach out and touch a man. And yet, even as she thought it, she realized that her body told a different story from her mind. It was Eremon. Her arms ached to hold him, and her body sang its deep need to press up against his skin.

She took a breath, and slipped her arms about his waist, burying her face in the wool cloak across his back. It smelled of sweat and salt and woodsmoke, and she closed her eyes, feeling the tension vibrating through his body. The muscles were coiled hard under her hands, and he seemed not to breathe.

'Eremon,' she whispered. 'What is wrong? Speak to me.'

At her words, his chest tensed even more. 'I am not a god.' His voice was harsh.

She released her hold and moved around to stand before him. He looked down at her, the tension in his body mirrored in his face. His fine features were set like stone, his mouth a thin line, with none of the softness she loved so well.

What was wrong? Was he angry? And then her eyes met his, and she saw what his body cried out. Beneath the reflected green of the sea, lay fear, naked and raw, and the words that he had spoken at last penetrated her mind.

'I am not a god,' he whispered again.

She smiled. 'I know. It is not the God that I love, and need. It is the man.'

He searched her eyes, disbelief warring with hope, and she willed herself to be as naked as he. Then she reached up and cupped one cheek with her hand. 'Eremon. Did you think I came here to find the God? Did you think that my kisses in the circle were for Him?'

His breath whistled through gritted teeth. 'I did not know. I thought ... perhaps ... that was all that called you forth, that night. All you wanted from me.'

In answer, she cupped his other cheek and drew his mouth down to her own. And the instant their lips touched, the same fire leaped between them; the same overwhelming hunger lit deep in her belly, and in the place where she had welcomed him with joy. And then his hands were buried in her hair, pulling out the pins so that the heavy tresses fell through his fingers.

'I thought ... you were not yourself ... that night ...' Between words, he showered her face with kisses, her nose, her eyelids, all along both cheekbones. 'That ... I meant nothing ... to you ... nothing as a man.'

She pulled back. 'Eremon, I was more myself than I have ever been! It was *I* who surrendered to you. It was *I* who showed you my dream ... that you are my soul-love. It was I who joined with you in the light.' Her eyes devoured his face, roving over the planes of cheek and lip and jaw that she had traced with her mind these last days, but not her mouth. Until now.

She brushed his lips with her thumb, slowly, watching the blood flow to fullness again. 'And all because I love you as a man – with your sword and your spear and . . . and your arrogance!'

He laughed shakily, but his eyes were bright.

She stroked his cheek. 'It was not you I ever looked for,' she said softly.

'Or I you.' He turned his face, and his lips found her palm.

'And yet you came,' she whispered. When his tongue touched her skin, the fire leaped in her belly once more, and she closed her eyes.

'I was led,' he murmured, and pulled her up against the length of his body, claiming her lips once more. She felt the burning of each touch, as his hands molded her curves to his own. And when the dizziness passed, and he released her again, she suddenly remembered.

'Your tattoos!' Her fingers crept under his tunic, edging it up so she could see his belly and chest. He gasped, but his eyes burned with something other than pain.

His skin was red and distorted with swelling, yet still she could discern the artistry, the lines of boar and stag and eagle. 'They are beautiful.' She looked up at him. 'But why do they not reach your face, your neck or arms?'

'In Erin, a king must be unblemished. I have taken oaths in two lands; I must retain my face for my own. The druids agreed, so that I can lead both peoples.'

At his words, a sliver of fear pricked at her heart. Is that why he agreed to such a commitment? 'You made your decision without seeing me.'

'I needed to.' His eyes were willing her to understand. 'This oath was sacred, and I wished to treat it so. I did not want to make the decision . . . because of my existing bonds.'

Her heart leaped. 'Bonds?'

'My lady's mind runs quicker than this!' He smiled

crookedly, but now the tilt of his mouth held no bitterness.
'My love for you forged a bond to this land long before I even
knew it. You play no part in my oaths to these people . . .
because I made mine to you long ago, in my heart.'

Relief swept through her, and she realized her breast was
pounding with fear and . . . something else.

His skin was as smooth as silks from the east, and the
muscles of stag and boar flowed as his own moved under her
hands. She leaned in and slid her fingers up his back, under
his tunic, loving the warmth and the hardness both. In
answer, his hands traced the bones in her spine, shaped the
indent of her waist, moved around and up her ribs . . . and
then his palm brushed her breast.

And she tensed. The reaction was instinctive, like a jolt of
pain in her chest.

But when she saw the dawning of the confusion in his eyes,
the hurt . . . she said to herself . . . *No.*

'Eremon.' She leaned back to look up at him. 'There is
something you must know about me.'

The fear was back on his face, and with a pang, she knew it
was about to deepen into pain.

'Nothing else matters,' he said desperately. 'There is only
us—'

'No.' She broke from his embrace and turned towards the
water, for the words were hard to say. And suddenly, her own
fear rose up that he might reject her.

Still she must say it.

'On the day of the raid, I came to the beach and . . . saw the
men slaughter my family. When they . . . died . . . I ran away,
up those rocks.' She pointed with one trembling hand. 'But I
did not tell you what came after. Three men ran . . . ran me
down. They took me, Eremon.'

There was silence from behind her; a silence that stretched
out for so long, that she bowed her head, unable to face what
she would see in him.

There came a smothered curse, a sob, she could not tell,
and his arms were pressing her face into his chest, fiercely.

'*No!*' His voice was broken. 'Not you. Gods! I will hunt them down and kill them, kill them all!'

She felt the quivering in his arms, and knew that he wanted to strike something, anything. But there was nothing to hit, and nowhere to escape to. So she stayed silent, gripping him with the same fierceness he did her.

After a long while, his hard, painful hold softened, and his breath shuddered from him. 'All along you carried this . . . and I never knew. You carried it alone.'

She heard the new note. He was hurting, but it was for her! He did not reject her! She was being smothered in his cloak, so she turned her head until she could hear his heart beating against her ear.

'My love . . .' he murmured now, an edge of rawness in his voice. 'I will never let you be alone in this again.'

She closed her eyes, suddenly troubled by his words. But with the release of the heavy secret, and its shame, a new knowledge was sweeping through her heart. Perhaps Nerida sent it, perhaps the Goddess-light still lingered, illuminating what she had been too blind to see.

Eremon had never been sent to save her.

He but offered me the gift. All along, I had only to reach out and take it.

She took a deep, shuddering breath, and raised her face. 'Eremon, I will need to be alone with this, at times, and that is as it should be. But with you by my side, it will be easier.'

He was quiet for a moment. 'That is why you wielded the knife on our wedding night. And I forced myself upon you . . . gods!'

She wiped her cheeks. 'You did not force yourself, Eremon. You treated me with honour.'

'No . . . I pawed at you . . . and then later I tried to kiss you, when all along a man's touch was hateful to you. Forgive me.'

'Eremon.'

His eyes were wild with pain.

'Eremon, you did not do this to me. *They* did. You cannot be responsible for the actions of all men, only your own actions. And you acted as any husband would, as any man should.' She put her hands on his shoulders and gave him a gentle shake. 'Your touch was . . . is . . . not hateful to me. Remember, after we rescued you, when you tried to kiss me?'

He nodded.

'I wanted to, Eremon. It was because I wanted to that I pulled away, not because I did not love you. I was so scared that if I gave in and you touched me and I flinched . . . that you would reject me. I did not want to let you down . . . not you. Never you.'

At those words, the pain in his eyes flared brighter.

'So you see,' she added, smiling wistfully, 'I am not the Goddess, either. Just a faulty vessel; a broken vessel.'

At that, he folded her in his arms again, gently this time. 'Faulty, perhaps – as am I. But you are still my fierce, loving, maddening Rhiann. That is all I need.'

Rhiann closed her eyes and let the warmth of his body hold the pain at bay. For now, there was just this moment, and she would savour it: the scent of the hollow of his neck, the beat of his heart, and the softness of his breath in her ear. Beneath their tunics, pressed together, she sensed the lines of power on her belly and those on his drawing them ever closer.

At that moment, a carnyx trumpet rang out from the wall around the broch, cleaving the air with a strident summons.

'Gods!' Eremon released her. 'Is there to be no rest for me? They call me back.'

Rhiann smiled. 'Many kings are waiting for you. This is what you have worked so hard for. Come.'

As they walked back up the glen, hand in hand, and drew closer to the shadow of the broch, Eremon stopped again. 'Will you stay close by my side this night? I need you there.'

She smiled, and leaned up on tiptoe to kiss him. 'The dream is alive, Eremon. We both saw it, that night of the rite. You and I have come together to do this for our people; all of them. My place is by your side, for this night and all to come.'

The boar-head trumpet cried once more, and was joined by

another, and then another, until the air all around rang with the clamour.

Together, they heeded the call.

EPILOGUE

Far in the east, in a city on seven hills, there was a room of gold.

The carved arms of the chair at its centre were gilded, the wall hangings were of cloth-of-gold, and there was a gold ewer of fine Gaulish wine on a small, ebony table.

From the marble terrace outside, sunlight poured into the room, and the blue sky beyond was pale with heat. The air was golden, too, heavy with myrrh and the scent of cedar, and dripping with the moistness of the River Tiber in late summer.

A stray reflection of sun caught the rings of the man in the chair, blazing on a ruby intaglio ring, carved with the head of the divine Jupiter. The man was young, with close-cropped dark hair and small, piercing eyes. He would address the Roman Senate shortly, and for this reason wore the purple on his toga.

A scribe crouched on a stool by a table, a sheet of vellum spread before him, dipping his stylus into a jewelled inkwell. The scratching of it was the only sound in the silent room, apart from the buzzing of a bee, which had ventured through the terrace doors from the gardens of the Palatine.

The scribe finished his opening paragraph, with its long formal address, and the man with the ruby ring continued his dictation. As he spoke, the stylus resumed its flight across the vellum, in perfect, cursive script:

. . . Gnaeus Julius Agricola, as well as greetings, I give you

confirmation of my ascension on the early and unlooked for death of my dear brother Titus, former Emperor of Rome.

Know then that on the fate of your forces in the northern realms of that province of Britannia, so rests the glory of the Empire.

You are hereby ordered to advance from your present frontier position as dictated by my predecessor Titus, and take all the territories of that land known as Alba from southern to uttermost northern, from sea to sea.

In accomplishing this, I confirm my faith in you as a staunch support of my father Vespasian, and our family for all these times past, and the military commander who has conquered so many new territories for the Empire.

In return correspondence, indicate your dispositions and campaign plans for the coming season. In all, you have my support and faith in your abilities, as always.

Farewell!

Domitian

Emperor of Rome

HISTORICAL NOTE

Any historical novel is a blend of fact and fiction. While I have stuck to the facts if they are known and widely accepted, luckily for me, as a fiction writer, there is so much we either don't know for sure, or is the subject of great debate among scholars. In these cases, fiction takes precedence. I make no apologies for that, since I set out to tell a good story first and foremost, which just happens to be set against a historical background.

While I've been as careful in my research as I can be, errors and omissions will have occurred, and these are entirely my own fault.

There is not enough space here to include all the detailed facts, but I wanted to explain here the major issues, and why I decided to use certain facts as I have. Also, Kilmartin in Argyll is well worth a visit, and there you can go to the actual sites of Dunadd and Crìanan (often spelt Crinan), the Dun of the Cliffs (Castle Dounie) and the line of 'ancestor mounds' and stones in Kilmartin valley. Kilmartin also has the best little museum I've ever visited in the UK, the Kilmartin House Museum, which houses some great interpretive displays – and does a mean coffee!

The Roman Campaigns

All of the basic information about the Roman army's movements, its fort building and frontiers, are taken from the biography Tacitus later wrote about his father-in-law, Agricola. Some scholars think it likely that Tacitus did in fact spend a short time in northern Britain as a young man.

Interestingly, although I had written my plot before I knew this, Tacitus does mention that Agricola entertained an exiled Irish prince and was considering the invasion of Ireland with this prince at the helm.

Dalriada

Also known as Dál Riata. Later Irish and Scottish annals speak of a people who came from Ulster in northern Ireland to colonize Argyll in western Scotland sometime in the sixth century AD. This colony of Gaels, as they were known, established their king's seat at the fort of Dunadd near Crìanan in Argyll, bringing the Gaelic language to Scotland. However, most scholars agree that, because of the close proximity of their coastlines, the northern Irish were probably in close contact with western Scotland centuries before the accepted colonization. So the first real contact between Argyll and Dalriada could easily have been made as far back as the first century, since I am not proposing a wholesale movement of people at this time.

Dunadd

Dunadd is now accepted as the royal seat of the kings of Scottish Dál Riata from approximately the fifth to tenth centuries AD, and became a centre of trade and fine craftsmanship. However, excavations have proven that people were living, or at least visiting the site for thousands of years before that, including the time around the Roman invasions of Scotland. It is unlikely that a prominent volcanic crag close to the sea would not have been used by the earlier Celtic peoples of the area. Excavations have focused on the stone walls built in the middle of the first millennium, and it is entirely possible that traces of timber buildings have either been missed, or were destroyed during later building on the site. To my knowledge, the plain around the crag's feet has not been excavated.

Tribes

The Greek geographer Ptolemy, writing in the second century AD, has left us a map of Scotland showing the names and placements of major tribes. It is possible that some of this information was gathered during Agricola's campaigns. I have included the tribal names and positions as shown on this map, although we don't know how accurate it is.

Some people also think that the tribal names relate to animals, and could indicate totemic affinities. Thus the Epidii might be related to horses, the Caereni to sheep and the Lugi to ravens.

A note on the Caledonii: On Ptolemy's map, this tribe is shown as the Caledones. However, by the fourth century, when the last book in this trilogy is set, the name seems to have become 'Caledonii' to Roman writers, so for simplicity's sake I've used that.

Picts and Gaels

The name 'Pict' is not used by Roman writers for the peoples of Scotland until the fourth century, and may come from a Roman term meaning 'painted people'. However, although my characters obviously 'became' the Picts, we don't know what they called themselves. So I've stuck to the old name for Scotland, Alba, and called them Albans. With regard to the 'Gaels', there is strong evidence that this is what the early peoples of Scotland called those from Ireland. Argyll, where the Dalriadans later had their centre of power, means 'coast of the Gael'.

Language

By the sixth century there is some evidence that the Picts (descendants of Scottish people) and Argyll Scots (descendants of the Dalriadan Irish) spoke a mutually unintelligible form of the Celtic language. However, languages can change rapidly, and we don't know how close the two were in the first century, although many people think it is likely to have been much closer. I've left them speaking essentially the same language, for simplicity's sake.

Personal Names

I don't follow one naming scheme, since we don't know what language the Picts/Albans spoke: was it closer to Welsh or Irish at this time? So some of my names are Irish, some Pictish, and some I have invented. The only records we have of Pictish names are lists of kings. As far as possible, I've used names from this list for major male characters, including Brude, Maelchon, Gelert, Drust, and Nectan. The one exception is Calgacus, which is Celtic and means something like 'great swordsman'. He is noted by Tacitus as leading the resistance of the tribes against Agricola.

We don't have records of female Pictish names, so in the book these are mostly Irish, such as Caitlin, Eithne, Mairenn, Dercca, and Fainne. Rhiann, though based on Welsh, is not a traditional name. All of Eremon's men have Irish names, although as Aedan sang at the wedding feast, Eremon is not a traditional name and in fact is the name of a mythological hero, the first Gaelic king of Ireland.

Gods

In a similar vein, since we don't know what the Albans called their gods, I've used a mixture of Welsh gods (Arawn) and goddesses (Rhiannon, Ceridwen), British goddesses (Andraste and Sulis), and Irish gods (the Dagda, Lugh, Manannán). These last two appear all over the Celtic world, from Ireland to Gaul. Manannán appears in Welsh mythology, often as the husband of Rhiannon, and gave his name to the Isle of Man as well as being one of the most important Irish gods. Taranis is known from Gaulish inscriptions and seems to be a god of thunder. Cernunnos, the stag god, also seems to have been widely worshipped on the Continent as well as in the British Isles.

The Sacred Isle

In the book, I equate the Sacred Isle with the Isle of Lewis in the Hebrides, purely because here, on a lonely headland facing the Atlantic, happens to stand the greatest stone circle in the British Isles after Stonehenge and Avebury: Callanish. The broch tower that is the site of Rhiann's raid is also mostly still standing nearby; it is called Dun Carloway. Interestingly, the historian Plutarch relates the story of a traveller, Demetrius of Tarsus, who visited a 'holy island' probably in the Hebrides, during Agricola's campaigns.

The Female Royal Line

One of the most intriguing aspects of the Picts (my Albans) is that there is some evidence that royalty was passed through the female line, rather than from father to son. If true, this puts the Scottish people out of step with what we know of the early Irish and British. This idea was one of the starting points for my story.

The Old Ones / The Sisterhood

Following on from the above, I began to muse that perhaps the reason why only Scotland had this strange custom could have been because an ancient form of Mother Goddess worship, which had died out elsewhere, survived there. In the book, I'm proposing that the female-centred religion of the Neolithic or Bronze Age people (the 'Old Ones') may also have involved an order of priestesses. The existence of the Druid order is well-known to classical writers, so I had the idea that, at this time, the two are still co-existing. A note to all boffins: I know there is no evidence for this!

Stones / Mounds

All of the standing stone arrangements and tomb mounds in the United Kingdom were built by Neolithic or Bronze Age peoples before 1500 bc, not by my Iron Age peoples in the first century AD. However, most scholars agree that Iron Age peoples probably venerated and possibly used older monuments for their own rites. Though there is evidence for this in other parts of Scotland and Britain, there is no evidence that the monuments in the Kilmartin valley or the great stone circle of Callanish on the Isle of Lewis were used in this way.

Pictish Stones

The most well-known aspect of the Picts is that they left behind extraordinary carved stones, mostly dating from the sixth or seventh century AD onwards. Although I'm aware that we have none dated to my time period, I had the idea that the same symbols were used to decorate wood, walls and bodies much, much earlier. Drust's few stones are an invention, but I'm proposing that the idea died out with him for a few more centuries. Perhaps his eagle stones are even now buried somewhere, waiting to be discovered!

One point of interest: I chose the boar as Eremon's family totem because at Dunadd there is a famous rock carving of a boar. Though it is of much later date, I like to think that it was Eremon who brought the boar symbol to Dunadd and that it became a sign of the Dalriadan royal house because of him.

Names of Landmarks

For some of the major landmarks, I've given the real meaning as far as we can ascertain. Thus the (existing) hillfort of Traprain Law, Samana's home, seems to mean the 'place of the tree'. The Leven river that flows from Loch Lomond probably means the Elm River. Lomond itself probably means 'beacon' so we have the Loch of the Beacon and The Beacon for the mountain Ben Lomond. The Clyde was known as the Clutha, but its meaning is not clear: the same applies to the Forth. Likewise, no one seems to know what Crìanan means, so I've left it in its original form. Calgacus's Dun of the Waves is an invention, but I've sited it at present day Inverness because it is at the mouth of the Great Glen, and because the form of the Moray Firth makes this site easy to defend from sea attacks.

BOOK ONE: Leaf-bud, AD 81

CHAPTER 1

These days at sea were the first peaceful time she had enjoyed in years, Rhiann realised, her cheek pillowed on the bow. It felt as if their little, open boat floated between the shining water and pale sky, its white sail a wing, suspending it in a void of blue.

As the journey unfolded, the drowsy sea had put her in a kind of trance, gathering itself every now and then for a listless roll against the hull, only to subside into a dark mirror all around, laced with drifting weed. The breeze had stayed westerly, a sea-wind to bring them home, but it barely roused the water to waves, or billowed the sail that rose from the centre of the hide *curragh*.

Rhiann loved *curraghs*, for they sat close to the water, and yet skimmed like a gull over the swells, and when the side dipped she could trail her hand in the cold sea, feeling its pull on her fingers. Mostly, though, she lay with her face along the railing, aware of few things beyond the tang of salt and tar, the creak of oars, and the sun on her eyelids.

And so she found herself, on another cloudless afternoon three days after leaving the Sacred Isle, when Rhiann at last registered the insistent pull that had slowly been turning under the surface of her mind, tugging at her senses.

'Beast! I'll get you . . . *there*, hah! Cold, isn't it!' Caitlin's defiant words, floating from over Rhiann's shoulder, were followed by an even louder screech, and Rhiann didn't have to turn to guess that Conaire, who had much bigger hands, had dashed another palmful of seawater over his wife. Either Rhiann's tansy brew had softened Caitlin's nausea, or true to character she was gamely ignoring it. A rumble of laughter

1

lifted from the others at the oar benches: those of Eremon's men who had come to the Sacred Isle with them, and the islanders who crewed the boat.

Rhiann's knees had gone numb, and she shifted on the willow ribs of the hull to ease them. As she did, she half-opened her eyes, her chin resting on one hand. Beyond the glitter of the sun on the water, the nearest island was sliding past in a fine weave of black cliffs thronged with sea-pinks, its green hills sprinkled with yellow gorse, the white surf edging bays of pale water. At the end of one spill of rocks a seal watched their passage, its head and tail curved into a bow, its eyes as dark and liquid as the sea itself.

'Hello.' Rhiann saluted to it with one finger, curling out from under her chin.

Below the seal's perch the sea was being sucked between rocks in a turmoil of white foam. And staring at the roiling water Rhiann made the connection, suddenly realising what she had been sensing from afar; a deep thrumming on the edge of her hearing, resonating through the air. *The whirlpool*, Rhiann thought, straightening with sleepy shock.

The whirlpool's spinning waters churned the narrow strait between the islands close to Dunadd, marking a boundary between Thisworld and the Otherworld. And Rhiann knew, with the refinement of her priestess senses, that she had only heard it from this far away because it was a sign for her. So she did what any sensible person would do: bit her lip, and futilely clamped her eyes shut again.

The sun prickled on her forearms where she'd pushed up the sleeves of her wool dress, yet inside Rhiann had gone cold. For the whirlpool was telling her she must wake from the sea dreams in which she'd been floating. It meant that her span of days must resume; that they were nearly home, and must face all that lay there. And by the Goddess, Rhiann didn't want to.

Instead, she wanted to hold on to the deep thrill of joy, the thread of gold wound all through her now that she had returned to the fold of the Sisters. Now that she had been filled by the Goddess light once more, in the stone circle. Now that . . .

'Ah, my sea-sprite.' There was a creak of the hull, as a tentative hand brushed Rhiann's cheek. 'And have you returned to me at last from the faery deep?'

Now that Eremon was hers . . . Rhiann completed the thought and allowed herself a smile, for although everyone else had known somehow to leave her alone, Eremon hadn't, nor had she wanted him to. 'Just now,' she replied, although she couldn't stifle a sigh as she stretched, blinking her eyes fully open in the bright, leaf-bud light.

'A wistful breath?' Rhiann's seat, a pile of leather packs and wrapped weapons, squeaked as Eremon flopped onto them. 'Were you pining for me from the depths of your watery abode?'

Rhiann squinted up at him from one eye, though in the glare she could only see a pale grin against a tanned face. 'Keep spouting such words, husband, and it won't be me in that watery abode, I can tell you.' Yet her hand crept out and laid itself on his warm, bare foot. Just to remind her he was really there, and laughing down at her.

'If I kept talking like *that*, I wouldn't blame you, wife.' Eremon grinned and hooked his arms around his knees, his green eyes catching the light off the waves. The narrow braids holding back his dark hair framed a face painted with sunburn across clear, brown skin. He had rolled his trousers up and cut the sleeves off his linen tunic, and even in this short time the sun had turned his bare arms as dark as oiled oak. 'Poetry makes my head ache, and it has only just cleared after all those Sacred Isle feasts!'

Rhiann rested her chin on Eremon's knees and toyed with one of his braids, dark as otter fur. 'I did wonder at the island chiefs . . .' She cocked one eyebrow at him. 'Going to all the trouble of proclaiming you their war leader, and then trying to kill you with ale . . .'

'Ah! As King Stag I must be able to do everything well, apparently . . . including drinking.'

'Well, I think your practice with Conaire stood you in good stead there.'

A shout drew both their heads around, and they saw their

3

friends gesticulating wildly at each other in what passed for them as conversation. Fiery Fergus was daring to provoke the much larger Conaire by twisting the end of his oar, spraying all of them with water. With another squeal, Caitlin cupped a handful from the sea and this time flung it at Fergus, as Conaire folded his huge, sunburned arms over his oar and rocked with laughter. With a long-suffering grimace, Colum wiped his dripping grey hair, even as the web of lines around his eyes crinkled.

Spying them thus occupied, Eremon slid his lean frame down the pile of packs until he was pressed against Rhiann's knees in the bow, his broad shoulders blocking them from the view of the others.

The clean lines of Eremon's face were still as hard as when Rhiann had first seen him two years ago, his slanted eyes still sharp, and yet nevertheless some tense hunger in him had softened this last week, his defenses lowering. And with their faces close together Eremon smiled now; his rare, true smile that Rhiann had rarely seen, for before the Sacred Isle one side of it was always lifted with bitterness.

Being on the receiving end of its full power was still a new experience for Rhiann, and she found her breath doing that trip in her throat again, which was most disconcerting.

'Rhiann,' Eremon breathed, as if tasting her name on his tongue. And, more confident now, he brushed back the tendrils of hair at her nape, his thumb moving in circles over her skin.

Somewhat shakily, Rhiann returned his smile. These last days, every time this look of secret wonder stole across Eremon's face – the look that said *I can't believe I touch you* – something fluttered at the base of Rhiann's belly. *No, lower.* Like warm fingers, brushing between her legs. And with it, not surprisingly, came fear.

For ever since those raiders on the island, desire had always been mingled with fear in her. Every reach and expanse of her flesh had preserved the moment when those rough men threw her down and took her, with the blood of her family still on their hands.

Sparing her life; but not her soul.

4

And though in the stone circle on the Sacred Isle – the first time she and Eremon ever lay together – the Goddess energy and the flaming stars and the *saor* herbs had swept Rhiann to some place of surrender, what would happen now it was just she and he alone in their marriage bed? What if the old memories crippled her again? What if she couldn't help shrinking from him, despite her love . . . and he turned away . . .

No. Gently, Rhiann endeavoured to take her racing thoughts in hand. Surely everything had changed now. The Goddess had at last returned to her, just like the connection she had always felt before the raid. Rhiann's spirit had touched the Mother in the stone circle; she had filled with light in the old way. And Eremon was hers.

Hers. To banish all thought, Rhiann reached out to touch warm skin instead, cupping Eremon's face, tracing one high, sharp cheekbone and then brushing his lips, fuller than those of the other Erin men. This was because Eremon had British blood, too, in his veins, giving him darker skin and a leaner build and those sea-coloured eyes.

Eremon turned his head now to kiss her palm, and then held the end of her braid up so the sun lit it to flame, a flash of mischief crossing his features. 'Did you know your hair is the exact colour of amber, Rhiann? The darkest amber, not the light . . .'

Grateful for the distraction, Rhiann laughed huskily. 'Yes, husband. And my eyes are like *violets* I believe – the bards have got there before you, I'm afraid.'

Eremon, though, was not to be distracted, pressing her hair to his nose to inhale the scent of the honey soap with which she bathed. 'You should always wear amber near your hair, against your throat . . .'

Rhiann closed her eyes as his fingers stroked the hollow below her ear. 'Then you may have to sail to the northern seas yourself, my prince,' she whispered, 'for it is far too rare for that. Even the amber for the royal jewels was traded long ago.'

'No.' His voice also dropped. 'Not the royal jewels. You shall have a necklace all of your own set with amber, so I can see it shine against your throat.' He paused. 'As a wedding gift.'

Her eyes leaped open. '*Wedding* . . .?'

Eremon's teeth flashed as he kissed her fingers. 'What a terrible memory you have, priestess! Our marriage was not to the highest grade, remember, and after a year and a day of the betrothal you were required to choose whether to permanently bind with me . . . or not.'

Rhiann's confusion dissolved in a hot flush across her cheeks. 'Oh, Goddess Mother! After all that has happened, I *did* forget!'

'I will try not to take that as an insult.'

Rhiann shook her head and laughed. 'Eremon, do you mean it, truly?'

'Certainly.' His brows knitted together in an exaggerated fashion. 'But will you have me? Now that you know I no longer command any people, beyond these few grumpy warriors . . .' He waved a vague hand over his shoulder. 'And I have no wealth, no home . . .'

'*Eremon!*' She thumped his chest, none too gently, and he caught her hand there at the neck of his tunic. When Rhiann felt the thud of his heart beneath her fingers she looked down, her cheeks flaming. 'Besides, my home is where you are, and yours mine. You were born a prince of Erin, but you are also of my people now.'

She glanced up to see him gazing at their entangled fingers, and the grim lines of old pain were back in his face. A few days of kisses could not erase these, even if she felt that everything inside *her* had shifted and settled into new curves and bends, like a river changing course.

'That is true, *a stór*,' Eremon murmured, 'and because of that I fear our wedding feast may need to be a trifle hasty.' A black-tipped gull passed over the mast, screeching as it spun, and Eremon looked up and tracked it over the sky, his neck curving. 'Sunseason is getting closer, and I feel sure Agricola will not have rested his soldiers while we rested on the Sacred Isle.'

The day darkened for Rhiann as if a cloud had sailed across the sun. Without volition, her eyes drifted south, towards the distant whirlpool. Ah, yes, there it was: the first mention in days of what waited for them at home. By unspoken agreement, each had sought to stretch out that interlude of peace on the island, knowing they weren't like other couples, free to revel in new feelings. They were pretenders; acting as if they had no cares beyond those of lovers. Rhiann's fingers pressed to the hollow of her throat, trying to loosen the sudden tightness. 'What will we do?'

Eremon was staring east across the sea, where the mainland was hidden by the long, blue islands, as if his gaze could penetrate the leagues that lay between the Epidii lands and those occupied by the Romans. 'This new alliance with the Caereni and Carnonacae, added to that with Calgacus, makes us a force to be reckoned with, at last. I think it is time to take advantage of that; to strike a blow before the Romans do.' His eyes came back and fixed on her face, dark with regret. 'Soon I will have to leave my bride and take to the field.'

Rhiann freed a hand to cup his face again. 'We knew that our partings would be frequent, *cariad*. Yet by the Goddess, if I'd wanted a quiet life, I would have married a cowherd, wouldn't I?'

Eremon snorted, his mouth lifting at one corner. 'Perhaps your council would have been better pleased with that! After all, they gained a war leader, but no gold or cattle in exchange for their princess.' A thought occurred to him, creasing his brow. 'Do you think they will refuse to make the marriage binding?'

'Eremon!' Rhiann raised herself up, pillowing her knees on her blue priestess cloak. 'You sail home with two major alliances, and you've trained our men so well we've already achieved one great victory against the invaders. How can you still doubt your position here?'

Eremon was chewing his lip, as he often did when thinking. 'Because it still isn't secure, and I can't make it so with a sword. Not when the enemies may be inside as well as out.'

The boat had drawn close to another skerry of rocks, just breaking the surface in swirling, sucking foam. The water rebounding off it hissed along the boat's prow as it dipped, and Rhiann's hand grasped for the railing, steadying herself. 'You mean Maelchon,' Rhiann whispered, her eyes fixed on the curling edge of the bow wave. They believed the dark king had engineered the shipwreck two weeks ago, but did not know his exact motives.

Eremon's mouth hardened into a straight line. 'Maelchon had left Calgacus's fort, so he couldn't be the only person behind the sinking of our boat. He would not have known we were leaving by sea, or when we sailed . . .' Suddenly he bit off his words, clamping his lips together with a hint of his old severity.

And although Rhiann had let the memory of the shipwreck subside, at Eremon's words something cold slithered up her spine. The plunge into the sea . . . the sucking of freezing water at her mouth and nose . . .

Eremon saw her shiver and curved his arm around her, lying back to press her cheek into his chest. His tunic was stiff with salt, and smelled of male sweat, although she suddenly realised how oddly reassuring she found this. 'I'm sorry I spoke of this now,' he whispered. 'Let me deal with it, *a stór*, my beloved.'

His voice vibrated in Rhiann's ear, yet she resisted closing her eyes and sinking into his strength. 'You said enemies inside. You mean within the Epidii; my own people . . .'

Eremon's hand stilled on her bright hair. 'Only the Epidii warriors knew we were setting sail from Calgacus's fort. No one else within the dun knew.'

Rhiann's mouth dropped open with instinctive denial, but just then all thoughts were banished by the sudden, startled shout of the boat's captain. He was a black-haired island man, and keen of eye.

'Lord!' he cried to Eremon, and when Rhiann raised her head she saw he was pointing at the mainland, his other arm clasping the mast, each tendon strung hard under the weathered skin.

Eremon leaped up so abruptly that Rhiann fell on her hands and knees across the packs, before scrabbling to her feet.

'Prince!' the sailor shouted again. 'Smoke! Thick smoke, in the air over Dunadd!'

8

CHAPTER 2

Driven hard by the now desperate oarsmen, the boat shot between the scattered rocks into the Bay of Isles like an arrow released from its string.

Yet once they rounded the great headland that sheltered the bay from the sea, Rhiann saw that the smoke staining the blue sky came not from Dunadd, but from the signal beacons, lining the high ground to north and south of the bay.

'They are burned out,' Eremon muttered to Rhiann, shading his eyes to look up at the ridges, cloaked in bracken and sheep-bitten turf, with hazel and oak trees spilling down the slopes, just coming into full leaf. There were no flames to be seen, only the trailing smoke of the huge bonfires.

Rhiann's breath was tight and high in her chest. She glanced at Eremon, wanting to speak, but the bright day was now reflecting in the hard glitter of his eyes. His mouth was drawn into a severe line, the tendons in his throat taut. The man who had cradled her so gently moments before was gone.

Conaire, Eremon's foster-brother, had laid aside his oar to join Eremon in the bow, his lithe leaps from rib to rib belying his great height and hulking build. 'Do you think it safe to land, brother?' Conaire swiped at his sweaty forehead with a massive hand, the bronze ring around his thick forearm flashing back sunlight.

Eremon was still, his dark head thrust forwards toward shore like a hound scenting the air. Ahead, the bay had opened up into full view: the broad sweep of marsh surrounding the mouth of the river Add; the river channels snaking over the tidal mudflats, and further towards the eastern horizon, the blue hills that cupped the plain on which Dunadd sat. Close on the shore was the cluster of roundhouses and jetties that made up the port of Crinan. A pall of smoke hung over the village, yet the buildings themselves seemed whole.

Across from Crinan, on a headland that curved around the bay like a sheltering arm, the black skeleton of an abandoned dun crouched. That fort had been burned by the Romans less than a year before, but of course it was the reminder of this attack that had terrified them; of coming over the hills to see smoke against the sky; the bodies sprawled among the ruins. Her blood was now pounding so hard that Rhiann's sight shook, and she wiped her sweating palms down the skirt of her dress, trying to calm her breathing.

Caitlin, Conaire's wife, now flung herself across the oar benches to reach Rhiann, her haste making her uncharacteristically clumsy. Rhiann grasped her thin arm to steady her.

'Wh-what does it mean?' Caitlin cried, her tiny hand clutching at Rhiann's fingers. Rhiann looked down into the small, heart-shaped face beneath a cloud of fair hair, plucked from its braids by wind and damp. Caitlin was drawn and pale from the nausea of the voyage, which though calm, had still affected her now she was expecting a child.

Rhiann forced a smile and stroked Caitlin's cold fingers as they bit into her arm, though she herself was fighting down a wave of panic. 'I am sure it is nothing . . .' she murmured. Just then the backwash from the rocks of the headland made the boat lurch, and Rhiann's hand leaped out to steady both of them against the single mast.

'There is no outward sign of trouble,' Eremon at last pronounced, his gaze on the shore. 'The fishing boats are there on the sand, unharmed. Look! The nobles' boats are also tied up, whole. There is smoke, but why?'

Rhiann peeled Caitlin's fingers from her arm and helped her to Conaire's side, moving closer to Eremon. 'Goddess, what of Dunadd?' Their fort sat in the middle of the marsh on a rock crag, and could not be seen from the sea.

Eremon chewed fiercely on his lip, and then glanced up at the taller Conaire. 'What choice do we have but to land? We are only a few, yet I can see no people at Crinan.'

Conaire was nodding as he curved his broad arm protectively around his wife, his bright gold hair a beacon in the sunlight. 'We can see nothing from here anyway, brother. If anything is amiss, we are few enough to land and approach Dunadd by stealth, in case there are scouts.'

Rhiann was feeling sicker by the moment, still trying to shake off the daze of the rocking sea and sunshine. It was still so early in leaf-bud, despite the fine weather. The marsh grass was new and green, yet the tops of the mountains that ringed the plain were still dusted with snow. How could the Romans have come so early in the season? How could they have been caught out again?

As soon as the boat grated on the mud beach beside the first pier, the warriors were splashing through the shallows, swords drawn. Above, on a spur of rock that guarded the river mouth, the scattering of roundhouses crouched silent beneath their pale thatch roofs. As Eremon had seen, the nobles' timber boats with their carved prows were bobbing unharmed on their weed-furred ropes. The little hide *curraghs* were drawn up in rows above the tideline, alongside dugout canoes. Yet there was no bustle of people coming and going, and no children crying. Only a lone dog, tied up against the first house, barked at them in a frenzy.

At Eremon's orders, Rhiann and Caitlin stayed in the boat with the Sacred Isle sailors, ready to push off at his sign. But no sooner had his warriors disappeared among the rocks, than Rhiann's eye was caught by a pale blur in the shadows of the houses. Her heart gave a great lurch as she recognised the shape; that of her mare Liath, led by a short, rotund man who stumbled past Eremon in agitated haste.

Drawing up her long robe with both hands, Rhiann put one foot on the railing and jumped down into the shallows, heedless of the freezing water that soaked her leather boots to the skin. 'Didius!' she cried, splashing free and breaking into a run.

In the middle of the sand they met, Didius stumbling and

11

yanking on Liath's reins, making the mare throw up her head in protest. Rhiann halted, her initial smile of greeting faded. Didius's plump cheeks were quivering beneath his straggly, black beard, and his nose, the only large, straight thing about him, was red and streaming. 'Didius?'

Suddenly Liath tossed her pale grey head, tearing the reins free to push her way to Rhiann's side. With nothing to hold, Didius stuffed his fingers in his mouth to halt the sob that rushed out, his black, Roman eyes shining with tears. 'Lady, I am sorry,' he gulped at last, the musical Alban speech thickened by his native Latin.

As Rhiann soothed the mare, stroking her cheeks, Didius snorted and wiped his nose on his tunic sleeve. All of his Roman clothes were long gone, as was his clipped hair and shaven face. If it wasn't for his swarthy skin and oval eyes he could almost pass for one of the Epidii now, though because of his girth, not a warrior.

'Didius, what is wrong? Where is everyone?'

Eremon stepped up behind Didius now, sheathing his sword on his belt, and the Roman glanced up at the prince with some of his old fear. Yet his distress got the better of him, and he grasped Rhiann's hand and pressed it between his own. 'Lady, we thought you drowned! All of you, in the sea!'

Rhiann drew in a sharp breath.

'Dead?' That was Eremon. 'Who said such a thing?'

'The – the chief druid. Gelert.'

Eremon's eyes met Rhiann's, and she saw the same terrible question dawning there. *How did the druid know about the ship going down?*

'Didius.' Rhiann strove to calm her voice. 'Tell us how this happened.'

Didius's throat bobbed as he stumbled through an explanation: that after returning from Calgacus's fort by land, the chief druid went into seclusion, and then emerged to announce that he had been sent a vision from the gods. Rhiann, the tribe's Ban Cré, the sacred Land Mother, and her husband the war leader had drowned at sea.

As Didius reached the end his breath caught, and Rhiann closed her eyes for a moment, knowing exactly what this news had meant to him, a Roman prisoner, whose only protector among the Epidii had been Rhiann herself. She reached out to squeeze Didius's callused hand. 'Go on.'

'Well, that was three days ago, and the mourning has been terrible. People burnt offerings in a big bonfire at the water – see, over there – and they lit all the beacons on the cliffs, and now many have gone to Dunadd, and the keening of the women has left no peace anywhere in the fort. The council of elders is at the King's Hall, and a mourning feast is being prepared. No one will speak to me, they are all so anguished!'

A chill crept over Rhiann's skin, for there was one other person who would be utterly devastated by this lie. She dropped Didius's hand and rubbed the goosebumps from her forearms. 'And what of my aunt, the Lady Linnet? Have you seen her?'

Didius shook his head until his chins wobbled. 'No, lady, she has not come.'

'Goddess!' Rhiann whirled to Eremon. 'I must go to her *now*; she will be frantic!'

Eremon laid a reassuring hand on her arm. 'Soon, *a stór*.' He addressed himself sternly to Didius. 'If this was the news, son of Rome, then why are you here unaccompanied, with my wife's horse?'

'Eremon!' Rhiann exclaimed.

For a moment, the single, buried thread of iron in Didius rose to the surface, in a compression of his wet lips. Yet then it sank away, and embarrassment stole over his plump face. 'I wasn't escaping – where would I go? I wasn't. I just . . . didn't believe it.' He gazed pleadingly at Rhiann. 'I *knew* you would return, and I've been sleeping here with Liath ever since the druid emerged. Three days now, and watching the sea every day.'

Rhiann pressed both hands to her mouth, and slowly nodded. 'Then you prove both your loyalty and your keen senses, for as you can see, we are alive and well.'

Above, the pale ovals of faces were now appearing at doorways, and there was a growing murmur of surprised voices from the cluster of houses.

'Rhiann, we must go,' Eremon ordered, jerking his hand at Colum and Fergus.

Taking a deep breath, Rhiann glanced over her shoulder at the boat. Conaire had returned to sweep Caitlin into his arms, depositing her gently on the grey sands as Fergus and Colum now sheathed their swords and began tossing their belongings to the beach.

Taking Liath's reins, Rhiann led the mare to Caitlin and explained what had happened. 'We must hurry to Dunadd,' Rhiann finished, 'and so I wish you to ride Liath, *cariad*.'

Caitlin swallowed hard and shook her head. 'Oh, no, Rhiann, I can't. You're the Ban Cré; if what you say is true the people need to see you entering at the gate with proper ceremony.' She tried to draw herself taller, with a bold toss of her fair hair. Yet though she was kin to Rhiann, she didn't share Rhiann's height, and the effect was less than defiant. 'I will walk.'

Conaire's blue eyes were shadowed with concern, and he bent his head close to his wife. 'Beloved, please ride. You got so sick on the boat . . .'

Conaire caught Rhiann's eye, as Caitlin set her lip and jutted her chin. Faced with no choice, Rhiann dropped her voice, wielding her best weapon. 'Do it for the babe, Caitlin. As your healer, I strongly advise you to rest yourself during these early moons.'

'I don't . . .' Suddenly, Caitlin clapped her hand to her mouth, her arm holding her belly. Her throat moved convulsively, as a fine sweat beaded her forehead, and Rhiann put her hand gently on the back of her neck.

Choking down the spasm, Caitlin dropped her hand and breathed deeply. 'I suppose I must then,' she conceded at last, and in a rare show of submission allowed Conaire to lift her to the mare's back. The crew of the boat offered to accompany them, but Eremon refused, telling them to ask for food at the port and return home.

Desperate with haste, they could spare only moments for the few fisherfolk who emerged from their houses as they passed, touching Rhiann's hands and Caitlin's legs across Liath's back. Throwing hurried answers to the questions coming from all directions, they took the trade path which led along the river, across the marsh to Dunadd.

The banter of the sea journey had been replaced with silence. Colum's face had set into even grimmer lines than usual, his blue eyes hard beneath his stringy cap of thinning, grey hair. Fergus was watchful, scanning the shadows beneath the river trees and the pools and reeds to the marsh side of the path. Didius's short legs made him the slowest, and though he must puff and pant with his head down to keep up, his black eyes kept darting to Rhiann's face, as if to assure himself she was truly there.

When Dunadd emerged into view above the banks of river alders and willows, Rhiann realised she had braced herself to see some sign of disaster on the walls. But from afar there seemed nothing amiss.

The single rock crag still reared proudly from the red marsh; the timber palisade of the village at its feet marching around it in stout oak stakes. The thatched roofs of the nobles' houses, high on the crag's crest, glowed like sun on ripe barley. And the scarlet and white banner of the White Mare, the emblem of Rhiann's royal clan, rippled from the apex of the King's Hall, set on the dun's highest point.

Something else was the same, too. The roofless circle of oak pillars that was the druid shrine still reared against the skyline beside the King's Hall, its squat, dark posts as threatening to Rhiann as ever. For the shrine was the chief druid's realm – from there Gelert must have announced their deaths.

And how? Rhiann wondered again. *How could Gelert know?* Yet Didius's words called forth a powerful memory that had been subsumed by the shipwreck and all that happened after: the unearthly glow in the druid's eyes when he stood on the shore above Calgacus's dun, watching their boat leave.

Glancing at her, Eremon immediately drew her close and raised her hand to his lips. *I know*, his look said. *I know, too.*

Even in the salt-stained tunic and trousers, with stubble shadowing his brown skin, still Eremon looked every bit a prince, and Rhiann resolutely tried to take comfort from that. The more plainly he dressed, the more his straight line of back and shoulders stood out. And when his face was darkened with sun and dirt, then the green of his eyes blazed all the brighter. He was a match for Gelert; she had to believe that.

And what about me? Rhiann thought, with a flare of fierce pride, closing her eyes to remember what lay within her own soul. In the stone circle she had felt the Goddess fill her with the light of the Source – the life force which ran through all things – feeling it clearly for the first time since the raid. In that sacred space, the connection between her body and the spirit world had been mended. Her surrender to Eremon had helped to reforge that silver cord, making the two parts of her whole again.

And as she summoned it, the wordless joy Rhiann had floated in that night now surged again, strengthening her spine and shoulders. Slowly, she opened her eyes, the after-glare of the sun dancing in spots before her nose. If she had that inner light to call on, then she could face Gelert and Maelchon and even Agricola. She could. She must.

They had not even fully crossed the causeway over the river when the first shouts rang out from people gathered on the meadow, digging the baking pits for the mourning feast. Then the cry of a horn soared up from the timber tower that spanned Dunadd's main gate.

They had been seen.